Readers Love The Books Of The Wode!

"Hennig's Wode series continues to reinvent the legend of Robin Hood . . . Thick with conflict and intrigue, this retelling turns a well-known legend into a fresh, earthy tale of human passions twisted by politics and ancient powers."
—*Publishers Weekly*

"There's nothing quite so exciting as an author taking an overused traditional narrative and breathing full and rich life into it the way that Hennig does with her retelling of the Robin Hood/Green Man stories in her Greenwode series. I was smitten, right from the beginning."
—*Charles DeLint*

"Hennig expertly weaves the threads together in seductive, evocative prose that put me in the scene as few others have ever done . . . An enthralling transformation of folklore and legend into something wonderfully original from start to finish."
—*Susan R. Matthews*

"An intensely emotional, breathtaking version of the Robin Hood legend . . . Beautifully showcases the cultural and religious upheaval between peasant versus nobility, oppresses versus oppressors . . . Highly recommended."
—*Bella Online*

"A complex, meticulously researched, and vividly realised re-imagining of the Robin Hood myth, which depicts Robin and Guy as lovers instead of sworn enemies."
—*A Swimming Pool Library*

"I can't recommend this book highly enough. The prose is poetic, powerful, insightful. Hennig has a masterful command of weaponry and battle-speak, as well of wode magic. This is a soul-plumbing, life-changing experience."
—*Historical Novel Society Review*

"It felt like discovering a fine wine. There was incredible tension: romantic, character-driven, and plot-driven. This isn't a light sip of a read."
—*Queer SciFi*

"Given the author's innate ability to take classic lore and make it new again through works of fantasy, fans of other genres or literature in general are sure to enjoy these."
—*Amazing Stories Magazine*

"With *The Wode* books, Hennig weaves Welsh mythology into the classic tale and reimagines Robin Hood and Guy of Gisborne as lovers and Maid Marian as Robin's sister–and all three entwined by magic and fate. The worldbuilding is intricate, the language is gorgeous . . . and the characters are achingly flawed. It's the best Robin Hood retelling I've encountered."
—*Pages below the Vaulted Sky*

BOOKS BY J TULLOS HENNIG

The Books of the Wode
(Tales of Robin Hood, a.k.a. Robyn Hode)

Greenwode

Shirewode

Winterwode

Summerwode

Wyldingwode

- BOOK TWO OF THE WODE -
Being a tale of Robin Hood (a.k.a. Robyn Hode)

J TULLOS HENNIG

FOREST PATH BOOKS

SHIREWODE

Published by
FOREST PATH BOOKS

SHIREWODE Copyright © 2013 by J Tullos Hennig.
All rights reserved

This is a work of fiction. Names, characters, places and incidents are products of the author's imagination or are used fictitiously and are not to be construed as real. Any resemblance to actual events, locales, organisations, or persons, living or dead, is entirely coincidental.

Forest Path Books supports writers and copyright. This book is licensed for your personal enjoyment only. Thank you for helping us to defend our authors' rights and livelihood by acquiring an authorized edition of this book, and by complying with copyright laws by not using, reproducing, transmitting, or distributing any part of this book without permission.

Forest Path Books publications may be purchased for educational, business, or sales/promotional use. For information, please email the publishers at:
info@forestpathbooks.com
or address:
Forest Path Books, LLC
P. O. Box 847, Stanwood, WA 98292 USA

Stay informed on our releases and news!
Join the reading group/newsletter at:
https://forestpathbooks.com/into-the-forest/

Cover design by Mahli (*bookdesignbymahli.com*)
Cover content is for illustrative purposes only, and any person depicted on the cover is a model.

Map illustration © 2013 by J Tullos Hennig
Pi Rho Runestones font © Peter Rempel (licensed for use)
First published in North America by DSP Publications, 2014

ISBN: 978-1-951293-57-4 (trade paperback)
978-1-951293-35-2 (hardcover)
978-1-951293-00-0 (e-book)

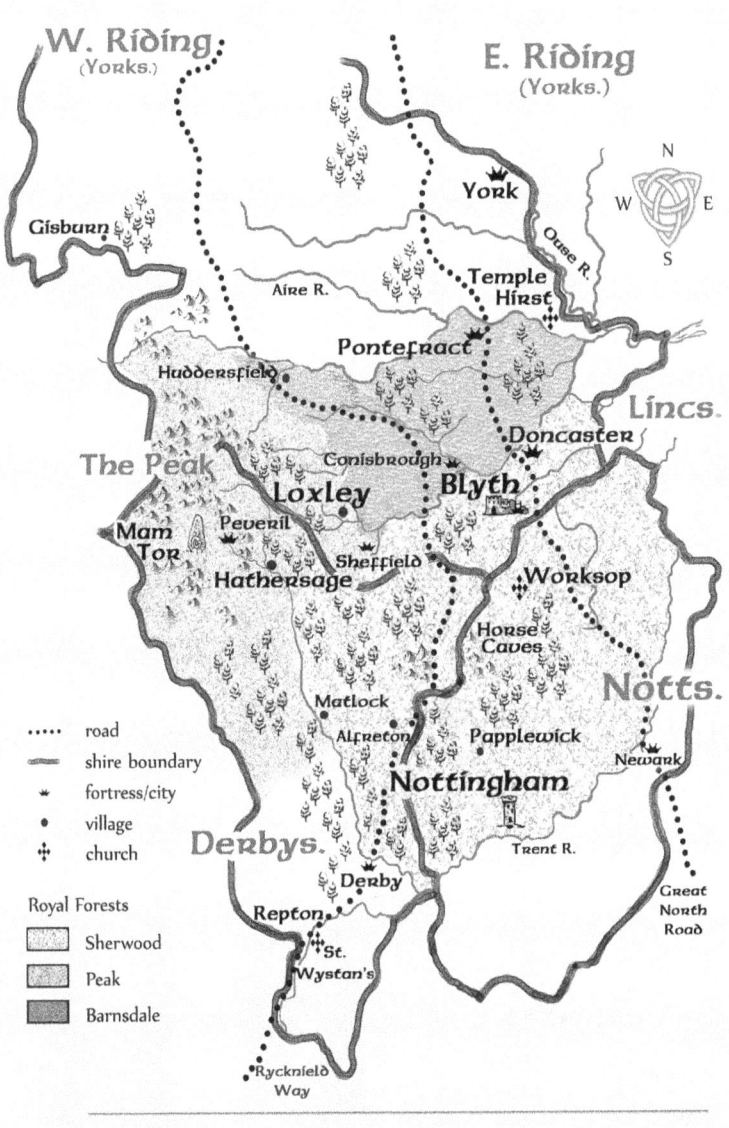

Map of the Shire Wode

For "Robin" & "Marionette" –

who have never tried to stifle *anadl tynged*.

Prelude

*Deep in the Shire Wode
Waning of Beltane, 1190 CE*

"I am a stag of seven tines."
 The old man sits at the fire, breathing smoke, invoking flame. Humming an elder bard's song of island magic, old when he was young.
 "I am a tear the sun lets fall."
 The young Hunter is flung at the old man's feet, sacrifice to the rocks, to the earth, to Mother. Nearly bled white, there is a great and gaping hole breaking the usual line of tensile muscle along his breast. The arrow has been cut out, but the damage is great. The poultice has been replaced, over and over, furs laid and the fire drawn hot.
 "You are a hawk above the cliff."
 But *tynged* lies still-quiet. A skein spinning outward, vivid sparks of warmth amidst the violated aubergine of viscera, into indigo and then fraying into the black against moonlight. The moon is waning; Her dance now has him, tripped and tangled. Her voice draws him down into the death spiral. She would take him back, set him free.
 The Horned Lord would foil Her, have his weapon back. And Cernun is the Horned Lord's: spirit and body.
 "I am the womb of every holt."

Cernun uses every wile, every healing mantra and simple, every bit of magic in his aging frame. Twice already has he drawn the shroud over the Hunter's face, sung the death song. Twice has the thin flax lay still then, impossibly, sucked inward, breath stirring, faint.

Blooded. Broken. Yet still the Hunter fights, knowing his fight is not yet begun. The magic would take him down and he would seem to have no choice but to let it swamp him—Death breathes his name even as She heats him with fever and infection.

Part of him welcomes Her.

. . .all of them dead. . . lost. . . mam!da!mari!. . . burning. . . hanging on the cross. . . death of me, deathofme. . . loved him. . . loved him!

. . .treachery. . . betrayer. . . murderer. . .

And despair leads to pain leads to rage back to pain . . . but rage is always the stronger, and pain but feeds the fury in his blood. The Hunter refuses to bow, to bend.

Incites the darkness. Shows throat, but with a snarl.

So the old man snarls back. Touches death. Tries to weather the squall. Breathes the spells to set the Hunter back into thisworld.

"Take my life for his," Cernun chants. "Mine for his. He is our future, our purpose, our hope. All that is left. You have his blood, Lady, my life is forfeit. I am but Your Hermit, old and spent. This boy has purpose, yet: he would be Your Darken King."

He is wounded too grave, heart and body. The Lady's voice is a soft echo within the caverns. *Would you countenance a crippled King?*

"Who walks unburdened in thislife? Together we can make him whole."

Are you so sure? Nay, my own, it is finished. All things must end.

It is not yet Our time! Her consort protests, muted thunder in the depths. *It is not yet* Our *ending!*

I am Death—

And I am Your spear roaring for blood. I am Time, the meaning *of Death. The meaning of—*

Life, She must concede.

"His blood is Yours, the teind paid, Holly King fallen beneath the Oak King's sword," Cernun murmurs. "He has been broken, bound, the Sacrifice endured. If You must hold a spirit's hem, grasp mine."

She turns great, luminous eyes upon him. *I shall. Never doubt that.*

Silence falls, truncated softly by the drip of water against rock, the crackle of the flames, the hoarse, faint breaths of the wounded. Even the presence of the lad who sits watch outside is magnified, held in thrall of the magic. Then:

What of the others? She asks. *The Pale Knight and the Maiden? They are taken by Our enemies, flung to wind and water, to barren stone. They are lost to Us.* The Horned Lord pauses, then says, fecund with meaning, *He is the only one who can bring them back.* The Lady Huntress concedes, bows Her bright head, turns aside. And the Horned Lord grabs his Hunter by the hair, kisses him, all passion and cold fire and indomitable will.

Breathe the fire. Breathe your destiny. Breathe, *Hob-Robyn.*

I am the tomb of every hope, comes the answer, teased wavering from the black. I have no breath. I am a ghost, howling in the night, disappearing in the trees, dreams of hope and love twisted into betrayal. Into nightmare.

You are. Breathe them. Anadl tynged, *my own. You are all of those, and more.*

You told me. Told me. . . told me he would betray us all. And I didn't listen. And now. . . I canna See. . .

Cannot, or will not?

It is. . . gone. All I See is the ending. The precipice. I hang with bloodied fingers over a thick, black void, and tynged is frayed, burnt beyond any hope. Burnt like Loxley. Like my heart. He. . . he let us fall, his Maiden and his lover both. . .

And you will take your vengeance. That I promise you. You will have what is yours by rights, and see the traitors writhing at your feet. The cowl upon your heart will also shroud your head. It will be your protection, your being. It will be how your people will know Hob-Robyn is not dead. The Hunter will never die. He is resurrected into the Hooded One.

The Hooded One is a spirit.

Aye, as you will be a spectre, a cry in the night, fae green Wode sprite, breath of nightmares and dreams. The Hooded One is Mine, My soul, you are *Me. My avatar and all of ours is both spirit and flesh, blood of the King who has bled and died and lives again through the love and tears of his people.*

The King. . .

The King of the Shire Wode. It is what they will call you. Rob in t' Hode.

Robyn Hode. Aye. That *is who we are.*

The coast of Normandy
End of May 1190, CE

"So this is the new one, eh?"

Dead. They're all dead. While he is alive.

There is an irony in it. Something twisted and injured, like an animal in a trap waiting for the coup de grace, the hand to break its neck, the edge to open an artery. The relief of ending.
He does not deserve relief.
"Sacre tête, boy, you look like hell. Your trip across the Channel was not so kind, eh?"

Gamelyn bowed his head lower, gave a small shrug. It had in truth been miserable: a high wind filling the sails and waves slamming the bow, which in turn had him heaving his guts over the railing for nearly the entire trip.

"I imagine once the *mal du mer* passes, you will be glad to finally see the land of your people." A grim chuckle. "Not that we will have much time to entertain the sights of Normandy."

Gamelyn should be awed. Respectful. His father had come from here, and some of his dam's people. They had travelled across the English Channel in the wake of Hastings and the one Rob's people still called Willy Bastard . . .

Rob. Marion. Their. . . people, dead. All of them, cut down like animals and none to mourn their passing, none to even express regret. . .

Even his own remorse was a silent and castrated hollow place within, one he had dug himself and kept backfilling with rage and grief. Over and over and *over.*

Now there was only a queasy gratitude that his feet were once more on solid land, Norman or no. Even if a sadistic little pig of a guard captain had nigh dragged a tottering Gamelyn from the gangplank and quick-stepped him, horse and all, from the portside to the encampment. Once there, Gamelyn had been marched through the chaos of soldiers sparring, shouting and armouring, to this tent where he now knelt in the chill, stomped down mud to meet *chevalier* de Gisborough, his new master.

Who just happened to be a Templar Knight.

Gamelyn had heard stories of the Templars. They were uncompromising fanatics, zealots. They put entire towns of Jews and Saracens to the torch: men, women, children—it didn't matter. If they were deemed to have offended God, the last sight beheld would be the white tabard and crimson cross. It was said Lionheart himself owed much of his working capital to what funds had been passed to him by the Templars: they held power over a *king.*

"Uncover before your lord!" The sadistic little pig, still behind Gamelyn, tangled hard fingers in the woollen scarf about his ears and yanked it away. Gamelyn grabbed it just before it throttled him. The captain seemed satisfied, did not press the matter. Damp oozed down Gamelyn's nape, and he caught a whiff of vomit. Mayhap he should discard it, but the wrap had been the only protection against the damp crossing, and now the crisp wind rattling the tent flaps.

A snort from the Templar. "Well, there's no doubt he fits the physical description here." He brandished the parchment; Gamelyn's gaze rose to it then chased away. "The hair alone . . . Leave us, Etienne."

"My lord, he came with a horse. A fine courser."

"And this is my concern how? Other than he's well equipped and I am grateful for it."

"He's a mere squire—"

"Who will likely earn his knight's spurs anon, as he is not baseborn. You are covetous, Etienne, and you will see the chaplain for it before night's end." An almost lazy threat lingered beneath the words, merely emphasised by the opulent baritone.

Gamelyn snuck a look at the sadistic little . . . at Etienne, and saw the threat blossom apprehension in the narrow face.

"I will myself come and ensure that you give such a valuable animal into the care of my own groom. *Va t'en. Vite!*" the Templar added as Etienne hesitated further.

Etienne obeyed, retreating from the tent. Gamelyn breathed easier—he had not liked leaving Diamant tied outside all packed up like a charcoal burner's nag—but only a bit easier, as he was left kneeling, alone, before the Templar.

"You're a quiet one."

Ah, but Rob would have laughed himself sick at that one . . .

And the great, aching hole opened up again, making Gamelyn sway sideways and put a hand to the chill, well-trodden mud to steady himself.

Enough. He would not do this anymore. *Enough.*

"Get up, lad. You will be my squire, not my serf."

Gamelyn resumed the relentless backfilling of the despairing rent in his soul, lurched up. Slow, wary, he watched his new master the entire while. The Templar was some inches taller than Gamelyn; his frame stretched lean, but built up, a power that gave suitable promise beneath the white tunic with its bloody cross. His brown hair, cropped short, had begun to grizzle; his beard was similarly greyed and well-trimmed. He met Gamelyn's gaze and matched it, edged keen and glinting pale by the flickers of lantern light.

But his eyebrows were drawn together, considering. He seemed . . . nonplussed.

"Well. No doubt I'll talk enough for the both of us." Once again the Templar consulted the roll of parchment Gamelyn had presented him. "It says here your father has but recently died. Your brother has given you a proper writ of lineage, stating you are Gamelyn Boundys de Blyth, third son to Sir Ian, mesne lord of Blyth and noble vassal to Huntingdon and King Richard. He states here your intent to pledge yourself to Crusade for absolution of your sins." The eyebrows drew together even tighter, then relaxed. One climbed upward. "Hard to know what sins a sixteen-year-old lad can truly claim." Gamelyn clenched his jaw, said nothing.

"Hm. I see that none of this *amour fraternel* kept your brother from sending you in lieu of the scutage he could have paid for your service."

Brotherly love? Again, Gamelyn clenched his jaw . . .

"*You were the one who cozened our father to send so many marks to Ely's monastery; now you will make up for that lack. Our king demands scutage; instead he shall have you. If we want to keep these lands our father worked so hard to gain, then sacrifices must be made. . ."*

Sacrifice. What will you sacrifice, Summerling? the velvet-deep voice of Rob's god had queried . . . then had not sounded again, not even in the depths of nightmare.

He was, truly, bereft.

The Templar still watched him, still seemed . . . curious? "No doubt, however you inconvenienced your brother, the worst of those sins was likely mere proximity."

Ah, yes. Sins.

If Gamelyn lived to see ninety-nine, he would never atone for what sins the fires of Beltane had wrought. Nightmare had become reality: all of them, dead.

Even his father. The illness had taken him that same night, and Gamelyn hadn't been there. Hadn't said good-bye. Everything lost, in truth wiped from Gamelyn's existence in that moment when Rob's hot, dark eyes had levelled down the arrow he aimed at Gamelyn and screamed: *Rival. Lover. Betrayer.*

They had dragged Gamelyn's unconscious body back to Blyth. He had woke, chained like a mad dog to the first convenient barrier—a buttress in the main hall. Otho had been the one to explain, painstaking and patient, how when they'd brought Gamelyn back to the castle and managed to revive him, he had, indeed, gone a little mad. Drawn a dagger on the Abbess, taken out several guards and nearly Johan as well.

Under the circumstances, what choice was Johan to make?

"*The church might be loath to take in a madman; the Crusade, however, is full of them. Otho has insisted you be given a choice,* petit frère. *This is your choice: you either ride to your new appointment of your own will, or I shall deliver you there tied hand and foot. But you will go and be gone...*"

"Well," the Templar said. "Not an uncommon predicament in these troubled times. You are one of many secondary sons marching with us. It is no cause for shame."

His throat still too tight and thick to speak, Gamelyn bowed his head, acknowledging the kind words.

"I knew your father, lad. Sir Ian was brave, fought in Palestine like a tiger. You could do worse than emulate him."

Strangely, this unclenched Gamelyn's throat, made it possible to say, quiet, "Thank you, my lord *Chevalier.*"

The Templar blinked, taken aback, and Gamelyn realised it was the first thing he'd actually said. Then the Templar shrugged. "I would hazard you've heard more than a few tales about your new master . . . or his Order, I should say."

It was Gamelyn's turn to blink.

"Eh, boy? Have you heard we sacrifice virgins upon the full moon, eat the hearts of our enemies? That we worship Heathen idols and lie with each other instead of women?"

Well, Gamelyn considered grimly, the last two should suit him. *Enough!* He slapped misery midwhine and tipped it into the never-ending hollow; began, again, to backfill.

"The women whom, I assume, we sacrifice." The Templar gave a derisive snort. "Hear me, Gamelyn Boundys de Blyth, you are now squire to *Chevalier* Hubert de Gisborough, *Templier,* Master and Commander to Hirst Preceptory of Yorkshire. I do not answer to Church, Crown, or any idle gossip. I deny nothing. I admit nothing. It is no one's business but our own, and if you have the leanings insinuated in this letter, then you might have the Holy Orders within your grasp should you act with humility and prudence. You will do well to keep your mouth shut. Which, I presuppose—" the Templar rolled up the parchment with a swift twist, "—from these past moments we have spent in each other's company, will not be a hardship for you. "So. I know enough of why you're here in Normandy, eh?"

Actually, you really don't, and that's just fine.

"You've been sent to me because, as it happens, my junior squire was killed in a bizarre accident. Run over by a loose tourney horse. A good lad, but stupid. Clumsy. And couldn't write a blessed word. Can you write, boy?"

"Yes, my lord *Chevalier.*"

The Templar's grey eyes lit up. "Really? Can it be possible you achieve more than a pathetic scrawl?"

"Yes, my lord *Chevalier*." Gamelyn was beginning to take note of more than the minimalist details of tent and Templar. All about, on tables and stacked in open trunks, were an assortment of tomes and parchments being packed. It loosened his voice even more. "I can write Latin as well as both *Langue d'oc* and *Langue d'oïl*. I used to pen letters for my father. He often remarked upon my steady and legible hand."

Pride, Gamelyn. Pride will be your death. . .

If only. Now, 'twas all he'd left.

"Bloody marvellous!" The Templar's voice made a smooth power of accompaniment to the slap of his hand against the table. "And you seem to know words of more than one syllable. Dare I hope your reading is as easy as your spoken vocabulary?"

"I can read, my lord *Chevalier*."

"But do you *like* it, lad?"

"Never liked reading. Too many thoughts gathered all ripe in one place, too many scrawls and marks t' make anyone's head full to bursting. You and Marion can have it, and welcome. . ."

"I . . ." And bugger and piss, but Gamelyn's throat was trying to close up again. "I do, my lord *Chevalier*."

"*Excellent*. You'll be a goodly improvement over my last squire—rest his soul." The Templar peered at him, searching, and when Gamelyn dropped his own gaze, uncertain, the Templar gave a sharp *tsk*. "Well. You've come far from home, and will be farther yet, anon."

"I'll go. Of my own will. There's nothing left for me here. . ."

"We'll see what you're made of. A few cautions, then. When you do address me, it will be as 'Commander', or 'my lord Commander'. In actuality, I prefer you not address me unless I speak directly to you. Again, I assume this will not be undue hardship. You seem not overly made of chatter."

"Yes, my lord *Cheva* . . . my lord Commander."

"Go, then. See that your horse and baggage are tended to, and report to Etienne. He is the sergeant in charge of the squires. He has taken up the duties of *Confanonier* since that unfortunate man was killed in a sortie north of here, but he is not of noble blood, so you will address him merely as Sergeant. It annoys him, but we all have gadflies we must endure. If you have questions, Etienne or your fellow squires are the ones you will ask. I am not your nursemaid. You are no peasant, so we will find a boy to see to your basic needs, but you are new and shall work your way into favour no less than anyone. You are not one of us yet, mind."

And may never be. What Holy Order would take me now?

"*Va t'en.*"

"Yes, my lord Commander," Gamelyn said and bowed out of the tent into the wind and the rain.

Worksop Abbey,
Autumn of 1190, CE

You will find the abbey a safe and holy place, the Reverend Lady had promised, and so she had found it. The stone walls had enclosed and clothed the mother-naked bairn that she was. Her life had truly started anew. No doubt for the better, or so Sister Deirdre would say, even if something about Sister Deirdre struck her as unsound, tainted.

No doubt 'twas due to such feeling that she had not quite trusted to drink the draughts Sister Deirdre had provided when she had first been brought to the abbey from the castle, bundled up and taken away in a cart not unlike the one used for the dead. The secrecy was necessary: an evil spirit roamed the castle, as the Reverend Lady had explained, an unfortunate man driven mad by the same evil ones who had tried to sacrifice her to their demon, and her spirit could not be contaminated with his. She had heard howling, like a demented wolf . . . and it followed her into dreams when she poured Sister Deirdre's draught into the piss pot instead of drinking it.

No, not just dreams. Nightmares. Of horned demons and naked worshippers, of blood and fire and a hooded figure leaning over her in the dark, as if to steal her, breath and spirit.

From that night forward, she took the draught, and the dreams stopped.

There had been talk of travelling, since she had recovered so quickly—a miracle, the Reverend Lady said, when they had found her in the forest. God Himself had smote the filthy pagans about her and it had been the Reverend Lady who had first put hands upon her, found her not dead, but healed of her grievous wounds. A miracle. Travelling had been an exciting thought. But when she went too far from stone walls, too close to the tangled horrors of the woodland surround, the headaches would start, and the half-remembered/half-nightmarish *things* would swirl about her, as if she held some sort of recognition for them.

As if she were unclean.

It would get better, Sister Deirdre promised. Once the spirits had found her unassailable by anything but God, they would cease their caterwauling, the Reverend Lady insisted. She should stay cloistered, and pray.

The barren stone would protect her.

She was eager to do so. The abbey of Worksop was a proud edifice to do God's work, but also held a private chapel for those who did not choose to open themselves to secular scrutiny, and a separate dormitory to the same ends. She'd been given a tiny cell, and a simple white shift to wear until the Bishop could come and witness her case. It was not so simple as taking oaths or vows, the Reverend Lady had explained. A novitiate needed to be in a state of grace to take communion, and considering the miracle, surely she was, but . . . It was a man's world, at the end of it, and the Archbishop wanted to see this wondrous nearly martyred victim for himself, to judge.

And when she asked for a name, at least—a name with which to cloak herself to meet this uncompromising Archbishop—the Reverend Lady told her she might choose herself. When she spoke the first name that rose to her tongue, it seemed to give them pause, but it . . . fit. Was hers, in a world where nowt belonged save the sound and feel of it upon her tongue.

"Marion," she said. "My name is Marion."

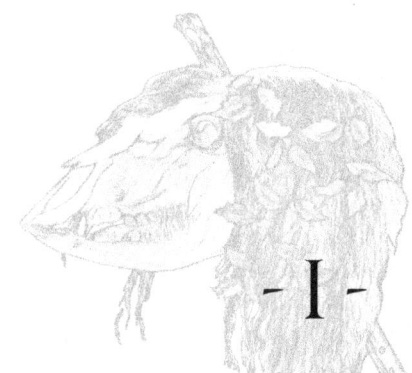

- I -

Near Wentbridge, Yorkshire
Waxing of March, 1192 CE

He scented into the wind, and waited.
A lean figure crouched on an oak limb twice as broad as himself, clad in a faded mix of leather and woollen that all but blended with the burgeoning, lush foliage. He'd a graceful curve of elm balanced on his knees and several arrows, fashioned for the length of his drawing arm, stuck in a thick knot of unruly black hair hanging over one shoulder. Another handful of arrows waited in a quiver hung upon a smaller limb, within reach.

The bow was strung. Ready.

Robyn shifted, snuffed the air again. His booted feet made careful purchase on the wet wood. It was raining, had been raining for two days straight in a light patter, and what the rain hadn't managed to soak, the mists hanging in the river bottoms had. The road, a wet ribbon threading past his perch and southward, wound slick as sheep dung, slow.

Aye, a good day for hunting.

"He just *knows* things, Robyn does."

"I've never doubted that. What the old *dryw* doesn't tell 'im, t' dreams do. You've known Rob only these past few seasons; I've known him since we were bairns, Arthur. I know when he's maddened on some hot scent."

"You're allus pushing it, Will. One of these days he'll answer yer challenge with more'n a clout upside that thick head of your'n."

The voices were soft, barely carrying past where they resided—another aged oak a stone's throw southward of the one Robyn occupied. Will Scathelock was less than happy with their intended quarry.

But then, Will had spent too much time hiding and keeping his head down. What spirit had moved him to hunt his mother's murderer had borne fat fruit, then withered for lack of light and direction.

"This is different, Arthur. 'Tis pure trouble, and you—"

"I can hear y' both, you know." Robyn pitched his voice just enough to carry to their tree.

Silence. Robyn could feel their eyes on him, but didn't take his own off the waterlogged road. A spray of water dappled the hood half covering his skull: tree-rain, always quixotic, building with the wet until weight or the wind unloaded a branch-full, usually when you were least expecting it.

And bloody *damn* but it had been a sodding long, wet and bitter winter. All of them were about as pleasant company as boar bears after hibernation; just as lean and hungry, trammelled too close for too long and just bloody brassed off.

They had begun these sorts of forays last spring. Obedient to Cernun's edict that they might be outlaws but they were not criminals, they had, until now, drawn the line at openly accosting travellers. There were other ways of warning intruders off their territory. Games and no more, well-timed and covert: an arrow through a cap here, traps laid there, delicate, drug-tipped bodkins shot merely to crease the skin and send the senses woozy, eerie sounds and balls of light and acrid smoke to foil the curious. Those games had been underlain with a grave purpose: Cernun's health was failing, had been since he began calling the rites and Robyn had made his first, faltering appearance at Summer Solstice. Everything had its price. The Horned Lord's chosen avatar, dead at the hands of his rival. Yet still, Hob-Robyn remained, a *dryw* who had walked the otherworld paths and come back to life with death-magic humming all crazed in his veins. The dark-cowled Green Man once more roamed the Wode.

And it was truth, all of it: the youth once known as Rob of Loxley had died. More than once he had hung, bound with bloody and tattered ropes to the Tree connecting the worlds, with the Horned Lord holding to him by the sheer, tensile fetter of his name and His Lady offering release.

If only. Robyn's lip curled into a half smile. *You truly didn't want me to take Her fine offer, eh? When have you ever sought release by a woman's touch? Touché,* as the Motherless Franks would say. Robyn's smile broadened. *Anyways, you en't finished with me yet. And neither are you, Hob-Robyn. Finished. This*—a soundless breath of approval, almost as if the Horned Lord scrutinised the terrain and their doings within it—*is more like it. No more hanging in the shadows like kicked dogs.*

Robyn snuffled a nigh-silent chuckle, considered the patter of rain on the leaves, then rotated his left shoulder in its socket. If he wasn't careful, it would stiffen up.

Games. The outlaws had moved farther north, none of them comfortable near the ruins of Loxley. Their relationship with the people here had begun cautiously, with trade. Game for crafted niceties such as bread and ale, a packet of beautifully fletched arrows for a measure of cloth to replace thin-worn tunics, furs and hides for grain and vegetables.

Then word had come, trickling along the byways and through the villages: things had changed. A king who had never truly held to his own kingdom now had even less reason to return. Richard, called Lionheart, was held prisoner in some far-off land, and a ransom demanded for his return.

One king were like to another as far as Robyn were concerned. Hang him from some foreign gallows and let the crows pick his bones, for all it mattered to a people winnowed of their homes and families.

But this had mattered, and brought hard change. The nobles were up in arms, jockeying for place and travelling the roads, flexing their muscles and making everyone's life miserable—including a motley group of outlaws who had fled fire and rapine to claim part of Barnsdale as their own.

On the wings of such change came the dreams: not in mists and possibilities, but realities razor-edged as any flail, merciless as any conqueror. Robyn had found his uncanny talents healing as his body had healed: scarred and not quite whole, powerful beneath the pain. And the wildness behind his eyes grew daily more unchancy, as if in dangerous tandem with a world that kept passing them by.

I did not keep you in thisworld to hide like a fawn in the thicket.

Aye, long past time the game should turn.

Several clicks and three dove calls came from upwind. Robyn alerted without thinking, plucking at his waxed bowstring. A lovely sound, the heavy strum and shudder, and the moisture shed with a spray of cool drops flung against his face. Almost as lovely as the sound of approaching hoofbeats. Eight horses, it sounded, and according to John's signal, only a quintet of guardsmen.

Even better. Lips curling again, decided and ruthless, Robyn pulled his hood forward to shadow his face.

Kept waiting.

He could see them, now, pushing through the mist. Wet, weary, and grim, even to the guards. The fore guards seemed somewhat alert, crossbows primed and shields slung ready. But the flank held their crossbows with little conviction; one even had it slung over his back. In their midst were four riders: the lord and his lady set apart by their well-bred palfreys and their tight-woven, expensive capes all trimmed with fur; their body servants, one an elder man and the other a girl, trailed on their own mounts.

Hopefully it was the retinue they sought. Robyn raised cupped hands to his mouth, blew a soft call: be ready.

The party drew abreast of their hiding place. As they did, a voice, seemingly from nowhere, ordered a halt.

The guardsmen leapt into action, surrounding their charges—but the hindmost ones were just that much too slow. Easy pickings. The rear guardsmen were flanked and fell to three grey-fletched arrows. The left front ended up with two arrows embedded in his shield, tried to return the favour and found he had no discernible targets.

"Show yourselves, villeins!" he bellowed.

"Whyever should we do that?" Another call wafted from the trees, and the remaining guards kept looking back and forth, trying to find its source. Robyn smiled. He knew exactly where Gilbert hid; could see him, in fact, right next to the gorse bush across the way, behind a nocked and held arrow. Gilbert was almost as canny with a longbow as Robyn himself; it had been Gilbert and John who'd levelled the odds by dispatching those extra guards.

"Drop your weapons," Arthur ordered. He had shinnied down to the gnarled, exposed roots of the tree he'd been perched in, nigh invisible. He could no longer shoot a bow, but his one remaining arm was murder with stave or axe. "You've no chance."

The guards kept trying to find targets. They were having little success; the heavy mists caught sound and held it, spitting it out far from its origins.

The head nobleman yanked back his cowl, spurred his horse forward and unsheathed his sword. It was not quite the shock Robyn had thought it might be; the man had changed but little.

It would be sweet, to see this one crawl.

"I am Sir Johan, mesne lord of Blyth and Tickhill by grant of the king!" the nobleman barked. "Whoever you are, I demand you let us go on unhampered!"

"You're in *our* forest, lordling," Robyn growled from his tree perch. "Are we supposed to be impressed—other than with your stupidity?"

The mesne lord of Blyth puffed up like a threatened goose. Robyn could feel Will's eyes on him, uncertain.

Robyn didn't let him founder in it. "Stupid," he confirmed to their quarry, throwing a grin to Will. "How is it other than daft t' tell me how important you are? I might fancy a ransom from your sainted hide."

"You wouldn't *dare!*" This protest, from the lead soldier, squeaked into silence as Robyn loosed his arrow and it imbedded, quivering, into the curve of the crossbow. The guard's hand jerked and the crossbow disengaged, the bolt flying wild into the mists. One of the women gave a small shriek.

"You've no idea, lordling," Robyn drawled, nocking a second arrow, "what I will and wain't do."

Neither did Johan back down. "*Un chien Anglais.* You'd think to lay claim to what is not yours, like all your kind."

"I'd say Franks are more the dogs!" Gilbert called. "Pissing on our territory!"

"We have women with us!" the fore guard protested. "None but a coward would threaten women!"

Robyn smiled and yanked the hood farther over his face, relaxed the push on his bow.

Leapt down.

"*Rob!*" Will never liked it when Robyn went off-plan—unfathomable, that, for Will should bloody well be used to it by now.

Robyn didn't answer. Instead, he sauntered onto the road. There was a rustle and shuffle, then a thud—only one of their own could have heard it—as Will hastened down to cover his leader's unprotected flank. And all about them, the sounds of damp strings creaking into full nock.

"Damn it, *Rob!*" Will's hissed rebuke was muffled by the scarf he'd pulled up to cover half his face.

Their adversaries were as surprised as Robyn's own men by what had occurred. Outlaws did not waltz into the middle of a wide-open road. They did *not.*

"I en't the least interested in your womenfolk, man." Robyn hid the snarl that wanted to curl his lips by pitching his voice mild, almost chiding. "I'm wanting information."

"Information." Johan, still flummoxed, had recovered enough to attempt to see his adversary. Between the mists and the shadowed dark of Robyn's cowl, he seemed to be having little luck.

One of the women wasn't so brave: she took one look at the lethal figures and crossed herself. The other woman—obviously her mistress—stayed still and shocked, much as the other two guards. The elder body servant had drawn up next to his lord, hand on dagger, more bravado than any real threat.

"Blyth, you say." Again, Robyn gave a soft, careless drawl to the words, though every sensation he possessed hummed and whirled. The Horned Lord's hot breath on his nape. The magic, waiting.

Take him. I have brought you to him, as I promised. Take him down.

Robyn bade it wait. "How fare your brothers, milord of Blyth?"

"My . . . brothers?" Johan's face twisted from anger to puzzlement. "I have a brother who is seneschal to my lands . . . and will see I am avenged, should I not return," he added.

Robyn raised his bow, aimed the bodkin at Johan's ribs. "I were understanding, milord, that you'd two brothers. And two powerful cousins—one as sheriff to our fair shire, and another who bides as abbess to Worksop Abbey."

Will let out a nigh-silent hiss; the emotion of the breath merely fed into the magics humming in Robyn's skull.

"What would you want of Abbess Elisabeth?" the noblewoman demanded.

Johan shot her a quieting look. "You've indeed been too long in the forest, *Anglais*, growing mould in your brain, to ask such things. Old news matters little, yet why should I tell you a damned thing?"

"Nay, stand down," Will uttered by Robyn's right shoulder. "I wouldn't, was I you." This to the lead guard who'd inched his crossbow toward Robyn.

"Take his advice, man. And as for you, *Frank*." Robyn stretched his bow tighter, smiling as it spoke to him with a soft groan. "I'd advise t' answer m' questions."

Johan stiffened.

"I can shoot your horse out from under you quicker than you can spit. In fact," Robyn raised his aim, slow and sure, directly between Johan's eyes, "I could shoot *you*, easy as that. And the beauty of it all? You'd never know why."

Aye, kill him. Is it not why we're here?

"Robyn." Will's voice was a warning, the only sound drifting through the tension. Robyn's faulty shoulder gave a stab and tremble, as if in response, but he didn't take his eyes off Johan, a bloody haze drifting through his mind.

"Answer me, Frankish dog. What news of the Sheriff? Or of the third brother and the cousin?"

Johan looked set to not answer, his offence at being held in the sights of a wolfshead trumping any sense, it seemed. Part of Robyn frankly hoped he wouldn't see sense, just for the excuse of watching his expression when Robyn did drop him off that fine palfrey.

The Horned Lord, also, seemed eager for excuses. *Would his pain not bid the night mare gallop softer through your mind? Is it not what you want? The blood of those who betrayed you?*

Again, Robyn's shoulder gave a quiver. Johan paled, obviously taking it for further threat.

"Oh, God!" the maidservant blurted. "Save us, he's *mad!*"

"Shut *up*, Winifred!" the noblewoman hissed.

"We have money!" Winifred was little more than a girl. "Milady, if you'd jus' give 'im the money, mebbe he'd let us go!"

Listen to the child. This one is not yours, Hob-Robyn.

This presence, lighter yet of a feminine steel that held none of the mercy it evoked, was one he had not heard in . . .

The scythe that shall reap him must wait for another's hand, another's right—and when the blood-heat has cooled, My Consort will know the truth of it. Revenge is sweet, but Mercy can give its own pain, collect its own rewards, after all.

Robyn hesitated. As if waiting for just that fragment of uncertainty, his shoulder stabbed and sent a painful spasm down his arm. Robyn gave a filthy curse as the arrow loosed and sang; its passing merely whiffled and snatched at the fur collar of Johan's cape, took out a patch of leaves, and disappeared into the dense growth on the far side of the road.

Bloody *fucking* damn.

Johan tottered sideways in his saddle, caught himself in belated understanding; he had not, after all, been hit.

"Milady" turned and swung her riding crop at Winifred. The maidservant shrieked as it impacted with a crack.

A second's distraction—but enough for the left fore guard to swing his crossbow about to aim at Robyn. Instead he jerked and fell forward, one of Gilbert's arrows through his throat. The remaining guard was cursing at his crossbow, still fouled by Robyn's first arrow. The body servant gave protest as Johan spurred his horse forward. As one, Robyn and Will split to let him pass. Arthur came running up, axe in hand, forcing Johan to haul on the reins and bounce to a halt.

"Come then, 'milord'. I'm a good Saxon," Arthur growled, wielding his axe. "And we love horsemeat."

"Enough!" Robyn had taken another arrow from his hair, nocked it lightly. His gaze still fixed on Johan, but the heat of it had been broken.

Broken by Her voice, one he'd thought never to hear again. The Lady had always been Marion's possession.

It stabbed him, worse than his brittle shoulder tendons, unclean and raw as a dagger left in a maggoty wound. He sank his teeth into his tongue, bidding grief and Voice both begone, just for the little while.

"Mayhap," Robyn's words were slow, considering. "Mayhap all we're needing is our own tax, after all."

"A *tax—*"

Arthur threatened with the axe once more. "Aye, and wouldn't *your* like tax us t' death?"

"You . . . poacher!" the noblewoman spat.

"Shut your face, bitch," Arthur warned her.

"*Enough!*" Robyn turned to Johan. "So, milord? The information?"

"Not that it matters," Johan spat, "but Sheriff de Lisle has been granted reeveship of Derby and Nottingham as well as York. As to the youngest of my brothers, he went on Crusade and I have not heard of him since! And the Reverend Lady is away far south, travelling on God's business, no doubt, and out of *your* foul reach, villein! Now, *release us.*"

Mercy, for a traitor? A murderer? The Horned Lord again, hot with bloodlust. The Lady was gone. *There is none in him, give him none. Kill him.*

Instead, Robyn relaxed his nock. Cocking his head, he ambled closer to the noblewoman. "So. This money. It's your dowry, is it?"

She started as if he'd pulled bedchamber secrets from her brain and stared down at him. The maidservant was still whimpering. The remaining soldier fumed, helpless as Johan.

"The question is, milady," Robyn continued, soft, "do you value yon coin more than your husband-to-be?"

"*You'll* regret this, I promise you." This from Johan, despite the proximity of Arthur's axe to his horse's neck.

Aye, you will. This will not end today unless you end it.

Will gave a grumble, and it sounded closer to Johan's agreement than the Horned Lord's.

"Oh, I regret," Robyn murmured, an abrupt singsong to still the magic dancing mad along his nerves. "But not as you will. You're the one who'll truly regret. You're the one who'll lie awake nights, wondering why. You'll find no solace, wine or woman, and your dam's blood will be the death of you."

Silence fell as the last echoed, breath grounding into promise, one Robyn could feel settling around them. The maidservant began praying again, throttling it with a whimper as her mistress threatened her again.

Johan's momentary unease at the words was reverting back to humiliated fury. "I refuse to give ground to a prattling, hooded bastard of an *Anglais!* At least have the stomach to show your face!"

"I've the stomach," Robyn snarled, and tossed his hood back. "Have *you?*"

Johan frowned. He plainly recognised something about Robyn, but he just as obviously couldn't place it—even though he clearly wanted to.

"Let me guess, we all look alike t' you?" Robyn had to laugh, even if it stung a bit. "Well, I'll confess the like, man, since you all smell of money t' me. John, find the marks for us, aye?"

As John seemed to appear out of thin air—though he'd merely been crouched all the while behind a bush with bow at nock—the maidservant's praying grew louder.

"You en't told me how much you value this man of yours, milady." As the noblewoman started to reply, Robyn shrugged and turned to Johan. "I'll not stoop to such tactics as your like, t' have a woman watch her man killed before her. 'Tis a dog's tactic, indeed."

On the other side of the two women, John was rummaging through packs. He shot a huge-eyed glance at Robyn. Robyn smirked in pure triumph.

"My lord!" the noblewoman burst out to Johan. "*Do* something!"

Not that His Lordship could do anything other than utter a string of curses, with Arthur's axe on one side and Will's longbow on the other.

"Marry the sod quick, lass," Robyn said, sibilant and sweet, to the noblewoman. "I think you're surely deservin' each other."

"You knew who it were."

Robyn threw up his hands and stalked to the other side of the fire. He nearly trod on Gilbert, intent on counting; instead he stumbled upon the silver marks piling onto Gilbert's woollen cape. They went scattering.

"Hoy!" Gilbert barked. "Have a care, man!"

Robyn merely snarled and kept going.

"All along, you *knew!*" Will insisted, striding after him. "And you never told us a damned thing. *Rob,* answer me!"

Robyn whirled on him. "I knew, aye, some but not the whole of it! It were a *dream*, Will. Would you—would *any* of you?—believe a dream?"

John was shaking his head, bending down to help Gilbert retrieve the scattered coinage. On the far side, Arthur sharpened his axe with brows drawn in an uneasy frown. Will seemed gobsmacked for a few seconds.

"Bloody damn, Robyn, d'you think there's a one of us as don't know you . . . well, you *see* things?"

"Then why d'you keep at me? If y' know what I See, then why're you always at m' heels—"

"Ach, Will, let it go!" Arthur said. "It went well enough."

"Well enough, for all of us having no idea what Rob were doin' and him saunterin' onto the road like he bloody sodding *owned* it—"

"Well, we do own it, and 'tis time they knew it!" Robyn snapped.

"They know, all right. They know they saw the outlaws who have, 'til *now*, been mostly unbothered in Barnsdale. And more, they saw their leader! 'Twere absolutely sodding mad, showin' your face!"

Robyn, primed for a retort, lost what wind he'd gathered. But only for the moment. "All right, he got t' me! The Motherless scum what had t' do with destroying m' family *got* to me, and if I wanted to rub his nose in it, surely you'll forgive me t' lapse! Not that *I* fetched any pleasure from it. All he saw were a pack of wolves, nowt more!"

"You knew who he were, and you were going to kill him. That's what you meant t' do. *Kill* him, and you weren't thinkin' it necessary to *tell* us? Threatening a noble, fer fuck's sake—have y' lost what mind y' have left?"

And that last stuck in the back of Robyn's throat, anger loosing the choke hold of injury. "And y' dare ask me why I didn't tell you? You dare ask me to explain when I bloody well canna?" How *to* explain; how to make plain a tangle oft not unravelled until he was in the moment, in the thick of it?

"Bloody *damn*, Rob, what if you had killed him?"

"Then we would have let the wolves have him."

"And the women?"

"Were part of why I laid the *geas* upon him and didn't kill him!"

Will grabbed at Robyn's hair, pulled him close, eyed him. "You're tryin' to get 'round me."

Nay, I'm going right through you, like a ghost, and I'm not even trying any more than you can see where I've been.

"I also know," Will said, subdued but stubborn, "what killin' that one would mean to you. Not to the Horned Lord, not to Robyn Hode, but to *you*, Rob o' Loxley."

"You say 't, Will Scathelock," Robyn murmured against Will's ear, "like you think there's a difference."

Will met his eyes, an uncertain frown quirking his brow.

"Things have to change, Scathelock." Robyn pushed back, turned from Will to sweep a quick gaze over all of them. "Do you *want* to hide in the Wode forever?"

"What else is there?" Arthur said, ever pragmatic.

One side of Robyn's mouth curled up, and he gestured to the pile of coins between John and Gilbert. "Tell me. Truthfully." He walked over and tapped at Arthur's chest. "Tell me how *good* it felt to twist their tails."

Arthur started to grin.

"Rob, 'twill—"

"Tell me, then." Rob turned on Will. "Tell me it *weren't* just short of lovely, grindin' them into the dirt."

Clearly despite himself, Will chuckled.

"Aye. Our like are worked to death, fed rubbish, and all we're doin' is offering bits and pieces to 'em, accepting offering like fae spirits—"

"We are fae, to these people," Will pointed out. "You're the god's face, his spirit. And that en't *enough* for you?"

"'Twill never be enough while we're nowt t' ones in power. The Horned Lord has waited long enough. His shade bided quiet, *tynged* soft as old wool in th' loom, wrapping some about me da and more tightly within Cernun, hopin' for peace. And since then, all the good it's done is let t' nobles rape our land, break our backs and bleed us dry!" Robyn knew his words were tangling but didn't care, threw his hands wide. "They're claimin' our sweet, wild Wode as theirs, think to cordon 'er—*tame* 'er!—with fire and steel. And all the while they cobble up more laws to banish us from her depths. They trammel our . . . our *spirits*, more and more, under t' barren stones of their bloody churches, by their taking of *our* sacred places, *our* hallowed things. They call *us* evil . . . 'pagans' and 'demons' for their church to curse at and pray away—and all the while we're *letting* 'em! Letting those sodding prayers have power over us, lettin' 'em *take*, an' all so they can whip us, chain us to their plough, cage us in the dark and burn . . . " His voice choked; he finished it, all too soft. " . . . burn our homes." Silence.

"Well, bugger that. I'm done crawling. 'Tis time we *fought back*."

Still the silence, hanging heavy about the spare camp, all of them in their own ways chewing it over, thinking.

"Robyn," Gilbert ventured, slowly. "What are we to *do* with all this?"

They turned to where he was seated, John across from him, and a hand-high pile of silver.

"I mean, it's a great deal of money. What are we to do with it?"

"Aye, right enough." Will knelt down, scooped up a handful and let it fall, then smirked. "More than even *you* could lose at knucklebones, Hob-Robyn."

Gilbert gave a loud howl of laughter—a bit too loud, as far as Robyn was concerned—but when the rest joined the mirth, Robyn gave a lopsided smile and a small bow, acknowledging the well-aimed jab.

"Well, 'tis a fair question." Arthur shrugged, going back to sharpening his axe. "If we're to be takin' on the business of beggaring those buggers, we can't exactly spend our pelf without more notice than even *you're* wanting, Robyn."

"Mm," Robyn agreed, pacing to the camp's edge and back. "You say beggaring."

Will gave a mighty groan and put his head in his hands. "Aw, *blight* me but when you get such a gleam in your eye, it allus means trouble."

John rolled his eyes and gave Will a shove, rolling him onto his back.

Gilbert was watching Robyn pace, a light kindling in his eyes. "If you're thinking what I am, 'twould be—"

"Proper sodding revenge, sure enough."

"Would one o' you lads kindly explain it to some of us as en't following?" Will protested.

Robyn nodded at Gilbert, whose grin was broadening by the minute. "Mayhap we should help our lot pay their taxes, eh?"

And Gilbert reached down, took up a doubled handful of the coins, and let them cascade back onto the blanket.

Robyn had watch, that night, and he was grateful for it.

The rain had finally ceased. Some distance from where they'd made camp, he'd found a likely perch: a crook in an elm, low enough for a nice, thick seat, high enough to keep suitable watch. Robyn had been there since night had fallen, watching the patch of sky above tear itself from sullen grey into swatches punctuated by stars. He had unlaced his tunic beneath the cover of his cloak, was alternately rotating his left shoulder and giving a steady pressure against the muscle beneath his collarbone. The damp always made it ache something fierce; the day's activities had merely made it worse. Not so necessary to hold a continuous bead on four-legged quarry.

They had retreated to a camp well-hidden, one of their favourites, a hollow deep in a copse of elm and black poplar a half hour's stroll south of Wakefield. Robyn could see the fur-covered mounds of his men, asleep around the steady, reassuring glow of a fire stoked to warm coals. A frown drew at his brows. Only three, where there should be four?

Ah, the fourth made an approach, the identity immediately apparent by the lightness of his step. Robyn looked down and met John's brown eyes, kept rotating his shoulder in the socket as John climbed up, crouched beside him. Immediately he reached out, stroked at Robyn's shoulder, running his fingers forward and down to the deep hollow there, and the thick knotting of scar tissue beneath. Gave Robyn a serious look beneath quirked eyebrows.

"'Tis not likely to get stronger if I coddle it overmuch." Robyn tried to shrug away as John pulled first his cloak then his tunic away from the aggravated shoulder, instead halted midmotion as John layered on a thick cloth, still warm from the firestones. Robyn gave a grateful sigh as the heat penetrated.

It had been the most gruelling, humiliating months of his life, learning to draw right-handed. He still wasn't even a fifth of the archer he'd once been, the bow he carried more suited to a boy of ten. He couldn't even contemplate trying to draw the old Welsh longbow his mam's da had left him.

Well, he were lucky to even be alive, let alone pushing a bow.

But he wouldn't let it break him, wouldn't lose this as well. He kept after it, fixated as a hound on the hunt. If Arthur could pick up things with the elbow bend of his stump, then Robyn would reclaim his left draw.

His archer's heart also refused death.

"You missed," John murmured, slow and . . . chiding?

John had his own reasons to want the lord of Blyth dead. Johan Boundys had been the one to put a price on John's head for aiding Gamelyn's escape on that long-ago Beltane.

Robyn looked away. John nestled closer and touched his lips to Robyn's temple, lingered there. *No blame*, it said without words. But the question remained: *Why?*

"I do miss, y' know. More than I should, what with *this*."

John laid his cheek against Robyn's shoulder. Robyn gripped

him close, too many tangled emotions clutching at his heart to even pick a one.

"He were marked, John. The Horned Lord breathed his name into the void, and it were my right. My *right*, and in the hot breath of the moment, I wanted him dead . . ." Robyn trailed off. "But the Lady spoke to me."

John tensed, looked up at him.

"Aye. She doesn't much care for me, that we both know, and She's been long silent, but She spoke, sure enough. She said Blyth's lord weren't . . . mine."

"The *geas?*"

"Washed through me like water from a hidden spring. It were what I had to do, of Her . . . bloody, damn, John, I can scarce hold t' the god's horns! Now I'm to be tangled in *Her* hair as well?"

John's answer came much as always: more kisses, touches growing intimate, then insistent. Unfortunately Robyn was hurting too badly, too distracted and spent with his own thoughts to be cozened. After a few tries, John gave a frown and an aggrieved sigh, gave it up.

"'M sorry," Robyn whispered.

John knew better than most what toll magic's workings took. What had come from such a deep place as the *geas* was no miniscule hex-breath. He shrugged and gave another kiss to Robyn's temple, settled for kneading Robyn's shoulder. For John, some form of touch was better than none.

Sometimes it overwhelmed. Tonight, it comforted.

"We canna kill all of 'em," Robyn said finally. "But we can castrate 'em. 'Tis a fair deal t' make with our devils, John, 'til we're strong enough to blood them."

A frown quirked at John's brow.

"Oh, aye," Robyn vowed. "We'll blood 'em all right. We wain't kill Blyth's lord, but we'll run ruin over him. The Sheriff will know of us before we're done. And we'll have the Black Abbess anon. But there's work on the way."

- II -

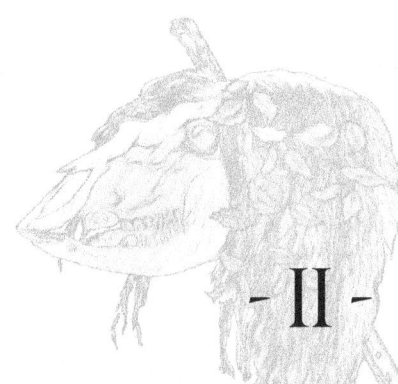

*Near Damascus, in the
Crusader States of Outremer
March of 1193 CE*

What is truth?
   Truth comes to him in dreams . . . nightmares. Truth is hinted at in a faint whiff of sea and brine, rendered more in full by the towering cliffs of rock and sand about him. The high walls of the city hold a reek of primal details: bodies hot-dank with adrenaline and fear, hearths left to gutter and smoke, torches spitting in the moist grip of gaolers. Of twenty-seven hundred human beings, shackled and herded like cattle in the courtyards below.

   They must die. Richard, anointed by God King of England, has given the order and Grand Master Robert de Sablé has bound his Templars one and all to it. The prisoners are hostage to Saladin's promise of surrender, and that promise has been broken.

   The breach hits close: the shield brother of Gamelyn's master is prisoner to Saladin, and hasn't been returned as promised. Yet . . .

   Just as strong as outrage, unease flickers though the ranks. These are prisoners, not fighting soldiers. There are men, aye. But also women. *Children.*

   This is not homicide, the priests insist, invoke forgiveness upon them: *it is malecide, the destruction of evil. It is not mortal sin, not*

murder. Demons must die. We are killing for Christ. This is the truth you must carry with you.
  Truth? What is truth?
  While Gamelyn's heart would weight him, his horror would stay him, when the prisoners turn upon their gaolers, fighting for their lives, years of relentless training do as they were designed. Another, more primal force is unleashed: the berserker blood-rage of his matriarchal Saxon forebears sucks Gamelyn within a mindless, merciful current, leaving nothing but the truth of that fury. Of the fight. Of *survival.*
  After it is over, after thousands have been executed, after Death has taken him by the throat, shaken then tossed him aside, Gamelyn drops his sword and walks into the sea. The wages of this not-sin are all over him: blood sinking into his pores, bits of grume beneath his fingernails, more blood soaking his newly bestowed white habit to nigh black, and spiking his short-cropped hair from ginger to crimson. It will not wash off. The coastal waters, once clean and sparkling, are clotted with gore. Bits of hacked-up limbs and entrails dip with deceptive gentleness alongside floating bodies; hair and clothes clinging thick with brine and brack. It seems never-ending, a perverted and rust-coloured foam swelling with the tide as the sun sets upon Acre.
  The destruction of evil is not murder. . .
  Gamelyn's eyes roll upward in his head. He lists sideways, topples forward into the water.
  But, nay. No way out there.
  A hand grabs him by the scruff of his tunic, yanks him up. A strong arm wraps around his ribcage and he spews copper-salt water from his lungs and down his front. It burns his throat, burns truth to cinders beneath the eye of a bloody sun.
  With the brusque flight of dreamings, truth has . . . changed.
  Not scarlet blood in the water, not water, not any longer. Flames. Flames in the dark, and green in his still water-logged nostrils, and Gamelyn no longer seeks cleansing in the bay of Outremer, but brings corruption to a burning forest.
  The burning of Loxley village. The strong arm is still about him, with two others holding his arms in some bizarre mockery of crucifixion—for he is being crucified, flayed from the inside out by what they are forcing him to witness. The body floating before him, black robes swirled in blood, becomes an abbess kneeling on the woodland floor, her fingers clutched in black hair. Rob's head hangs from her grip, eyes open: sightless, ebon reflections in the flames of what was once Rob's home.

"*God has punished him. Pagan filth, as unnatural a beast as you, who would rut with boys and demons. This is truth, Gamelyn. This is how demons die."*
Demons must die.
What is truth, Gamelyn?
And it all sucks away into the sunset, leaving him struggling in the warm, blood-filled water, fighting his companion's fierce hold. There is only the sand and the thick brack of blood filling his mouth, and nothing but his name, over and over, humming in his ears and fading into the screams of the dying and the injured. There is no cleansing to be had. No absolution. No *truth*.
Aye, and what is truth?
It is not possible, but Rob bends over, nuzzling his ear, alive and real. Impossibly *there*, with him, in the bed. *There is no truth but this: you are mine. Mine, and it's past time to come home, Gamelyn.*

◯

Jolting upright, one hand instinctively curling about the graceful curve of the dagger always—*always*—beneath his pillow, he saw the dark head nestled into the bedding beside him and wondered if it had all been some horrific nightmare.

Yet dry air pinched at his nostrils. There was the dull flap and flutter of tent fabric in a gust of hot wind and, as he licked dry lips, there was the grit of sand in molars that no amount of liquid could rinse out. He smelt and felt the heat-sweat skimming his bare skin.

Dreams were death.
This was truth.

Beside him, his companion turned over. The eyes sliding his way were ink-dark, but they contained no insolence. The boy's skin wasn't pale and freckled, but dusky as almonds, and his manner contained all the deliberate courtesy his race tendered the *Ifranji*—the Franks.

No blame to them, if they hid a shiv beneath it.
"Is everything all right, Master Templar?"
He didn't answer, kicked the light linens from him and rolled to his feet.
"Master?"
Once there had been some pretence, at least, of engagement; now it was one more lie cozening the night, and unbearable in harsh sunlight. They were all liars. All whores. The boys he

sometimes took to his bed; the priests with their blood-soaked endorsements of slaughter as salvation; the king who had proven no less a soulless murderer than himself.

Aye, himself. No less the whore and certainly no less the liar. Even his name was not his own, taken when he'd staggered from the bloodstained coastal waters of Acre and made a new penance, a new vow: not God's, but his own.

Yet that last was no lie. Gamelyn Boundys had indeed drowned, a newly belted Templar Knight overpowered by the stinking rot of too many flung-aside corpses.

Pathetic innocent, to think to find absolution on Crusade.

Guy de Gisbourne knew better.

Behind him, the boy-whore was making quick work of clothing himself. Ducking as Guy flung a wadded-up kerchief at him, nevertheless the boy caught it with the reflexes of a town pickpocket. Concern turned to a smile when the boy saw what tender of coin had been twisted in the fabric. He broke into a soft babble of Arabic. "*May all the blessings of the prophet be upon you, and your sons, and your sons' sons—*"

Guy interrupted him with a polite response—also in Arabic. Curtness was one thing, but it was never a good idea to insult a Saracen, even a whore. He jerked his head and repeated, "*Out.*"

As the boy made a speedy and discreet exit beneath the back tent flap—amusing, the pretence, seeing as how his ilk serviced half the Templars and a goodly share of the Hospitallers as well—Guy stepped into thin cotton braies. Taking note of the still-empty cot on the other side of the small tent, he padded barefoot over to the entry and flung it back to greet the morning.

Nothing less than a boiling caldera, the landscape beyond, bubbling from sand and rock and a scorching spume of reflected, undying sun. It greeted his eyes, harsh and bright enough to make them water and his skin once again remember the sick-making fire of those first weeks, spent in days upon days of horrific sunburn. Blood spilled upon this earth—if it could truly be called earth—quickly baked into a congealed sludge. Taking a piss sent steam rising from the flat, rocky pan as soon as the stream hit the ground. Some distance northeast, past the mountains of the Jabal ar Ruwaq and into the Hamad desert, drifts of sand could sink the legs as insistently as water, a quarter mile of it like five miles over solid turf. Horses or camels were the best transportation. The air here lay thick as any blanket— not soft with moisture and green, but with a harsh, gristly heat that scraped at the lungs, set up residence and seeped out the pores in a thin, never-ending sweat.

It was hell, no question.

No question but he deserved every second of it.

And God!—he'd not had a nightmare like this in a very long time.

"*Confanonier?*"

No doubt such foul dreams had been brought on by the contemplations of his commander. Denied Jerusalem, Hubert had but yesterday confessed to a wish to return home. And so his faithful second must follow, an imp kicked out of hell to return and wreak havoc upon mankind.

"*Confanonier?* Sir Guy?"

Guy tilted his head, looked to the young squire approaching, hesitant.

Of course the squire was hesitant. A *Confanonier* was the standard bearer and whip hand of their Master and Commander. He had the power of life and death over the squires and horses in his charge. *Confanonier* de Gisbourne had come to his place through the killing of the one before him. Or so it was said.

This squire was too new to remember any realities of why Guy had sent to hell the murderous little swine who had been his predecessor. Just as well. It was merely common sense to fear and mistrust one who had such control over your life.

"What is it?"

"The Commander would have you break your fast with him, milord *Confanonier*. Right away."

Guy nodded. As the squire made a swift retreat, Guy knelt in the harsh sunlight and bowed his head.

The regular soldiers and people surrounding them thought it prayer. The Saracens of Alamut thought him either a promising infidel or a practitioner of *sihr*, the sorcery of the red and black *djinn*. The Templar squires and servants—even some of his fellow knights—thought him devout and, therefore, dangerous.

The last held, perhaps, the most of any truth. As to the rest, he was merely the servant of destiny, and destiny's mask oft worn by the Master of the Chastellet stronghold, Hubert de Gisborough.

Guy looked up to find a familiar figure standing beside him with an also-familiar, considerable patience. Much's head-covering, protection against the relentless sun, darkened his face further— save for several thick scars running from temple to jaw and down into the *keffiyeh*'s wrap about his neck. With that, and the two fresh-filled water jugs slung over his beefy shoulders, the Saxon peasant looked nearly more Saracen than the whore who'd but recently vacated Guy's tent. Much's eyes even had the deceptively mild cant to them, and if they were light-coloured, well, Guy had seen many a Saracen with lighter ones.

He and Much had come across each other on Cyprus quite by accident—or perhaps not, since Much had fled the same set of circumstances at Blyth, and to his only option as well: Crusade. It had not been overly complicated to see to a reassignment to the Commander's service. Some favours had been owed.

"Where did you sleep, Much?"

"I had guard duty, milord. Just as well, I thought."

That was as close a mention as Much ever came to Guy's business. In fact, Much commented little on his master's business, often aided Guy's minimal penchants, be they for dark-haired boys or the bubble pipe.

Guy rose. "I shan't be joining our brethren at breakfast this morning."

"Aye, milord, I heard." Much went over to his own cot and unloaded the jugs on a table beside it. Guy watched as Much began the familiar ritual of opening the trunk and laying out gear, preparing his lord for an important conference. "The horses are well this morning. Diamant needs a good run."

Not for the first time, Guy marvelled at how Diamant refused to stay down when he was felled. The grey stallion had almost as many battle-scars as Guy himself.

"Talk's all over camp how Himself has orders from on high. It's hoped we'll be going home anon."

It's time to come home now, Gamelyn.

Guy tottered slightly, reached out and gripped a tent pole.

Much started forward, eyebrows drawing together. "Are y' all right, milord?"

Guy shook his head, dismayed. "I . . . didn't sleep well."

"Th' dreams again?"

Guy shrugged, released the pole. He turned from the door and meandered over to where Much was shaking sand from several tabards.

Good luck with that.

"Y' en't the only one, milord. I've had nightmares passing understanding for several nights. There are many as hoped they could walk the holy streets 'afore we left, seek forgiveness there." Much shrugged. "It en't right, they should ban only us."

Even two years ago such a statement would have flared outrage in Guy's breast, prompted a like response.

Now, he was just very tired.

"Salah ah-Din does not trust Templars any more than he trusts the troops of *hashishin* the Old Man sends down from Alamut to treat with us." Guy pulled on his linen tunic, stained with sand and sweat. "And Salah al-Din is no fool—why turn your back on a venomous snake? Here we sit in the wake of Lionheart's Crusade, privy to the front line of his slaughters but with our own, tangled agenda and no less intent upon our goals than any Saracen bowing toward Mecca. We fight where we are directed and kill as we are ordered to kill, all at God's bidding and the only slightly lesser commandments of our Grand Master."

Much grunted—his preferred response when his own master lapsed into the rhetoric of cynicism—and remained silent as he helped Guy pull the black tabard over his thin tunic. He set to straightening the crimson cross upon Guy's breast, then with equal care placed the belts: two of them, one slung at the hip to hold the long, curved falchion in its leather scabbard, the other at the waist.

"'Tis too much for the likes of me, such thinking," Much finally said. "I would've liked to see a holy city, but I'll be glad to go back home to me own gods. An' begging your pardon, milord, but I should think 'twould be better for you as well." Much ventured this with no little caution and a good deal of reverence.

Of course, Much didn't know all of it.

"I'm not sure we deserve to return home, Much." Guy held out his forearms as Much tightened the lacings on his boiled leather vambraces. "Any more than any of us deserve to enter Jerusalem."

"I'm not sure deservin's the word I'd use," Much replied, quiet. "But we sure don't belong *here*."

◯

"You en't welcome here, Robyn Hode."

A tense affair, approaching anything resembling civilisation, with the outlaws at all times wary for soldiers, or clergy, or anything, truly, that seemed abnormal or dodgy. And it if wasn't exactly abnormal for Huddersfield's village headman to be waiting for them at the outskirts with a small group of his cronies, neither was it customary.

But this?

Robyn came to an uncertain halt. His four companions gathered close behind him, also unsure. They knew the headman, of course, but didn't interact much with him—usually they dealt with the village's cunning-woman, Marget, for herbs and simples and the like.

"What's this about, then?" Will protested.

"It's about harbouring outlaws," one of the other men said.

"An' what Sheriff's promised will come t' those as does," the headman stated.

"I don't understand," Robyn said, frowning. "You've welcomed us—"

"Aye, let you share our bread and ale and all we've t' show for it is soldiers breathin' down our necks!" another of the villagers protested.

"All to... show?" Robyn repeated it, sure any moment someone would correct him, say it had all been a big mistake. Something.

John peered at him, brown eyes puzzled. Robyn peered back, then at Will, Gilbert, and Arthur. All of them, fairly gobsmacked, and no less than he himself. For the first in some time, he wasn't sure what to do.

Save make the protest, "You've had plenty to show. We've brought game—"

"The king's deer!" the headman shot back. "If we're caught wi't—"

"Not just deer!" Will growled. "We paid your bloody tithes last quarter. We've helped you more than the once."

"That were before" was the stolid insistence. "It's en't just the soldiers, neither, but the priest. He says th' bishop's up in arms for what you've done t' him, and will excommunicate any who truck wi' pagans."

John bristled.

Robyn started for his dagger, forced his hand to relax. "Funny, that," he growled. "I seem to recall a few of this village enjoying the last fête of Beltane."

"And we're feeling God's wrath for 't. 'Tis one thing to mind t' old ways, another to—" The speaker broke off as another elbowed him.

"It's done, Robyn Hode," the headman insisted. "Y' should consider yourselves lucky we're giving you the chance to leave, and not turn ye all in for the price on yer heads!"

"I'd like t' see y' try it." Arthur stepped forward, scowling, his hand on the axe at his belt.

The huddle of villagers stepped back, muttering. The face-off was no less on edge for their fear, however.

Fear would make even a sane man do something mad.

"So it's come to this, has it?" Robyn broke the silence. His words were soft, almost monotone.

The headman refused to meet his eye. "That's the way it is. You need to clear off. Now. I wain't be responsible for what happens if you don't."

"What will happen," Robyn said, "is nowt. Don't 'spect Huddersfield'll be heard should any of you cry out."

Then he spun around and started walking, didn't stop even after he reached the sparse tree line past the fields.

The others followed quickly enough, murmuring amongst themselves. Robyn said nothing. The others weren't so shocked silent, was all he could fathom.

Even if he wasn't exactly sure *why* he felt so shocked. Surely it shouldn't be so . . . unexpected. Like a slap in the face, or a gobbet of spit hawked at one's boots.

They were fearful.

Yet, still. This felt too akin to betrayal.

"Bloody . . . ungrateful . . . *serfs*!" Arthur spat as they went deeper into the trees, bold agreement with Robyn's whirling thoughts.

"You were a serf," Gilbert reminded—and ducked as Arthur grabbed an arrow from his quiver and swung the nock end at him. "Hoy, mind the fletching! I just mended that!"

"Damned cowards, the lot of 'em!" Will sneered.

"Robyn!"

The voice, breathless and hushed, made them whirl and grip at their weaponry. It was Marget, face flushed and grey hair unbound, shawl flapping behind her.

"Robyn, please. It en't all of us."

"'Twas enough," Gilbert pointed out. "None bothered to speak up. Not even you."

"'Tis hard done to go agin me whole village. They're good folk—"

"Aye, and we're seein' the good in 'em the now," Arthur snapped.

"They're fearful, nowt else," Marget said, and held out a bag. "What I promised t' you."

Robyn shook his head. "We'll take nowt from your village again."

"I *want* you t' take it, Robyn." Marget kept holding the bag out. "It en't so easy, what's happening in the villages. Granted, I c'n go me own way sommat, but the new priest is a right single-minded bastard, and the soldiers have hard orders. You've made some powerful people angry of late."

"So 'twere well when we just were playing games?" Will snapped.

"En't no game anymore, lad," she chided. "Surely you knew that when you started poking the bear."

"We take t' consequences, every day!" Will retorted.

"Nay," Robyn said, soft, peering at Marget. "We aren't tied down. We can vanish, into thin air should we choose. Your village, not so much."

Marget returned his gaze, nodding. "I'm warning ye, Hooded One. You're in for some evil times if they have their way. Take the bag; y' know you need it. Then vanish for a while."

Robyn relented, took it. They did need the simples. None of them were skilled at herb lore. Another reason of the many to mourn his mother and sister's absence.

Of course, if they were here, would *he* be?

Too many questions, this just the last atop a pile of growing uncertainties. "We wain't be here again," he told her, and motioned for Gilbert to give her the brace of rabbits they'd brought.

"I understand. I'm sorry." Marget took the rabbits, gave a quick curtsey, then returned the way she'd come.

◯

"You know what we must do."

Cernun still wandered, but the frailties that had started to catch him up from his efforts with Robyn's healing were tasking him sore. Cernun had found a bolt-hole, a cave not far from a Templar stronghold called Hirst. Strange thing to call it, in Robyn's estimation, for it held no Templars—whatever *those* were, Cernun didn't elaborate and Robyn didn't ask—only villeins maintaining it. Cernun knew some of them and had, it seemed, known their masters. If an old man was comforted by a place and people he'd once known, then it was enough. Robyn hunted for Cernun, provided him with whatever he needed and, with John and Will, exchanged a constant attendance upon their elder.

"Huddersfield is the first, but it shall not be the last." Cernun huddled by his fire, though the weather was warm enough, drinking a hot posset from Marget's stores. "The Church has taken fierce hold here, and these people have not been overly thwarted by that hold. Not like Loxley." His gaze rose and held to Rob's.

Not the first time Cernun had raised the possibility of returning south, either. Rob looked down and away, did not raise his eyes until Cernun turned to pour from a sack into their blessing bowl.

"The meat you brought to my fire is ready, Robyn Hode. Share with me the drink." He handed the bowl over. "*Bendith.*"

Robyn repeated the blessing, drank and handed it back, watched as Cernun drank.

Then said, hoarse, "Loxley is gone."

"Loxley is a symbol amongst the *dryw*, amongst the *wicce* and cunning-folk. Martyrdom is a powerful force, and the Shire Wode is filled with those who would be our people. They have no love for the corrupted ones who burned our covenant."

"Yet de Lisle is sheriff there, as well. Not only Derby, but now Nottingham." Robyn took another drink: mead, sharp and sweet-thick on his tongue.

"You think to run from him, then? His soldiers nearly took Stronghelm and Janicot"—Cernun always used their coven-names—"from you, but you took them back."

Robyn well remembered the day, only a fortnight previous. The inevitable finally occurred: they got careless, or Sheriff de Lisle had been given one more incentive by Yorkshire's nobles to curtail a ragged pack of wolfsheads—or, as Gilbert remarked, more likely both together. Sheriff's men, led by several mercenaries who knew exactly what they were doing, staked out several prime spots along Watling Street and captured Will and John. Instead of taking them back to York, the guard captain decided to hang them both from a stout tree then and there. The latter was the soldiers' undoing: the road where they'd chosen an adequate tree had more sparse cover than the high Saylis wood.

The outlaws had riddled the soldiers with arrows before they could so much as tie the nooses.

Robyn shook his head, passed the bowl. "I'd but go to ground for a while. Strike elsewhere 'til they've forgotten us. I've no wish to run too far from de Lisle. He's kin to the Black Abbess. One way or another, he will lead me to her."

"Revenge is costly, Hob-Robyn."

"Sometimes," Robyn said, his eyes on the flames, "'tis all there is."

Cernun fell silent for so long that Robyn looked up, concerned. The old man was peering at him, expression unfathomable. He held out the bowl.

Robyn took it, drank again. "Worksop is on the edges of Nottingham's Shire Wode."

"As is Blyth."

The castle's name, so seldom spoken, echoed hollow within the cavern. Robyn drank again and said, licking at his lips more from apprehension than appreciation, "Cernun. So many . . . *ghosts* bide nigh t' Loxley."

"Those ghosts are your *strength*, Hob-Robyn, and you know it.

They would welcome their son back. You stood in the stones at Mam Tor, newly back to this world. But then you faded from ones who would honour you."

Robyn looked away.

"None could blame you. Your heart needed healing even more than your body, and time away from the ravages of loss. Barnsdale has been well enough. But now?"

True enough. The northmost edge of Barnsdale had less wild woodland than the forests farther south. It was proving, more and more, to have too many places vulnerable to discovery, too many waylaid Importances shrieking for restitution. Skirmishes were escalating into all-out war. What support system they had garnered had begun to wither.

"It is past time, too, you looked to finding a Maiden."

Sweet Lady, not this again. Robyn shook his head. "For Will, mayhap."

"Will is not the one who bears the horns."

"Will has more horns than I could ever—"

"*Robyn.*" Cernun was frowning.

"I once told me mam," Robyn said into the cup, a hoarse echo, "twere wrong t' take such things lightly. If we blame the Christians for blightin' our earth into sommat . . . *corrupt*, for mocking our ways of blood and flesh, then how are we different if we force such a thing, set it all t' meaning nowt?"

"There are many kinds of love, lad."

"'Ceptin' mine, is that what you're saying?"

Cernun looked down, sighed. "Nay. All I'm saying is the land cries out for the rites. The *whole* of the rites, not part."

"That's what *I'm* saying!" Robyn shot back. "Is it my fault, now, that my . . . that they're gone and I canna . . . that I mourn 'em?"

Silence fell between them, neither sure of what to say.

"It is past time we returned home, Hob-Robyn." Cernun reached out, poked at the fire with a stick, his eyes rheumy and shadowed in the golden light. "The time comes when I will not be able for such a journey."

◯

They arrived to Loxley Chase upon the eve of Summer Solstice.

Robyn and Will led. The others, silent, hung back along the narrow path, giving willing ground. Even Cernun, bundled on a sturdy jennet for the journey, didn't press forward into the territory once his, let himself be steered in their wake.

Unsure of what to expect—they had been long away, after all—Robyn was humbled by what they did find. Woodland had blossomed, sent tendrils over the charred ground, taken over the fallen-in husks of stonework, covered the ploughed lands with a thick carpet of green.

Will was smiling, just as surprised by what he saw. For all his wanderings while outlawed in the Shire Wode, he'd stayed farther south, mostly in Stafford and Leicester, and never ventured here.

"We come, and go," Cernun said. "The Wode remains."

Robyn had thought to breathe a blessing upon the place, to instil what magic he could, a gift to ward off the destruction. Instead he knelt down, put his palms flat to the burgeoning earth and closed his eyes.

"The eternal return," Gilbert murmured. "Look at it."

"Aye," Will whispered beside him, and when Robyn looked up, he saw all of them, even Cernun, had knelt, asking.

Robyn stood. "We're going deeper into Shire Wode."

"Are we hiding, then?" Will asked, unusually solemn.

"Nay," Robyn answered, just as solemn, then grinned. "What'd be the point of that?"

◎

They'd been camped near the caverns of Loxley Chase a bare se'nnight, when John came running into camp as if a pack of wolves were at heel.

Robyn lurched up from where he was dozing, back-to-back with Gilbert, who bent over his work of fletching a new cache of arrows. Gilbert went falling back and cursed as quills went flying. His curses stopped midthroat as John spoke. "Cernun."

"Go find Will and Arthur, Gilly," Robyn ordered. "We'll be at the caves." Then Robyn followed John as he disappeared back the way he'd come.

He'd known it was coming; they all had. Cernun had been growing weaker and weaker, as if his return to the Shire Wode had been the last thing he'd left undone. Robyn was grateful that he had brought Cernun home, sorrowful it had not been sooner, glad the old man did feel as if he could, finally, let go.

But it didn't stop the ache, the rue of losing yet another tie to ever-vanishing summers past.

"Robyn. Robyn?"

"I'm here," he said, gentle, and knelt beside Cernun, lying on his pallet by the fire. The caverns echoed their voices, muted them and, hopefully, took their magic to the otherworld, to welcome the ones coming.

Particularly this one.

Lord?

I am here. I will see him safe to Her.

"Robyn." A sigh, wavering but echoing the tones of the god he'd once borne. "I'm glad you're here, son."

John bent over, kissed the old man's forehead. "*Bendith, Arglwydd.*"

"And you, Janicot. You will take care of the Hooded One."

"As he lets me." John slid his gaze to Robyn, gave a sly smile.

Cernun patted John's shoulder, let the hand slide down to where he'd nestled in his bed of thick-heaped boughs and warm wolf furs.

With another look at Robyn, John left them alone.

"You *are* my son," Cernun said fiercely. "The only one I could ever claim, even if but a little."

"You've been a father t' me. To all of us. Even as outlaws."

Cernun gave a frown, mock-disapproval that faded into a chuckle, then into coughing. Robyn held Cernun's hand through the fit, fetched him fresh water, propped him up in his lap and helped him drink it. Once he drank, Cernun lay against Robyn's chest, panting.

"I've been a burden of late. You should have taken me into the Wode, left me to Her mercy."

"'Tis no burden," Robyn murmured into the lank, white locks, "but honour t' do this for you, Horned One."

"Honour," Cernun whispered. "Mine."

He grew heavier in Robyn's arms, his breathing coming slow and shallow.

"A good journey," Robyn whispered against his ear, and did not let go.

Cernun jerked. "Journey," he slurred.

"Shh," Robyn told him, stroked his face. Of late Cernun had been less lucid, the death-dreamings coming more and more. It was the way of things. Even a dying buck would twitch and dream before death sank him into the Lady's arms.

"Journey," Cernun muttered against Robyn's hand. "They are coming. Water and wind returns him. The stones are singing."

"The stones bide quiet, old man," Robyn told him. "They honour you, also."

"Nay," insisted Cernun. "They sing along the roads and paths, to the cold white places . . . Sing him home, sing our Lady's lament, wake Her sleeper with the pale knight's kiss." He took in a deep breath and let it out, hanging in the darkness. "Pale knight . . . Templars. Returning. To seek the treasure."

"Templars?" Robyn repeated it, puzzled-soft. The word seemed to make Cernun restless, his limbs twitching, so Robyn began a gentle back and forth motion, soothed, "Nay, *Arglwydd,* their like are gone, remember? Gone to fight the Lionheart's bloody wars, you said once."

"I am no longer *Arglwydd,* no longer lord and king of the Shire Wode." Cernun opened his eyes, looked at Robyn. "That has long been you."

Then his eyes closed. He grew heavy. His breath slowed, stilled; the thrum of the pulse in his throat weakened, also stilled.

Robyn began the death-song, breathed the web of magic from its start to finish, then went silent, tears leaking into Cernun's hair and soft spasms taking his chest.

He was there for some time. When the others arrived, he angled out from beneath the shell his mentor had left behind, backed away so the others could pay respect. Then he knelt down again, kissed Cernun's hands and crossed them on his chest, bent to lay kisses upon his eyelids, then his mouth. Said, low, "*Bendith, dryw.*"

"The king stag is dead," Will said, soft. "So lives the king."

- III -

Crossing the Channel Sea
Summer of 1193

The final leg of any journey was always the hardest. The crossing from Normandy lived up to that reality, the ocean tossing their ship like a child's toy. There was, perhaps, never a good time to cross the Channel. But summer winds had proven capricious: nonexistent for over a fortnight, then blustery. Nevertheless, the Templar galley had unfurled her white-and-red sails, taking the chance when it came.

And now, with the shores of England beginning to peek through thick, grey clouds and wind-driven rain, Guy felt more emptiness than relief, more dread than any stray thrill of homecoming.

There were ghosts in those mists.

What would happen when he did step foot ashore? Would the ghosts come for him, recognise him, take him down as he deserved?

Nonsense. Guy pulled his cloak tighter about him, grateful for the oiled wool and the thick insulation of the cloak's cowl keeping his scalp relatively dry. Ghosts! So what if it had been May when he had last departed the shores? Mere coincidence. And nothing bided here that he'd not already faced off with on the battlefield, or stolen in on silent feet and suffocated. He had left here a child, was returning as a man. He had made a way and a life for himself, had relied only on the sword at his hip and the comrades at his back. Had spent his loyalty upon one who thoroughly deserved it. Hubert had treated him in kind—rewarded him with a name and a place he'd earned and, in the end, a comradeship tested with blood and battle.

"Guy?"

He turned from the railing, dipped his head in welcome. "Commander."

Hubert also wore a thick cowl and cape; his cross-emblazoned white tabard, in contrast to Guy's black, made a beacon in the rain. "Quite a difference, eh? The first time you made this crossing, I did fear that from the look of you 'twas mostly on your knees."

"Praying *and* heaving," Guy agreed.

"And now your man is below, heaving and cursing."

Poor Much. "I tried to tell him it would be better above, but he refuses to believe me. He says his god is punishing him for being so long away."

Hubert moved to stand beside Guy, putting both palms to the railing and sucking in the chill wind. "I am glad to be home again. Though it feels *cold*. I fear our first winter will be hard on sun-drenched bones. *C'est ça.*" He shrugged, turned his gaze upon Guy. "And you?"

Guy blinked. "Me?"

"I know you were not overeager to return. But there are things here waiting for us, things we have both left undone far too long. You have earned your absolution, wholly. I say again, I would give you an honourable discharge should you wish it. I would give you back the white mantle, should you wish *that*."

"Nay, my lord," Guy said, earnest. "I have all I need. What vows I made I will keep to."

"I am not sure you do not keep some of your truths, as well, still altogether close." Hubert's eyes were piercing, not unkind, upon Guy. He looked away, into the rain, toward landfall. "May it happen that here, Guy, in our home, you will find it in your soul to tell me."

Perhaps. But some things had no words—and some, to give them speech would merely lend them too much power. "*C'est fini,*" he said, quietly. "As I have said, my lord, there is no other life that can exist anymore. My life is with the Templars, and in your service, if you permit."

"Permit?" Hubert laughed into the rain. "I am grateful, Guy. We will go home to Temple Hirst together, then. There is much our Grand Master has bidden me to, and therefore much reliance I shall place upon you."

Guy nodded, and continued to watch the shore with some trepidation as it loomed, closer and closer.

Once a broken boy had spent his days backfilling a hole where his all-too-fragile soul had once lain. That empty place no longer existed, in fact had grown into a stone rampart a castle architect would envy.

When Guy stepped ashore he felt nothing, and smiled.

᚛ᚱ᚜

First he was treading the branch lightly as a squirrel, bow drawn, backing Will and Arthur . . . then something slammed into him. For mad seconds Robyn thought he'd been shot—he'd felt this before, had once before looked down to an impact against his chest, seen an arrow sprouting from his body like some alien tree growth . . .

There was nothing.

There was *everything*.

Robyn wobbled on the branch, fingers suddenly numb upon his bowstring, then it struck against him again. As if lightning had hit the base of the tree with an upward convulsion then a thick-hot collision into his heart and, behind his eyes, a wave of indescribable and soundless *noise* ramping up in his skull.

It was . . . familiar.

Then it took his senses from him.

Robyn toppled, nigh boneless, off the branch. Experienced every moment of the fall, nearly twenty feet of it, as if floating, not plummeting. Heard the solid, dull sound of his own body hitting the ground, the hoarse heaving cough of air knocked from his lungs, the slip-halt then hammer of his heart against his breastbone and the wash of pulse behind his ears and eyes.

But none of it drowned out that pulsating, deep-set *presence,* a recognition seeping up from the earth's very bones. From jarring impact to humming senses to the raw tendrils sucking him downward, and the sparks of his own power fingered outward, *seeking*.

Tynged reared up like a barely broken horse, screamed like a *baen-si*, scattered then spun about him and took him into night's grip. Left him there, small and naked and—

Thrown down, grounded. Back in his own body, breathless and numb, surrounded no longer by the silent, soundful presence but the cries and the ring of steel and the hum of arrow-flight against his ears.

"Gilly—*watch* y'rself!"

"What's happened? He—"

"He can't've fallen. He never falls."

"He bloody *fell.* Sweet Lady, Will, he— Get that one! Watch it!"

Robyn wanted to say sommat. Anything. But he couldn't draw air to make a single sound. Every breath he had, would take, could take—

"Fetch Robyn! I'll cover you—*fetch him*, Will! Get him to saf—!"

More arrows, steel against steel, shouts and curses and heaving bodies. Footfalls, stumbling and running. Hoofbeats.

"Let 'em go! Arthur! Let 'em—"

The sounds of retreat.

"Are you all right?"

"What's—?"

A slender, hard hand brushed the hair back from Robyn's forehead then placed itself there, cool and *sane.* Robyn looked up, slung a line from John's calm gaze and hoisted himself back into sommat resembling his right mind.

"He's alive," Robyn panted. "He's alive, and he's *here.*"

That set John back into confusion, set them all to looking about, still on the edge of panic. Will leaned over and grabbed Robyn, shook him.

"*Who's* here?"

"N-nay," Robyn husked out. "No' *here,* but . . . the land. She knows him . . . knows his steps, knows . . . " Some lucid part of his brain informed Robyn that he was babbling, but it was altogether hard to breathe, let alone make sense.

Will's ire confirmed the "not making sense" part. "Bloody hell, Rob, what're y—"

Just as sudden as it had overtaken Robyn, the pressure left him. Where it had dug in and set fierce talons about his vitals, it gave a violent heave then ripped free, unforgiving as a barbed arrow, as a bandage left stuck to a wound, thick with dried blood and pus.

And this? An old, festering wound thought long gone, forgotten. It had only been buried.

The pain of it doubled him, nose to knees, then slithered away into the dark corners of his consciousness and dissipated.

"Rob!" Will kept shaking him. "*Damn* it!"

With a sudden growl, Robyn shook Will off and rolled to a crouch. Panic still threaded through the lot of them; they were too vulnerable, too close to the open, and who knew if their marks would make good an escape, or come back. He had to get upright, had to regain control of not only himself, but them.

Had to bury it again, at least for now.

He forced himself upright, swaying. This time when Will held out an arm, Robyn took it until the pinwheels stopped whirling behind his eyes.

"Was it . . . " Gilbert hesitated. They had come to know, all too well, the Horned shadow that traced their leader's steps, but speaking of Him was not something any of them did lightly.

"I'm all right," Robyn insisted. "We have to go. It's not safe, here."

The return to command, even snappish, reassured; they all fell in and followed without another word.

But Robyn could feel John's eyes upon him, brows drawn together, sombre.

®

At camp, Robyn watched his men watch him for as long as he could, then grabbed up his longbow, knotted a handful of arrows into his hair, and said he was going hunting.

Alone.

The emphasis was necessary, for every one of them had started for their own gear. At his qualification, they'd stopped midmotion and went on to do some other chore, looking somewhat abashed at being so caught out.

Robyn didn't go hunting. Instead of taking down some hapless game—their larder was stocked well enough, anyway—he ended up taking out some aggression on scraps of cloth hung against a tree.

Considerable archery practice—at sheriff's men as well as target clouts—had rehabilitated his left arm to nigh his old skill. He felt a man—his *own* man—again. The old monster of a Welsh longbow that had lain sleeping in Cernun's care rode at his back again, her spirit submitting gladly instead of struggling and besting him. The feel of nigh two ells of yew giving to his push and sighing at his pull like a satisfied lover was, sometimes, better than sex.

And this release had its own satisfactions.

Right now, he was imagining a ginger-haired hillock of heartbreak at the end of that release. The arrows sang, hit and hummed, one after the other, deadly accuracy and economy.

I thought you were dead, you Motherless sod. John told me they'd sent you to war, and we all know the odds of a young soldier surviving. It sounds all of danger and hot glory to fight for king and country, only our king is a Frank who refuses to even speak our tongue, so how much would he value our Mother's sons?

Another three arrows, lining up, one next to the other and the other.

So long... years of it... first Marion then you, ripped from me, always wondering how and why, never feeling whole... the pain there but not... like Arthur, with his missing arm aching in the damp.

Two, in between the three, a finger-length upward. Then four below, two fingers down. The clout was edged with Gilbert's goose- and peacock-fletched arrows.

Had Gamelyn... felt it? Could it even be possible he had not?

Robyn stalked over to the tree and pulled his arrows from the clout. Several of them had pierced altogether deep. He tugged the clout away and tossed it aside. Working the bodkins from the rough bark, he exhaled a soft, healing benison, saw the white-blue sparks dancing about the trunk and knew the apology had been accepted.

Not for the first time, he wondered what the world had been like when everyone could see these things, could feel and sense the other realities hovering just beneath this one. For surely it depended upon the day whether he himself thought such a possibility either wondrous or one flaming mad.

Realised, suddenly, the tree he had spitted then caressed was an oak.

Always the slap with the kiss...

Memory ripped at its old, festering scab once more, so merciless that it made his knees wobble. Robyn clutched at the tree, found tears, sudden and hot, filling his eyes.

Found the demand burning through his mind: *Why didn't you tell me?*

The answer, when it came, was slow, almost as if the Horned Lord spent his thoughts in aimless drift through the trees. *There was nothing to tell.*

"Nowt to—"

He was dead to us. Beyond my reach.

The sense of it trickled through, cooled Robyn's outrage as swift as it had risen. "And now... he is not."

Now, he has returned.

"Will he come?" He didn't dare hope—didn't *want* hope—but it warbled through the words, nonetheless.

He will not be able to resist. A dark, eerie satisfaction edged in the words, telling Robyn the Horned Lord had spent much energy into the wait.

A wait that, until this moment, Robyn had not acknowledged.

He is not the lad you knew.

"Neither am I," he whispered. "I'm not sure I know me, most days."

Summer has returned to our land, my own. We must make sure, you and I, it cannot leave again. However that must be.

There was a threat beneath the words, stirring resentment in Robyn's belly. "I were told he didn't mean—"

It does not matter. He was cause for betrayal and would do so again in a heart's beat. He has turned his face from me. From you. The tynged *that would swirl about him is foreign, dangerous.*

"But I *felt*—"

He is your rival. You forget that at your peril. You played well, but you lost, little pwca. *Do not presume you can game so recklessly again.*

As the consciousness faded from his own, warning, Robyn smiled.

"What else, O my lord, does a *pwca* do?"

- ENTR'ACTE -

Nottingham Castle
Autumn of 1193, CE

"I want them found, do you hear me? I'll raise the bounty and double that should any of my own men catch the bastard!" Brian de Lisle, Lord High Sheriff of Nottingham, York, and Derby, threw a half-full goblet at his guardsmen. He was aiming for the captain, and would have hit him, by God, if the fellow hadn't ducked. "Though Christ help me, it seems my own men are as incompetent an army as a cloister of nuns!"

At table beside de Lisle, a tonsured man in velvet black gave a pointed cough. Next to him another, dressed in sumptuous dark blue, eyed his priestly companion and hid a smirk beneath one hand.

De Lisle ignored both of them, intent upon the bearers of what ill news he held—a missive from Geoffrey, Baron de Ros and the latest unlucky traveller up the Great North Road. "Find him and bring me his head! Or your heads will be looking out from the gatehouse spikes! Get out!"

The hapless guards retreated. Even the guards within the chambers inched closer to the doorways as de Lisle kept pacing, muttering.

"Brian," the priest at the table began, "you'll have an attack of apoplexy—"

"Look at this!" De Lisle turned and thrust a roll of parchment at his nearest companion. "Just so you don't think you're the only one favoured with this wretched wolfshead's attentions!"

Prior Willem, youngest son of the de Lisle household, took the missive and perused it. "Good Christ. A hundred marks. I count myself lucky to only lose ten."

"I count myself lucky I've not had the pleasure." Roger, once de Lisle and now the Baron de Lacy of Pontefract, shook his head and perused his empty plate with some dismay. "What does this villein look like, anyway?"

"Tall, I've heard. But scrawny. Villein, no doubt, with a dark hood laced close. I'm not sure any have ever seen his face." Willem was still finishing off his own dinner.

"He's half a dozen men, at least."

"And shoots like a wild Welshman," de Lisle growled. "Left-handed to boot!"

Willem shuddered. "If *that* isn't a devil-spawned—"

"Devil!" de Lisle snorted. "What I'd give to catch this 'devil' in an open field with a good warhorse."

"You know, Brian, I would be happy to send soldiers down—"

"I know the cost of your generosity, Roger, and I cannot afford it," de Lisle growled back.

"I can barely afford the bloody soldiers myself!" de Lacy replied. "I'd lend them to you for the cost of board alone—"

"It still costs, Brother." De Lisle tossed down the missive. "God in Heaven! Between the Queen Mother milking every unfreshened cow she can find for King Richard's ransom and this damned pack of mangy outlaws who insist on terrorising decent citizens . . ."

"Mayhap you should inform Queen Eleanor of this wolfshead's rampages into her son's ransom coffers," Willem suggested. "She'd be after him like a whirlwind." He held out his emptied cup. A serving girl hurried to fill it and the Baron's. She then approached her master with some caution, offering the pitcher.

De Lisle started to shake his head, then gave her a brief smile and held out his cup. "Find the honeyed breads, girl, and bring them if you would. My eldest brother will start licking his plate anon."

"Aye, milord Sheriff." A quick curtsey and she was gone.

De Lacy snorted. "Where do you find them, Brian? Are all the prettiest girls in three shires here, serving you?"

Willem shrugged. "Our dear brother has always had a gift."

"Better me than you, Willem!" De Lisle smirked.

"Our sister is right. One day God will punish you."

"Why should pleasure be punished? A man deserves some comforts other than mouldy manuscripts." De Lisle tilted his head to Willem, then de Lacy. "Or tournaments."

"Women are for the bedchamber," de Lacy stated. "A good charger is better friend outside it."

Willem shook his head. "God is punishing you for your wenching ways, Brian. Likely He's sent these outlaws to torment you."

De Lisle scowled. "How kind of you, *little brother*, to remind me."

"Well, your table is no torment. My compliments to your cook." De Lacy shoved his chair back and kicked his boots onto the table, gave the Sheriff a toast with his mug. "But as to torment, one of my mesne lords is in for it. One of our cousins, old Uncle Ian's eldest?"

The maidservant brought in the pastry. As she set it on the table, she gave de Lacy's prominent boots a chiding glance, which he ignored.

"Torment?" Willem asked, snagging a pastry.

De Lacy took two. "I was at a tournament at Blyth—ah, but Tickhill has the best mêlée field in England—"

"You said 'torment'," Willem pointed out, "not 'tournament'."

"For a religious man, Willem, you have no patience whatsoever," de Lacy's reproach was halfhearted. "The 'torment' is for poor Johan Boundys, who has the King's brother in residence. Count John attended the mêlée and settled into residence. Supposedly overseeing the finishing of the chapel his royal mother the Queen dowered there."

"The key word," de Lisle said, "being 'supposedly'."

"*That* one, unlike his mother the Queen, would be happy did Lionheart's ransom disappear into the coffers of this wolfshead of yours," de Lacy pointed out, leaning back in his chair and chewing. "Mayhap you should treat with this . . . 'Robyn Wood', is it?"

"Robyn Hood, sir," the girl supplied.

"Do you know of Robyn Hood, lovely one?" De Lisle ventured suddenly, walking over and putting his arm about her.

"Oh, aye, everyone knows about him," she replied, colour rising into her cheek. "But know him? Nay. There's no knowin' a spirit."

"A spirit?" De Lacy guffawed.

De Lisle growled, "Don't mock your betters with such nonsense."

"I meant no mockery, milord," she said, wincing as de Lisle's grip pinched her shoulder. "I only spoke what's said. It's said Robyn Hood's the Green Man, possessed by the Forest Lord's spirit. 'Tis why 'e can disappear in the Shire Wode, milord."

"Shire Wode?" Willem mused. "Old term. How quaint."

"Superstition!" De Lisle snorted. "You see what I deal with?"

Willem shook his head, crossed himself. "There are things in Sherwood Forest that would horrify any man of God."

"Even from my own family. Devils and ghosts! Christ, Willem, you sound like Elisabeth—"

"Elisabeth is... prideful with her piety," Willem agreed. "It will take her far in the eyes of our Church. But it is impractical. If every pagan was riven from this isle, then we'd have no villeins to work the fields. You'd have no bedwarmers."

"Nay, Father, I en't no pagan, I swear—!" The girl broke off with a small yip as de Lisle's grip pinched again.

"You're too eager to answer your betters," he growled then, with a sudden laugh, released her. "Get out, girl. Save that quick tongue for other uses."

She made good her retreat.

Willem watched after her. "You'd do well to heed your villeins in this, Brian. There's been witchcraft in this shire before—and a burned village to their cause. Most of the peasants mean well, making their little charms and offerings. No harm in them, as long as they pay their tithes and baptise their children as Christian. But this wolfshead... if he believes he's what the wench claims he is, you could have more trouble than you think. Witches have no true power against God. But they have altogether much claim against the minds of men."

"Loxley. Bloody sodding Loxley, and I didn't have a damned thing to do with it!" De Lisle walked over to the table, snagging a pastry for himself before his brothers ate them all. "Our dear, devout sister spun old FitzAaron in her pious web like the fool he was, and I'm still paying for it."

"In more ways than one," de Lacy pointed out. "She still hasn't forgiven you for denying to let soldiers to her for her little private peasant crusade."

"It was bad business," de Lisle groused. "Just as this Robyn Hood is. Bad business."

De Lacy reached for another pastry; midreach he hesitated, then snatched it up and sprang to his feet. "Crusade," he repeated, snapping his fingers. "That gives me an idea."

"Well?" Willem sighed as his elder brother kept silence. "Must we have an announcement with lute and horn to hear this?"

De Lacy pointed a finger at him, scowling. "Surely you've heard Temple Hirst is swarming with its Hounds of God again."

"Templars." Willem shuddered. "God save us, yes."

"Of course." De Lisle took another pastry. "Months ago, wasn't it, they passed through? Didn't bother to stop; not that I wanted them *to* bother. I just hoped they would resist torching any villages on their way through. Elisabeth looks a proper moderate next to those fanatics."

"Monsters, all of them," Willem insisted. "Priests should not take pleasure in killing."

"I'm not sure Templars take pleasure in anything," de Lisle said.

"That's what makes them dangerous." De Lacy was pacing, tapping two fingers against his chin. "Listen to me. You've two choices, it seems. You can bargain with this peasant hero of yours to aid Count John—"

"And find my arse handed to me with greens on the side when King Richard is finally ransomed—"

"Or," de Lacy stopped and gave a mild swat to the embroidery on his brother's tunic, "perchance Elisabeth's little crusade can work for you instead of against you."

De Lisle was not amused, brushing at his tunic as if a dog had mussed it. "Roger. That latest tourney—were you wounded? In the head?"

"Listen to your elder brother, Brian," de Lacy chided, "he's Baron of Pontefract for a reason."

"Yes. He's eldest and old Uncle Robert died without issue, leaving our mother the holding of which the king ... ah ... *relieved* Huntingdon. Oh, and that minor issue about the thousands of marks you paid into Richard's coffers to *ensure* said holding—"

"Blast and bugger you." De Lacy scowled at him. "*Successful* Baron of Pontefract for a reason, then. You and Willem might be sticking your heads up your arses in fear of white tabards on supposed mad monks, but I've been paying attention. The Master of Hirst Preceptory is actually *not* the Devil Incarnate. I've had some dealings with him since his return, and while I wouldn't call him altogether trustworthy, I would say he's reasonably sane. For a churchman."

"God will punish you too, Roger," Willem threatened.

"For tormenting you? He's likely to egg me on, if the Almighty has the sense of humour He must have."

"Don't encourage him, Willem," de Lisle groaned. "We'll never get to the point."

"The point," de Lacy emphasised, "is that Temple Hirst's Master has been my guest at Pontefract twice now. He has consulted with me upon several matters. One of architectural interest, a stolen artefact the Templars were looking for. And found, I might add. The other was a matter of ... well, of inconvenience. Several mercenaries—scum— terrorising the Priory of Kirklees."

"*The point*," de Lisle reminded, "is a wolfshead my men seem unable to kill."

"Both of you, impatience personified. See here, the Templar Master's banner waver . . . bodyguard . . . well, whatever he is, I can't remember now. But *he's* the one I think might be of help."

It was de Lisle's turn to sit down and prop his feet on his table. "You *were* struck in the head at your last tourney, weren't you? Of what use would some Templar Knight's lackey be?"

De Lacy rolled his eyes, came over and sat beside him. "This lackey has a hellish reputation, and he lived up to it. I was witness. He took care of those mercenaries within a few days; took them out in a pub and brought their heads to me hanging from the back of his saddle. Word has it the man is a defrocked Templar Knight, serves the Master as penance for whatever horrors he committed on Crusade. Templar trained, obviously, but it's said he spent time as a thrall of the Saracens. Dresses like one, a bit. Carries one of those great falchions." De Lacy's hands described the sword, curved and lethal. "For all that, he's a deceptively mild-looking fellow, and *young*. I should swear he's not much older than my lad Henry. But a frosty-eyed killer, no question."

"A twenty-year-old Templar assassin!" de Lisle scoffed, pouring more wine for all of them.

"Poor lad." Willem shook his head.

"Poor lad, my arse. I suspect he could hand all of us *our* arses." De Lacy took a drink, grabbed another pastry. "Without trying."

"You'll need another tourney to work that lot off." Willem grinned.

"I've one next week. Anyway, this man. Assassin. The Templar Master points and this man of his just *does*. Without question. We should all be so lucky to have one like him. But it seems to me you could hire him if you sent word to his master. I'll help, if you like. Let this Templar know some Godless Heathens are running riot in Sherwood Forest and he'll take care of it. No torchings, no mass slaughter of valuable peasants . . . "

"It might," Willem said, "just work."

"Implore God not to punish me then, yes?"

"With proper penance, all things are possible."

"With you, that always means money."

"I never thought to hire a Templar." De Lisle sat back, pondering. "But you're right, Willem. It just might work."

"Bask in my brilliance," said the baron, handing out his cup, "and pour more wine."

- IV -

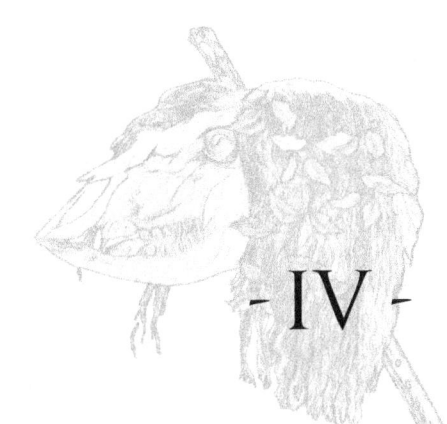

*Temple Hirst, Yorkshire
After the Feast of St. Denis, 1194, CE*

There was satisfaction to be had, in the practice. Strictly scheduled, like every other aspect of a Templar's day, it consisted of at least several hours of sweat-breaking intensity after morning observances. The armoury at Hirst in actuality made up a huge gallery on the ground floor opposite the refectory. It was set with every device of battle imaginable: archer's clouts and rush-padded wrestler's matting; quintains bearing anything from strips of dangling cloth to short spikes imbedded in leather; axes and lances; battered shields and practice swords; maces and misericordes; flails and horseman's picks.

The open practice remained noisy, even with the normal strictures against unnecessary conversation, but it mattered not to Guy. Solitary or communal, he rarely spoke during his practice, focus absolute.

There was pride in it, certainly. One of his Brother Knights had once called him on it. *Proud as Lucifer,* the man had accused to the Master. *He thinks himself above us, and he does not even wear the white.*

Guy hadn't cared. The man had not even been to the Holy Land. But Hubert had motioned Guy forward. Had sent him and the challenging knight into the courtyard and watched, impassive and unsurprised, as Guy had, just as impassively, bested the angry Brother.

Pride is an empty thing, desperate to be filled, Hubert had told the watchers as Guy had held out his arm to the Brother, helped him up then bowed and backed away. *The pride of Lucifer? You forget Lucifer, Iblis, Inanna—such stars of morning all braved the underworld to come back with knowledge others did not understand. Those others were also proud: too proud to listen.*

Aye, the practice was its own prayer, one more useful than an empty and egocentric plea to an indifferent deity. A haven, an assoilment of movement, sweat, and breath. When his duty would break him like a hart being readied for the table, there was the practice. When the dreams—the utterly damned nightmares that had invaded his sleep since he'd come back to the isle of his birth—when those would rack him limb to limb, he had the practice to wash them from him.

"Brother Guy?" The voice wafted into his consciousness, the forceful tone suggesting it wasn't the first time he'd been so summoned. Guy turned, blowing and sweated, twirling the two steel blades to unthreatening positions. The sergeant waited, mindful, of course, to stay just beyond sword's reach.

"Yes, Brother?"

"Our Master guessed you'd lost track of time." The sergeant gave a slight tilt of head and tiny smile to Guy's state of dress. "The horse dealers are here. Master de Gisborough asks that you attend him at the stables."

"Of course." He *had* lost track, Guy realised as the midday bell began its peal. He had wanted to be at the stables before now. Guy spared himself a cursory glance: barefoot against the chill stones, clad only in muslin braies and the thin girdle twined around his hips that no sworn Templar ever removed, his forelock dripping into his eyes and the tail of his braided-back hair clinging between his shoulders like a damp, frizzly rope. "Kindly tell him I'll dress first."

⓲

Hirst had been short of horses since its crusaders had returned. It was not necessarily a horrible plight. The Preceptory was known for raising both fine grain and hot-blooded horses, what with the river so at hand and the bottom lands so fertile. But the matter had become more urgent. They'd several fine young stallions up and coming, but it was a lengthy process, training a warhorse, and they needed to fill their shortages now. Richard still languished a hostage in Europe, the nobles were restless, many of them power-hungry vultures hovering in the void of a king's absence. And there was Count John.

The Templars needed to be ready. Always.

But finding good mounts was no easy task. They'd already dismissed the offerings of three dealers.

A newly clad Guy strode through the stables, snuffing the homely, reassuring smell of fodder and enjoying the rhythmic sound of content, chewing beasts. Squires were busy readying the horses for the afternoon's work, nimble and swift shadows in the dim, tossing brushes, wringing stable rubbers, humming and speaking to their charges or each other. The day had held to morning's fair promise: light streamed through the windows and the open far door, where the Master of Temple Hirst stood. Arms crossed and feet firmly planted, his silver-bistre hair and white habit limned him brilliant in the noonday sun.

There were several others with him, knights and sergeants and the Preceptory's Seneschal, of course, advising the finances of such a purchase. The sound of prospects' hoofs clopped back and forth on the stones of the yard, led by a bow-legged freeman and his four sons. A few other horses were tied to rings on the outer wall.

"A promising group, at least," one of the elder knights was murmuring as Guy approached.

"Ah, Guy. Can we dare hope this lot will find you a suitable replacement for Diamant, eh?" Hubert acknowledged his arrival, then, "Well, not a replacement, but a worthy successor."

Replacing Diamant was like worrying at a bad tooth. The stallion had survived sand, storms, and Saracens, had been injured so many times and not died; it seemed impossible Diamant would be lost on the voyage home to a foul, chancy slip on the deck and a broken right foreleg.

Guy had sobbed like a child as he'd held the horse's head, looked into his eyes, and put him out of his suffering with the keen edge of his dagger.

His Brothers had mourned, too, standing behind him as they'd heaved Diamant's body into the Mediterranean. Even Hubert's inscrutable face had been seamed with tears. They had all grown to love the great horse—a mascot, almost, a charm representing survival in a mad world where a full two-thirds of Templars did *not* survive—but Diamant had been much more to Guy. The immeasurable sorrow as they'd consigned the ivory body to the deeps had been accompanied by a guilt-ridden, perverse sense of release: Diamant represented the last tie to Gamelyn, the last bereavement, the last . . . reminder.

It meant Gamelyn was finally dead, as well.

"We might have to venture to London, though," Hubert was saying, eyeing the string of mounts. "There's a few here that look quite promising. But not enough. How many do we actually need?"

"At least a dozen," another knight guessed.

"By my last count, we need a remount of sixteen," a sergeant put in, folding his arms across his black habit.

Hubert chuckled. "Then it's well enough we've had several outside obligations to fill our coffers handsomely. Flambard and Charles's bodyguard stint for Chester's wedding, for one. And those, ah, problems that you and your man solved for Roger de Lacy, eh, Guy?"

"I like that bay with the white hind." Guy watched as the horse strode out strong from his haunches and shook his head, all bluff to his handler. "He looks a fighter."

"I'd my eye on him as well," the aforementioned Flambard said with a grin. "But you spoke first."

"Yes, I did." Guy shrugged with a return smile.

"Speaking of Baron de Lacy," Hubert ventured. "Guy, walk with me for a moment, if you please. Brothers, will you excuse us?"

The others murmured assent, attention upon the horses.

"Please saddle your bay," Guy told the lad who held him. "I'll give him a try."

"And the blaze-faced bay for me," Hubert said. "We shan't be long."

Hubert headed for the small copse of trees on the far edge of the stable yard, his pace almost leisurely. The only trees within an arrow's flight of anywhere in the fortress, they offered some respite from rain or shine, a seeming luxury with a purpose when one spent hours on end in the yard on drills. Guy followed, unable to contain a tremor of curiosity but willing to the wait, putting his hands behind his back. Behind them the ring of shod hoofs echoed against the stone walls of the yard, their Brothers' low voices comparing the horses as they were trotted and walked out.

"Your reputation has preceded you, Guy."

"Pardon?"

Hubert gave a small smile—the one that usually meant Guy was in for it—then stopped beneath the dappled shade and pulled a roll of parchment from the inside of his tunic. "My lord de Lacy was undoubtedly pleased with your . . . peculiar skills."

"I hope I can continue to serve you well with them, my lord."

"And I well realise you look to my advice for what obligations you take on. The baron has recommended you for another task. I have been mulling it over for a few days. It is . . . interesting." Hubert handed over the parchment, peered back the way they had come. "I think I rather fancy the dark chestnut as well. This man has some fine animals."

Guy fingered open the note and perused the cramped script, first with curiosity then with growing scepticism. "Interesting," he echoed, flat, and slid his eyes up to meet Hubert's. "You would sanction me going to Nottingham to service his need to kill a *wolfshead*?"

"A *notorious* wolfshead," Hubert pointed out. "I've heard tales of this one, even if you have not."

"My lord, surely—"

"Yet before we give full discussion to Nottingham, there is another matter I must broach to you, my faithful bodyguard and *Confanonier*. Thus the need for . . . privacy, eh? Some of our Brothers might not understand." Hubert's gaze met his and held, all sly diffidence gone. "I know the dreams are getting worse."

So much time and effort spent controlling his complexion, yet Guy felt heat suffusing his cheeks and gave a soft curse. "Mayhap, then, Much should be my new sparring partner if he finds it so difficult to keep his mouth shut."

"Do not blame him, Guy. I walk the dormitories sometimes when I cannot sleep myself, checking upon all of you. I saw you, not merely once but several times in night travails. Much bided with you, loyal as any hound, so I pressed the matter with him. It is as surely my fault as his. I did not appreciate you were still possessed by such things."

Possessed. What an . . . apt description. Guy become conscious of how he'd clenched the parchment into a ball, peering out over the yard without seeing it. "I shall send for Much straight away. I'll likely need to see how the bay palfrey takes to dragging men behind—"

"Guy, you are uncharitable to one who has only the greatest of concern for your well-being. I am myself saddened that you would not trust me with this."

"My lord Commander, I—"

Hubert held up a quieting hand. "How long have you been with me, lad?" It was soft, fond, not the taut fury Guy had expected.

For surely he deserved that fury; he had, after all, kept silence with one who well deserved nothing but trust, one who had given him a new life, a new purpose . . .

It was not your life to give away. Just as some silences are not yours to break, "my lord". . .

Guy sucked in a quavering gasp, throttled it midbreath. Began backfilling with every scrap of denial, reason, and pure fear he could muster.

"Are you all right? Guy?"

Guy nodded, gathering the shreds about him, a fortification that, more and more, seemed to be cracking from its base. This was not acceptable. He would not be weak, not again. He did not want to be this . . . this fragile *thing*.

"Listen to me," Hubert said, stern. "We all have secrets we must keep. Some for our own sanity, some for the sanity of others. I am not angry with you. I blame myself; my blindness. I knew some sort of . . . mark had been placed upon you—"

Guy closed his eyes, gritted his teeth. The clench of the parchment in his fist tingled his fingers.

"—but I'd no concept of what form it might take."

Guy had been foolish to believe himself adroit enough to hide anything from Hubert. Hubert was a Templar Master, hallowed and studied, adept of the Inner Mysteries.

"You have seen but a few of the Temple's holy secrets, but scratched at the uppermost layer of what they mean." Hubert's concurrence was unnerving, considering. "You should not be ashamed, or dismayed by such . . . ah, visitations. Neither should you shy away from such a gift—"

"It is no gift! It is a curse! I have been cursed, and deservedly so." Guy crossed his arms, shook his head. "I never should have set foot back in England."

"What if divine purpose has brought you back here?"

"And which divinity would that be?" Guy retorted—the very snappishness of it another admittance, another *weakness*. Yet he could not stop. "So many devils, so many gods, and most would claim to be the only one—"

"A subject upon which we have had many a discussion. And so it comes, full circle." Hubert motioned to the crumpled parchment still in Guy's fist. "To that."

"My lord, please. I cannot see how." Guy looked down, his shoulders hunching up in a manner he thought sloughed away years ago.

And then Hubert delivered the *coup de grace*. "You cannot ward away the past forever, Gamelyn." It was soft, but no less a blow.

Gamelyn wasn't dead, damn him, not if Hubert could but give

him such mention and give rise to this . . . this . . . sinkhole of uncertainty."

"You wrong me, Commander!" Guy husked out. "That is *not* my name. Not anymore."

Hubert didn't answer for some moments. Well used to such silences—contemplations, really—Guy tried to gather his composure, re-attended to the horses still being exhibited in hand. One was being saddled; another stood quiet while one of the sergeants mouthed him and ran steady, searching hands down his legs.

Guy realised, mortified, that he was shaking. With no little fury, he set himself to conquer it.

"I would have you take this commission," Hubert finally said. "For there is another, more urgent matter lying beneath."

"So you do not send me just to kill a wolfshead." Guy had succeeded in regaining some control. It would do, for the present.

"It is true: beneath one matter lies the beating heart of another, a difficult one, brought to my attention upon our return." Hubert no longer contemplated the horses, but peered upwards, seeming fascinated by the thick leaves sheltering them from the late summer's sun. "There was once a Heathen covenant in southern Yorkshire. Its influence spread much farther, however, reaching from the bottom edges of Sherwood Forest to the upper valleys barely south of here, through Barnsdale and the Peak." Hubert slid a glance sideways. "But you know that, don't you, Guy?"

Guy only thought Hubert had delivered the final blow. Yet this, a faithless misericorde, gave no swift mercy but a slow, barbed slide into his ribs to hang, then gave a twist. Guy had no words. Literally could not make a sound.

Even the hoofs and their comrades' voices had faded into a tense, thick-muffled tension. Guy couldn't fight, couldn't flee. Instead he stood and let the knife slide deeper.

"They were killed," Hubert continued. "Not in honourable combat, but in a cowardly fashion, like nobles with their games they call hunting. Not need, not necessity, but engineered cruelty and torture for the mere sport of it. The covenant was cut down during their most holy of rites, by a fool fanatic woman and a sheriff who let superstition overcome what wisdom he might have had." A pause. "I see this is no news to you, either."

"Loxley." The last time that name had passed Guy's lips had been in his last confession to Brother Dolfin, made in the same hour he had ridden away from Blyth, never to return. There had been no question, then, that he was penitent. That he had endured the worst punishment he had, at the time, thought possible. That he had been damned to live, just as Rob, and Marion, and all their people had been condemned to die.

It was over.

The sins upon which he had spent hours upon his knees, fasting and dry and begging for clarity upon the eve of his knighthood, were another matter. A bare fortnight before the siege of Acre, he had made willing and public confession to Master Hubert and the gathering of Brothers. Had consented to be stripped of everything that made him of those Outside the Temple, even to his hair and clothing. Had let his measure be taken, marked with his own blood, sputum, and semen, suffered it wrapped around his hips, never to be removed. Had made proper obeisance to his Masters and the sacred things of the Temple, rising to be clothed in scarlet and white, to be girded with a Templar's sword.

Beauseant.

To be whole.

All he'd wanted—all he'd *ever* wanted. Nothing of what had come to pass in the Wode had surfaced, had needed to surface. It was *over*.

Or so he'd thought.

"Yes. Loxley was burned to the ground, its people butchered like cattle. There was also a stone circle desecrated. Horrible doings. The leader of the covenant was a wise man. A high priest of the old religion. A *dryw*, he called himself."

You knew Adam? Guy thought wildly, but again, could not speak. Inconceivable, how any of this was known to Hubert.

"Older than my father, this druid, but still hale as an oak. We had . . . a meeting of minds."

Not Adam, then. Faint, like a whiff of wet from a tree rained on days previous, the memory wafted: The crème-coloured stag, transmogrifying into a white-haired, straight-backed old man . . .

Hubert kept speaking, either did not truly ken what his words were doing to his *Confanonier*—or did not choose to care. "I'm sure the old druid was killed with his people. A tragedy. He knew things. Dreamed." Hubert's gaze met Guy's. "Like yourself. But unlike yourself, he submitted to his ride upon the night mare, could back her if not tame her."

Guy would have closed his eyes, but it gave no respite. Once so bidden, it would no doubt picture itself against the backs of his eyelids.

The dreams had grown worse, an endless over-and-over of destruction. The bloody massacre at Acre. The fire and arrows of

Loxley. All of them a never-ending nightmare, one in which no submission to God's will, no interment into the role of unfeeling instrument of Purpose, no amount of blood and sweat and ice would give enduring erasure.

Nothing forgiven, or forgotten. No . . . *absolution*.

Hubert was just as relentless. "And the dreams are taking you back there, yes?"

"Yes." A hoarse whisper. *When I let them. I cannot let them. I cannot let this. . .*

Damn you, until we came here, it was finished! Over!

It will never be finished. Faint, deep as a fathomless pit within him. *The dance is never over.*

Then it faded. Thank God. Guy controlled his instinctive flinch. There must have been some . . . some other *thing* shining in his gaze, for Hubert reached out, gripped his shoulders.

And, God save him, he nearly flinched from that as well. Not because he feared punishment. Because he saw the sudden compassion in Hubert's face.

"Dreams." Hubert was nodding. "I must apologise for taking you back there awake as well as what night brings, but we must speak of this. It is all too plain to me what is happening."

Looking down, away, anything to not have to meet those fierce grey eyes, Guy shook his head.

"The old druid said you would come to me." Very soft.

It was a good thing Hubert was holding to him. Guy's legs were suddenly refusing any support. He clutched at Hubert's tunic, fingers hanging to the bloodied, white-backed cross. Speech came, truncated. Aghast. "I . . . you . . . you *knew* what had . . . what I had—"

"No," Hubert admitted. "I did not. But *he* knew."

"I . . . I don't understand."

"Neither did I, at first. I will confess I thought him slightly mad. Of course, then I did not grasp the price of such gifts. Here, in our Temples, such things are taught differently, our ways more . . . circumspect. Yet now I see, within the masks and mirrors of control, what could be released. Now I begin to understand. And you have given me *that* gift."

Guy knew the Temple held secrets to which he was not privy, paths upon which only Masters and the most Adept could tread. He had hungered for the knowledge, but had made himself turn from any prideful hope of one day having access to such paths. There was safety enough in that he should vow himself set apart, one of the Temple yet never fully so: living in hell yet serving Heaven.

"Guy." Hubert grabbed him by both shoulders, shook him. "Command yourself, now. You must listen to me."

The sharpness, after the gentle compassion, slapped his face. Guy was thankful for it.

"This old druid acted as not only caretaker of the forest and his people, but as protector in possession of ancient and valuable artefacts. He spoke of two of those with no little reverence: the Horns of the god, and the goddess's golden Arrow. I fear a usurper has found these things. I fear there is a man in Sherwood wielding a great power. One he has not earned, merely found and profaned."

Guy fell silent for long moments, regaining his thoughts, re-girding defences. Then, "You believe this wolfshead playing games with Nottingham has usurped the rightful place of the old druid."

"Cernun would have never let an outlaw into his covenant. And all of those are dead; indeed you were witness to it. And now, this." Hubert motioned to the parchment still clutched, tight-white, in Guy's hand. "It would seem you are meant to redress this injustice. You have more rights to these sacred relics than any filthy outlaw. *Gamelyn.*" Twice in one day he'd spoken the name when, after Guy had been sworn to the Templars, his Master had said it perhaps twice in as many years. "In the name of She who holds the life-thread of us all, you know I only speak the truth."

You are meant to spread your wings across the Summering...

The memory crept in on silent and predatory feet, nearly gutted him on the spot.

"I'm not... I... I... *violated* any rights I had long ago—"

"You speak of having no rights, yet this is what the old druid said: 'A boy will come to you. Teach him well, for he must be the sword-arm and shield, must wend the serpent's path of myth and memory to join a rift rent in the world.' And I had no idea. There were so many who came to us for the Crusade. And after Acre, when you came to me with your pain, wished to make your penance, I stripped you of your tabard in acceptance of it. I have only ever wanted to give you the ways of our Order. *Beausant.*"

All he had ever wanted. An answer. Redemption. To be *whole.* Guy ducked his head, repeated its power. "*Beausant.*"

"It worked for the both of us, in truth, that you should not wear the white. But there was more to it than denying you a Knight's purity of dedication and setting the penance upon you. You are more dedicated in your heart and body than many of our Brothers, yet your soul remained... aloof. I suspected there another mark, another *claim* upon you. That you were still tied to some other fate and you could not fully be ours. Then we returned here and I saw what this place fed in you—"

"Fed? In me?"

"Do you still think to deny it to my face, Templar?"

Another verbal blow, more whipcrack than slap. Again, Guy was thankful.

"It seems I cannot, my lord Commander. But neither shall I give to it." Through his teeth. "It is *over*."

"Clearly it is not. Listen to me, Sir Guy de Gisbourne." Hubert's voice turned, silk into steel. "You will go to Nottingham. You will take his commission, and you will heed your true mission in doing so: go into the Shire Wode, find this usurper, strip him of this power he has not earned and take him down."

What choice did he have? Guy closed his eyes, nodded. "Yes, my lord Commander."

Hubert was silent. When Guy opened his eyes once again, he found his mentor peering at him, gaze strange and opaque.

"I will pray, Guy, as I always have, that this will set your ghosts to rest at last."

- V -

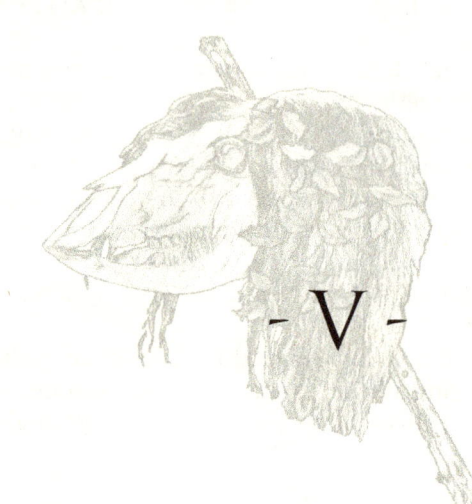

They rode, bold as brass, the Great North Road from York to Nottingham, hoping for outlaws. All they saw was rain. And more rain.

"*Any* outlaw would do, the temper you're in, milord," Much muttered.

"Mayhap, since Blyth is only a few miles away, we should stop and take out my brothers?" Guy sniped back. "Since you're feeling so cheeky."

Much raised his eyebrows and shut his mouth.

They didn't stop at Blyth to avenge any sins—imagined or otherwise—just put spurs to their horses and headed on south. Guy's mount, the bay stallion he'd so fancied, wasn't as trained as the sellers had imagined; that, or Guy held an unfair comparison to Diamant. The bay, whom he'd named Falcon, was big and bold and had some fancy cues on him, but was very unseasoned, and did seem altogether inclined to take to the sky when things startled him.

Perhaps it was just as well. It gave Guy something to focus on besides the all-too-familiar terrain.

They arrived in Nottingham as the rain let up, the clouds drawing back enough to reveal the sun sinking in the sky. The gates were being closed and the torches lit. The guards had gathered, pikes at the ready as the two riders approached, clopped over the bridge and drew up to the gate. As soon as they noted the distinctive gear and uniform of those riders, the head soldier galvanised the remainder into efficient greeting and action. The gate, halfway lowered, was raised. One guard was dispatched to let the Sheriff know he'd important guests; another took their horses. The one in charge said he would personally escort the Templars to the keep.

Much insisted on taking the horses as they dismounted, shaking his head vehemently when Guy suggested they both go at once to the keep itself. "I'll see t' things, milord, and wait for you to send for me."

Not that Guy had imagined otherwise. Humble to a fault, Much rarely chose to be in the company of his "betters," though Guy would stake his reputation on the fact of his paxman being a damned sight better than any noble he'd broken bread with outside their Templar Brethren.

Guy smoothed at his hair, gave a brush to his clothes and a twitch to straighten his sword-belt, and motioned the head guardsman on. Short temper had given way before the reality of work stretching out before him: it might be an uncomfortable purpose, but it remained a sacred one, charged by his Master. So he took in every detail, ticked off anything important—and not so—with quick and deadly efficiency.

Nottingham's keep was well-defended, both in construction and arms. A full two-thirds of the inner wall hunched on the edge of a sheer cliff; the other third had a tributary of the wide moat that bordered the outer bailey. The drawbridge was in good nick. Yet still there were signs, here and there, of the castle's disrepair. As always with such fortresses, construction remained ongoing. A particular project was in progress along the west side of the keep, and the top ramparts were in fact crumbling. Woodland had crept within a stone's throw outside of that wall: a definite sin in the book of defensibility. Of course, Sheriff de Lisle had three shires and several castles to choose from. He'd only recently taken up an extended residence at Nottingham. The "why" of the latter could prove important. Accessibility to this gadfly of an outlaw? Or merely that it was well known as one of Count John's favourite castles?

As they were passed through the stout wooden pickets of the outer barbican—not without a few props and snorts from Falcon— one of the blue-clad guardsmen leapt on his horse and cantered the several furlongs to the main gatehouse. Another, at a slower pace, escorted the mounted Templars across. Both scorned notice of the wide-eyed glances trailing them; instead Guy strafed his own gaze across the open green. It was strikingly quiet. Not a market day, then, and residents settling in with the sun's setting. Only a few people—very few—here and there, intent on some purpose, and a few horses and cattle let to graze on the common.

The guardsmen at the moat's gatehouse were conferring as they approached. A lad scurried forward to take the horses as they dismounted. Much scorned the help, but with a tilt of eyebrow at Guy, followed the lad toward, presumably, the stables.

"My lord." The head gateman bowed Guy over to a man who had appeared just inside the lower gate. "If y' please, this is Robert of Lewes, seneschal to Sheriff de Lisle."

Lewes was well past middle age, tall and cadaverous. He bowed, an ink-stained hand politely at his breast. "Milord Templar. I had not been told you would come yourself."

"I am Sir Guy de Gisbourne, Brother to the Preceptory of Hirst. Who were you expecting?"

"Please excuse any discourtesy, my lord Templar. I was told to expect a servant of your Order, not one of your rank. You honour us, my lord."

"All Templars are servants of our Order." Guy tilted his head up to look at the sky and let his tone edge into long-suffering. "I do hope the honour extends to admittance before night falls?"

"Of course, my lord!" The seneschal gestured Guy forward, led him across the muddy ground. "Please. I will take you to the Sheriff right away. He sits to table as we speak."

More buildings here within the walls, but passersby were still few—and curious. The travel delay had been favourable, it seemed, for a relatively unheralded arrival. A hint of savoury herbs came from a long, low building beside the north wall—the kitchens, no doubt. They were heading for one of the few stone buildings—likely the Great Hall.

"My lord Templar, have you . . . " The seneschal paused, a bit delicately, as they reached a narrow side doorway . "Are you . . . erm . . . I was under the impression that you travel in small groups?"

"Only my paxman, who is seeing to our horses. I would appreciate your oversight and assurance that Brother Much will be fed and shown our billet whilst I do business with your lord."

"Of course." The side hallway, lit sparingly, had begun to grow chill with evening's approach. An arch some paces down spilt brighter light—and several voices. They headed for it.

"If you will wait here, my lord?"

"No need for ceremony," Guy demurred, and walked on in.

Predictably, the seneschal gave a squawk.

A smirk tugged for admittance at Guy's lip; he denied it and strode forward. His eyes missed nothing.

The voices fell silent. The hall was dominated by a large dais and a wide oak table covered much of that dais. The two at the table were bent, looking at a parchment—a map, likely—while several serving lads and lasses brought in trays of food and drink. One, a young blond man, seemed not much older than Guy himself, and therefore not de Lisle. The second man, approaching his prime though his dark locks showed little grey, straightened. A frown was gathering on his brow and, no doubt, a sharp-whet reply honed itself on his lips. He bore Nottingham's chain of office—and some intelligence, for as he took in the telltale of Guy's black-and-crimson tabard, one could almost hear the gears turning, akin to a trebuchet being carefully wound into firing position.

The seneschal scurried in. "My lord—"

"I am Guy de Gisbourne, Brother *Confanonier* to Temple Hirst," Guy interrupted, and dipped his head respectfully. "Please forgive my intrusion, my lord Sheriff. I am not one to stand upon too much ceremony."

Not to mention, so much more could be kenned when people were caught off guard.

"I am Brian de Lisle, Lord High Sheriff of Nottingham, York, and Derby," the elder man said, stepping forward around the table and hopping down from the dais in a sudden, graceful move. The velvet of his robe fluttered, belled as he pulled it close and lifted his chin. He didn't need to; he was a goodly height, his eyes nearly level with Guy's. "I bid you welcome to Nottingham, *Chevalier*. This," he gestured to the younger man, "is my steward, Sir Edward."

Again, Guy tipped his chin. Edward bowed, tried not to stare and failed miserably.

"We were . . . " De Lisle's gears were still turning. "We were not expecting you before tomorrow, so please let me apologise for this poor welcome by inviting you to sup with us—"

"Brian, when do you . . . Oh. Forgive me. I didn't realise you were . . . " The female voice wavered to a halt, from behind them and by the door.

Guy met de Lisle's gaze curiously. The Sheriff raised his eyebrows and tilted his head as if in apology. "My pardon, *Chevalier*. Allow me to introduce you to my sister, if you would."

Sister. Alarm bells jangled in Guy's skull.

The Sheriff gestured past Guy's right shoulder, expectant. Guy drew in a deep breath through his nostrils, let it out. He had expected his past life to raise a brutal head and test him. He had *not*, however, counted on it doing so in such a precipitous fashion.

It had been several years. He looked nothing like to the boy she had known, and not only because he wore a beard and had longer hair.

"Guy de Gisbourne, Brother Templar to the Preceptory at Hirst . . ." De Lisle had already started the introduction.

There was nothing to be done for it; Guy turned. Every thwarted bit of fury he had ever possessed ramped upward, threatened to spill over as he locked eyes with one of the worst of his enemies. It was everything he could do to not draw his sword and take her head on the spot.

"Please to meet Elisabeth, Most Holy Abbess of Worksop Priory."

She seemed little changed, perhaps smaller, her black robes hanging heavier. It did not make him want his hands about her throat any less. Her dark eyes had gone wide, more from confusion than any recognition... and yet, beneath it, something sniffed at familiarity.

This was not good.

"Do you two . . . erm . . . know each other?" De Lisle's voice broke the almost-rapt uncertainty, scattered it and gave Guy another focus.

He wasn't here to settle personal scores. *Not yet, anyway,* fury hissed from behind his eyes, and with chill determination he shoved it back, cordoning it into one of the many small and airtight corners in his heart.

Instead, he tilted his head, all grave, diffident courtesy. "I think not," he told the Sheriff. He pointedly did not address the Abbess. And thanked the God of his fathers for the popular and misogynist misreading of why Templars usually refused to directly address women: contempt.

Not that contempt even began to explain what he felt for this particular woman, though it had little to do with her sex.

"Are you sure, Brother Templar?" Elisabeth was frowning. She had her own gears, this one. "You seem . . . familiar."

Guy once again addressed the Sheriff. And tried not to feel too pleased as his disregard plainly annoyed the Abbess. "I often come up against all sorts of prejudices against red-haired persons. One seems to be that we all look similar." He shrugged. "One of the more harmless of them, granted."

And if doubt had taken seed, the roots of it seemed to stunt at his cavalier negation.

"I will admit, my lord Sheriff, to some surprise that you have an abbess attending your office. Almost as much surprise as you seem to find at *my* appearance. I daresay the latter has little to do with the colour of my hair."

De Lisle's nostrils flared. Good. Keep him annoyed and he would be more focused on his own importance than anything else. "As the Holy Abbess Elisabeth is my sister, she comes here to visit. As to my surprise . . . well, yes. I will admit I am surprised. I had heard Gisbourne worked for the Templars, not . . ." De Lisle's thick eyebrows went upward as he gestured to Guy's black tunic with its crimson cross, his pause as delicate as the seneschal's had earlier been—and just as telling.

"Not that I *was* one?" Guy abandoned any pretence at subtlety. "Allow me to make things clear. I am a knight of noble birth and styled *Confanonier*, standard bearer and personal guardian to Hubert de Gisborough, Master and Commander of the Templar Preceptory at Hirst."

The Sheriff's nostrils flared again. The Abbess was watching him very carefully. Her doubts were clear, but also her uncertainty: she could not place him.

Certainly not with her uncle's son Gamelyn Boundys.

"Therefore, my lord Sheriff, you will address me as not merely 'Gisbourne', but Sir Guy or my lord de Gisbourne. Or my lord Templar, for I am indeed a Brother of the Templar Order and thus your only authority over me—by not only King's grant but Papal writ—consists of what I choose to give you. Rest assured you will receive all due deference and respect your coffers have gained you regarding this little assignment. Though"—another shrug—"I'm not terribly convinced deference has gained you overmuch thus far."

De Lisle had been puffing up like a bantam cock since Guy had informed him of the faulty mode of address; this last pronouncement was obviously not to be tolerated without some rebuttal.

"You forget yourself, my lord!"

"I merely," Guy returned, "acknowledge the facts as they stand, my lord." *And am enjoying it far more than I should.* "If you were capable of ridding your shire of this particular wolfshead, no doubt you would have done. You have not, so I am here. *Non?*"

Ah, Hubert was right. Reputation remained far more effective than any actual blows dealt. A power more priceless than any gold: watching the Lord High Sheriff of three shires have to seethe . . . quietly.

"How do we know the Brother Templar is who he says he is?" The Abbess purposefully addressed her brother and clasped her hands, peering at Guy with all the demure comportment of a new bride.

He remembered her as formidable. But holding to righteousness against her uncle's late-gotten son was one thing; holding to it against a Templar?

Remarkable, indeed. Or patently stupid.

De Lisle did not find it at all remarkable. He shot her a quelling look and Guy had the sudden urge to laugh. Albeit with a hysterical tinge.

"It is not an unusual request, surely." The Abbess's words were, again, directed to de Lisle. But her eyes were still narrowed upon Guy.

"My lord. I and my companion have travelled long today. Surely my habit and this," Guy held out his hand, where a gold signet glinted, "the seal of Hirst and my Master, shall at least gain me a meal at your board? Then I will gladly return to my superiors, let them know Nottingham Castle is run by a cloistered woman instead of its sheriff, whom we were mistakenly informed had the hiring of me—"

"Enough!" De Lisle had obviously decided upon which horns of this dilemma to impale himself. "Please. Sir Guy. I see no need to go to such lengths. My sister can be . . . overzealous in her views. And if she cannot exhibit decent manners, abbess or no, I will ask her to take dinner in her chambers." The vicious look he shot the Abbess made it plain he was serious. As to Abbess Elisabeth herself, she did not bother to hide the ugly and thwarted expression claiming her face as she turned and walked, head high, over to sit at the far end of the table. A point of pride, nothing more.

Which was fine by Guy. Anger would keep her off-kilter, as well. And hopefully she would be insulted enough to leave.

"Please, my lord," de Lisle insisted. "Sit at my table. Too much time already has been squandered upon this filthy outlaw."

ᚴ

"Too much, this latest insult. The thieves took a wagon holding a full third of the Archbishop of York's treasury. They killed the guards before anyone saw them—as silent and deadly as the old greyfeather Saxons who tried to oust William—then they set the horses free, gave the archbishop and two monks escort to Nottingham in nothing but braies."

A mere thief, but a clever one, it seemed. A jumped-up and belligerent cutpurse with the charisma to persuade a small band of killers to his biddance.

"This wolfshead and his mangy followers roam Sherwood like it belongs to them. The peasants call him Robyn Hood, when they're not muttering nonsense about green men and magic. Fae tales and witchcraft... all sorts of like nonsense! There were hints of him in Barnsdale, but he seems to have followed me, and all the bolder for it."

A romantic villein with a peasant's weapon. A pretender to the Hunter's place. A spirit. A ghost in the green Wode.

Nay. Nothing more than a ragged bastard who had stumbled into a power not his own, a thieving villein who had stolen druid artefacts so he could wield that power.

Usurper to a demon lad, dancing in flames.

Guy gritted his teeth and kept walking the parapets, steps measured. It was not for enjoyment of the still night and the forest's surround, with black fingerlings of branches reaching to a thick-clouded and starless sky. He did not want to feel the Wode's beauty; he needed more to suck in the moist air, clear his head, ponder. Go over what he'd been told. Consider the options.

Stop mourning for what was gone.

Much had stayed in their newly granted quarters, ensuring to their comforts. He'd sworn to have warmed brandywine when Guy returned. And Guy was going to need it. He'd truly not prepared himself well enough for any of this. He'd thought it would be ... if not easier, at least not so ... insidious.

Dead. They were all dead. Rob's bones mouldering beside the ruins of what had once been Loxley, Marion's body flung from Blyth's dead cart into the common grave there. Eden lay no longer in the black Shire Wode.

Still, he called it the Shire Wode. Not Sherwood, as the conquering race—his father's race—had deemed it. He had seen the Abbess's odd look when he had called it so. He could not afford many mistakes like to that. It was Sherwood Forest, one of the finest royal hunting preserves in England, with thousands of tangled, dark places to hide murderers and thieves. He could not afford sentiment. Guy shook his head. Kept walking. Pondering.

Murderers. Thieves. *Wolfsheads.* And this particular wolfshead was not worth mere pennies, nay. He had the cunning of an alpha wolf, this one, and the luck of the fae. The common folk had raised him up—as if their superstitious twaddle had anything to do with the will of gods. As if prayers and pleas would move a power that would still a babe's heart even as it bawled its first breath; that left men to die racked with agony, their intestines strewn over the hot sand; that would let earthly emissaries murder towns full of hostages, or *be* murdered by treachery and a lover's naïveté.

The sound of his teeth gritting echoed against the nearest merlon, apropos in that he quite needed a place to shelter from the flung arrows of his own inner siege. An unwelcome reminder: he was not in control. Not in the least. Guy laid a clenched fist against the upthrust bit of wall, took in a deep breath. Enough. No more weakness.

No fear, Gamelyn...

It slithered up from memory, fire and heat wrapping itself about his throat. If Guy could have spitted the sudden-soft voice with a keen blade, he would have. Instead, he spat into the flames:

I hate you. Stay dead, damn you. Leave me be.

And no more remained: only blessed, blessed silence.

He kept walking.

This sheriff, unlike the one he'd replaced, was a cool one. Not overly burdened with either belief or a conscience, de Lisle refused riot, would never indiscriminately burn villages or murder peasants—not because it was "unjust," but because it was sensible. Crops must be gathered; cattle must be driven. To hold no value to his villeins' existences would mean inadequate labour to work his fields, no food for his table, no income with which to secure his tenure. Brian de Lisle had not gained the reeveship of three shires by being hotheaded or stupid.

Footsteps rived Guy from his thoughts—at first faint, then more regular, approaching. He came to a stop with hands at his sides, seeming no threat but in actuality close to both sword and dagger, and waited. Presently two guards came around a turret, one armed with a pike and the other with a crossbow. They hesitated upon seeing Guy there. One started forward, weapon to hand and the other following close suit. Their job, surely, nothing more or less, but the challenge died in the guard's throat as he strode closer, saw through the mist and murk Guy's tabard—and the crimson cross upon it.

"Your pardon, milord," the guard quickly muttered, his companion following respectful suit. Weapons and heads lowered, they both gave Guy a wide berth as they passed.

After, Guy hesitated. He thought he'd heard another set of footsteps echoing on the stones. But not boots, not strong or heedless with the right to be there . . .

But nothing. Guy frowned then shrugged it off. Likely an echo. The mists were creeping over the parapets from the sheer drop of stone and the bottom lands beyond, gathering thick upon the paving and gusting about his knees as he moved. Sound was chancy in such conditions.

He kept walking the stones, slow and nigh-silent, once again deep in thought.

This latest move merely betrayed how indeed quick-witted de Lisle was. Hire an independent agent to do the work, however filthy, and wash one's hands of the cost while reaping the rewards. And while de Lisle might have been expecting more common bounty hunter than sworn Templar, he had quickly become aware of the doubled blessing. It might throw a wild card into de Lisle's control of the situation, but it also meant success. Whatever Guy must do to bring the situation to heel, he could not be called to account for it by any power in this land but his own Master.

First, to do some intelligence: a canvass of the castle, certainly, and then one to the villages skirting the Shire Wode, including some adroit and undercover questioning. The villeins might be afire with rebellious hope, embers stirred to a flare by this new "hero" of theirs, but surely they didn't value an outlaw more than their own. Why would they? And if they did chance to think themselves inclined to altruism . . .

He well knew how ultimately fragile *that* was.

Another step yanked him from his musings. This one more hesitant. Quieter.

Sneaking.

Guy leaned against another merlon, again all-too-casual, but ready.

Another slide of step. Another hesitation. They were very quiet, whoever they were, with an instinctive grasp of how regular sound bided as much a giveaway as volume. This might have been a bird, or a tree branch.

Guy knew it was not. He touched his fingers to the dagger at his hip, but otherwise made no move. Waiting.

He saw the curl of mists, moving ahead of the figure before it came around the corner, and Guy rocked forward on his toes, put a firm grip on both dagger and sword and started to action. Then he witnessed the nigh-silent, wary intruder's appearance: clad head to foot in a dove grey that fanned the mist and gleamed even in the clouded dark. Guy uncoiled himself from the preamble to attack. His stalker wore a novice's habit.

Though she had made an error in assuming he no longer remained, surprise did not make her lose that eerie and quiet grace as she turned to flee.

"Wait!" he hissed after her.

She hesitated, half turned.

"I mean you no harm, Sister. Please, don't go on my account." Even as Guy said the words, something within him wondered why.

Perhaps her stealth puzzled him so. Perhaps it was the sideways slide of her eyes, gleaming like a trapped hind in the dim.

He knew that look. Had hunted it. Had *felt* it.

"I should no' be here alone." It was muted.

"But you are not alone," Guy protested, also soft, again unsure of why he did so.

A downward dip of the veil, a hint of a smile beneath it. "I should suppose, to have the company of a Templar Knight is to be well guarded indeed."

Guy was surprised. Surely she had not looked at him enough to see his clothing.

"I am sorry," she said. "I were watchin' you." The grey-clad shoulders lifted and dropped, and the novice went over to the parapet's edge, laid her hands on the stones and looked out over the mist-shrouded shadows of fields and forest.

Watching him? Even more intrigued, he stepped closer. "If you were watching me without my knowledge, then surely you need rely on none for protection."

Another hint of a smile. The novice's profile seemed young in the shadow of veil and clouds, but not a child's no matter the soft hesitancy. "I thought you were here for the view. 'Tis a lovely one." She had the burr of peasantry rippling through her voice—Yorkshire, certainly, but also perhaps the North—a mélange of familiarity to soothe his soul yet also twist his heart. He'd believed both impossible. "I've precious little chance to see the forest in this way. All the beauty, 'tis there. All the . . . danger." Her head cocked sideways, as if curious, the veil laid a whisper across her cheek. "But you weren't here to look. It . . . surprised me."

Guy's turn, now, to cock his head, curious.

"Such things could surely snare anyone's gaze, but not you. You'd hardly a glance for it. Your attention bided . . . confined, by stone and your own thoughts."

"Are you chastising me for ignoring the forest's beauty? Or heeding its danger?" *Or for talking to you. Why* am *I talking to you?*

Neither did he turn and walk away, as he should have done. Instead he moved slightly closer, trying to see her face.

"I merely find your concentration admirable." The thick veil fell behind her shoulders as she shrugged, lifting her chin. There was an ease about the gesture that rang an alarm deep within;

there was . . . *something*, something indefinable about her profile, now bared to the faint light. "You so easily shrug away the world, set yourself on your meditations. For myself, I find such diligence . . . difficult. I do envy you, Templar."

Guy's ears were ringing. No, not *ringing*, more like a deep-set hum, a breath of sound trickling up his spine and behind his ears . . . it made no sense. His words were gruff to cover it. "I assure you, if you truly knew me you would not. I have done . . . terrible things."

"You are modest, as well." She turned to face him. "Terrible things bide all about us, Sir Knight. If you . . . " She trailed off, brows drawing together as their eyes met. As if she knew him. As if he knew her.

He knew her.

But it was impossible.

The name came bubbling up from his chest and he couldn't stop it had he tried.

"Marion?"

It was a whimper, hoarse. A child's plea.

It was *impossible*.

"How do you know my name?" Her brows drew together, one canting slightly upward. He knew the expression, *knew* it. "Do I know you, Sir Knight?"

I know you. I know you and this. . . this can't be happening.

"They said you were dead." His voice was barely a whisper. "They took you aw—"

Away. In the dead cart. The villeins saw it, I know because I asked. . . when I could ask, when. . . I kept asking and asking and they all told me. . . after. . . even Brother Dolfin in the confessional. . . and I knew it had to be true, you could not have survived.

Her eyes, clear in the half light, would be grey in sun or sunlit shadow, pale-lashed. A wisp of wiry hair tried to escape the wimple's confinement, but 'twas the half smile, both curious and clever, that he would have known anywhere.

"There is a familiarity about you," she said, more cautious than curious. Yet no recognition sparked her eyes. "Please forgive me. I have not been allowed to venture out much. I should think I would remember a Templar, of all things, but Reverend Lady Elisabeth says I should be careful what—"

Guy lunged forward and grabbed her by the shoulders. "What has *she* done to you?"

Curiosity turned to alarm. "She . . . what? Let go of me!"

"Don't you know me? Why can't you—"

"I don't . . . don't know any . . . you're *hurting* me!"

"Marion, it's me. *Gamelyn—*"

"I *don't know you!*"

The force of it was as a welcome slap, erecting reason out of a sudden and utter chaos he wasn't equipped to handle, not anymore, for he had sublimated it into nothingness and surely that was why . . .

Why? *How?*

He loosed her, backed away as if she had burned him.

But she didn't run from him. Nay, she stood there, arms crossing and fingers clutching to where he had gripped her, shaken her, and her eyes were no longer clear, but clouded. Confused.

Walk away, Sir Guy. Walk away whilst you still can. . .

The sound of boots echoing against the parapets, running down the walk toward them. More out of instinct than anything else, Guy whirled and drew his sword, stepped in front of Marion . . .

Was it Marion?

It had to be.

Three soldiers, no doubt drawn by the shout, rounded the curve. It was rather amusing, actually, to see them nearly haul backwards in their haste to stop, piling into each other—the walk wasn't narrow, but they were startled by what waited there.

Small wonder they couldn't catch a thieving wolfshead.

"M-my lord," one stammered. "We heard a shout."

Guy straightened, made some show of putting his sword back in its sheath at his hip. "Well. Do you hear one now?"

One of them actually listened. Guy had to restrain himself from putting his palm to his forehead. Instead he made a shooing motion. "*Va t'en.*" And when they blinked at him, repeated it in the Anglic tongue. "Go. *Away.*"

"Aye, m'lord," the one who'd spoken first gave a quick bow. "Our apologies for disturbing you."

Guy dismissed them from his thoughts, turning back to Marion . . .

But Marion was gone, as if she'd never been there.

- VI -

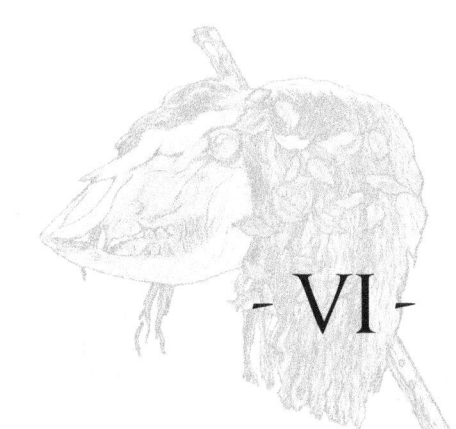

Every night before she retired, Marion had the duty of removing the wimple and veil from her mistress's hair and throat, the pectoral cross from where it hung against her breast—which Marion put in a small box—and brush the nape-length fall of wheat-coloured hair into some order.

It had taken a while for Marion to handle the cross without a shudder. Sister Deirdre had once made an injudicious comment about wicked memories, and the Abbess had spoken sharply to Deirdre. But then, Marion and Deirdre had never gotten on. If it indeed meant some wicked memory, Marion was glad to not have it, from the feelings it garnered. But this, the tending of her mistress's hair, stirred some small, pleasured place in the ebon blank of Marion's recollection, and she was glad to do it.

"I fear my brother has jettisoned sense in his battle against this ridiculous outlaw," the Abbess said with a shake of her head. "Bringing in a Templar, of all things!"

"Aye, I saw him! On the parapets, while I were walking—" Marion bit it back. The problem with having such a shortened recall? Sometimes she was so pleased to have something actual to recollect, her tongue was unwise in what it babbled. She hadn't intended to mention her night's walk. It would only worry the Abbess, and Marion surely caused her benefactor enough worry.

The Abbess gave her a frown, then turned back around with a sigh. Marion knew it would not end there, and it didn't.

"You should not have been walking the wall alone. After dark, in the fog. It was foolish, Marion. You have God's grace in the miracle of the life He granted back to us, but you cannot ever forget what evil would still claim you. You must be wary, and vigilant. You must be protected." The Abbess leaned back in her chair, angled her head. "Not to mention this Templar. Gisbourne. It is my understanding he has a particularly ruthless reputation." A pause. "Did he bother you?"

"No. We spoke, but—"

"He *spoke* to you?" The Abbess seemed surprised.

"Reverend Lady, he did. He . . . "

Said he knew me. Called my name, in a. . . a voice I've heard before. A voice I've dreamed.

Surely that was why the words stoppered in her throat, went dull and dead. For the dreams were evil. Pernicious ravages from a life she could not remember, yet was never allowed to forget.

They had tried to kill her and steal her soul. It had been a miracle, her survival. Even the archbishop from York had agreed it was nothing less when the Abbess had told him what she had witnessed. Not that Marion had been allowed to hear their conversation, in case it should damage her fragile mental state. But after, the archbishop had spoken to her personally, blessed her and assured her that, even if they did not have the requisite witnesses to make it official in the eyes of the Church, her presence was nonetheless a miracle. Marion bided in a state of grace and was to be allowed—in fact, encouraged—to continue her novitiate.

How could a Templar—one of the legions of Christ's Cross in the Holy Land—be part of any evil dream?

"Marion?"

Realising she had paused in her tending, Marion shook her head and once more resumed running the horsehair brush through fine strands. "'Tis too long, Reverend Lady, tangling 'neath your veil so. Shall I fetch my scissors?"

The Abbess's hand, slender compared to Marion's but nonetheless strong, reached up and took hold of the brush. "*Marion.* What did this Templar say to you?"

Dutifully, Marion tried again. Something different, perhaps. "He said he were . . . " Again, the strange constriction of her throat, as if the Templar's name literally would not sound.

"What?" the Abbess turned, eyes narrowed. "Was he forward with you? Rude?"

"He's a *Templar*, Reverend Lady!"

"He's a man," was the Abbess's flat reply. "And *those* particular hounds of God fear no laws made by King or Church."

"They say the Templars do God's work in the Holy Land."

"I see precious evidence of it here. Little better than moneylenders. Hired killers and fanatics. They consort with Saracens and heretics. It's even said they worship a Heathen idol."

Marion fell silent. It was hard to believe that ruddy-haired, quiet man worshipped idols. That he feared nowt?—aye, *that* she would believe. For all his face looked to be younger than hers, his eyes were *old*. Opaque as a serpent's, chill as the steel at his belt . . .

Except when he'd grabbed her. Feeling had blossomed within those flat eyes then, altogether malleable and . . . *vulnerable*. And all because he thought he'd recognised her?

Dangerous? Neither did she not question that. She would no doubt have marks on her arms to hide from the Abbess's critical gaze come morning. And why she would hide them, when she likely could have him chastised for treating her so?

"Give me the brush, girl. Your mind is plainly elsewhere." It was chiding.

Cheeks warming, Marion did as bidden.

The Abbess laid the brush on the table and pushed away, rising to make her way across the chambers Nottingham's sheriff had granted them for their stay. "Dawn will be upon us anon. Prepare yourself for bed."

"As you wish, Reverend Lady." Marion went over to the far wall, where a narrow cot had been placed and rushes piled high. Her own hair needed a good trim and a scrubbing, lying crinkled against her skull as she removed her wimple and coif, gave it a good scratch.

She was glad Deirdre hadn't come, this time. It had been so recent, after all, that Marion had been allowed outside Worksop's confines, only since the Abbess had returned from her travelling. Once Marion had been glad of the safety of her cell and the kitchen garden. She had a way with plants, and the abbey's herbalist was very glad of a skilled student. But lately, she wearied of her protective cage.

Marion had been surprised when the Abbess had offered to take her on this trip. On the surface a peacemaking venture with her brother, the Abbess never had merely one goal in sight. There had been talking—well, arguing, mostly—about kings and heirs, estates and barons. And the wolfshead no one could catch. He was of particular fascination to Marion, forbidden fruit of a life beyond her reach. As the perpetually present novice—not unlike the servants ghosting through the castle, ignored unless needed—Marion had heard much of it. Had listened avid and invisible, hungry for news of the world. Much of it she also hadn't understood very well, due to her lack of outside contact.

All of it necessitated regular trips to the chapel; Marion knew she should pray for release of her unseemly curiosity. But she had little talent for praying and none, seemingly, for the remorse she should feel at such subterfuge. It felt . . . more survival than sin.

"*What has she done to you?*"

The Templar's vehemence had not, as it should have, made her want to flee. It had made her want to sit with him, take his face in her palms as if she knew him as a brother, or lover, and ask him the same:

What have they done to you, *Gamelyn?*

Only that wasn't his name. The Abbess had said it: Gisbourne, not Gamelyn. Had she misheard? Gamelyn was an ancient name; it meant *the old man's son*.

A small sliver of pain burrowed behind her right eye. Marion dove into bed, pulled the coverlets up close. She wasn't about to admit to the discomfort; the least sign and they would bung her back up in the abbey.

How did she know him?

"Marion. Stay away from the Templar. He seems—"

"Sad?" It burst from Marion, curiosity and dread overcoming the tightening of her throat that said, plain as plain: *Say nowt. You cannot tell her about him.*

And she could not even fathom *why*.

Silence. Then, "I find him cold. Proud. Whyever would you think him sad, Marion?"

The sliver broadened into a knife-sized stab. Marion bit her lip, said, "I don't know." At least it was the truth. And it made the pain ease.

Silence, only their breath in the dark, and the call of a dove from outside the window.

"I don't know either," the Abbess said. "But I intend to find out."

ᚴ

Black. Black, and cold, and laughter wisping through the trees like tendrils. . . like tendrils, wood and leaf, creaking, vines of ivy sidling up, grabbing him, taking him down into the black and still, the laughter. . .

Then a hand on his cheek, warm and firm, lifting his face up to meet Marion's. The trees have not taken her, after all; she kneels down before him, smiling. Soft. Mocking.

"Fool. Do you think you can fight this?" She shakes her head. "You should never have come back. . ."

He lurched up, writhing and struggling before he became conscious of what clung to his arms and legs: not vines, but merely the coverlets. Guy kicked them away regardless, lay there panting, naked and a-sweat, until every sense came to the realisation he was here, in bed, in the roomy chambers the Sheriff had granted to himself and his paxman, in Nottingham Castle. His breathing, hoarse and grating, filled the stone walls like a bellows. Hopefully the terrors hadn't found voice before he'd woken and strangled them.

"Milord?"

Putain de merde. Guy closed his eyes and sighed, then lurched up to a seated position, put his head in his hands. If he'd woken Much in the connecting alcove, then aye. A shout or two.

"Milord, are you all right?" Much came padding in; Guy could see him through loose-laced fingers: only half-dressed, short-cropped hair sticking up at odd angles, eyes blinking against the lit candle he held up.

Nodding, Guy took another breath, kneaded at his temples, which were pounding fit to burst. "I'm sorry to wake you. I thought . . . " He swallowed. "I don't know what I thought."

Much leaned against the bedpost, brows furrowing as he gave Guy a critical onceover. "They're getting worse, en't they?"

He didn't want to answer, some little superstitious voice in the back of his head protesting that to give it voice would merely let it in, so Guy placated it by merely nodding again. Admitting, only not.

For someone who'd thought himself well done with a sublimated past, Guy was certainly spending a lot of time in the re-conjuring of it.

"Shall I fetch the pipe for you?"

Guy nodded. He had to *sleep*. He had a feeling he'd need every scrap of endurance and brains about him in this little war.

It was a war. Not as strewn with blood-soaked sand, corpses, and the litter of men's souls, true . . . but, in its own way, proving just as chaotic. Just as internal as external.

Just as necessary to temper any weakness into hardened steel.

He thanked Much as he brought the pipe, brazier, and tin, watched as Much first lit another few candles, then coaxed the brazier into life. Guy waved him off from hovering further. "Go back to bed."

"I've to admit," Much said in his cautious way, "the beds here're bloody comfortable."

"Then no sense to both of us losing any more sleep than we must," Guy chided, soft. "On with you. I'll be well enough anon."

"If y've need—"

"You'll know."

A mantra, almost, one they knew as well as the calluses on their sword-hands. A comfort, calm within whatever storm would rise. Its own proof of tempering in the trust of comrades-in-arms.

Tempering. So many methods, and Guy had tried them all. First it had been the scourge. He still had scars on his ribcage from his short stint of experimenting with that particular method of penance. Only he'd miscalculated when he'd found himself fancying it if he didn't lash hard enough; applying it hard enough meant he was crippled up for several days after. Good enough for a monk in his cell; not so good for a squire to a soldier who might be called to duty at any moment. There was enough arse-whipping handed out in battle without giving in to self-indulgent flagellation. His knight needed him in the field, depended on a squire fully capable for anything, sound in wind and limb.

Likewise with any other form of self-torture. Not only unfeasible, but suicidal. A danger to his lord and everyone who looked to him.

Better Guy be very, very careful in what he chose to feel.

Lying back down, he took up the pipe and inhaled, held it deep, felt it quiver then knock against his lungs, insistent. It had to be when he was this keyed up.

Sex had not proven enough. He had no business indulging whilst on a mission, anyway. His vows precluded any physical congress with a woman, of course. That had proven no true hardship. Though he liked women well enough, he'd never, by chance or design, lain with one. Perhaps it was true, that one never missed what had not been experienced. Lads were a different matter. If not openly encouraged, neither was it vilified—and the company of one's brethren greatly preferred over swiving any female. Such pleasure had proven in itself a curious form of self-torture—acceptable in that it left no lasting pain. None physical, at any rate.

The lines of acceptable strictures had blurred even further once Gamelyn had been sent, with several other young Templars, as trade and emissary to the Saracen *imam* who ruled over the *hashishin*, the assassins of Alamut. They had joined the boys who were training as *Fida'i*—counterpart in many aspects to the Knights

Templar. Those dark lads had fought him, at the first, had scorned his infidel race and been in awe of his hair—after all, it was rumoured Mohammad himself had possessed such a blessing/curse. They had fought alongside him once they had found the *Ifranji* to be nothing less than an avenging angel in battle-heat. There had been sex, there; lots of it. Throwing a gauntlet at death's cavernous face had a way of tearing down the wages—and faces—of sin. In the aftermath of that had lain introduction to another insubordination: the hashish pipe. Under its influence, the Saracen lads had once again changed their assessment of the *Ifranji*: more *djinn* than any angel—one of the cold, smokeless beings conjured from fire. They'd called him *hariq aljinni alsheer alghaba*. The fire-haired *djinn* from the forest . . .

As smoke filled the dim chamber, Guy conjured that *djinn*, over and over. The past would not help him now. Only the present. Only *now*, cleansed with fire and sword.

Finally, he slept, without dreams.

Morning found him, as usual, at matins.

There had been a time when prayer had given ease. He had been a dutiful supplicant, willingly offering up soul and mind in exchange for security, reassurance. Structure. Now Guy knew: life was none of those.

Now it was habit, nothing more and nothing less: an expected routine twining itself tight with the rest of the day, marking off the hours and allowing him, if not comfort, at least a blank space where he did not have to think, or do. The past was anathema. The future lay unwieldy, either a mixed mutilation of days stretching out endlessly, or a mildly intriguing possibility of progress throttled midbreath. The present hung between—*he* hung between—like some bloodied avenging angel welcoming both the solace and the snare, dealing equal measures in pain and pleasure with a grimed sword and tattered, fouled wings.

It had taken some time, but now he could kneel at the altar of his father's God and spill neither bile nor begging. He could just . . . *be*.

Only . . .

Now the past was rearing up beneath him, a blood-maddened destrier. Now there was *Marion*.

Guy found himself routed, in retreat, falling into familiar habit like a deep abyss. Found himself kneeling, laying his head into his hands, *praying*, as if he actually still believed absolution could be had in such abject surrender. And when, just before dawn broke outside the Nottingham chapel, he felt the presence at the door, he held his breath. Did not leave.

For the same instincts that had saved him, time and time again, that had given him no choice in ducking assassin's dagger or enemy's sword or sneak attack, whispered to him the identity of the newcomer.

Silence, filled only by the shallow, halting breaths from the chapel's entry, by his own exhalations into his clenched fists. Then footsteps, steady and quiet, as Marion trod the chapel's centre aisle and halted beside him, a bare pace away.

Then she knelt beside him, clasped her hands and bowed her veiled head.

Those hands had dirt-marked calluses, yet were moon-pale even against the ivory-and-grey of her habit. The cheek within the veil was freckled, but those freckles were washed out, as if the sun had rarely touched her—unlike his own skin that still bore an insistent bronzing beneath uncountable copper constellations: years of enduring a desert sun.

He didn't stop to wonder at why she looked more a newly freed inmate of some sunless gaol, or why she had not simply turned and fled his presence, or why she had chosen, of all the empty, pre-Matins chapel chamber, to kneel within his reach.

Instead he leaned closer. And when she didn't retreat, leaned closer still and whispered, into his hands, "I did not do it. I *didn't*."

Silence, again. Guy slid a glance toward her; she had not moved. Seemed lost in her prayers, as if she hadn't heard.

Guy closed his eyes, shook his head against his folded hands, then crossed himself and started to rise.

One of her hands reached out and gripped his tunic, stayed him. He halted midcrouch, looked down. Her brows were furrowed. Her gaze had risen to meet his, grey reflecting crystal against the scattering light of the lit sconces.

Those eyes settled his doubts—and raised new ones. She seemed confused. She'd absolutely no recognition of him in her expression, yet . . .

She remained here, beside him. She had approached him.

He should have kept silent. Something was wrong, and he should have held his tongue.

"What did you not do?" Her voice came low, almost hoarse. "Why tell me?"

"I . . . I am sorry." Gaining his feet, Guy reached down and gently disentangled her hand from the hem of his tunic. "I am inconsiderate. Both last night and this morning. Please." He settled her hand back atop the other, still resting on the altar board. "Continue with your devotions, Sister, and I shall leave you be—"

"Do we know each other?"

"Sister—"

"Please." She dipped her head down. "You must understand. I don't know your face. But . . . " She hesitated, took a tiny, tight breath and continued, "You seem . . . familiar, somehow. You see, there are things I . . . en't exactly remembering."

"There are many things better left forgotten," he murmured. "Memory is not always . . . kind."

Again, the grey eyes sought his. The expression in them sent him back to his knees.

"Memory." Her head dipped. "What," she murmured, "of dreams?"

"I don't believe in dreams." He shrugged. "Well, maybe nightmares."

"Nightmares." A whisper, this time. "Aye, I think you know nightmares, Templar." With head still bowed, cowl still shadowing her face, Marion rose. A slow, graceful motion, the grey habit shifting around her like clouds.

More out of ingrained courtesy than anything, Guy also started to rise. Her hand shot out, grabbed his shoulder. The hand clutched with a peasant's work-laden strength; it also possessed an exact, learned science of knowing which fibre of neck muscle would easily send him, once again, to his knees. Guy gave way with a grunt, peered up in surprise.

Marion's eyes gleamed beneath the cowl, but they were blank. Dark.

There is much hidden. Much you need to know.

Marion's lips had not moved. Her eyes were still pools of soot, sepia smudged beneath. There were splotches of scarlet livid upon her cheeks; that and the faint dusting of freckles, made up the only colour to her face, white as the underside of her novice veil.

You have slept long enough. All of you have. Will you hide forever, Gamelyn?

It was not Marion's voice. Nor was it the deep, male voice that had once and long ago violated his being. Guy stared up at her, agape. He had no words, had no *thoughts*.

Find them, Gamelyn. Find the wolves in the depths of my green Wode. For when you do, you shall find yourself. The sleepers will wake, and. . .

The pinching fingers released his shoulder. He sucked in a sharp, almost involuntary breath and She smiled.

"Aye. *Anadl tynged.*"

Fingers rose to his eyes, folded them closed. Then Marion's fingertips—Her fingertips—slid to his forehead, traced there. He could see the sigils, like fire burning behind his closed eyes. First the sign of the cross, then five points of a star, then the horned crescent of the under-waxing moon—

"Marion! What is going on in here?"

Guy leapt to his feet and drew his sword, all in one smooth, dangerous motion. Mere instinct, unstoppable reaction. Yet somewhere beneath instinct, a rational voice screamed at him: *What are you doing?*

"This is a chapel!" Framed by the entry door, the Abbess gave furious protest. "Put away your sword, you murdering . . . "

Guy could no more respond to the protest in his brain than he could avoid stepping between the Abbess and Marion, serious threat speaking in the language of swordsman dip and dance. "I am not the murderer here," he growled.

"Sir Knight." Marion's voice broke the sudden . . . possession, madness, whatever it was. *Marion's* voice, *Marion's* hand—not any phantom of whatever waking nightmare Guy had just entertained—taking hold of his sleeve. "'Tis all right. 'Tis merely the Reverend Lady."

No, a beast within him snarled, *it is not all right, and will never be until that bitch lies dead—*

Oh God. . . shut up! Guy ordered, silent and uncompromising, as if kennelling a beast.

And the beast, not without another snarl, did as bidden.

Guy turned his gaze from abbess to novice, back again.

Then rammed his sword into its sheath and quit the chamber.

"Templar!"

Guy kept walking. The sound of footsteps, rapid and in pursuit, merely encouraged him to lengthen his steps.

"Templar! You will stop, now!"

Oh, will I? He kept walking.

More steps, and a hand laid upon his sleeve, yanked so unexpected and fierce that Guy did stop. He slid his gaze to the Abbess's hand clutching to his sleeve, then to the Abbess herself, with all the regard he'd give a body insect. "You really don't want to do that."

Her cheek going pale, she let go. "I want to know what you think you are—"

"Woman, you are impertinent. Do you truly think that because you can harass your brother, *I* will tolerate it?" He turned away.
"You should have no interest in me. I certainly have none in you."
"But you seem to have interest in my novice."
He halted midstep, immediately regretted it. Did not turn.
"What do you want with her?"
Guy shook his head, started walking again.
This time, when she raised her voice in more questions, he didn't stop.

Marion heard their voices, started forward several times, shook her head and remained where she was an equal number of times.
Her fingers were tingling where she had touched him.
How did she *know* him? Even the question made her head throb, the blood pounding through her temples, and for the first time she welcomed it, wondered at it.
Questioned it.
She turned back to the altar, peered up at the cross. At the peasant king who had died for his people . . .
"Holy son," she whispered. "You, I have always known. Somehow."
The footsteps came, slow, advancing upon the altar. Marion turned to her mistress, expecting a sharp rebuke.
She received none. The Abbess's face was wan. The hand she lifted to smooth at her pectoral cross shook. "I told you Templars were mad. Did you see what he did? To *me*."
Marion did not feel the least penitent. Despite the fierce ache pounding at her skull, she felt . . . powerful. "I think you startled him. He has been long at the wars, so you said. He probably canna sleep without a dagger to hand and a beast's instincts."
"A beast, surely," the Abbess said, peering at Marion with a frown. "Are you all right? You should not have been in here alone with him."
"He . . . " What had just happened? She had bowed her head, speaking of memory, and the next thing she remembered was him kneeling at her feet, and her fingers tingling upon his forehead in a . . . "He asked for my blessing, Reverend Lady." She couldn't *remember*.
Still, the usual sense of helpless frustration at it was . . . muted. Nor did she want to turn aside, hide.
Sleeping. I have been. . . sleeping?

"I will speak to my brother about this!" the Abbess said. "He will have to do something. Surely the Templar can stay elsewhere. I am fearful for your safety."

Her mistress's concern always reassured. At this moment, it did not. Neither did she know why.

That *was* unnerving. What *had* the Templar done to her?

"Come." The Abbess lowered herself to kneel. "We will pray for him."

Marion's fingers tingled. She peered at them, surreptitious, as she bowed her head and began a Paternoster.

She had prayed for him. Had traced several signs upon his forehead, but try as she might, Marion could only remember the last one. And it had been a crescent, not the cross.

ᚴ

When Much came back from seeing to the horses, Guy had all his belongings spread over the bed, searching. Much stopped in the doorway, letting his rucksack drop through his fingers and to the floor.

"I need a smoke," Guy said. "A smoke, then to bed. We start out at first light. I've a few ideas."

Much didn't move. Guy looked up, saw the frown, the concern. Moreover, Much kept *looking*.

"*What?*" Guy finally asked, none too patient.

With a twitch of his broad shoulders, Much retrieved his burden, continued inward. Said, mildly, "I've wrapped it wi' the cleanin' rags in me sack, here. Padded, like. Bloody things en't breaking that easy, but they do. Break. I weren't 'spectin' you'd need it again before we were on the road."

Guy held out his hand for the rucksack. Much slung it on the wide, rush-padded bed, pushed Guy's hands away when he would have opened it, and started rummaging himself. In next to no time, he produced the pipe—and the small, waterproofed pouch holding its fuel.

Guy kenned his hands were shaking. He slapped the weakness into submission and sent it crawling into a corner. Was satisfied as his hands steadied, just like that.

Not that it would last long. Not with what was happening.

"The horses are well. That new bay needs a good gallop. He's antsy as a lad waitin' for a go at his first whore."

Guy had to chuckle. It was rare when Much didn't have a common, well-salted analysis for every imaginable situation.

Much started laying the things out on the thick, scarred table beside the bed, and lit the tiny brazier, letting it warm. The light flickered on the wall, catching the glimmer of silken thread in the hung tapestries. Outside, the night hung close, cloudy and growing chill. Autumn, waxing into full fruit.

Harvest looked to be bountiful. A good time to catch outlaws. Particularly these, who seemed to be taken with their supposed munificence. It was easy to forget largesse when food coffers were full.

Much never let Guy prepare the pipe, even though it would be ease to strung-out nerves. Guy spent the time picking up the results of his harried search. "Would you care to join me, Much?" Guy's words were quiet, though he knew what the answer would be. Mere camaraderie, courtesy, the suggestion.

"As y' ken, this en't the safest place," Much replied, but his eyes met Guy's and he smiled, accepting the spirit if not the offer itself. "One of us needs a clear head. And *my* head's no' so troubled tonight."

ⓚ

"*Alive.*" Much sat beside the bed, leaning against it. "The Maid, the Lady's vessel. Her power bound by a . . . " He obviously had no fitting word in English, growled an Arabic gutter curse beginning with "daughter of jackals" and ending in a reference to carnal knowledge of pigs.

It was some time later. How much, Guy had lost track—but the fat candle had burnt lower, the moon risen and disappeared from the window's frame, the sounds of habitation gone to silence.

There were many things Much didn't know—this he deserved to know. Much had survived many things, and, to Guy's continual bemusement, Much's faith had survived with him. Perhaps it was the utter pragmatism of the Heathen outlook, forced to accept nature in both Her bounty and Her indifference.

Guy wished he could see Much's face. All he could see was the strong, broad profile, barely delineated by the candle.

"'Tis beyond belief, milord." A whisper, strangely tight. Then, like tiny, glittering snail-trails, Guy saw the tears trailing down his companion's face.

A frown gathering at his brow, he rolled onto his side and reached down, lightly traced Much's cheek. Much lowered his head and, when Guy would have retreated, grasped Guy's hand, held it to his cheek, kissed the palm. Released it and rose.

Guy raised his hand before his face, contemplated the moisture there almost in bewilderment. "What is it like, Much? To . . . to believe in something so fierce it brings tears to your eyes? To be so grateful to receive the mere emotion of it?"

Much had turned to him, face—and silvery tears—in shadow. "I think you knew once, milord." Strange, how his voice seemed to shake all the more.

"Mayhap I did. Mayhap I was just an idealistic idiot."

"You're many things, milord, but never that."

"Mm." Guy took another inhalation of the pipe. Everything felt wonderfully stretched, as if time itself lingered in fog and fugue. Even the past had little power over him, at this moment. The hashish was almost gone. And so was he, thankfully.

"Mayhap, milord, 'tis merely that both our gods are laughing at us."

In itself the concept amused. "Well. After all, what else is there for gods to do?"

Much still watched him, eyes a-glitter in the shadows. "An' now this . . . aye, no laughing matter. She's been held prisoner, Her powers sleeping. Even as the Shire Wode has been, sleeping."

"There's little sleep in the Shire Wode now. This wolfshead seeks to set it afire."

"Fire in the forest, 'tis a healing thing. But it destroys, also. The likes of outlaws, they destroy."

"This one seems to want to set the world on fire."

"All of it sleeping. For you. She's your Maiden."

Guy snorted, sending the breath of smoke outward in a burst that settled, floated and curled about the bedposts. "I'm not even sure what that means."

"She were Maiden to t' Wode."

"Much—" A warning, albeit lazily given: *Here be dragons. Go no farther.*

"Milord, the dreams. *Your* dreams. Even Master Hubert sees."

"Master Hubert sees . . . " *Too much in me*, Guy thought. *I will disappoint you, as well, my lord Commander. Betray your trust, in the end. It's all I've ever done.*

"He sees what you *are*. If the Maiden calls—if the Lady calls—you wain't—"

"I am not the Hunter!" It was strangled.

"The Hunter is dead, milord." Much went over to the far wall and his own bed, his soft voice trailing behind. "I know 'twere grief to you, but such things are as they are. The king died for his land. Long live the king."

- VII -

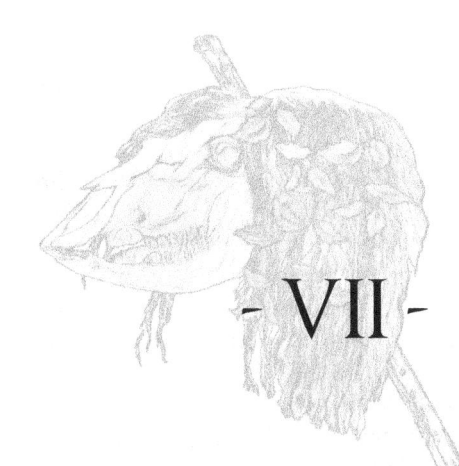

"Sommun's askin' after Robyn Hood."

"Fancy that," Robyn answered. He scarcely gave a glance to the older man who had sidled up to him wearing a dirty hat with a torn brim, instead kept leaning against two comfortable supports: Will Scathelock's brawny left arm and an equally sturdy hemlock. The outlaws had just arrived to Matlock with a prize. Already the villagers were gathering round, the headman relaying directions to those unharnessing the sorrel jennet from the wagon. They'd have the grain unloaded in no time, Robyn knew. As to his own . . .

"Arthur, leave off the horse; John doesn't need you fussing. Best take Gilly and David and set watch."

"And Will?" Arthur raised his eyebrows.

Next to Robyn, Will flexed one arm and winked. "Nae doubt I'll have the wagon."

"A proper ox, you are," Gilbert quipped, and took off with a yip as Will strode forward and aimed a half-hearted boot towards his backside. Robyn gave a small stagger at the impromptu desertion, realigned himself against the tree trunk, propped a foot for good measure.

"Sommun has t' do work for the pretty ones," Will quipped back.

Robyn laughed, gestured with the strand of hay he was

twiddling in his long, callused fingers. "Aw, Scathelock, 'tisn't so bad. *I* think you're pretty."

"You would, y' tunic lifter."

"Skirt chaser."

Will smirked and Robyn grinned back, watching the villagers unload the grain sacks.

"Robyn," the man with the dirty hat tried to wheedle.

"Leave Himself be, Cedric!" Matlock's headman, Wulfstan, came over, frowning.

"But there's sommat he should *know*, Wulf—"

John caught Robyn's attention just as he considered turning it to Cedric. A few hand signals and a dip of his dark head toward the setting sun, and John had made it plain he was ready for a cask of mead to warm the night with.

Robyn agreed. Matlock was known for its honey and, of course, the mead rendered from it. Surely Wulfstan would spare them one in recompense for the nicked grain.

"Same again?" Will asked Wulfstan, who nodded.

"We'll pour it off, give you t' auld sacks, and will thank the Horned Lord for his gift of the gelding for however long we have 'im." Wulfstan grinned. "There's none'll grudge us a good animal what just came walkin' up loose. They'll take 'im back should they ever find him, and curse Robyn Hood."

One side of Robyn's mouth tilted upward. "Fancy that."

"We'll take the cart and sacks a ways east," Will agreed. "Your folk rarely have business that way, and the less they've to do with it, the better. Aye, Robyn?"

"Aye." Robyn twirled the hay stem, lightly furthered, "John's wanting a bit of mead, Wulfstan, should you have it t' give."

The headman grinned. "Fancy that," he teased, in the same tone Robyn had just used, and Robyn chuckled. "I think we can spare a firkin for t' King of t' Shire Wode," Wulfstan continued, walking over to take the horse from John.

"Our little John gets more with a twitch of his eyebrows than any of us with a round o' beggin'," Will complained.

"Fancy that," Robyn arched his own eyebrows and elbowed him.

"Not my type. *You* fancy that," Will retorted, with his own elbow knock.

"Mm. As I can, aye."

"*Robyn.*" Cedric had skulked closer, a distinct whine edging his voice. Of course, Robyn considered, the best method of communication Cedric could muster usually involved whining. "I tell ye, 'tis *important*."

Will gave a sigh. "Look, man, if we jumped every time sommun gave Robyn's name a mention—"

"This 'un en't just mentioning. He's *questioning.*"

Robyn shrugged, transferred the stem of hay to his mouth, began chewing one end. "There's some as are sayin' the Sheriff's hired hisself a man, see?"

"Does the Sheriff fancy boys, now?" Will snorted, and gave Robyn a shove. "Mayhap you two need a chat!"

All right, *that* was not in the least bit funny. Robyn gave him a hard fist to the ribs. Will gave an "oof!" and went staggering— more than satisfying, considering he nearly made two of Robyn.

"Hoy! *Rob—*"

"Scathelock, if you don't shut your yap, I'll bloody well shut it for you—"

"You have t' listen, Robyn!" Cedric made a grab for Robyn's sleeve, which Robyn deftly avoided. "This 'un's askin' all sorts of things about Robyn Hood, and he's some *nobleman*—a killer from 'crost the sea, I heerd."

"A nobleman killer!" Will scoffed. "En't they all?"

But Robyn was watching Cedric, the strand of hay stilling between his teeth. "You've actually heard the Sheriff hired this man?"

"Aye, Robyn, 'tis what I've been trying to tell you!" Cedric's already protuberant eyes were bugging out further. "My cousin Edgar—as works in the Sheriff's kitchens?— aye, well, *he* said one o' those Templar Knights had come to Nottingham Castle, sniffin' about sommat fierce—"

"A Templar!" Will grunted. "*Jay*sus, Robyn. What in hell have you done to brass off one of *those?*"

Robyn shot him a quelling look; he wasn't about to flaunt his ignorance in public. He'd heard of Templars—mostly in Cernun's last days, words and warnings he hadn't understood. "And what did Edgar have to say about this . . . Templar?"

"Edgar'd heard all th' tales, y'know, about how those lot have horns and a tail and no soul—"

"Right, that's what the nobles say about Robyn!" Will snorted. "There y' go, Rob, there's a match made in t' otherworld for you!"

Robyn gave Will a black look that promised serious damage; it thankfully shut him up. "Did Edgar," he said, taking the hay from his teeth and examining it, "say owt useful?"

"I know, Robyn, I know. I were just sayin' all that to let ye know what Edgar were expectin'. Only 'e weren't getting it, see? Said the

Templar broke bread with the Sheriff and his sister like any normal—"

"Sister?" It twined Rob's nerves taut as any bowstring. "The Abbess?"

"Bloody damn," Will growled. "*She's* back?"

"Aye, Edgar said she'd been away down south, or th' like, for some time."

Surely a paradox, that a weasel of a cutpurse with a wagging tongue should so casually utter the name Robyn had cursed since he'd emerged from Cernun's caverns with a nigh-crippled arm, his world shattered and his heart full of unspent fury.

'Twere no surprise, the fury, forced to simmer but rising hot and wilful at the prospect of finally locating one of his enemies. Had Cedric known the impact of something he'd thought no more than an embellishment for his tale, no doubt he would have spun it out for the drama. Even now his goggle eyes were taking them in, back and forth, measuring the import of this latest. Robyn throttled every murderous impulse he had—if nothing else, he'd learned to listen to the cagey side of his instincts—and gave Will a warning look as well. This went too personal, too deep—a sharply honed weapon that could not be blithely handed to any outside their own.

"The Templar." Robyn's voice was flat; his eyes must've been moreso, considering how Cedric's open, eager mouth shut itself with a small "pop" and he immediately dropped his gaze. "Did the Templar come with the Abbess?"

"I . . . " Cedric, desperately trying to gauge the waters, finally had to speak plain truth. "Truly, lord, I dunno."

"But you did see him, aye, Cedric?"

Cedric's eyes bugged farther. If he only knew how much he gave away in mere expression and body cant, surely he wouldn't be worrying so much on any arcane powers the Hood might possess. Robyn didn't even have to waste a half sigh in the reading of Cedric.

"Well, lord Robyn, to be truthful—"

"'Tis better to be truthful, Cedric," Robyn pitched his voice deceptively mild.

Cedric gulped. "I en't so sure. I were in t' Brewhouse. Nigh t' Underkeep, y'know?"

Robyn did know. The Underkeep was a familiar nomer for the collection of sandstone caverns beneath Nottingham Castle, notorious throughout the Midlands for their stench—not only from the tannery pits maintained in one section, but the assortment of lowlife that frequented the remainder of the caves. The Brewhouse remained a particular favourite, the oldest and largest of several pubs, brothels, and dives scattered throughout the caverns. Robyn had certainly done his share of supporting the Underkeep's various and questionable attractions—an oblique "sod you" to the Sheriff in his castle above— until the price on his head had risen so high. The band as a whole had gotten all nursemaid-y and insisted he had to quit risking his neck for a few drinks and dice rolls, the latter of which he kept losing anyway. He always won his share at the dart pricks, though, and with the knives—unless John was playing the latter.

"But this man what I saw?" Cedric continued. "He didn't look t' be no knight a'tall, let alone dressed as that sort. I've heard y' en't missin' a Templar, what with their white clothes and th' scarlet cross on 'em. But this one? He were dressed plain as plain, wrapped up in a brown cape and a woollen shawl. Y'know how dark th' Underkeep is. His face weren't none too plain. I wouldn't've even suspected 'im as Edgar's Templar if it weren't fer me seein' the colour of 'is hair and beard. He were redheaded, had it braided out of his face all fancy-like. Just as Edgar said the Templar did."

"Probably en't no Templar, then," Will scoffed. "They're monks, right?" he protested as Robyn slid a sceptical gaze his direction. "They shave their heads." He snorted, yanked at one of Robyn's tangled locks. "Run in horror from *your* mop, they would!"

Robyn bared his teeth and pretended it a smile. "Monks."

"*Fighting* monks. One of that lot could likely rout us all. This en't good."

Robyn wasn't too sure he believed Will, but again, he wasn't ready to put his own ignorance on open display.

"Edgar said this 'un kept going t' chapel, regular-like, and that he wore the blood cross, but 'tweren't on white!" Cedric protested. "And th' man I saw had a great fancy ring on his hand like Edgar said the Templar had. Had a poncy sort of speaking tae him. He didn't speak just plain talk, like he were speaking Frank, or some other language as those nobles do when they don't want us to ken."

"So you *spoke* to him."

Cedric jumped as if Robyn had ensorcelled his innermost thoughts. "I meant nowt by't, lord." Cedric's use of honorifics always increased in direct proportion to his self-reproach. His gaze abruptly occupied itself with anything but meeting Robyn's. "I . . . well, I . . . "

Robyn turned, leaned until his face lay a mere handspan from Cedric's and said, very soft, "What did you tell him, Cedric?"

The man was sweating, now. "Just enough to earn a few pennies, milord, I swear! Nowt important!"

"Why don't you let me be the judge to that?" Robyn leaned closer. "What did you tell him?"

"He just asked me about what I'd already said tae th' potkeeper!"

"You were talking our business in a *pub*?" Will queried, deceptively mild; he'd already flanked Cedric.

Which Cedric only then noticed, and started stammering. "I poke around, like. There's several g-g-good pubs in the Underkeep, and the potkeepers t-t-tell me things just as Edgar does f-from the castle, so's I can bring 'em tae you—"

"You're babbling, Cedric." Robyn took hold of the filthy tunic, pulled Cedric just that much closer. "Stop telling me what I already know, and tell me what I need. You told him we were raiding the north road—"

Again, Robyn's knowledge made those bug eyes pop wider. "I told 'im nowt, lord, he weren't already knowing. He just—"

"Wanted confirmation 'twere us." Robyn met Will's blue eyes, saw his own dismay echoed there. "How many raids did he know about, then?"

"All the ones done ower the past two moons. Even th' ones the sheriff didn't know! Like th' prisoners y' set free on th' road t' nowhere—the one t' Derby, I mean. And he spoke o' ones I'd nivver heard. He ticked 'em all off, cool as if they were on some list in his head. I didn't tell him, I swear! He already *knew*, and I saw nowt in agreein' with him fer tuppence worth—"

"You little—" Will started forward. Robyn held him with a look, said, silent and clear: *Nay. Worse than any enemy's a loose-tongued idiot with a grudge.*

Robyn jerked his head to back Will off, then loosed Cedric's tunic, made a show of smoothing it. "This man were there when you arrived. How long did he stay?"

Cedric seemed to think about this. A frown drew his brow thicker as he answered, slow, "Y' know, lord, I en't sure. He were there, then he weren't."

"Robyn," Will began.

Robyn shook his head, leaned back against the tree, and shut his eyes.

A fighting monk. A fighting monk who could supposedly hand their arses to them, but asking seemingly useless questions of a man who clearly wasn't to be thoroughly trusted. A bigger jumble of contradictions Robyn had never heard . . . only perhaps not, if the questions were indeed meant to confirm what information this monk had already gathered. If the questions were a-purpose, scouting unfamiliar terrain, using a skiving drifter's language—spoken and unspoken—to test them.

Which meant the information had already been gathered, and that bode troublesome enough. To what purpose? Merely to kill Robyn Hood for the Sheriff? Or was there more? —and Robyn's instincts were screaming the truth of that, no question. The few times Robyn'd questioned said instincts had fetched him thoroughly buggered and nearly dead.

Perhaps if he actually really knew what a Templar was, it would make more sense. He'd never run across one, had never thought past Cernun's oblique warning, because Cernun had warned of so many things.

Will thought he knew what a Templar was. Marion would have *known* what a Templar was about. Robyn's throat tightened—the ache never went away, never would.

One more reason to bleed you like a pig. The thought sped towards Nottingham, an arrow seeking the Abbess's heart. *I'd lay marks on this being your doing. You've come back into my territory, you and your fighting monk. You're more dog than most of your kind, a craven bitch sniffing out the least hint of good, clean magic and seeking to kill it.*

Ah! Such a one would make a fine gift, the Horned Lord steamed behind Robyn's eyes. *Summer draws nigh, and his blood might buy the Lady's favour.*

Robyn frowned, sensing layers upon layers in the low inner Voice. He began to query, was diverted as Cedric started to creep away.

"Cedric!" Robyn said. "I've full tuppence for you, and a measure of corn, should you choose to do *me* a favour."

(ᚴ)

"That's preposterous!"

"I swear t' you, as mad as it sounds, I saw it!"

Guy rolled his eyes, leaned back in his chair and put his boots up on the scarred table. The alehouse was a particularly squalid one, even as such things went. He'd found the caverns below Nottingham castle to be a thriving industry of vice, and as long as it stayed below, the Sheriff showed common sense in letting it just sit there, stew, and rot. Better the devil you know, and all that.

"He disappeared right afore me eyes, I tell you!" The old man was well into his cups, garrulous despite the glares being sent his way. Some of those glares promised dire doings. Guy always watched his back, but the old drunk likely had no such caution.

Well, the more drunk, the more informative. Guy had learned long ago even the most inane babble had a tale to tell, should someone care to decipher it. He'd about done all he could within Nottingham proper, anyway. There was a distinct knack to it: just long enough to make a few patrons comfortable; any longer and they'd start becoming uncomfortable, wondering why.

Giving a yank to where the frayed ends of the damp wool cowling his head had kinked itself too tight around his throat, Guy pulled it down over his forehead. More akin to the Saracen *keffiyeh* than any hood or shawl, yet thick enough to shed the wet, he could wear it draped, depending on his surroundings. Here, it made adequate disguise, and shabby enough to pass for common. He'd first adopted a head wrap, like so many of his fair-skinned companions, as simple protection against the fierce sun of the Holy Land. The linen covering of self-preservation had morphed into a useful habit, a woollen cloth more useful to England's weather, with the side benefits of many affectations, still protective.

It was certainly more useful in this company than a bare, eventually recognisable head or the blatant cross on his black tunic and cloak; the former hidden beneath a dull brown overtunic, the latter hung discreetly on a hook in his allotted chambers in Nottingham's keep above. It wasn't quite time to drag those out for a last trip through. The uniforms would set a few more tongues loose and wagging in their wake, but it was better as a last resort before moving on.

"It's said auld Robyn's nowt but a spirit hisself. A ghost of vengeance from the old religion, old Hornie incarnate . . . huh. If 'tis true, then he's come into this world pissing fury, I'll tell ye."

"He's a temper, then." Guy looked around, caught a few surly-looking men several tables over, gave a friendly shrug that, plain as plain, said: *"Do you believe this fool?"* The raised hackles smoothed, but not as much as Guy would have liked. Definitely watch his back—and make sure none here saw his front too plainly, either.

"Aye, and he'll use it. Anyone hunts him, they're likely to come back riddled with arrows. Sheriff's lost more men to Shire Wode and Robyn Hood's men than dysentery. And those arrows are spelled, mark my words. No mortal archer has that many kills to his credit."

"So he can be invisible, he shoots faery bolts instead of real arrows, and he's some forest devil behind him." The latter made

Guy seethe, deep in some forgotten, forlorn place. He had to find this outlaw, carve every lie from him with the sharpest blade in his possession. Not only for a blood oath to a murdered lover, not only in obedience and gratitude to the man who'd given him a name and place and reason for living, not even to perhaps find some peace in what remained of his soul. Now there was also Marion, who had lost . . . everything. Including her self.

He pitied her.

No. He *envied* her.

He raised his jar to the old man. "I'll give you this, friend: 'tis quite a tale you're spinning."

"No tale to't!" the old man protested. "Robyn's uncanny. He put a curse on a man who'd crossed him, and the man died a week later, jus' fell down dead."

"So." Guy contemplated the chipped rim of his jar. "Such a man, such a powerful one? He must have enemies."

An affirmative grunt. "As many as are with 'im, there's those as fear 'im." The old man drained his pot, looked mournfully at the maroon slick on the bottom.

Guy's mouth twitched sideways. He finished his own then motioned to the potkeeper for another round. The wine was cheap and had little kick to it; he could drink it all day and just sweat and piss it away. The old man, however, was obviously unused to anything stronger than coarse ale.

The potkeeper came around, liking the coin the quiet stranger tended but somewhat uneasy of its effects. He touched his pate, put a firm hand on the old man's shoulder. "Shall I chase off this old fool? More drunken spew than sense."

Guy shrugged. "No harm done. I've never heard such things— have you heard of this Robyn Hood?"

A long shot, and it fell as expected. The potkeeper shrugged, ducked his chin, and hurried away.

Whoever this wolfshead was, he had the way of it. The ultimate secret of power:

Fear.

Word trickled back to the Shire Wode: a pair of strangers kept approaching outlying villages, on a broad sweep from east to west and sniffing for outlaw fodder. One cowled and menacing silent, obviously outranking the thick-hewed, swart man who couldn't stop saying "milord" out of obvious and long habit.

Cedric had done well—but then, he always did when paid well.

Upheaval had resulted when Robyn announced his intent to go alone; first to the Underkeep to find out more about the Abbess's visit, then on the trail of the two strangers.

"I'm going with you." Will was pacing back and forth across the campsite.

"Nay. You're not." Robyn sat by the fire, seemingly unaffected by Will's rant. And he had been ranting. Their companions, well-used to such an occurrence, had cleared the area about the fire. Several were clearly and vocally in support of Will's objections.

Arthur, of course. Arthur had teamed with Will not long after Will had first been made outlaw. It had been first Will then Robyn who had kept Arthur on despite a missing arm these past years; if Will said jump a tree, Arthur would likely do it. And David, a newer addition to their band, had objected. He didn't like going to Nottingham, didn't like *any* of them going to Nottingham, since he'd spent time in the gaol and still had nightmares over it.

Gilbert and John were staying out of the way, scraping fat from a hide, preparing it for tanning. Still, they made it plain they didn't like this idea, either.

Too bloody bad.

"One's more chance of not being seen." Robyn poked at the fire, sending sparks upward. "I'm going. Alone."

"Have all those dreams wakin' you lately caused what brains you have to squeeze out your ears?" Will demanded. "You en't going alone!"

"Robyn," Gilbert said, quiet to Will's thunder, "if you are seen, then one's more chance of never coming *home*."

"This Templar has all of you skittish as orphaned fawns. He's likely not what you think he is—"

"I'll guarantee he's more!" Will growled.

"You don't know that. All you know is rumour—all anyone knows hereabouts is rumours!"

"All right, then," Will acquiesced. "Leavin' off the Templar, then. You're not thinkin' of him, anyway. You're set on having that bitch of an abbess. And when it comes to't, I've as much rights to see her in my sights as you!"

"Nay," Robyn growled back, "you don't."

"Bloody hell, Rob, you know—"

"I know." Robyn lurched up. "You should've, would've, but you didn't, Will, and I once told Marion the same thing—you're more the liability because of it!"

"Like *you'll* just walk up and ask her t' dance?

"You weren't there, Will, none of you were *there!*" His voice broke as he caught John's eyes, dark and huge, watching him.
I were there, after. I know.
Robyn looked away. *You do, but not all of it. There's only one other alive who knows what I do... and he's refusing to know. Gamelyn's lost, and I pray I never find him.*
Will had no answer for that, so he avoided it and kept on. "You've spent these past few years sniffing her trail. You've spent sacks of mead and whisky debating what you'd do to her when you finally hunted her to ground. You talk about me being liability for me vengeance. You'd slit her throat, Robyn Hood, and laugh—"

"Because I *am* Robyn Hood!" It purled about them, a growl/threat/promise echoing through in the trees. "D'you forget? I am *the Hooded One*, the Horned Lord's avatar, and when 'tis time for her death, I'll know. I'll give it. And I'll *enjoy* it, because the bitch needs no more than killing."

Silence fell after he'd spoken, the others turning away—showing throat like any proper wolf challenged by their leader—even Will, looking away even though he was gritting his teeth.

But John, head down, nevertheless kept watching Robyn, kept *looking.*

Robyn held his gaze. Said, quiet into the remains of thunder, "If I take John, can I count on the rest of you t' do what's needed here?"

The others all tried speaking at once. John dropped to his haunches, lowered his gaze.

"We've commitments here!" Robyn raised his voice to cover theirs.

"Robyn," Will said into the sudden quiet. "Y'r talking the Underkeep. John's better at sneaking and knife-work than an ugly hand to hand. And t' bow, we're all crafty with a bow, though mebbe not as you or Gilly White-hands."

Gilbert preened, and it broke the tension. A little.

"Seems to me sneaking with a dagger and bow will do us better," Robyn answered. "Our days of walking in and starting pub brawls are over, Will. We're too known."

"Hoist by our own notoriety." Will made it a lament—again to ease the tension.

"Sounds to me," Arthur murmured, "you've the way of it, Robyn."

"He's right, Will," Gilbert pointed out.

"We canna all go and you know it," Robyn furthered. "There's talk of the nobles bringin' back t' geld, and already taxes coming due. Too many of our people are cryin' for help. I need the rest of you *here*."

"Too bad there's no rendering some fat from some churchmen," Will growled, nodding to where Gilbert and John were still working. "All right, then. You know best. And it's sure John'll not let you do owt daft."

"Neither will you do owt daft," Robyn said. "Keep t' the agreement, Scathelock. If y' start thinkin' *you* know best and come traipsing after? I'll render *you*."

Will looked as if he were about to make some quip; after a look at Robyn's face, he merely shrugged. "Aye, Robyn."

Robyn kept looking at him, making sure of his capitulation. Satisfied, he squatted down. "Will knows a bit about Templars, but Gilly's the one amongst us who's the book-learning. Do you know owt about that lot, Gil?"

Gilbert slung excess fat from his dagger into the bowl, shoved at his curly forelock with the pommel. "Some."

"Well, then, you need to tell us. I don't know enough, that's certain, and all of us had best arm ourselves with whatever we have, if it's as bad as Will thinks."

"Aye, it's as bad," Gilbert murmured, almost to himself. With a lift of his eyebrows, he started to explain.

- VIII -

Nothing to see in his corner. Only a lanky peasant nursing a jar, hood pulled over his head and feet propped on another chair. Nothing interesting, move along, no reason to even pay attention.

But the lanky peasant was paying attention.

"Two bloody long watches, back t' back on the hindmost wall watching trees grow. And Cap'n wonders why I fell asleep against the turret!"

"Yer lucky he weren't tossing you over it!"

Robyn couldn't have timed it this well if he'd tried—his luck was definitely holding. The Hammered Anvil was a likely place for soldiers to slip their leashes for the while and, sure enough, two tables over a clutch of soldiers were drinking and joshing. Most wore the device of Nottingham, but there were several in the Abbess's colours.

He remembered those, all right.

"Aye, well. Better the back wall than th' west edge. That sorcerer monk wanders there along the cliff face, just walkin' and mutterin' to hisself."

"Aye, that 'un gives me the willies. He an' his dog both, sniffin' about, an'—"

Two others shushed him, looking about anxiously.

Sorcerer . . . monk? Robyn frowned as their talk grew muted. He shifted in his chair and pulled his hood back just enough to uncover the ear closest, tucking the hair behind for good measure.

A shadow fell over him; he slid his gaze upward, expecting the potkeeper. He gave a lopsided smile, recognising Meg.

"I thought it might be you," she murmured, leaning a hip on the table and fisting one hand in her skirts. Already tucked up, she tweaked them up just that much higher, propped one foot on the chair where he'd propped his own.

"Am I so obvious?" He peered up at her, letting the smile quirk his mouth farther sideways.

"*Ronald's* obvious, to one as knows him. He thought 'imself a proper clever boots, sneaking his best scrumpy to the grotty yeoman in the corner. But I saw 'im, right enough. 'Tis been a while, eh?" She leaned closer. "Best act interested, pet. Me brother's in the pub tonight, and you know how he is if I waste time on sommun's not interested in the goods."

Robyn angled forward. "I keep tellin' you, lass. If Martin's getting above himself with you, I'll be happy t' teach him some manners. I lie with a fair rough crowd, aye?"

He really wished he could talk her into letting them whack sense into her brother. A pimping piece of work who more often than not demanded a full third of his sister's earnings, that Motherless clot was one Robyn would just as soon use for target practice. And clean his bodkins in lye, after.

"Nay. He is me brother, all's said and done. Speaking of brothers, you en't here alone?" She looked concerned.

"Nay. I've a . . . brother, waiting and watching. But take this, so that useless lump of yours eases up." Robyn took tuppence from his pouch and flipped it to her, then sat back. "How 'bout a drink for us both, then you can sit in me lap and gi' us a story, eh?"

"I'm still no' so sure iffen yer lap's torment or comfort," she murmured as she pocketed the tuppence and gave a tug to a lock of black fallen from his hood. "There's somethin' takes the heart from a lass, t' ride a cock-hoss that en't risin' to her wiles."

"And here I thought I were a blissful rest for you." Robyn grinned wider. "Fetch our drinks, woman."

She chuckled and walked away, a sway to her hips he swore every woman born must know from the cradle, like. Meg was too smart to be a whore, and worth ten of Martin. But as with most of Robyn's people, there weren't a lot of choices in life. You met the hand you were dealt with a lift of your chin—and a sly marking of the cards so you had *some* say in the game.

Sure enough, Martin was blustering by the taps. Loudly. "What're you doin' with that 'un, Meg? He en't got nuthin', look at 'im."

Shut it, y' daft sod, shut it. I want no notice from the likes of you.

"Well, that's funny, en't it," she retorted, "'cause he bought me a drink, fer starters, with the coin you say he don't have."

Ronald the potkeeper reached out, gave the brother a shove. "Shut yer trap, Martin. I've tol' you afore—"

It was drowned out by another raucous burst of laughter from the soldiers at their table. "Hoy!" one of them shouted for Ronald. The potkeeper threw an apologetic glance first Meg's, then Robyn's way. Pitcher in hand, he hurried over.

Meg turned away, rolling her eyes and waving a hand in the air. Martin followed her over to Robyn's table, still haranguing.

Anger was quickly trenching a great hole in the sense of staying quiet. Scum, Martin was. Treating his sister like—

And then Martin had the ill luck to bend over and shove himself into Robyn's face. "Me sister's no time for the likes of you. Have your drink and clear off."

Robyn met his gaze. Purred, "I had a sister. Never would I've treated her as you do Meg. Nor lived off her back like a grubby wean."

"You sonova—!" It throttled into a tiny yip as Robyn's dagger appeared at the tip of Martin's chin.

"I'll pay m' way." Robyn had barely moved. "To Meg. With no interference from you. Now, leave off. You smell."

Another cheerful roar from the soldiers. Robyn kept one ear tuned that way, just in case. Otherwise, he still didn't move, didn't lower the dagger.

A tiny nick oozed down Martin's chin. Recognition also began dawning in the rheumy eyes. Martin dropped them, backed off. "Aye, lord."

Thankfully no one save the potkeeper and a drunken duo of lads—who quickly turned away—took note of what was happening in the back corner. The soldiers were talking about some horse race. The alcove closest to Robyn held another whore with her client, far too busy with each other to notice . . .

Wait. Another pair of eyes lingered upon him. Across the cavern, at another ill-lit corner table, a burly loner with a beard and a close-shaven head. He had the way about him of a soldier— only moreso, if possible—all wire-strung tension, looking everywhere. His gaze held on Robyn without any blatant notice. Only Robyn's senses weren't exactly the dull acceptance of a villager, either, so he knew he was being watched. Not curiosity, not quite. It almost seemed . . . antagonistic? Nay, not quite that, either.

"My hero," Meg murmured, handing him his jar. Robyn took a sip, gaze wandering but attention fixed on the lone soldier-type who, thankfully, began watching the door instead. Looking for someone. The respite allowed Robyn to finally taste the liquor on his tongue: good scrumpy, laced with mint. As he took another gulp, Meg gave a perfunctory hike of her overskirt and straddled his lap. She didn't smell so sweet herself. All town people reeked, to a nose used to clean air. One of the reasons he hated the towns: fine-tuned senses blocked by too much smoke hanging in the low ceilings, by rank bodies packed in too tight beneath, and dung and piss-pools seeping into the dirt.

"I've not given you too much trouble, have I?" He sat back, taking a surreptitious whiff at his hood. Unfortunately he didn't smell much better, about now. But there . . . a hint of bark, loam, and leaf. Home.

The lone soldier's eyes flitted back over toward them; he shrugged at the whore on Robyn's lap then lifted his jar in a wayward toast. *Comrade, I salute you.*

Robyn wasn't thrilled that the soldier-type had realised any comradeship. *I don't like this. I don't belong here, never have.*

"Nuthin' I can't handle," she assured. "So. We both know you en't here for the ride, eh?"

He spoke the first thing that came into his head. "Those soldiers. I heard them, too, talking about a sorcerer."

Meg snorted. "Those lot can't see one when he's walkin' amongst them." She frowned, leaned slightly closer. "*You* be careful, aye? There's none of us as wants to see you strung up and burnt, or yer head on a pike over the gates."

"*None* of you?" he teased. "You're sure of that, are you?"

"En't nuthin' to fool about! Y' take a chance, coming here y'rself."

"Life is chance, nowt more." Robyn took a drink and shrugged, eyes giving another wander about the smoke-filled cavern.

"There's been a lot of jabberin' about one o' those Templar Knights, here with 'is servant. Come t' see the Sheriff; nae doubt what that lot's on about. There's all sorts of nasty talk about their like, y'know. Cold-blooded killers, the lot of 'em and I've heard tell this 'un's the worst. Half the people are fearin' he'll set a crusade on Nottingham. The other half're hidin' so he can't hex 'em. Or spit 'em for sport and eat 'em. Th' tales I've heard . . . " She grimaced. "He sounds a right nasty brute."

"Have y' seen him?"

"Not a bit of it, pet." She leaned closer, started rocking up and down.

Aye, Will Scathelock weren't one for this job—he'd be thinking more with the nether brain than the one in his skull, have Meg on her back in a heartbeat. Too distractible. Whereas Robyn's strung-tight nerves could only focus on the sense-numbing surroundings and Meg's words as she continued. "All I know is, that one's bad for business. Sorcerer or monk, I wish he'd go back to hell or his convent."

Speaking of convents . . . "Bugger the monk, then. It's a nun I've come to see you about, anyway."

"Nun?" Meg rolled her eyes. "What would a nun be doin' 'ere?"

The soldier-type was still, occasionally, watching. The hair on the back of Robyn's neck started to rise. He dropped his chin, let hood and hair drop farther over his face. "I heard one's stayin' here, with the Sheriff."

"Aw, sure, them I know about. Not just one, there's a couple of 'em. I think one's some abbess or the like, that and the Sheriff's sister, eh?"

Robyn's gaze rose, slowly, to fix upon hers. The subvocal growl he felt building in his chest—just the *thought* of being in such close proximity—must have transferred somewhat to his eyes. Meg went wide-eyed, swallowed, stilled.

He dropped his chin, closed his eyes and took a soft, deliberate breath then let it out, a bare murmur: "Meg. Do you know where these nuns stay, pet?"

Meg started rocking again, slowly. Good thing her face was hidden from everyone but him—the pale apprehension there might be a dodgy thing. "A coupla those soldiers're hers. The abbess's. I could likely find out. I 'spect she's in the main tower, close by the Sheriff." Her voice turned concerned. "You've no plans on going *in* there, aye? 'Twould be—"

"Madness," he agreed. "But I need to know . . . "

He trailed off as he gave another glance about, and frowned. The soldiers were still carousing, the two in the next alcove coming to the grand finish—or not so grand, perhaps, from the look on the whore's face—and . . .

The soldier-type had gone missing.

Every instinct Robyn had buzzed, mad as a jiggered wasp, setting heat behind his eyes. He felt . . . slow. Sick in his head and stomach both, waves of sensation and motion breaking over him though he was stock-still.

"Robyn," Meg whispered. "You look as though you've seen a h'ant."

Aye and didn't that proper describe what was walking into the pub, smooth and soundless and *there*. It had to be a ghost. Yet Robyn heard him. Saw him.

Knew him.

The soldier-type had returned, had obviously been waiting for *him*, gesturing with no little courtesy to the table where he'd been sitting, where he'd tipped his mug to Robyn. The ... ghost was scanning the pub cavern with a quick, flat gaze, shrugging back a woollen wrap from a braided-back length of hair that gleamed gilt and russet in the torchlight. The cape wrapped about him was heavy, dark; he flung it over one shoulder and it seemed for moments he'd blood on his chest, scarlet splashed new and broad over the ebon of the tunic beneath.

Real or no, there was blood *in* it. Robyn felt it drawing at his nostrils, could nigh choke on it, hot-thick, at the back of his throat, tasted the metallic edge of it upon his tongue. So much blood. So much, swirling into the black ...

The other soldiers lowered their heads and their voices. The young lads had vanished. The pub sucked itself into quiet. Ronald the potkeeper hurried to assist such a distinguished guest.

"Lady save me." Meg had followed Robyn's gaze and stilled. "That's *him*, en't it?"

Him. The cross floated before Robyn on a haze of smoke, winking as if encrusted with jewels, all too like another cross, swinging above his body as he'd lain in his blood, in the ashes of Loxley Chase. He *had* died that night, the last thing in his sight a *cross* ... only now it shone more akin to beacon-fire than jewels, heating a scarlet brand on the Templar's chest. As if in some odd spectral tandem, Robyn's breath filled the blooded chest, made it move, made it *breathe*.

It was no ghost. He wasn't lost; he was alive. *Here*.

A *Templar*, in Nottingham. *The* Templar.

The Templar was *Gamelyn*.

Fingers snarled in his hair, the other hand brushing the hood back from his face. "Robyn?" Meg hissed.

Robyn lurched forward, yanked the hood down nearly to his eyes. He shoved Meg back, tottered to his feet. The movements seemed slow, as if he were drugged, but instincts held true. Anything quick would attract attention. He couldn't be seen. Not here. Not *now*.

"Out. I need to get out," he pleaded. "*Quietly*."

He was afraid, deathly afraid for the first in a long time ... pinned like a hare in a smoked burrow with dogs at the exits, afraid to move, to *breathe*, for surely it would be sniffed out. *Felt*.

Even as Robyn himself could *feel* the Templar's breath, *feel* his heart pounding, strong and heated-steady—

The Templar stiffened, frowned and blinked, as if someone had said his name. His eyes were quick as Robyn's own, a sharp gaze sweeping the pub.

Desperate, Robyn whispered the magic along the edge of the knuckles he only then kenned he had been biting—hard—and twisted it into being: *You canna see me. You canna feel me...*

"*Nyd wyf yma i,*" he breathed. *I am not here.*

Those juniper-green eyes were familiar—yet not—as they peered directly at him.

Blinked again, shook his head. Frowned harder.

Then passed over.

Perhaps it wasn't Gamelyn. It couldn't be. Surely Gamelyn would feel the magics writhing, would *know.*

Surely he is blind, your Oak-clad brother. We knew he had returned, but it has been long. He has denied us, again. Betrayed *us.*

Robyn actually felt his hackles rise, snarled and started a slow, feral stalk forward. The Templar had dropped his gaze, considering a remark from his companion. Then he tucked a sly smile to one corner of his mouth, and the weight of it made Robyn stagger against Meg.

For Robyn knew that smile. Had done his damnedest to coax it forth, had covered that mouth with kisses, had let that mouth cover *him* . . .

He half stumbled, half ran from the cavern, let the glamour thin then unravel into the bare, shiny threads of a worn tunic. They slipped out the back corridor and into the night.

Meg propped him up against the wall, peered at him. "I think we'd best to check that last batch of scrumpy. It might be off—"

"Nay, en't the cider," he whispered. "On with you, Meg. I'd best go quickly."

"You're sure you're all right?"

He nodded, gritting his teeth. *Let me go. Now.*

"I'll see what I can find about that abbess for you," Meg said, then slipped back the way they had come.

He stumbled out, made a tottering halt for just that much too long, recollecting his bearings. When a hand laid on his back, he nearly jumped from his skin. Dagger in hand, Robyn recognised John a spare second before he struck.

John's hands clenched at his wrists, brown eyes wide with shock then distress. "*Robyn?*"

"It's him. Here. He's . . . " And blight and bugger it, Robyn could do nothing but prattle. "John, he's *here*."

John gripped him tighter; Robyn gripped back, hauled him away from the small cavern, out into fresher air and towards the trees. Cover. They had to get to shelter.

John shook Robyn. Hard. Pointed to the sandy soil beneath their feet and the obvious tracks they were leaving.

Had Robyn lost *every* sense he had because of . . . because of . . . ?

With an angry, half-muttered curse, Robyn led John in running strides down the sandy terrace leading to the castle. The small path lay deserted; most of the activity centred around the entrances on the other side. Only people who wanted to not be noticed came this way. And the one person they did pass was puking his guts on the stones, no danger.

"I seen nuthin' but a trick I were turnin', milord. One you scared off!" Meg's voice echoed out from the back tunnel, high with fear but game with denial.

It was adequate impetus. As one, Robyn and John backtracked, keeping on tiptoe to the tread of their footprints in the dust.

"Get back to yer work, lass!" A male voice, rough with fear. "Women, milord. They don't know nuthin'—"

"I'm not sure you know anything, either."

Robyn would have known that voice anywhere. His feet wanted to stumble; he cursed again—silently—and kept his feet just as silent, true.

"Yer man were right to think Meg's trick no common one. But *she* didn't know any better, milord, I swear."

The huge stone keep of Nottingham Castle loomed over them, shrouded with a black and starless night that sucked them in as they dove into the thick undergrowth not a stone's throw from the back exits. Only the one torch threw faint light along the terraced lane. The sounds of the heaving man down the way were very plain, then covered by voices exiting into the still air.

Robyn and John burrowed beneath the thick bracken. Went still. Barely even breathed.

"I would swear tae ye, milord. It were him. Robyn Hood."

They were but a stag's leap from the back entry, and saw them come out: the Templar and Meg's brother, Martin. John gave a tiny growl, low in his chest. Treacherous *sod*.

The Templar said something unintelligible, then headed down the terrace, long strides swift upon the tracks they'd laid. Martin was left waiting there, shifting uneasily back and forth. Robyn saw

John's eyes, gleaming with the torch flickers, marking the man. Bringing his dagger upward, John touched it with his lips and drew back, ready for the throw.

The sound of leather and metal, boots covering ground with long strides: the Templar returning. Robyn reached up, covered the betraying glint of John's eyes with his fingers, dipped his own gaze. John twirled his dagger into his palm, covering the sheen of metal as the Templar came back into the clearing, voice soft but commanding. His hair gleamed pale beneath the gibbous moon, his cloak flung back so the scarlet cross burned, floated in the dark like a torch held aloft.

I will be the death of you.
Traitor. Destroyer. Rival.
Gamelyn.

Nay, Robyn muttered to the fever-pitch flaring behind his Sight. *Nay, not now. Not. Now.*

As if the Templar had remembered his coppery head could prove a betrayal in the dark, he pulled his cowl forward. One lock escaped, trailing down his breastbone. "Are you sure you saw him retreat down the terrace?"

"Aye, milord."

"Well, there's another with him. And they've doubled back."

John tensed in surprise; Robyn felt it himself. No one should have been able to follow their trail. They'd barely left one.

Perhaps, after all, Gamelyn also couldn't help his own instincts. Perhaps he felt an imperative akin to what still roared a fiery path deep into Robyn's brain, leaving trails of ash and char.

"They're long gone, no doubt." Again, that *voice*, so familiar yet . . . not. As if something thick and chill had been slurried down Gamelyn's throat, given the gentle tenor an inexorable whisper of cruelty. "We'll go back in. No point to waiting."

The duo returned, walking the path not a stone's throw away from their hiding place. The Templar—*Gamelyn*—went with a more considered pace, quiet as any denizen of the Shire Wode. Wherever Gamelyn had been, he'd learnt sommat. As they passed, John laid another silent kiss to his blade, opening his eyes to follow Martin, a promise: *Later*.

They disappeared into the Underkeep's entrance.

John started to rise; Robyn grabbed him, stayed him before he as much as twitched. Flicked his eyes, ever so slightly, toward the cavern entry.

Only there if you looked close; 'twould almost be easier to smell it. But there, seeming merely another shade within the entry's shadow, it bided. Holding too still against the flickering torches. Betraying a glint of pale.

A stray, long lock of ginger hair.

Very slowly, his eyes on Robyn, John lifted his dagger. The thick haze of crimson not-sound swelled upward, a crescendo behind Robyn's eyes. An obligation, twitching along every nerve he possessed:

He belongs by right to no cross, no barren conqueror god. He has returned, and he is ours. I care not how you take him, but you will do it.

Not... like... this...

Robyn shook his head. John's eyes betrayed no emotion, disappointment or otherwise, but they held to Robyn's. A different question, this time. This time, Robyn gave an affirmative.

Still silent, John nodded and handed his dagger to Robyn. Opened his palms, mouthed the charm and let the breath wisp toward the stand of laurel a pike's throw south.

The laurel rustled, dipped downward.

The speed with which the shadow reacted was astonishing. Darkness catapulted past them, a glitter of bared steel edging it. In a mere few strides, the Templar had reached then leapt the laurel, a graceful, swift spring not unlike a deer clearing a fallen log.

It was terrifying. Powerful.

Breathtaking.

John's hand touched Robyn's back. Robyn jerked, silently cursed himself for gaping like a daft idiot as another, muted curse rose from behind the laurel.

"Milord?" A low call; another figure coming from the back entry. The soldier-type.

Again, John and Robyn froze. John's arm curled tight about Robyn's ribs, slender fingers splayed at the bottom of Robyn's sternum, and holding firm. The last in particular was shockingly welcome. Robyn realised he'd angled forward as mindlessly as bracken in spare sunlight.

"They were here." It was thwarted, but cool. Almost amused. "Now they're not. Tricky bastards."

Despite himself, a smirk ticced at Robyn's lip. A heartbeat later he was thoroughly grateful for John's embrace, the calm *sanity* of it.

John's other hand snuck up Robyn's spine, grabbed his hair, tugged. It was not gentle. Robyn turned to him, saw the question in his eyes. Robyn nodded answer and, all slow-quiet, put John's dagger back into the fingers clutched to his waist. It bled chill through Robyn's tunic: another path leading back to his right mind.

And he'd accused *Will* of being a liability.

John slid the flat of the blade across Robyn's ribs, still slow, and gave him a tiny push. The meaning was obvious: *Go on. I'll finish, follow.*

Robyn gritted his teeth, turned away and melted, silent, into the trees.

ⓚ

Much was not best pleased. "I were watchin' from the front. They couldn't've gone that way."

"No matter." Blade lit fitfully by the torchlight, Guy came back around the laurel. "They're gone."

"But you heard 'em? It weren't no animal?"

"Oh, it was an animal, all right." Guy sheathed his sword at his hip with a dull rasp and ring. "A two-legged one who's either daft or arrogant enough to waltz into the bowels of Nottingham and swive a whore." He shifted the cape more comfortably over his shoulders. "If, indeed, that's all he was doing."

Much's lip curled. "What else *is* there t' do with her like? I told you, milord—no doubt t' man were suspicious. He never stopped lookin' for trouble, like, even when he thought none were watchin'. But she did nowt but her trade."

"You're sure?" Guy pressed.

Much crossed his arms, pursed his lips. "Huh. Thinking on it, milord, she did take overlong. She were talking, a bit."

"Talking. To a trick." Guy lowered his head, gave a chuckle that had absolutely no mirth to it, then shook his head and started back the way they'd come.

Much followed, silent.

ⓚ

Robyn made several twists and turns—sometimes running and sometimes walking, silent and listening all the while—before he entered the unremarkable copse where he and John had, the previous night, made camp.

He sank to his haunches, put his face in his hands.

His hands shook. In fact, his entire body tremored as if with some ague, tiny shivers crawling up and down his spine. All his senses—all the subtle ways to touch and be touched, to block and turn aside—screamed. As if the skin had been flensed from him and he was raw, turned inside out.

Once Robyn had careful plans as what he would do, should he ever see Gamelyn again. They had not consisted of being bloody sodding useless, of being ripped from the inside out by a . . . a *recognition* he wasn't sure he comprehended, nor of having his feet kicked out from under him by a treacherous need he'd thought long dead.

An arrow to the gut, a knife to the throat—and those the more merciful of the myriad ways Robyn had planned to kill the one who had betrayed him so. His sister dead, his parents butchered, the people who'd trusted them murdered or maimed, his home torched and laid waste . . .

He'd wanted Gamelyn dead, wanted to bind him on the violated stones of the Horned Lord's altar and take his heart from his body, still beating. Wanted to turn the knife on himself for being so daft, for trusting, *believing*.

John had been with him, all the while. Had been Cernun's shadow and helpmate through summer's end and a foul winter and into summer again. John had watched, waited and agonised in silence as Robyn had tossed in fever, as Robyn had died and come back more than once, fighting beyond sense or sanity with vengeance the only focus—the only *weapon*—he possessed.

Finally, John had spoken to that focus. He had spent more words on Gamelyn's defence than Robyn had ever heard from him.

The truth had given him an even more valuable weapon: Gamelyn had not intended to betray him.

Yet . . . now Gamelyn hunted him at the Sheriff's request. Gamelyn, seemingly of his own accord, bided with one who *had* betrayed them all.

The Abbess. *That* was one Robyn wanted to see writhing in death throes, with his hand delivering the blow, and no power on earth would stop him.

Yet he felt, at this moment, did the bitch walk up to him and say "By your leave" he'd not have the strength to so much as lunge at her. This had taken him broadside, spun him, and made him question. Hesitate.

He could not afford such uncertainty. There were too many depending upon him.

But neither had he expected *this*.

Robyn curled up into a ball, arms wrapped about his knees. He was rocking back and forth on his haunches in a motion any madman would know all too well, all the doubts and denials rashing over his skin like fever-pox.

Denial. Aye, my own, your Summerlord has twisted his denials into a fearsome power.

Even the voice of the Horned Lord felt akin to molten metal pouring through Robyn's brain.

"He is not"—through gritted teeth—"mine."

Oh, I'm afraid he is. Things have come full circle, o pwca. Never doubt he will come after you. Shall we enter the game in full, you and I?

"He rather has t' advantage!" Robyn challenged, throwing the hair from his face and looking up to meet the glowing eyes of the Horned Lord.

You were caught unawares.

"Fancy that," Robyn sniped. "And how were it I were caught unawares?"

You expect me to warn you? What's next, that I suckle you like a babe?

"And you wonder why I'd rather be arsy than compliant."

Nay, my heart, I do not wonder. Compliant would be boring.

Robyn uttered a few choice curses into his knees. "No doubt, now I've felt t' worst of it, I'll know better."

You speak some truth, aye. But what you've felt is not the worst he can dredge from you. You've no concept of what he is now capable of.

Robyn remembered the offered feints so far: Gamelyn's stillness in the alcove, coupled with his reaction to John's diversion. The stark speed of it. The *beauty* of it.

"Nay, I think I really do."

Assume nothing, Hooded One. You do not know what hunts you.

"And you do."

I do not know enough. His soul lies closed, deep and darker than any oubliette; even I cannot easily prise my way in. He is. . . scarred. And while scars can strengthen, they also bear weakness.

Robyn grimaced, put fingers to the deep divot in his left pectoral, and nodded agreement against his folded forearms.

The question is: will the Oak come willing? You once dared me to throw the bones and trust your belief in him. But now he is your rival in truth: a warrior monk shrouded in the barren cross, to contest the King of the fecund Shire Wode. No longer the innocent boy you cozened with pretty words and a limber body. 'Tis time to throw the bones again, sweet Hob-Robyn. He denies us, and we will take him back. We must. A pause. *Would She help us. . .?*

She. Meg? The Abbess? The Lady Huntress? Robyn clenched his hands against his forelock, started to speak.

"Robyn."

Instead he chased those hands back through his hair and raised his eyes to meet John's.

John gave a grim nod.

Robyn kept looking at him. "I'm sorry. It wain't happen again. I wain't *let* it happen again."

John knelt down, then reached out and gripped Robyn's tight-folded hands, stilled him.

Robyn hadn't known he was still rocking back and forth. He let John unlace his fingers merely to twine his own about them, put his head down to rest against their hands. They had always been quiet together, comfortable and comforted by their simple animal nearness. Will was his link with the past and his strong arm, disinherited Gilbert the scholar, David the herbalist and scavenger, crippled Arthur the cynic and reminder of why they kept going. But John was their heart, their conjurer—not only of the charms and protections he wound about the outlaws of the Shire Wode, but of *tynged*'s pulse: John believed in Robyn even if Robyn had no belief to spare for himself.

So it was past understanding how Robyn felt he had to explain, to wrangle words into being when there usually was no need for them. "I were . . . proper upskelled, thrown off me game and no question. I weren't expecting—"

John put his fingers against Robyn's mouth, leaned forward.

"You en't understanding," Robyn protested against John's fingers. "It were—"

"I know," John murmured against his ear, "who it were." Then he removed his fingers, replaced them with his lips.

Robyn shuddered, then closed his eyes and opened his mouth.

ᚲ

Guy waited, watched as Much passed through the pub's main cavern and gave the whore's sleeve a tug. Passing a tray of drinks to what remained of the group of soldiers, she scrutinised Much, then the silver penny he held up between two fingers, then shrugged and nodded. When she tried to direct him to an alcove nearer the bar, Much insisted on the far alcove closest to the back corridor. Another shrug, then she followed him.

It was easy—too easy, in fact. The whore walked into the alcove readily, her only hesitation when she saw another there to sigh, proclaim, "If you're wanting double, it'll cost you . . ."

Her voice faded as Guy stepped into the faint light of the torch spitting in the corridor. Eyes widening, she started to sidle sideways. Quick, but not quick enough. Her attempt at escape was blocked by the immovable breadth of Much, and when she thought to cry out, Guy had already snagged her by the hair, spun her around to slam her up against the alcove's back wall. He slapped a hand over her mouth, shoved that forearm against her sternum, and one thigh hard against her pubic bone.

He put a quieting finger to his own lips, then to the hand he had clapped over her mouth, then dropped it downward. Outrage guttered into fear as he raised it once more, holding a small, thin dagger. Her eyes searched frantically past him, widened and returned to his as he repeated the shushing motion with the flat of the dagger.

"I'd prefer you give me no reason to permanently silence you. However," he continued, still soft, giving a tap of the blade against his silencing hand, "please believe me when I say I shall indeed silence you if you are too . . . troublesome."

Eyes still wide, the whore nodded. But she was, ever so slightly, moving one hand. No doubt searching for something to use as a weapon.

Predictable. "I would assume you wish to keep all those fingers you're moving?"

She stilled.

"Better. Put both hands behind you and grab your elbows, now. Keep them there. My man is watching the corridor for us, so the more you tell me and the less you evade the inevitable, the better for you. And me." He removed the hand from her mouth.

"I don't know nothin'," she murmured, sullen beneath the fright.

"I don't like liars. I despise traitors."

"I'm not—" She broke off as he tapped her nose with the dagger.

"Quietly, now. You're a liar because you lied to me about the man you serviced then helped escape. You're a traitor because that man was a wolfshead. In fact, I'm certain you not only know he is a wolfshead, but that he is a particularly *notorious* wolfshead."

"I don' know what you mean!" she retorted, but it was quiet.

Good. She at least had some modicum of intelligence. Which translated into one fact: she knew exactly what he meant.

"Your brother knew the man."

"Me brother sees outlaws in every tree." Her eyes gleamed. "And he's not likely to let you keep me here longer than it takes for a quick fuck—"

"My man's not likely to let your brother anywhere near either of us until I'm finished with you." Guy tilted his head. "Whether it takes longer than a . . . 'quick fuck', was it? That depends on you."

"I've nuthin' to say t' the likes of you."

"The likes of me." He smiled, bent slightly closer. "You have absolutely no idea what that is, do you?"

"Yer a monk, en't you? Never changes," she mumbled. "Monks are th' worst and th' dirtiest."

Guy had to chuckle. It was no more surprise to him than to her. "I suppose you would know. Well, then." The chuckle had relaxed her, slight but there. He raised his hand to rest lightly at her throat. "Be assured, there will be nothing sexual in this for either of us. Unless, of course, you happen to fancy pain." He clenched his fingers, hard, and her eyes bugged out. "Listen to me, woman. The foulest monk for whom you've ever opened your legs is going to seem a love song compared to what I have for you if you don't give me the truth.

"Now." Guy loosened his grip and started twirling the dagger between his fingers. She watched the blade like a mouse snared in a kestrel's gaze. "Let's dispense with all this righteousness, shall we? The man's a wolfshead, when all is done and said. And a valuable one to the Sheriff. Just to bring in his head would gain you a tidy sum, so something has to be keeping you from turning him in. It can't be the pittance you acquire in servicing him. I mean, surely he can't be so much better at the simple mechanics of rutting than any other trick you turn."

"It's not like that!" she shot back.

He'd judged her adequately enough: meeting with the outlaw gave her something she deemed important, something she would protect. Indeed, something *virtuous*. Which was somewhat laughable, considering. "How is it, then?"

"You wouldn't understand."

"Likely not. Does Robyn Hood come to see you often?"

"And if he did . . . " She started off defiant, trailed off into uncertainty.

And fairly intelligent, for her type. "Come, woman. I knew it had to be Robyn Hood, and you knew I knew it. Now we have no more lies between us. All you're telling is what I already know."

Her eyes were pinned to the ground.

"Does he come just to see you?" He tipped his voice into amused. "Mayhap he fancies you?"

The whore gave a flat chuckle, peered at him. "Fancy me. And you say I'm the one with no idea. You're the one as knows nuthin' of who *you're* dealing with. *Monk*."

"If I knew everything, then what would be the use of you, eh?" He cocked his head, watched her flinch as he twirled the dagger to a stop just above her jugular. "Does he keep his silence through fear?" He turned the blade against her neck from flat to edge. She winced as it pinked her. "I'm sure you'll agree, fear is a most excellent deterrent. *Are* you afraid of him? I imagine if you're afraid he'll put a spell on you, or curse you, money likely wouldn't—"

"I'm thinking 'tis sommat the likes of *you* would more set your hand to!" she sneered.

He shrugged, then snugged his hand, hard. The sneer dropped from her face even as the air gave a shocked huff from her lungs.

"I must confess, this man, this *Robyn Hood*,"—he dipped a pleasant nod—"continues to amaze me. So many are calling him the commoner's hero. Quite a paragon, it would seem. Yet he slaughters soldiers and churchmen, terrorises the countryside with the threat of his so-called 'magic'." He tossed the dagger into the air, caught it, and once again began flipping it in his fingers. "And swives a filthy whore in a squalid little cave."

She nearly spoke before she thought, strangled it. Smarter than the average, no question.

"If he's such a hero, then where is he now?"

"Running from *you*, I'd hope."

Guy stopped the dagger in his fingers, tilted his head to give her a too-patient look. "Oh, he did run. I saw him. Actually, there were two of them . . . " He trailed off as her eyes widened. "See? I told you. I know a lot of things you don't."

"You en't caught 'im," she insisted. "If you had, what would you want with me?"

"Good question." He nodded, leaned closer. "Tell me what I want to know, and there actually might be a point to keeping you alive."

She believed him. There had been doubts before, but as he brought the dagger to her throat, she had no more.

"Do you think your hero would give himself up for you if I dragged you into his forest and began to cut bits from you in front of him?"

"You en't got him. You en't." She was starting to whimper.

"Why should you care? He'd not care so much for you, you know." He trailed the dagger upward, halted just below one eye. "Unless you're saying he does care? In which case, should he care, somehow, for a whore, then how many pieces should I slice you into to make him come after me?"

"You don't want him after you," she said, no defiance, this time. "You don't want *any* of his people after you. Please."

"Why was he *here*, woman?"

"Y-*you!*" she blurted out. "He wanted to know about you. And . . ."

"And?" He let the dagger's tip slip into skin, welling a drop of blood that trickled down her cheek like a tear.

"And . . . a nun. In the castle."

"A . . . *nun.*"

It threw him, utterly.

It plucked some lost chord on a thrown-aside instrument. It formed a reaction where there had been nothing but objectivity. Guy angled back, blinked in pure confusion. He wasn't used to this. Wasn't accustomed to feeling *anything* in this space, this function.

It sucked a small, hesitant breath into his lungs and swirled it, let it escape in a tiny, silent whisper:

Marion.

What does he want with Marion?

The whore was indeed no fool. She took the offered chance, shoved at him, nearly twisted from his grip and sucked in air to scream.

Instinct, pure instinct bade him grab and pull her back against him, clench his hand over her face and yank her head back at the same time he raised the dagger and sliced. She wrenched back with a harsh, thick gurgle, hands flailing at his, feet thrashing as blood gushed forth, soaking her dirty tunic front and his blade-hand.

Instinct had saved him more than once. But this was no war zone and no battlefield; no room here for anything but calculation. He gave a snarl as her feet kicked and twitched, more feebly with every passing second, but not at her. At himself.

Killing her was a mistake, fed by a reaction he'd had no business having.

Closing his eyes, Guy held her close, whispered a final unction against her ear as her life drained onto the floor.

Much rounded the door—he knew the sounds of killing as well as Guy himself—but he merely gave the body a spare glance, said, "You need to see this, milord."

Guy blinked at him, then picked the woman up and carried her where Much led, down the back corridor and to the exit they'd but recently chased two outlaws through.

The whore's brother lay across the back threshold, blood

seeping into the limestone and sand. A neat, efficient slit at his jugular gave the only sign anyone had been there, and gone.

And all of it, done in absolute silence, with Guy himself questioning the whore only a few twists of tunnel away.

"Well, well," Guy said softly, toeing the carcass and looking off into the green. "It seems you don't tolerate traitors either."

Then he lowered the whore's body down next to her brother's. Closing the man's staring eyes, he knelt beside them, murmured a quiet prayer.

Much stood with head bowed as Guy finished the prayer then made the sign of the cross on both still foreheads. Guy didn't immediately rise; instead he remained kneeling there, looking off into the trees, eyes narrowed.

Something. There was something. A faint hum, a twitch behind his eyes.

An inhuman whisper laid bare in some feral and forgotten place . . .

"Milord?" Much asked, when the moment stretched into several.

Giving his head an angry shake, Guy lurched up. "Go and tell the potkeeper there's been murder done. I suspect Robyn Hood put paid to these two for telling me too much."

"Aye, milord." Much started off, hesitated as Guy reached out, touched his sleeve.

"There's no excuse," Guy said, soft. "I bungled this, and badly."

"Surely it en't as bad as you think, milord."

"I hope your optimism proves correct. But I would wager my scabbard this Robyn Hood knows what I am. We're going to have to make a change of tactics."

- IX -

Returning to Nottingham the next day, even to the Underkeep caverns, was out of the question. Robyn didn't sleep, but stayed curled up next to John. Let him sleep. And brooded.

Robyn spared a thought for Martin, but not much of one. He thought more on Meg, who had often said she would smile a little did Martin trip on a stair and break his neck, but she would also mourn a little, because she was that sort. If nothing else, Robyn owed geld to her. Martin would no doubt be worth more dead than ever alive.

He would have to talk to Meg again, the sooner the better. The Abbess—that one was worth more than a few thoughts, and none of them pleasant. To be so close... yet it might as well be a hundred miles for all the good it did him. 'Twere like gleaning from a field already picked over by desperate serfs and hungry birds.

And *Gamelyn*. That made up more than one thought—a hundred, like. All of them, ripping shreds into his composure.

Nay, they'd no business in Nottingham, not now. Better to ford the Trent and head east, regroup, make plans. John would not be best pleased at no breakfast—Robyn raised a hand, stroked light fingers through the brown hair—but there was an inn at Stapleford. Run by a widow who'd worn out three husbands, it had by

Will's reckoning the best food in Nottingham's east-most hundred. Better yet, no one in Stapleford knew them by sight.

Robyn felt the dawn approach, gave John a gentle shake, and rolled to his feet, ready to be gone.

(Y)

Outside Nottingham's armoury, rain pattered, light and soothing music to lull any to sleep. Tonight, Guy didn't fancy sleeping. The dreams would not stop coming. The whys of it were unfathomable. He had been taught the means to lock such troublesome spirits away.

Have you? And do you really want to?

It was Her. Lately, it was always Her.

And he would lurch up, heavy with too little sleep yet sleeping just deeply enough to panic beneath the formless, nameless, *insane* insistence.

Such a path led to madness; he'd learned that lesson long ago. So now Guy slept only when Much was awake, and after smoking himself senseless. It was akin to being on campaign. Which they were, after a fashion. A campaign that meant enemy territory in ways uncountable. Guy knew he couldn't do such a thing for much longer. The Saracens warned of too much reliance on the fierce *djinn* in the bubble pipe, and rightfully so. It would eventually wear at him, make his nerves clumsy and anxious instead of taut steel.

Yet for now, 'twas better than no sleep at all. So he smoked the hashish.

Or, he set himself to the practice.

The falchion in one hand and a long, curved dagger in the other, he described forms in the air, danced in place one moment then advanced, brutal power and speed, in attack.

He sensed the eyes upon him before he saw anything. Tempting, to whirl and feign attack; instead he kept working. It was more the insult, though he was unsure his stalker would appreciate the irony of it.

However, it became more and more obvious he was going to have to speak. It would not stop, otherwise, and she would continue to congratulate herself for being so clever.

"Surely you have something better to do than watch me sweat."

A sucked-in breath. For a moment Guy was uncertain she would not skulk away. Then the Abbess stepped into the doorway. "Don't flatter yourself, Templar."

"I'm not the one watching you." The words were a broken

staccato edging the slick glissade of his movements. He refused to halt, one motion sliding into another, the curve of the falchion arcing through the air like a glittering angel's wing then the dagger following, smaller and quicker. "I want nothing to do with you, yet you keep following me. You were lucky, two nights ago." Another twist, as if his joints were greased, and into a sudden halt. He peered at her over his blades. "Lucky that when I returned, I knew exactly who followed me as I entered the castle and went to my allotted chambers—"

"My lord de Gisbourne, surely—"

"Kindly tilt your piss-pot of empty courtesy elsewhere." Guy sheathed his dagger at his belt, swung the sword one last time to slap, flat, against his upheld palm, then let it swing down again, flipping it to hold, relaxed but ready, at his side. "Had I thought you any real danger, you would not be here having this conversation. You must take care, woman, that a weapon does not turn on you when you think to parry yourself against it." He slid a narrowed gaze to her, saw she had paled, and had to force himself to not smile.

"I don't believe you are exactly who you claim." She folded her hands into her sleeves. "Even now, you speak to me. As you spoke to my novice. I thought Templars were not allowed to speak to women."

"What you know of my order could no doubt dance on a pinhead with twenty angels." Shaking his head, Guy turned away and started swinging the sword again, this time in larger, heavy arcs. "*Va t'en, si'l vous plaît.*"

"I will get out when I have said what must be said. I will continue to watch you. You are not what you say you are. You claim nobility, yet you wear the dark colours of one base-born, not the white robes of a true Knight. You go unshaven, yet your hair is too long for your order. You wear the tabard and the crimson cross, but your clothes are more reminiscent of a Saracen, even your sword is of—"

Guy laughed; he couldn't help it, and it stoppered her words as nothing else would have. "*Bêtise du femme!* Has it come to pass that you have never seen the return of one who has taken up the Cross? Of course," he added, not bothering to hide the bitter lacing beneath the words, "not many return, do they?"

"Come, woman. What do you *really* want? It is unfathomable that you should want anything from me but, mayhap my head on a platter. Like Solomon." His teeth showed, more snarl than smile. "How apropos."

"Do not bother my novice again, Templar."

You seething hag, if it wasn't for your novice, I would see you shoved out the window of the tallest turret in Nottingham.

Guy went back to practicing, listening for the sound of her retreat. It came, finally.

The exchange had been foolish. But satisfying. It had, in its blunt fashion, solidified his resolve. He'd gathered enough information. He knew what he had to do.

And Samhain was approaching.

The Voice crept in, soft and dangerous: *You'll find more than you bargain for, o Templar, should you follow that path.*

This one would not leave him be. "What do you want of me?"

Prove to me you have not betrayed Us.

"You know I did not. You *have* to know."

I knew Gamelyn. At Guy, I do not begin to guess.

The only way that made any sense to Guy, considering all of it, was to protect Marion, somehow. Which unfortunately put him in league with his enemy—for the Abbess did in truth care for Marion's safety. And as to his other nemesis...

I am going to find you, Robyn Hood. Phantom or no, you and I are going to do some business, Guy vowed. *And then you are going to get very dead.*

(Y)

"I felt certain, by now, that you'd have news for me."

"I wasn't aware you'd hired me to gather gossip."

"Nay, I hired you to bring me the head of that cursed wolfshead."

Had de Lisle possessed a sharp stick, he would be poking it at the Templar. It was like watching ten-year-old boys taunting each other, one trying to get in what licks he could before he had to retreat. More than once she'd seen the lads try it with—

Marion wobbled in her chair, grabbed the table and took in a sharp breath. The suddenness of it, like a rippling spike on the inside of her skull, seemed ill combined with the strange, humming lassitude after, in which she tried to capture what memory tried to blossom, then retreated.

"Marion?" the Abbess murmured. "Are you all right?"

Giving a quick nod, Marion took a soft, deep breath and held it for a moment. She didn't know any ten-year-old lads. Ones she remembered, anyway. Again she tried to grasp the notion, the idea she might have known such. Perhaps in a village where she had grown up. Perhaps had cousins, or brothers.

"Milord Sheriff, I did tell you the matter might take as little as a few days, or as much as a month. Unfortunately it looks more the latter, as I'm having to work through the remains of what, so far, has been a massive and inefficient disaster."

The Sheriff turned back to his plate, rather sullen at the defeat. It was plain he resented having so little control over the situation. Neither was the Templar being terribly forthcoming. Since his arrival, the Templar had, with little grace, accepted the duty of sitting to his host's board—on the few days he had been in the vicinity—but he spoke only when he had to and seemed intemperate when that silence was broken.

The Templar ate no meat, Marion noticed. It wasn't Lent, or any other fasting days— he'd been glad enough of the goose at last night's table, she remembered. Perhaps they had strange eating rituals to go along with the supposed idol-worshipping the Abbess insisted they entertained.

And his name was Gisbourne. Guy de Gisbourne, but somehow the name didn't seem to fit, like an ill-cut tunic. Better than "the Templar." Or Gamelyn—*the old man's son* or whatever it meant—a name he'd given her in a moment of weakness, at that. She felt truly uneasy with that one.

If it came to it, she wasn't too sure herself about the meat placed before her. De Lisle had hunting rights in the forest, of course, but venison hadn't been something the abbey often saw at board. And if Worksop was gifted royal meat, it certainly didn't grace the novices' plates.

This was daft. She liked venison, and since the Abbess had, of late, insisted Marion join them in the main hall for the evening meal, Marion should take advantage of what benefits followed.

"And your plans forward?" the Sheriff persisted. "Not that I care there's a whore or two less in the caverns"—he made an apologetic gesture as the Abbess crossed herself— "but it worries me, Robyn Hood coming so close. It worries me more that you failed to catch him in my own basement."

Gisbourne's face was not as pale but just as freckled as Marion's own, and those freckles seemed to stand out more vividly when he became annoyed. Not that anything else on his face told anything—not even a tightening of jawline betrayed his thoughts. This time, however, he gave into a roll of his green eyes and pushed back from his plate.

"My lord Sheriff, whatever plans I might have, I'm not about to voice them here."

"I assure you, Sir Guy—"

"You may think your walls are inviolate. I assure *you*, my lord, they are not. And it's a certainty at least two, likely three, of your table villeins are connected in some way to this wolfshead's cult."

De Lisle dropped his knife with a clatter of steel on pewter. "My villeins?"

Gisbourne shrugged and drained the last of the drink from his goblet, set it down with a mild *clink* on the board. Marion noticed that none of those aforementioned villeins ventured close to refill it. They were milling about rather uneasily—only a fool thought they didn't listen.

Only a cruel man would know they did—and taunt them with it.

"I'll find them, have them hanged!"

Marion found herself clutching at her skirts, her nails digging into her thighs. *And I thought you sad? You're a bastard!*

Gisbourne snorted, tossed from his face a lock of ruddy hair that had worked loose from the braid holding it back. "Aye, *that* would be wise. Take a leaf from your predecessor's book and execute half the villeins of Nottingham." The green eyes, no longer emotionless, cut down the table . . . surely it wasn't at Marion . . . nay, they touched Marion, then the Abbess, bent over her plate and chewing as if they were discussing the weather. "Or burn an entire village just to prove a point." He gestured with his mug. The villeins still hung back, then a younger man squared his shoulders and took the pitcher from a girl, came forward and poured.

"Never take for granted what you have in the moment," Gisbourne furthered, and it seemed he spoke more to the young villein than the Sheriff. "Someone can always take it from you on a whim. Particularly if you don't take care with what you say."

Or maybe he spoke to the Sheriff. Marion frowned, stabbed at a piece of venison, and began chewing. And chewing. Tough, the meat, despite salting and stewing. The bucks were in rut; if some fool had not killed with one shot, then fear would have merely added to the animal's lack of composure . . .

She hesitated midchew. How did she know *that*?

"I imagine, however, we might find some answers by Samhain."

"Samhain?" De Lisle snorted. "I'm surprised you use the term."

"It matters little what I 'use'." Gisbourne tipped his goblet, oblique thanks to the young villein even as he watched him return to the small group. "It's what it is. Interesting concept, don't you think, my lord Sheriff?"

"I was unaware it possessed a 'concept'," de Lisle scoffed. "Other than an excuse for a bunch of superstitious louts to prance about in their skin and wear masks so they don't have to face their neighbours after a night of drunken idiocy."

"Hm." Gisbourne contemplated his mug. His eyes kept flickering, hard and glittering as the jade on Abbess Elisabeth's cross, from the villeins muttering in a small group on the sidelines to back down the board. "Samhain is an unholy time, yes? A time when the door between the worlds is thin, and spirits roam. Perchance they roam the Shire Wode . . . *Sherwood*, as well."

The Sheriff had plainly decided his guest was speaking nonsense. "And how will that capture Robyn Hood?"

"This talk of pagan ritual is souring my stomach!" the Abbess stated. "It is not a fit subject for mealtime discussion."

Gisbourne kept contemplating his goblet. "Your sister has the option, of course, to leave the board. It might be better, my lord, to have no women prattling when there is serious business to discuss."

Cold, arrogant, bastard in every sense of the word—she had heard Templars renounced everything for their order—still sommat bided there. Sommat *else* . . .

This time the pain in her head knocked her sideways in her chair, spun the hall about, and sent her wilting into blackness.

ᚤ

"Marion?" the Abbess said, then, "*Marion?*"

Guy had seen Marion reel in her chair as if she had been struck, had leapt out of his own seat as she slid down to the dais and nearly over the edge; he caught her just in time.

Her head lolled over his arm as if her neck had been broken.

A hand pounded at his back. Guy turned, hefting Marion as he did, to find the Abbess whacking at him.

"Put her down, you—"

"Don't be foolish, Elisabeth," de Lisle countered, grabbing her arm. "He's the stoutest of us here."

As if any real strength was needed. Guy didn't remember Marion being this thin, this . . . insubstantial. She felt as if she might break if he held her too tightly.

Several villeins were milling about, trying to assist. De Lisle grabbed one of the women and told her something, low and urgent. She made a quick retreat.

"She isn't choking on anything," Guy said. "Has she been ill?"

The soft query seemed to confound the Abbess. After a pause she shook her head, said, "She's never been strong."

That made no sense; the Marion he'd known had always had the constitution of a draught animal and twice the energy. Of course... Guy gritted his teeth, peering at the wimpled head against his shoulder. This wasn't the Marion he'd known.

"Bring her this way." The Abbess was already heading for the doubled doors of the dining solar. Guy and de Lisle followed, out into the hallway and toward the winding stair leading to the inner bedchambers.

At the top of the seemingly interminable stair, Guy paused, shifted Marion; she was long-limbed and unwieldy despite her lightness. It would have taken a soldier used to odd burdens to carry her up the stair. Much was there on the upper storey, seated outside the door of the chambers he shared with Guy, sharpening one of his knives. He rose, questions in his blue eyes. Guy gave the tiniest of head-shakes. With laconic ease, Much lowered himself back to the stool he'd been propped on, resumed his sharpening. The rasp and stutter of it followed them as they went into the end chamber, across from de Lisle's own expansive solar.

"I've sent for my own physician, Elisabeth," he was saying as Guy lowered Marion to the indicated cot. "I know she's dear to you."

I'll wager that, Guy snarled as he straightened and looked down at Marion. *A trophy, is she? Look at the Heathen I tamed and brought to God!*

"The girl should be taken back to the abbey." He could scarcely believe he was saying it. Take her back to live with the woman who had killed her family?

But Marion seemed... content. She was not whole, but after all, what living soul could claim to be? If she had no memories, was it such a bad thing? What he would give for that sort of blindness!

The Sheriff started to reply, then the Abbess answered, curt. "We still have business here."

The business of political manoeuvring, nothing more. When not listening to improbable tales in pubs or camps, Guy had been paying attention within the castle walls as well. He always did whenever he left Preceptory walls, in order to more easily report the pulse of the countryside to his masters. Guy had lived within his own sphere for so long, he had little fortitude for the petty schemas within which nobility—church or secular—would occupy themselves. But neither was he oblivious to the necessity of knowing which way the wind might next blow.

The physician came in, paying no attention to any of the

importances in his path. In fact, in short order, Guy and de Lisle both found themselves shooed from the chamber and the door shut in their faces.

Guy eyed the door with a distinctly ferocious expression, caught de Lisle peering at him and shrugged, turned away. Across the hall, Much was still sharpening his knife; he started to rise.

"Gisbourne."

The edge to it, the lack of honorific, both were delivered like a test parry. No doubt intended to prise further open whatever the Sheriff had, unfortunately, seen in Guy's expression in the past minutes.

Guy was good at being invisible. Good at making threats. Bloody good at maiming and killing. Good at listening, discerning motivation. And the Sheriff's motivation was plain as a stream of piss aimed at Guy's leg. De Lisle was looking for a weapon—which meant, at some point, he intended to use it.

This was *not* good. Guy's skills did not overly extend to the type of fencing offered by a master gamesman who had gained control of three shires and covertly plotted against his king.

From against the wall, Much exchanged a long look with Guy and lowered himself once more—to a ready crouch, not a full-out seat.

A smirk twitched at Guy's mouth, then he turned back to the Sheriff, face impassive. "De Lisle."

The mockery on the Sheriff's face fell only slightly at the return snub. "You're a young man, Templar. I'd say you're even younger than that novice you just so tenderly tucked into bed."

Damn. No, not good at all.

"How old *were* you when you were conscripted into your order? A wean?"

Ah, yes, he knew exactly where this was going.

"Must be quite a shock to the system, eh? To come from your little sterile encampment, all pure and virginal and righteous. I imagine you've done more killing than fucking. Assuming, of course, you *have* done any fucking. You *are* very young, monk."

Christ, but you've no idea, have you? Guy crossed his arms, straightened until his head topped de Lisle's by just that much.

De Lisle was not put off. "I understand you can get into all sorts of trouble even talking to a woman, and here you've had one in your arms." Feigning camaraderie, he leaned closer, said, "Was it nice, Gisbourne?"

Not as nice as lopping your head off. Right now.

"Not just any woman, either. A nun. Another professional

virgin." He gave a *tsk*, shook his head. "What a tragedy. Doubly so, for I've heard Templars prefer boys."

"Templars," Guy said, very soft, "prefer killing unholy bastards who would think to make them into lackeys."

"Gisbourne, I'm paying you." De Lisle leaned into him, hands on hips. "That makes you my lackey."

Guy didn't move, didn't so much as shift his arms or his weight. He knew he could have this puling, manipulative bean-counter against the wall with a blade to his throat before he could draw breath. "Funny, that. For I've yet seen no silver in my palm."

"I've seen no outlaw's head on my postern, either."

"Then quit pissing about and leave me to *catch* him!" Guy growled.

"I'll leave you when you do indeed manage to catch him. Perchance you'd stop making eyes at my sister's novice long enough—*unh*!"

All right, then, the Sheriff *did* manage to take a breath before Guy had whirled, grabbed him, and slammed him against the far wall.

"A *reaction*, Templar?" De Lisle's acerbic query twisted upward into alarm as Guy raised the dagger he snaked from its sheath and put to de Lisle's throat.

"Is this, then, a reaction you see on my face?" Guy whispered. "In my *palm*? Or is it just my way of telling you to belt up?"

"I can have you *hanged* for this!" De Lisle grated out.

"Oh, I'm afraid you really can't." Guy leaned closer, ever so slightly, and smiled as the Sheriff paled. "You're not this stupid, Sheriff. Don't threaten me. Let me do my job and go play your little head games with someone who gives a damn. Like Count John."

He probably shouldn't have said the last, but the sick-white, mottled expression spreading over de Lisle's face was frankly worth it. Flipping the dagger back into its sheath, Guy released de Lisle. Then turned away and walked back to his chambers.

Much gave a lift of eyebrows as Guy passed, and kept sharpening his blade.

Ⓨ

"Did'ja hear, Robyn? 'Twere bloody business done at the Hammered Anvil two nights ago."

Cedric seemed out of sorts, had come late, running and out of breath. This meeting had been pre-arranged at the same time

Robyn had paid Cedric to seed some rumours for them. For a bit of extra coin, Cedric met them here at the crossroads well and, if necessary, took a message from Robyn to Matlock or Hathersage. From there it would make its way to the others.

John looked across the well at Robyn, who gave a suitable frown and dipped into the drawn bucket, drank of the cool water. "I've heard sometimes things get out o' hand there."

"Things is outta hand, awright." Cedric said. "Two killed, throats slit ear t' ear."

Robyn choked on the water, coughed out, "Two killed?" as John stiffened.

"Aye, one of the whores and her brother." Cedric's eyes were not just goggling, but popping wide. "Word is *you* did it."

Two? Robyn slid his eyes over to peer at John, who looked just as dumbfounded as he himself felt.

"Not that I believe it fer a moment. Ronald don't, either, though he durst not tell th' Templar so. He knows you were friends with Meg, though he en't mourning Martin none. Says that one could've gone t' hell any time with no loss."

Robyn closed his eyes, whispered the breath of a small charm toward Meg's spirit. Then the rest of Cedric's words sank in. "Durst not tell the Templar?"

"Aye, Robyn. Ronald saw Martin talkin' to him. He thinks 'twere about you. But he thinks the Templar done the killing," Cedric hastened to assure.

He saw me with her. He killed her for it. Gamelyn. . . killed her.

This was getting deep, too deep for a light swim. Surely Robyn had never doubted Gamelyn could kill did he have to—there had always been a deep, dark undertow of ice in the still pool that made up Gamelyn's being.

But there had also been a clarity within that ice: bright-fierce, artless and addictive . . .

You do not know what hunts you. . .

Perhaps he should be afraid. Instead Robyn was angry. Perhaps he should feel a betrayal. Instead he felt a . . . fascination.

If I don't know what hunts me. . . does he know what he hunts?

"I heard his name," Cedric was saying. "Edgar told me. It's Gisbourne. Sir Guy of Gisbourne."

Robyn more felt than saw John's puzzlement, with his own repeated, "Gisbourne. You're sure."

"Aye. And Robyn—here's sommat else. Edgar said this Gisbourne were at the Sheriff's table, talking about Samhain. 'Magine, Robyn, one o' Christ's Hounds should know our ways."

"Fancy that," Robyn murmured.

"And the Templar were speaking later to one of the pot-boys. Asking questions about Samhain. The villein seemed taken wi' him, all friendly, so Edgar kept an ear out. Edgar weren't all pleased th' lad were so easy charmed, but . . . well . . . he's one of those."

"Those?" Robyn repeated blandly.

"You know." Cedric rolled his eyes then spat. "One of those what likes doing lads. I'd 'spect it of one o' those Templars—a lot of men, all together with no women? Bound to be some tunic-lifters in that lot. Unnatural, it is."

Cedric was useful, so no use in giving him a good hiding. Or in killing him. There was no killing ignorance, anyway; it just bred more like itself, and without the benefit of rutting.

John drank from the dipper, noisily. A smirk twitched his face, a glint lit his brown eyes as he cut them at Robyn. *You unnatural animal, you.*

Aye, well, takes one knowin' one. Biting his tongue against the sudden wish to laugh, Robyn put himself—and Cedric—back on task. "What were he asking about Samhain?"

"The lad?"

"Nay, y'daft git, the Templar. Gisbourne." The latter tasted strange on Robyn's tongue—as well it should, considering.

"Too much, according t' Edgar. The lad is one of our'n. His folks live around Alfreton, come to the fêtes as they can."

"So this Templar—this Gisbourne—is looking, mayhap, t' crash t' party."

Cedric's face sagged with sudden fear. "He en't . . . I've heard his like burn whole villages. It en't gonna . . . en't gonna be like Loxley?"

John's hands clenched, taut-white, on the stones of the well. The voicing of it set a tiny thrill of horror along Robyn's own nerves. Gamelyn had been at Loxley, had seen the fire, the bodies. Surely he wouldn't. Not *Gamelyn.*

Only it wasn't Gamelyn, was it? It was the Templar, the bounty hunter hired by the Sheriff. Sir Guy of Gisbourne.

You do not know what hunts you. . .

Was Gamelyn still in there? Was the name just another mask? Because sure as Gamelyn's heart still beat, albeit cold beneath that bloody cross, no question Gamelyn had been proper sodding brilliant at charming up a mask for every circumstance.

"It wain't be like Loxley," Robyn said softly, leaning his forehead upon his hands, those folded atop the well rim. He gathered his senses—all of them—and let out a long breath over those hands. Seconds later, he saw it touch the water, stir it. Saw *tynged* rippling out, the breath breaking up into myriad futures, glints and laps of possible outcomes and actions. The black place lingered, a void which seemed to haunt any future he ever entertained in connection with Gamelyn, immeasurable tiny whirlpools sucking into the glimmering warp of *tynged*. One in particular roiled widdershins to everything else. Counter and cross-purposed, this lay indefinable, an oddling sense all twisted and drowned, the eddy going deep and trying to pull him in, desperate . . .

Robyn took another breath, held it in his lungs to quiet the shivers in his limbs and the sudden, forlorn ache sinking to his bones. The Sensing had been deeper than he'd meant, but then the emotions went hard and deep.

And all the while his spirit had roamed, his brain had been humming, planning. He looked up, found that the timelessness of such things still continued to surprise him. John knew what had happened, but to Cedric, Robyn's stance had been mere hesitation and a gesture of frustration.

Just as well.

"I'm going to need more, Cedric. Mayhap the lad who fancies the Templar can be charmed in another way."

ⓨ

"Do you think 'twill help, milord?"

"It can't hurt." Guy considered the tiny silver cross, bound with its chain and set precisely in the middle of the four candles. Just extinguished, wisps of smoke crawled from the blackened wicks, with melted beeswax still lingering, fragrant, in the air.

Beneath the necklet, several sigils had been drawn with care upon the floor. As Guy reached out and took the necklet up, he smudged the heel of his hand across the signs, leaving an unremarkable scuff of soot on wood. A bead of scarlet quivered upon the silver and began to slide; he used his thumb to smear the blood over the cross, and whispered a few words of Latin. "I'm just glad I had this. It was my mother's. I'd like to think she'd not begrudge the use of it." He raised it to his forehead, then put it to his lips.

"Too bad Johnny en't here," Much ruminated. "He'd know the right of it in a heartbeat, set a spell 'twould put our paltry conjurin' to shame."

"I remember," Guy said, a bit hoarsely.

Once John had threaded a leather necklet over young Gamelyn's head, hung with a wooden stag's head—a charm of making, humming with sheer sensate power—and whispered, *'Twill help you find him...*

Nay, John's ability had been nothing like this ill-cast novice working Guy kept trying to perfect. Hubert had found him a poor student. The workings of tool and craft had never spoken to him; the neophyte ceremonials with which his Master had tested him, one by one, had never sunken into his soul as they'd both hoped.

There was another mark upon you.

Perhaps this was why the mark had not been blooded clean. *She* still lived.

Is this why I'm here, Lady? To protect her?

You are My Summerlord. It has always been your tynged, *to defend My honour and, in doing so, give honour to your Maiden.*

"She'd be safe in th' abbey, if they'd just send her back."

Guy contemplated the charm, then began polishing it with a silk kerchief from his pouch. "I . . . I'm not sure, right now. She was the Maiden. Still is."

Much was staring at him. "I en't heard you talk like this before."

"Which means I'm not making any sense."

"Huh. Mayhap y'r making more sense than I've heard in too long."

Guy gave a grim chuckle. "I'm glad one of us believes that." Their voices were already low—their chambers searched for any kind of spy-holes or suspicions—but he lowered his tone further. "One thing is sure. The outlaws are looking for her. What if their leader knows, somehow, what she was? Is." Guy shook his head. "Bloody hell, this really is making no sense. But I can't help thinking, Much . . . you know why we were sent here. What if, somewhere, locked inside, *Marion* has secrets? Secrets this wolfshead wants? If that's true, then nowhere is safe for her."

"Which," Guy straightened, curling his fingers gently about the amulet, "is why I shall go to the Samhain gathering alone. You'll stay here."

"Milord," Much protested. "Nay."

"These are *your* gods, Much. She is . . . *your* Maiden."

"And you are my lord."

"Much—"

"There's been hard things t' happen when we didn't have t' other's back."

They peered at each other, remembering. It had been Much who had dragged Guy from the coastal waters of Acre. It had been

Guy who had carried Much, leaking blood all over his shoulder, from the losses of Jaffa.

"And what will happen should this outlaw find Marion?"

Much, gathering wind for another reply, fell silent, the air whistling from between his teeth.

Guy held the cross up to the light, eying the dull sheen of old silver and drying blood. If his blood had any worth in the Lady's eyes, then hopefully this would give some protection. "The serving lad fancies my attentions, has sworn to take me there. I've done my best to cozen him—"

"Milord, begging your pardon, but there's nowt alive who's *that* good a fuck."

Still dangling the charm from his fingers, Guy shrugged. "When I was this lad's age, I fancied there was."

"You were brought up t' think such things wicked. I'd wager me best dagger this lad en't so ignorant as you were. He's likely proper Heathen—"

"Oh, I've no doubt he is." Guy smiled.

"Then he might be tryin' to play *you*."

"Indeed he might." Guy untangled the necklet from his fingers, wrapped it in the silk kerchief he'd prepared. "The question is whether he's more scared of Robyn Hood than a Templar. Should prove interesting."

Much sat back, muttering to himself.

"I'm not leaving for another day at least," Guy offered. "Why don't you let off a little frustration yourself? Buy one of those whores who happen to fancy you a drink or three and show her how good a fuck *you* are?"

Much kept muttering. He was never pleased when his master decided, amidst riding the lion, to let go of one ear and pull its whiskers.

But neither was Guy willing to let Much risk more than necessary. "Listen. If the Sheriff gives you any trouble—"

Much snorted. "Did I change me clothes, he'd not be knowin' me from the ratcatcher. Y' forget, milord, how your kind en't altogether observant of mine. Meaning no offence, o' course."

"Of course." A grim chuckle. "Then change your clothes when you have to. But watch her."

"An' the amulet?"

"I'll give it to her myself, before I go."

"An' if they do take her back to Worksop?"

"Follow." Guy tucked the amulet in his tunic. "And if anyone comes after Marion, kill them."

- X -

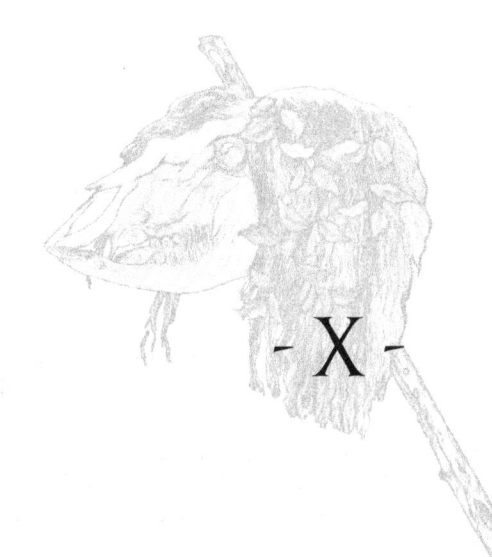

She woke the next morning with the worst headache in a very long time, and the feeling that she was caught in a whirlpool, swirling in the black, drowning . . .

And the worst of it, the Abbess held her beneath the water.

Tempting, to lie there, curl up on her cot, and never move again. Instead, Marion rose and dressed, ran a comb through her short mop of curls and veiled them. Even if this morning the familiar fabric felt heavy, more shroud than veil.

She shuddered off the anxiety—the dream, nothing more, and she was tired of being the fragile one, the sickly charity case! Miracle or no.

The Abbess's bed lay empty but rumpled. Marion put on woollen stockings and boots against the chill of the floor stones, then tidied both beds and the chamber. Finally she worried down some bread and fruit, and started for the outer chamber. Voices halted her as she raised a hand to the thick-hewn door.

" . . . will he be coming?"

"He's meeting with Roger at Blyth just before All Saints—"

"Roger agreed? I thought he had no use for the count—and no stomach for the consequences."

The Abbess. And Sheriff de Lisle. Marion appreciated, from the timbre of their voices, that she should turn away and mind her own business. Yet a small and subversive inner voice bid her hold her place.

There is too much already you do not know, it chided. *Will you continue to surround yourself with stone and consent to your own ignorance?*

The reproof in it set flame to her cheeks. Marion took a slow breath, held it, then leaned forward to listen.

"Our dear brother wearies of being taxed to death by a king who looks to his kingdom as nothing more than mortgage for his slaughters. Roger is willing to listen, at least, to John's bid for his support. Richard has no heir and looks likely to rot a captive in Germany. And . . . " The Sheriff's voice dropped. "It's said there are men in place to ensure that, does the king win free, he will not return to England."

Marion's stomach gave a fierce dip and wobble. Ignorant she might be, but she understood all too plain what was being said.

Treason.

And if they caught her listening to such talk . . .

"So, God willing, John will be king, and Eleanor likely locked back up in her ivory tower with her boy-minstrels and sonnets to courtly love." The Abbess's voice curled scornful.

Courtly love. Marion had heard of such things—several of the other novices were quite taken with the Queen Mother's ideals, and why not? Love for love's sake, and not as geld to some man you'd barely seen thrice, and likely twice your age?

Their talk had merely confused Marion, at the time. She'd no experience that she could conjure to match theirs. All she had felt was an odd scorn that they should think such ridiculous things about a natural function. Of course, so many of them were repulsed by their own bodies' blood-time. Didn't they recognise in it a powerful thing, a gift from the Lady?

This time the dull ache in her skull flared like heat. Pain, yes, but not horrific, or stabbing. Nevertheless it was chancy; if Marion hadn't been holding to the door, she might have fallen and given herself away.

Lady, she wondered, putting a clammy hand to her face. *What Lady? The Virgin Mary? And what gift?*

The Sheriff was speaking again. "So you plan on staying, then, until he comes here?"

"Since we don't exactly know when he'll arrive, then it might be best. If I leave for the abbey, then return upon the Count's heels, it could be suspicious." A pause. "Nor am I sure my novice is up to the travel."

"Mm. She seems sickly."

Annoyance gave way to curiosity as the Abbess replied, "With what she went through before she came to us, it is no surprise." Unfortunately, she said nothing more on that topic, but after another pause, said, "And what of the Templar?"

Marion's eyes narrowed at the raw dislike in her mistress's voice.

"My, you've a bee in your wimple over that one." The Sheriff's voice held amusement.

"I know him, Brian. I don't know where, or how, but he is familiar—"

"Bah. If you do know him, what could it possibly matter?"

"His attentions to Marion are unseemly."

"Bah, I say. You grew up in a houseful of brothers, Elisabeth, you should know better. That Templar might be a killing machine, but he's also barely twenty, has been away to war and likely never so much as touched a woman. So he's decided yon pale victim of a novice is a fair and unattainable object. Chide the Queen Mother's romantic notions all you want, you cold baggage, but young people lap that stuff like fresh cream."

"I will not have this conversation with you! Disgusting!"

"Sister, really!" The Sheriff's laugh soured too quickly. "If only we were so lucky that he'd try something overt with the girl. 'Twould give us a weapon to contain him. Arrogant little shit. He'd better catch this wolfshead, and soon. I'd rather have that business done before the King's brother decides to grace us with his presence, thank you. And—"

A firm knock on the outer door, and steps outward to answer it as the Abbess said, "Who can possibly . . . " She went silent as the outer door creaked open.

"Forgive the intrusion, my lord Sheriff, but your man said I might find you here."

The Templar! Marion's eyes widened—was it possible that *he* had heard anything of what had been said?

"Well, Sir Guy?"

"I will be absent from the castle for a few days. My man, however, will be about, gathering more information. I hope our mission is coming to an end."

"Not half as much as I," the sheriff retorted.

"I also, if I might, wish to apologise directly to *you*, Reverend Lady." Gisbourne's voice came gentle, deceptively so when one considered, well, everything. "You must understand, the rules of my order are explicit, and it is hard, sometimes, to discern what is permissible and what is not."

Deceptive indeed. Marion's lips quirked. An indefinable quality lurked beneath his voice, subversive and cunning. She could almost smell it.

"Well." The Abbess obviously could not. "That's quite... surprising."

"Laudable, even." The sheriff's voice was wry; he wasn't fooled.

"I also would like to offer a token of my good wishes to your novice's health." A pause.

This, perhaps, made a fair time for an entrance. Marion opened the door, then swung it gingerly open just as the Abbess was saying, "I don't think..."

Gisbourne had noticed Marion immediately; his eyes were upon her, gauging, even as the others turned.

"Marion?" the Abbess queried. "How long have you been awake?"

It held a layer of not-quite-threat. Marion calmed her resultant trepidation with the reminder: this was not the first time she had heard questionable things. She made light of it. "Not for long. I were having my prayers. I didn't ken anyone were here—the chamber is proper quiet."

Gisbourne's cool green eyes were still gauging her, as if he knew she, too, was hiding something. "I hope," he said, "you're feeling stronger?" He held, gently yet firmly, a folded piece of gauzy silk caged within his long fingers. She had only seen such costly eastern fabric upon the Abbess's robes. "May I?" He gestured with the cloth, gave a minute dip of his head to the Abbess. Despite the courtesy, his eyes were chill.

He loathes her. The realisation came to Marion, made her eyes sting and her stomach roil uncertainly. *She is his enemy.*

Why?

"Oh, what harm can it do, Sister dear?" Beneath the sheriff's reproof lurked, very obviously, a reminder which chilled Marion: *a weapon to contain him.* "It's even a cross."

And why had all these things started to rear their heads, so obvious? It made no sense. As if she had been wandering in a dumb fog.

"It was my mother's, Reverend Lady, given to her by the Archbishop many years ago for her health. Many prayers are bestowed upon it."

"How... romantic," the sheriff drawled.

Gisbourne shot de Lisle a look that surely belonged on the business end of a crossbow sight. "I mean no disrespect," he insisted, "only that your novice should do my mother the honour of wearing it."

"I will accept," Marion said, meeting his gaze. "With your permission, of course, Reverend Lady."

The Abbess demurred, and Gisbourne came forward, with a bow offered the tiny silver cross on its bed of silk. His hands were callused, browned and freckled—seemingly more comfortable with live steel than any silken finery, yet he extended the gift in his palms as graceful and reverent as any knight of the Queen Mother's courtly romances. Marion's heart gave a tiny lurch and slip against her breastbone and, as if in answer, her head twinged warning. She hesitated. Gisbourne's eyes slid to hers, a tiny frown quirking between his brows—warning? concern?—then went flat and studied the hem of her habit.

Hiding. In plain sight, she comprehended, feeling not only the Abbess's eyes upon her, but the Sheriff's. Quickly, she reached out and took up the offering. The silver strangely warmed her fingers, and lapped a lulling heat around her neck as she threaded it there, fumbled with the catch, then fastened it to lie at her throat.

Gaze still downcast, he had made no other motion toward her, had clasped his hands behind his back. *Twenty-year-old killing machine*, the memory taunted, but the presence of him now was stronger, in more ways than one. Tall and broad-shouldered, girded with sword and metal, ruddy hair braided back from his face and a lock of it trailing over his shoulder and down, gilt on midnight . . . no doubt he was a man. A proper handsome one, at that.

He knew her, somehow. His name was not just Gisbourne, but Gamelyn, and it was not a name he wanted revealed. He had done sommat . . . nay, had *not* done it, but feared she would think he had.

"Please do not take it off, my lady." Gisbourne's voice was still very quiet, controlled. "It is small, easily lost."

Then he turned from her, gave a dip of his head to the Sheriff. "I will return. Likely with your outlaw's head on my saddle, if all goes well."

Killing machine. Marion watched him depart, felt both dismay and remorse.

He'll find more than he would bargain. This time the Voice came soft, and deep. Feminine.

It seemed, oddly enough, to further heat the silver cross at her throat.

"Wellaway! Sommat's coming."

As Robyn uttered the quiet murmur and froze midmotion, the outlaws all, to a man, tensed and drew their weapons. As they started for the caves carven into the hill, Robyn peered at them. He took a few running strides to jump up on a large rock set out from the hill. "And aye, look!" he hissed. "It's the wagon of ale 'n mead, comin' to slay us all in our sleep!"

Will let out a filthy curse and swung his staff upward at Robyn. As he gave a quick hop, avoiding the blow, the others were growling just as angrily. David threw a handful of dirt at him. Even the ferret tucked into David's tunic chittered angrily.

"What in hell was that in aid of?" Arthur complained.

"You're a right Motherless git, you are!" Gilbert seconded. "Get us all worked up like that!"

Will was still cursing. John glared, pretended to throw a knife at Robyn.

"Aw, leave off!" Robyn snorted. "You're all jumpy as a doe with twin fawns!"

"In case you forgot, you've a murderous sod of a Templar after ye," Arthur reminded. "And we en't sure when he'll grace us with his comp'ny."

Robyn shrugged. "The lad says he were asking all about the rites, so I'm guessing then?"

"The lad," David snorted. "One of Nottingham's villeins!"

"Whose parents are fine Heathens," Gilbert pointed out. "The boy's more scared of Robyn than the Templar, anyway."

"Fear can be a fine thing, in its place," Robyn murmured. "And we'll be ready for the monk, when he comes."

The monk. The Templar. He had to keep using those words, keep reminding himself.

Has twisted his denial into an awesome power... His soul lies closed, deep and darker than any oubliette... He denies us, and we will take him back.

A gamble to be sure, and this time 'twere one involving not merely Robyn, but others in the mix.

'Tis time to throw the bones again, sweet Hob-Robyn...

Aye, he agreed, crouching down on the rock and looking out over the black and busy river. *But I'll throw them in my own way.* Something more powerful than any denial twisted deep in Robyn's chest—fierce and forbidden. *I have to believe he's still in there. I have to try.*

Below his perch, the wagon rolled to a creaking halt between the river and the hill. In the box rode Wulfstan with his contribution to the fête, with the headman of Ingleby beside as guide.

"This is bloody amazing!" Wulfstan alighted from the cart.

It truly was, Robyn had to admit. It had been an old shelter of Will's when Will had first fled into the Wode on his own, a cavernous hollow possibly dug out when the Trent, a good arrow's flight beyond, ran higher. There were Saxon runes carved into the walls, and faded paintings even older.

"Wait 'til you see our hermit's cavern alight with fires and torches. 'Twill beckon our people to gather. And all good godfearing Christians will huddle in their homes, fearing the darkness whilst we claim it." Robyn smiled, hopped down from the rock. "'Tis a ways you've come, Wulf, and we bid you welcome. *Bendith.*"

"*Bendith*, Hooded One. We'll honour the spirits together, as was once done when your ma and da were still alive. Surely they'll be with us come the summoning of Samhain, proud to see their son now."

ⓨ

Guy rode for Derby at sunrise on Samhain eve. There he found lodgings for not only Falcon but himself, and gave orders that he was to not be disturbed, even for meals, as he fasted for All Saints.

The innkeeper volunteered little and asked few questions—odd for his trade, but not unexpected. In Guy's experience, people were either overly curious or made uneasy by his presence—truly rare to find an in-between reaction, and unease usually preferable. Guy was led to a small chamber that could not have been more tailormade for his purpose. It was small and reasonably clean—not that the latter had any import; he'd not be there long. Likely the place had been storage at one point, off to itself and, even better, adjacent to a hall that led to a back entry. And it had a lock.

As the innkeeper lit a tallow lamp, spilling faint illumination into the dark cot, he made uncomfortable apology at the mean offering—all he had available to ensure his guest's request for privacy. Guy prevented him from lighting a second lamp and, once the innkeeper handed him the key, handed over a few coins more than had been asked for the lodging.

"It will do nicely. My thanks."

The innkeeper blinked at the offered tender, snatched it up and retreated, closing the door behind him. Guy tossed his bag onto the rush-piled bed; one of the closing ties gave way. Horsehair went spilling sideways, a boot-length of black tumbling after a grey carapace. Brows drawing together, Guy took it up.

Rather grotesque, actually: the thing had been fashioned to resemble more a horse's rendered skull than a living head despite being covered with grey hide. There was a capelet—also of grey horsehide—with it. The key over-the-top aspects to its grotesquery were a predator's sharp canines amongst the normal grazer's molars, and a lower jaw with a mechanism to make it snap. There was an irresistible irony in it; from the moment the Underkeep merchant had shown Guy the mask, his decision had been made.

A capull-hide, the merchant had said, then handed the mask to him with an odd bow. *For a* capull-coille—*a horse of the Wode.*

Nottingham's serving lad—Peter—had been the one to insist upon a mask; in fact he'd had several ready when Guy had met him two nights previous. When Guy had demurred, the lad had assured him: all who came to Samhain wore masks, some more elaborate than the one he'd chosen for Guy. He'd been openly disappointed when Guy had said he'd find one for himself.

"Aye," Guy murmured. "A very helpful lad."

And too eager. That Peter was part of a trap, Guy had no doubt. And thus had Robyn Hood made a costly mistake, thinking such a young lad wouldn't let an important task turn his head. But now the wolfshead wouldn't know how Guy would be dressed, and Guy would make sure Peter would be unable to reveal anything.

Guy was to meet the boy on the road to Repton midday. A brisk walk should have him there quickly enough. And . . . He angled the mask over his head, didn't bother tying it at his nape but flicked the silver-shot ebon mane out behind, and nodded. More than adequate to cover his own hair. The capelet would hide the glint of chainmail, its weight still the jingle. He'd debated going without the chainmail, but venturing into enemy territory without some protection was pure foolishness.

He made a sinister silhouette against the wall, the lamp backlighting him in fits and starts. Walking over to the lamp, he flitted his fingertips back and forth, setting the flame—and the pantomimed wall-ghost—to dancing.

Shrugging off the mask, Guy peeled from every hint of Templar gear and weaponry. The cord tying his hair back from his face would be adequate, or one of his knives. Sneak up on the man, do the job quick and silent, and none the wiser.

If all went well, he'd need no sword.

Ⓨ

Dusk descends over the stone circle, mists rising and caressing the grass, the trees, the stones splayed in the clearing as if some giant has thrown them, mere jack-straws, heedless and chaotic.

She walks into the circle, barefoot, dressed only in her thin, white undertunic. The grass is damp and chill against her feet, the breeze brisk, the mist clinging and slicking over her skin, setting wiry ringlets in her hair. It is not merely discomfort, it is also agitation, a nigh-forgotten surrender to sensation. The susurrus of thick air and thin linen sets the breath tight in her chest, heats her cheeks, fills her loins with humming pressure. Her skin contracts into tiny little pinpoints of shivers, of dread/thrill/chill that cloth merely agitates instead of warms. She raises her hands, cups her breasts, shivers as her palms brush taut nipples and clutch at thin, damp fabric. Her breath escapes, a soft moan wavering then spreading to all points. A call.

The waning sun turns parts of the landscape into grey and violet and, with a trick of the last light, into the dark scarlet of blood. Dusk to night to dawn to day, and then back to dusk. It is an omen. A reminder. The blood she sheds, every moon. The blood which her Lord will dedicate for the land, for his people, to give his life upon the altar of renewal, the cycle never-ending, the wheel turning.

That which must be given, in service of hers and what it bestows. . .

"Milady!" A powerful hand gripped her arm, snug and sure, pulling her back. A man's voice. "Lady, are y—"

It choked off as Marion turned on him, wrenched her arm from his . . . impertinence!

She was not helpless, she was not fragile!

A dark-clad man with short-cropped hair and grizzled beard held up his hands, making quick apology. "I'm sorry, but y' looked likely to tumble down those stairs, 'stead of walking 'em."

Peering past his mailed shoulder and down the long flight of stairs beyond, Marion realised that she did not know how she'd come to be here. And that she knew him: the Templar's servant. His brown tunic also bore the crimson cross—a smaller one, set over his heart.

"I . . . I should be the one sorry. I . . ." Marion hesitated, took a deep breath and tried to reach for her scattered thoughts.

It had happened. Again.

"Lady?"

"I'll be well, anon. I don't know what came over me."

The man was peering at her chest even more than she his, his brows tight-knit together. She frowned back, raised a hand to her throat in both affront and uncertainty. Blinked at the heat searing her palm.

The tiny cross, given her by the Templar, felt as if it had been lying in fire-coals instead of around her neck. As Marion lifted it, the old silver seemed to glimmer with the rusted black of dried blood.

Blood. That which must be given, in service of hers and what it bestows.

"The charm," the soldier murmured.

The charm.

"Where did he go?" she asked.

It was the soldier's turn to blink. "The sheriff? The—"

"Nay. Your master. The Templar. He said he went to find an outlaw, but where?"

Again, the soldier blinked, then shrugged. "Where indeed? 'Tis the moon of Samhain, so he goes t' chase a ghost. He's done too much of it, since we returned." Seemingly unperturbed by the illogic of what he'd just uttered, the man stepped closer, peered at her. Concern scrawled itself across his face. "Are ghosts chasin' you, Lady?"

She nearly answered, nearly said *Yes*, but turned her face away, focused on the more sensible of her reactions. "Ghosts do not exist. And I am no lady . . ." She trailed off, realised she didn't know his name.

"You are *the* Lady," the man answered, with a dip of his head. "Her form as walks upon our land. My master, Sir Guy, bid me see t' your protection, and rightly so. On such a night, spirits walk and ride wild."

Riding wild the Samhain night. A surge of conflicting emotions rose within her breast, culminating in a tussle between allure, horror, and indignation. The veil thinning between the worlds, and dreams coming even in waking hours. The aloof courtesy of the Templar, a charismatic and improbable suitor with his silk-wrapped gift. The plain and home-spun comfort of this man, one of her people . . .

Her people? His . . . *Lady?*

What did she need *protection* from?

"My name is Much," the man said. "My people are of Auckley Mill."

"I am Marion, Much."

He knelt, picked up a thick pile of woollen fabric heaped at the top of the stair. "I know, Lady."

"Marion!" A call from the stairwell. "If we're to see them arrive, you'd best hurry!"

The Abbess's voice set the world, slightly tilting sideways, back into straight and strictured focus. Count John was arriving, a se'nnight early at that, and Sheriff de Lisle was having a conniption—the premature arrival meant more money he would have to spend for a royal guest's entourage. The Abbess had sent Marion upstairs to collect their capes. The day had turned cold and clear. It would behove them to be there, to do honour to their king's brother as he arrived to Nottingham castle.

It was then—and only then, though it was somewhat disturbing—that Marion perceived she had dropped the cloaks on the upper stair. Those were what Much rose with in his arms and held out to her.

"Much," Marion said, abruptly unsure. "Will he return?"

"He allus does," Much replied. "Even if he en't wantin' to."

ⓨ

Night had well fallen. Perched up in the highest of the carved-out openings of the Saxon cavern, Robyn kept watch. On the perimeter beyond—a circle cast wide with fire and blood, smoke and sigils sketched into the air and charmed into protections—were the bale-fires, warning and beacon of the protected place. Some of the lights seemed to move: people approaching with hobby lanterns and will 'o wisps, gourds carven hollow and set alight as protection and guide for the masked revellers. The stationary lights were small bonfires, contained with stacked and daubed stone.

And before Robyn, the grandest light of all: a great bale-fire halfway between his perch and the river beyond, the southmost and northmost points of their circle. Sparks flew upward as someone—Will, clad only in breeks and the length of fair hair glinting beneath his wolf mask—tossed on another log.

The drinking had already started, and a few brave souls had begun the dancing. Robyn smiled. First the play, and then the more serious matters. The moon was rising, huge and yellow between the trees, and the veil between the worlds was drawing ever thin. He had a duty tonight. But first his own offerings, his own silent homage to those gone on ahead, to his most ardent memories amidst the many. Cernun. His mother. His father. His sister. He could hear them whisper in the night, feel their breath on his hair . . . except Marion. He had walked with her in *Annwn*, the otherworld, but since that night of firelit dying, he had never so much as felt her breath on his cheek.

I'm sorry. It was what he always said to the silence. *I tried. I failed you.*

He did not look for the Horned Lord, or the Lady. On such nights they did not speak. On such nights he *became* them, so, no need...

Instead, he rocked on the cavern ledge, and crooned into the night: *Come, then. All ye who would go before, or go after, come by and see this wheel's ending.*

ᚢ

Who would go before, or after?

The voice tickles at her mind, like a soft breath against her ear. It questions. And she gives answer into the night:

Ardhu. Arglwydd.

Black one. Lord.

And he comes to her call. First visible as a tall, ebon shadow in the dark trees, the hart's antlers come ablaze with Samhain's sunrise. He walks into the circle of stone. Dark eyes glitter, full of barely contained heat as he comes to a halt beside the centre tabletop of the altar. He stamps, lets out a blast of breath that swirls in the morning mists, threads out, seeking. As if alive the mists twine, tangle then split; several tendrils wander near her, still seeking but never touching, never finding. The other tendrils have purpose, and aim, flying like arrows to the edge of the stones.

His call, too, is answered. A great, chestnut warhorse breaks through the trees, feathered hoofs grounding in a light precision both belying and revealing his strength. He shakes his mane as he comes to a halt, stands his ground and returns the stag's blast. Though he has not the great, spreading set of tines the King Stag has, the stallion has those massive hoofs. And, as he opens his mouth in a ringing neigh, he bares the long-sharp canines of a predator.

The stag waits, patient...

"Patience is overrated!"

As if the sunset carpet of dusky green had been yanked from beneath her feet by a jongleur's troupe of tumblers, Marion jolted back to where she stood. Once again she was merely leaning against the cold stone of the great hall, behind her mistress's chair upon the dais.

The small cross, hanging against her throat, tingled warm.

"Surely my solar is suitable, my lord Count, whilst you wait for yours to be aired and cleared?" Sheriff de Lisle's apology persisted, relentlessly logical. "I beg your forgiveness, we did not expect you so soon, and—"

"My favourite solar should not have been left to founder in the first place!" While Count John was enjoying the banquet given in his honour, it was plain he was not as enamoured of the chambers de Lisle had prepared for him.

To his credit, de Lisle was not giving up trying to be reasonable. Yet even Marion could see that logic couldn't win, here. She'd never seen a count before and had already decided they were the most spoilt of brats she had ever encountered. Perhaps that was the way of it, when you were appointed by God and received everything as if you had divine right to it.

The Abbess's cup was nigh empty. Marion set herself to fill it.

"I again beg your forgiveness, my lord Count. I did not know the east chambers were your favourite. The castle has been neglected and I am doing my best to make repairs, but as you know, the coin for such ventures is not always easily obtained—"

"No doubt it goes into my brother's war-making instead!" Count John snorted and, to the sheriff's obvious relief, left off his previous harangue to stew on a new one.

Count John was also, and obviously, a late-gotten son. An uneasy place to be in any power struggle, to be sure.

Marion blinked. Again, sommat she knew. Like the thing that had come to her when they had watched the count's arrival.

A strangely low-key affair, and Marion had imagined a royal arrival to be heralded with the swell of trumpets and dancing horses, an entourage of banners, of wagons draped in velvets and silks. She obviously knew nothing about this sort of thing. There were banners, and an entourage, and wagons. The horses showed no inclination to dance; indeed, the count seemed an indifferent horseman. The banners were splendid, the soldiers well turned out, but the wagons were worn and commonplace, filled with nondescript chests and some furniture—though one was populated with a half dozen maidens who were dressed very prettily indeed, in those velvets so absent elsewhere.

The Abbess had not approved of that wagon, not at all. Marion contented herself with a smirk—even if Count John was no man as an equestrian, he seemed to have enough manhood for another kind of riding. She kept watching the giggling, richly gowned girls with some wistfulness. They looked not much older than Marion herself, but they also stirred no recognition in her—she was always searching, these days, for it— and she was sure her own work-hardened hands had never known the touch of brocade or velvet.

It was, at least, another piece to the puzzle. Like knowing about late-gotten sons . . .

The old man's son. Gamelyn.

She raised her fingers to the tiny cross resting upon her habit. It lay cool, now, though it would warm with no understandable provocation. Where had the Templar gone for Hallows?

Why did she *care*?

And what did any of it have to do with a black buck and chestnut warhorse fighting upon a pagan altar?

ᚣ

Who would go before, or go after?

Guy paused, looking off into the darkness with a frown. Lights flitted through the trees like fae lanterns. The drift of smoke met his nostrils, commingling with the mist-damp rising from the fens, and the soft roar and coppery illumination bespoke the former's origin: a large bonfire.

He and Peter had stopped to don their garb for the fête. Peter seemed unsure—in truth had seemed antsy since they'd met earlier in the evening. Guy was unsurprised to feel a light hand on his back as he bent down, but he was rather surprised by the kiss Peter gave him as he turned in question.

So, Guy mused. *You're not so new to the game of courting, but leading the ox to slaughter is not so to your tastes?* The thought should have hardened his own intent. It could have been easily and quickly done, the lad dealt with then and there. Instead Guy broke from the kiss, pulled away.

Peter kept kneeling there, watching as Guy once again bent to his bag, pulling out the *capull*-hide and mask. As Guy shook out the mane of the mask, he heard the lad suck in a quick gout of air, slid a gaze to sideways and asked, quiet, "What is it, lad?"

"A *capull-coille*," Peter breathed. "Wherever did ye find such a thing, milord?"

"That's what the merchant told me it was." Guy felt a quiver of disquiet at the look on Peter's face, half dread and half wonder as he raised a hand, touched fingertips to the mask. "What is it?" Guy asked again. Not for the first time, he missed Much. Much would have known what this . . . *horse of the Wode? . . .* truly meant.

Peter shook his head. "Nowt the likes of me should speak to. Merely 'tis . . . a powerful figure." His gaze took in Guy once more, held. He held his own mask—a mouse—loosely in his lap. "I wonder," he murmured.

"Wonder can be a good thing."

"Nay, I mean . . . I don't think you're as bad as they say."

"They?" Guy said, just as quiet.

Peter frowned.

"Peter." Finishing with the *capull*-hide, Guy turned to face his companion. "I'm afraid they're right. I'm afraid I am as bad as they say."

Peter's eyes went wide. He didn't have time for any other expression. Swift, ruthless, Guy grabbed him, twisted him around and against him. The lad hadn't time to so much as struggle.

It should have been easy. The dagger was in his hand. The boy was a traitor and had led him here, to a trap.

Instead, he knocked Peter's temple with the pommel of the dagger. Peter let out a grunt, then crumpled.

Guy should have killed him. Should have left no loose ends, not this close to the end of a long hunt.

Calling himself ten kinds of cowardly, Guy dragged the lad behind a bush and left him there.

- XI -

Firelight everywhere, turning the place into a velveted spill of copper and gold with black edges. It illuminated small, hollowed-out gourds, lit the way with beacons in stone fire pits, frothed up into the sky from the main bonfire. And defined, against the cliff-face, tens of openings, large and small, into a deep cavern beyond.

Guy could see, the closer he came, the runes and sigils carved into the well-lit walls. The Templar Masters would surely want to know of this place, if they didn't already.

And people. It could rival a market day in Nottingham: individuals drinking, eating, sitting and standing and dancing. All masked, from the simplest of things to elaborate and detailed, limbs bared to the firelight, most garbed with some outlandish overtunic or tatterdemalion cape. Guy relaxed the closer he came to the main fire, noting everything.

Including the fact that it was roiling up into one amazing revelry.

A woman bumped into him by accident, turned to apologise. Her eyes went big as they met his, and for a horrific and nerve-twining instant Guy thought he was somehow discovered. She started laughing and let out a whoop.

"Th' Hob! The Hobby!"
Hob? Guy remembered the name all too well, and it shook him. *What?*
At first none heard the woman. Guy tried to back away, lose himself in the crowd from whatever had amused her—probably drunk, nothing more. But as he retreated he found others turning to him, and soon the woman's cry began to shift through the crowd, and they were turning to him with the same glee. "The' 'Ob 'Oss!"
"Th' *Wode* Horse! The Tup!"
The Tup . . . The Wode Horse . . . It hissed through and over the crowd, excited murmurs, echoes in the trees.
"Aye, the Tup! An' he's brung seed to th' dying ground!"
Within a matter of moments, Guy found himself amidst a small crowd of masked revellers, their dance twining and spiralling about him. The ones coming closest were mostly females, all laughing, each trying to shove the other toward him.
Guy had to forcibly make himself not turn tail and run. Inconceivable, that a bunch of maidens would nearly rout him when he had faced down desert armies.
Abruptly he remembered the teeth on his mask, groped at his chest for and yanked at the string. The teeth snapped together with decided effect: the lasses shrieked, darted away. But they were laughing, and they kept coming back for more.
Fairly soon he became the epicentre of laughing and hollering folk, who pulled him into the dance. He went along. Thoroughly exhilarating, the wanton energy of it, a familiarity that must be speaking to his mother's Saxon blood.
Another mark on you. . .
Hubert's voice, reminder and sobriety.
You have the right. . .
Nay, I really, really don't.
And just like that, Guy was back in himself, the detached weapon looking for something to cut into.
The dancing line swung past the river, curled about, and came back to the caverns. Guy played his part, every sense he had waiting. *Waiting.*
"'Tis time for the horseplay, aye?" A growling purl of a baritone, its common accent not dodging its power in the least. Everyone turned, expectant. If Guy hadn't known who he was, the surge forward and murmurings of the surrounding people told him.
Waiting was over. It stood, limned in the largest of the cavern openings. A man . . . a *beast* . . . unbelievably tall with an immense fourteen-point rack seeming to sprout from the cowled head. Caped

with furs and feathers, rags and leathers, it was impossible to see body shape, or to discern if there truly was a body beneath. The sight of it stirred the unlikeliest of fears in the deepest places. Guy barely caught himself from angling back in sheer instinct. It was the gilt on the tines, and the glint of chain—bronze and silvered— dangling from the rack of antlers like the scrapings of velvet, which pulled him further from superstitious instinct, from reaction to rational.

No simple pilfer from the king's deer, this . . . the horns held upon them more wealth than any of these peasants would see in a lifetime. The Horns of the god? Was Guy looking at part of what his master had sent him for—one of the artefacts that this murderous wolfshead had stolen?

The beast-man's fire-lit eyes locked on him. Guy abruptly found himself in the midst of the circle, the masked revellers parting around him. He was left solitary, ringed by masked faces and glittering eyes.

"Did you think I'd let you do this, Gisbourne?" Full of some deep emotion, the beast-man's mellifluous voice slapped Guy sideways and, inexplicably, traced shivers across his skin. "*Take* him."

They fell on him, silent and purposeful.

Guy didn't go down easily. His knives came to his hand, and he shook them off like a bear attacked by wolves, teeth gritted and silent, blades flashing in the dim to the sounds of cries and curses, the warm spatters of blood-letting. But there were simply too many of them, like a hive of ants all over him, bearing him down, shoving his face into the dirt.

And some of them knew how to fight. His knives were wrested from him—he still had others, well hidden, but could not reach them. Hands hard upon him, twisting his arms behind him until they creaked. He was hustled closer to the caverns, where the hooded figure stood, horn-crowned, limned in firelight and shadow.

"Robyn Hood," Guy snarled. "It isn't yours, do you hear? Not yours, and I'll kill you for it! I'll *kill* you!"

Robyn Hood—it had to be he—gave a sudden leap down from his perch, lissom and frighteningly quick. An audible gasp echoed in the glen, a hiss of warning from somewhere behind Guy's left shoulder. The horns and cowl made an adequate mask, shadowing the outlaw's face and leaving nothing to be seen but those gleaming eyes. He bent over and grabbed the mane of the *capull*-mask. Digging deep to tangle in Guy's own hair, Robyn Hood yanked Guy's head back.

"Not mine? Truly? Then whose is it? Yours?" The voice dipped, went dark as the night around them. "You've no concept of what is mine, Templar. P'rhaps you need t' have a drink on me. We'll see who has what."

Guy tried to lunge for him, nearly succeeded. More people piled against him, immobilised him. A burly and bare-chested figure with a length of fair hair and a wolf mask bent over him, fastening a rock-solid grip on Guy's nape, forcing him to his knees. Another figure, in a weasel's mask, came forward, a goblet in his hands.

Robyn Hood was back on his perch, waiting.

They had to force Guy's mouth open, pour it down. It was thick, grainy, like unstrained and scummy water.

"Aye," the man holding his nape said, curse and admiration, "he's a tough one."

Guy knew what it meant to be drugged. Knew his tolerances, what he could do, how long before such things would take him down.

Unfortunately, this was unfamiliar. *Strong.* The world started to spin before he'd made a silent count to ten. Some of the hands had relaxed; he gained one arm free and flailed outward merely to have it gripped again, and with pathetic ease. No small firepan of bubbling brown or powder or pipe. It expressed itself not with smoke-filled ease and fugue, but in an indefinable *presence* that yanked his wits sideways and took them dancing.

He kept fighting it, with jerks of coherence amidst lulls into the spiral. But soon all he could see, obscured by the mask and doped out of his mind in a torch-and-soot-filled night, was the dancing shapes, the gleaming eyes. The tall, bestial figure coalesced beside him again, seeming to appear from nothing. He had great, golden eyes shining from the darkness of the hood—the hood was living, made of fur, holly berries, and ivy. The great rack of gilded antlers was not artefact or headdress, but sprouted from his forehead. He reached for Guy with a well-corded, blue-painted arm, one hand empty and the other holding a knife. Guy reared back, bucked and fought, but there were tens of hands upon him, holding him down.

"Coward!" he spat. "Let me free! I'll fight you!"

Or at least, that was what he meant to say; it came out much more garbled, his tongue taking its own fancy.

"You'll fight me, all right," the hooded stag-man said, in that *voice* again, ringing inside Guy's head and shivering him. "But at Samhain?" A tsk, as if chiding. "You were waiting in t' Shinin' Lands ower long, my lord. *I* rule the Wode, and I say what is proper. And I tell you, 'tis not our rightful time. The spirits would take us, burn us t' cinders."

The knife and hand came closer. Guy snarled, struggled. The hand curled beneath the muzzle of the mask, took Guy by the beard as if he were a recalcitrant he-goat, forcibly stilled him. The knife edge was brought to his temple, paused there. It flicked sideways.

No pain, not even a sting, and the hooded man-stag yanked the *capull*-mask from Guy's head. Both the surprise and force of it yanked Guy forward. Only the tens of hands restraining him kept him upright. The urge to struggle tensed every muscle he owned; instead Guy set his jaw, glared upward. The hooded man-stag held the mask aloft, its mane flying. He let out a sudden howl; triumphant, blood-curdling, it sent another inexplicable and visceral quiver up and down Guy's haunches. Answering cries split the night, echoing against the cliff, out over the Trent: wild yips and howls and shouts. A pole was extended, the *capull*-mask stuck on it like a severed head upon a pike. As Guy watched, blinking stupidly, the pole was lifted into the night sky, the "head" paraded back and forth. Its jaw kept snapping, as if it were grotesquely still alive without him.

Then the hooded man-stag turned on him, tines sharp against the firelight, knife brilliant in his hand. The shouts throttled into silence: heavy, black.

Beast-eyes glowed, amber fire beneath the horns. Guy held those eyes, unblinking, as the knife came closer. Refused to flinch as it laid, chill, upon his cheek. Mere insult— the flat, not the edge—and a snarl curled Guy's lip as a smile flashed, mocking, beneath the shadows of hood and horn.

"D'you crave the pain so much, Gisbourne?" A whisper, sibilant, smooth as the caress of the blade against first one cheek, then the other. "Have you so forgotten what it means to be alive that you need the reminding?"

"You *filth*—"

"Kill him!" a voice cried into the din, and several took it up.

"Kill!"

"Kill the traitor!"

"Nay!" Their leader turned on them, snapped, "I forbid it."

Forbid. Forbid. The voice seemed to penetrate Guy's ears, still shivery and deep, to burrow inward and into his blood, echo in the great, suddenly empty space of his brain.

"Then the Hunt!"

"The Hunt! Set the Hunt on him!"

Aye. Hunt him. Hunt *him!*

Guy was losing his battle with the drug, losing sight, losing his focus.

Lost. *Lost...*

"Run, little lost palfrey," the hooded man-stag whispers, and the tattoos on his arms begin to coil, hissing snakes of indigo. "Give us some sport, now."

And suddenly, Guy is unencumbered. Free. With a snarl, he leaps at his enemy.

But there is no one there. Nothing. His surroundings are as pitch. The fête is a mere murmur of sound, far away. There are night birds calling, and the wind far above, rustling the tops of the trees.

Then a chuckle, rippling into the night. From his left. "Gisbourne? Over here, Gisbourne."

Guy spins, lurches in the direction of the voice.

But there is no one there.

He stumbles, falls, gets up. Takes out his sword—he has his sword? How?—swings it, whirls, swings again.

Falls. Again.

Voices. *Laughter.*

"Damned... cowards!" he hurls into the black.

Nothing answers. Only the darkness, heavy as a woollen cloak, with no light from moon or stars.

Only a rhythmic, nigh-silent tread.

Only a figure walking towards him, dark and graceful and *familiar.*

Only the forest closing about them, dark and wild and tangled.

Only the feelings within him, rising just as wild, just as tangled.

"No." A mere whisper on the wind, his voice gutters, an echo. Tiny. "You're... dead."

And if I wasn't?

A gesture from the... shade, and Guy's sword wisps into nothingness. Shade... shadow... all shadows, but Guy *knows* the sculpt of these shadows, knows the warmth, *remembers...* and it is there, forming from darkness into light. *He* is there, black hair tumbling wild over pale skin, nimble hands cupping Guy's cheekbones, trailing down over his chest.

Remember. Remember this...

A lithe body moulding to his, and whispers in his ear, and breath commingling with his.

And aren't you ready for some real horseplay, my fine stallion?

For the longest moments of his life, Guy wants to believe it. Wants to obey. Wants nothing but *him.*

It's time to come home, Gamelyn.

But it cannot be him. Of all the cruellest, vilest things they could do...

"*No!*" Guy tears away, kicks out, screams, "Lie! Filthy, sodding whoreson... *Fais pas chier!* Leave me alone! Stay *dead*, damn you!"

Again, silence, this time heavy and filled with a sudden despondency, pressing against him, rolling him on the ground like a turtle on its back, and just as helpless.

No.

Not helpless.

He has to get... up...

On your feet! Hubert's voice booms at him from the dark, lurching him to his feet just by the power of voice and scorn alone. *God in Heaven, are you a Templar, or a puling boy?*

A boy. Always. The old man's little boy, mama's gadelyng... *Watch your back, petit lapin, or the wolves will get you!* Johan taunts in Guy's ear, and Guy swings around with the back of his fist. Should connect...

But no one is there. More laughter—Johan's laughter—echoing off into the trees. The rhythmic resonance of hoofbeats sounds, retreating in the distance at a gallop, and Guy tries to scream more abuse...

Can make no sound.

Instead a wolf howl splits the night, solo voice soon accompanied by another, then another. Around him. Gathering.

The moon reveals herself and he sees them: a pack of wolves ringing him, snarling and tussling and trotting back and forth, back and forth.

Go! their leader growls, a black-maned he-wolf. *After him! He's your meat. I'll give him to you. But you have to catch him, you clot!*

The wolf lunges, snaps at Guy's heels, and Guy wheels, chases after Johan. Finds nothing; keeps running without any knowledge of how or why or where.

Run, my pretty scarlet capull-coille... *Run!*

The wolves howl at his heels... nay, at his hoofs... because somehow he is no longer man but palfrey, with four legs and a tail as if the *capull*-hide torn from him is once again his, only this time married to skin and sinew, transforming him as he flees the wolves. The trees grow arms, reaching out to hinder and claw at him as he makes a tearing, panicked flight, twisting and leaping and ducking and diving and, above all, *running,* the pack slavering at his heels.

Water. He scents it before he sees it—can see nothing, really, in this black, the moon-goddess has once more closed her eyes behind clouds. Water will hide him, will lose the scent, throw the hunters off his trail.

He lunges for it, dives forward, finds himself thigh-deep—

human again—and breasting in river water. He half swims, half treads/walks, but finds his feet sliding into nothingness and goes floundering deeper. He flails, fights, but his chainmail tunic sinks him quicker than he can think, and he finds himself carried, finds himself dragged into a swift and frigid current . . .

Found.

And the cold water shook him back, somewhat, into his senses. It tossed him up and down, barely allowing a fierce sucking in of air before pulling him back down into foam and noise. But the air became harder to fight for with each gasp. Mud and rocks dragged and tugged at his heavy clothes, scraped against metal—protection and confinement and taxing weight.

He was going to drown.

Another eddy spun him upward to take a gasp and heave of breath . . .

A solid, cold object slammed into his solar plexus, driving the wind from his lungs and knocking him nigh senseless. More from instinct than any rational directive, Guy clutched at it, spitting and coughing, found himself nearly bent in two against a thick tree that had fallen into the river.

It wobbled beneath him, creaking and cracking. Again instinct bade him climb—not toward the top, but for the roots still clinging to the bank. He had made it halfway—all the while the river pulling at him, trying to take him back—when the tree gave a mighty crack and groan, gave way.

Guy lunged for the bank, felt mud and sedge in one hand even as he loosed the collapsing tree and it pulled itself out into the current—and Guy nearly with it. The hand upon the bank seized, clutched; he felt the sod try to crumble and he used the last of his strength to kick and flail and fight and, finally, land himself on the bank, retching and shuddering.

And all he could think was if the wolves came now, they could have him, and then maybe Rob would kiss him again on the way to hell . . .

"Good Lord! Who are you?"

It seemed survival beyond sense when Guy lunged upward, heavy with water-spray but nonetheless ready to meet this newest foe. Instead there was a blur of motion, a heavy *thud* that sent stars in upward arcs behind his eyes, then the stars fell in a shower of flares and sparks as he plummeted with them, into silence and darkness.

O

They wait. Dark hart and fiery warhorse both: the first patient, the second eager, barely contained.

There is a bow in her hand. The wind picks up, rustling her damp, white kirtle about her knees. She knows she must take care with this shot, must gauge well both draw and release, into that wind.

She knows that she knows how.

The arrow flames as she puts it to string: a beacon, a turning point. It flares as she draws, then spins into smoke and sparks as she looses it, an arc over the altar where two forces wait, a-tremble.

A beginning. A signal.

Like demons from any hell ever imagined they leap forward, charge with a thunder of bare hooves and metal-shod hoofs, and they collide with the darken brilliance of angels in a war on earth for heaven and hell. It is a battle never-ending, set up, fixed from the moment two infants came into air and breath. They love each other. They hate each other.

They need each other.

Yet they are too caught in the bloodlust to know that they need. Too tangled in what-has-been/what-will-be to see what is.

She sees what is, finally. She needs them as they need each other, as they need her. She knows them. They are damh Righ and Capull-coille—the King Stag and the Horse of the Wode—they are her brothers, her consorts. They are the kings who would battle for the right to be her lord, her twin, her lover, her son. . . suddenly she is walking toward the altar. Striding with a purpose, and one which reveals she does belong there, is merely and explicitly another player in this collision of mummers' plays, of celestial creatures given earthly form.

Ivy. Holly. Oak. Winterking, Summerlord, Maiden.

Ceugant.

It reverberates into the air about them, halting the battling beasts-cum-men. They turn on her, snarling and bristling.

They are both wounded. Their blood, mingling on the altar; their breath, commingling in the air.

She steps on the altar between them, and they hold.

In the way of dreams, they are no longer fae beasts in a tilt for dominance, but change: shape and form and weapons. Horse to belted knight, Stag to hooded archer; beast to demon to angel, angel to fae spirit to man to god then man. No mere pawns in a cosmic game, but Hallowed Lords of a broken Realm. Kings of a Wheel spun wildly widdershins.

She holds out her hands to them. The knight sinks to one knee, his sword point-down before him. She reaches a hand for him, strokes *fingers through his copper-gilt hair and down his cheek, lifting up his face to meet hers. Eyes green as the ivy in her own cinnabar curls peer at her, cool and considering, then he hefts his sword, offers it to her. Upon it a serpent twists, an eight of electrum coils never-ending.*

She kisses the serpent on its flat, smooth head; it shimmers like a bronze torc then. . . sinks, moulding and melding, into the sword. The gilded swath coils about the knight's hands, travels up his arms, wreathing his head and sliding back into the serpent-blade as she claims the knight with a name.

"Gamelyn."

He lowers the sword to the altar, bows his head.

Beside the silent knight, the hooded archer waits, still standing but head lowered. When she turns to him, he lifts his hands; in them he offers the arrow that she loosed. It burns, blue-white, in his palms—but it does not burn him, and as she reaches for it, it flares and disappears. In its place is a long, thin arrow forged in gold. It is fletched with the iridescent tips of peacock feathers, their eyes watching, always watching.

"So you will always see me," the archer whispers, eyes meeting hers, ebon reflecting indigo. "Always know me, even when the hood must take my Sight."

She pins the arrow into her hair, a token. While she does so, the knight rises, sword in hand, and comes to stand behind the archer. With a lover's tenderness, he furls the hood back; with the stern grip of an executioner, he pushes the hooded archer down to kneel and tangles strong fingers in black hair, pulls the archer's head back. Sword in hand, the knight awaits her bidding. Both of them, now, patient. Waiting.

She reaches out with both hands, runs fingers along the knight's cheek, down his breast and to where his hands grip the archer's hair. Breathes upon them.

The breath wreathes about their clasped hands, wafts, moves, head to tail one singular, sinuous link, soft snakeskin and gilt illumination. It undulates, over and under their fingertips, cowls the black hair with green and gilt mist, pours down to wreath the archer's throat, a living necklet: noose. . . garrotte. . . torc of a barrow king.

Her fingers linger, relaxing the knight's hold, then trail down farther, close the archer's eyes. Her lips move, say his name. "Robyn."

And her brother whispers her own back. "Marion. . ."

She shot upright on her cot, darkness clinging to her and the sound of her name still threading out past her senses.

Her name, spoken by her brother's voice. Her name.

Her brother.
Rob.
Marion was choking, choking on *memory* as it nigh drowned her, visions fading as mist in sunlight into reality, a scream gathering behind her eyes like a storm.
Loxley. *Loxley*, crumbling, and flames licking at the stars, trees groaning, the earth crying out. Running. Rob leaning over the neck of their horse and urging more speed. The feel of the bolt as it had outsped them, taken her in the back, and how she had been unable . . . unwilling to say anything because Rob would stop the horse and they would be caught, killed . . . only it didn't matter. None of it mattered, their parents were dead— murdered— and the soldiers would murder them, too. The soldiers had cornered them, Rob using every arrow he had until the last one . . . Rob lay dead, *dead* . . . and Gamelyn screaming a shrill-hoarse denial into the night . . . even above the roaring flames, she could hear his *screams* . . .
No, *she* was the one screaming, keening like a *baen-si* into the darkness and the moonlit chamber, a red-black haze filling her eyes. Hands took her by the shoulders, shook her.
"Marion!" someone was saying. "*Marion!* Wake up!"
A slap came out of the red haze, snapping her head sideways and throttling her screams.
Just as Gamelyn's screams had strangled silent when they'd shoved him to the ground and she thought they'd killed him too.
And the Abbess's voice: *"It's a miracle she's alive. God has given her to us, a sign. A miracle."*
The *Abbess*.
"Marion." It was the Abbess's voice, and the Abbess shaking her, and Marion looked up.
Stone walls surrounded her, and echoed empty. A fire crackled in the hearth. No burning forest. No carnage of fallen bodies, of Gamelyn or Rob, because that had happened . . .
Years ago.
And now she remembered. All of it.
With a mighty heave, a strength nigh forgotten, she swung. Her blow connected— somewhere, somehow, she didn't care—and she shoved, kicked out, lurched sideways. "Get *away* from me!"
"Marion?"
Marion dove for the foot of the bed. Her legs fouled in both the coverlets and her ankle-length linen undertunic; with a grunt she went tumbling over the bed-foot and onto the floor stones. The breath seizing at her lungs, she tried to stumble back to her feet.

Instead, she tottered back over her boots, nearly fell again. Her dagger, normally placed in her boots whilst she slept, skittered across the stones. Her eyes followed it like a predator tracking prey.

"*Marion!*"

Marion leapt for the dagger, snatched it up, and rolled to her feet. One hand gathering her skirts so they didn't trip her, the other palmed and flipped the dagger into a comfortable hold. For the first time in . . . it *had* been years, Marion kenned, since she had felt so at ease, so secure in her own being. She stalked across the chamber toward the woman who'd destroyed everything she'd ever loved—including her self—and saw that ease mirrored—darkly—in the sudden terror scrawling itself over the Abbess's face.

"Marion?" It was a whimper, a plea. The Abbess matched Marion's pace, step for step—only backward. "Marion, what are you—"

"I know what I'm doing. I know what you've done. I *know*."

"Marion, my girl, you had a bad dream." The Abbess was trying to regain some control over the situation, but every step backward took that much more of what kept slipping from her grasp. "You need to wake up—"

"Wake up?" Marion hesitated. The Abbess heaved a quick breath of relief, leaning against the foot post to her bed. It turned to a gasp as Marion merely bent over, taking the dagger in her teeth so she could tie up the loose edge of her skirt into a knot. Assuring one less thing was in her way, Marion palmed the small dagger once more, continued talking—and advancing. "I am awake, now. I've been sleeping. You've kept me bunged in stone, hoping I'd . . . stay . . . *sleeping!*"

"You cannot . . . you aren't thinking rationally," the Abbess stammered.

"Nay. I'm not. But it doesn't matter, for I'm awake. I'm awake, and *I remember.*"

"Reverend Lady?" The voice came muffled, from the far door. Marion froze, just for a second.

The Abbess took it, screamed, "*Help me!*"

She screamed again as Marion snarled and leapt for her, scuttered around the bed end just in time. Marion ran up against the wall near the headboard, twisted around just as a clunk and rattle sounded from the entry—someone trying the outer door.

"You locked it," Marion told the Abbess, and flipped the dagger in her palm. "You *allus* lock it. What d'you fear so?"

The Abbess made a dodge, trying to get to the door. Instead of going around, Marion leapt up on the bed and ran across it. The Abbess was taken by surprise, and Marion snatched at her sleeve, missed. Ran after. The Abbess nearly made it to the door before Marion reached again, this time fisted the woollen fabric and yanked. The Abbess stumbled, tried to retaliate with a swing of her unhampered arm. She didn't have enough leverage to do serious damage, it nevertheless left an open-handed strike of red against Marion's cheek.

Pounding, in terrific earnest against the door, with excited voices on the other side.

Marion snarled, gave another hard yank at the handful of dark fabric. It ripped, the robe pulling down over a linen-clad shoulder and causing the Abbess to lurch sideways. Marion pulled again, hauling the Abbess backward. The Abbess screamed again, raw and terrified, as Marion, in silent fury, shoved the Abbess against the wall with a dagger at her throat.

The pounding on the outer door had only increased, with muffled shouts and curses. The Abbess's cry wavered to silence as the blade pressed close. Her eyes were wide. Terrified.

Good. Marion leaned closer.

"Please," the Abbess whimpered. "You don't know what you're doing. You can't . . . " She trailed off, and her eyes went wider.

Hands, hard and merciless, laid upon Marion at nearly the same time, dragging her from the Abbess. It broke her silence, pulled a cheated howl from her, and she twisted, struck out . . .

Much deflected the blow easily, grabbed her wrists, twisted her around and hugged her close. "Lady, nay, please, y' can't be—"

"Let me *go!*" Her voice rose to a shriek as the Abbess, free, sped to the locked door and frantically tugged at the bolt. "Nay! Let me *be!* Let *go of me!*"

She slapped, kicked, scratched, tried to bite, and almost won free. Much merely ducked his head, took the blows, and hung on like a pit dog.

"I'm sorry," he kept saying. "Y' can't do this, Lady, I'm sorry, I—"

The Abbess struggled with the lock. Marion lunged forward, was foiled. Instead she sucked in a huge gout of air, let it hiss from her lips, serpent's wisdom and kiss and *tynged.* Just as the bolt flew open, she lunged forward again, cried, "I will use every power you denied me to kill you, do you hear me? For every breath my brother has not taken, I will flay a strip from you—"

Much's hands dug in, fingernails scraping. "You must be quiet," he hissed against her ear. "Listen to me, Maiden, I *beg* you . . . "

Maiden. He knew her. Knew her, yet *still* tried to stop her?

The door flung open, let a bevy of guardsmen rush in.

"I will hang your skull from my portals and spread your bones to the four winds, that you will never know rest, never—"

Soldiers fell on both of them, and though some lucid part of Marion realised Much could have dispatched them easily, for some reason he let them take him, pin his hands behind his back. Let them take her, though she fought with all the frenzied strength singing through her veins.

Kill them. Curse them all.

It took two soldiers to hold her as the Abbess approached. She held a hand to her throat, where a crimson stain marred her white gorget and streaked her trembling fingers.

"Marion." She was obviously trying to regain control. "My child—"

"I'm no child of yours, you barren hag!" Marion spat at her. "You had my mother killed, my father. You *murdered* my brother. You had my village burnt, my people slaughtered like pigs. And when my brother gave me my life back—"

The Abbess was white, her voice starting to crack. "*God* gave you your life back—"

"*My brother* gave his last breath to save me, and you shot him down like an animal!" Marion snarled. "You held me captive, kept my mind from me, kept me prisoned like a pet dog!"

"You *were* a dog!" the Abbess shrilled back. "A demon, spawned of demons. I *set you free!*"

"And for every day I've spent rotting in the murk of your piety, you will endure twofold—" Marion writhed against the hands holding her, almost won free again.

"Let me go! Let me—!"

"What in hell?" The sheriff was the last to enter. Marion barely had a chance to glance at him, the guards had forced her to her knees.

"She's gone mad. *Mad!*" the Abbess cried.

"What is *he* doing here?"

Marion looked up, saw that the sheriff had walked over to where Much stood, quiet in the hold of the guardsman.

"That man saved my life!" the Abbess answered.

"The door was bolted. How did he get in here?"

"Through t' window, m'lord," Much offered. "I heard . . . well, I heard it. My master said I were t' keep an eye, like, on things, as I could."

"The Templar said that?" The sheriff's tone turned sceptical.

Much looked away, as if discomfited he'd said anything.

Master. Templar. Memory struck again, white-hot behind her eyes, and Marion tried to lurch up. "Where is he? Where is Gamelyn?"

Much's eyes widened, then narrowed, seeking hers. "I know no Gamelyn."

"Gamelyn?" Almost silent, the murmur from the Abbess, and something within Marion said, *Take care... take care, child...*

But every sense scraped raw, untuned. All she knew was the one constant, from vision to reality—the one being still living who would... *know*... "He is your master!" she screamed at Much. "Do not lie to me! Where is Gamelyn?"

"My master is Guy de Gisbourne." Much was shaking his head. "Poor lass," he told the sheriff, "she en't makin' much sense, is she?"

"You have *betrayed* me—" Marion's hiss fled upward into a yelp as the soldiers yanked her arms up behind her back.

Much closed his eyes, still shaking his head.

They were all against her. All of them. Marion's gaze turned to Abbess Elisabeth. She hadn't finished the *geas*. Had to finish it, if it became the last thing she ever did.

"You will *breathe* darkness. For what 'protection' you smothered over me, your breath will throttle. You will walk in your hell feeble and ignorant, while the—"

"*Silence* her!" the Abbess shrieked.

Marion heard the blow before she felt it, a slap against her temple that flung her sideways and to the floor. She saw Much, pinned against the far wall with eyes wide and shocked, then a grey veil came down and shrouded her in silence.

O

Dawn had broken over the Trent, clear and cold. They had kept the fire just outside the hermit's cavern fuelled bright, against the dark of Samhain and to light the retreat of their people into the Shire Wode. Now the darken-crowned king of that Shire Wode warmed cold hands by his fire, waiting.

His men had insisted on going, to look. To make sure Gisbourne was gone: drowned or lost, they didn't care. Robyn had consented; he wanted to be alone.

The *capull*-mask lay beside Robyn where he sat, legs propped and bent, chin resting on his knees. The mask's nonexistent eyes seemed to stare through to his bones. Frankly the empty sockets were more familiar than the juniper-green eyes which, only last night, had been behind them.

"Guy." He tasted the name, swore with it, ever so softly, "*Gisbourne*. I don't know you. *You* are the enemy. You've... killed him, haven't you? Gamelyn is dead, and mayhap he consented to his own death, but still you killed him. Just as you would have killed me, last night. Even in the arms of the rite, even when you... *saw me*, you... you refused to see."
He is too far gone, Hob-Robyn. You played well, but the game is over. You will have to kill him.

Separate again from his god's presence, hearing His voice instead of *being* it... and Robyn wanted to howl loud enough to drown out the morning-chilled sense of it. Instead he burrowed into his own confusion all the more, folded his knees against his chest and wrapped his arms tight about them as if to ward it all away.

What if he is in league with the Black Abbess? Would that be enough motivation for you?

"Gamelyn would not—"
Are you so sure?
"Are you?" he shot back. "Sure?"
Silence. Then, *Do not be a fool, my own. There are ones who need you. The boy you loved and lay with and hated... he is long gone.*
"I know!" he growled into his forearms. "I know, I *know!*"

He sat there, tossing bits of bark and bracken onto the fire, watching them turn to char until he heard his men returning.

"No sign of him, Robyn," Arthur said.

Robyn hadn't imagined they'd find him. Nay, the dog had gone to den, to lick his wounds and contemplate his next action. It would not be pretty, whatever it would be.

And that was his fault, too. He'd thought to drag the boy from the man, the lover from the rival. All he'd done was humiliate a Templar.

His five companions all gathered about the fire, warming chilled bits.

Robyn picked up the *capull*-mask, peered into the hollow eyes. "He's out of our way for the now. But he's still alive."

"You sound... glad." Will peered at him, brows drawn, eyes piercing.

Robyn didn't answer. Couldn't answer. He merely leaned forward and tossed the *capull*-mask onto the fire, watched it burn.

- XII -

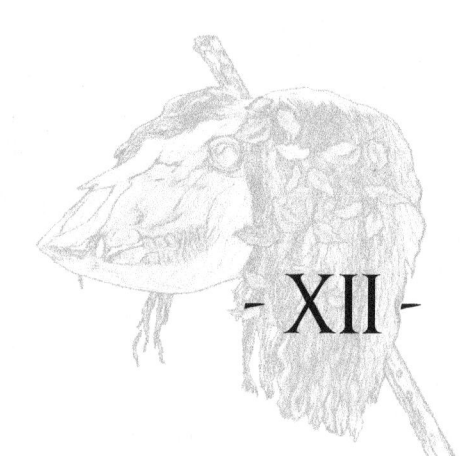

He was dry, was the first thing Guy realised as the dark began to recede. Dry, and warm . . .

And unweaponed.

Exploding upright from a pile of woollen and furs, Guy landed in a crouch, ready for whatever came. Heard a growl, then a hiss.

His eyes were assaulted by bright light, and his skin by chill. There were stones, even colder, beneath his bare feet, echoing his breath in heavy silence. No danger; merely the quiet, broken by a soft refuge of a voice.

"Be easy, Brother."

Guy whirled to find a hearth of stone at the end of a hall lit by high windows. A barefoot, brown-clad monk was leaning over that fire, cassock tucked up into his belt. A yellow hound clung, persistent as a cocklebur, to the hairy leg bared beneath the cassock. The hound kept growling, a soft buzz barely audible over the fire's crackling. The monk, with one thick-fingered hand upon a long-handled spoon, stirred a cauldron, which . . . well, it smelt heavenly.

"You're safe here, in God's house," the monk continued. "Get back under the furs and I'll lend you a robe; it's turned chill and your clothes are still drying."

Guy peered down, noted that yes, he was naked, and yes, it must be cold because he was shivering, gooseflesh rashed over pale skin.

Nevertheless... "Where am I?"

"You are in my cell at the church of St. Wystan's, Gamelyn."

That last set him back on his heels, but no more than the face of the monk as he turned about.

It was Brother Dolfin.

▶

"They called it punishment. I called it Heaven on earth."

They were sitting by the fire, perched at a small table on two somewhat rickety stools, making inroads on an excellent pottage and fresh bread. Even the yellow hound had decided Guy was harmless, if a bit unpredictable. Of course, the bowl of pottage Guy had been passed as canine peace offering had a bit to do with that. The hound hadn't taken his nose from the bowl yet.

"I mean, look at this place. Full of light, with a fresh-running stream to hand. Politically speaking, it is exile, of course. But they mistook me for one who cared, and I did not abuse them of their notions. My flock is small," Dolfin admitted, "and they tend to varying degrees of lesser piety, granted, but they seek my advice and aid. Most even come to mass. And I managed to salvage my books from the chapel at Blyth when your brother had me sent away."

"It's a lovely place," Guy admitted. Once he'd dressed, Dolfin had given him a quick tour. The church was small, of Saxon origins if not older, with runes and carvings that a young and pious Gamelyn would have found iniquitous, but a world-wearied Guy knew for what they were—a deep and ancient magic fiercely untrammelled by the new religion's claims. No wonder the pagans had chosen nigh to this spot for the revels of Samhain. There lay a deep trough of sacrosanct attendance here, scratching at fraying nerves.

Surely it all must shut up eventually. After all, unfed hungers would, with enough neglect, shrivel into the merest of dull aches.

Once the hungry one is dead, aye. She was laughing at him, no question. *Will you die for me, Gamelyn?*

I almost did, last night, and where were you?

Of course, no answer. Guy kept eating. It was quite good, the pottage, seasoned with herbs that cleared his airways, thick with tender gourd-meat and salted mutton. He'd been well-clad, not in his own clothes but an extra cassock obviously belonging to Dolfin; even on Guy's considerable height and well-muscled frame, it hung like a sack. But it remained a warm sack, and Dolfin had added woollen hose and several furs to the mix. No sense, he cautioned, in taking chill after nearly drowning in the Trent, after all.

"You're lucky I found you," Dolfin reiterated. "Not many venture out upon the sabbat of Samhain; fewer still can find a fordable place mid-night to carry an unlucky pilgrim to shelter."

"You... carried me across." An impressive feat, but not impossible. Dolfin was, as the large cassock attested, quite a sturdy fellow.

"You were on the wrong side of the river. And nigh drowned." Dolfin shrugged and grinned.

When Guy spoke again it was slow, feeling his way with words. "How did you know who... well. Who I was?"

"Few men can wear a mask waking *and* sleeping." As Guy met his gaze, Dolfin looked away, continued, "Though I will say, waking merely re-conceives the mask."

"You're making little sense." Yet all Guy could focus on was the word, *mask*. The insult of the previous night: the hand that had gripped his chin, the dagger that had cut the *capull*-mask from his face and been drawn, flat-bladed, across his cheek. The slow fury rising at the mere thought of it. The *humiliation*.

"I was your confessor. It's likely I've seen you in direr straights than most. I was... sceptical, at first, of my own suspicions. The cord about your waist made it all plain enough, but still. A *Templar*. Yet, the more I thought about it, the more it made sense. After all, you'd nothing but God left, had you?"

"One should think that would be enough for any man, wouldn't one?" was Guy's muted response.

Silence, then, "I'm sorry. For many things," Dolfin added as Guy quirked a puzzled frown at him. "One being, I do feel a need to apologise for that bump on your skull. I had to hit you pretty hard."

"I imagine you did. I didn't know who you were, after all."

"Mm. Exactly. You've grown into a proper soldier, while this old soldier is merely growing." Dolfin grinned and patted his belly, which had indeed gained a bit more breadth in the past several years. "I was lucky enough to get the drop on you."

"More than mere luck carried me, wet and all, across the river," Guy demurred.

"How chivalrous of you to defend my middle age." Dolfin

grinned wider. "I only hope that good food and a warm fire is adequate recompense."

"It's . . . good to see you." Guy said the words gingerly, not sure until he'd voiced them that they were, in fact, true. After all, it was another reminder. Of all the rude shocks he'd been in for over the past weeks, however, this held an odd . . . comfort.

Dolfin processed this with a nod, offered up more pottage. Guy accepted. They both ate in silence for a while.

"What were you doing there?"

Guy chewed, food and question both, then gave the basic truth. "I've been sent to kill an outlaw."

"So," Dolfin mused. "Gamelyn Boundys is the Templar hired by the sheriff to kill Robyn Hood."

"Nay, friend." His negation was altogether calm, flat, as if the name did not in truth hollow him all empty and colder than the Trent. "Guy de Gisbourne is that Templar, and he has come not only to kill a wolfshead, but to take from the villein what he has stolen."

Dolfin took this in with a rise of thick eyebrows. "Interesting."

Interesting? Guy met Dolfin's eyes. "Do you know him?"

"I am not about to betray any confidences, Sir Guy."

"Is it betraying a confidence to tell me what you know of a thieving wolfshead?"

Dolfin frowned, then relented. "I know nothing more or less than anyone hereabouts knows. He is not of my congregation. Nor likely to be, I'd guess. But it would not be betraying any sort of confidence to say there are some who think him no mere thief."

"Do you know him by sight, then?"

"Robyn Hood?" A snort. "Only a few have even glimpsed his face." A smirk, and a pulling up of his own cowl. "His namesake is an altogether common mask—crude, almost. He gives it new and effective significance."

"Effective, truly. I would unmask him, all right. With a sword hewn through his neck. I knew where to find him on Hallows, but they thwarted me."

Dolfin cocked his head, a silent question, and rose, taking up the well-scraped bowls. "I heard the Wild Hunt abroad mid-night. Tag, there, went running after; 'twas why I ventured out myself."

"The Wild Hunt?"

Going over to a bucket in one corner, Dolfin bent over and deposited the bowls into it with a *plish* of water. "When the Horned Lord runs through the green Wode with the wolves, on the hunt for stray spirits. It is said only the Green Man can summon the god to do his bidding at such a time. Some even maintain the Green Man is the one who rides, possessed by his god. I have heard Robyn Hood is a powerful witch."

"There was no witchcraft. Only tricks and games of shadow. I was drugged, nothing more; a jongleur's jape that anyone skilled with herbs could play."

"Hm. But it worked, and you put out of commission without them having to so much as cast a spell in your direction. Seems to me efficient. If magic is real, then 'tis likely not an easy thing, its use. Why would this Robyn Hood waste what power he has on a rabid dog set to bite him?"

"I am no rabid dog," Guy snapped. "Neither has this wolfshead any real power— what he did but proves it."

"So you would have taken him down, amidst one of their holy rites." Dolfin swished the bowls in the water, left them to soak, and straightened. The hound, Tag, stuck his nose in, began lapping at the water. "Do you not see what you're doing, Templar? The lad I knew would never stoop to the same tactics once used to murder his lover's people—the people of Loxley."

Guy rocked to his feet, the stool falling to the floor in the wake of his ascent. "Do not dare speak to me of that!"

Tad growled; Dolfin shushed him. "And if I do 'dare' such a thing, will you then call Crusade upon my small church?" It was all too mild. "Seems your mask has a mar upon it, after all. And that pride is still a drumbeat you are prey to."

For long moments Guy refused to speak, uncertain, in fact, that anything coherent would voice did he find words to express. It was violent, and debilitating, and nearly foreign; he'd all but forgotten the taste of it, the tang souring his belly.

He subjugated the odd, painful mix of dread, pain, and fury, wrapped it in ice, let it harden into a slurry of indifference.

"It has come to my understanding," Guy retorted, "that pride is indeed the cardinal sin of my order. Nor am I any longer that boy who was too weak to face the consequences of it."

"So you *are* prepared for the consequences, should you be the one to begin a slaughter of more Heathens?"

"It is *not* the same." Guy's fists kept clenching. "I was not there to make a wholesale slaughter upon innocent people, only to take out this power-mad wolfshead who has misled them all—"

"Worksop's abbess thought she had a righteous cause, as well. Robyn Hood's people do not believe him false."

"He cannot *be* anything other than false!"

"How would you know?"

"I would *know!*" It thundered through the stones of the chapel. "Have you *forgotten* what I saw? What I told you . . . *confessed* to you, sobbing in your lap like a child? How *she* had them all killed, like animals rounded for slaughter. How she had me dragged over to where *he* lay, forced me on my knees to look at him, like some hound having his nose shoved into a pile of shit he'd left on his master's bed." Guy closed his eyes. "He was dead. His sister lay beside him, dying. He'd tried to save her."

And he did save her, I know this now.

"I remember." Dolfin's voice murmured quiet, full of compassion.

Guy was unmoved by it, kept wielding words like jagged, dull blades against his own flesh. "I keep trying to forget. He had a crossbow bolt rammed in his chest, and blood everywhere . . . but I've seen so much blood since then it's not *that* I remember . . . it's his *eyes*. Every nightmare I've had since I came back from Outremer, every waking dream sneaking up on me unawares . . . it's his eyes I see. There was absolutely no life in them. As if everything he'd been had . . . gone.

"I killed them, Dolfin. I never meant to, but I betrayed them, and it killed them. And now a usurper holds to a power not his, wields precious artefacts my masters have sent me to take from him. And you expect me to feel *remorse* for what I must do? I *have* none, Dolfin, not for this. I will do as I am ordered. I will find this wolfshead and kill him and I *will feel nothing!*" Guy turned away from Dolfin's stricken face and said, again calm, "Save relief. I will feel that."

Silence. It stretched out, wavering and thin. Guy took a long, shallow breath, then padded over to the hearth, felt his clothes. Nearly dry, though the chainmail would have to cool for a short while; it had been placed closest to the flames to bake out moisture.

"I don't know anything of Robyn Hood." Dolfin came back over, silent with his bare feet. "I spoke the truth when I said he does not come near my church. I was surprised he came this nigh to Nottingham proper during Hallows. I fear I can be of little help to you."

"You have done enough," Guy answered. "And I have ill-repaid your kindness with my . . . pride." He turned to Dolfin. "As always, you've slapped it back into the gutter where it belongs."

Dolfin frowned, more concern than displeasure, then sighed and moved closer to the hearth. He took up a poker and removed the chainmail tunic from the fire, began to pull down the dry clothes from where he'd hung them.

"Do you have anyone who can take a message to Nottingham?" Guy asked as he dressed.

"I've several lads from the village who do for me. Or I can myself, if it's urgent."

"Not so urgent, but important." Guy smiled. "Do you remember Much?"

"The soldier lad? The one who came to Blyth a miller's son?" Dolfin blinked. "Are you telling me he's with you? With the Templars?"

"He's my paxman. He has a duty in Nottingham he cannot leave, but if I don't return by this evening, he will worry. It would leave him to that duty with a clearer mind if I let him know my continued absence is purposeful."

"I'll fetch parchment . . . wait. Can he read?"

"Some. We've signs we use, to be sure."

Dolfin brought quill and parchment; upon it Guy merely scripted the sign he and Much used for *"still hunting"* and rolled it up. "You have my thanks," Guy said as Dolfin took it.

"I understand why you must do this thing, Gamel . . . Guy," Dolfin corrected himself. "I only ask that you be very sure of what you are doing."

"I wasn't when I started," Guy answered. "Now I am."

"That's the biggest gourd I've yet to see!" Robyn laughed, backing away with a shake of his head as one of the stouter villagers challenged him silently to try lifting it. "Nay, I've no doubt *that* beast would win a wrestling match with this skinny archer. P'rhaps you should have Will or David give a go."

Will, however, was otherwise occupied. He had bent his neck and scraped his fair hair to fall down his front, walking away with one of the gourds balanced on the back of his neck. The children were screaming with laughter, and some of the smaller ones with a bit of fear—Will looked to have no head, only a gourd for one.

One of the little lads, running and screaming, ran smack into Robyn and clung desperately to his leg. A mere breath later, the lad seemed to notice to whose leg he clung, and jumped back as if Robyn had been a brand fresh from the fire. He and Robyn peered at each other with like trepidation for long moments, then the little one stuck his finger in his mouth and ran the other way. Robyn wasn't much better: he retreated to the well in the village centre and put his buttocks against it as if the children were sheriff's men hoping to attend his wake.

"If you weren't so skairt of 'em, they'd not run from you,"

Arthur said, coming by and bumping his shoulder against Robyn's. He then ran after the children, growling like a bear.

And the little beggars *loved* it. Robyn shook his head and crossed his arms. Some people just had the way of it, with bairns. He didn't think he was all that daunting; he'd been told more than the once he could be pleasant enough to look upon, frightening only when he'd his hood up and the blood hot behind his eyes— and likely with an arrow at full nock. And it wasn't as if he had to tie his hood forward, over his face here, in the village of Hathersage, fierce friend to Robyn Hood and his men. John's people had lived here for generations; they'd drunk from this sweet well and laid runes and sigils upon the stones to bless it. Many of the people who had survived Loxley had crossed the river and come to live here.

Bloody damn, even John got on better with the little ones. Sure enough, he sat in a corner, doing silent tricks with knucklebones for an equally silent bunch of goggle-eyed children.

"I hope you'll take some gourds with you," Gunnora said. "We've a bumper crop, mind." Hathersage had no headman, instead a cunning-woman ran things. It was not unheard of, even in the more Christian districts, but more usual in the North, where pockets of the Old Religion still held firmer sway. Gunnora sat firmly on the waning side of middle age. It had been she who'd had the teaching of John in charms and making. Seeing as how John maintained that his mentor had more talent in one little finger than he in his entire body, Gunnora was a powerful cunning-woman indeed.

"In fact," she said, a grin on her face, "you'd likely take some of the children wit' ye and we mightn't be the wiser."

Robyn gave his head a vehement shake, kenned his protest was too telling, shrugged and grinned at Gunnora.

She grinned back. "The children are in awe of you, Hooded One, nowt more. En't fear what makes 'em look t' you all big-eyed. Y'r a story come to life. You added to it by unhorsing that knight proper under Hallows' moon. Aye, you did, and those of us as witnessed it told the story all the long journey home, to those as greeted us and amongst ourselves."

It was funny how such things spread, truth be told—and not always in a comfortable way.

"No matter." Gunnora gave his shoulder a pat. "You'll have yr'self a Maid, anon, to give you children, show you both t' wonders and terrors."

Robyn tried to smile and nod, but failed miserably.

"Well," Gunnora chuckled, "mebbe later rather than soon, but surely you're t' choose a lass for the summering next year. There's many would be your Maid just for the rite, y'know. You're fair to look on, good shoulders and teeth, a cunning smile. And a comb through that lovely black hair would only shift your chances t' t' good."

"*Sweet Christ, but you clean up rather nicely. It's amazing what a comb can do. . .*"

The memory came out of nowhere and gutted Robyn before he could so much as raise a guard.

Had it only been a brace of years ago that he had been so young and besotted, making himself all proper to visit the mesne lord of Blyth, his true intent to cozen that lord's son into wanting him all the more?

Robyn silently repeated what Gamelyn . . . *Gisbourne* had spat his way only a matter of days ago. *Stay dead, damn you. I don't still care. I canna. I* wain't.

"Robyn, are you listening?" Gunnora's hand on his shoulder gave a shake. "Will you all do us t' honour of stayin' to sup?"

"I'll have proper mutiny if I don't," Robyn answered, grinning as Arthur ran by with a clot of children after him.

Then Gilbert came up, holding two sizeable gourds before him like breasts, and Robyn seriously thought about smashing one of them over his head. Would have, too, if Gunnora hadn't started laughing.

"They don't look half right on you, lad!" she protested between guffaws. "An' ower large, at that. Wishful thinking?"

"Nay!" he protested. "Robyn's always saying I'd be the one to shave and wear dame's drag, did we have to. Just trying it out."

"Or John," Robyn reminded. "Least we'd not catch *him* feelin' himself up."

"Well, it's not about to be *you*." Gilbert pretended to pout. "Since you can't shave to last the day. Hairy sod."

"At least 'tisn't on me back and bum, like to Arthur."

"That un's a bear, no question," Gunnora agreed, then added, "Robyn's too tall, 'tennyrate."

"You're tall, Gunna," Gilbert protested.

"Aye, but not *that* tall."

"Still, if it weren't for the hairy bits—"

"Can we talk about sommat other than my hairy bits?" Robyn complained. "Or sizing me up for a skirt I en't likely to wear?"

Still chuckling, Gunnora went over to rescue Arthur from the mob of children. They had decided he was a bear, all right—and one to wrestle to the ground.

"Hoy, he loves it!" Gilbert protested, then tossed Robyn a gourd.

Robyn grunted and snatched it midair. Putting it down, he squatted and perched his bum half on it.

Gilbert did likewise, leaning all comfortable against his leader. "There's been no sign of that bloody Gisbourne."

"Aye."

"Not a smell, not a sausage. P'rhaps he's terrorising the south?"

"Could be."

"Or p'rhaps he went back home with his tail betwixt his legs!"

"*That* en't likely."

Gilbert sighed, propped one elbow on his knee and rested his chin in his palm. "They're breaking the hind we brought, planning a feast. We're staying to sup, aye?"

"Aye."

"You're as talkative as John, about now."

Robyn shrugged. "A bit on me mind, about now."

Gilbert cocked his head, pretended to peer at a leaf between his toes. Said, quite casually, "You're not still off to the Tor, what with all the goings-on?"

"Why wouldn't I?"

"Well . . . " Gilbert eyed him.

"Did Will put you up t' this? He seems to think I canna tie me own cod-wrap, most days."

"Nay, 'twasn't just Will. He's stomping down the old biddy-hen better than he used to. He just . . . he lost you once, Robyn. All of us worry, not just Will. That Templar isn't fooling about. The price on your head's been raised again." Gilbert's grey eyes were troubled. "When *John* is all broody-like . . . "

Aye, well, John knows what I've not scraped up m' nerve to tell the rest of you. Pardon, lads, but this Templar what's after us? He and I used t' rut each other senseless when we were lads. If 'twere only that there'd be nowt to worry, but hearts were shared and broken amidst all the tupping, and I'm bloody sodding terrified *of what he's able t' conjure up in me even the now.*

"Gilbert. We're moving camp more often. We're taking every precaution. I e'nt leaving off Mam Tor because of some bloody damned *monk*." The last came out too forceful, too telling. Robyn stood up.

"I'm going, as always, and I'm going alone. As always."

Her thoughts were more her own, now. But 'twas plain no one else believed so.

Marion had watched, through a high window slit, the sun rise and disappear over the keep to sink beneath another window slit on the opposite side of her tiny cell. Some body servant's cot, no doubt, hastily vacated for a novice nun maddened by Samhain's evil wind. A pallet hunched along one wall, thankfully free of lice, with reasonably clean blankets, and a small piss-pot in the far corner, accompanied by a bucket of water. The latter bucket held a skim of ice—no hearth, of course—but they had thrown her woollen cape in with her, and her thick hose. Meals were also brought to her. They obviously didn't mean her death—not yet. But neither did they seem to know what to do with her.

The guards were unresponsive, giving her the bare courtesy demanded by fear. It wasn't fear of the Abbess; Marion could all but hear their thoughts: *What if her madness is catching? What if she is a witch?*

They had no idea.

She was beginning to.

Her mother and father, *all* of her people . . . dead. They'd been dead several years. Her brother had given his last breath to her. But the magic had been interrupted, and her spirit had fled with Rob's into the otherworld merely to be torn from him, lost and wandering, when he . . . died.

She was no longer lost. But she was totally alone.

Marion had spent the first hours of her confinement curled up on the bed in alternate fits of rage and fear and grief. She had cried herself into exhaustion, slept more soundly than she would have imagined and, upon waking, had both drunk of and splashed her swollen face with icy water, and waited.

The wait had been spent in gathering those thoughts that now fully belonged to her, gleaning and winnowing like the crofter's child she was. There was much—too much— to fathom all at once. But she had to try.

Why had this Samhain been so different from the ones that had come before? What had finally called her strayed spirit back to her body? The answer lay about her throat, in the sparse but powerful slick of blood on the tiny cross the Templar had given her. Gamelyn's blood.

Rob was gone, so Gamelyn held the power of the Wode by right.

Only he was not Gamelyn, not anymore; he was Guy de Gisbourne, a Templar. But what Templar knew the basic ways of a blood rite? How could a devout Christian have learnt the ways of such magics?—a boy who had only known the Lady's face in the Christ's Maiden/Mother.

He knows Me now.

Marion closed her eyes, laid her forehead upon her drawn-up knees. The Lady had been drifting, in then out, as if She knew that Marion could not yet bear the full weight of possession. After all, Marion had spent several years . . . empty. Magic was not a thing borne easily, without will or skill.

He understands little, but he has seen My face. He listens. Not that he has a choice.

All of it, too much. Too much to take in. Too much to waken merely to find that reality was the dream. The nightmare.

Voices, outside the door. Then the sounds of metal: keys banging against the door and one turning in the heavy lock. Marion rose from her curled-up position on the bed as the door opened, clutched her cape tight to her.

Four guards, and one bearing shackles. She couldn't help but back a step, her head giving a wary shake.

"The Reverend Lady is t' see you," the one bearing the shackles said. "Sheriff insists, for her safety and yours, we must bind you."

They were chary, but adamant—that there were four of them attested to that.

So she submitted to it, ankles and hands both bound, with the promise of a gag should she even try to breathe a hint of a curse. All this for a novice nun several stone under her best weight—any of those guardsmen could likely pick her up and break her in two at present. It should be amusing.

Marion did not smile. She was going to get another chance at the Abbess.

Go carefully, Maiden. All is not as it seems.

It seemed to Marion that only one option remained. She had bungled her first chance, wild and disoriented, but she wasn't about to do so again. There would be no rest until she saw it through.

I demand it, demand her blood to cleanse my own, by wind and fire, earth and sea!

You would take upon the rights of the Hooded One?

He gave what he was to me. So I claim this, for him.

And the presence runnelled away, just as Marion's own senses were stretching, raw and overwhelmed.

As if on the draught of that leave-taking, the Abbess came gliding in. Behind her lurked the sheriff. A sardonic expression twitched at his face, yet he seemed unsure of whom to direct it toward. The Abbess looked more than a little disconcerted.

Something in Marion's heart heeded it, felt pity for it. The rest of her heart, however—indeed her soul—frankly gloried in it. Sang: *Gaoler. Murderer.*

"She is chained, milord Sheriff." One of the soldiers bowed. "Reverend Lady."

Lifting her hands as if to demonstrate, Marion inclined her head with all the mockery at her command. "Am I so dangerous, then?"

"Marion." The Abbess approached, steps measured. "It grieves me to say this, but I fear the demons have returned to your spirit."

She does not know the half of it, does she? The Lady sounded . . . amused.

Marion was not.

"There has been the danger, always, the danger your memory would return . . . oh, Marion." The Abbess was wringing her hands together, her eyes keen . . . sorrowful? "Please. Let me help you. You do not have to let this happen. You can fight it. We can fight it, together."

"Help me?" Marion retorted. "Like you helped my village? My family?" She started forward, inexorable despite the clink of manacles, despite a firm hand on her shoulder trying to dissuade her—one of the soldiers.

"Marion, you speak in fear and blindness."

The hot breath of vengeance tickled her neck. "I speak the truth. At last. Tell me, *Abbess*, did you have that same sad look in your eyes as you had my brother *murdered?*"

"Your brother was a sorcerous . . . sodomite!" the Abbess shot back. "And is no doubt burning in hell even now!"

"I'll give you your hell!" Marion choked out. "Hell, and burning, and you wain't have to wait until you die to see it!"

"Silence that insolent *puterelle!*" de Lisle ordered with a roll of his eyes.

The soldier wrapped a beefy arm over Marion's face. She started to struggle, but his voice mouthed, nigh silent, in her ear, "I am yours, Maiden. I've sent word to m' master; he will come. Y' must take care."

Marion tensed, slid her eyes sideways, found recognition in light blue eyes above a newly shaven face. It was the Templar's man—Much—dressed in Nottingham's colours.

"This is ceasing to be entertaining," de Lisle said from where he leaned against the wall beside the entry. "You're wasting your breath, Elisabeth."

The Abbess's gaze had turned, from distressed to a flat, nearly furious edge. "There is nothing God cannot help, with proper . . . inducement."

"Inducement," de Lisle repeated, then shook his head. "With the Church, that always means property damage." His eyes cut to the Abbess. "You will not make me complicit as you did with FitzAaron, Elisabeth. No indiscriminate torching of my villeins."

"She is not one of 'your villeins'." The Abbess's gaze was still flat. Marion wanted to sneer back, but something there stayed her; blind and tenacious, it set a-chill any defiant heat. "She is mine, of my Church and my bond. If she will not repent, there is only one way to cleanse her soul."

De Lisle angled off the doorway, a frown quirking at his brow. But it was not anger, or even concern . . . nay, mere puzzlement. "Hm. Might make a fitting spectacle for our liege, at that. Mayhap we should ask him. But until then?" He sauntered over, by a curt nod indicated Much should release Marion. Much obeyed, not without a warning look her way.

De Lisle came to a stop before her, arms crossed, feet set apart. "She's reasonably clean, anyway." He reached out, took her chin in one hand, angled her face back and forth.

From over his shoulder, Much held Marion's gaze, still warning. Marion clenched her teeth, looked away. She saw the Abbess, watching her brother with no little distaste and drawing up with indignation.

"Well, Sister. I've always wanted to have a redhead. Give her to me for some sport, and I'll let you burn her. Fair enough?" He threw a smirk over his shoulder, the ploy suddenly obvious.

He didn't want Marion, had no intentions of bedding her. Some childhood taunt, no more or less, playing itself out even now between a brother and sister.

One she would never have a chance to play with *her* brother.

Fury rippled through Marion, and before she could as much as consider any rational response, she spat at the sheriff.

He turned back to her just in time, then stood frozen, spittle dripping down his nose, hardly believing what had happened any more than she. Without even a change of expression, he lashed back. Not just once, but twice.

The first blow took her in the gut, the second in the temple, flinging her sideways.

She hit the floor, rolled, tried to get up . . .

Then knew nothing more.

- XIII -

The child was five or six, playing on the village outskirts in a pile of leaves. She had leaves clutched in grubby fingers, several tucked in tangled, chaff-coloured hair, had obviously been rolling in a pile all raked up for play.

It really didn't matter what side of the blanket one was born on; leaves were fun. A faint memory of brothers and the laughter of leaf-burial made him smile as he walked over to the little girl.

She had blue eyes in a round face that turned up to him in surprise, a tunic which, perhaps, had once been fawn-coloured. The bare legs below the stained tunic were grey with cold beneath a layer of dirt and wood-smoke. Other, older youngsters had been here with her, but had fled upon sight of an obvious nobleman: learned reflex of peasantry. Once it had made him angry on their behalf, then it had saddened him, now there was merely bone-weary acceptance. And any niggling, traitorous emotions that would prompt any weakness, that would whisper Rob's name in his ear, or suggest that Marion had certainly looked after her baby brother better than this . . .

Someone had forgotten their little sister and would deservedly catch trouble from home.

"Hullo," Guy said.

"H'lo," she chirped.

Surely she was old enough to be afraid; either she was enraptured with her play or perhaps a bit simple. Or, as he'd been told more than once, he had a deceptively pleasant face.

"I've leafs," she informed him, quite gravely, holding them out for inspection.

Just as gravely, Guy squatted down beside her and did the courtesy of inspecting them. "You do indeed."

"M'name's Lizzie."

He took up a leaf, held it backlit by the setting sun, twirled it. "I'm Guy, Lizzie."

"Brofer says'at . . . " She looked around, began to frown. "T' others . . . left . . . "

"They're likely back at the village," he said then, as her face started to show puzzlement, "Here. Come with me. I'll take you back. I'm going that way myself." As he held out a hand, Lizzie held up both arms, plainly expecting he should carry her. One eyebrow rising into his forelock, Guy bent down and picked her up. With startling strength, the thin arms and legs snugged about him, ribs and waist. He received a further surprise when the child tucked her head into the hollow of his shoulder and laughed.

"Hm," he said, going back to the road. "What's so funny?"

"Your hair's same as this leaf." She held it up in example.

Well, he had to give her that—it was. Guy bent over and snatched up another leaf. She gave a shriek—half pleasure, half fright—clinging as fiercely as one of the simians he had seen caged in Alamut. She didn't smell as rank, though she whiffed of smoke and leaf-mould.

"Ah," he said, holding it up to her hair. "Seems to me your hair is the same as *this* leaf."

"Brown." Lizzie was plainly put out.

"A very nice gold-brown," he corrected, and let the leaf fall, fluttering down to the path.

"I want orange hair, likes t' you."

"No, you really don't. It just means you have too many freckles."

"We all gots *those*." She gave him a sceptical look, then blinked. Leaned closer to his face. Both hands rose and landed with a tiny smack against Guy's cheeks. "*Lookit* all!"

He'd survived sneak attacks from Saracens and Cypriots and thieves, but this peasant child had slapped him unawares, and sharply. A smirk tucking into one corner of his mouth, Guy shrugged. "I did tell you."

"They's all *freckles*?" Lizzie shoved back, peering at him—and as her hands were still clutching his face, his head rocked back slightly. "You en't got pox?"

"Oh, now, you can't possibly know what pox is," he chided.

"Do so!" the child insisted, rubbing at his face. When she licked her thumb and would have applied that, he grabbed her hand.

"They don't come off." He gave her a light shake. "Promise."

Surely someone in her village had his complexion. It wasn't *that* uncommon.

"Y'r like to Dickon, then," she gave the answer. "His en't pox neither."

The village was becoming visible in the distance, the trees opening out to show ploughed fields claimed from forest. There were three villages of the Shire Wode in particular, found to have the most contact with the outlaws: Calverton, Matlock, and this one, Hathersage. He had worked his way through them, outward from Nottingham. This one lay closer to the ruins of Loxley.

He'd never had the wherewithal to revisit Loxley. But this village . . . Hathersage . . . it was all the more a suitable place to throw a gauntlet down.

The word had already been spread; there was no one in sight. The road he trod barely met the description of such, leading to a small clot of hovels. The fields were orderly, well-kept. Stooks of grain stood proud, and goodly produce basketed, hung from eaves, or stacked in a lean-to, proved a plenteous harvest. A well made up the village's centre, older stones with, Guy noticed as he drew closer, runes tracing the upper lip and the base.

"Come out!" he shouted. "I need to speak with you!"

Lizzie decided to help. "Hoy, ever'one!" Her reedy voice nigh split Guy's head in twain. As she drew breath to shriek again, he put two fingers to her lips, shook his head.

Anyway, they were coming, singly and in small clumps, from various places around the village. One woman—obviously the mother of the child Guy held—let out a gasp. An older man grabbed her as she started forward.

Lizzie started to wriggle down; Guy held on, told her, "In a moment."

"I wanna—"

"Be still, Lizzie."

His tone must have warned her; her eyes went big and she quieted, ducked her chin obediently. Guy hefted her higher and pitched his voice to carry into the village once more.

"Is this how you serve your master? Hiding in your cots with the sun still in the sky? Where is your headman?"

"No headman here, milord." A tall, grey-haired female stepped forward, lifting her chin. "If milord Templar will deign to speak with a woman."

Guy's mouth twitched sideways. "You know who I am."

"Lately there en't many in t' Shire Wode as doesn't, Sir Guy."

The—headwoman? Cunning-woman, mayhap?—took a step closer. "If you'd put the child down, I would offer a meal and rest for the night. 'Tis time for supper hereabouts."

Guy gave her a long look, took Lizzie with him as he trod over to the well. Resting his backside against it, he said, "There's no need for hospitality. I won't be staying. Let's make this simple, shall we?"

The woman frowned. "Milord?"

"If you know who I am, then surely you know why I'm here."

"Nay, milord, I'm sure I don't."

Several of the villagers had come closer, albeit hesitant, behind the headwoman; the others stayed behind. The woman who must be Lizzie's mother was eyeing the well, then her daughter, then Guy, panic beginning to sprout behind her eyes.

Lizzie began squirming again, discomfited no doubt by her mother's distress. Guy gave her a tiny shake, smiled when she looked to him, and whispered, "See if you can find the lad who has freckles like me. Would you do that for me?"

Distracted, she began to look.

"Why no' put the bairn down, milord Templar?" the headwoman said. "What need do you have of her?"

Guy shrugged, took a stray leaf from the little girl's hair. "I could ask you the same thing. What need should you have of an outlaw who will only bring injury into your village?"

"We don't shelter outlaws, milord. We know the law."

"And living so close to Loxley, you know what happens when those laws are broken?"

A rash of mutterings rose up from the small group, some protesting, some fearful.

'Twas adequate proof: the outlaws were indeed a force in this village. Villeins did not normally even raise their eyes to their betters. Revolution did not flare into being without some spark.

"Loxley were unlawful," the headwoman replied, unmoved. "They replaced the sheriff as did such an evil thing."

"I assure you, woman." Guy met her eyes. "You have no *concept* of evil."

Her clear gaze flickered, retreated from his, and Guy smiled.

Still clinging to his black tabard, Lizzie muttered, "He en't here—"

"Keep looking, then," Guy told her, soft. "It would be very helpful."

The one who looked to be Lizzie's mother started forward. Guy held up a warning finger, shook his head. She threw a frightened look to the headwoman, who shook her head, her wary gaze never leaving Guy.

"Were you there?" Guy asked her, blunt.

The headwoman started—small, but there. "Were I where? Milord?"

She tacked it on, an afterthought. Proud.

Yes, I know how to deal with you.

Guy savoured the thought, said, "Loxley. Were you there, woman?"

"If I were, would I likely tell of 't?"

Not her, but someone she knew well had. "Have you ever seen anyone burned? Not the aftermath, but the during?"

The headwoman kept staring at him. The others were silent, soft and heavy-thick as lead with it.

"It's a horrible thing, to burn. You don't die right away. The pain is . . . indescribable. If you're lucky, you faint and don't come to. If you're unlucky, you know every second of it. Your nerves trying to tell you . . . screaming at you, really, to make it stop, just *make it stop*. And all the while, your flesh crisps and chars, and your blood boils. You cook before you die. And it can take a very long time to die."

Lizzie let out a small and sudden yelp. "There!" Everyone save Guy leapt in place like startled hares. "Dickon!" Lizzie ordered. "Come here."

Dickon stood behind several older villagers, a lad nearly grown and indeed possessing his unfair share of freckles as well as a thick thatch of fair hair tinged russet. Dickon shook his head, backed slightly.

"Come then, boy," Guy said. "Surely *you* can tell me what I need to know."

First Dickon peered at the man standing next to him, then the headwoman, clearly uneasy. The man took his arm, protective. The headwoman was frowning.

"Dickon, I'm losing patience," Guy drawled. "I only want to ask you a question or two. Then I'll let you take Lizzie back to her mother."

Something flared in the youth's eyes, all too familiar; another that had managed to not yet have the spirit beaten from him.

It'll do you no good. Guy's thought etched itself in acid. *They'll just take you down for it.*

Lifting his chin, Dickon came forward, albeit slow.

"So. Lad. Tell me. How old are you?"

"Fifteen, milord."

"Nearly old enough for your own children, eh? When I was your age I was—"

Running wild in the forest and lying with a lover.

"—being taught how to use a sword properly, squire to my brothers."

"I en't no sword, an' no land. That's for *your* like, milord." The undercurrent of acid matched Guy's own. The surrounding villagers responded to it, various shades of fearful and petulant. Guy smiled, saluted it with two fingers to his lips then outward—a mockery of a kiss.

"Dickon c'n be mean," Lizzie told Guy, serious.

"Now, Lizzie. Mean is sometimes the only way to survive. Eh, Dickon?"

Lizzie shrugged and started playing with Guy's hair, humming. Dickon's face twisted. "Give her t' me. You said you would."

"I said I would, what?"

Another twist on the lad's face. "You said you would. *Milord.*"

It gave its own strange contortion in Guy's belly, but immediately—and not unlike the dried leaf he had held to Lizzie's hair—crumbled into dust. "Do you know what it means to pray, boy?"

Dickon frowned, tipped his chin in a vague nod.

"I should think you would, if this is a good Christian village."

"Milord Templar." The headwoman stepped forward. "We have a priest here, regular-like."

"One of the Old Religion, or a Christian?"

He'd nailed her with that one. She was quick, however: her cheeks paled but her mouth was already moving. "The priest from the church t' Sheffield comes, milord. You've no call to chide us for not seeing to the proper education of our folk."

"Whatever is bound on earth shall be bound in Heaven; whatever is loosed on earth shall be loosed in Heaven," Guy quoted softly, returning his attention to Dickon. "Do you know what that means?"

"As above, so below," Dickon countered, then flushed as Guy nodded, said:

"So the Heathens say, yes."

The lad swallowed, hard.

"So. Has this priest told you what excommunication is?"

Dickon nodded.

"Tell me, then."

"Surely you kno—"

"*Tell me.*"

Dickon shot a look at the villager who'd grasped his arm, likely his father. The man frowned, but still gestured the boy to do as he was told. "'Tis when the Church says you don't exist."

"Close. Very close." Guy leaned forward, as if imparting a confession. "*Res sacrae, ritus, communio, crypta, potestas, praedia sacra, forum, civilia jura vetantur.*"

Dickon blinked. "Milord?"

"I could spell it out for you, but there's no point, truly. To be excommunicated is, indeed, to not exist. Not only to the Church, but to everyone about you. Unless you want them to be shunned along with you. It means hell, Dickon. Do you know what hell is?"

A nod, slow.

"No, I don't think you really do." Guy shifted on the well, slightly closer to the lad. "Hell is like burning, all the time. And you can never escape the pain of this burning; never a relief, never die, never rest." Guy stroked a finger over Lizzie's hair, picked at a strand of it. Said, "Hair burns first. Like tinder set to flint and steel."

Dickon's lip trembled, brows drawn together. "You said you'd give her to me if—"

"People lie, Dickon. Every chance they have, they lie. You just have to figure out why. What's at stake." Guy hefted Lizzie, then stood.

The lad flinched but, to his credit, didn't back away. Lip still trembling, he held out his arms.

Guy raised his eyebrows, then, keeping his gaze on Dickon, whispered in Lizzie's ear. She shook her head. Guy gave a stern repeat, then passed her, pouting, to Dickon's outstretched arms.

Dickon was no fool. He turned and fled, Lizzie complaining all the way.

Guy brushed himself off, said, quite casual, "I'll return in a day, maybe two. Mayhap there's one—or more—of you who might find your memory more . . . agile."

The villagers gazed at him, seemingly dumb. Not that he expected anyone to leap forward and offer him assistance. No, this had to be a subtle thing: extend the suggestion, let it stew.

Nevertheless Guy took care, turning his back on them to leave. But the only step coming after him, if properly hesitant, was accompanied by the headwoman's mulish voice.

"Iffen we knew where Robyn Hood were," she said as he turned, "it'd matter nowt. When he finds out you've been here, he'll find *you*. Like he did on Samhain."

This wasn't some passive game of effrontery; this was ballsy beyond belief. Guy paused, then strode back to her. The villagers had started forward; all but a few men tottered back. Guy halted that much too close to her, pitched his voice so they all could hear but nevertheless spoke to her, sibilant menace.

"Your village seems overly blessed with children. Does it make them any less valuable to you?"

"Not likely," she retorted.

"Good. You might want to think on that. On whether you value some jumped-up thief more than your own people. On what *I* am. On burning. And hell." As her cheeks paled again, Guy smiled. "Quite a lot of responsibility you have, woman. I'd consider it carefully, were I in your place."

↑

When she woke again, it was to darkness. A stench rivalling a carcass left to blow and rot stung her nostrils—that, and mouldy straw, and rat urine.

A tickle at her nose. In pure reflex Marion lurched up and struck out. Her hand hit something small and solid; the rat squeaked and went skidding across the earthen floor, dirty straw in its wake.

There was more than one rat squeaking. Now that she had moved, however, not a single one remained close. Her eyes became accustomed quickly, picking out the dust motes in the sheer, spare light skimming in from the opening above, then the movement across from her on a rickety bench.

Another prisoner? For this was prison, the oubliette spoken of with such horror in the crofts, the dead man's hole. She tried to speak; all that emerged was a small croak, which closed in on itself as she saw what lolled on that bench.

A dead man, very dead, and the rats were still feasting on what remained of his entrails.

Marion let out a sound between a cough, a retch, and a cry, and half crawled, half scuttered backward on her rump across the floor. She didn't stop until she hit the wall behind her and pressed against the solid, scummy stones, panting.

A howl of sheer panic crested the back of her throat, begged release. They had put George in Nottingham's gaol, and he had died there . . .

Stop it, she told herself. *It canna be George, this fellow's but a few days dead at the most, and George died. . .*

How long ago?

Years.

Again, she felt the press and passage of time, moving not with her, but past her.

Years, it had been. They were, all of them, long dead.

And likely, she would soon join them.

⟰

"He were in Hathersage, then."

"Aye. And Matlock." David had just returned from there, visiting his grandmother.

It was hard to maintain any semblance of calm. Hard enough to fathom that anyone could track the "safe house" villages—they'd been so careful—but. This.

"He threatened to *burn*—"

"Aye, lessen they give him what he wants. 'Tis sure they'll face the interdict if they thwart him again. The bastard said nothin' less than you or your whereabouts will stay him."

Robyn couldn't believe it. Couldn't believe *this*.

John couldn't either, it seemed. He wouldn't meet Robyn's eyes. He and Arthur had come back from Hathersage with their own story. One wouldn't think interdict would threaten a village not in spiritual sway of the Church. But there were more and more villages who had fallen away from the old ways, and no matter how self-sufficient a village, if they were shunned by every other connection they held . . .

They'd be as near outlaw as could be gotten. As villeins, they were still worth more alive than dead, but still, no light matter. And to threaten the torch?

Robyn let out a tiny groan, had to lower himself to the ground on wobbly knees that wouldn't hold him. He wondered if he might heave his guts. Surely Gamelyn would *not* . . .

Nay, Gamelyn was surely dead. This was proof.

You do not know what hunts you. The memory slunk in on cat feet and hissed at him.

I know now, he told it, and put his head in his hands.

Thankfully—oddly—the Horned Lord stayed quiet. But his presence glided, a shade flickering, back and forth, just outside the small copse where they'd made camp. The others saw him, as well. They kept throwing wary glances behind them.

"This is my fault," Robyn said into his hands. "I humiliated him—"

"We all," John said, slow, "did it."

"I thought . . ." *Thought he would know me. Thought he were, somehow, still in there. Somewhere. And now. . . I have to stop him.*

Clenching fingers in his hair so tight it stung, Robyn took in a halting breath, then let it loose. Closed his eyes and spun inward into thought while his more abstruse senses spiralled outward, seeking.

"All right," Robyn said. "Here's what we'll do. I've duty t' Mam Tor—"

"Not alone," Gilbert spoke up, and the others agreed.

"I go alone t' Tor," Robyn said. "That en't changing."

"Robyn—"

"I'll not bend on this one t' any of you," he growled, stood. "There's none but you as knows where I go then, or *why*. If any of you had borne witness that night, you might have the right. Even John en't allowed, and he saw what came after. The Lord and Lady forbid the place on moon-dark to any who have not touched those deaths. Madness lurks there for any t' trespass. Which is why none can ever know.

"But," he allowed, "three hours past the dawn, you can be there. We'll make Mam Tor a stop-off. You'll meet me there and we'll go on to where we'll move camp—"

"We're already moving as much as we ever have," Will pointed out.

"This time we're moving out, more in th' open. Let 'im target us instead of the villages." He gathered them all by eye, found every one of them in accord. Aye, they were angry enough to push the fight, now. "We've gone to a bit of trouble, setting up our contacts all over, not just those few villages he's after. And we know there's likely to be some . . . well, some loyalties more agile than fast."

"None's likely to help, not with this happening," Arthur pointed out.

"They'll be with us, should we show them the way out of it." Robyn looked up, a grin tucked in one side of his mouth. "Once he catches me—"

They all yelped various negations. Even John.

"Listen. If he catches me, then we all know where he is. We can turn the tables on him—"

"Like y' did at Samhain?" Will interrupted.

"The Trent got in our way, nowt more. An' we made the mistake of not givin' the river sprites their due, despite bein' on their bank. They took Gisbourne and he's damned lucky they spit him out."

"He is," David bemoaned. "But we en't."

Robyn shrugged. "We'll take our luck back from him. How much ransom d'you think the Templar's top pit dog would be worth?"

"Bloody damn, Rob!" Will burst out. "Surely you really en't thinking . . . !"

Robyn smiled.

– ENTR'ACTE –

"Brother?"

Spoken softly, the question echoed through the stones of the chapel. Much had waited, had bent his own head while the monk had finished his devotions, but once he had risen, waiting was over. He'd no time for pleasantries.

Aye, and Much recognised Dolfin as soon as he turned. The bright blue eyes, the too-strong jaw, the thick-hewed body that had broadened and softened with regular eating—and the tucked-up cassock, the sandals hanging at the belt, the bare feet heedless of the cold stones.

Dolfin, though, didn't have the same advantage. "May I help you?" He came forward, curious, but the language of his body claimed a readiness for trouble, if need be.

Much smiled. Once a soldier, always one. "I'm hoping you can, Brother," Much quieted as Dolfin came forward, espied the small, crimson cross on the shoulder of Much's brown cape.

Dolfin hesitated. "You're here looking for Gamelyn."

"I'm here looking for Brother Guy," Much amended. Ingrained, the rebuttal; he well remembered the day that name had been taken. He'd no wish to relive it himself, much less parade the memory about. And sure enough, it was proving itself the one rent in his master's otherwise-flawless armour.

"Of course. My error which, I hope, you'll forgive. You're Much, aren't you?" Dolfin closed the remaining distance between them, no less ready for trouble but this time with a welcoming smile. "It's been a long road for both of us, it seems, to this place. I barely recognised you. Or him. Both of you have been longer than you should in the wars."

"The boy y' sent with milord's message told me where it came from," Much said. "You might speak to him of that, should you not be wanting him to gab."

"It was of no matter." Dolfin shrugged. "But I have a feeling you're not here to be social."

"Nay, Brother. Those wars you're speakin' to, they en't done by a long shot. I need to find Sir Guy." Dolfin's face fell, and Much felt his own gut sink. "You en't seen him."

"Nay, I'm sorry, lad. I've not seen him since we sent the message to you at Nottingham, and that's been . . . hmm . . . "

"Just ower a se'nnight," Much finished and went silent, leaning harder against the curved stone wall at his back, thinking.

"He did speak of heading north, of having pinpointed several villages that were overfriendly to the outlaws." Dolfin shook his head and sighed. "I fear for those villages, in truth. Your master is a very driven man. And the outlaws humiliated him."

This set Much's nerves a-jangle. He stiffened. "They *what?*"

"Hm." Dolfin peered at him. "It does speak to the cunning of this outlaw. But anyone is susceptible to being outnumbered. They drugged him, so he said, and fell upon him. The Wild Hunt rode Hallows, and he fell beneath its force."

"Bloody hell!" Much burst out, then shook his head, clenched his fists. "Forgive me, Brother, but . . . did I hear you t' rights? The Wild Hunt, y' say?"

"You know of it."

Much nodded, trying—and failing—to still the sudden thumping of his pulse. Anyone ill-fated to get caught in the Hunt was seldom fortunate enough to come out with their mind intact. "Bloody . . . He's all right?"

"He was when last I saw him," Dolfin assured. "He fell in the Trent and, while it nigh drowned him, it also saved him. I found him there, waterlogged and still fighting. I brought him here, saw him to rights."

Perhaps the Hunt had no sway over Much's master—even if Guy didn't understand . . . didn't *want* to understand what he was, surely the Wode knew its own.

"You've my heartfelt thanks, Brother." Much made a go at

pacing the width of the chapel. He made it only halfway before stopping. "You're sure he were all right? I mean . . . the Hunt."

"He was. I swear to you." Dolfin still peered at him. "The only ones I've seen this petrified of such a thing are . . . You can't possibly still be Heathen, but you grew up one, didn't you?"

Much nodded. "The ways of my ma's folk are still close t' me." Then, as Dolfin's eye flickered to the cross on his cape, Much quoted, soft, "'There are many mansions in my father's house.'"

A smirk chased across Dolfin's lip. "Just so. Though I'd never expected one of the Templars to think so."

"Well, neither am I a fully sworn Templar. But you'd be fair scunnered, Brother, what the Preceptory holds to its heart. I were, and I don't know the half of it." Much ran both hands over his close-cropped head, then crossed his arms with a huff. "You en't seen him. He'll be heading north, for the heart of the Wode and those villages . . . and I can't be going after. I thought, maybe . . . " He shrugged. "Eh, 'twere a rubbish thought. A desperate one, more like."

Dolfin was watching him. "Much, can I help? I will, you know."

Guy had obviously trusted Dolfin—the note alone proved that. And Much had never known the priest to be anything but forward in his dealings. Much hesitated only a moment, then described his predicament: set to guard Marion—who she was and why Guy meant to protect her—and how Marion had been thrown in Nottingham's gaol, with talk of witchcraft buzzing in the corridors.

"And that Abbess's like? You were in Blyth, you saw the cursed doings she put in motion. The Lady has set Her Maiden's memory free, but I en't sure th' timing's so fair. I en't sure I should even be here, but what else could I've done?"

Much was used to having orders, used to following and doing without such havering about to it. He preferred it that way, not . . . this.

Dolfin must've been an officer. Or a mercenary, used to his own counsel, for he didn't seem the least dismayed by the open-ended situation. "These villages, then. You obviously know which ones were friendly to Robyn Hood and his followers . . . and these were ones Gam . . . Guy planned to exploit in his search?"

Much nodded.

"Then I'll go. Find him. You need to get back to Nottingham as quickly as you can, make sure they don't do anything worse than lock up that poor lass. They're giving you no trouble?"

"They don't dare. But I'm being proper careful," Much added. "That sheriff, de Lisle, tried a few pissing matches with Sir Guy. He en't daft enough to push it the more, I think, but I en't my master, neither. And now Count John is here, all rarin' for the burning, and with him . . . " Much shook his head. "That Sir Johan, *he's* the one as worries me most. I have to warn Sir Guy of 'im, so's he can be on his guard. Of all of 'em, a brother would be more like t' ken another brother, and he'd make trouble just t' have it. And to tangle it further, th' Maiden were babbling me master's old name. You should've heard her, she were nigh mad—"

"I'm not sure I blame her," Dolfin interjected. "That young woman has spent several years in a dream. To wake up, so sudden . . . it must be horrific. Everything she thought she knew—everything she knew then—it's all gone. And to find herself in the hands of her worst enemy?" He reached up to rescue a candle guttering in an alcove. "Poor lass."

"Aye. She were in a state, and no question. But I told 'em my master had asked me to keep an eye on her."

"That mightn't be so bad. 'Twill give you an excuse to stay nigh." Dolfin poured wax away from the drowning wick and onto the alcove's shelf. "But did they wonder why?"

"I think," Much said, careful, "*they* think my master's smitten with her. And I s'pose he is. Just not as they think." Just talking about it, he felt he'd been gone too long. No one else had seemed to notice what was trying to unearth itself in Marion—save, perhaps, that bloody-minded Abbess and she didn't really *see* it— but Much had seen, had felt the raw power behind the *geas* that Marion had pulled up from the earth and tried to fling at her enemy.

Aye, Much was never one to question a goddess's ways, but he couldn't help but feel She'd not chosen the best time to stir Herself. Unless . . .

Abruptly, he'd thrice the worries. What if something had happened with Guy? The cross Marion wore had Guy's blood on it, and even if Guy didn't want to know what he was—had always been—to the Wode, Much knew. Mightn't the Maiden know, if her Knight became . . . compromised?

"I have to do sommat!" Much burst out. "If he's in trouble I wain't just—"

"I'll go." Dolfin's words were calm, buoying. "Much, I'll go find him. Travelling is, after all, part of my duties. I can leave my lad here to tend the chapel, ask a fellow Brother to hold mass—only once or twice a week, here in Purgatory." He grinned. "I'll be on the North Road by morning. Surely, the path your master's bent on, he'll leave a trail."

"Of bodies, if nowt else," Much muttered.

Dolfin crossed himself. "Let's hope not. Truly, you've come to the right place. I know the people hereabouts. They trust me, and so must you. We'll find him. If anyone can get that poor lass out of Nottingham's dungeons, it's a Knight Templar on a mission."

Much almost didn't dare to hope. He didn't like placing his master's life in other hands. But he had been given explicit orders. Even now, he was likely disobeying the letter of them.

"It's gots t' be quick, Brother Dolfin. There's no telling how much time before they do sommat about th' Maiden."

"I'll go to Temple Hirst if I must, but I'll find him."

"Mightn't be a bad thought. Master Hubert would send help in a heartbeat, should we need it. But Sir Guy might take it amiss; he's used to having t' job done his way." Much shrugged. "Leastways, with Himself the King's brother in residence, everyone's all distracted, waitin' on him hand and foot."

"Aye, that's true enough," Dolfin acknowledged. "So. Think of anything you want me to say to your master, and I'll write it down whilst we have a bite."

"I should get back, Brother—"

"And you will, anon. But you need to gather your thoughts, and food is the best cure for that. Anyway." Dolfin gestured into the chapel. "No sense in going anywhere on an empty stomach."

Much relented to the sense of that, but couldn't help a glance to the exit, both wary and impatient.

- XIV -

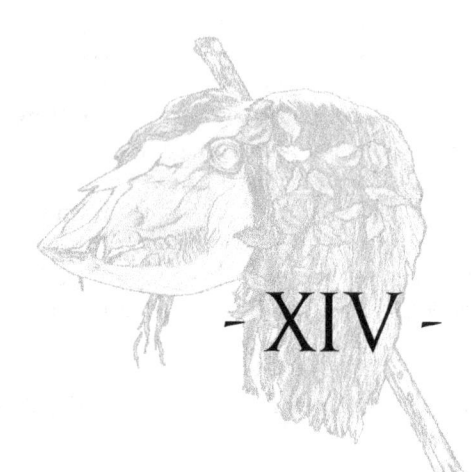

Truly amazing, what a combination of coercion and coin could accomplish. It would buy and sell belief, in the proper circumstances.

Not that these circumstances were optimal. One could scarcely stand up in the tiny, squalid hut. Guy had tied Falcon within a copse of trees some distance away, and a good thing. The stallion would no doubt have turned up his well-bred nose at the accommodations: a side-shed to a scarcely larger cot seated on the farthest edge of Matlock, well within floodplain. It had been a byre until the cow had died, his host informed him, and his sister had persuaded her husband to give him the space when he'd made his way here several months previous.

"She said I could stay as I needed, too, even once they could afford a new cow," the villein prattled as he spread an ill-tanned hide, padded it with straw for his distinguished guest.

The sister and husband were conspicuous by their absence—out at the fields, no doubt. And this man, though hale enough to work, had shrugged away the notion Guy had put forth—he'd be missed, surely?

Guy knelt at the man's request but did not sit. It didn't help: several fleas jumped hopefully onto his bent, leather-clad legs.

"Your friend told me you could assist me," Guy reminded.

"Aye, o' course, milord, I know who you're lookin' for. There's no' many who don't, milord Templar. It's become a proper tale—"

"Tale."

"Aye, milord. About your hunt for the outlaws." The man kept babbling, but seemed to ken the barely concealed impatience on Guy's face. "Beggin' your pardon, milord, but word travels hereabouts like a fart in a close room."

How apropos, Guy considered, then smirked at himself. He was getting too soft and dainty if fleas, old cow shit, mould, and a foul-smelling, worthless villein could make him twitch. He left the smirk on his face, let it go slightly south of vicious, and eyed the villein. "You're beginning to bore me, man."

The villein's eyes popped wide and he bowed his head, crossed himself.

"Neither do I need a prayer before we begin. Though if you keep me waiting any longer, final unction might be appropriate. For you."

"I . . . I'm sorry, milord. You're a much more holy man than even my priest, and—"

"Robyn Hood." It was flat. Guy flicked several persistent fleas from his boot.

"Aye, milord. I were getting to—"

"Then get to it. Now."

"Well, I came on him once." He paused, seemingly for emphasis.

Guy waited for about two breaths. On the exhale of the second, he reached out and grabbed the villein by his tunic, jerking him forward. "For every flea bite I receive while I'm waiting for you to tell me something of import, I will give you a cut with my horsewhip. Start. *Talking.*"

"It were nigh to the old stones at Mother's Tor!" the villein babbled. "An unholy place, like."

Mother's Tor. Guy cast back in his memory, found a scabbed-over remembrance that started to bleed as he picked at it. One would think he'd be used to the constant reminders by now.

"You mean Mam Tor. Those stones were pulled down." *And the surroundings burned, fertilised with tens of bodies*, his memory supplied helpfully. *The same night they burned Loxley.*

Die, he told it. *Die and be buried.*

"Well, some of 'em still stand, like. It's said ghosts walk there. I'd gotten lost, else I'd never have gone near it. An evil place, all silent and still—"

"And Robyn Hood was there."

"He must've heard me coming. He were . . . waiting for me. Appeared out o' nowheres and grabbed me. Told me if I breathed to a living soul where I'd seen 'im, nightmares would be a pleasant alternative to what he'd bring down on me. That it were a sacred place.

"Me daughter laid upside and down me with the rough side o' her tongue, said I'd trespassed where I'd no business. That I belonged to the White Christ, not th' Horned Lord, and 'twere Christ's people as had done the desecration. That the Hood would do me proper if I showed me face there again. I did some askin' . . . on the quiet, like. No one knew nothin' 'bout the stones, but I heard sommun saying as the Green Man goes off by hisself, 'specially on the dark of the moon." The villein lowered his voice. "I think he goes to that evil place on the dark moon to consort with his devils. Speaks with 'em, and changes hisself into a horned devil. Rides with a pack of wolves. You saw 't." The villein leaned forward, on all fours in the mouldy straw. "They say he called the Hunt on you, and the only reason you're alive is God came to you and beat the demons back."

If only. Guy considered the awe commingling with terror on the informant's face. *No god comes at my beck and call. The wolfshead let me go because he* chose *to.*

It still galled.

"He scared me spitless. I'm no' so sure he's even a man. But you said you wanted anythin' 'twould help you find him."

"If you're so scared," Guy murmured, watching another flea jump from his leg to his forearm, "then why are you telling me all this?"

The man looked troubled. He was scared, no question.

Good.

"I'm a good Christian soul, I am," he murmured. "I don't believe all the stories they tell about you. I asked the priest about you, and he says Templars're God's warriors. I believe him. He says th' Horned Lord's of the devil and Robyn Hood one of his demons. I used to go to the rites, but I don't no more. I don't want to burn in hell."

Mam Tor. Fury started a slow, crimson-black burn behind Guy's vision. Was there nothing this wolfshead would not do to usurp the power of what had come before?

He rose, remembering just in time to not rise to his full height, and started to leave.

"Milord . . . " Wheedling.

Guy tossed him the promised coins, hesitated, then hunkered

back down again, watching in silence as the villein dug in the flea-ridden straw for his money. Waited, until the villein looked up.

"All those stories they tell about me?" Guy leaned closer, and the sallow face blanched nigh-grey. *"Believe* them. Because if I find you've been lying to me, I will come back here and gladly send you to meet God. Without your head."

⬆

Hours, it had been.

He'd left Falcon the previous noontide at the nearby keep of Peveril, with the lord's promise to see him well grained and groomed. He'd come here directly, stayed into evening. Night, too, had come and gone, the dark moon further obscured by the clouds still hanging, low and sullen, just above the top of the tree he perched in. Dawn was making an unwilling and perfunctory appearance, its light more grey than rose.

Guy waited, underfed, dry, and stiffer in his limbs than he would have preferred. Well, so be it. Stalking had its merits, true, but this animal had proven himself too wily. A stand was a better way to go, no question. He gave a careful shift on the pad of his cloak hem, setting the dense leaves rustling. Only slight—it might have been a breeze.

Even if there was no breeze. *Clever, this wolfshead,* Guy reminded himself. *Take every care possible. Stay in silence.*

The stones lay beyond him, looking like a thrown set of thick, grey bones across the clearing. The far copse bordering them still bore traces of blackened, fire-stunted trees, but the green Wode covered man's follies as she always did, a steady encroachment upon the scarred land. She seemed to wait, silent patience.

Weakness, nothing more, to let the place unsettle him, even in a vague way.

The rain that had been hanging, thick and heavy over the forest, began to fall.

Guy leaned back against the trunk and shrugged closer into his cloak, pulled the dark grey *kaffiyeh* farther over his forehead, and laid his head back against the thick burl. Spent a few moments entertaining what it might be like, to hang the most holy Abbess of Worksop from this very tree, in sight of the stones. Folly, certainly. Vengeance made a self-indulgent juggernaut, one that rarely met its hopeful target. He was a weapon in this pursuit, nothing more; he had not been given leave to gratify personal satisfactions.

Save that Hubert wanted you to lay your ghosts to rest, a small, angry voice reminded.

Unlikely. All he'd done was brass them off and wake a sleepy, ravaged child who, all the while, mewled pain and whinged outrage.

Had someone found out what the filthy villein had told Guy? More likely than the man lying to him. Guy had heard every sort of lie, had learned through many errors— some life-threatening— how to sift untruth from honesty, how to cozen the latter from shadows. He'd wager the Damascus steel hanging in its scabbard over one shoulder that the villein had been truthful. If he had lied? He'd have to die, of course. Let one take advantage, and it would cascade like an undercut sand bank.

Guy paused. He'd heard something. Not much—more a quick breath, a pause in the *tap-tap-tap* of rainfall, a rustle on a stray breeze.

Only there was no breeze.

And then there was a hooded man walking into the clearing, as simple as that.

Guy angled forward, with slow stealth gave a twist of his scabbard so it lay nestled in its rightful place between his shoulder blades. Still silent, with as much consideration as a hunting lion, he lowered himself along the branch, almost supine. The leaves didn't so much as stir. Taking a long, quiet breath, he held it, willed: *I'm not here. Not here, and you can't touch me.*

Laying his chin upon his hands, Guy watched.

And was mightily unimpressed.

This was the notorious Robyn Hood?

Lanky as an adolescent boy, this one. From what fear and awe surrounded him, from the hints and suggestions of some magical means, from the *presence* of that figure lit by Samhain's witchlights, shadowed with hood and horn . . .

Guy had expected some huge-thewed, disgruntled soldier, or a charismatic ex-jongleur, or perhaps even one like to himself, a dispossessed noble with more brains than political savvy. This fellow looked more beaten serf than any wild-eyed fanatic.

His step came halting, his frame slumped, his mien wary. A monster of a longbow lay strapped to his back, but he frankly looked incapable of pulling it. Even his clothes spoke of poor circumstance: his tunic was thin, as nigh to a rag as could be considered clothing. Surely someone who'd stolen more than his negligible weight in marks and goods would possess better. As to the rest of him, he sported leathers like some barbaric northern hill tribe chieftain, with tall boots, a long overtunic, and breeches over thin hose, the hides soft and finely tanned. Probably from the king's beasts. The hood—namesake and camouflage—sagged sideways, a weather-stained ebon that unfortunately continued to obscure the villein's face, even as he paused at one upturned dolman, placed a leather-wrapped hand against it, and angled his chin up. A dark scruff of beard was all Guy could truly see, then a glint of teeth—smile or snarl, who knew which?—before the outlaw bowed his head again, placed it against the rock, and held motionless.

Guy kept waiting, hardly daring to breathe.

The outlaw remained there for long moments, almost as if he were praying against the crumpled stone. Guy waited him out; no sense in rushing this, and maybe this wasn't the right fellow after all. Maybe this was some scout, a ne'er-do-well boy who'd hitched his poor wagon to an unlikely star.

However it became clear, soon enough, that no one else was coming. The outlaw pushed away from the dolman stone and made his way with halting, heavy steps to the broad, flat rock in the centre. As he approached it, he shrugged the bow from his shoulders, the flat quiver filled with arrows, his leather overtunic. The latter clinked as he laid it aside. Chainmail on the shoulders, likely stolen from a murdered soldier.

He stood there for a moment, face upturned to the rain, head . . . cocked, almost. Guy stayed still, wondered what in hell the outlaw was doing. Then the outlaw tilted his head back down, brought his hands to his face and gestured outward. It misted forth, a visible exhale of breath joining with the fog beginning to rise around his feet and drift across the stone circle.

Guy frowned. A quality, foreign and forlorn, imbibed the slow manner of it, yet also oddly . . . familiar, the gesture, and the hands tending it. A too-full itch of sensation teased behind his eyes, a recognition of . . . something. And the fog, crawling across the clearing.

Toward him.

Guy froze, wondered for several taut moments if he'd somehow been found out. It was too akin to what had risen up on Samhain in the bottom lands of the Trent, the elements themselves seeming at the outlaw's beck and call. Then he noted the fog, rolling outward from the middle of the stones in several directions. Cool logic skewered further any superstitious fancy as the outlaw knelt, oblivious to any watching eyes, and lowered his head as if in prayer. The mists swirling about him were doing so merely on the breeze of his movement, not from any arcane manipulation.

Guy snarled at his own folly. The outlaw—if he was indeed Robyn Hood—remained quiet, unaware. There might never be a better time. Rain began coming down in a steady patter, giving him at least some cover to get the drop on the outlaw. Creeping down the trunk, Guy was cautious of his footing, doubly cautious as he drew his sword from its sheath. Its muted rasp made his only sound, and that no greater than a tiny breath.

It was ridiculous, in fact, the ease of approach. More and more, Guy considered, this fellow kneeling in the rain next to the stone altar, unweaponed and oblivious, could not be Robyn Hood.

Well, then. Guy could take out some of his frustrations by beating the Hood's whereabouts from this gaunt hanger-on.

Repressing a sigh, he reached out, tapped the fellow's shoulder with his sword. "Get up, you."

As if a badger had exploded from its den, all teeth and growl and sudden, vicious movement, the outlaw twisted, grabbed the blade of Guy's sword and yanked, hard.

Guy lurched forward, cursed. This sort of move was unexpected . . . foolhardy—but effective, as the outlaw swung a kick at Guy's legs, still gripping tight to the sword blade. Guy leapt over the kick, landed lightly, grounded himself then tightened up as the outlaw yanked again, trying to pull him further off balance. Instead of swinging the sword sideways—a novice tactic—Guy gave a mighty heave. The blade should at least slash the man's palm to bone, at best remove a few fingers.

No fingers went flying. The motley scraps of leather and cloth wrapped around the outlaw's palm split instead—not, however, without a gratifying spatter of blood and a surprised hiss from the ebon cowl.

The outlaw fell back, blood seeping through his clenched fist, and made another arc with his foot—which Guy leapt over again, then still again as the outlaw brought his other foot through. The outlaw rolled with the motion, away from the stone, then leapt to his feet. Two daggers glinted in his hands: one the length of his forearm, the other a short, thick skinning knife.

Guy followed, sword ready. They circled each other, light steps on the wet grass.

"Robyn Hood," Guy said, quiet.

A pause, a dip of that dark hood, then, "Guy of Gisbourne." It was low, almost hoarse.

"You fight two handed," Guy acknowledged. He feinted to the right, then tossed his sword from right to left hand, gave a swift lunge forward. "So do I."

The outlaw wasn't there. He'd ducked and rolled sideways. The roll was accompanied by a ripping sound. As the outlaw gained his feet, part of the threadbare tunic hung. He'd clearly not expected the switch of sword hands, had ducked the wrong way.

Teeth flashed—again, snarl or smile, hard to discern—as the outlaw crouched, ready. "Well done you. *Templar*." It was plain he'd not make the same mistake again.

Neither would Guy. He'd intended to wound but merely grazed. This was no beaten serf or untested boy—the man moved quick as a mad ferret.

"You've no chance. *Wolfshead*."

Several more feints, several more engagements, quick and brutal. No more words, taunt or test. In grim silence they fought, circumnavigating the stones but in particular the altar stone. Higher ground, but tiny rivulets beaded and runnelled over it, assuredly more treacherous a footing than even the sodden grass, already slick as sheep shit.

The outlaw was quite tall, and he moved as one more accustomed to a knife fight than the sword. Indeed, they were dancing rather than truly fighting; the outlaw used his knives only when a blow came too close, and then to aid the parry and a sideways retreat. The dagger once came altogether close to Guy's face. He ducked, his *kaffiyeh* yanking sideways. Another duck, and a twist; the wrap came free, fouling his opponent's dagger.

The outlaw let out another soft curse, tried to twitch it free, ended up tossing the long dagger aside as the sodden cloth merely fouled it further.

And how, Guy wondered, blinking the wet from his eyes and tossing his sword from hand to hand, did that bloody black cowl stay put? Did he have a bald pate underneath, and glue to hold it in place?

Time to find out.

Guy lunged forward, sword flashing then cutting sideways, back and forth, over and under then a thrust. A more ponderous opponent would have been eviscerated then spitted. The outlaw had no sword. Only one short blade, lightning reflexes, and quick endurance—small defence against a long, razored curve of Damascene craft wielded by an expert.

Of the outcome there was no doubt, but it came sooner than Guy had imagined as they backed toward the altar. The outlaw, fully occupied with not getting sliced from neck to knees, lost track of where he was. Only for a second, but a fatal one.

His heel impacted with the altar rim, sent him stumbling

backward. Guy took the opportunity: flipping his sword back and behind, he kicked out. It hit the outlaw square in the gut. With a windmilling of arms and a sharp "*Unh!*" Robyn Hood hit the broad stone flat on his back.

Guy leapt onto the altar and stood over him, sword braced flat on his forearm. His opponent lurched upward, more from instinct than sense as he promptly almost skewered himself on the sword held to his breastbone. Just as quickly he contracted, not unlike a turtle into its shell, chest going all hollow. The hood jerked forward—lacings held it drawn close, Guy noted, as the keen edge of his sword caught on them, sliced.

The damned hood, finally, fell back.

A tangle of black curls falling into his face, the outlaw scooted, frantic retreat, on his backside across the altar. Guy followed with several quick, smooth steps, crouched over him, put sword to the pale throat, counted the beats in that jugular as they ramped up, rapid with adrenaline and fear. Entire body curling in on itself to avoid the sword-edge, the outlaw slipped as his injured palm made contact with the wet stone and skated sideways in its own blood.

It came from nowhere, a sound that was . . . *not*. More pressure, or the beating of a heart echoing into the trees and behind Guy's ears.

A hoarse grunt came from Robyn Hood's chest. He gave a backward arch and fell against the stone, lay there as if pinned with a bloodied nose and hair flung back and black eyes widening up at Guy . . .

The *eyes*.

Guy froze.

He knew those eyes, had seen them in nightmares, over and over—haunted, hunted . . . *dead*. He knew that face turned up to him, a revenant dirty and leaner, scruffed with black fur. Knew intimately the cheeky glint that fired in the black gaze, the crooked, slightly malicious smile that made quick work of any reflected fear and shock—all of it. All of it, part and parcel of a mocking insolence Guy had seen a hundred times . . .

A lifetime ago.

And the sound/not-sound/*reverberation*, piercing his eyeballs and throbbing behind his ears.

"Do it, then," the revenant said. "Do it, but don't tell me you en't feeling *that*."

The sword wobbled in Guy's hand. His knees buckled. He tottered and nearly fell atop his enemy, and all the while: *Feel . . . that. Feel . . .*

"*Putain de merde.*" It was foul, but warbled upward into faded. "You're dead! *I saw you die!*"

"I saw *you.*" A growl. "*Watching* me die."

"Rob." A whisper. Worse, a *whimper.*

"Nay, *Gisbourne.*" It was derisive. "I'm the one you've been lookin' for, eh? *Robyn Hood.*"

Robyn lurched forward and brought both arms up, one to slap at the sword, the other to punch at Guy's ribs. After both blows, lightning-quick, Robyn then rocked back and rammed both heels into Guy's crotch.

And Guy, unable to so much as muster a defence, *let* him. Agony scoring bloody furrows behind his eyeballs, Guy stumbled backward, fell off the altar and onto his side. The humming-pulsing *something* had grown fainter, and with it seemed to fade part of his consciousness. Guy wondered, for agonised seconds, if he was going to pass out. Throw up.

Or, more likely, get skewered.

"I heard y' comin' a mile away. Felt every footstep you made into my stones and my circle . . . and never have you heard *me*. Why is that, *Gisbourne?*"

Guy's vision still pulsed with black pain, but part of him watched as Robyn wiped at his nose, rolled to his feet and strode over to the far side of the altar. Bent over, picking up something.

Get up, a little voice yammered at Guy, barring sight and sound. *Get up, you idiot, he's going to* kill *you.*

So? he snapped back.

Robyn padded over to him, still silent. Leaned over him. Guy could only lay there, fists stuffed between his legs, felled like a hamstrung ox ready for the slaughter.

Of all the ways or means he thought would bring him to death, this hadn't even made the list. And how apropos was that?

"Let me guess, pet." Robyn crouched over Guy, held an object before him, glinting dull. "You've finally come back for this, have you?"

For seconds it looked to be a cross. Improbable. More like impossible. Guy blinked, and it came into focus, glinting in the half-light.

A dagger, nothing more, the long one Guy had tangled in his scarf and not even thought to recognise. Now, however, it was quite familiar, delicate and deadly, thought as lost as the impossible and lovely reverie that it was reminder of, a time and place and person better left forgotten . . . yet which he had never been able to forget.

Eden.

Rob had kept it. But what memory did he aid?—that of lover, or of betrayer?

The unpleasant light in those black eyes, the abrupt and sideways smirk, gave an answer. Rob . . . *Robyn* rose and walked a few steps away, flipping the quillion dagger end over end with no little ease.

"Aye, well. I think you've left it a bit late, eh?"

Anger flared, and Guy started to lurch up. With the speed of a striking cobra, Robyn whirled, sent his elbow smashing full into Guy's face. Momentum and blow both sent Guy arcing backward into heavy impact against the ground, and *at least he didn't stab you with it* was the only thought he had before oblivion claimed him.

- XV -

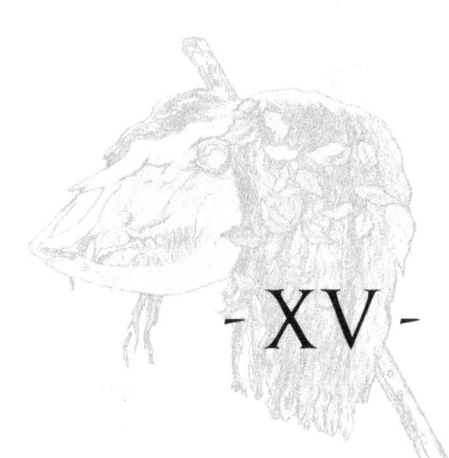

When Guy crept back into consciousness, he found himself sodden, upright... and bound hand and foot to a large tree. He only opened his eyes a small slit, looked through pale, wet lashes. Rob—nay, damn it, Robyn Hood, he could not afford to forget that!—*Robyn* had seated himself, cross-legged, on a great gnarled root not two ells from Guy. Hood thrown back, a narrow gash clotted dark along nose and cheek, his eyes downcast and shoulders hunched with effort. His left hand was wrapped with a bloodstained scrap of linen. He was sharpening the quillion dagger.

Robyn didn't look up. Neither did Guy move, but kept his eyes barely half-mast and took quick inventory. His jaw was killing him, but a tiny wiggle confirmed nothing broken. Three sets of rope. One about his neck of plaited grass, thin, guaranteed to cut if tested too sorely. A second pulled his arms back around the tree trunk, thicker and stronger and knotted about each hand for good measure. The third wound about each ankle and, again, around the tree trunk.

"I know you're awake," Robyn said.

Guy opened his eyes, pretended a stretch that tested the ropes. Just as he'd figured: sturdy hemp, already damp so they'd not loosen overmuch. He could likely saw at them with the rough bark of the oak to which he'd been trussed, given time.

If he was given that time. The notorious outlaw leader was certainly attending to his dagger with all the tender conviction of an executioner with his axe.

Not to mention, Robyn Hood had proven as unfortunately thorough with his cautions as with his rope tying: Guy's weapons were gone. *All* of them, including the familiar stiffness of an inside seam of his tabard's cross—a thin stiletto—as well as the tight brace of three throwing knives strapped to his arm and the inseam sheath in his boot with its two shivs. Even his hair fell loose: the tight-braided cord he used, not only to braid back his forelock, but more importantly as garrotte, had been looped over the hilt of his falchion. The curved sword itself was stuck in the ground within arm's reach of Robyn's left knee; the litter of destructive implements lay in a small pile beneath.

The thought of being so thoroughly searched was as humiliating as the knowledge of who had done the searching.

"No doubt they'll make a proper jongleur's tale of it all," Robyn said, eyes not leaving their scrutiny down the length of his dagger. "It's already over the shire how Sir Guy of Gisbourne donned himself a *capull*-hide on Samhain and lost his head a-hunting the outlaw Robyn Hood. I find meself wond'rin' . . . shall they be mentioning how a Templar ended up with his arse tied to a tree?"

"You're assuming," Guy ventured, "that either of us lives to hear any tale."

"You're a rare opponent, I'll give you that." The black eyes met his. "Tell me, Templar, were you truly so ignorant of the tup?"

"The . . . tup." Surely the man wasn't talking about what it sounded like.

Robyn snorted. "Nay, an' that's wishful thinking—not *that* kind o' tup. The Hob's horse. Though your mask were more t' *mari lwyd*, the grey skull fit for Samhain, t' bid the light's waning and th' gleaning of souls, seeding whispers of a comin' year." One black eyebrow crept upward. "Certainly 'tis a fine ballsy tupper of a stud who can sneak up on the King Stag in full moonlight."

Robyn's voice had deepened, but it still commingled the lilt of the west Marches and the drawling purl of Yorkshire . . . and could put more sly and prurient innuendo into a comment than anyone Guy had ever known. Including Much.

And bloody hell, but Much didn't even know where to find him did he disappear, though he'd know *whom* to hunt. *Don't come after me, old friend. This old. . . "friend" will likely kill you without a qualm.*

"Why did you let me live?" Guy countered. There were a thousand meanings underlying the simple question, yet all of them leading to the one, unacceptable vulnerability: *Did you know? Know it was me?*

As impossible a question as the one Guy almost immediately asked himself: *And if* I'd known Robyn Hood was... you?

"Tweren't your time." Robyn shrugged.

"And you know... 'my time'."

A smile, quick and feral, accompanying another scrape of steel against whetstone. "Some things I ken, some I don't. You've gained a bit o' knowledge yourself, since last our paths crossed."

"I'd little choice in the learning." It was not what he would have elected to say, but words were all tangling at the root of his tongue and, in the process, useless.

"Aye, 'twould be a nobleman, to speak of choices in this world as rights we all could claim."

That sounded more like Rob. Only this was not Rob, not anymore. No more than Guy himself was still Gamelyn. Or maybe more had been left of Gamelyn than he'd thought, for one thought troubled—and in the trouble, unfamiliar. Odd.

Guy de Gisbourne *would* have killed Robyn Hood without the least compunction, would have not known the truth until a boyhood lover lay dead by his hand. Robyn Hood, on the other hand, had known who Guy de Gisbourne was—that much was obvious—and still would have killed him. Still might kill him. So what did that suggest?

Did you know?

What Rob... *Robyn*... knew? Guy didn't possess the key to his own thoughts at present, let alone the means to parse a brassed-off sodomite Heathen of a wolfshead. Assuming he was still a sodomite.

Of course he was. Guy felt a fiendish, thwarted desire to laugh. After all, the whore had told him, hadn't she, when he had suggested Robyn Hood fancied her? Even the Lady...

You were laughing at me, too, he snarled inward.

Again, She remained silent.

Because your tynged *is Mine to decide*, another Voice growled, soft thunder. Over by the altar, a faint glimmer formed, horns and hide the colour of crème. *You have come, of your own will, to the appointed place. To Her womb, to meet My justice.*

Guy blinked against the wet framing his eyelashes, and it faded into nothingness.

Meanwhile, satisfied with his blade-work, Robyn Hood had taken up the hair cord-*cum*-garrotte and...

Putain de merde, was he actually tying his own hair back with it?

"And here I thought 'twere vanity, those pretty braids in your hair." One side of Robyn's mouth quivered and tucked itself, mocking. "Does it do t' job, then?"

Mayhap then, *this* was penance. Absolution no god, no mentor, no pain could give. Death at the hands of the one he'd inadvertently betrayed. The amusing part?—there had been a time he'd *begged* for it.

No more. Guy wasn't sure he wanted absolution, not like this. Wasn't sure he was entirely pleased to see the dead brought back to life and intent on slaughtering him, however deserved. Wasn't sure of *anything*. He had grown so accustomed to a lack of response that he wasn't sure exactly what this—this sensation, this feeling, this . . . need?—was.

Frankly, the only thing Guy knew for sure? He was thoroughly and nauseatingly buggered.

With a shrug, Robyn pulled the tie from his hair, threaded it back over Guy's sword hilt and gained his feet. The lithe, animal grace had only intensified with maturity. The boy had been occasionally clumsy—the man, not at all so. Guy found himself wondering if it had all been a set-up: from traitorous villein to ring stones. This bore no resemblance to the hunched, uncertain individual who had entered the stone circle.

"How long did you know I was here?"

Robyn peered at Guy, tucking the dagger against his forearm. "Long enough." Which gave no answer.

It was starting to rain harder. Though the oak offered some shelter from the worst of it, they were both wet, getting wetter. Still, Robyn didn't redon his hood, his black locks drawing up into ringlets, forelock dripping tiny runnels of moisture onto his cheekbones, tracing thin pinkish streaks where Guy's sword tip had cut the hood and, it seemed, Robyn's nose and lip. The rest of his hair, longer than Guy had ever seen it, clung in spidery strands to a carelessly laced tunic. That tunic, indeed thin, slicked in spots nigh transparent to pale skin and long, tensile muscles—and those muscles made it obvious he could pull that monster of a longbow. The forearm cradling the quillion dagger was brown, also tensile with muscle. He was shivering, his breath steaming in the chill. Animal . . . Guy had used it in contempt, and yes, Robyn bided nearly that, antithesis and turnabout of everything civilisation stood for be it foul *or* wholesome.

Truly, this indeed made some hellish and raving lunacy to stumble into. That he should be looking the possibility of death in the face, yet want nothing more than to shag it stupid . . .

The black eyes were still peering at him. They seemed... curious. "Tell me, Templar. Managing t' faff your way into th' fête were no easy task. We've become proper careful. But *this*." A gesture, encompassing the stones behind them. "Who'd you maim, kill or threaten with interdict to find me *here*? 'Tis no little secret, me coming here to honour my dead."

Suddenly, the hunched uncertainty took on new meaning. The low voice held little emotion; it was unnecessary. The emotion hung there, between them, edged.

Instead Guy focused on the realisation: this hadn't been a trap. "All it takes is finding the pattern," Guy replied, soft. He knew he should keep silent—he was, after all, a prisoner—but he couldn't stop the words any more than he could stop watching Rob... *Robyn*. And all the while, told himself 'twas merely sensible—this animal could turn and rend. "The one tiny habit within random chaos—that's the objective. And secrets?" He shrugged. "The more careful a secret, the more it betrays."

"Fancy that. But then you'd know all about betrayal, aye?"

The closest either of them had dared to dance to *that*, and why did Guy feel outrage? He hadn't *any* rights to be outraged, but he was, and it answered for him, just as venomous.

"Not as much as you know about playing games."

Robyn's nostrils flared. Then he smiled.

It was not a pleasant expression.

"You'd rather not talk games?" Guy sneered. "Then shall we talk about enemies? You've just as many who'd pocket the substantial price on your head as you've zealots who'd sing hosannas to your infamous and sinister bow-arm. Or do you think you're above brassing people off?"

"*I'm* no' the one wearing monk's clothes." Robyn's eyes glittered. "Who told you, Templar? Who desecrated *my* church?"

"*Your* church?"

"These stones and t' Shire Wode are as close to any holy place as we need or want, and your people would destroy it. Aye, 'tis my *church*, by any words you'd ken. My *forest*—"

"Your forest. Our king might have something to say about that," Guy ventured, deceptively mild.

"*Our* king?" Robyn stalked closer. "That one's off fighting wars with *your* lot. All of you, pissing on each other's legs, scrappin' like dogs over a bitch in heat, and all the while what Motherless scum *our king's* left to hold the laws use those laws t' bleed my people white, rape them bloody, and burn their homes!"

Again, dancing too close to what neither of them would say.

Had Robyn taken up one of Guy's shivs and thrust it home, it might give less pain.

"When I was there, I prayed for you," Guy said, quietly. Not exactly what he'd meant to say, and while he expected a reaction, it wasn't quite the one he received.

The blow nearly took his head from his shoulders.

It was mildly satisfying to see Robyn grimace and shake his bandaged hand. Guy gave his head its own shake, clearing away sparks and stars, tongued his lip. "You've been practicing."

"Aye. With your face on th' clout." Suddenly Robyn leaned close, murmured, "Don't waste your breath, pet. Or your babblings to your god." Then he reached up, knuckled the trickle of blood from Guy's mouth.

First the slap, and then the kiss . . .

Abruptly, it was all Guy could do to not lean into the touch and purr.

No. Oh, God, *no.*

He pulled away, as far as the thong about his neck would allow. "I didn't mean it quite the way you're thinking."

"And you surely know what I'm thinkin'." Robyn shrugged and turned away. Guy watched him start to pace, thoughts racing. Chaos. Unbearable . . .

I hate you. What you can still do to me. What you make of me. . . Christ, I wish you'd stayed dead! Better that than. . . this.

"You'd do well to let me go."

Robyn gave an incredulous snort. "Chance'd be a fine thing!"

"You must know I'm not alone. My man will expect my return—"

"And *my* men'll be coming, another hour t' most. We're shifting camp again, thought 'twould be easier to just go on from here. We've been on the move a lot, lately. I hear tell," Robyn shot a sideways glance at Guy, "some mercenary scum is hunting us. A Templar with a proper reputation. They say he's a cold-blooded sod. More weapon than man. Rumour has, he came back from the Holy Land and got bored when he'd no one left to butcher for his god—"

"You have no idea what happened there, or what war is like!" Guy snarled back, was immediately furious for rising to the obvious bait as Robyn smirked.

"What d'you fancy you've walked into the middle of?" He was still pacing, back and forth, barely contained as any caged beast. "Enemies. You've no idea what enemies I have, but still you make yourself into one of 'em, use what rights you once had to prance into the place *your* kin sowed with the burnt corpses of mine. This is my forest, Guy of Gisbourne. Mine. You've profaned my place, and if you've the sense your god would give a toad, you'd best start praying for y'rself, for you'll be answerin' t' *mine*, now."

Again, Guy saw it, shrouded in the fog that clung to the surrounding trees. An ivory spectre by the altar, waiting as the stalking, hot-eyed King of His Shire Wode pronounced sentence. Horns gleamed, wet with rain . . . then wet with blood as the man-creature knelt on the rock and rubbed his antlers into the blood— Robyn's blood—pooling on the altar.

Fear runnelled heat from Guy's damp scalp and down his spine, drawing up his groin and haunches, humiliating as the fear-release of urine upon one's first battleground.

It took refuge in fury. "So I'm to just *let* you and your pack of thieving bastards cut my throat?"

"I'm no' sure I wain't be better paid cutting your throat."

"Filthy *wolfshead—*!"

It cut off into a gurgle as Robyn spun, took him by the throat. Leaned close.

"An' so y' keep callin' me. *Guy*." A whisper—a caress, almost. The sloe eyes went lazily half-mast, yet seemed to look through Guy, sparks flaring beneath the soot of lowered lashes, as if Robyn saw through skin and bone, could read his thoughts. Then Robyn raised that too-familiar quillion dagger and laid it against Guy's jugular, tightened his fingers against Guy's windpipe, breathed in his ear. "Say it again. *Please*."

No fear, Gamelyn. . . It came stealing out of the past, a lesson he thought well learned and done. *Fear does y' no good. You show throat, they'll only sense it, and then you're nowt to 'em.* A sloe-eyed companion teaching him the stalk. Another voice. Another boy. Another *life*.

It seemed forever they were there, held in some stasis of body and mind. So close—*too close*—with Robyn's breath sending shivers down his nape, and Robyn's hard, callused hand beginning to relax its stronghold on his throat, letting Guy suck in small, urgent quavers of breath. But when Guy thought to move, ever so slight, the dagger bit, a warning sting of blade and blood.

"Bide still, now. I might be so overcome by your nearness after all these years that me hand would slip," Robyn murmured, still soft. "My god wants you dead, *Templar*. What does yours want?"

"We're not," Guy gritted out, "exactly on speaking terms."

The dark eyebrows arched even higher. "Truly? Aye, well, that should make this fair interesting."

"*Int*erest—"

"Yours has abandoned you, and mine have taken me by the throat. It's not just the Horned Lord, you see. It's Her. Any gift of flesh taken by Him is graced by the Lady's breath. This," Robyn jerked his head towards the stones, "place is Her circle, Her womb. Blood is what She knows, better than any of us, birth to death." The mellifluous voice turned, an edge steely as the blade at Guy's throat. "I'd give you to Her right now, and who t' say I were unjust? Cry your innocence ower Loxley to the bloody stars, but what came of it? How many of my people have you terrorised? How many peasants have you killed on your little self-indulgent road to salvation?"

"And you?" Guy spat back. "What's *your* body count, Robyn Hood? What arrows have you loosed with Loxley's mark upon them? What vengeance have *you* wrought? How many unarmed monks have you ambushed? How many soldiers have you shot in the back? And those men—surely some of them had families, *lovers*." The black eyes flickered—perhaps Guy was getting to him, after all. Or perhaps it was the way the rain had started to fall harder, misting their breath into yet more camouflage, more smoke to foul any mirrors. "What about the man you left in his blood behind the Underkeep, the brother of that whore you seemed so fond of?"

"You mean Meg?" The feral gloss returned to Robyn's eyes once more. "The woman whose throat *you* slit? She had a *name*, Gisbourne."

"*Untie* me!"

"Why, so you can slit *my* throat?"

"So I can die a man, at least, and not be shot in the back or have *my* throat cut like a common thief!"

"Aye, the worse sin would be to do owt like a commoner, would it?" Robyn leaned back in, though his fingers didn't resume their choke hold. "Your definition of sin has changed, somewhat. *Monk*."

Rage quivered, demanding release. The bastard. The filthy whoreson of a *bastard*.

"Untie me *now*."

"Don't give me orders, Gisbourne." A snarl.

"You have no—"

"Shut the bloody fuck up. *Gamelyn*."

It was as if he'd been punched in the gut. It was mortifying, but Guy could literally not make even a sound.

"Aye, well then, you've a name too, don't you?"

The bastard was laughing. *Laughing,* behind those velvet-dark eyes.

"And it's mine, now. You're in my kingdom." The snarl slid into a smile. "*You* belong to *me,* here."

"You have finally gone round the twist!" Guy rasped. "You're *insane.*"

"Fancy that," Robyn said, still smiling. "You've been trailing after insanity for all these years. I'm thinking you've finally caught it up."

The fingers still wrapped about Guy's throat moved, didn't soften, not one whit, but slid to curl around Guy's nape. They tangled in his hair, tightened then gave a brutal yank, scraping Guy's skull against the oak. Guy looked down his nose at Robyn, a snarl quivering at his lip. Robyn merely leaned into him, closer still, and the breath fluting from his nostrils heated Guy's rain-slicked cheeks. The black eyes were pinned to Guy's own, so steadily that Guy could nigh see the reflection of his own, wide and shocked and furious.

Then Robyn closed his eyes and put his lips to Guy's forehead. It started as a mere brush, barely a caress, but Robyn lingered there, mouth giving a tiny, rain-slick slide toward Guy's temple.

Inconceivable. Unbearable. And so *close* . . . the fingers on Guy's nape tremoring, slight, and the touch against his brow seemed to whisper . . . *something*—a familiarity a young, ginger-haired naïf would recognise, yet one a soulless, Temple magician's weapon could not begin to comprehend. Nevertheless, the breath vacated Guy's lungs with a devastating thump and hitch, and when Robyn pulled back, away, Guy could only stare, twitching and trying to take his breath back.

It stirred, again: that deep penetrative *not-sound* hanging about him, hot breath and cold talons, tines glinting in the night, slick with blood, as slick as the sweat and blood beading in the dark stubble on Robyn's upper lip, as the glimmer in ebon eyes, and behind it, *pain,* a pain to wrench the stars from a clear night sky.

Kill me. Now. Death is preferable to—

"*Anadl tynged,*" Robyn murmured, and the band denying Guy any source of air seemed to snap with the words, the not-sound behind his ears dipping lower. Expectant. Again, a smile quirked at Robyn's mouth; again, it was not a pleasant one. He raised the quillion dagger between them. "Aye, take my breath, my Summer-lord, and I'll have yours, though we'll *both* choke on it. For there's no choice left to us, no dance but the last one, no Maiden to gi' us balance in the game."

Every shred of sanity Guy possessed ricocheted inside his skull; it focused on that last, all savage desperation and little sense. Game. *Maiden.* Was it all some vengeful game? All of it, hanging over him, bringing him back to this place and these demons—and had Marion been part of it, somehow?

Ask him, the Lady whispered at his shoulder, and Her sudden presence from the silence no demon but an angel, Her wings a faint susurrus in the wind and rain. *Ask the King of the sweet Shire Wode of his Maiden fair.*

"All the time . . . you knew. *She* knew."

Robyn's brow furrowed. "She."

"The Lady. *Marion.* Did you *know?*" It came out a strangled cry, spittle flying. "Because if you did I swear I'll—"

It made Robyn rear back, even if slight. "And you say *I'm* mad? What in bloody sodding hell are you *on* about?"

Guy started laughing, then; he couldn't help it. Here was this ghost prancing about in the forest wearing gilded antlers and a hood and bloody well knowing . . . knowing *everything.*

"Was it worth it? Your little game, you and your god? No games, you said then, you 'don't play games with your heart' . . . "

Robyn's eyes widened, white in the dim.

"*Fuck* you bloody, you black-hearted, lying whoreson of a peasant! Your god wants me dead and sings to me of betrayal and lust and death while *you* flirt with it, play me like a poppet on tattered strings and all the while . . . and all the while *your sister*, is she nothing but a pawn in this game of y—uh!"

Choking Guy silent, Robyn's hand once again turned to iron. "My sister. What about my sister?"

Guy tried to speak, could not, settled for glaring.

Robyn shook his head, leaned forward. "What could you know about my sister, other than your kin took her from me! Took her as they murdered me mum and da, lopped *their* heads off and I only hope they were dead before 'twere done. And Marion . . . I tried, but I couldn't save her in time. They left us all for dead, half the bodies unrecognisable, or so they told me. I were dying and the last things I saw were you, then her, lying there. Left for dead as they left me . . . " He trailed off. Backed off.

"Marion?" A hoarse, raw whisper. "*Marion.*"

Guy stared at him, air—and sudden sanity—returning. "You . . . *didn't* know she was . . . alive."

As Guy voiced it, Robyn stumbled back several steps. His eyes had gone from mad sparks to a flat, empty void. He looked as if someone had just walked up and stabbed him: the same, empty disbelief, the weakening knees, the colour draining from his cheeks.

Guy knew, all too intimately, what it looked like.

"Nay." Another whisper. "Should I, then?"

A sting at Guy's throat and a gag betrayed his lean forward, as surely as a wrench upon his wrists betrayed how he'd tried to reach out. Utter madness that he should, as inconceivable as what he next said, and why.

"You weren't to know."

"Yet I knew of you." Robyn's words were quiet, too considering. Puzzled, even as his speech thickened and tangled in on itself. He took another few and staggering steps of retreat; he bent over, propping against his thighs as if he was going to vomit. With some effort he straightened once again, but seemed . . . enervated, as if every bit of tensile grace and spirit bled from him. "I felt you from th' time you returned. *In* me, in m' blood, rushing and halting and there . . . I didn't want you there. Nay, didn't want what you'd become, a taunt behind me eyes when t' memories would come like firescorch."

It should not have mattered. The words should not have even scratched the surface of Guy's well-polished carapace.

But they did.

"She's me *sister.*" Robyn's voice, so bewildered-calm, began to tighten and fray. "Blood, heart, breath—I gave it all to her. I knew 'twere over. I knew they were set on killin' me and I hoped I'd at least give her th' chance . . . before I died. And when it were over, when I walked t' otherworld and felt her there beside me . . . then she were gone and all that brought me back were finding you, taking you back with me." He shook his head, as if to break the rising fury in his voice. "But I woke to . . . nowt. Both of you, *gone.* I felt it in me bones: you were lost and she were dead. Only you came back . . . and I knew . . . and how didn't I know she were still *alive?*"

"How could you know? You're not God, Robyn—"

Those eyes rose to meet his, snapped into hectic, obsidian brilliance. "Oh, but I *am.* You are. Don't you see, all of us can be gods, *are* gods. We create. We destroy. We deal death in ways'd sicken any sane man, and we bring life into a world *we've shaped* into horrors t' rival any hell or heaven our sick, twisted brains can fathom."

Guy started to speak, found himself struck mute as Robyn glided over to him, an all-too-familiar mockery touching his lips. He raised his hands, placed them light to Guy's shoulders, trailed downward to his chest. Halted there. Clenched bow-hardened fingers into Guy's tabard, twisting crimson into black, flesh straining white.

"We even create our own truths, don't we?" Another hoarse whisper.

What is truth, Gamelyn?

And Guy couldn't bid it silent, not this time. Not this time.

"Your god didn't create people; people have created him—and look t' what you've created, o Templar. Look t' me. You want justice and order—you'll make it happen, wain't you? Even if you have to hack my head off to see it done."

"I think," Guy gritted out, "you need to look in a glass for that."

Robyn laughed at him. *Laughed.* "Glass? I'm looking at one, right now. Look at what we've made of ourselves. Of *each other*. Our gods made you my rival, and I would have made you my lover, and you would have of me a memory. The Lady would have me Her sacrifice, and the Horned Lord you, and *tynged* would have us twin sons suckled by different dams and fighting back to back with our Maiden. Only it's all gone wrong, en't it? Because what world could ever exist that I wain't want *her* in? My *sister*, Templar."

"It's not—"

"Likely the same world where you're a monster killin' for your Christ, or where there's nowt left for me but killin' the woman who killed us all. Or seeing bled on m' god's own altar one who once ripped th' heart from me body and called it love."

What do you think you did to me?

It wouldn't voice itself. Couldn't: the habit of self-preservation lay too deeply entrenched.

The fingers clutched harder; Guy scarcely felt it. "*Where is she, Gisbourne?*"

"Untie me, and I'll tell you."

"Tell me"—the dagger whipped to his throat, quick as an adder's strike—"and I'll let you live."

"Bloody *damn!*"

The blade at Guy's throat jerked, stung. Robyn whirled. Surely neither of them should have let anyone sneak up on them. Yet Robyn didn't seem surprised.

There were five of them, dressed in assorted motley leathers, furs, and rags. Heavily armed, Guy noted, though only one of them bore a sword; most had well-used staves, knives at their belts, longbows strapped to their backs. One even had an axe.

"Bloody *damn*, Robyn!" This from a fair-haired, handsome

fellow, not so tall as Rob—Robyn—but made about two of him around. All of it muscle. Hero-type.

"Don't let us interrupt you," said the axe-wielder who, from the missing hand, was undoubtedly a poacher. Next to him, a slight figure pulled his cowl back and peered at Guy.

Surely Guy had been punched in the gut enough for one lifetime, let alone one day. The slight man was *John*. From Blyth. The same John whose absence he and Much had, a bare se'nnight before, bemoaned.

Is there anyone else you'd like to warn me of? Guy sent out into the void. Not that he expected an answer; therefore, disappointment was not rife when he received none.

John's brown eyes were wary upon Guy, unconvinced of anything wholesome connecting the man tied to the tree with the lad he'd helped escape Blyth's cellars. Indeed, John walked up right beside Robyn, gaze not once straying from Guy, and put a hand to Robyn's back.

It lay between them, unmistakable: *If you've hurt him again, I'll do you, son.* But then, John had never needed his voice to get a meaning across.

"It's him, en't it?" Another fair-haired man, thick-bearded and eldest of the lot save perhaps the poacher, taking in the crimson-and-black telltale of Guy's tabard. "Gisbourne. You caught the bloody-minded sod!" Part of the man's beard writhed, then slithered a serpentine over his shoulder and burrowed in, beady black eyes winking at Guy. A hunting ferret.

"Robyn's bested a Templar, by sweet fuckin' Christ!"

"How'd he find you?"

"Jaysus, Robyn, I told you. Told you 'tweren't a good idea, comin' here on y'r own—"

"He caught him, though, so may happen it was!"

"G'wan, I say," the poacher said, sneering at Guy. "Don' let us get in the way of you killing th' bastid."

All this time, Robyn had been taciturn, his attention flickering to each speaker. "We're going," he suddenly growled. "We've been here long enough." His eyes met Guy's, a blow. "Too long."

"You can't just leave him." This one had a mass of curly hair, but his brown beard was carefully trimmed; added to his sword and his voice, it all betrayed a former class status which none of the others possessed.

"You gettin' soft, Gilly?" the poacher retorted. "Leave 'im all right, y daft pillock. Food for th' wolves."

"We wain't kill him," Robyn said, but it was soft, and obviously only John heard, for John's hand clenched, and the soft-hard gaze went from Robyn, to Guy, then back again.

"And what if he escapes?" the hero-type pointed out. "Kill him, I say, and leave him for th' wolves *that* way. You let him go, and he and his kind'll hunt us over the earth."

God, but they nattered like crows—however did Robyn stand them?

"Nay!" Robyn burst out, white fury. "I tell you we *wain't* kill him!"

The others fell silent, obviously taken aback.

"Ransom, then?" the noble-born one—Gilly?—stated, as if a foregone conclusion.

"We'll decide anon," Robyn snapped. "Let's be off." He made a few curt hand signals and jerks of his head, then leaned over and pulled Guy's falchion from the ground, rested it carefully on one mail-padded shoulder. Watched.

There was no more nattering. A tense discipline fell over the small group and held, tighter than many knighted units Guy had seen in war. John and Gilly fanned out, scouting. The man with the ferret eyed the blooded bandage wrapping Robyn's palm, touched fingers to Robyn's bloodied nose and lip, cocking an eyebrow. Robyn gave a light shrug and wiped at it. Answering the shrug with one of his own, the man with the ferret extended an elbow toward Robyn; the little animal undulated down his arm, grabbed Robyn's hair, and burrowed in as if it were some old routine. Then Ferret-man produced a coarse sack from the carryall on his shoulders, began to gather up Guy's confiscated arms and bag them up with a care that bespoke appreciation for good weaponry.

The hero-type and the one-armed poacher flanked Guy and began to rearrange his bonds—also carefully. Guy didn't bother struggling; he knew it would be futile. He was compromised—not only by the tingling of blood-starved limbs but the ebon gaze, which never left him. Robyn watched from the sidelines as the two pulled Guy away from the oak, but not before they'd re-knotted every binding. His arms were bound behind his back, between his legs and up to his neck. His feet were shackled—enough to walk, but he'd pay hell running. The thin cord about his neck was fashioned into the worst of humiliations: an impromptu collar, complete with braided hemp leash.

And Robyn kept *watching*, wary and expectant and ... wounded.

Guy groped within himself, thumbed through his underused

lexicon of emotive ability for words—any word, any description—
of what that wary gaze made him feel. It should be triumph. It
should be smugness, or gratification. It should be bloody fury. Yet
all Guy could come up with?
Empty. Weary.
Lost.
As lost as the confusion behind Robyn's black eyes.
Names were power, indeed. The question: was it a power either
of them could manage to wield?

- XVI -

Names *are power*, he'd taunted, and then Gamelyn... Gisbourne... *Guy*... and oh, sweet *Lady*, who *was* he anyway but fury and hate and need and longing all thrown together and shaken, then sifted separate again? How could everything the Templar now was turn Robyn as widdershins as what Gamelyn had been, then?

Marion, alive.

Alive.

Robyn wanted to curl up on the altar and bleed himself out onto it... finished. Because he knew. *Knew.*

Had he died as he ought, perhaps none of it would have happened...

Writhing self-absorbed in guilt ill becomes you, my own. You did die. It was finished. Cernun brought Hob-Robyn back, but for Rob of Loxley, it was finished.

The Horned Lord's voice, for a wonder, sounded calm. Pragmatic, even.

You knew, you heartless sod, you knew!

The only heart I possess is in my possession of yours.

And if *that* wasn't fair nigh to a jab, Robyn didn't know what was.

Yet even then, gods cannot know everything. Particularly when thisworld *holds a* pwca *like to you.*

Robyn slapped his hands to his ears and refused to hear. For all the good it did him.

'Tis the Lady who holds the hem of your sister's spirit. She also has rooted the mighty Oak. She has played well, and you yourself set into motion things I never would dream.

She knew, then.

There is little She does not know. She is, after all, Mother of all things.

They'd nearly reached their next campsite. Woodland surrounded them, damp, muted-quiet from rain and fog. Robyn walked point, but John kept inching farther ahead, exchanging looks with the others. All of them knew their leader walked but half-aware.

Of course, they'd all come to some understanding of it by now. Part of the price of their success lay within Robyn's oft hag-ridden state, waking as well as sleeping. But their prisoner was not so blasé; more than once Robyn felt Gisbourne hesitate, felt that gaze—concerned? unlikely!—strafe him.

Aye, and Robyn felt *everything* when this was happening to him. *Stop* looking, *like you care or it matters t' the likes of you what's happening to me. Leave me alone. I hate you. I never want to see you again. I should have died that night, should have—*

Enough! the Horned Lord growled. *Had you died, your consorts would have been lost to us forever.*

You say't like you think they en't still *lost.*

They would have gone on, blinded by a light that would enslave and blind others. We would never have raised the Ceugant *into this world.*

I don't care. A silent whimper into the black. *I don't care, don't care!*

For the sake of all you were to each other, for all you could still be, you must care. They need you. Both of them, prisoned. Both of them jessed, hooded. You *are the Hooded One. They are not.*

So I'm the prisoner, then? And that's to be right.

You're the one who can bear the bindings.

Nay, I canna. Not this. Not anymore. Go away. Leave me be!

Meanwhile, their prisoner shuffled in his bonds—he could be heard a mile away. Robyn spun on Gisbourne, gratified by the stumbling halt and the slight buggy cast to his expression. "If you en't about t' walk quieter than that, *Templar,* how'd you survive being on Crusade?"

Beside Gisbourne, Will smirked and lifted his staff, hoping for some action.

"*Desert,*" Gisbourne pointed out, clipped. "Sand and scrub and flat pan. Neither was I tied like a mad dog!"

"Don' know how they do it in those barbaric places," Arthur sneered, "but we put mad dogs outta their misery, here."

"Barbaric." Gisbourne sneered right back. "You've no idea, you ignorant *poacher*."

Arthur hefted his axe. Will puffed up like a fighting cock.

Robyn growled, "*Enough.*"

The two obeyed, not without a glare each for their captive.

"Aye," Gilbert teased Will, "*you'll* be the one to carry the murdering sod, should you lay him out."

Will chuckled and put his staff back on his shoulder, giving it an "accidental" swing close to Gisbourne's head. Tied or not, Gisbourne's reflexes were prime: he dodged with a roll of his eyes.

Robyn wanted peace. Answers. Robyn wanted to reach out, wrap his calloused fingers about that arrogant Templar's neck, particularly wanted to press his thumbs into that one dark cluster of freckles upon Gisbourne's windpipe and squeeze until those juniper green eyes popped. Robyn wanted to wipe the sadistic smirks off his men's expressions, in particular to shove Will's face in the knowledge: 'twas the "poncy ginger paramour" they were dragging through the Shire Wode. Robyn wanted to turn, run through that self-same Shire Wode until his heart stuttered and seized and stopped. *Anything, anything, just make it bloody stop!*

None of those options were possible, so he kept walking.

The camp, scouted by Will—whose knowledge of this part of the Wode remained unmatched—was a particularly good one. The hollow lay shielded by brambles on one end—no way in there unless the trespasser possessed a remarkably tough hide—and a grove of wych elm and willow, the latter in particular betraying a plentiful water source.

Gilbert and David were the best at seeing to their comfort in camp; the others knew by now to get out of their way. Will, of course, had made much of tying "that Motherless clot Gisbourne" to a stout elm, and left Arthur standing guard. To do him credit, Gisbourne maintained a stone-hard composure despite when, after a few leering comments didn't get a rise, Arthur started sharpening his axe not an arm's reach away.

Robyn left them to it, climbed another elm and burrowed in to keep watch, knees to chest and back to trunk, staring off into the distance.

It wasn't much longer before John sent David—with little Tess tucked in his hood as normal—on to scout toward the nearest road, northeast of them, in this case. Robyn watched him go, sometimes just a wriggle in the green, other times a silhouette against a clear place, then lost sight of him.

David had already insisted upon seeing to the injuries Robyn had accrued during his struggle with Gisbourne. The cut on his face made a mere sting, but the hand had begun to swell up proper, with an unmerciful throbbing. Robyn would have to pack it fresh again tonight with some drawing paste. It should ease off soon enough, but for now he was fair crippled up. Considering their prisoner's abilities, Robyn supposed he'd gotten off lucky. Anyway, the throbbing in his palm took away other discomforts. Sodden from the morning's rain, Robyn's warming shivers were turning to shudders, and him up in the tree where the wind was most likely to chill him the more.

But he wasn't going down. Not likely, and not yet.

He started to question the wisdom of that a while later. He was feeling a distinct shade of icy blue. Pride didn't see fit to warming him up, nay, not in the least. A nice fire crackled below, and several furs warming by it, and . . .

A trill wafted through the trees, then the stuttering, harsh sound akin to a pheasant cock—recognisable to the outlaws as their own—and quickly followed by another trill. It seemed impossible, so soon into the territory, but there was game afoot on the road, and David was letting them know.

Below, Robyn's men had broken the lazy aftermath of making camp into an industry of gathering weapons and preparing for action.

"Robyn?" Will pitched his voice just loud enough to reach the treetop. "Shall we go on? With that hand, it's unlikely you'll be of use today."

At this point, Robyn was too miserable and conflicted to even mind a miss of the encounter. He nodded. "Your game, Will. I hope it's a few fat churchmen; little trouble save for whinging, and we'll need a bit of extra brass to feed our important visitor." Shooting a look through the branches, Robyn saw Gisbourne roll his eyes as Arthur flipped him a rude gesture. Robyn couldn't help but smirk, met Will's gaze and nodded reassurance. "I'll watch the Templar, make sure he wain't slip his tether. Off you go, then."

One by one, they vanished into the trees toward David's watch. Robyn didn't miss how John lagged behind. Still shivering, Robyn started downward.

"If it's a big lot, they'll need you, John," he said. "I'll warm myself and keep watch so you can go with them."

John waited until he came down, brows drawn together as he saw Robyn shivering.

Robyn's lips quirked. "All right, mama hen, gi' us a fur and be done with your fussing."

An answering quirk chased itself across John's lips as he snatched up a fur and tossed it at Robyn, who slung it around his shoulders and sighed. Toasty-warm. Bliss. Sometimes, Robyn considered, he were right sodding daft. A body needed some comfort, after all, even if the pain would often clear your head.

"John?" It was oddly hesitant. John turned as Gisbourne voiced it, gave Gisbourne a level look, one Robyn knew he himself would not fancy being on the other end of.

Was it . . . *remorse* that Robyn saw twist its way onto Gisbourne's face?

Nay, he couldn't believe that. Wouldn't. Such a path lay strewn with more dangers than he could imagine.

Liability. No god-voice taunting him, this; instead 'twere his own self-reproach. *You're the liability now, Robyn Hood. King of the Shire Wode, aye, you and your skinny arse! Just have a good long look in that reflective brass, for you're bein' taken down by t' Hob's other face.*

Gisbourne didn't speak again. He watched, silent, as Robyn came over to the fire. Not without an inner groan, Robyn shrugged from the fur and lowered to one knee, unlacing then shucking the sodden tunic. Gisbourne didn't stop watching as John knelt beside Robyn. Kept watching even as John kissed Robyn and ran one hand down his chest—always John did it as if he wanted to feel the quickening of Robyn's heart as they exchanged breath and caress. Just as Robyn always put a hand to John's throat to feel the same thing. Reaching for life, in the midst of a death always snapping at their heels.

Then John rose and followed the others into the trees. Gisbourne was *still* watching, with something resembling more a cool amusement than anything else. It made the hackles on Robyn's neck stiffen and quiver. Instead of striding over and giving the bloody damned Templar a bloody damned good clout in the jaw, Robyn gritted his teeth and focused on propping his wet tunic on sticks nigh to the fire. *Aye, well, me little John's here and you're not. Even now, you're not here. Even if you were. . . here. . . John would still be here. Sod you, nobleman.*

As if he'd heard, Gisbourne dropped his gaze.

"Where is she?" The query escaped Robyn, staccato and harsh.

Gisbourne didn't answer, still looking away.

Robyn held his hands to the fire. How could Marion be alive

and him not know it? Not be able, now he did know, to so much as reach out and touch her spirit . . . only perhaps he'd never developed the skill. What magic he'd been born with remained his by right and instinct and gift; what magic he had now had come with the doing and the honing of those innate abilities. So perhaps it was that simple: he'd never had to consider a time when Marion would be near but out of reach.

Where was she?

Hooded, steamed the reminder. *Prisoned.*

With Gamelyn . . . Guy . . . *Gisbourne,* Robyn reminded himself angrily . . . only nay, it had been Gamelyn whom young Hob-Robyn had loved and been petrified of losing. He had always known Gamelyn's presence as a chancy thing, and Robyn's instincts had honed to that inevitability, seeking sun in darkness.

Robyn *knew,* blood and bone and spirit, where Gamelyn lay, only he too was prisoned, smothered beneath the jessed and furious raptor that made up Guy. Was it madness to think his Summerlord still there, stark and withering without the sun?

"Where is my sister? Do you even know?"

Still no answer. Gisbourne's eyes kept sliding to him, then chasing away.

Robyn shook his head, held his hands over the fire. He was all prickles and gooseflesh, and much of it from inner, not outer, chill. He didn't like being in this place of not doing, forced to inaction when time and reality kept trying to slide from under him. He had to find his sister, and instead he kept barking all mad at the moon like a lonely wolf who'd lost his mate.

That mate was dead—*dead,* and a revenant walking with Gamelyn's body, breathing Gamelyn's breath, speaking with Gamelyn's tongue. Those green eyes were still smudged with gilt, but of more bitter frost than bright fire, mere hints of sunrising over an iced field. The ruddy hair was still smooth and thick, but lay longer than Robyn had ever seen it, edges bleached pale, as if the sun had runnelled copper from them and onto bronze-tinged skin. Gamelyn's skin would never not be freckled but was no longer so pale or smooth, his jaw hidden by more copper—a well-trimmed beard. The outlines of his body beneath chainmail and blooded cross still possessed more flesh than bone, grown from boy-softness into broad-hard aggression, with curves and angles that made Robyn's fingers tingle with the need to touch them.

And what was the sense of that, then? Like as not he'd draw back frozen stumps. Better still Robyn should hack his own hands off and never draw bow again than make the try.

This was not Gamelyn. This was a stranger, a killer. He had come from everything Robyn ever had rightful cause to hate and, while the lad would have turned away from those hated things, the man was drinking his fill. Had long ago pricked Robyn's heart with a lovely, poisoned bodkin, shrivelled it so that even John could never hold the full-blooded weight of it in his hands, and Robyn *loved* John.

Gamelyn was dead. Guy of Gisbourne had all but murdered Robyn's gentle-fierce boyhood lover, had truly become one with the race that had shackled Robyn's own. Aye, Gisbourne was a Hob all right—a hobhoulard, a quisling hob-thrush sent to fly a dart through the hob-robin's heart. Such a fetch needed nowt but killing.

But first, Robyn had to know where he could find Marion.

"Rob."

Nay. Don't call me that like you've t' right. Leave me alone. I hate you.

"Rob." Then, louder, "*Robyn.*"

A small and tender part of Robyn was shamed by the fact that here he stood, cut into a million pieces merely by what his enemy *said*. The rest of him threw back its head, snarled, said, "Are y' happy, then, to see you can hurt me? Only that's no news, is it, because you've always been right practised at it."

There were marks on Gisbourne's throat, scarlet stripes livid amidst the coppery freckles and beard—he'd been leaning against the thin binding—why?

"I didn't know," Robyn said. "Don't you understand, I didn't *know* she were still alive, and I should have."

"I didn't know *you* were still alive."

"An' if you had? Known?"

Gisbourne peered at him, then dropped his gaze to the fire. "There is no profit in 'what if.'"

"Profit." Even the sound of the word rang chill; it roped runaway feelings as if they were the feral fell ponies of David's homeland and latched tight, as unforgiving as the hemp cord about his rival's neck.

It would be so easy, to tighten that cord, to watch the Templar struggle for air, to take his last breath. Easier, in this moment, than kissing him and tasting it.

"I thought you might be coming after her. After Marion," Gisbourne said, and in his juniper-green eyes there flickered . . . sommat. Not flat. Not dead.

Neither did it make any sense. "Of course I'd've come for her!"

"I thought," Gisbourne said, soft, "you were someone else."

Again, layers upon layers beneath the quiet words. Robyn grappled with them, silently peering at Gisbourne. Normally he didn't overly contemplate what to feel, or how. Such things were what they were, passing through him like mist, piercing or covering then wafting aside.

In fact, the only times in his life when Robyn had been unsure of what to feel, and how, had been with Gamelyn. Gisbourne. Whoever the bloody sodding hell he was.

"I don't even know why I'm here, anymore," Gisbourne muttered. "It's all gone. Gone, and you aren't who I thought you were."

"Get in the queue, Templar."

"Neither is Marion."

"Neither is Marion, what?"

"She's not . . . who she was."

Robyn rose, stalked over. "What are you talking about, Gisbourne?"

"Look." Gisbourne shook his head, met Robyn's eyes. "She has no memory of . . ." Gisbourne jerked his head, grimaced as the injudicious movement bit the thin rope into his throat once again. "This. The Shire Wode. Her life."

Robyn kept shivering, a bone-deep, insistent tremor. He clenched his fists. "I don't understand."

"She didn't know me. She knows her name, but she doesn't know who she is. She doesn't remember anything about her life before." Gisbourne fell silent. His gaze chased out, fixed on the fire. "I don't think I did her any good, speaking to her. She seems . . . content. I should have left her alone, to . . ." He trailed away, frowning at Robyn. "You're cold."

"Not even half as cold as you, Gisbourne, if you're sayin' what I think you are."

Gisbourne closed his eyes, still frowning, and took in a sharp breath. "What do you think I'm saying, then?"

"I think what you'd be better off saying is where she is. Where I can find her."

A smile, bitter with no hint of sweet, and Gisbourne opened his eyes, peered at Robyn. "And what if she doesn't know you, either?"

If Gisbourne had his hands free to punch Robyn in the gut it would have been a softer blow. "I'm her *brother*."

"And you love her."

"What kind of question is—"

"And you love her so much you'll make her remember what we've been spending all this time wishing we could obliterate from our own minds." The green eyes looked more the opaque gaze of a serpent, no part of a human being. "Feel free to step in and contradict me if I'm wrong."

"Wrong or right, it's not yours t' say."

"I think, in this case, it just might be. Would it be so much better for her to remember all of it?"

"Better for her? Or better for *you*?"

Gisbourne frowned. "You don't really under—"

"Oh, I think I really do." Robyn leaned closer, still shivering, and said, all too quiet, "That's what *you'd* want. That's what *you're* all about."

"It's not so simple."

"Not simple, never simple when it's you, pet. But 'tis truth." And bloody *damn* but Robyn was freezing his nibs off.

"And what is truth, after all?" Gisbourne murmured, as if curious.

Robyn strode back over to the fire, snatched up a warming fur and swung it around his shoulders. "One thing's not changed, and that's *your* truth. It's much simpler, en't it, to live in your little world of right and wrong, killin' and savin'. Always, always lookin' for your little *Garden*, all the while terrified of what would happen did you find it."

"You don't under—"

"Don't tell me I don't understand!" Robyn shot back. "Don't tell me what I see or feel when you're so far away from it you'd not sense it did it bite you."

"Far? From what? Pain?"

Robyn barked a laugh. "Oh, aye."

"I've walked every deep-rutted cart path, knelt in purgatory and thought it Heaven, limped through every muddy, piss-stained, bloodied street in hell—"

"Fancy that," Robyn murmured. "Never t' once did I see you there."

The brief moment of response drained away, akin to cupping water in spread-fingered hands. Gisbourne leaned back against the tree, shook his head, again gave that odd little chuckle: not cheer, rue and poison instead of cheer.

"Where *is* she, Gisbourne?"

Gisbourne closed his eyes, said, "At this moment, I truly don't know. I saw her in Nottingham, before Samhain. She might still be there, she might not. If they took her back to the abbey—"

Robyn reared back like a spooked horse. "Abbey?"

"She's a novice nun."

Robyn's voice didn't want to work. His mind surely didn't want to process any of that, either.

A couple of nuns at the castle, Meg had said.

Robyn's teeth gritted in the silence. Gisbourne's eyes flickered to his.

"She's with the Abbess," Gisbourne said and yet again gave an empty chuckle. "I thought you were after Marion, and all this time, you were after the Abbess." It was matter-of-fact, only a slight quaver betraying any uncertainty—if uncertainty it was. "What *would* I have done, had I known?"

Robyn still couldn't speak.

"I suppose we could have drawn lots for the right to take the bitch down."

Oddly enough, this gave Robyn his breath back, and words to shape it. "She's mine, Templar. She owes me. My village. My family." *You,* he thought but did not say.

Gisbourne held his gaze. "My father's peace in his last days. My right to ever go home again. My faith in a good, just God." He hesitated, looked away then spoke again, eyes still opaque. "Marion. *You.*" He spoke the last word as if it held a foreign taste—not frightening, not humiliating, just . . . other. "All of it, gone."

It was its own force, pushing at Robyn's solar plexus—no blow, but firm, unyielding, and it sent him to stagger, just a step or two.

Gisbourne peered at the fire. "My man is guarding Marion. I've told him to kill anyone who tries to take her."

Again, it gave Robyn the wherewithal to reply. "He wain't stop me."

"I'd prefer you didn't kill him." A slight, rueful smirk. "It's Much."

Robyn lifted his chin, lip quivering in an impossible smile. *And sod the gods, look here at what is gatherin' in the sweet Shire Wode, bedded enemies all.*

"So you go after her anon." Gisbourne's voice sounded so . . . dispassionate. Considering. Again, he lowered his gaze. "And if you get through Much—which won't be easy, I'll tell you—what if Marion doesn't know you?"

That one hurt. "I'll take the chance," Robyn avowed.

The green eyes rose, no longer so opaque. "Have you ever tried to get into a castle? Nottingham has been neglected, true, but it's still one of the best fortresses in the shire. The guards are overworked and underpaid, but word is, Count John is coming for a visit. They'll be on their toes, if they want to keep their heads, and they'll catch you, Robyn."

"Then *take* me there." Robyn hadn't even considered it until he spoke, but as he did, *tynged* rippled past his vision in unfrayed agreement.

Gisbourne blinked.

"That's why you're here, en't it?" Robyn paced close, searched those flat eyes for something . . . *anything*. "To bring in Robyn Hood. Dead would be fine. But alive would be better, wouldn't it?"

Gisbourne peered back at him, silent for long moments. Then, "You're mad. I'm in hell, and there's a mad wolfshead in it."

Robyn threw back his head, barked a sudden, shocked laugh. He just as quickly sobered, propped a hand on the tree above Gisbourne's shoulder and leaned in, their noses almost touching. "Take me, then."

A tilt of the ruddy head, then Gisbourne tucked his beard toward his chest—evasion or aversion?—and mused, "Mayhap that's not quite the statement you should make, standing nigh on my boot toes and stripped from your tunic. Last time you were bare-chested and had my arse against a tree, it ended up in more turmoil than either of us could bargain for." His eyes slid upwards. "Whatever will your men think?"

It made the spit draw tight in Robyn's mouth, made every nerve he had—that one, too, damn its eye!—stand at attention. "I know what my men think, most times," Robyn returned, low. "Time were, I could make out what you thought."

Gisbourne shook his head but, this time, didn't drop his gaze. "Don't go there, Robyn Hood. You won't like what you see."

"I've liked little of what I've seen so far, Guy of Gisbourne. 'Tis what I *don't* see that holds my thoughts."

Again, Gisbourne shook his head. "You can't—"

A sudden commotion wafted over their heads, bouncing and tossing from tree to tree. Shouts, the clang of steel, the buzzing of not only bows but crossbows loosing—the latter a sharper, more high-pitched noise.

"Bloody *damn*." Robyn shoved away, nerves twining further taut. "What—"

A few more shouts, then silence. Robyn twisted his hair into a knot, snagged up his bow and quiver, and slid a few arrows into the knot. Painful hand, perhaps, but if he could get the bloody bow at least strung, then . . .

He stopped, his eyes meeting Gisbourne's. With a frown, Robyn cocked his head to one side and let the longbow slide through his good hand to rest on his boot. "I don't suppose you'll just wait for me, should I leave you on your own."

Gisbourne took in a breath, released it. "I don't suppose you're enough of a fool to find out. Even if you are daft enough to go into a live-steel fight with no tunic."

Robyn leaned on the bow. "And so me mam's people did. Naked and painted indigo. They also knew when to let their mates take the fight." With a shrug, he lowered his weapons to the ground. "I'd chin any of my lads who left a dangerous sod as yourself on his own just to have a chance at a good row."

And he was cold again. Picking up the fur, Robyn slung it over his shoulders, grimaced as it caught on the arrows still stuck in his hair. He unknotted them, slid them into his quiver.

"You still . . . do that."

"Eh?"

"Put arrows." Gisbourne seemed puzzled. "In your hair."

"No doubt they'll bury me with 'em." Robyn eyed Gisbourne, said, sceptically, "Do captive Templars eat?"

"They do. If—" Gisbourne shrugged, odd puzzlement retreating "—they're offered food."

- XVII -

A troublesome procession trailed into camp, just about the time Robyn began to study the nearly ready stew, debating whether or not to go after them. Will was limping and swearing, leaning heavily on Arthur. David, Gilbert, and John all ringed a figure who, despite a slender build and average height, had been bound with the same extremity of attention with which they had treated Gisbourne. Some boy, perhaps—a ransom?

Robyn lurched to his feet. "What in bloody . . . Will?"

Will was cursing, not so softly, but a smirk twitched at Arthur's lip as he jerked his head toward their prisoner. "That'un nailed him proper."

The wound was plainly not serious, or Arthur wouldn't be trying—and failing—to hide the grin in his voice. Nor would Will have the wherewithal to give his leaning post a whack on the head. As he did, Robyn saw where the arrow was—the middle of Will's right arse cheek.

Robyn bit his lip, refused to smile.

"Aye," Arthur nodded, as if kenning Robyn's thought. Then he snorted. Even the others, guarding the new arrival, seemed to think the situation less than serious.

"*That'un* nearly nailed *all* of us!" Will protested, with another smack at Arthur's pate. He swore as the movement twisted at the lodged arrow, consented to let Arthur and Robyn help him to lie on his side by the fire. Robyn checked the wound with a practiced eye; the arrow had hit glancing, thank the Lady's grace, and had pierced right through. The bodkin was a fierce one, pronged, and thankfully wouldn't have to be dug out.

David, John, and Gilbert were still ringing their newest visitor. Whoever-he-was had skin as dark as the flank of a wintering hart. Likely dark-haired, then, but an intricately wound cloth hid that, one matching the wheat-coloured tunic and bloused braes tucked into short boots. The garb seemed just slightly off centre of normal, the cut of it hanging differently, the fabrics edged with costly colours. John held a hide belt with a fine dagger, and a strange-looking shortbow with a quiver of arrows, ones matching the dart in Will's bum. All of it odd, quality accoutrements.

Definitely a prize to ransom, then.

And not a lad, Robyn realised as the prisoner's soot-lined eyes rose to meet his. Not only those painted eyes; a closer look revealed a definite curve of breast and hip beneath the loose, bloused-out tunic. The woman—girl?—how old was she, anyway?—gave him a straight-up inspection that held little trepidation.

The timbre of her voice gave her sex further away, as she let out a burst of speech that in no way sounded familiar, curling and tumbling from her lips. When her captors merely stared at her, uncomprehending, she threw her bound hands in the air and peered about. Her gaze fell on the wych elm to which they had bound Gisbourne, and widened. Gisbourne's closed expression had given way to an odd frown.

"So," Robyn said, curious, as woman eyed Templar. "What's the story?"

"Four travellers, three men and this one," Gilbert said.

"Only four, and you fetched y'rself shot?" Robyn slid a look to Will.

"I en't seen a girl shoot t' like since Marion!" Will protested.

Marion. It sank talons down deep, shook Robyn. *Alive. She's alive, and Will doesn't know. He needs to know.*

Not now. Robyn couldn't think on it now.

Maybe he should take lessons in denial from Gisbourne. Who was still staring at the girl like he knew her, or something.

"The men refused to give in," Gilbert put in. "One of them was dressed sort of like her. The others were soldiers, but . . . different. Will's right. They all fought like bloody mercenaries. Her, too. David nearly had her once, and he might be the best amongst us with the wrestling, but the bint did some weird trick and landed him on his arse. When she finally strung her bow, the wind was all kept spoiling her shots."

"Assuming she weren't *aimin'* for Will's arse," Robyn said, and smirked at him. "Y' should've opened up your tunic a wee bit more. I hear lasses fancy th' like."

"The only way you'd know is by hearing!" Will growled into the furs, gave Robyn the archer's salute—two fingers, straight up, of "sod you." Then Will gave a yip; David had left guard duty to bend down and inspect the wound. Tess—none the worse for wear—was chattering at both David and Will, all the world like some bossy ferret wortwife.

Aye, their big lad wasn't going to live this down for a while.

"Twasn't until John popped her bowstring with his knife and we'd taken out the others that she gave up," Gilbert added.

"I've not seen the like of them on our roads, for sure." David rose, going over to the hollow log where he'd stowed their bag of medicaments. "Bloody tough, they were, and th' lass fighting like a brassed-off Kintail wildcat."

John shrugged several pouches from off one shoulder. They were filled, and one clinked with the sound of marks—or weaponry. The woman let out a torrent of sound in his direction.

"So, girl." Robyn stepped closer, and her dark eyes riveted back to him, turned wary. "What am I to do with you, then?"

She shook her head, shot more of the strange, tangled language at him. It didn't seem friendly, whatever it was.

Robyn spread his hands, shrugged at her, said, quite deliberate, "I . . . don't . . . understand you."

"Christ's blood!" Gisbourne's voice sounded, clearly exasperated, from across the fire. "As if merely speaking slower and louder is going to make her comprehend a language she doesn't know!"

"Who asked you?" Arthur snarled.

Robyn peered sideways at Gisbourne.

"She says," Gisbourne said, eyeing Robyn, "that the pouches you have taken are hers, since you killed their original owners."

"Oh are they, then?" Gilbert snorted. "Cheeky!"

Robyn glanced at Gilbert, then turned his attention once more to Gisbourne. "You understand her talk?"

"I understand Arabic, Turkish, some Berber and Persian. She happens to be speaking Arabic."

"Poncy git!" Will scoffed, then swore as David, medicaments out, started sawing at the arrow's shaft just below the barb. Robyn was tempted to agree with Will.

On the other hand . . .

"Can you talk to 'er, then?"

Gisbourne shrugged, then threw a few words toward the woman. Or at least, Robyn considered, they must have been words, though not anything the like of which he'd ever heard.

The woman's dark brows drew together, clearly considering. Then she answered. After a pause, Gisbourne replied.

And oh, bloody *damn* but Robyn made a rampant daft pillock twice over, with a particular emphasis on the rampant, as the thought came to his mind on what an agile tongue it must take to speak those syllables. And the soft quaver to Gamelyn's . . . Gisbourne's voice as he did speak . . .

Stop it. Die. Now.

"Robyn," Gilbert was frowning. "How do we know they aren't plotting something?"

Robyn shrugged. "We don't." He pitched his words to Gisbourne without looking at him—wasn't about to look at him, not right now. "Tell her if she'll stop pricking bodkins through our arses, she can share a meal with us. In fact . . . " He took the dagger from his belt, walked over to her. She tottered back a few steps, halted when Gisbourne quickly said something else. But she looked like a deer stilled by a wolf's advance; she stuck out her chin as if to deny it as Robyn took up her bound wrists.

Blinked, startled, as Robyn exchanged a glance with both men flanking her—Gilbert beside, and John behind—then cut the rope. She kept rubbing at her wrists as Robyn walked over to the fire and took up a bowl and a skin of water. Pouring water into the bowl, he brought it over to her. "Y' must be thirsty, lass. Have a drink, then sit by our fire. Maybe 'twixt your Templar friend, there, and a meal, we can find out what and who you are."

The dark-lined eyes blinked again. A small smile stretched her mouth, but she didn't reach for the water. Robyn put the bowl to his mouth, took a sip, offered again with a slight dip of his head. "See? Water. 'Tis safe."

The woman shot a bemused look over toward Gisbourne. This time Robyn did look over, convinced he'd committed some offence. But the quirk playing about Gisbourne's lips was not mocking. It seemed . . . admiring? He uttered a few more syllables of the wonderfully erotic-chaotic speech.

She nodded, then turned back to Robyn. "*Assalaam Alaikum,*" she said, slowly enough so the sounds were more akin to words than mere sounds. "*Na'am.*"

"She said," Gisbourne translated, "yes."

"All that for a little 'aye'?" Robyn asked.

"She also gave you a blessing."

"A . . . blessing."

"You gave her one, after all."

Then the woman smiled, took the bowl from Robyn, and took a long, deliberate drink.

☙

If he lived to his father's grand age of sixty-eight, Guy would never decipher why a certain peasant from Loxley should behave as he did.

No mere peasant, that one. Your Holly Lord is a riddle wrapped in a cipher, the Lady purred to him, as close as if She were sitting beside him.

He was still bound to the cursed tree whilst the Saracen female—who had shot one of them!—sat beside Robyn, using gestures to show him the finer points of her bow. At least they hadn't untied the woman's feet. And both the poacher and the hero-type—the latter lying on his side with his wound well dressed and antagonism sticking out of him like hedgehog prickles—were watching every move she made. They clearly were as gobsmacked by Robyn's actions as Guy.

The bow, a lovely and quality Turkish shortbow, had lighter filigrees on the dark-burnished wood, and curved supple as a young lad's upper lip. He could see why it fascinated Robyn, used to the deadly simplicity of a longbow. The possession of such a thing made the Saracen woman a bit of a riddle, herself. Granted, it was not unheard of, a beweaponed female in Saracen lands. Less rare, actually, than one in Christendom. And obviously, in Robyn's pedigree there were the Pictish queens and the likes of Boudicca; indeed, Guy's own dam-line could boast such. Nor could Guy forget the Queen Mother, Eleanor, who had ridden to Damascus and had a torrid affair with her uncle while wed to Louis of France—then had divorced Louis for love of an Angevin . . . if one forgot that she had spent much of her married life with King Henry locked away because she'd proven *too* powerful.

You're learning, She approved. *Your fascination with women, untutored though it is, remains part of what endears you to Me. Your rival respects us, loves us. But he does not have the requisite hungers. It is . . . irksome.*

Why didn't You tell me? he snarled back. *Had I known it was . . . him . . .*

I warned you, but it is My fault you did not see the full scope of My warning? Ah, little gadelyng—

And that appellation still had the power to set him snarling in a flat second.

—you and your leman seem to dance beneath the misapprehension that I and My Consort are obligated to you when it is, in fact, the other way around. Your precious Hob-Robyn would not be alive to torment you, had I not consented in his return to Abred, *thisworld.*

Guy found himself wondering if She thought him happy with the situation, but Her presence sucked through and away from him like a mistral, leaving him chill and, somehow, empty.

But not as empty as the glances Robyn kept giving Guy.

"I think"—the noble-bred was leaning over the cauldron, giving it a taste—"that Robyn has, for once, made a decent stewed rabbit."

"I cook fair enough!" Robyn protested.

"As long as it's venison," several of them said, almost by rote.

Robyn grinned, then rose. He motioned to the woman, who shot a look at Guy then shuffled after Robyn.

Why was she being so biddable? Was it much the same as Guy himself, just biding her time, waiting for her chance?

What was she doing here?

Robyn pointed to a pile of furs, well-padded with rushes and fell. "You can lie here, on my place. It'll be warmer, and I'll likely be keeping watch on . . . " Robyn trailed off as she stared at him, obviously wondering whatever he burbled on about. Robyn shrugged and turned to Guy.

"Can you help me, here? I want her to know she's a good place to sleep before we sit to eat."

And the Lady thought Guy "untutored." Robyn obviously hadn't spent enough time around women who weren't his sister or his mother or some nurturing wortwife type. Guy, meanwhile, didn't have to ask a single question, only watch the chary cant of the Saracen woman's eyes, gleaming with the firelight.

"You should know," Guy ventured, "straight up, she thinks you plan on bedding her."

The others started laughing.

Robyn's eyes went wide as saucers. "She thinks . . . bloody damn!" Robyn shook his head. "That en't what I meant!"

"Robyn's a brave man," the one with the ferret swore, fervent speech betraying him more of the wilds of Scotland than Yorkshire. "I would no' sleep with such a wildcat; she'd cut me bits off ere I slept."

"Tess would bite her for you." And with that, the noble-bred named the ferret, if not the ferret's owner, who gave her a scratch.

"I'd give her a go," the hero-type put in with a lift of brow.

"You'd give owt a go, Scathelock," Robyn snorted.

Warned the ferret man, "Best keep an eye to Tess; she's a lass, too."

"Hoy!" Hero-type protested. "I don't do things wi' four legs! No more'n I do things with *three*." He glowered at Robyn, who chuckled.

"Nay!" the noble-bred protested. "Will gets all the lasses . . . let me!"

It hit Guy, suddenly, who the hero-type was. Scathelock. Will. Robyn's childhood friend who'd been outlawed.

"Our little John en't put in his bid." The poacher gave a ruffle at John's hair; John repaid him with a wry, sideways frown that said, plain as plain: *You are joking, right?*

The Saracen woman clearly didn't care for the sound of any of it.

"Aye, that's enough!" Robyn snapped. "All of you. She's a guest, and a lone woman in a bunch o' men. Our mams would clip our ears, treatin' any woman so. She's a face of our Lady. We killed her protectors, so it falls to us."

Guy wasn't so sure the woman had needed those protectors. While the outlaws had discussed her disposition, one of her hands had dropped to the outseam of her breeks and the slight bulge of a thin knife. The outlaws had obviously missed one. Or, with the Heathen hearth-courtesy that Robyn seemed to demand, likely had left off body-searching her until they knew what was allowed.

Chivalrous, true, but unwise. A cornered female could prove more dangerous than anything on earth. If the woman knew how to use that knife—and Guy wagered she did—then she could have several of them bleeding and escape all too easily. Guy nodded. That was likely what she waited for.

"She'll stay hobbled," Robyn was clarifying, "'til we know what she's about, but none's t' share her furs 'less she asks you for it. Even then, you're taking a chance she'll slide a dirk in your belly as you're mounting her. So don't."

Or perhaps not so unwise. Guy's own relief at this reassurance of Robyn's sense . . . well, it made no sense. Other than being a thrall to one's anatomy was a weakness—and a likely fatal one.

So it was less than sensible—in fact, pure idiocy—how as he started to mutter a further reassurance to the woman, his hackles rose as he saw she once again eyed up Robyn. No longer wary, watching Robyn speak with that authoritative growl deep in his voice, it was plain she wasn't the least displeased with what she saw. Of course, she wouldn't be, would she? The lanky boy had matured into a very lovely man, and the power of that unbroken spirit running just below the surface had merely grown more . . . fascinating.

Inconceivable, where Guy's thoughts were wandering. Not just no, but blast and damn his soul to eternal hell, no.

Not a difficult decision, choosing which horns of the dilemma upon which to impale himself. "I would wager, Robyn Hood, you might get more than you bargained for if you share a bed with that one. She rather fancies you."

Again, his men found this far too amusing. Guy wasn't sure if he agreed.

Robyn backed off that like a well-trained destrier. "You like her so much, *you* bed her!"

"I didn't say I liked her. And my vows preclude—"

"Monks!" Robyn snorted, and it gave an odd twinge in Guy's chest. "Well, *monk*, tell her. Tell her I don't tup lasses." The black eyes cut Guy's way, then Robyn moved closer, murmured for Guy's ears alone, "Tell her what you should damn-well know yourself."

"Things . . . change." Guy turned, spoke to the woman, listened to her response. "She says, neither did her father, but here she is."

More chuckles from the others, and Robyn's cheeks darkened. "Look, lass, you've nowt to fear from me. From any of us. You owe me sod-all but an explanation come the morning. All I'm offerin' is a place by the fire. 'Twill be cold tonight."

Dutifully Guy translated. As she replied, a smirk began to curl at his lips.

Robyn obviously saw it, for he demanded, "What's she saying the now?"

"Coy wench," Guy murmured, shaking his head. "She would prefer to keep warm with one who can understand her when she asks them to move over."

Robyn approached, silent, peering curiously at the woman as she spoke. A frown, then his eyes slid to Guy, held. "I thought you said she fancied me. Are you tellin' me now she *wants* to sleep with a monk?"

He *was* a monk. Not a very good one, but still. Why did Robyn constantly calling him one slide a brined blade beneath his skin?

Guy shrugged. "You don't have to believe me. But I will also tell you, she is curious as to why I am tied, and why here, away from the fire. She says it is no way to treat a guest."

"You en't no guest," the burly poacher growled.

Guy shrugged. "I am merely repeating what she says."

"Sounds like a trick, Robyn." This from Ferret-man. "She probably knows him. You untie him and they'll both be slitting our throats. Or making his escape back to the bloody-minded sheriff and turning us in!"

John, as usual, added nothing to the vocal conversation. But he gave the rest of the outlaws a forbidding look and they fell silent—some less than happy about it—as Robyn stalked toward the tree where Guy was bound. John followed, watching both Robyn and Guy with what could only be termed as deceptive acquiescence—one hand lingered behind him, likely on a knife.

Robyn also peered at Guy—peered *through* him, in truth, and the strange intimacy of it threaded warnings all along Guy's spine.

As a lad, Rob had meant sheer, nerve-twining danger in so many ways . . . his adult avatar, even moreso. A surety filled him, a subtle power backlit his eyes, and those eyes narrowed first at Guy, then the woman.

The woman also watched, from Robyn to Guy, then back. She arched one eyebrow, said, softly, in Arabic, "I see."

"What do you see, woman?" Guy's query was sharp.

"What have you done to displease your lord, o Templar, that he would tie you and deny you his bed?"

"You will," Guy hissed, "be silent."

She looked away, ducking her head and draping the part of her headwrap that hung at her nape over her nose and mouth. Hiding a smile, no doubt, for her exposed eyes were tilted with amusement.

Robyn stood silent, watching it all. Behind him, John was frowning, and grouped behind him, the other outlaws also waited, with more patience than Guy would have given them, considering.

"What's her name?" Robyn asked.

Guy relayed the query.

She slid her gaze to Robyn, the scarf still tucked over the lower half of her face, and said, "Siham."

"What is this?" Guy queried her sharply in Arabic.

She shrugged. "It is the name I bear, Templar."

"And?" Robyn prompted.

"It means 'arrow'. I was confirming that it is, indeed, her name."

Siham kept watching Robyn. "Tell your master—"

"I have no master but the one who holds that title at Temple Hirst," Guy said. "Should I tell this wolfshead you keep fucking with your eyes that you carry a shiv in the seam along your left leg, and a bodkin—likely poisoned, because it is wrapped—tied at your ribs?"

Her face went slack with surprise.

"Do not play games unless you are prepared for the consequences, woman. What are you doing here?"

"I might ask you the same." A smile replaced dismay, her attention sliding again to Robyn. "Or do I already know? He is pretty, isn't he? Lithe as a gazelle, and no doubt as wild. Though you have the gazelle's eyes. In more ways than one."

It had been a long time since Guy had found himself literally speechless with fury.

"Come now, flame-hair, can you not take a compliment? Such a shame, two such fine-looking men who scarcely see the woman standing between them. Do his followers who hate you realise that he looks to you with his heart in his gaze?"

"What," he hissed, "do you want?"

"They're talking too much, Robyn." The poacher had skulked closer. On the "fury" scale of measurement, he ranked a close second to Guy.

"Sayin' nowt, though," John murmured.

A smile chased across Robyn's face and disappeared, leaving a twitch in one corner of his mouth. "Aye, that. She's taunting him."

All right, then . . . John was John. And Robyn . . . knew things. But now this woman was also making too-shrewd guesses about Guy as well as Robyn. Guy knew he'd let too much of this circumstance slip from his grasp if that much had been parsed despite the language barrier.

"Why would she taunt you, Templar?" Robyn asked, and crossed his arms.

"As I don't know her, I have no answer for you."

"What does he want?" Siham asked him. "Besides the obvious."

"What do you want?" he growled back.

Suddenly, Siham dropped her gaze. "Tell him that if I can outmatch him at the bow, I will take his place by the fire." She smiled, then once again peered up with kohl-smudged eyes, this time at Guy. "And so will the Templar."

Guy raised his eyebrows, tilted his head. Then gave up and translated.

Robyn, to his surprise, snorted. "She wain't have ower hard a job if she's keen as Will says she is." He held up his injured hand.

"If he is the one they call the Hood," Siham told Guy, "then he owes me that much of a handicap."

Guy shrugged, again translated.

"Prettily said," Robyn's reply was sardonic.

"She's a Saracen," Guy agreed. "They sweat and excrete poetry."

"I think he's lying, Robyn," the poacher challenged, then addressed Guy. "Your people killed her people. I heard about it. Templars put whole towns to sword and fire. Why would she help you?"

"You speak as though you went on Crusade," Guy retorted, soft-edged. "But your words betray you don't know shit from a sword."

The poacher lunged forward. Robyn whirled on him, said, very soft, "Arthur." The term "slain with a glance" more than fit the situation; Robyn didn't raise a finger, but the poacher—Arthur—halted as if whacked with a staff.

Robyn turned to Siham. "Nay, I think not. I'm not so sure you two en't acquainted from Crusade."

"Truly, I do not know her," Guy told Robyn.

"Truly," Robyn told him right back, "I don't know *you*."

The threat beneath the words quivered, one known only to the two of them. And John, Guy amended, watching the mild brown eyes widen, then narrow.

"You're as close to any fire as you'll get this night, Gisbourne," Robyn continued—again, a layered threat. "Tell the woman she'll sleep in my place. Alone, as I'll be keeping watch, with John. And," he added, turning away, "tell her I'll have that knife down her breeks, and the one in her bosom. It'll be no chore for me to take 'em off her meself, but I'm thinking it's not the way she'd prefer I put my hands on her, strip-searching her for whatever weapons she has."

This message was one Guy found himself altogether too pleased to convey.

Ⓕ

The forest held a darkness rivalling any oubliette, particularly now, with the moon dark and only a patch of stars showing between the thick treetops. The only source of illumination was the fire, and it merely revealed more shadows: sleeping figures, close by.

Fire was not only necessary for survival here, but for sanity, Guy mused. Even in the farthest reaches of the deserts beyond Outremer, he had never seen a night this dark. There was always the sky, wide and open, drenched in moonlight and pocked with stars. Celestial light had in turn made its own, reflecting and refracting against mountains and plains, rock and sand. Even the few alpine woodlands he had traversed had been filled with light.

Here in the Shire Wode, night made a never-ending cavern with a ceiling of heavy mists and tree boughs, a thick, soft floor of rot and fermenting growth. Guy had ... forgotten. The dappling of diffused greys and greens, the drip of moisture, the breath and blood and living soul, pulsing about him. The utter blackness of night. The confines of Her womb.

He could only hope She would see fit to expel him soon. *Marion?* he reminded into the silent dark. *I'm supposed to help Marion?*

There was no answer. Not that he expected one. Not that he was sane to expect one.

Nor did any surety of sanity persist in the one who suddenly descended from the trees. There was something indubitably set left of reasonable in that Robyn seemed not only at home in the darkness, he revelled in it. He all but danced through the shadows, a spectral mix of menace and bliss; he ascended the trees and walked their branches in the pitch as if they were earth spreading solid beneath his toes. Alighting from his perch as easily as a bird to ground, Robyn padded over to the fire just as silent and tangled fingers in John's hair, comfort and fondness beyond any words.

All of them, really, so open with their affections as if they'd nothing to hide, nothing of shame, only comfort and reliance despite their snarls and growls.

Trust.

Of course, if they didn't trust each other, they'd be dead. Like with himself and Much. So there was no reason that witnessing such a thing should put a knot—a foreign stigmata he'd no business heeding—deep into Guy's belly.

I don't know you.

Robyn peered about, missing nothing from his new vantage point including the female sleeping—weaponless—in his furs by the fire, and the fact Guy was awake, watching.

With another gentle tug to John's hair, Robyn walked over to Guy. His footsteps were just as silent as his descent; the only way to see that he truly walked on the earth was the tread of his feet, marked in dew.

"I could do with a piss." Guy's words were barely above a whisper. They still seemed to echo throughout the camp.

Robyn halted, stood there for a moment. His face, a shadow

within the nimbus of firelight backlighting him, was unreadable—but his voice betrayed chagrin. "You should've said sommat." Then, with a shade of what might have been humour, "I mean, it's been since we were on the road. I confess to having a wonder at whether you Templars had some extraordinary training."

Guy snorted, shook his head. "Hardly. And talking about it isn't helping matters."

Robyn turned to John, made several motions too swift and guarded for Guy to fathom, then came around the tree, seeing to Guy's bonds. John crouched a stone's throw away, watching with seeming nonchalance—but Guy saw a knife glint, ready, in his hand.

"You've been sawing at these, I see." Robyn didn't seem surprised. "Just so you know, John has his orders. The others can wake in a heartbeat. Should you take me out, there'll be no stopping 'em from killing you."

"If they can."

"Oh, they can," Robyn's voice remained matter-of-fact as he knelt to free Guy's feet. "So I wain't try owt, were I you."

"You would, were you in my place."

"Fair enough." Robyn rose, freeing the last rope and pulling Guy from the tree, giving enough freedom so Guy could shake his numbed hands. "I'd run like damn and take out as many as I could in the doing. Which is why"—Robyn's eyes, gleaming all of a sudden against the firelight, met Guy's in oblique warning—"if you so much as twitch, I'll take you down meself."

- XVIII -

He were fair distracted and upskelled—otherwise Robyn wouldn't have let this slip past him. Now he had to escort their ... guest, in the middle of the night, with everyone asleep.

Mayhap the Templar had planned on just that.

Well, if so, then Robyn would have to admit to his own ideas forming, weave and warp plaiting itself and extending before him into the black. Letting the man have a quick piss was only part of it.

And there were things needing to be said. Robyn was going to have enough trouble convincing his merry lot of hardheads as to the sense of this, let alone have to yammer on with the enemy about it in front of them. And right about now, there were too many flaming "ifs."

If the Templar was serious about trying to help Marion.

If Gamelyn still somehow lay beneath the Templar's façade: earnest, innocent Gamelyn, who'd craved knowledge and honour even more than he'd feared his god.

If the Templar had told the truth about not knowing who "Robyn Hood" was . . .

Nay, he'd not known, that much was plain. When he'd been faced with it, he'd let Robyn take him down and lain there beside

Mam Tor's altar as if praying for Robyn to finish the job. Looking back on it now, it gave Robyn a wrench and shudder at what that had surely meant.

Aye, no question Gamelyn had been a new-scrubbed apprentice in denial compared to Guy of Gisbourne, who had taken fierce hold of the whip born within his reach. He was surely liking the wielding of it overmuch; other than that, he might well have been formed of ice on the Trent. In February.

How thick was that ice?

'Tis what I don't see that holds my thoughts...

What do I call you? Robyn thought, watching Guy flex his hands as well as he could within the bonds. *What do I* dare *call you?*

Those green eyes slid Robyn's way, chary. No question but that Guy merely bided his time. Fastening a length of rope through the wrist-bindings—a simple but effective slip-lead that could pull Guy's wrists together at the small of his back with a mere tug—Robyn gave a jerk of his head and a display of the dagger in his bandaged left hand, motioning his prisoner on.

They went a ways into the trees, far from the fire and the sleeping outlaws. The trees closed tighter around them, damp and black, but Robyn, well used to it, could cast his senses about him and nigh see through the Wode's pitch. Every time Guy would hesitate, Robyn would push him on with the butt of his knife-hilt, guiding him around obstacles and down faint deer paths. Soon they were descending into a small hollow, camp a fair distance behind, farther than necessary. Guy's expression grew more and more uncertain, and Robyn himself wondered why he'd brought him so far.

Other than here, in this small hollow, they wouldn't be heard.

The bottom squelched beneath their feet; Robyn kept going until they'd crossed the boggy turf into slightly higher, firmer terrain, then halted beside a gnarled old apple tree. The tree had some companions, Robyn noted—their telltale spiky branches etched against the dim. Not only was there deadfall dotting the mossy ground, but the tree beside them still held a goodly bit of fruit. They'd have to come by later and do some picking.

"Well?" Robyn prompted as Guy kept looking at him, and played out just enough rope for Guy to do just that. "Get on with it, then. Or does being watched put you off, bein' a proper tight-arsed monk? I en't turning my back on you, either way."

With a grimace and a soft snort, Guy started unlacing his breeks. He didn't seem overly hampered by the short leash. "You've obviously never been on a long campaign."

"I prefer fighting for things I believe in."

"And now who's talking like there's choices to be had in life?" If anyone could use having a piss to make a point, 'twere this 'un. Robyn gave his own snort, reached up, and popped an apple from an overhead branch, fingers inspecting it for rot. "You're telling me you *didn't* choose to be a monk?"

"I'd choices, all right" was Guy's sarcastic mutter. "As a sodomite *and* a bewitched madman who'd proven traitor to his lord—and there's a choice for you, which of those remained the most damning, eh? In the wake of that, my dear brother informed me I'd two choices. Either be taken—bound hand and foot, of course—to where Richard was massing his crusading armies, or accept his extraordinarily munificent gift of a horse and gear, and ride for the coast, take ship to Normandy of my own will."

Robyn took a bite of apple, hazarded it fairly sweet, and moved a small step closer, taking up on the rope. He knew the motion as well as his silence gave a form of assent. He knew he wanted to hear more.

Even if he shouldn't. Want.

"They gave Arthur a choice," Robyn offered between chews. "Being a soldier or losin' his hand. He preferred a slow death ower dying in some rich man's pissing contest for lands not his own."

"I note, however, he's still alive." The chainmail tunic gave an absent jingle as Guy, finished, began refastening his cod-wrap. "Mayhap even a Heathen doesn't want to die when . . . faced with . . . " It trailed off, as if conceding what he'd just said, and to whom.

"Mayhap," Robyn returned, ever so soft, "unlike the Christians, who greet and wail at death despite all those promises of heaven, we fear neither death *nor* living."

Silence.

"Living's the worst for you, en't it? But you're not likely t' seek death, because your god and his priests wain't allow you any say over the one thing rightfully yours: how much your spirit can or wain't take in."

"You have no concept . . . " Again, it faded away, as if, amidst the rote protest, Guy again perceived exactly to whom he spoke.

"An' mayhap you're right, Gisbourne," Robyn allowed. "This is one thing about you I've never kenned."

Guy blinked, frowned. "What?"

"How Summer can be so bloody cold."

Silence, again. Guy's expression but proved the point. It might have been carved from the chalk of the Barrow-line caverns beneath the Shire Wode.

It made Robyn want to lash out, breach it. "I'm no' the one who's all set on being pure and untouched. Whatever the bloody hell *that* is. I want t' be touched. I like it. My memories slay me in m' tracks, run a salt-laced dagger over my skin over and over and over again, and that's what living is. While *you* . . . Does your heart even bother to beat 'neath that bloody cross?"

Finally, a ripple and clench of jaw.

Robyn's mouth tucked to one side in abject satisfaction. He held out the apple. "Have a bite?"

Guy peered at Robyn, then the apple, then off into the darkness. His face smoothed, and his voice was wry when he answered. "How thoroughly apropos."

What was that supposed to mean? One of Robyn's eyebrows lifted. "Y' want a bite or nay?"

"I think . . . not."

Robyn kept peering at him, the apple still outstretched in his palm. "Aye, well. Here you stand. *You're* still alive, too. But I'd think you'd have had enough of being afraid."

More silence, and those eyes meeting his, familiar yet *not*, unblinking in the faint light.

"En't that what all this is about?" Robyn prodded.

"You've said, several times now, that you don't know me." Quiet, with an underlay of menace, tensing Robyn's nerves in an agitation somewhere between resistance and roused. "Given that, don't you think you're assuming quite a lot about my motivations?"

"For someone who's so smart, who's all that book-learnin' and travellin', you're bloody sodding thick."

The fair head lifted, ever so slightly, gleaming more gilt than copper in the faint light. The broad shoulders tensed.

"Tell me sommat, Templar. You were set to protect Marion from a wolfshead. One you thought might hurt her. Why?"

"Why does it matter?"

"It obviously matters to you." Robyn fancied he saw a quiver, down deep, in the hard-muscled frame. He finished the apple with quick bites, tossed the core aside, and licked the juice from his fingers. "You know what I think?"

"Hardly." Guy once more looked past him, into the darkness.

"I think Gamelyn is still in there. Somewhere."

Another quiver, barely there. "Well. Thinking too much always did get you into trouble."

"I think we have to find him."

"'Finding' implies someone is lost."

"Aye, it does."

"So mayhap *you* should leave the thinking to those who can." Tosser. "Fine, then." Robyn stepped even closer. "No more thinking. Let's *do* it. Take me to them, Templar. Do the sodding *job*, since you're so good at it. Take me to your masters, help me fetch my sister away from that bitch who's stolen her from her rightful place."

"You think you can cheat death again, Hob-Robyn?" It was flat, colourless. All the while, Guy absently fingered the slip-lead.

As if this one did anything absently. Robyn's mouth twisted in a lopsided smile even as he warned, "Don't try it, lad."

"Don't call me lad." Quicker than an eye blink, Guy grabbed the rope, slid just enough slack through his hand to foil Robyn's reactive jerk on the line. Guy spun, jerked his wrists sideways to pull Robyn off-balance.

Robyn was already there, too close for leverage, the rope sagging limp between them. He lurched closer still, reared back, and slammed his head against Guy's.

Guy staggered back. Robyn saw a few stars himself, if truth were told— though he wasn't about to tell it. Instead Robyn flung the loose end of the rope around the tree's trunk then, in nearly the same motion, caught it and leaned his full weight against it. Perhaps that weight made no true deterrent, but the muscles developed over a lifetime of bending a longbow were. When Guy merely dug in and leaned right back, Robyn smirked and gave a fierce haul at the rope. Astonishment, then a fleeting grimace as Guy's bound wrists were yanked sideways from his back and he was forced along. Instead of allowing himself to fall, Guy twisted, stumbled over a root, and regained his feet, letting the next tug pull him along.

Robyn merely followed, taking up the rope's slack. Apples rolled and squished underfoot, making the footing into a treacherous, ankle-twisting hazard as they circuited the tree.

Abruptly, Guy changed direction, lunged at Robyn.

He nearly caught him, too. Only a quick dodge saved Robyn being bowled over. Rope still in hand, Robyn grabbed a low-hanging branch, swung up and over the leap. Guy went sprawling, cursed. Growled, "I've seen apes that find climbing more difficult than you!"

Robyn dropped to the ground. "Climbing's no' so hard," he said, panting. "Getting you to hold still for two breaths is much, much harder." He backed a few steps, tottered as he trod on an apple.

Guy took the opening, exploded upward. Twisted again, kicked out. The momentum nearly felled him, but the well-aimed boot caught Robyn in one hip with a dull smack and flare of pain. Still doggedly holding the rope, Robyn let the impact spin him, sucking in a quick breath against it. Young Gamelyn had indeed learnt sommat in his time away; if things came to a brutal hand-to-hand, a skinny archer's tricks and leverage stood little chance against a warhorse Templar. As Guy staggered up again, Robyn took his own chance, lunging forward to slam Guy face-first against the tree.

Several apples dropped; one gave a sharp clip to Robyn's shoulder, but as Guy hit the tree, he let out a grunt that made any pain simmer down to satisfaction. It was almost as satisfying as the sudden reality of Robyn's body shoved up against Guy's. And the realisation that his adversary's arse had also improved with age. Quivering with muscles, round and hard as one of those apples clinging, nigh ripe, overhead . . . hard as Robyn himself, suddenly, rising to the challenge of this "tight-arsed monk" and wishing nothing more than those bound-back hands would slither down and take hold.

Bloody *damn*. Will was always claiming that Robyn's liking for a quick wank in the teeth of danger would kill him, someday.

Templar. *Enemy.*

Yet you aren't so sure of that, are you, my Hob-Robyn?

Well, and if this wasn't a damned inconvenient time for Herself to show up. Particularly since She wasn't altogether fond of talking to Robyn in the first place.

Robyn gritted his teeth and pushed away from Guy, yanked him around. Whatever retaliation Guy was gathering himself to make, it stopped midforce as Robyn whipped the quillion dagger from his belt and against the black-clad belly. Robyn took a quick wrap on the rope and shoved the end between Guy's bound wrists, threading it out, effectively binding him against the apple tree. And all the while, Robyn had a half smile quivering at his mouth.

"Nice try, that," he acknowledged. "You've a flaming hard head on you, Templar."

And more than the one, from the tilt of that tunic. Surely it wasn't from the dagger in such close proximity.

Or mayhap it was. Mayhap Robyn wasn't the only one who fancied a bedding blade amidst the sharper ones.

"That makes two of us," Guy retorted, somewhat strained. "You can move the dagger away from my bollocks, now."

"Anon, but not just, I think." Smile broadening, Robyn took another wrap on the rope. "Surely you don't need 'em anyway, being a proper monk and all."

"Surely it wain't be yer place t' decide." Guy's mimicry of a Yorkshire burr had but improved and a scathing overlay included the Marcher lilt Robyn still held from his dam. A cut no less deep than Robyn's dagger, and Guy looked to be preparing more; yet almost immediately, it wound down. "Stop calling me that."

"What? Proper? Or a monk?"

"Neither. I'm certainly no proper monk." Guy suddenly looked down, eyes flickering as they fastened to the dagger. Not only recognition—but something else.

That something flashed through Robyn like heat lightning, the sudden . . . admittance of it. He didn't move the dagger—nay, not one bit—but he leaned in, ever so slight.

Muttered, "Bloody damn. You *are* there."

The green eyes slid up and met his. "And where else would I be?"

"You tell me, Gamelyn Boundys."

"You can stop calling me that as well."

"It's your name. It's the one your mam gave you. It's the one you kept insisting was yours the first time we met in the woods when your horse dumped you against a tree. Remember?"

Guy looked away.

"It's the one Marion would call you. Only she'd nigh sing it— 'Sir Gamelyn'—and you'd stare at her all big-eyed and smitten as a lovesick sheepdog. And though I loathed myself for 't, I'd fancied what might happen should you stare at *me* so."

"Stop playing with me, *wolfshead*!" Guy snapped out.

"Do you still love my sister then, *monk*?" Robyn snapped right back. "Enough to take me to her?"

"You can't possibly—"

"You've no concept of what's possible here, in t' Wode. You've forgotten. Or . . . " He touched the tip of his dagger to the knot risen between the riding vents of Guy's tunic, smoothed the blade's flat down the growing length of that knot and sensed more than saw the shudder taking the black-clad frame. "Or mayhap the memory's . . . rising. *This* remembers, aye?"

"Such reactions mean nothing." Guy's retort sounded more a rote lesson than any absolute protest. "Only the animal in us, refusing restraint."

"Nowt wrong with animals. They don't lie, or bother pretending, 'less they're in fear for their life." Robyn took a sharp wrap on the rope, looped it fast. "So. Are you in fear for your life, Templar? Or does it happen your like fears nowt including the Christian god?"

"I'd be fool indeed, if Robyn Hood had me tied to a tree with a knife at my testicles and I didn't fear for *something*."

Robyn chuckled. "Always trying to find a way around it, or without it. And now you just refuse to look at it. But it's there. I've seen it." His eyes never left Guy's. "Lain with it."

Was Guy . . . *snarling* at him? Aye, just a slight curl of lip, more telling than any open curse or shout. As if he sensed it, Guy looked away.

"Aye, and look at you, I'm thinking there's some fire under all that chill. Bodies don't forget. 'Tis like riding a horse, once you learn the rhythm."

"No one's that good a fuck."

"Keep telling yourself that, pet." Robyn's smile faded. "Or have you just poured all that thwarted passion into my sister? Only now, it seems she's a novice nun who canna even remember her own name, let alone the name you've discarded? Plenty safe, that. And nowt left for the memory of *us*, then."

Those words hurt—more than they hurt Guy, it seemed. Robyn drew the dagger up and back, over his shoulder and ready to strike, wanting nothing more in the moment than to see pain . . . fear . . . *something* in those eyes.

But nothing. Guy kept looking aside, as if baring his throat to the knife.

Robyn smiled—snarled—and thrust the dagger into the bark right beside Guy's nape. Ruddy-pale hair measured the wind of the blade's passage, but Guy didn't so much as twitch.

Robyn hissed into Guy's exposed ear, "Aye, nowt left. So no need to decide what to do with a dead and damned love that sweet Gamelyn held for a peasant lad, one who had the bloody cheek to go and return from the otherworld."

Or, mayhap the pain bided mutual. Guy's profile was still turned away, but his jaw roiled, his breath venting through clenched teeth, the too-rapid rise and fall of his sternum pushing it into the night. Slowly his eyes returned, large and furious— and . . . glimmering?—to hold Robyn's.

The thwarted power of that glare. The glittering, dangerous edge.

Barely a second later, Guy twisted and tried to knee Robyn in the crotch. But he hadn't the proper distance to make it count. Robyn merely swerved, leaned all the closer, once more whispered against Guy's ear, "Aye, you remember. Or there wouldn't be all this pissing fight in you. You've done nowt but fight from th' time I skinned you of t' *mari lwyd* and tried to snare you with those memories floating on Samhain's breath. I spoke your name then. Just like I'd whisper it against your nape when we were lads, reminding you of it when I'd tup you so hard you'd forget—"

"Please." It was a hoarse whisper, but this time Guy didn't look away, as if he couldn't. "Don't."

"So." Robyn put another wrap in the rope, tied it off. "Is this 'don't?'" He raised his free hand and spanned it over Guy's breastbone, feeling the hammer-pound of the heart beneath it before following the lines of the blooded cross down. And down farther. "Or 'don't stop'?"

If the hard knot lurching upward between the riding vent of the ebon tunic didn't answer, the harsh, stuttering gasp Guy gave, as Robyn curled his fingers about that knot and squeezed, did.

"I want you back. I want to find you. And if tying you to a tree and rutting you stupid's the only way to do it—"

"Robyn." It was low. And desperate. "*Think.*"

He breathed a chuckle against Guy's neck. "*Now* you want me to think?"

"We . . . we can't do this."

"Aye, and that sounds like the Gamelyn I know," Robyn purred, and ran his tongue up the cords of Guy's neck, slick-rough against prickles of new-grown beard. "And I'll tell you what I only ever told him. We *are* doing this."

"*Rob!*"

Robyn fastened his mouth against Guy's, cut the protest into a rattle and choke, gripped his chin when he tried to swerve sideways, held him through it. Tried to nip Guy's mouth open when Guy would clamp his jaw, gave another twist of his hand as Guy tugged at his bonds, felt fabric strain and flesh lurch against his gripping fingers at both motions, a betrayal all too eager. And when Guy opened his mouth in another, strangled and forced-silent gasp, Robyn sounded him, lips and breath and probing tongue.

And the fact that he might just get bitten for his pains just made it all the better, somehow.

Guy's jaw tightened—contemplating, threatening—but Robyn merely rocked up against him, dared him, hand curling in another hard twist and squeeze. Teeth bared, all right—nipped hard, but not too hard—and fastened to his lower lip. Robyn snaked his hand up beneath Guy's black tunic, finding flesh and fine hairs and . . .

Robyn sucked in a breath—his, Guy's, he wasn't sure—and wondered if ball lightning had rolled from sky to tree branch and through them both. Guy shuddered against him; what started to be a full-fledged bite into Robyn's lower lip quivered, fell open. Flinging his head back against the tree, Guy gave a desperate heave at the rope. All it did was arch his body harder against Robyn's.

All it did was roll the cord—twining fire into Robyn's nerves and Guy's skin— across Robyn's palm.

Another jolt echoed through them.

Robyn pulled his hand back, shoved up Guy's tunic to peer at the braided cord slung at his hip bones. "Sweet Lady," he breathed. "'Tis no fancy strangler of a hair-tie, this." Robyn once again reached for it, smoothed the sting and spun the intoxication of it through his fingers.

Guy sucked in a strangled groan, and the sound of it runnelled up and down Robyn's spine like fire-heated water.

"So the Templars are sorcerers, after all," Robyn murmured.

"What"—a gasp—"are . . . *uhn*! How—"

"'Tis your measure, aye?—counted and bound about you, marked in your blood and seed and sweat." Robyn bent, smoothed first his hair then his lips over it.

"Oh, *God*."

Robyn rose to lick the shiver of sound from Guy's lips, ran a heated line, back and forth, over the cord twined in his fingers, over the smooth, faint-furred flesh beneath the cord. Felt the throb of craving/ache/want clench at Guy, felt more than heard the shudder of breath at the raw intimacy.

"Aye," Robyn whispered again. "This is why my people 'ware keeping ours so close. You've felt only a judder of what another with the magic can do to you with such a thing in his hand."

"God," Guy groaned again. "*Don't.*"

"Don't?" Robyn purred. "Or don't stop?"

Guy opened his eyes, held Robyn's, shuddered as Robyn shoved against him. Tugged at the bindings, threw his head back against the tree, twisted . . . *whimpered* as Robyn slid his teeth up the pale cords of his exposed neck. Licked. Nipped.

There rose something dark and glorious in it: a hot breath heavy upon Robyn's nape, urging the taking and breaking both. Pulse pounding, commingling, and the heated whiff of blood just beneath the surface, all bound up in that throbbing cord in his hand—*his, all his*—sending every sense Robyn possessed on the trail and the capture and the kill

Take him. You have him. Take him. He is begging *for the breaking. . .*

Even the Horned Lord's voice faded into the black as *tynged* took Robyn, flayed him, and he wasn't going alone, not into this dark. He tightened his fingers on the cord, watched those lips part in a soundless, suppliant sigh, and tasted triumph, heated as the skin sliding against his.

"So, 'tis turned at last, Gisbourne. The whip's in my hand, now, and all your power means nowt here in *my* place. You're stuck, my brother-rival, and the longest night upon us anon, and a thousand little deaths into the void. You canna do a damned thing, and you're mine again, *mine—*"

"*Robyn.*" It was desperate, hoarse. And beneath it, surfacing through it, a soft, shattered memory:

Three children running free in the forest, tears and tussles and laughter . . . love and hope and heartache, a breath of passion in the sweet green Wode . . . and *tynged* weaving three fates into a skein of possibilities, back to back and hearts innocent with one accord . . .

As long as you stand together, none can stand against you. The Lady's voice . . . yet not quite. It tickled at the base of Robyn's skull, teased him from the black of *tynged* and once more into the pitch of his own gaze, of his own mind and memory, of his own body pressing a line of heat and hardness against Guy. His fingers relaxed upon the cord.

And like an arrow loosed from commingled tension of bow and arm, Robyn was released, staggering against Guy, sliding down his body to huddle at his feet.

Silence. Even the Wode paused about them, stilled. As if the wind did not whisper movement into branches, or cause to drip wet chords of sound and silver to the thick-mossed ground.

Robyn reached out, grabbed hold of the rope binding Guy to the tree, and hauled at it. The first try was unsuccessful, and the second and third not much better, but finally, slowly, he tugged and tottered upright.

"Robyn?" Still hoarse, and barely above a whisper. "What has . . . what is . . . *Robyn?*"

Robyn shook his head then, with shaking hands and fumbling fingers, pulled Guy's tunic back into place. He was careful—*so careful*—and once done he pushed away, with a tiny stagger in his step.

Then he reached up, took hold of the dagger, with one swift yank freed it from the tree.

Held it up between them.

Guy watched everything Robyn did with a mute *waiting* . . . and one that unsheathed talons, scored Robyn to bone. As if Guy expected nothing but, having found the means to break him, Robyn would fulfil the rest of the sacrifice.

Don't you see, we've both been broken. Found light and spent it wallowing in darkness, and the dawn is coming. It's done.

Robyn put the pommel of the dagger to his lips, then, with a quick toss and snatch midair to change his grip . . .

Cut the rope.

ᛘ

Guy could scarce believe it as it was happening—the latest quandary in a tangle of them.

The cord. He'd never liked for others to touch it—never truly understanding why, though sometimes it couldn't be helped—but since the day Hubert had knotted it about his hips he'd not felt this . . . *this* . . .

The dagger, not taking his blood but giving him his freedom, and the . . . whimpering need, hot-eyed and acquiescent, surging up from the soul Guy had forgotten he had, *wanting* that dominance, protesting that freedom.

The *nothingness*, the blank-black rent behind Robyn's eyes kindling into flames, ribbons and skeins of a thousand starless nights and sunless days in a second's passage.

The reality of yet another thought darting, a vengeful and authoritative shard splitting a frozen rent through his brain: *Take him down. Now's your chance. You have your orders.*

Guy staggered forward the few steps, reached out.

Robyn's eyes wheeled, catching the dim light, like flame held to a wolf's night-sight. But he stood his ground as Guy grabbed him by his tunic front, yanked him close—so close their breath commingled in the chill air . . . so close he could see it wiffle the stray ebon strands at Robyn's temples. Another breath, and the silver-threaded forelock stirred, strayed across the narrow bridge of Robyn's nose.

It wasn't enough, to be close. Guy had to do what the bindings hadn't allowed, inner or outward.

He had to *touch.*

Guy raised his hands, raked fingers through wind-snarled curls, clenched. Saw Robyn's full lower lip part from its mate, quiver damp and expectant, as Guy leaned in.

This kiss was his to create and execute, bruising, absorbing, requirement and demand and, ultimately, surrender. Robyn *took* it, softened and whimpered and invited Guy to take even more, and Guy finally had to break from it, overwhelmed, if only for the moment. He rested his forehead upon Robyn's shoulder, tasting the heat of him, still, on his lips, then put his face into Robyn's hair. Wild mint and bark, woodsmoke and must; Guy breathed him in, juddered, and couldn't believe what he was doing.

Hard, shaking fists clenched in the breast of his tunic, tried to shove him back. Should have been able to, but Guy had all but burrowed in, and it was as if every bit of strength had fled from Robyn's sinewy arms.

"We . . . canna," Robyn admitted, a husk against Guy's temple. "I fear for . . . There's too much . . ."

"I know," Guy answered, low. "And I don't care." No less a resistance, no less acquiescence, but this time pitted twofold. "Say my name," he pleaded. "Just tell me . . . tell me who I am."

Another shudder, and a sound, almost a sob, from Robyn's throat. Then . . .

"Gamelyn." It was soft as swan down, Robyn's whisper against russet hair. As soft as the caress Guy laced, breath and tongue, across Robyn's temple, over his cheekbone and past his jaw to the spot of his throat where the pulse beat, steady-strong. As Guy latched his teeth there, it quickened.

"Gamelyn," Robyn said again.

Guy pulled him down. Robyn said it again as Guy's hands rucked up beneath Robyn's tunic, tugged down to unbreech and bare him. Yet again as Guy's tunic, so carefully replaced, and then his braies were tugged away, as Robyn grabbed at one still rope-wound wrist, twisting the frayed hemp about his wrapped hand and giving a yank with that insanely strong bow arm. Guy found himself, hands, face and knees planted in the moist, chill loam, with Robyn curling against him, a lean line of heat and hardness following the further arch of his spine. Robyn whispered his name again, a feathered trail of fire along the braided cord just above Guy's buttocks, lingering to feel the shock tickling at the base of Guy's spine.

Feel. He could *drown*, in this much feeling.

"Do it," Guy breathed. "Oh, God, just . . . *Please.*"

It hurt. It had been too long, and only spit and sweat to slick the first thrust, but once the first became a second, then a third, the pain twisting sharp and sensate then flowering deep into his belly, a warm knife stabbing and shivering every sense into utter abandon.

And Robyn said his name at the last, a lingering groan, as he hunched over Guy, plunging and shuddering, his teeth raking Guy's shoulder and his fingers splayed and rolling against the cord, and finally Robyn flipped Guy onto his back for the last strokes. Drove him down into the earth and grass, lean, pale body and midnight tangles blocking out the stars, copper-gilt hair and body spreading, *sinking* into the black-green Wode, amidst the deadfall of apples and the ruin of everything they had so carefully constructed.

※

"I canna tell them. Not this."

They had lain, spent and shivering, tangled tight as the ropes still abrading Guy's wrists, until the moon had climbed past the trees.

Finally Robyn had extricated himself, retreating behind his own eyes, to sit naked with his arms curled about his bent knees, as tight-wrapped alone as they had been together only moments previous.

Then he'd spoken, and it . . . *Was* it shame Guy heard in the low voice?

It was something he'd not thought to hear from Robyn. Ever.

"John. John will know, he likely does already." The dark head shook. "I should have told them who you were. I kept trying, and trying. It never seemed the right time. I meant to tell 'em when they returned from the raid, only they had the Saracen woman, and Will wounded. All of it." Robyn ran hands through his hair, fingers snarling tight. "But I wasn't sure of the woman . . . Siham." The black eyes moved to Guy, held. "If you knew her, *would* you tell me?" Then Robyn shook his head. "Nay, don't answer that. All that puzzles me is why a Saracen woman is travelling the road, knowing no English."

"King Richard speaks no English," Guy reminded softly.

"Aye, and en't *he* a fair king to have over my people?" Robyn murmured, though it sounded more a growl. "One who wain't even be arsed to speak our language—"

"Robyn."

"They'll have to know about Marion. What I'm doing."

"Robyn, you can't—"

"I can. I will. And you'll not hinder me in this." His voice shook. "You have to help me. Take me in. Sweet Lady, we have to get her *out* of there!"

And Guy had no denial to voice to that. "I know," he whispered.

"We'd best get dressed. Go back. They'll be wondering. Or sending out Arthur with his axe, looking for me and aiming at you."

"Robyn—"

"It's so easy, in the middle of it. So easy, when you're at my mercy. But what happens when I release you?"

Guy held out his arms, exposing the cut ropes—and nipped flesh. Said, low, "You have."

The words were not easy to speak. So many truths in that simple one, the precision of it skimming a slow, deceptively deep gash. His impenetrable mask, marked for all time, disfigured. Everything he'd made—tried to make—of himself spilling to the floor, exposed for all to see, as if he viewed his own evisceration.

Robyn was shaking his head, brows knit tight, eyes lustrous with pain. No, not mere pain.

Evisceration.

"Aye." Assent came dubious, hoarse. "And I nae more can trust you with your bonds cut than you can trust I'll not fall into t' black and choke you with 'em. We're . . . predators, Guy of Gisbourne, *rivals* on opposite sides of a war not only in thisworld but th' others, and we *feed* off it, glut on the rush of the stoop, the wind and blood on our feathers. What happens when I en't in the middle of you but once more on th' edges looking in?"

"*Robyn.*" It shook, forceful and weak all at once.

Black eyes riveted to his own, and they sat in silence for long moments. Then Robyn stood up, started gathering his clothes.

"You . . . you mix me up, you allus have. You make me *think* on too much, make me hesitate, get all confused, make me question me own instincts . . . Sweet Lady! Why do I *have* to question, to fight back? Why can I not just leave it *be*, like me da did? Nowt will ever change because of Robyn Hood—babes'll still starve, and my people feel the whip, and we'll still hack our way through the ones who'll hurt us and ours! Why wain't it all just *leave me be*, and then none of it would matter but what we could take from it! Instead here we stand, on opposite sides of our *world.*"

Robyn fell silent. Guy stared at his back—surely Robyn knew better than to turn his back on Guy, but there it was, another instinct bypassed . . . or perhaps not. A tremor racked the broad shoulders—and Guy felt it run down his own spine. He *knew* . . . and had turned anyway.

"I don't even *know* the questions anymore." Guy's voice quavered against the dark. Against that pale, whip-scarred and muscle-corded back. "I thought I had all the answers. My life was my own . . . or at least I thought it was." His voice abruptly deepened, guttural. "One night, Robyn. One night that shaped everything I did after it . . . and two days ago I found that night to be . . . well it wasn't a lie. 'Twas the only truth I've ever known, what I saw and felt . . . God!" he burst out, a sudden blast of fury set to scorch the trees. "It *wasn't* a lie. But it's all turned into one, somehow, and everything it shaped has become a deception that's made its own truth!"

"Truth. You keep sayin' that, truth, like it's owt you can snare and tame."

"I'm saying I don't know what truth is!" Guy retorted. "I never have, and the lies keep piling atop each other until I don't even know what I am, anymore!"

"Truth is," Robyn muttered, "there *is* no truth. Not as you'd have it. Not as your people'd have it."

"You're talking anarchy. Madness."

"It's a mad world. You should know that by now."

"I should. I did. And then . . . " Guy laughed suddenly, laced with rue and sharp-sweet poison. "Ah, but She'll have Her way, won't She? One way or another."

Robyn had leapt like a startled hare at the laugh. He turned to Guy, eyes wheeling ebon and white in the shadows, watching his lover/rival as if he feared his descent into what surely must seem a madness. Moreover, Guy couldn't stop it, couldn't . . . *shut the bloody fuck up.*

"She'll have us tilting each other, to lie hamstrung . . . *vulnerable* . . . oh, *God!* You say I turn your world inside out. Bloody damn, Robyn, what do you think you've done to *mine?*"

Silence, again. Unfathomable, painful, knotted tight as the ends of Guy's braided cord belt—and just as tingling-tender.

"And what do we do, now?" Robyn murmured. "We've soul-deep oaths sworn in this battle, both of us. I'm the last of my kind, the Shire Wode my kingdom, the only power my god still claims. You were sent here to strip me of that power. Likely you're the only one as could. So tell me, Templar. What happens should your masters tell you the peasant lad from Loxley en't fit to hold the Horns?"

"They won't. They thought—"

"They thought a wolfshead took the covenant. And they were right."

Guy fell silent. He had no answers. The trees waited about them, never truly silent. *The Wode always speaks,* the peasant lad from Loxley had once told him, *if you know how to listen to Her.*

Oh, God. The first thing akin to a prayer that he'd uttered in years—and he wasn't sure, even then, exactly to whom he uttered it. *Oh, God. . . I. . . can't. Can't. . .*

Guy was the one to speak, finally, into the Wode's melody. "We cannot do this again."

It would have been easier to tear out his own tongue. Robyn's gaze met his, still wild, still gleaming, yet part and parcel of the night about them. It made the utter calm of his response all the more unreal.

"Aye," he murmured. "We canna."

- XIX -

John was waiting for them. His gaze slid upward beneath his brows, gleaming in the fire's light, taking it all in: Robyn's uncommon hesitancy . . . the fresh weight seeming to drag at his heels; Guy's bent head . . . and the ropes dangling, severed, from his wrists. Then he returned his attention to what he had been doing as they'd approached. Within his slender, callused fingers dandled a small chunk of oak heartwood, a form taking shape within it, beneath the sure edge of his smallest knife.

As they reached the fire, Guy hesitated—he wasn't sure but he'd end up tied to the tree again—then gave to the small directive, sitting down but leaving goodly space between himself and John.

John's brows drew together, his expression troubled as Robyn sat between them, noticeably closer to John than Guy. Instead of John's expression smoothing into what Guy would expect—some inkling of triumph, perhaps?—John merely ducked sideways into Robyn, his temple resting against Robyn's shoulder. One hand curving up to hold John's head tightly against him, Robyn gave a strange shudder then released John, who straightened and bent back to his carving.

Guy watched, mystified as to their feelings but even more to his own. The cord about his hips tingled, warm, while the rest of him felt cold. It should be . . . of some comfort, the chill.

It was not.

You're afraid of dying... but you're more afraid of living.

Guy stared at the ropes still dangling, beginning to fray, from his wrists. They were beginning to ache, with the odd ferocity of all shallow wounds; it was something he refused to process. Firelight revealed stains darkening the hemp, and a further smear amidst freckles and gilt hairs. Blood. Hardly surprising. More surprising, how those hands tremored—and the only way Guy made that discovery was by the shudder and sway of the rope's frayed ends.

He didn't want to unwind them.

I'm afraid of what this means.

Meaning. Consequence. A peasant lad and a nobleman's son had once turned their backs on their respective worlds, only to see those worlds torn apart and scattered to the winds. Had bridged the divide separating them at birth with an oath, one sworn on one another's bodies and carved into one another's hearts with the blade stuck in Robyn's belt: that they, with Marion, would go away together, wield the Ceugant with three powers merged and not two battling for the one, leave loyalties behind, trust only to each other.

Now there were other trusts. Other loyalties.

The Templars.

Marion.

Robyn Hood's band of outlaws.

Guy looked up to see John, once again, watching him. Only there was no challenge in it, no threat perceived or given.

Robyn sat, elbows resting on crossed legs, staring into the fire with eyes both too empty and too filled.

John had to know. If nothing else, surely he could smell the heat and sex-sweat traced over Robyn. Guy could, past even the leaf-mould and the thread of woodsmoke rising into the night, could swear that he still felt the fingers tracing it over his own skin, trails gleaming like burning phosphorus.

Had their lives *ever* been their own?

That in itself was betrayal: a question Guy de Gisbourne had never thought—or wanted—to ask.

That question—and others—spun through his head even as false dawn began to conjure dim ghosts from the Wode's green-black shadows, even as John left off his carving to repair and replait the rope that Guy had—slowly, finally—unwound from his abraded wrists.

Robyn, still, remained between them. He had fallen into a

stunned and exhausted sleep—not in Guy's arms, as some tiny need within Guy yearned for but knew he had no rights to, here and now, but with his head pillowed on John's thigh, his hands curled, lax, into John's cloak. John would, every so often, caress the black hair spilling into his lap, hand so light that Robyn didn't so much as stir.

Guy peered at his own hands. They wouldn't stop shaking.

How Robyn could sleep, when the boundaries of their existence had been so shattered and pieced so crudely back . . .

It was as much a marvel as the open tenderness of John's touch upon his sleeping leader. A betrayal of too much, a liability—a luxury—that Guy had to scorn, to deny. Survival, no less instinctive than Robyn's own . . . but undermined. Had in truth been slowly undercut since a faded dark hood had flung back and exposed a part of himself thought long dead and gone.

He didn't know how to live with all this . . . furore.

I en't the one who's all set on being pure and untouched. Whatever the bloody hell that is. I want t' be touched. I like it. My memories slay me in m' tracks, run a salt-laced dagger over my skin over and over and over again. . .

Memory? Madness, more like, flung in his face, laughing as he *felt* it . . . over and over and over again.

There was only one way to survive it. Only one way he knew to contain it—*deny, hide, mask it, draw an icy, remote cloak about it*—and now he was passing that on to Robyn like an infection, a sickness, a . . . leprosy of spirit.

John put aside the ropes for the tiny nugget of wood, held it up with slender fingers to scrutinise his shaping in the faint light. His other hand kept combing gentle, almost negligent fingers through Robyn's snarled locks.

He's better for you, Guy thought, and knew, with that thought . . . it wasn't done. Wasn't finished. It would never be finished, no matter what they'd said to each other after they'd fucked each other senseless.

Senseless, indeed. More than senseless, to think it could be anything but done. Too much lay between them. In myriad ways.

Guy had often been proud that the man who had become Gisbourne, the Templar weapon, had survived. He'd been so scornful of the innocent he'd been, of how Gamelyn had merely lingered, small and pathetic, a broken shade of the warrior Guy had become.

Now he knew: Gamelyn had merely been biding his time.

Aye, Summerling. Who is the stronger now?

Guy put his head in his hands, cursed Her manipulations for craven and cruel theurgy.

Oh, come now. Manipulating you and your leman is like grasping wind. It was a laugh, a scold. *I do not play the games our Lord prefers; He is more the gamesman than I ever pretend to be. Thusly He is often thwarted and unfulfilled. Like you, a lover/son who has found fulfilment and turned away from it. I must confess to surprise that he*—Her breath stirred Robyn's hair—*has agreed to your denial. But then, he does love his people so. . . and you, my Knight, are a serpent in your own Garden. With two heads. You have made the Hooded One afraid*—*afraid with which head you shall strike. Afraid of his own.*

It's why we. . . cannot.

Of course. A chide, mockery. *You are rivals. It is sin. One of you must die for Me. How ever shall you do it, Templar? You have your orders, do you not?*

Orders to kill a usurper. Are You saying Robyn Hood has usurped a power not his?

He was mad. *Mad.* Sitting unbound at an outlaw's hearth, arguing with the Divine Feminine.

Laughter whispered on the wind, faded into John's voice. " . . . to you?"

Guy had heard John's voice so seldom he was unsure it was, in fact, John's voice. Tautening his fingers against his forehead until they bled white, Guy opened his eyes. "Did you say something?"

A small quirk touched John's mouth, disappeared in the next instant. "You hear Her," he murmured.

Guy didn't need to ask what John meant. "I'll trade the privilege with you any day," he replied.

Over in a tangle of furs and woollen, Gilbert stirred, back to back with David. From beneath those furs something gleamed— the eyes of the ferret, watching the ones by the fire.

"Mm." John was eying Guy, as well, then said, even more remarkable, "So that's where She's been."

(M)

Gilbert woke first, sprang to his feet upon seeing Guy unbound by their fire. Tess's irate chitters over having one-half of her toasty bed disrupted soon woke David, as well—and the same sight had him to his feet, drawing a dagger.

Tess, in tiny and sinuous mimicry of her bedmates, charged a threat toward Guy, arching her back and hissing.

John hissed his own warning, jerked his head to where Robyn

still slept, sprawled between John and Guy. Guy merely sat very still and kept his hands where they could be seen.

Slowly, obviously puzzled, David put his dagger away. Gilbert, gaze flitting from John to Robyn to Guy, then back to Robyn, gave a curious shrug then padded away, presumably at nature's beckoning. Only when he returned did David leave—as if, Guy mused scornfully, they hadn't spent most of the night *not* watching That Bastard Templar.

Both of them came to the fire and hovered there—uncertain, silent, firmly planted opposite the two waking and one sleeping.

The drama repeated itself as the others woke, of course, sans ferret. And sans dagger, in Siham's case. Though the outlaws were so set off guard by the man sitting unbound at their fire—*as if he'd the right*, Guy distinctly heard Arthur mutter at Will—Siham likely could sneak away and take a horse and they'd never have noticed.

John would have, though. Guy would bet his sword arm on that.

Siham, surprisingly, didn't take advantage of their befuddlement. But she was the only one who came and sat to Guy's vacant hand. Gilbert had been the one to cut her bonds, after a tense and twisty silent conversation by hand with John.

The resultant silence, all of them sitting about the fire not looking at each other, was even more overwrought.

Robyn woke into this hellish discomfiture with a stretch and shudder. His hair scrunched in four different directions, his eyes puffy, he peered around then yawned. "Where's breakfast, then? I'm famished."

(M)

"I tell you, we should enter the archery tournament," Gilbert was saying in between bites of breakfast.

Several grains had been boiled down together, Guy noted, along with some fruit, to make quite a tasty porridge. He cupped the wood-burl bowl and took judicious sips—it was also extremely hot.

"He's off again," Will snorted. As his gaze fell upon the two additions to their mealtime, he scowled harder.

"And why not?" Gilbert persisted. "'Tis easy marks. Robyn and I could take on all comers with one hand tied. Eh, Robyn?"

"What?" Robyn started; he had been peering at Guy and Guy knew it, those eyes burning against him like a brand and Guy afraid—*afraid!*—to meet them.

"Kind of hard to push a bow one-handed," Arthur pointed out, with a wave of his missing one.

Siham, still seated beside Guy and held, seemingly, by his own strangled quietude, suddenly murmured, "What are they saying?"

"Not anything important. Mostly the archery tournament being held for Count John at week's end."

She frowned at her bowl, which was nearly empty. Guy wasn't sure why—he'd assured her there was nothing unclean about the food—then she stated, "This Robyn Hood. He is their . . . *imam*."

Religious leader, holy man, guardian; it fit more than Guy found comfortable. "I . . . guess he is. Yes."

"And you?"

Guy frowned sideways at her.

"I saw him take you from here, last night. Yet this morning, you are still here. Untied. He has set you free, and you do not want it."

Guy's frown wavered, gaze falling to take in his bruised wrists. Something juddered, small and nigh invisible, in his belly. The frown regathered itself and swerved into a glower, angling back to Siham. It was more than enough to silence her, so he continued to make silent inroads into his meal.

"Not to say," Will was pointing out, "Robyn's push would give 'im away, sure's iron needs fire."

"Aye. Not many know his face, but the bow arm sinister is just a wee giveaway." David rose, taking the cauldron from the fire. "'Tis a chance, Gilly." Walking over to Siham, he silently offered her more. She shook her head, smiled brief thanks when he took the bowl from her. She kept looking from Guy to Robyn and back again.

John, again, was the one who kept surreptitious tabs on her.

"Life's all chances." Gilbert shrugged, hands spreading. "Fifty marks, mind you. Won out from beneath the Sheriff's nose!"

Guy felt as the hart must, surrounded by hungry wolves just waiting for the first twitch to fall upon and rend him. It was not a reaction to which Guy had accustomed himself.

He was accustomed to none of this. The hands that kept up an occasional tremor, the bruises on his wrists that should humiliate and instead captivated, the barely stoppered rage that kept rising into his throat as if to choke him, the sweat trickling down his nape and the shiver—*not* fear, *not* weakness—it would give.

What are you, a Templar or a puling boy? Hubert's voice growled from memory.

Guy needed a sword in his hands. That would steady them.

"You need to shut yer daft face, Gilly," Arthur growled. "You flap it when it en't safe."

Now, the ill-disguised, ill-tempered sneers Will and Arthur kept giving him?—that, Guy was accustomed to.

"We're not going to the tournament," Robyn said into the resultant quiet. "The day before, Gisbourne will take me in."

Well, and if *that* wasn't incendiary thrown against a fortress gate.

There were several beats of pure, aghast silence, then as one the men rose to their feet, an eruption of denial.

"*What?*"

"Robyn, you en't—"

"What in bloody—"

John hadn't moved, seated, seemingly unaffected, next to Robyn. Neither did Guy move a muscle—albeit for very different reasons. He did spare a flash of thought for Siham as she jerked next to him, instinctive retreat, then put her from his mind and tensed, prepared for just about anything.

It was a relief, actually.

"There's no way you can poss—"

"I must be deaf, I thought you said—"

"You heard me." The words beheaded protest with a sharp edge and held it up, dripping. Robyn rose to his feet in one agitated, aggressive motion. "Gisbourne is taking me to Nottingham, and I've m' reasons, if you'd shut your bloody yaps long enough to listen to 'em!"

Truly impressive, the thin-spun trigger Robyn wielded on this particular and deadly crossbow. There was no question in Guy's mind that several of the men could have taken Robyn out by sheer bulk alone. Yet in this moment, not a one seemed willing to challenge his right to stand them down.

Guy had to look away, fix his hands against the bowl as, again, they shook. If only he could so easily still the sudden and insane stirring in his groin, responding to the feral command as readily as it had mere hours before.

Only hours before, every control he had remaining to him taken, bound and broken by a black-eyed demon's hands and voice—silken, merciless insistence...

"My sister's alive," Robyn said, curt.

There were a few mutters, choked off as Robyn glared their way. He did not, however, glare Will into silence as Will spoke, his voice rough.

"*Marion?*"

"Marion's *alive*, Will. She's in Nottingham Castle."

"How do you—"

"Gisbourne saw her."

"And you believe him?" Pain threaded beneath the query—one unwilling to slide into full-fledged agony. Guy knew the symptoms well, had a flicker of sympathy for Will.

Only he shouldn't. Feel. *Any*thing.

"I do. I have to. And I have to let him take me in."

"You . . . have to?"

"'Tis the surest way of getting her out, to be taken to her!"

"What is happening?" Siham hissed at Guy. Guy's first impulse was to snarl Siham into silence; when he looked to her, the impulse faded. Her dark eyes were wary; she mightn't understand the words, but she would have to be blind and deaf to not ken the explosion that had just occurred.

"I thought your sister died with Loxley." Gilbert was frowning.

Will's sun-browned face turned ashen. Arthur's hand alighted on his arm. David sighed, shaking his head and lowering the cook-pot back into the coals. The little ferret was nigh hidden beneath the folds of his woollen cowl. John had risen, watching dark-eyed and resigned.

"They now speak of a woman, a novice nun," Guy told Siham, quiet. "The Hood means to free her from Nottingham Castle."

Siham considered this, then nodded. "I see. Yes. This woman I know."

Guy froze, slid his gaze to her. "You . . . know."

"And how would some Motherless Templar Knight know Marion?" Will demanded. The words were shaky, still unwilling—and they rived Guy from his attention upon Siham. Arthur's arm had stolen about Will, obvious support and strength. But the poacher's eyes stayed riveted to Guy, dangerous.

"He wasn't bloody *born* a Templar," Robyn said, flat, and Guy knew what was coming, wished there was some way to stop it. "He's *Gamelyn*, Will."

Will's eyes widened, slid half-unwilling to take in Guy. The others followed suit, though some of them seemed less aware of what that name meant than Will obviously did.

"Bloody fuck!" Will exploded then, his voice softer but scaling upward, tight and incredulous, "Bloody . . . the poncy ginger paramour?"

An angry retort wanted to voice itself to this; Guy swallowed it, promised it he would pay Scathelock in kind later, then put half his attention back to Siham. He did not even consider taking the other half off Robyn, or his outlaws.

"And how long, then, have you known who Guy of Gisbourne

was, *Robyn Hood?*" Will's voice shook. "How long have you known about *Marion?*"

Robyn looked down, said, low. "Not long enough."

He wasn't speaking to the first, Guy knew, but the liability of the second raked bloody furrows along Guy's nerves. He forced the pain into its own small gaol, locked it, threw away the key. Said to Siham, again, "You know of the novice?"

Siham's notice, while divided, naturally stayed more intent upon her own conversation with Guy. "Indeed. The word went out by courier—mayhap two days ago? All the wayhouses and villages from Blackburn south were buzzing with it. A novice nun was gaoled under charge of witchcraft. They plan to burn her at the tournament." Her lip curled with disgust. "As part of their . . . entertainment."

Guy still didn't move, not so much as a breath of threat, but from across the fire, Robyn sensed . . . something. His gaze slid from Will to Guy and Siham, quietly measuring.

Arthur had also noticed the conversation if not the tension of it, had left Will's side and taken a few steps toward them. "What are y' saying to her?"

Guy ignored him, ignored them all; Siham's words had flared within him that wild, forlorn *anger*. He was glad to whip it into service, put his focus to a task, a necessity. With the light and pleasant mien of a torturer preparing the instruments, he asked, "What other secrets do you bear, woman?"

Siham gave a huff. "Secret? News passed in a wayhouse is no secret. And it is no secret I intend to win the tournament."

The tournament? What did the tournament have to do with it, other than a venue for . . .

Entertainment. Fury and outrage did battle within Guy's chest; he throttled them and leaned closer, ever so slightly. "Why?"

Siham flicked a glance at him, either did not see the murder lighting behind his eyes or was foolish enough to disregard it. Or mayhap didn't give a damn, Guy considered, as she continued, "My mother was burned. They said she was a witch, even as this woman supposedly is." Her eyes went shiny-flat. "Nottingham offers, to the winner, the 'honour' of loosing the first fire-arrow onto her pyre. I plan to shoot it into her breast. A fire is no quick or pleasant way to die. It does not matter whether she has the way of sihr or no, it is a pact I have made to her, woman to woman. We are sisters in this wrong, and she will know my mercy as I give it."

It seemed . . . obscene, speaking of Marion in this fashion. But he could not fault Siham's motivations—or her intent.

"Right, enough of that!" Arthur was suddenly standing over them, pawing at Guy's shoulder. The hand upon him, the demand, the stealth that had taken Guy by surprise—all of it demanded action.

Before Arthur could so much as register surprise, Guy leapt upward with the spring of a crouched predator, grabbed the poacher, and spun him into a headlock. Guy's free palm slapped against Arthur's jaw, ready to jerk his neck sideways.

It was all done so swiftly, the outlaws were stunned immobile. Then, as one, they lurched forward. Even Siham. Gilbert grabbed her arm.

Guy's muscles responded before his brain kicked in, backing a step, tightening the grip on Arthur. Arthur let out a fierce grunt—pain, surprise, shock—and Will in particular started forward again.

"You really don't want to do that," Guy snarled. "I can break his neck before any of you can touch me. *If* you can touch me."

"I can touch you." Robyn's voice sounded, low and hoarse, from beside the wych elm Guy had been tied to.

Guy kept most of his attention upon Arthur and the other men, let the rest of it slide towards the voice. Robyn held his longbow at full nock, an arrow aimed as absolute upon Guy as the black eyes staring down it.

"You'll back off," Robyn said. "*Now.*"

Guy hesitated for a mere second, heard the creak of the longbow arming further, then snarled again. Shoved Arthur away. To do Arthur credit, he didn't make the same mistake twice: he staggered a retreat, wheezing and choking his breath back.

In the resultant stunned silence, the only sounds were Arthur's coughing, and the tensile sound of Robyn relaxing his push on his longbow.

Siham yanked her arm from Gilbert's hold, lurched forward a step, shot Guy a query of outrage and concern. He answered it by holding up a hand and shaking his head.

"And you'd think t' trust *him?*" Will burst out, thrusting a finger towards Guy. "Trust Marion's life to a rabid dog of a monk what'd tear your throat out and not so much as break a sweat?"

Robyn gave a snarl and turned away. He twiddled the arrow back into its quiver— and left his bow blatantly strung.

"For nowt more than a boyhood memory what betrayed you *then,* you'll give him proper chance to do it again?"

"This is not open for discussion."

"No, you're right, it en't. We'll *not* be discussing owt puts you in that Templar's hands so's he can drag you back to the Sheriff and chain you up with your sister! *If* the bloody sod doesn't decide you're too much trouble to take back alive and 'stead chops off your head on the way!"

Robyn leaned his bow against the tree with a gentleness that belied his hands. White-knuckled, they shook. His eyes met Guy's, blazing, and Guy's own barely kennelled . . . *whatever* was all too happy to meet and match it.

Taste it, like blood spattered from a sword strike. "It doesn't matter," Guy said, gritting his teeth. *Down. Stay.* "It's done, and I'm—"

"You're what?" Arthur rasped out. "A bastard from a race of bas—"

"Arthur," Robyn said, wooden. Was Guy the only one who smelt the fury beneath it? Who suddenly saw, behind Robyn, a horned figure of molten pitch and black heat? "Belt up, or I'll do you m'self."

"But *Robyn!*" Will protested, taking a step forward. "This is madness!"

Madness . . . aye. Did no one else see the madness running beneath Robyn's skin like blood? Did none of them hear it, like a heartbeat, and one Guy couldn't purge from demanding his own to heat and beat?

"You can't—"

"I *can* shut you up." Will spun on Guy. "This en't your business."

"Will." Robyn, warning.

"You can try," Guy hissed. *Take me on, then. Leave him, and take me.*

Will's eyes narrowed, his gaze on Guy but his words to Robyn. "*Damn* it, wain't you see what's going on, Robyn? He's *one* of 'em—a murderin' monk, a nobleman killer! He en't that boy no more, I en't, you en't—'cept you're actin' as foolish as one with this. D'you truly think any of us'll let you do this?"

John let out a tiny noise—it could have been a groan, or a sigh.

Almost in the same breath, Robyn whirled, strode forward. In the next breath, he'd swung. The openhanded blow caught Will off guard, sent him back on his arse in the dirt with a stagger and slide. Robyn leapt on him before he could regain his feet, crouching over him, one hard hand at his chest and the other drawn back, prepared to do it again.

"Are they mad?" Siham demanded. She had come up behind Guy, unnoticed. She did not speak Arabic, but *langue d'oc*, and Guy answered her, unthinking, in the same tongue.

"Shut *up*, woman!"

Siham gave a soft curse, but not at him, so he put her from his mind. He also dismissed Gilbert's sudden frown and glance.

"So you'll *let* me?" Robyn marvelled, his voice oh-so-soft. It fooled none of them, this time—least of all Guy, who could feel each breath like talons compressing his own lungs. "So now I'm a fool, a helpless fool who canna be trusted to make a proper choice?" Robyn's fingers tightened. "I'm not so helpless I canna knock *you* over, Scathelock. If you'd your way, you'd keep me wrapped in a doe-skin cloak!"

"You're not understanding! You never have done, you *wain't*. You're my brother in everything but blood," Will husked back. "You're all that's left."

"But I'm not all that's left, am I? *He's* left." Robyn jerked his head toward Guy, standing in the midst of a loose semi-circle of staring outlaws.

Every bit of Guy's own fury was runnelling away from him, as if the watching ebon figure had drawn the furore from him, like a poultice to a pus-pocket.

And it was a *relief*.

"He's *nowt*—!" Will choked off as Robyn's fingers tightened on his throat.

Guy raised his eyebrows; he knew that hold by now. Akin to prying a limpet from a ship's hull, breaking it.

"And *Marion's* left. That's what this is about, you know. Not me. Not Gamelyn." The slip was telling—too telling. "What about Marion, then? You once said you loved her! What would you have me do, leave her there?"

Will's eyes dimmed. Robyn angled back, loosened his hold.

It was a mistake. Will hadn't given in; Guy could see the eagerness quivering in his hands and thighs, waiting. Guy started forward; a hand grasped his sleeve and he stiffened, slid his eyes sideways, and started to tell Siham to mind her own business . . .

It was John, eyes gleaming. Plain as plain, if Guy interfered, he would have to go through John to do it.

So the moment came, quicker than Guy expected but much *as* expected. No less a fighter—and likely a better one—once Robyn eased any leverage, a matter of mere brawn for Will to heave up, flip Robyn onto his back, and sit on him.

"Have they gone mad?" Siham muttered again.

Guy could only hope. And hope all this wouldn't end in a massive, snarling wolfpile. He exchanged a troubled glance with John, followed that glance to where Arthur and Gilbert and David were standing, looking remarkably helpless.

"Get off me!" Robyn spat.

"You en't *going!*"

"You have no—"

"I should be the one!" Will retorted, shoving Robyn back down, hard, against the earth when he tried to rise. "There's none to say as I en't Robyn Hood, and if any of us're to die, it can't be you, *Ardhu*. I can see that even if you wain't!"

Robyn glared up at him, silent. Then he took in a soft breath, released it in a cold command. "*Rhyddau fi.*"

Release me.

Guy *saw* it, like a fingered, thick mist. Felt the words drop like stones. Sensed the pressure of them behind his ears and eyes, chill cold, putting a tense wobble to his knees. It was suddenly hard to breathe, as if the air had been sucked from his lungs. A hand took hold of his sleeve. This time, neither John nor Guy exchanged worry or threat; Guy felt only a sudden apprehension, and John's face had drawn in an odd, puzzled concern.

Everyone had stepped back, even Siham, who had no idea what was happening. Will was no less affected. It clearly took everything he had, to resist the breath as it wrapped around his face and then his chest, barely seen fog of magical duress. His hands shook, pressed against Robyn's shoulders, fought. The veins stood out on his neck, his eyes staring, defiant. But in the end, he had no choice. He broke away with a gasp, fell back.

Released.

It released Guy, as well. He clenched his fists, refused a stagger for a step toward Robyn, then two.

The others predictably, bristled. Not that he cared.

"This is ridiculous," he growled. "If I behaved to my master as you do to yours, I'd be hanged."

"I'm not their master," Robyn growled right back, and flung the hair out of his face, just spoiling for another row.

"I think you've just proven you are," Guy pointed out, clipped. "But this time you need to listen to what they're saying. You need to listen to Siham even more."

"Listen to the girl?" Arthur started.

Gilbert peered at Siham. "She speaks Frank."

Robyn's eyes widened, and in quick demonstration, Gilbert shot a Frankish query at Siham.

Her eyes also widened, and she answered, rapid.

"And?" Robyn was terse.

"She says she thought we were commoners, without the Frankish tongue."

"It doesn't matter, it doesn't . . . all of you just bloody well *shut up!*" Guy strode forward, ignoring the threat that oozed from just about all the men as he did so. "Robyn. I was listening to what she had to say to me about the archery contest. Your men spoke of monetary prizes. But there are . . . others." He met Robyn's eyes. "One in particular."

Robyn's brow furrowed.

"They're going to burn a witch at the archery tournament. The winning archer is granted the right to shoot the arrow that will set the pyre ablaze."

The confusion on Robyn's face was transforming into horror with every word Guy spoke.

"I don't know what's happened, but time has caught us up. We have to decide what we're doing. Now."

Ⓜ

The decision came easy, in the end—and one agreeable even to the wariest of the outlaws. Guy insisted upon it; Gilbert put it in terms his comrades were comfortable with: if the Templar indeed seemed intent upon aiding them, then why not let the Templar use his influence to do so?

Guy also pointed out that, if influence didn't work, he'd the means—and the run of the place—to free Marion, and easier than any outlaw with no knowledge of castles and a price on his head.

Robyn was aware of Guy peering at him for much of the discussion. He did not return the favour, merely kept his attention on using the quillion dagger to trace designs in the rich loam between his crossed knees.

Guy kept looking at the dagger too.

David spoke up, then, sketching his own experiences with being imprisoned in Nottingham. Gilbert also had valuable input; he had visited the castle, but in the upper levels as a guest with his family. Between the three—Gilbert, David and Guy—rough possibility firmed into solid offensive. In the end everyone had their say—which from the look on Guy's face, he wasn't used to. Happens he was more used to just shooting orders and having them obeyed, Robyn figured.

The escape plan furled out, elegantly simple, tight-hewn. Foolproof.

And Robyn didn't trust it.

If it were a horse, he'd be wary in the saddle, and he didn't even understand why. Nay, he did, but there were too many questions, too many answers they just didn't have, too many futures and possibilities swirling in and out of his Sight.

Or mayhap he was being the fool that Will had accused him. For truly, 'twere the plan he didn't trust, not Guy's execution of it.

Robyn nodded absent compliance, and kept his own counsel.

John would go with Guy, a link with the world outside the walls. Siham would go as well, continue her delayed journey to the archery contest—and good luck to her.

At least Gilbert had answered Robyn's questions as to why she was taking the loss of her party with such equanimity. They were mere escort from Pontefract, charged with seeing her safe delivery to the archery tournament for her sponsor, the Baron de Lacy. Once she had discovered Gilbert's fluency in the Frankish tongue, she had willingly spoken with him. Finding him, no doubt, more willing to hold conversation than a sullen—and conflicted, Robyn could smell it—Templar. Gilbert fancied talking, no question.

They were still talking several hours later, Gilbert and Siham, seeing to the horses the outlaws had liberated from Siham's party. A light mist had begun to fall; a good day to ride, as long as it didn't start pouring.

"It's a good plan," said Guy, as if he sensed Robyn's hesitancy. He kept ducking Robyn's gaze—not that Robyn blamed him, doing his own share of the avoidance dance—and kept busy checking over the chestnut rouncey he'd chosen as mount. They would fetch his warhorse from Peveril on their way south. Robyn shrugged, one hand fingering the dagger at his hip, the other combing through the horse's red-flax tail, and contemplated how bloody sodding daft it was to wish he was combing Guy's hair, instead.

It bided the same colour, even.

Not just daft. Pathetic. It was done. They'd had one rut-crazed night to settle old frustrations. It was enough. It had to be.

He is your lord, and you his. It will never be enough between you, one death or the many little ones, aye? The Horned Lord's voice seemed to waft between them, a hot breeze. Robyn found himself listing toward Guy, had to step back, recover some sense of distance.

A foe to our foes is friend, not enemy. The Horned Lord, capricious as ever, had obviously decided that Guy, alive and being rutted senseless into the ground by Robyn, was more amusing than Robyn ensuring Guy's blood was duly spilt over that same ground.

The tupping's done, damn you, Robyn hissed into the black.

The Horned Lord merely chuckled.

"It is an old Arabic proverb: Mine enemy's enemies are my friends," Guy said, strangely serene for all that he intended to ride into Nottingham castle and possibly commit treason.

Perhaps he, like Robyn, had grown quite used to it by now.

"You heard." Satisfaction filled Robyn as his voice remained as calm and controlled as the Templar's ever was. He could only hope he'd not heard the entirety of it.

Guy hesitated, fingers stilling at the girth billets, then continuing to roll the buckles upward and snug. "It . . . wasn't you then, was it?"

"He doesn't sound like me."

"Oh, He does," Guy said, tight and almost inaudible.

Robyn found himself once more angling forward, ever so slight; instead he backed off, shooting a self-conscious glance over to where Arthur, David, and Will stood around the fire, making quiet conversation—and keeping an eye on That Templar, particularly since Robyn stood within reach. It was a welcome distraction to see John approaching, holding a longbow—albeit a sobering one. John's face was mournful; he kept caressing the bow with gentle strokes.

Robyn started to turn away, instead hesitated, his fingers once again finding then lingering upon the hilt of the quillion dagger at his hip. Guy turned to peer at him, curious, and tensed as Robyn drew the dagger from his belt. Robyn saw the green eyes flicker to Guy's own sword, tied athwart the chestnut gelding's saddle—instinct, nothing more or less.

Robyn put the dagger to his lips, then took a deep breath. Handed the dagger, hilt first, to Guy.

Guy's composure had bled into open astonishment. He started to speak.

Robyn forestalled it. "'Twere yours, after all. In the beginning. Still yours, here at the end of it."

"The end." The breath hummed into the air; Robyn fancied he could feel it lift his hair. "*Robyn . . .* "

"Take it, y' ginger-haired git," Robyn insisted, still holding out the dagger. "I think"—and bloody damn, but his own voice creaked like an ill-strung bed—"think you might be needin' it."

Wordless, Guy reached out, palmed the dagger, and stuck it in his belt.

John came over, still holding the longbow. Robyn turned from Guy, met John halfway. "Don't forget," Robyn murmured. "Papplewick."

John's gaze met his, firm confirmation. Then his face turned once again lugubrious. He handed the bow to Robyn. John had made it, a spare for when Robyn did not wish to risk harm to his grandsire's great Welsh longbow. On this spare were the telltale marks of the Shire Wode covenant. Between that and the immense length and pull of the bow . . . there simply were no others in the midlands of England who wielded such a bow. It was weapon, friend, battle comrade . . .

Statement.

It took several tries and a boot added to every bit of Robyn's considerable shoulder strength to break it. It almost broke his heart in the doing. But he and John had agreed— this was the final proof, and they weren't about to let it go whole into enemy hands. It, even more than any bloodied trophy, would be verification that Robyn Hood had indeed been slain. It would buy them time, not only to free their Maiden—but to escape with her into the green Wode, see to whatever she might need, disappear.

"That's my part done, then," Robyn said, as Gilbert put the pieces in a sack, wrapped it tight and handed it up to Guy.

"I know exactly what to do for mine," Guy said, grim. He fastened the broken longbow to his saddle pommel, then vacated the near stirrup, held an arm down to John. With lithe ease, John mounted behind him, turned his eyes to Robyn.

"*Au revoir, ma chérie.*" Gilbert blew a kiss to Siham, and she actually flushed.

"Cheeky," David warned.

Guy peered at Robyn, solemn. "I'll bring Marion back. However I must. *Allons,*" he said to Siham, then wheeled his horse and cantered away. Siham followed, the remainder of the horses on a tether behind her.

"I don't trust him, Robyn," Will said, coming up from behind.

"This far, I do," Robyn said, very quiet. "After?"

After, the Horned Lord breathed along his nape, *he will be ours. One way or the other.*

ᛗ

Mist worked itself into a steady rain. Nevertheless, Guy gave no explanation as they detoured slightly east, passing from forest road into fields. The ending of harvest was evident: those fields were thickly populated, villeins hard at work to bring in the crops despite the rain. They passed through the nigh-deserted village of Matlock—again, every able-bodied worker in the fields—and picked their way through the marshy outskirts, moving to the cover of a copse of trees. There, within sight, hunched a familiar and flea-ridden hut.

Familiar to Guy, anyway.

When John started to slide down, Guy gripped his arm. "Stay here," he ordered, eyed Siham as well. "Both of you."

Flinging his off leg over the horse's neck, Guy handed the rein to John and unbuckled his sword from its scabbard, pulling it free with the hard, sweet rasp of fine-forged metal.

Finally. Something to take the edge off. Action. Righteousness, in its most basic form.

The villein lay curled up alone on his vermin-infested mattress. Sleeping off the pleasantry of a well-scraped plate beside him, possessed of all his limbs—in short, skiving whilst his kin worked like dogs. And . . .

You handed me a secret you had no rights to, you puling traitor, and of that secret you will tell none else.

This would be pure pleasure.

Guy toed the mattress, gave a growl. When that didn't work, he kicked the bony haunch protruding from the tattered blanket. "Up."

"G-gi' off me!" Still groggy, at first the villein didn't recognise him. Then he did. "M-my lord?"

Guy grabbed him by his grubby tunic, dragged him up and out through the squat door of the hut into the rain.

"Milord!" the man howled, staggering along. "What? Please, my lord!"

Guy said nothing, pulled his cowl over his face, and kept dragging the villein by his tunic over the sodden ground. The villein's howling diminished to a moaning whine, his staggers to resigned stumbles and slips. Guy didn't stop until they came to another stand of stunted trees and thick eelgrass. He gave a shove; the villein went sprawling in the tall, sharp grass.

It was more than adequate, this place.

"M-milord." The villein dragged himself over, grovelled at Guy's feet. "Please. I didn't lie, I didn't. *Please*, I didn't—"

Guy hefted his falchion, a curve of silver glittering in the rain.

"This," he informed the villein, "is quite personal. I'm sorry."

The villein didn't even have time to scream.

- Entr'acte -

It had been a long and frustrating hunt. One would think a tall, red-haired Templar would be easy enough to find—if nothing else, through the trail of corpses he would be wont to leave behind.

But, not so easy. Dolfin had as yet found no corpses—well, none a Templar had given cause to. He had been asked to give the last rites at several villages he'd passed through: one an old wood carver who'd dropped over his bench—not a bad way to go, at that—and the other a premature birthing of twins that had also cost the father their mother.

No sign of Guy, however. And to confuse the matter further, there were a lot of people on the move, travelling to Nottingham for Count John's tournament. The news travelling with them made Dolfin realise anew how imperative it was to find Guy.

His progress lagged slower than Dolfin would like, to boot. He hadn't taken such a purposeful trek in some time—obviously been indulging in too much comfort, fresh bread, and "just one more" postprandial ale. His jennet possessed a comfortable gait, and his saddle had been well-padded with sheepskin, but he still spent the mornings gimping about, saddle-sore.

Then he came upon the telltale corpse.

The people of Matlock were staggered—the man had been a useless clot, but to die in such a fashion! Random butchery. Senseless. It was what happened when all sorts were travelling the roads and not staying where they belonged like proper folk.

Save that the man's sister, helping Dolfin prepare the body for burial, kept murmuring about her brother giving offence, sacrilege. Bit by bit, Dolfin had finagled the whys and wheretofores from her, such as they were. Her obvious hesitancy at confiding her true beliefs to one of the Church was disarmed by Dolfin's unautocratic responses. She seemed positive her brother had offended the Horned Lord with his unwise tongue. Robyn Hood's justice was not to be trifled with. Likely her brother's skull hung in the Shire Wode on a sacred oak, offering to the Horned Lord. Templar? Aye, there had been a Templar pass through not long ago, but everyone knew that. Looking for Robyn Hood, he was. She could only hope her brother hadn't opened his yap to *that* one. Word was, the Templar'd been threatening the villages as had ties . . .

Her eyes went big, then, and she shut up. Even innocuous queries got Dolfin nowhere. When he left off speaking, busy with the rites, she departed for a short while, but came back almost immediately.

When Dolfin finished, rites and anointing, she held out a ha'penny in offering for Dolfin's service—no doubt what she had gone to retrieve. He took it, unwilling to offend her grave courtesy. And then gave it back to her, doubled, in exchange for a meal and a bed for the night—the sun was sinking quickly in the sky, and Dolfin knew better than to chance the forest roads at night. Outlaws.

He woke the next morning to find a stranger seated beside his bed, watching him with a patient, if intent, gaze. The man looked as if he'd been travelling, damp with rain and his boots and breeches spattered with mud. He had a short, thick dagger in his hands, flipping it between his fingers in some negligent—and rather threatening—game. His cape, flung back and patchy with wet, exposed a broad, leather-clad frame, sandy hair and several days' scruff of beard. There was a strange bulge beneath the left breast of his overtunic that kept . . . moving.

Dolfin rose to sit up—albeit slowly, keeping his hands in view the entire time. "Might I help you, my son?"

"I'm no' your son," the stranger ventured, mild. The bulge roiled again, then two beady eyes and a pointed, whiskered nose popped up over the vee of the man's tunic.

Dolfin started, then couldn't help the grin quirking at his mouth. A ferret.

But the grin faded quickly, as the stranger pointed the thick knife at him. "I hear you've a curiosity on you. About Robyn Hood."

The ferret chittered, as if laughing at Dolfin.

- XX -

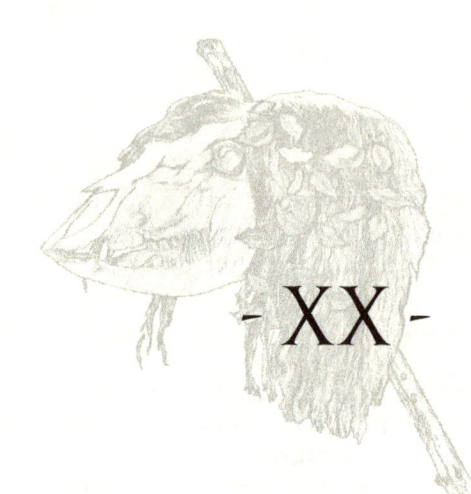

"I'm not terribly certain of any of this."

"Hm. That makes three of us."

Siham spoke first; Guy repeated it in English for the benefit of his passenger, gave an eloquent shrug as he halted Falcon. Turning in the saddle, he held out a supportive arm to John, mounted pillion. "Best to dismount here. There's still goodly tree cover."

John eschewed the offered arm, leaned his forehead against Guy for a trace of seconds. Then John's hands came up to Guy's shoulders, warmth against sudden tension, one sliding upward to curl about his neck.

Siham watched, dark eyes narrowed—suspicion, or deliberation? Either way, she put a wary hand to her knife. It didn't put John off, no more than the stiffening of Guy's shoulders. Siham had already expressed reservations when Guy had told her that John, unlike many peasants, was a fine rider.

"Why, then?" Siham had eyed John, who had ignored her as he'd done all along. "Why ride behind you?"

Guy had shrugged. "Who knows, with John?"

Now, however, it made abrupt sense as a warm weight dropped upon his breastbone and a leather cord brushed his throat. The amulet lay heavy with presence; John had been, all during the ride, wrapping Guy's power into his own, their physical touch the final magic of all. John leaned closer, pulled Guy's hair from his nape and kissed it, then tied the amulet as he breathed a soft tangle of words. Most of them Guy did not know—the old tongue, for the magic of the heath—but he shivered, and John spooned closer, furthered:

"Remember who you are, what you've been, what you shall be."

John kissed his ear, this time, lingered at his pulse point, whispered, "Save her, but don't forget *him*. Don't forget *yourself*, Gamelyn."

Guy shivered again, raised his hand to his throat, and traced the amulet with his fingertips. The oak heartwood John had been working the night before had been shaped into a series of curves and angles, akin to a broadhead, yet with hollows and interlacings. The tiny thing warmed at Guy's touch, and his frame gave another strange and resultant little shiver. He started to turn, but John merely pushed away and, swinging his leg over Falcon's croup, dropped to the ground. Giving a satisfied lift of brow to the bloodstained meal-sack hanging next to Guy's boot, John went over and, with a nod to Siham, took the reins to the three horses she led. His gaze moved to Guy's, held, a few breaths of silent avowal before John turned away, made his retreat into the trees, the horses ambling behind.

Siham's gaze had turned perplexed. "Robyn's men," she finally said, "are all riddles."

"Parlez le français," he chided.

She obeyed. "It is . . . sorcery."

"Once," he reflected, "I feared it was."

"But now, you are a Templar."

Not for the first time, Guy wondered what she knew of Templars—and how she knew it. Instead he shrugged it off as inconsequential, focused on the task at hand, cued Falcon to walk on.

After a brief hesitation, looking after where John had disappeared, Siham followed.

"Are you sure we should separate? I—"

"Keep to what we agreed." It wasn't the first time, for offer or denial. Guy fixed a steady gaze on his unlikely compatriot. "I do not impugn your bravery or skill. This is not your fight." She started to speak again; he shook his head. "Your patron is a fair man, of his kind, but believe me, he will see little honour in this. Go to the archery tournament, win your marks then leave Nottingham and don't look back. You'll have a few tales to tell—and most important, keep your head."

Siham eyed the burden tied to his saddle. "Indeed."

"And if you have the ear of your god this day, pray."

"We all have the ear of God, Templar," Siham replied.

"Aye," Guy said, putting a leather-clad calf to Falcon's ribs for a canter. "But which one?"

Ⓜ

"I tell you, this one means no harm," David insisted, still panting slightly from his run across the fields.

"What is it, monks fallin' from the sky, next?" Arthur groused. "We can't be shed of th' bastards."

"We're nobbut a lot of pagan outlaws to their sort," Will agreed. "Moreover, Robyn is supposed to be a *dead* outlaw. That's why we're s'posed to be staying clear."

"Enough," Robyn said from his perch. They'd all climbed into a broad-beamed willow overlooking the marshlands nigh to Matlock. "We were passing, proper easy to wait while David went t' see his gramma. And glean information, if any were t' be had."

"Aye, true enough. At that," Arthur pointed out, "a corpse minus its head is pretty informative."

"You knew the family?" Gilbert cocked his head.

David nodded. "But not the corpse. Some skiver half brother from west of here. His kin were trying to do right by him, but he didna pay them half the same courtesy."

Robyn took it in, musing. Guy had laid a few dark hints as to what head he would substitute for Robyn's. Fair enough; the scum had lain his faithless tongue to what he shouldn't.

"Talking to some vulture of Christ, man!" Will shook his head. "Are y' daft?"

"This one's fair enough, I'll wager."

Will scoffed again. "What, a little bird told you so?"

"P'rhaps a robin?" Gilbert quipped, then shut it as the bird's quasi-namesake rolled black eyes at him.

David ignored them, climbed up to sit beside Robyn. "Look. I'd little time to pry overmuch from him, but with what he did give, I knew I had to come and tell you, Robyn."

"So," Robyn said, "tell me."

"He's not really looking for you. He's looking for the one looking for you. The Templar."

Robyn stilled. The others watched, intent.

"Interesting, aye?" David prompted.

"Proper interesting," Robyn concurred.

"He's determined to find Gisbourne. I told him precious little, mind, but he didna tell me much, either. Canny bugger. Speakin' all proper. His name's Brother Dolfin."

"Dolfin." Robyn mouthed the name. It was familiar, somehow.

"He did let slip enough that I think he knows what's going on at Nottingham," David furthered. "He's come a ways with the news, too—from that old church nigh where we gathered Samhain."

Faint memory teased into a skein as Robyn pulled it. Brother Dolfin. From Blyth. Gamelyn's confessor.

Sweet Lady, old acquaintances were popping out of the ground like earthworms charmed by rasp and stick.

"I want to meet this monk," Robyn said, and leapt down.

Ⓜ

No doubt but a royal personage was in residence at Nottingham—and one who fancied himself considerably royal, since he'd staged a tournament within an unlicensed fiefdom. Nottingham made a particularly odd choice since Count John already held a chartered tournament ground as his own—Blyth's honour, Tickhill.

Or, Guy considered, not so odd at that. King Richard had been the one to set up the tournament charters—what better way for Count John to negate his sibling's sovereign influence than openly defy it? Not to mention the satisfaction it would hold: brassing off a too-powerful older brother was, after all, a ploy Guy himself had once participated in.

In consequence, the castle approach stayed busy with comings and goings, the road to the bridge dusty with many feet and the castle a-hum with industry. The surround leading up to the outer bailey wall was already peppered with not only simple campsites, but the showy tents and colours of visiting knights hoping to vie for prizes. There was an energy to it, a buzz ramping upward into an almost physical rush like, yet so pleasantly unalike, the precursors of real battle. As if a safety net were cast, somehow, in taunting death cleanly, facing down not villagers and innocents amidst a warrior enemy, but skilled knights hungry for the challenge. Guy hadn't seen its like since his last several years at Blyth, could remember with a mixed stutter of emotions the tournaments held there. Neither his father nor his elder brother had permitted him to take part in the main events—Sir Ian had proclaimed him too young, and Johan had proclaimed him too unskilled. Now Guy was neither, and even though he still mightn't be free to indulge sudden fancies, he knew himself capable. And, perhaps, knew his father would have stood in the lists, proud of his last-born son.

The taut expectancy in the air held more welcome remembrance than not; Guy turned his face to it like a fair wind and smiled.

Beside him, Siham rode quietly, lost in her own thoughts. On the walls looming up before them, the normal dark blue of the sheriff's guards were peppered here and there with red tunics, and the corner turret had a familiar banner flying. The slick of adrenaline firing Guy's veins ramped up even more, quickening his breath at the sight of the rampant Angevin lions that had overseen so many of the battles he'd fought.

Kenning his master's agitation, Falcon danced beneath him, black hoofs pounding hollow as they went from turf to the moat bridge. Guy had his hands full for a moment as the horse gave an excited leap sideways on the bridge, scattering passersby then propping on his front end at the last minute with bowed neck and bugged-out eyes as they came to the edge. Guy caught a grin on Siham's face as he careened past her, but others were less amused. Several were flat unlucky, falling into the water below with a sharp cry and splash. Guy gave Falcon a boot in the ribs, sent him forward through the gate and past the guards before he again took hold and headed back to the gatehouse at a prance. The guards were grinning. Siham, awaiting their permission, hid a smile that Guy was hard-pressed not to return. Instead he took adrenaline—his own and his horse's—to stern task and commanded Falcon to a halt. The young stallion obeyed, not without a wheel of eye and a champing of his bits.

"He seems a handful, milord Templar," the eldest of the guardsmen spoke—and it was admiring. "This lad says he came with you?"

"He has come for the archery contest, a lone survivor of his party. They were victim to outlaws—of which there is one less in Sherwood today." Guy nudged the sack at his knee, watched the guardsmen's eyes widen in varied shades of pleasure and anticipation. "Tell the Sheriff's seneschal that Sir Guy has returned, if you please. And kindly show this fellow to a decent lodging for himself and his horse—I have fulfilled my duty in seeing him safe to Nottingham. He has no Anglic, but speaks Frank."

"Aye, milord Templar; we'll see him put to rights." The elder guardsman turned, gave quiet orders to two of his underlings; one ran to do his bidding.

Guy nodded a terse farewell to Siham; her gaze met his, held there then turned away as a guard came up to her. Guy loosened his rein and turned Falcon's nose to the keep. The horse had started to settle down. Action was always better than the anticipation.

He noted several of Count John's men there, eyeing him with a suspicion they didn't dare express openly. He peered stolidly at them until they looked down, furthered, "And find my paxman. Send a lad to meet me at the door and take my horse."

"Aye, milord," the guard acknowledged, and Guy let Falcon move on.

Both the lower and upper baileys were crowded with more than the usual complement of vendors, taking advantage of the extra visitors, no doubt. Guy threaded the crowd—most of whom gave way as they saw horse and rider—and further contemplated his strategy. If he was lucky, the only hitch to his plan would be in delivering his prize to Count John as well as de Lisle. Not a bad hitch, at that. In the process, Guy might well glean valuable information for his masters and Temple Hirst.

He had to find Much. And from there, find where they held Marion.

The lad who waited for him up the mound seemed familiar, but had no help for Guy as to Much's whereabouts. There was no sign of the seneschal yet, either. Guy dismounted, gave Falcon a pat. The lad watched with a mix of fascination and trepidation as Guy scorned his saddlebag for the one at his cantle, and untied the burlap bag slung from the saddle skirts.

"Give my mount a good graining, and have my other saddlebag brought to my chambers," he told the lad, and gave him a ha'penny to sweeten it. "I'll likely have a task for you."

The lad smiled, bobbed his head, and led Falcon off. Guy watched him go, considering. Depending on the situation, he might be able to outright demand Marion's release, claim she had value to his masters. If that claim was acknowledged, then 'twas likely he could simply and openly ride away from Nottingham with Marion. No risk, no possibilities of foul.

"My lord Templar?"

Guy turned. The steward, Sir Edward, approached the doorway's massive arch. Dressed in much more state than Guy had yet seen, his manner was harried. "My apologies, my lord Templar. Count John is seeing royal petitioners today."

All of this—the monarch's flag flying, the guards, and now "royal" petitioners? It smacked of liberties beyond the realm of even a king's brother. The frown begging a twitch at Guy's brow must have been more visible than he thought—either that or Sir Edward was in tacit agreement, for he nodded, ever so slightly.

"It is unusual, my lord. But my lord Count is . . . an unusual man." Sir Edward hesitated, then said, "I informed Sheriff de Lisle of your arrival. He has requested, should you have what he hopes, I am to immediately escort you to where he and Count John are holding court."

What Guy had expected, though his nerves were hyped and tensile enough to be wary of every twitch of the steward's frame.

"No doubt," Guy drawled, "Sheriff de Lisle also gave you instructions that I should cool my heels until he said otherwise if I did not have what he hopes."

"My lord . . . " Naked panic crept over the steward's face.

Guy almost chuckled, quickly turned it into a conciliatory smile and held up his burden. "By your leave, I do indeed possess what your master requires."

"That is most excellent, my lord!" Sir Edward's relief was palpable. A little older than Guy himself, yet altogether young. He'd need to toughen his hide to survive this post. "The seneschal made me come. Frankly, he feared you might have disappointing news, and—"

"Of course," Guy said, then prodded, "He did say immediately?" *Let's have this mummers play, shall we?*

Ⓜ

The outlaws waited until Dolfin, mounted on his jennet, left Matlock and headed north. They tailed him for a while, silent and swift, then cut across on a switchback and got ahead of him. Robyn sent his 'muscle'—David, Will, and Arthur—onto the road proper, waiting in the trees with Gilbert.

They waited, their attention fully bent on the bend of road. And waited. Finally hoofs resounded from up the road, coming at a brisk trot; they all made ready.

The jennet came around the bend, trotting for all she was worth. Riderless.

Gilbert swore. "Bloody—!"

Robyn sensed rather than felt the *whoosh* of air; he ducked purely by instinct as the staff came down from behind them. Gilbert also ducked, but just that much too late; the staff, wielded by a dervish in brown, clipped the back of his head and he fell forward with a grunt. Robyn sprang forward, aborted it just in time and spun sideways as, with remarkable speed, the staff came flying again, whacking the tree trunk just behind where he'd been standing.

"Think to ambush a man of the Church, do you?" Brother Dolfin not only stepped light as Tess on a hunt, but wielded his poor man's weapon with pure fury in his eye. "Well not all of us are easy marks, I'll tell you!" With a cry, he pressed in again. Robyn leapt over, then ducked under, rolling to one side.

A shout from the road—Will—but Robyn had no chance to answer it. The monk really was murder with a staff. Robyn saw the others loping in from the road—Arthur hauling along the jennet, David with his staff, Will with an arrow at nock—and shouted, "Don't shoot! See to Gilly!"

Another flurry of blows, Robyn using every bit of agility he possessed to avoid them. Finally he clambered up a tree, padded across a broad branch, and leapt to the next tree—closer to his men—and swung down.

"Robyn! Here!" Will came to the rescue, grabbed David's staff and threw it. Robyn whipped it around twice, making sure he had the weight and heft of it, then faced off against the monk.

But the monk—Brother Dolfin, Robyn reminded himself—was staring at him.

"Christ's blood. You're Robyn Hood."

Robyn took the momentary advantage, lurched forward and swung. His first blow connected briefly, sending Dolfin staggering back with a grunt; the second met a block of resounding strength. Back and forth, attack and retreat, the staves cracked and knocked and slid, echoing through the trees. It seemed they were fairly matched, blow for blow—but Dolfin was tiring. Well-muscled beneath his brown habit, but soft.

"Too much ale and not enough walking, then?" Robyn said, all too sweetly as he danced back from an attempted clip to one shoulder.

"More than enough to deal with a scrawny lad," Dolfin growled back. "I think the King of Sherwood needs a new crown." He flipped one end of his staff toward Robyn's head, deadly emphasis.

Robyn dodged, spun back to face Dolfin. "We call it the Shire Wode, here." Robyn punctuated his correction with a feint, then a swing. "*Monk.*"

Dolfin hopped back. "*We* prefer to be called 'Brother'." Followed it up with a whirling riposte and advance.

Robyn ducked just in time—the monk might be soft, but bloody *damn* was he fast. "There's none o' your like I'd trust with me back turned, let alone call 'Brother'." He lunged forward, laid a barrage of blows—right-left-under-under—felt a smirk playing at his lip as Dolfin blocked them all. Fair play to the monk, then.

Dolfin saw the smirk, misinterpreted it, lunged forward with a growl. He feinted under, then swung over. Robyn spun, flung his own staff up. The blow deflected, it then swerved, a purposeful ricochet that gave Robyn a sharp rap on the shoulder, then slid down and barked his fingers. His staff flew from his numbed hand.

"*That*," Dolfin said, "is repayment for nigh drowning a friend of mine." Then he opened his hands, let his own staff drop to the ground. "Kindly tell your friends not to shoot me."

Robyn, shaking his stinging hand, shot a quick glance over his shoulder. Sure enough, Will still had an arrow at nock, covering him. Arthur was helping Gilbert to his feet.

"I shan't be offering any more harm. Unless,"—the monk's blue eyes went hard—"you've done further harm to my friend."

"By your friend, I assume you mean the Templar you're looking for," Robyn said, bending—carefully—to pick up the staff. As Dolfin nodded, Robyn furthered, smirking again, "Your friend, Guy of Gisbourne, who was once Gamelyn Boundys."

Dolfin's face went slack. He tried to speak; it took several times before any words would emerge. "H . . . how does Robyn Hood know that name?"

"Mm." Robyn tossed the staff back to Will. "I had a slightly different name meself, once. Rob of Loxley. Mayhap Gamelyn mentioned me to you?"

Ⓜ

"Gilly's a proper noble's brat, 'm afraid."

"Hoy!" Woozy, but a definite protest. Will and David had muscled Gilbert farther into woodland cover and against a sturdy tree.

Robyn grinned from his own seat—a large stone—and continued, "He's no' the staff in his blood like us peasants. You gave us the proper slip, Brother."

"Which en't easy," Arthur added, with no little chagrin. "We was watchin' the road too hard, Robyn," he made excuse.

"All of us," Robyn admitted. "Surely you didn't hear us?"

Dolfin shook his head. "But I must confess I expected something untoward, once your Scots friend with the ferret here showed up and vanished."

David grinned self-consciously from where he stood next to the monk. From the pouch hanging at David's belt, Tess burbled at Dolfin and gave a friendly nibble to the fingers he extended.

"I didn't expect the Hood himself," Dolfin said, serious. "Or to find Robyn Hood was the young man who . . ." His eyes flickered, uncertain, over the small group of outlaws.

Ire licked behind Robyn's eyes. "'Tis only in your religion that sex is a wicked thing, monk. You think these men—my brothers in all but blood—en't knowing what sort I choose to bed?"

Dolfin started to speak, peered at Robyn, then fell silent. "I'll admit I were wary of sayin' owt about Gisbourne. Not because he has tackle out 'stead of in, but because of what he is. What power he stands for—the least of which is making it some crime worse than murder for a man to love another man."

"There is nothing wrong with seeking a higher path."

"Nay," Robyn replied. "But who are you, monk, to say what's rightful part of any *higher* path? And what right do your people have to make filth from nature's ways? Or make an innocent spirit hate themselves for it? *Like Gamelyn.*"

Dolfin, to do him credit, looked down. "I don't have an answer for you, lad. I'm not here to judge anyone. God knows I've my own failings, and I've no rights to belittle what people find holy." His gaze rose again, met Robyn's. "This is a discussion I would gladly have with you another time. Peace, for now?"

Robyn inclined his head. "Peace, then. Between you and us, at any rate," he added. "I wain't promise the same for the rest of t' White Christ's followers."

Dolfin angled forward, hands on knees. "Considering what some misguided souls in my Church have done to you and yours, I can't say as I blame you."

Robyn leaned back on his stony rest, propped his heels on it and rested his arms on his knees.

"Why are you looking for Gisbourne, then?" David asked. He was tending to Gilbert's scraped pate with one of his salves.

Dolfin frowned. "Does he . . . Has Guy—"

"Seen me? Oh, aye," Robyn answered. "We've had 't out several ways." Dolfin looked confused, then worried.

"We en't killed him, if that's what's eating you," Will said.

"Not for lack of wishing!" Arthur put in.

Gilbert, rubbing his head and eyeing Dolfin with no little respect, added, "It's . . . complicated."

"It would . . . seem so." Dolfin kept watching Robyn.

Robyn peered back, unruffled. "What has sent you after him?"

Dolfin suddenly frowned. "The girl. Heavens. She's *your* sister."

Robyn leaned forward. "And you know sommat about her, aye?"

"You would need my message as much as Gam . . . Guy would. I'm sorry, it's not so easy to forget the past."

"I never forget," Robyn said, flat. "Neither can I shrug off what exists now. If you've news of my sister, damn straight you'll tell me."

"One way or t'other," Will seconded, soft.

"There's no need to threaten," Dolfin chided, mild. "I'll willingly give you what I know, but I also need to find Guy; I swore as much to his paxman."

Robyn shook his head. "Gisbourne's gone to retrieve Marion. He means to fetch her away before those Motherless sods try to burn her to death. So." He rose from his seat to a crouch on the rock. "Tell me. What do you know?"

"He's . . . gone? To the castle?"

As a sudden light of dismay leapt into Dolfin's clear eyes, it was everything Robyn could do to not grab the monk and shake from him whatever he knew.

"Aye," Gilbert answered, a bit light-tongued and unwary from his head knock. "He can fetch her out better than any of us, but we're going after. Always better to have a secondary plan, and none of us trusts him enough t—*Ow*, that *hurts*!" This as David firmly—and with some intention, to be sure—slathered salve against his injury.

Robyn left off shooting a glare at Gilbert—the others were doing it adequately.

And the monk lurched up, dismay turning into full-fledged alarm. "Sweet *Christ*. We have to stop him."

Robyn stiffened, wary.

"Not likely," Will said, leaning on his staff. "He left yesterday, a-horse. We wain't catch him."

"But we have to. Somehow," Dolfin said. "There's fearful treachery lurking within Nottingham for him!"

Ⓜ

"So. This is . . . was . . . your troublesome wolfshead, de Lisle." Count John stared at the head, seemingly fascinated. "Doesn't look so imposing now, does he?" He snorted, then gave a loud laugh.

Guy peered sideways at the Sheriff, who'd made much of inspecting the broken pieces of the longbow, and peered at the head, frowning. No way de Lisle could possibly know to whom the head actually belonged, of course, but the stakes were too high to not feel a tremor of disquiet.

And Guy still hadn't even caught a glimpse of Much. Surely he would have heard of Guy's arrival by now. It further disquieted.

"You see, girl?" Count John had a plump, fair-haired lass on his lap: one of the kitchen villeins and a former favourite of the Sheriff, if the looks he kept trying—and mostly succeeding—not to give were any indication. "This is how Our officials punish those who fall afoul of Our law."

He used the Royal Capitals like one truly needing the undeniable proof of their power.

The lass gave a small nod, staring at the grisly trophy. She had been feeding the count dates when Guy had strode into the Great Hall and bent the knee to the impromptu throne; now she had shrunk behind her lord, looking somewhat sick. But it wasn't recognition—or lack thereof. Once again, Guy breathed silent thanks to whatever would listen that Robyn had gained more recognition for his left-handed draw than the face his hood kept so successfully hidden.

"This is . . . outstanding!" The Sheriff straightened from his scrutiny with a genuine smile; Guy gave an inward sigh of relief. "I will confess, I had begun to think my brother overstated your abilities. I've never been happier to be proven wrong."

"Aye, well, he's a Templar, isn't he?" Count John rose from his seat and threaded his arms into his surcoat in one, catlike move. All those present knelt. He trod two of the four stairs of the dais with quick ease, his arms gesturing expansively, voice filling the hall. "We needn't remind this court of a Templar's reputation? Untouchable, ordained by God! Bloody miracle workers, all of them! God incarnate in red and white tunics!" Then, a bit quieter, "According to Our dearly departed father, anyway. And Our brother, who certainly couldn't manage his massacres without you lot."

Guy said nothing, kept his head lowered.

But Count John wasn't finished, his words derisively etched—just so much and no more. "And not just any Templar has graced Us with his presence. We have heard a great deal about you, Gisbourne . . . say, you can put the head away for now. No doubt de Lisle will pop it atop the gate for Our further viewing pleasure."

Keeping the count in his peripheral vision, Guy slid the head back into the burlap and laid it on the bottom step, hoping that would be the end of it.

Unfortunately, he was entirely too optimistic.

"Sir Guy de Gisbourne." Count John nigh crooned it. "No white tabard for you, but the black of the baseborn and the half-sworn. Which are *you*, Gisbourne?"

A thrill ran along his nerves. Was this a danger sign, or merely a younger, less powerful son trying to get his own back in whatever way he could?

For again, Guy well understood that last.

"We do have a special visitor, indeed." Count John pitched his words, sly and insinuative, to the court. "Rumour has it, my lord of Gisbourne was actually possessed of the dubious fortune of fighting alongside Our brother on Crusade. Pity about Jerusalem."

Pity. Guy thought of the uncountable bodies washing up on the shores of Acre, of a war lost long before he'd even arrived, of the Brothers he'd buried—and not buried—of Diamant bleeding out on the decks of a Templar galley. He gritted his teeth yet again, still said nothing.

A slender, strong hand gripped his chin.

"My lord!" Sheriff de Lisle murmured, taken aback by the liberty.

Guy disallowed himself any reaction whatsoever, and allowed that hand to lift his face.

"Tell me. Guy. Wherever do men like you come from?" Count John had hazel eyes, piercing and alive with the gilt of a canny, altogether random intelligence. As dark as his brother was fair, the overhead windows betrayed a glint of chestnut in his hair. "Nothing to say, then?" His gaze narrowed. "Up, Templar, and look me in the eye."

Guy obeyed, clasping his hands behind his back. Count John stood taller merely because he still perched on the dais stair; had he been on a level with Guy, he would have been a full head shorter, yet he was burly, barrel-chested. Adam, Robyn's father, would have said in his quiet, no-nonsense burr: *Aye, and that 'un covers the ground he stands on.*

It was another gentle memory, one Guy had to steel himself against. He'd no business thinking of such things. Now was no time to go soft, in any fashion.

You. . . you mix me up, you allus have. You make me think on too much, make me hesitate. . .

And what do you think you do to me?

He throttled supple confusion with sword-hard fingers, told it: *Die. Be buried. I've no time.*

"You're not very old after all, are you, Templar?" And in what version of hell did Guy ever find himself grateful for the sneer in Count John's voice? "Not as old as those eyes of yours would try to convey. All young men, even monks, have some sort of passion. Some sort of thought, opinion. Where would you stand, then, on the question of rightful inheritance?"

Guy thought fast. Very fast. "I have no inheritance, my lord Count. No family, no honours other than what my Order has given me. I am merely a poor Knight of Solomon's Temple and, as such, I have no opinion worthy of voicing in such matters."

"Poor?" Count John leaned closer. "Your Temple owns half the land of this bloody country! How is that 'poor'?"

"I cannot speak for the Temple, my lord Count. That is for my betters."

"We thought Templars had no betters." It curled, sibilant and dangerous.

Ah. That was it.

"God shall render us all in the end, my lord Count."

Count John's eyebrows rose. "And when We are at last crowned King?"

"God's will be done."

The count stared at him for a long moment, then unaccountably burst out laughing. "You double-tongued bastard!" It was more approving than angry, and Count John clapped Guy's shoulder. "You will not be the first of your kind to kneel to Us, mark Our words." It seemed jovial—indeed, he seemed quite pleased—but none could deny the underlying threat.

Though Guy couldn't help but wonder, if he had a few more of his Brothers at his back—or better yet, Master Hubert—how smug and overreaching this pretender would be.

"Are you sure you won't stay for Our tournament?" Count John leaned forward, grip tightening, a pretence of intimacy. "You'd stand a good chance."

"You do this poor knight honour, my lord Count. Pray forgive me, but without my Master's leave, I fear my participation would be unseemly. At any rate, I am expected to Temple Hirst."

"Even if We were to tell you there's a witch for the burning? There's an entertainment worth any religious zealot's time!"

The rage swelled, this time nearly shredding his composure to ribbons. For a mad, drawn-out instant, Guy drew himself tight, preparing to spring and intending nothing more than to see if Himself the Count could come up with sarcastic quips around a sword impaled in his gut. Placed carefully enough so it would take a long and agonising time to die.

Guy slapped the rage down, bade it heel, and added another chain to its neck. Now was not the time.

But it was beginning to look as if swaggering in and demanding Marion's release would not work. Guy needed to see Much. Talk to him. Find out what was really going on.

Instead he repeated, light as if discussing a game of quoits, "You honour me, gracious lord. Yet I fear I cannot."

"We could make you, you know. We might yet." Count John smiled. "Everything is beginning to come together, eh? Beheaded rebels and God's own monks serving Our cause. Wonderful!" Still smiling, Count John turned away and remounted the dais, settled back in his chair.

The Sheriff, somewhat flustered though he hid it well, gestured to Guy. "A word, Sir Guy?"

Guy nodded, followed a pace behind.

Behind them, Count John waved a hand. "Next?"

- Entr'acte -

The alcove was well hidden—curtained off, an exit to the kitchens often used by the staff. People came in and out, stood and watched from this spot with some regularity; no one would notice two more waiting for their lords to summon them. Not even Count John.

Of course, that one was too busy slobbering over his latest acquisition, a serving girl who kept feeding him dates and suffering his caresses. No doubt he'd bed her at the end of the day, if he didn't decide to do it right there on the high chair. He'd done everything but raise her skirt. Surely England faced the direst of consequences in considering this lecherous, disgusting Lackland as candidate for kingship. Nevertheless, John remained a better choice than the warmongering sodomite he called brother.

Abbess Elisabeth fondled the cross upon her breast, watched events unfold in the Great Hall beyond. Her face remained impassive, though her nose gave a fastidious twitch as the Templar revealed his trophy—it seemed impossible he should have fulfilled Brian's's ends, but she was not going to brush away a God-sent blessing even if delivered by questionable hands. Brian was actually smiling.

The audience ended. Sheriff motioned to the Templar, pulled him over to the side, speaking with him as they moved closer to the draped alcove. The watchers tensed.

"You have my gratitude," de Lisle was saying.

"I'd rather have guerdon, my lord."

It had always struck her, the mild tones of the Templar's voice. Always had this one been as falsely innocuous as the Serpent in the Garden, no more and no less.

"I plan on leaving at first light."

"Certainly. I will have it delivered to your chambers before sundown."

"The morning will be suitable, my lord Sheriff. I understand your time is not your own, at the moment."

"I will confess, Sir Guy—"

Was she the only one who heard the captious tone to her brother's voice? Of course, she had heard it since childhood. Brian couldn't pull much over on her.

"—bringing the bow was good insurance. Pity it's broken."

"I beg your pardon?"

De Lisle shrugged. "There aren't many in the midlands who carry a longbow like to it. Without such a prize, it might have been any peasant foolish enough to get in your way."

A smirk crossed the Templar's face and vanished just as suddenly. "My lord Sheriff, what would be the point of that? I could take your money for a common villein's head, but it's simply bad business. You'd know within a fortnight I'd not fulfilled my charge." He paused, the smirk returning. "Or would you? Scripture has given us a goodly lesson in the distinct problem of making martyrs, my lord. They always manage to resurrect themselves in some fashion."

Blasphemy! Elisabeth crossed herself, slid a glance to her companion, who peered past the curtain, intent.

"Well, let's hope, for your sake and mine, that Robyn Hood doesn't come back from the dead." The threat hung between them.

"That would be a blessing for many, I should think." Unmoved, the Templar dipped his head. "I beg your leave. I must find my paxman, prepare for morning's departure. Good even, my lord."

De Lisle bowed, stiffly, and settled for expressing his anger with a silent snarl at the Templar's black-clad back, before turning to stride back to the dais and Count John.

Abbess Elisabeth hoped she could ease that humiliation, just a little. Of course, she herself was positive, but it took evidence and proofs to convince her sceptical brother of anything, let alone this.

"So." She turned to her companion. "Do you agree?"

"It's my brother, all right. I'd swear to it." Johan Boundys's voice was flat. "Moreover? That"—he gestured to the burlap-bagged head still balanced on the bottom step of the dais—"is *not* Robyn Hood."

- XXI -

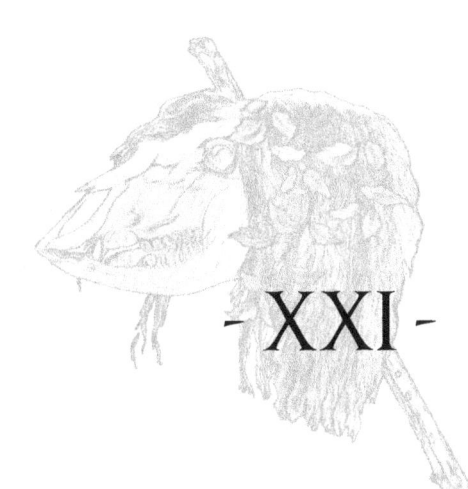

Guy sped up the stair. Just beneath the surface a cauldron of raw instincts and furies, too long subdued, were bubbling, hissing, screaming—*find her! find her, now! Get out of here!* The more-developed instincts slapped the primal ones across their mewling, gaping mouths, demanded some self-control.

He had to find Much, first. He had to wait. He had to go carefully, else it all would be lost.

Stopping at the stair landing, Guy put a hand to the wall, realised he had been holding his breath. Tiny bits of red were flitting before his eyes.

"Milord?"

Guy whirled, grabbed the villein by the throat and had him against the wall, knife in hand, before he recognised who it was.

Much, minus his beard, thankfully didn't seem overly concerned by the knife to his new-bared throat. "I'm sorry, milord. I know better than t' sneak up on you, like. But sweet Lady, 'tis good to see you!"

Guy released him, merely to grab the broad shoulders as Much did the same, smiling.

"'Tis all ower the castle, how th' Templar returned with Robyn Hood's head athwart his saddle."

Guy started to speak, realised he'd too much to explain and very little time— and they were still in the middle of the landing. Several passersby were already peering at their reunion, wary but attentive.

Indeed, Much's eyes were darting about; he kept hold of one of Guy's sleeves, led him in a different direction from their allotted chambers. "We moved quarters," Much explained. "With Himself the Count here, things are all t' sixes an' sevens. Did good Brother Dolfin find ye, then?"

Guy blinked, halted. "Dolfin?"

Much frowned. "Aye. He brought me your message. I knew you trusted him, so . . . Did 'e not find you? When the Maid . . . " He trailed off as two fine-dressed men, talking loudly, came around the corner. One a prior, the other a high-ranking nobleman, they paused midsentence as they came toward the stair—and the two Templars—with a double-take.

"Brother." The prior gave a quick nod and would have kept walking but the nobleman, whom Guy abruptly recognised, came forward with a smile.

"Sir Guy! A pleasure to see you again! My brother tells me you've delivered on your promise and then some!"

"My lord Baron." Guy greeted Roger de Lacy with a courteous bow. "I am pleased to hear it. And I understand I have you to thank for this commission, so I am doubly pleased. This is my paxman, Brother Much."

"And this is my youngest brother," de Lacy said in turn. "Prior Willem of St. Mary's of Newstead. I tell you, Willem, if this man is intending to take part in the tourney then I might as well lame my horse now—it well might be the least humiliating way out from under defeat!"

"My lord of Pontefract does me grace." Guy inclined his head, flawlessly polite; meanwhile, all he could truly focus upon was what Much had just said. "But I fear I cannot stay for the festivities; I have business elsewhere. Might I nevertheless wish you the best of luck?"

"I'll take that wish, and smile a little at your absence." De Lacy gave a graceful bow. "Do not judge me over-harshly for it. I truly would be honoured to cross swords with you at another time."

"And I, my lord."

Guy watched as the two retreated down the steps, the baron once again making an animated speech. De Lacy's ebullience hid a canny and inventive brain—what was de Lacy doing here, then? Had he decided to throw in his lot with Count John? Had . . .

Not now. Later. Now, he had to know about Dolfin. Guy switched thoughts as quickly and easily as sword hands, turned to Much.

"Milord—"

"Not here," Guy murmured back. "Are our new chambers safe?"

"Nowt's safe, milord, you should know that."

Much led him down the hallway and a back stair to another chamber, smaller but no less well-appointed. Much waited until Guy had entered and inspected their surroundings, then closed the door behind him and locked it.

"I've been keeping a low profile. For the most they've not noticed me, other than when we had t' shift about. The steward's a fair fellow, like. It's nowt as bad as might be. Everything's mad, like."

"Including 'Himself the Count'," Guy muttered, looking about. Everything was in its place. Much settled next to the window drape, peered out to ensure none lingered, then pulled out his dagger and a good palm-sized whetstone. Guy came over, unbuckling his swordbelt, and pulled his sword from its scabbard, offered it for the task. Much nodded, and put away his dagger—already honed. Guy's blade sincerely needed the work. The steady noise would, of course, help mask their conversation. Guy heaved a sigh, started to peel from his filthy clothes.

"There's water in t' bucket." Much jerked his head to a corner where, indeed, a bucket sat. "I can see to a bath; you look as if nowt but a good soak would set you t' rights."

"For now I'll use the bucket. Tell me of Dolfin . . . nay, not yet. Where is Marion?"

Much spat on the blade and gave it a fierce swipe. "In the hole."

Tunic open, Guy paused amidst unlacing his vambraces. "They put a *woman* in the oubliette?"

"Aye. She were trying t' curse the Abbess. They keep sayin' it's for fear she'll cast a spell on 'em, should she be in a cell up top." Much eyed a nick in Guy's sword, spat again and resumed scraping. "And *that* were nowt good, I'll tell you. I heard th' commotion and screamin', tried the door, ended up scaling t' outside wall to their window. She looked wild as the Lady Herself chasin' the Hunt, skirts grubbed up about her thighs and a knife t' hand, stalking that cursed Abbess. I tried to stop her, milord. I even dressed as one of the guards—I know several, friendly-like—so I could get nigh to her." He rubbed at his naked face. "I told her you were coming, and we'd help her. 'Twere all I could think to do. It did no good in the end." Much looked . . . shamed.

He'd no reason for shame. Guy walked over and cupped a hand at Much's nape, gave him a long look. "I'm sure you did all you could."

"Aye, well, you en't heard t' half, yet." Much reached up, took hold of Guy's wrist. Guy winced, surprised, and Much blinked, released him to take a closer look. "Bloody hell, milord, what did you do t' yourself?"

The rope burns on Guy's wrists had, since his retrieval of his weaponry, been disguised beneath his vambraces. Guy had all but put it from his own mind; now it leapt to the fore, and the fierce sting and ache it revived wasn't just from pain.

"You say I've not heard the half of it?" Guy took a deep breath, peering at his wrists as if they might grow fangs and bite him. "Neither have you, my friend."

Much's eyes slid beneath his brows to meet Guy's, concerned.

"We have a lot to tell each other." Guy turned toward the waiting bucket, began stripping from the rest of his clothing. "A lot of plans to see through. And not a lot of time to do either."

"Aye, well," Much said again, and squinted down the length of his master's sword. "That's things back to normal, then."

The outlaws went quickly despite the busy roads, made it to the camp just south of Papplewick as dark settled onto their shoulders. An old abandoned hut stood there— or leaned, more like. It was rumoured to have belonged to an old witch whose ghost would curse anyone who came near. An effective hideout, for none did come near. Save Robyn, whose dam had brought her young son and daughter along on her visits to Maud. The Witch of Papplewick had been, in truth, a Heathen wortwife, one who had entertained two wide-eyed children with her sleight of hand, and taught their mother Eluned much of simples and draughts both magical and practical.

Dolfin travelled with them. He had insisted—and so had Robyn. There was trust, then there was madness—and it would surely be madness to just let Dolfin go on his way until they'd finished their business with Nottingham. The explanations and stories given on both sides left no question in Robyn but that the monk cared for Guy's well-being, and whilst he seemed tolerant enough of the outlaws . . .

But when Dolfin offered to go into Nottingham, Robyn forbade it.

By now it was done. Either Johan had recognised Guy or he'd not. Either Johan would remember Robyn's face or he would not. Guy would either break her from the gaol tonight or come riding boldly from the gates come morning with Marion a-pillion . . .

Marion. Robyn could scarce credit his senses, numb and unresponsive save for the tickle in his gut that flared and spasmed. She was alive. She was coming home.

And if they didn't show by tomorrow's morn . . .

The morning after that was the archery contest. They might have to use it, after all.

Robyn started to brood.

(♪)

The bell had, long ago, rung Compline. Guy and Much slipped through the levels of the castle and managed to skirt not only the guards, but those guests sleeping in alcoves and halls as well as what few servants were awake and working. The outer edges and lower levels were not so simple. Much had kept tabs on Marion as best he could, but there had been no way of ensuring her condition—short of getting himself thrown in with her. So they had to leave their way out clear; mere avoidance wasn't an option.

Therefore, working like the well-oiled team they were, the two Templars took guards out as necessary, singly or in twos, even once a quadrille of Count John's soldiers lounging about a dice game. The bodies, dead or unconscious, they dragged into whatever hiding holes they could find.

Two guards were in the alcove above the keep's singular oubliette, one snoring, one watching—if sitting and using his dagger to draw aimless, bored sketches in the dirt floor could be remotely considered watching. Only the one entry, and two nigh-guttered torches in the windowless semicircle barely lit the guards' watch. Much had warned of the possibility of being unable to sneak up on this final redoubt.

Guy slid a gaze at Much, then shrugged and straightened. He strode in, brisk and self-assured, and kicked the chair out from under the sleeper.

"Is this how you ply your charge?" he demanded, soft but furious.

The awake guard yanked himself to attention, falling back against the wall and stammering excuses; the other scrabbled to his feet, groggy and grovelling both.

Perfect.

Guy bent over and hauled the downed one to his feet, shoved him up against the wall next to the other. He gave them a level glare . . . then smashed their heads together. The sleeper fell like a stone; the other was stunned, but not knocked out. Suspicion dawning in his eyes, he took a swing at Guy.

And he was a tough one. It took three blows to lay him out. Guy stood over him, blowing and shaking his fist—the man had a jaw like granite—and peered over at where Much leaned against the wall, watching with no little satisfaction.

"And?" Guy pressed when Much kept watching.

"Aye, well, y' looked to be doing fair enough on your own, milord," Much drawled.

Guy smirked, mimed a blown kiss at his companion—and left the two fingers upright, meaning plain. With a snort, Much sidestepped to the grating on the floor and bent over it, inspecting it. Made of a heavy iron, it covered a narrow hole leading down into pitch darkness, a horizontal gate to its own mouth of hell—with few guards and no locks. No need, with whatever prisoners out of reach in the smooth-walled pit below. Much pulled the heavy pins from the fastening hinge and gave a haul upward. The grating creaked as it rose, teetered; Much gave another heavy yank and it fell with a dull clang on the opposite side.

"Fetch the ladder." Guy knelt, peering into the dark, dank hole. A stench greeted and gagged him: excrement and rot and mouldy, fly-blown corpses. His gorge rose further at the thought of Marion down in it. Gritting his teeth against the reflex he hissed, "Marion?"

It echoed around the opening passage and into the pit below. But, nothing.

He tried again, louder. "Marion?"

"W-who . . . ?" The voice lifted for a split second, then warbled away into silence, as if Marion wasn't sure she wanted to know.

Much finally found the ladder, thrown against a back corner. "I were ready to unwind me rope," he said, as Guy snatched at the other end and helped him angle it into the dark hole.

"You might use it yet," Guy answered, then, as they lowered the ladder, pitched his voice down after. "Marion, it's G . . . Gamelyn." Midword he changed it: to her a name familiar, less forbidding. "I'm coming down."

A harsh intake of breath answered him. Exchanging a quick glance with Much, Guy took hold of the ladder rungs and descended into the dark.

It stank even worse, below; no question in his mind there were dead things, likely vermin though he'd seen places like this where they bunged away prisoners and forgot about them. Not for nothing was an oubliette called a "starvation hole." The thick air clung to the inside of his nostrils, a fetid skim of rot. The only bit of light in the pitch darkness was the faint torchlight from the exit hole a good seven ells above. His lead foot landed in a thin layer of straw, slipped on the scummy stones beneath.

"Gamelyn." It quavered from the dark, barely recognisable as Marion's voice. "Sweet Lady, it *is* you."

A grey ghost came into the shaft of dim illumination, one hand clutching to the front of her shift, the other raking the straw-strewn curls back from her face. The novice habit hung about her, a sack of ragged, filthy rents, and something altogether like blood smeared, dark and dried, upon her pale, bare legs and feet. He sucked in an uneasy breath, wondering what had been done to her and if Much had told him everything.

A squeak and skitter made them both jump—merely rats, scuffling in a corner. Marion's eyes met Guy's, all too willing to give in to whatever panic must have been chasing over his face. He shut it down, all of it—no time and not the place—and extended a hand, said purposefully light, "I'm here to rescue you, fair maid." With his other hand, he threaded the water skin strap over his head. "And I have water."

Marion came closer and took it, hesitant, as if not wanting to believe any of it truly existed. He had to pull the stopper from it for her, but once she tasted it, she gulped at it, frantic and thirsty.

"We'll have more for you above if you can keep that down," Guy said as she finished it, and took it from her. "Is there anyone else here?"

Marion shook her head. "No one . . . alive." It stuttered and choked, and she reached for him. Her hands, shaking but strong, clutched to his tunic. "Gamelyn, is it really you?"

"It is, really."

And suddenly she was listing up against him, holding tight with her head buried against his shoulder, her body vibrating against his in thick, crazed shudders.

Sobbing.

"I thought I'd rot down here. All alone, in the dark, and—"

"You're not alone. I'm here." Surely it wasn't his voice, murmuring to her ever so soft, gentle comfort. Guy de Gisbourne didn't know what comfort was, or how to give it.

Her hands fisted at the small of his back, beat a futile tattoo there. "I didn't know you. Know it truly *were* you until . . . it were a dream, and I woke . . . here. Only I'd no concept of what here *were*."

Neither did he know what to do with his arms; of their own accord they crept around her, pulling her close. "It's all right."

"Much tried to help me but I . . . I think I went a little mad."

"I know." Particularly he didn't know what to do with his heart, twisted and wrung with something he thought dead. *Gone.* "Much knows. It's over."

"I'd only just . . . just fetched myself back, and they . . . they . . . threw me down *here.*" It lurched upward into a clogged and waterlogged hiccup.

Marion's knees buckled. Guy caught her, swung her up and cuddled her close, murmuring things he'd forgotten he'd ever known, rocking back and forth the whole while. He'd . . . *feared* it for so long, lived with the weakness of it like his own heart and breath . . . only this wasn't a weakness, somehow, but an intensity seeping into his pores, twisting itself into something altogether foreign. Extreme. Incomprehensible.

"Milord?" Much hissed down.

Marion's sobs stopped, so abruptly that it drove a lance of fright through Guy. But Marion was moving, breathing. She shifted slightly in his arms, leaned closer. Guy felt dry, cracked lips brush his cheek, linger there, then her breath misted his ear.

"Thank you. Thank you for coming for me."

"What else was there for me to do?" he whispered back.

Marion hung, almost limp in his arms for a few more heartbeats, then sucked in a huge breath, let it out. She angled back and her eyes met his and clung, gleaming in the dark.

"I'm going to kill her, Gamelyn. You have to help me. You understand. You know what she's done. We have to take her down."

Still, no weakness. Only strength, and fury pouring heat into his veins. "We will. But first we have to get the bloody hell out of here. Yes?"

She took a deep breath, pushed back from him, and nodded.

"Milord!" Much hissed down again. "We're takin' too long!"

"We're coming."

Guy gripped Marion's shoulders and peered at her, considered the shaky hands that kept raking the hair back from her face and the thirst she'd had—she'd likely not had much food, either. If any.

"You'll go first. One rung at a time, and I'll be right behind you if you slip. Can you do it?"

Marion nodded, quick and tight, gave one last shove at her hair, then reached for the wooden rungs. With Much steadying the ladder and Guy as support behind, several times holding firm as she tottered back against him, they made it. Her limbs shook, unsteady. How she managed, Guy wasn't sure; he wasn't convinced he could do the same under like circumstances.

As he gained the top, Marion peered down into the hole, wild-eyed again.

"Rats," she muttered. "They kept skulking about me. I started my courses and no one would so much as throw me a rag!" Another sob, albeit behind her hand. "I've been ripping scraps from my habit, and throwing it to the rats so they'd stop sniffin' at me."

"Thank God for that!" Guy blurted out then, as she shot an exasperated look at him, felt he had to explain. "I thought . . . well. Your skirts were all ripped, and there's blood on your legs. I've seen enough of what happens to women on campaign."

"Nay, not a one touched me. I'm well enough. Just smelly-dirty. And lousy." She leaned forward, kissed his cheek again, then kissed Much as well. "Nowt a good bath and a fine-tooth comb, and"—her mouth went grim—"a good knife in my hand wain't make better. I've my own thoughts back in my own head."

And why was she comforting him, for the love of Christ? Guy grabbed her hand, laced their fingers together. "We'd better go, if we want out of here."

"I'm for that!" Much vowed.

♪

The castle rose about them, dead-quiet. Too quiet for Guy's liking. Much's discomposure showed; he kept casting about, waiting for the shadows to erupt into guardsmen.

Because they would. It was too bloody *quiet*.

Then a shout lifted into the stillness, followed by several others. Guy almost wanted to shout himself, with relief.

Marion leapt like a startled hare. Guy tightened his grip, still in hers.

"No doubt a lot of drunks leavin' the pub," Much reassured, barely audible.

Sure enough, one of the shouts lifted into song, woefully tuneless.

"I know that song." Marion breathed it like a prayer. "I *remember* it."

Her hand clenched in Guy's, and again the foreign, fatal pang pierced his chest. As if the touch had burned—and it had—Guy snatched his hand from hers, wrapped it around his sword-hilt.

"Gamelyn," she whispered.

"Don't call me that." And when she hesitated further, he growled, "Keep up."

Guy had a sense of real relief as Much moved to her, took her arm, and gently urged her forward. But the regard of her gaze followed Guy, solemn and confused; with another growl, this time at himself, he shook it off. She'd either understand or she wouldn't. And it wouldn't matter either way unless they fetched her out.

Bad enough that this fight really, really mattered. Perhaps Robyn Hood could wave his fury like a banner when he fought, but Guy de Gisbourne had not been primed by the random and quicksilver heat of moments colliding. His had been the slow, immaculate layering of experience and control. And every frigid cloak of restraint he settled about his being merely made him the more efficient.

Any time he had fought with emotion as spur or shield, he had lost. Badly.

They crept along the walls of the keep, heading for the back parapets where the trees had grown too close. The east postern gate was their first recourse—Much had used it often, and either bought drinks or outright bribed guardsmen for the information—wearing his distinctive tunic, of course, which tended to loosen tongues well enough on its own. The wall itself could prove a second option—in which case the rope Much had wrapped about his waist would serve them as bridge from one of the merlons to the nearest tree. Hopefully it wouldn't be needed; Guy wasn't sure Marion could withstand another climbing stint, even as passenger. But it remained a good second chance. None would expect them to go for the wall—easy prey to crossbows and a sure trap unless one fancied a long drop and a debilitating swim to meet more guards.

The security breach of the overgrown, too-close trees would be their safety net. And John would be waiting in Sherwood with the horses.

Guy entertained a fleeting hope: that Siham was well out of the way, asleep in some corner, her dreams of nothing more than accolades for her archery. Then he moved on, once again claimed by the present.

And the castle *still* lay entirely too quiet. Every instinct Guy had . . . *itched*, was the only way to describe it. Nothing of nature worked against them—had they conjured it, they couldn't have asked for a better night to break open the gaol. Fog had rolled in from the fens to the north, occasionally skimming the bow-sliver of new moon: faint light, but not enough to reveal them should they have to retreat to the wall. A brighter moon and clearer night would have betrayed their silhouettes.

Movement, beyond. Guy froze, swallowing his breath and

melting back against the shadows of the keep, sidling between a pair of vertical pilasters framing an unused, heavy wooden door. Much followed in quick tandem, and Marion as well, though her time in the hole had done her little justice. She made no sound, but leaned heavily against the door, trying not to pant too hard. Thankfully the mists hid much of her exhausted breath. They'd wrapped her in a warm cloak. The bare feet couldn't be helped. Adrenaline would only take over for so long. Over her bowed head, Guy exchanged a meaningful look with Much: *Watch her.*

Movement became more: two figures walking several ells beyond, one carrying a torch that hissed and spat as it parted the mists. Guards, their breath wafting in thick bursts behind them as they marched, intent. Purposeful. Again, Guy's instincts started their persistent, nagging prickle.

He waited until the torchlight faded into spastic orange flickers, then started forward.

A hand placed itself on his back—not Much's—and Marion leaned close, said nigh soundlessly into his hair, "Wait. Two more."

It shivered his nape—her voice, yet somehow not—and when he turned in mute question, an answer had risen within her eyes: a soft-eerie manifestation of the moon's bow. Behind her, Much had drawn back, eyes gleaming white in the faint light as he looked from her to Guy. Trepidation . . . but also bemusement.

Further contemplation quashed itself as boot heels made sharp cadence upon the cobbles. Almost as one, they lurched back between their concealing pilasters with the wall firm at their backs.

Two guards, approaching. Guy watched them, tensed as they paused, one swinging the torch back and forth. He could feel Much drawing up beside him. No question these guards were on search. One started to turn toward the wall, and Guy crouched, ready to spring.

You can't see us. We aren't here.

"We are not here." As if his own thoughts spoke into the air, yet in actuality Marion leaned forward to speak again, the Barrowtongue curling the magic about them like the mist from her breath: "*Nyd wyf yma i.*"

The guard was looking directly at them—

Guy coiled like a tight-drawn spring, ready to strike.

—and saw nothing.

Tense seconds, Marion's breath echoing into the sudden-still air, and both Much and Guy frozen, mute and quivering—*waiting*—like leashed tigers.

The guards turned, kept walking.

Marion's gaze was once more merely her own, but she did not seem surprised.

"I don't think I can do it again," she husked. "We should go now."

Guy blinked at Much, whose bemusement had ramped up to besotted. Guy briefly entertained the scenario of Much beating up Scathelock-the-hero-type for Marion's hand. Then considered, if Much wouldn't, Guy might himself.

And wouldn't *that* set the Pagan King of the Shire Wode all bolloxed.

Guy gave a fleeting smirk and put his mind back on business.

Down the wall, to the corner of the keep. Peer around, scan the bailey—thankfully not as wide here as going toward the gatehouse—and also breathe silent thanks to whomever would listen when it proved deserted. And *run*. Footfalls nigh silent on the turf, Marion stumbling to keep up, yet still her own innate skills held. Guy kept one ear behind, one ahead, attention split because it was easy, all too *easy*.

And then everything went spectacularly wrong.

There were not three, but twice that number of guards at the postern gate, all with swords at ready.

Guy exchanged a narrow look with Much, eyed the guards, and nodded. He turned back to Much, made a few hand signs—*I'll go. Watch*—then started to step towards the postern.

A hand grabbed Guy's tunic. He turned to see Marion shaking her head, eyes wide and frightened. Quicker than rational thought, his own hand snaked out to snatch her wrist, hard enough for her to wince and recoil.

In the next instant he loosed her, culpability stabbing at him. And in the next, Guy let that go as well, shooting Marion a grim look of warning when she thought to reach for him again. Much was at her ear, nigh silent, likely telling her to back off.

If you want out of this, I warn you. . . leave me to do it.

Nevertheless, Guy hesitated, off-kilter and conflicted as he moved from the cover of the wall, and surely that explained how what came next was more surprise than the inevitability it surely was.

The guards all came to attention as he stepped closer, but they did not stand down as he threw his cape back from the crimson sigil on his breast. Guy slowed, folding his sword behind him, seeming capitulation but in reality a coil into further readiness.

As he did so, another four figures detached from the wall, and from the foremost one came a voice, familiar and mocking.

"We've been waiting for you. *Gadelyng.*"

- XXII -

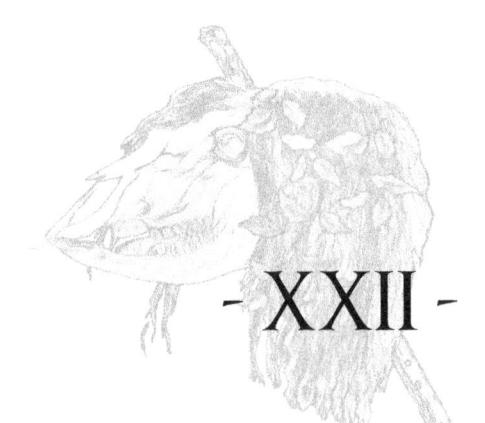

GADELYNG. The first time Sir Ian had heard Johan call his youngest brother what essentially translated to a gipsy's bastard, he'd given him a thrashing. Which merely meant Johan had taken care when and where he had used it, whetting it like a familiar and covert blade.

This time, however, it raised no pain within Guy, barely even a sting. Only fury—at himself, for allowing the trap to so easily close.

"Ah, of course. My apologies." Johan came forward, hand on his sword hilt, guards flanking. "It's Guy de Gisbourne, now, is it?" There was, of course, no regret in his face.

Guy considered the odds. He'd seen worse. But he'd surely seen better ones.

Time for the backup plan. "By what right do you gainsay a Templar?"

"I have royal authority for prowling the bailey this night." Johan beckoned the guard forward, to close in. "Can you say the same, little brother?"

"You seem to be beneath the misapprehension that I need authority." A small sidestep on the balls of his feet, away from the wall where Much and Marion were. "*Brother.*"

"You always were an arrogant little shit." Johan said. "I should think the Templars would welcome one as you. Sodomites and sorcerers, all. But even then, I find myself wondering. Are you truly one of them? What Templar would risk such a thing"—his gesture took in the guards, the castle itself—"because he wanted a peasant girl? A witch at that." He shook his head in poor feign of sorrow. "Give it up, *petit frère*. What woman is worth all this?"

Will you die for Me, Gamelyn Oakbrother?

In answer, Guy met Johan's eyes. Smiled. Flipped his sword, the sculpt of it heavy against the damp air.

Then, still silent, leapt toward the advancing guardsmen.

There was satisfaction to be had, in the practice. And pleasure— one of the few he allowed himself—to be had in putting practice into action. A twist, a turn, back and forth and repeat it twice. The falchion flashed in the fitful light and three men had fallen, dead or dying, before the others had moved to attack. Two pike bearers fell as they rushed Guy, one with a thick-bladed knife blossoming from his chest, another with a narrow shiv through his throat.

Much. Guy smiled again.

Johan drew his sword, shouting orders as, akin to some ebon bird of prey, Guy swooped down on the two knifed guardsmen, snatched up his paxman's blades and disappeared into the dark.

The alcove where he'd left Much and Marion lay deserted as he passed it. Good. Much was already on plan, and Marion, thankfully, not buggering with it. Behind Guy trailed more shouts, harsh questions and feeble answers, the sound of boots sliding and tramping in belated industry.

"After them! Sound the alarm! *Find them!*"

Surely Guy shouldn't feel this much raw pleasure at the panic in his brother's voice. He strangled it, promised it free rein later. He'd a job to do, now. An escape to see done.

Much waited in the alcove leading to the wall's inner stair. Guy began to demand an explanation, then saw Marion's hunched form and profile, pale and sweated in the sparse light.

"Can y' now, Lady?" Much was saying as Guy slipped in beside them and met his eyes.

Marion nodded, her gaze rising to Guy's. He jerked his head toward the stair. Much grasped Marion's hand, pulling her upward.

Guy followed. The stair ascended narrow and steep, quiet as any tomb. Marion's breathing echoed harsh within the wall, her footfalls stumbling. Guy sank inward just that much farther, growled a silent demand of the Lady: *Look to her, damn you—she's made it this far on heart alone; surely just a little longer...*

And She answered, to his surprise. *Your Maiden will survive. You will see to it, my knight.*

Which was no answer, if he thought about it.

They were nearly to the top before Marion's body flat gave out on her; she stumbled, went down. Much started to turn; Guy barked a negation—"Keep going!"—and without wasting a moment or breaking stride, Guy bent down, flung Marion over one shoulder. Thankfully she didn't struggle—a feeble protest, nothing more—and he carried her up the stair in Much's wake.

They surfaced from eerie quiet into open air and hellacious noise. Madness reigned in the courtyard below: shouts in the dark, the flare of torches, the sounds of running feet, and the incessant *clang-clang* of the alarm bell. Much was already across the wall-walk, crouched and waiting against the shelter of one of the merlons.

Guy dove across, crouched both for shelter and to let Marion down. She wilted against the stones, hunched and panting.

"I'm sorry. I'm no use . . . I'm sorry—"

"Stop it, now." Guy ordered. "Save it for when we're in the clear."

Marion gave him a wide-eyed look, but shut up.

"They come up here, milord," Much muttered, "and we're trapped."

"They'll come up here, Much, but we won't let them trap us. Fetch the rope."

Much started unravelling the rope from his waist before Guy had finished speaking. Then, digging into the pouch at his hip, Much took out a deceptively slender iron piton and started to knot the rope through it.

"She won't last for a hand over hand," Guy warned.

Marion obviously wanted to protest, took another look at Guy's face and remained silent. Much merely grinned and dug into his pocket, displayed a looped ell of rope, its midsection purposefully wrapped thick with rawhide.

Guy grinned back.

"*What is going on here?*"

It rang from the upper bailey, a literal shriek of rage. Marion tensed, Guy growled a curse, and Much, for a second, stopped working the rope. They all knew the voice, and what it meant.

"Aye, well, now you've gone and woken Himself the Count," Much groused. His fingers flew even faster, knotting and testing.

"Brassing off the royal brethren?" Guy tossed back. "Merely a fine end to a perfect day."

Marion peered at them both as if they'd gone mad.

Much tried to make a throw over the merlon from his squatting position. "Bugger!" he hissed as it fell short. Then, "By th' Horns, lookit the trees!"

Guy rolled on the wall, peered outward. The trees, utterly still before, were starting to fetch and toss. Fallen leaves, scattered over the parapets and walk, seized and roiled in the sudden wind.

"I'm making the try to snag the tree end," Much said. "The wind's in our favour."

"Do it. If they see you, they see; nothing for it, now."

Much rose, piton ready in one hand. The wind tugged at his tunic as he moved to the opening and, measuring by gaze, swung the rope overhead once, twice, thrice . . .

Let it go.

It made a lovely, almost-slow arc outward. Tangled in the trees with a shower of bark and dying leaves, whipped around the sturdy branch exactly where Much had aimed it. The piton slid, scraped, then bit and held.

"That was brilliant!" Marion burst out.

"You've never needed a crossbow to sink a rope," Guy said, fierce satisfaction.

Much grinned down at them, a flash of teeth in the dark, and flung the near end about the merlon, started snugging close their escape route.

And from below, the inevitable shout of discovery carried on the wind. "On the wall! They're on the wall, milord!"

The report of crossbows heralded more trouble. Much dropped to the walk just as a flurry of bolts came sailing. Marion gave a gasp as one hit the stones just above her head and dropped, shattered, into her lap.

"You imbeciles!" Johan's shout. "Stop shooting! Your sheriff and my lord Count want them alive!"

"That's it, then." Guy pulled Marion to her feet, put her behind him.

"If only I'd a bow—"

"Too long since you've pulled one, milady." Much had regained his feet as well, busily snugging up the rope, ensuring it wouldn't come loose.

"'Tis like riding a horse," she replied, tart. "Bodies don't forget."

Bodies don't forget. And it wasn't just Marion's voice Guy heard . . .

Guy had to smile; it was either that or howl. He hefted his sword. Voices were beginning to sound, up and down the parapets.

Boots and the ring of steel bounced off the cobbles from either side—guards advancing, no doubt, on the wall-walk toward them—and shouts echoed upward as Johan gave orders and the men-at-arms all piled into the narrow stair.

Only the one choice, now.

"'Tis ready, milord."

Guy took Marion's arm, shoved her at Much. "Get her out."

"Gamelyn, n—!"

Much's hand clamped down on Marion's arm, halted her. "My lord!" It was low, urgent.

Guy turned, held Much's eyes with his own. "They won't touch me."

"You don't know that!" Marion protested.

Guy didn't take his gaze from Much, brought his fist up to his mouth then flung the gesture out into the wind tearing through the trees.

Much gave a quick tip of his chin downward. "Aye, milord." He tightened his grip on Marion, started to pull her away.

Guy twirled his sword, drew the quillion dagger from its sheath, and started for the stair.

"Nay!" Marion tried to jerk away. "Much, we canna just *leave* him."

A steel-helmed head broke upward from the stairwell's darkness.

"My orders stand, damn you!" Guy snarled over his shoulder. "Get her *out* of here!"

Marion was gathering breath for another protest. Much clapped a hand over her mouth and dragged her backwards toward the merlon just as Guy turned back to the stair and gave a powerful swing of his falchion.

The helmed head went flying back the way it had come, its body toppling sideways on the stair. There were curses from within the stairwell. Another guard exploded upward. Another body went down, headless.

Guy smiled. Enough of those would plug this hole soon enough. They kept coming, and he kept swinging his sword. No helm, no shield gave adequate protection. It was like picking off tied goats. Another five, six, seven unerring strokes, and—yes! He'd finished with this entry point. For the moment.

A good thing, too—those others on the wall-walk were coming into view from both directions.

With several light, dancing steps, Guy went to the merlon, took precious seconds to peer out into the night. The wind, whipping his tunic and hair with such fierce abandon, had just as quickly calmed to a light toss of breeze. Marion had obviously capitulated; Much was already more than halfway across, Marion clinging to his back like a bairn to its mother, both of them whizzing down to the tree line on his rawhide-wrapped rope.

Several dark-clad guardsmen came running down the walk to Guy's left. One espied the two escapees, slowed and brought crossbow to bear. Taking his quillion dagger between his teeth, with one motion Guy slid a shiv from his brace, aimed, and threw. The guard gave a strangled cry as the shiv sank into his jugular. He fell forward over the wall just as Much and Marion disappeared into the shadows of the trees. One of the remaining guards gave an angry shout; he and his compatriot rushed Guy, and the ring of steel on steel resounded shrill within the trench of stone. Rage made them careless. Guy dispatched them as coolly as with the others, grabbed a shield from one, and looked for more.

None at the moment. Respite, brief but welcome. He could hear voices approaching, but he'd something to do now. His sword arm arced up and made swift descent with another steely cry—this upon rock. Sparks flew and the rope, severed, dropped into the trees after Much and Marion.

Guy swung about as more guards ran up. He leapt forward, his falchion a blur in the faulty light. The men didn't fall back at his approach; they fell upon him with threats and insults.

One got through his guard, cut a nasty furrow down his sword arm. Guy merely switched hands, dagger for sword, and kept going.

This did set them back, but only momentarily. Dressed in the royal colours of crimson and gold, these were Count John's soldiers—better paid, well-experienced. They worked him in teams, came in and out while he was only one. But they were still homebound fighters, more bodyguard and show. The few who had obviously seen the combat of war still weren't Templar-trained weapons, hadn't been further tempered in the fires of Alamut's fanatic legions. Guy lost himself in the slash and parry, the resistance and pull of flesh giving beneath steel, the grate of mail deflecting blows, the wind of a blade's passing as it just missed him. There was nothing but himself, the fever-pitch of combat and the cool ripple, spreading outward, of movement. He felled the sixth of the soldiers and whirled, ready for another opponent, to find himself alone on the wall-walk.

Only then did Guy look about him, take note of the bodies flung hither and yon on the stones. With such information penetrated other realisations: the odd stillness of the elements in the aftermath of precipitous wind; the alarm still clanging with tired insistence; shadows darting like disturbed ants in the bailey below; muffled shouts coming from the body-clogged stair. Above it all were Count John's stridulous demands.

Guy's arm was bleeding too freely, but not spurting, at least. He bent down and ripped at one of the soldiers' tunics, wrapped it into a makeshift bandage about his slashed bicep, tying it off with the aid of his teeth. He berated himself for slashing the rope—he could have followed—but in this commotion, he could keep them busy as Marion and Much, with John's help, made a clean getaway.

Once he saw Marion safe, Much would wait. And then, should the unthinkable occur and Guy not emerge soon enough, not only protocol but Guy's own orders would dictate Much ride hell-bent for Temple Hirst and let their masters know what had happened in Nottingham.

If for some reason Guy was detained . . . He peered about him and considered that, yes, the number of men he had killed aiding a prisoner's escape made likely enough reason to detain him. But it was all they'd dare.

Flipping his sword point down against the stones, Guy knelt down and put his forehead against the pommel. He whispered quick unction to aid the slain souls along, bid his own adrenaline back to stillness. To lull himself back to the calm, and the core of readiness. It wasn't over, not by a long shot.

He didn't have long to wait.

More came, armed with torches and swords, crossbows and pikes, pairs and triads at a gallop down the parapets. Their steps slowed considerably as they saw what awaited them: a Templar kneeling in devotions, surrounded by slain opponents.

As their pace staggered down to a creep, a struggle sounded from the stairwell. Curses, then several guards came stumbling up, Johan behind them.

The guardsmen lurched to a halt even as they poured onto the wall-walk. Johan was forced to stop. He cursed, shoved his way through merely to stop again, staring. First at the bodies, then at his brother amongst them—all of it lit in the eerie, barely flickering orange relief of the upheld torches.

One pulsebeat. Two. Guy counted six of them, pounding slow and thick behind his vision.

"Well, what are you waiting for?" Johan demanded of the surrounding guards. "Take him!"

They inched forward. With deliberate ease, Guy rose. His

sword still pointed down toward the ground, but the guards slowed.

In times like this, it was actually possible to *smell* trepidation, hesitation.

"You're making a very big mistake." Guy tossed a stray lock of hair from his eyes.

"I think not." Johan jerked his head at one of the guardsman. "Take his sword."

Guy slid his gaze to the guard so ordered. The man halted in his tracks. Guy smirked, then hefted his sword. This time the man actively backed a step.

"This is foolishness!" Johan spat. "Stand down, *Gadelyng*."

"Foolishness, indeed," Guy concurred. "I'll take that name from you, gladly, and for what price? You'll spend yet more of your men. Did I hand you my sword—which I cannot do—you will never hold me."

"Oh, I think I will. The throne of England has ordered your arrest for treason."

"A fine one to talk. Our king is not on this island, Johan, and certainly not warming the high seat of Nottingham."

"If he is even in this world." Johan's eyes gleamed. "So. Treason. I'm sure, considering, we could add sodomy. More than enough reason to see an animal like you in chains. Lower your sword."

"I cannot. Neither can you prove a damned thing."

"That's what you think," Johan sneered. "Stand down. *Now*."

Another commotion by the stair, and Sheriff de Lisle appeared out of the depths, holding another torch. "What in hell is . . . " He slowed, and Guy could see the tableau reflected in his eyes: twenty-odd men being held off by the one.

De Lisle was not overly possessed with the need to gloat. He lurched forward, bellowed, "*Take* him, you idiots!"

The guards leapt without thinking. Guy reacted—but an instant too slow. Hesitation, the faithless bitch, had turned on him; the guardsmen sensed it, like dogs—and like a pack of maddened, fearful dogs, they fell on him. Guy took several out, but even as he'd been overwhelmed within the fire-circle of Samhain, he was outnumbered here. They pressed close, with blades and fists and kicks, and proceeded to exact punishment for their fallen comrades.

De Lisle didn't let his men go at it for long: soon he was bellowing for them to desist. Johan added his orders to the mix, but the guardsmen took their time obeying. Before Guy found himself pinned against the stones of the merlon by several of the burliest guards, he'd had his head knocked against the stones, taken a few more choice blows to the ribs, had a bloody nose, a split lip, and a wrenched arm from not easily allowing his sword to be taken.

All accidentally, of course.

For now, the guardsmen took great pleasure in tying his hands behind his back. He supposed he would do the same in their place.

"If all else fails, sheer numbers will do the trick, lord Johan," the Sheriff said, terse, then, "The others. Have they been apprehended as well?"

Johan hesitated. "We have the Templar—"

"Whom you *didn't* have until *my* men took him. What of the others?"

"Long gone, my lord Sheriff," Guy interrupted. "And this . . . *lackey* insists upon spending your guards in an attempt to detain me."

Johan puffed up like a toad at the insult—which afforded Guy entirely too much satisfaction. Johan deflated as de Lisle rounded on him.

"Gone? You allowed the others to escape?"

"I told you who this man was, my lord. I personally spoke with Count John about him. We agreed—"

"This is not some personal vendetta! *We agreed* to capture all of them!" the Sheriff replied in a fury. "*All.*" Turning to his guards, he barked out, "After them! Every moment you wait is another they flee deeper into Sherwood!"

"Milord," one of the captains spoke up, "'tis night, and—"

"I have eyes!" de Lisle bellowed back. "You let them go! So you'll be the ones to go into the night and capture them! Or would you rather explain to my lord Count why you didn't *bother?*"

A good number of guardsmen broke for the stair.

"And shut up that alarm!" de Lisle shouted after them. Growling under his breath, he turned upon Guy. "You can explain to our liege why his entertainment has gone missing, Templar, and then—"

"You *agreed* to my capture?" Guy interrupted. His brother's motivations he understood; it made too much sense, Johan wanting to see him thwarted. But the Sheriff?

The alarm bell ceased clanging with a heavy, tuneless *thunk.* Beneath them the walls rumbled as the outer gate lifted.

"You seem surprised, *petit frère.*" Johan came forward, picked up Guy's falchion and the quillion dagger. The first he handed politely to the Sheriff; the latter he paused, examined. "You still have this pretty thing, I see. I would have thought it broken long ago."

Guy lunged at his brother. There was no thought to it, no calm reasoning, only obedience to an imperative that stabbed, foreign and furious, through his gut. It did for him what most inconsiderate emotion did—nothing. Unless he wanted to count the snigger from Johan and the blow to his solar plexus from an overzealous guard.

"Well, this bauble's luck has run out. As has yours. You have done nothing but play Nottingham false, from who you are to why you're here."

And bloody *Christ*, but it felt like Guy had broken a rib. Mayhap two. "My lord Sheriff," he warned, "surely you see this is a dire mistake."

"The mistake"—de Lisle stalked over to him—"is yours, Templar. Sir Johan is correct. You have played me false. I fully imagine your masters would agree that I am well within my rights to hold you until we contact them, as you have broken an accord I made with them."

Guy listened, stony, then pulled from his backside a twisted masterpiece of denial that would have had Hubert grinning with sheer delight. "I have broken no accord. I said nothing to you of my intentions toward the woman. I knew you would not hand her over to me, and I'd orders to free her, so . . . " He shrugged. "Release me, my lord, and there will be no more said to this—"

"You arrogant little *shit*."

Guy contemplated how it had been twice, now, that he'd heard the accusation levelled at him. It no more surprised him coming from de Lisle than from his brother.

"It wasn't the witch I meant." De Lisle said. "You brought me a broken longbow and a head, but that head did not belong to Robyn Hood."

Guy combated the sudden, sick lurch of his stomach with bravado. "What proof do you have of such an accusation?"

"I've seen Robyn Hood's face," Johan leaned against the far wall, pretending to focus upon his dagger. "The outlaw is a young man, with dark curly hair and eyes black as sin, whilst the villein you presented had lank brown hair and jowls like to a man in his prime. Not only that." He looked up, smirking ever so slight. "Once I truly pondered it all? The witch. The outlaw. *You*. It wasn't long to the realisation that I've seen this infamous outlaw before. In rather more revealing circumstances than I'd prefer. Wouldn't you say so, *Gadelyng*?" Guy blinked. Tried not to stare.

Failed, miserably.

"Ah, that does surprise you, I see." Johan smiled.

Surprise wasn't the word, actually. Guy was dumbfounded. Clumsy, leaden—as if he were stumbling toward a steep cliff, unable to halt, with the ground running out, slow but sure, beneath his feet.

"Where in the name of God are they?"

The bellow echoed up from the bailey, stilling all of them.

Count John.

Several voices rose in answer. De Lisle exchanged a meaningful glance with Johan, who turned at his place against the inner wall and called down, patently respectful, "We have the Templar here, my lord Count."

A low growling string of curses. "Well? Bring him down!"

De Lisle shrugged. "Take him to our lord. Now."

And, numb with shock, Guy let them.

*

Bad enough they'd had to leave Gamelyn . . . Guy—and Marion was not going to get used to that quickly enough—but when the rope had fallen after them, not long after they had come tumbling to the forest floor . . .

Much had watched it, a spasm of pain crossing his face to be replaced by comprehension, solidifying like forge-hot iron being dunked, steaming, into cold water.

Rather like the terse, frost-eyed Templar snapping orders and demands had seemed nothing like the ingenuous boy who had spent lazy days with her and Rob, wandering the green Wode.

Or, she reconsidered as Much grabbed her hand again, pulling her up, maybe Gamelyn hadn't changed so. The man who had picked her up, given her comfort in the pit—that had been the youth she remembered.

She. *Remembered.*

"All right?" Much asked—even though it was a moot point, in the end of it. What else could she do but nod and let him lead her at a half trot, shivering and limping, into the trees? When he thought to hesitate, to bend and heft her up, she shook her head.

"I can do it."

He gave her a chancy look, but allowed her that much pride. At least until she gave out again, and hopefully not until they reached . . .

"Where," she panted after him, "are we off to?"

The castle alarm was still ringing, accompanied by shouts and the clash of steel atop Nottingham's ramparts. It began, however, to mute as the trees closed tighter about them. Even with most of Her leaves being shed, the thicket of the Shire Wode lay formidable.

"Horses," Much said, and kept going.

Horses, for their escape. This had not been some passing fancy, but a planned invasion.

"Much . . ." she tried and failed, voice faltering, even more than played-out, shivery limbs and the painful burn of lungs no longer used to running free in the Wode.

It sounded like whinging. She would not whinge, not when so much had been incurred for her escape.

Much didn't say a word, just turned and scooped her up in his thick-muscled arms, kept going. And Marion couldn't begin to protest though she wanted to; instead she lay as quiet as she could, unwilling to throw off his headlong progress by even a shift.

Much halted. A strange shudder went through him, and he eased Marion down with a consideration bespeaking no more urgency than what they already moved beneath.

She saw them, then: several horses in the gloom, and a figure beside them, small, surely no more broad nor tall than an adolescent lad or lass. The figure moved into a stray shaft of the moon bow's faint light—a lad, then. Nay, a young man Boyish and slight to be sure, but he'd the neck and broadened jaw of maturity. There were also telltale muscles, beneath his loose tunic, of a seasoned archer.

Much seemed stricken in place.

"I called the wind for you," the young man said, slowly.

"Johnny." Much's voice clogged thick with emotion. "*John.* He said 'twould be you waiting for us. I . . ."

Much lurched forward, and the two were embracing, a fierce and joyful frenzy that raised a choke thick in Marion's throat. Just as swiftly, they shoved apart and eyed each other. There were tears upon the smaller man's cheeks, and as Much turned back to Marion, she saw the same glimmer in his eyes.

The smaller man—John?—turned to Marion as well. His gaze touched hers, dark and soft and fierce all at once. Taking his hands from Much, he put them to his face and bent his head to her. "*Bendith y mamau.*"

"You're . . . our people," she murmured, wondering.

"Aye," Much said softly. "Johnny, we have to go."

John turned to him. "Guy?"

"They have him."

The liquid-dark gaze went hard, then considered Marion once again. "Does she know?"

"I know who I am, now, if that's what you mean," Marion answered.

"Nay," Much answered, "she kens nowt. No time. And none now. 'Tennyrate, en't our place."

John's brow furrowed, then he nodded, turned to the horses, tightening up girths.

Marion knew something remained, something she should be paying attention to, yet she hadn't the wherewithal to give it more than a scant thought, much less anything resembling comprehension. Her knees kept trying to buckle beneath her.

Abruptly Much gained her side, his stout arm shoring her up. "Can y' ride, milady?"

"I can" was her reply. "I will."

"Fair enough, then," Much replied, bending down, and before she could protest he'd hefted her upward, carried her over, and slung her up into the saddle of the near horse. It turned a white-splashed face to peer at her curiously, but merely sighed and nosed its neighbour as if to say, "Fancy this, mate."

"Here. Take some more water. And some bread, a bit of meat." Much gave a slight smile when her stomach growled, loudly, as she took the food. "Go easy on it, mind," he further advised. "I'll lead yer horse."

John clearly agreed, eyeing Marion with some concern as he handed the rein to Much and then mounted the far horse, turning away from Nottingham even as he settled into the saddle. Much swung up onto the horse next to Marion's.

"Where are we going?" Her voice wouldn't stop being raspy. She gulped more water, took another ravenous bite of bread.

Much shrugged. "I en't the slightest, milady." He put spur to his mount and, beneath Marion, her horse lurched. Marion grabbed leather with her free hand, hung on.

They followed John into the murk.

- XXIII -

"My, but you have caused Us a great deal of trouble, Templar." Count John paced back and forth, wrapped in a heavy, sumptuous robe. The Royal Capitals were in high form indeed, leaving Guy in no doubt: he was in a very dicey situation.

He had been manhandled down the stairs, despite offering up no further resistance—no longer any point to it, after all. Once there, in the sharp wind still sweeping across the cleared bailey, they didn't bother taking him up to the keep but forced him to his knees on the damp, close-cropped hillock. Thirty armed men surrounded him—give or take a few—and a few dozen more looking on from the pitch-lit parapets. Johan stood, hand on sword-hilt and chest puffed out as if he'd single-handedly taken down the Templar. He stood just out of arm's reach, Guy noted with some chagrin. The Sheriff waited just beyond Johan, off to one side, and once peered up toward the keep. Guy saw her, then, a black-shrouded silhouette hovering in a well-lit window. The Abbess.

Quite an auspicious gathering. Guy wasn't flattered.

Count John's robes smelt of roses, a drift of sick-sweet above the tang of torn-up earth and the sweat-reek of the soldiers. In his hands, he held Guy's quillion dagger, gesticulating with it, had been doing so, actually, since Johan had offered it to him. Johan taking it had been enough to incite murder in Guy's soul; this continued . . . desecration surged even more inexplicable, furious and primal. It was an emotion that Guy had already decided he could not afford, here and now.

Only it kept returning, filling his throat and eyes like water with a drowning man.

"And what a story Our subjects have told Us, Gisbourne," said Count John. "If Gisbourne is indeed your name. If you are, indeed, a Templar."

Guy didn't look up, didn't acknowledge the words by so much as a clench of jaw. Repeated an old mantra, words to cool his blood when he saw that quillion dagger brandished by another's hand and didn't want to know what such rage meant:

You can't touch me. I'm not here.

"Nay, but We think that last is indeed truth. We have seen your kind fight and plot; it is a mark upon you. A scar. Schemes are part and parcel of a Templar's habit. We understand you are Our sworn man's brother." He gestured to Johan. "Sir Johan, Lord Boundys de Blyth, has proven faithful to Our cause. He claims that not only are you his brother, but a youngest brother, and therefore of no consequence."

"This is where he proves himself a short-sighted *bricon.*" Count John's voice suddenly turned edged. "Even youngest sons can prove themselves of consequence. Isn't that so, Gisbourne?"

Guy slid his eyes up to look at first Johan, then the count. Johan had paled; it made Guy's lips twitch—almost a smile.

Count John saw it, and chuckled. "Aye, late-gotten sons. Elder brothers heap scorn and mockery upon younger ones, always think themselves better." His voice tautened, scaled upward. "But We don't forget. And when We do strike, it is with *years* of humiliation behind Us!"

Johan was very pale now.

"So." As quickly as the disproportionate anger had risen, it quieted. But the formality did not return, a device practiced but not yet perfect. "You became a killing machine, and I became an intellect my lumbering brother could never match. You seem to have intelligence yourself, Gisbourne . . . mayhap you can claim more names than most, but as it is the one you now bear, might I call you that? Gisbourne?" Count John didn't wait for permission, just went on. "But I think you're not smart enough. You've made some enemies, here. Sheriff de Lisle claims you have breached a contract, given him false goods for his investment in your services."

"I took no money from the Sheriff," Guy retorted. "I warned him of making martyrs of mangy wolfsheads."

"You'll have to take that up with him, of course." Count John ran one finger down the dagger. "Speaking of wolfsheads..."

Guy tensed; he couldn't help it.

"Your brother claims you lie down with them. Literally, I mean. He says you and this Robyn Hood indulged in a bit of boyhood rumpy-pumpy." A low laugh. "Of course, every order of monks in the civilised kingdoms has outlived accusations of such vices. And your little tête-à-tête, it was long ago, yes? I mean, if We had every sodomite put to death, a full third of the male population would be lost, including Our fair-haired brother." Count John snorted, half laugh and half derision. "But then, Lord Johan has also informed Us that the witch you set free is also a boyhood... acquaintance. That the Reverend Lady of Worksop suspected you from the beginning, due to your—what was her word? Ah, yes—'unseemly' interest in a novice. Surprising, from a misogynist monk. Though the woman was fair enough—a bit of a peasant workhorse instead of a dainty flower to pluck, of course." He snorted again. "And obviously, the red hair wouldn't put you off."

"My lord Count," Guy finally said, soft. "What is the purpose of all this?"

A hand twined in his hair—tight—and gave a rough yank, pulling Guy's face up to meet Count John's.

"Our *purpose*, Templar, is to find out exactly what you're doing here. There are too many coincidences, colliding like soldiers on a battlefield. Seemingly random, but soldiers follow a plan. What is your plan, Guy de Gisbourne?"

"My lord Count," Johan spoke. "He did claim his masters had ordered him to aid the witch's escape."

Too many things colliding... it was no exaggeration. How in hell, Guy considered, had this tangled mess twined itself into such a slippery and fast braid and then, snakelike, turned on and bitten him in the arse?

"One more piece to the puzzle, then." Count John released Guy and took a few steps to one side. He kept twirling Guy's dagger.

Robyn's dagger. *Give it back, you miserable...*

"There is," Guy grated out, "no puzzle."

"So it is all, then, mere coincidence? Must We remind you, Gisbourne?—We are not at all stupid. We don't believe in coincidence." Pitching his voice into a near falsetto, he traced the next words like a jongleur telling a tale. "The novice just happens to have no memory, and just happens to regain it when you show up, and just happens to be a witch from a family of them, and it just so happens the novice is also the sister of a man, thought long dead, who just happens to be the most notorious outlaw terrorising the midlands—*my fief* of Nottingham!" His voice rose tight once again. "Who just *happens* to be an outlaw who, as your brother suspects, *just happens* to be the same peasant lad you used to fuck like a confused and desperate dog?"

Surely even the Lady Herself had not imagined this. Guy kept his eyes down. Surely She had not even imagined how this whole thing would be so spectacularly and thoroughly buggered.

Did we really need all this? Just to bring us all back together? Wouldn't a nice fête have done?

You had Samhain, did you not? And you denied it.

Not Her, but another, deeper voice.

Aye, it has been long, Gamelyn Oakbrother, since you have opened yourself to My voice.

Perhaps now, with Marion safe—and she was, Much and Robyn would not let her down—the Lady no longer had need of him. But the Horned Lord . . .

Are you still jessed by the god who belongs to the sand and heat? Yet even there, you were of my realm: the fire-haired forest djinn.

"*Hariq aljinni alsheer alghaba,*" Guy whispered.

"What?" Count John whirled on him.

Guy shook his head and ducked it lower, gritting his teeth. Reminded the Horned Lord that now, mayhap, was not the best time for distractions.

They have no right to tame you, claim you. Would you die for Me, Gamelyn?

He gritted his teeth harder.

Count John started pacing again, twirling Robyn's dagger. "So tell me, Gisbourne. Is this some wide-reaching plot? Who is this Robyn Hood? Does he have Templar backing? Is that why none can seem to catch the wily bastard?" He stopped. "I'm sure your masters would like nothing better than to see my brother back in England. I've heard they plot against me. Richard was always thick with your kind—his tame executioners and butchers, all of you!"

"He did say," Johan pointed out, "we would be making a mistake, capturing him. That his masters would come for him."

"The Templars?" Count John quickly asked. "Or the outlaws?"

"*The Templars,*" Guy said through his gritted teeth, "will not suffer me to be unlawfully detained. There would be no stopping it, did we let such a thing start."

"Yet I've heard no Templar will ransom another," Count John

riposted, and stepped toward Guy, light and rapid, to come to a halt before him. His fine, short boots were more fit for floors than turf, Guy noticed, mud-splattered and fur-lined. "So why should your masters come for you? Or . . . " He bent down, closer, and grabbed Guy's hair again, tilting his head up. "Are you working for this Robyn Hood? Is *he* your master?"

Funny, how now two had said the exact same thing. It was no less annoying coming from a jumped-up count than a too-discerning female. "My master," Guy gritted out, "bides at Temple Hirst."

"And he will, against your Order's policy, ransom you?"

"Are you demanding marks for my return? Are we at war?" Guy met Count John's gaze. "Have you officially declared yourself in rebellion against your king?"

He knew he was baiting a mad bear, but the grip in his hair hurt, damn it! The count let go his hold merely to draw back and smack Guy full in the face. More a slap than anything; it stung, but more with insult.

Bad dog.

A failing, granted—part and parcel of pride—but Guy had never taken insult well. He glared up at Count John, a snarl twitching at his upper lip.

"We are king in all but name!" Count John snapped. "Our brother is lost, and as his heir—"

"So we are not at war," Guy said, soft. "And my masters shall be quite interested to learn how a mere regent thinks to imprison one of our Order."

Hubert had always warned Guy that his sharp tongue would slip and cut his own throat someday. Count John actually raised the dagger, lashed out. At the last minute he twirled it, clenched his hand about the pommel. No mere slap this time, but a fist wielding an iron pommel, connecting with his jaw and snapping his head back. Count John might prefer using his brain, but he was no slouch with a right cross, either.

"Insolent cur!" Count John screamed into his face, delivered another blow and drew back for yet another. "I am no regent! I am the king's brother and in time? Who knows wh—"

"My lords!"

Count John turned, furious, as several guardsmen came tearing across the bailey. They slowed to an uncertain, milling trot as they beheld the scenario being played out and started looking, rather desperately, for their sheriff.

"What is it?" Count John demanded.

De Lisle shot a wary glance at the count, walked over to his men. "Yes?"

The lead soldier seemed nervous. "No sign, milord."

"No sign?" Count John's attention fully swung and focused. "No sign of *what?*"

"Th-the others, milord," the guardsman stammered. "Th-th woman and the T-Templar's man. There were horses waiting."

"And?" de Lisle growled. "Did you *follow*, man?"

"We couldn't, milord Sheriff. 'Twas no sign of them. Not a smell, not even a trace."

"*What?*" Count John's voice rose up into a shriek. Then, with another shrieked negation, he whirled with the speed of a pouncing lion and struck at the most vulnerable thing.

Or so he thought.

His booted foot caught Guy in the temple and sent him sailing back. The guards started for Guy, merely to scatter as their lord count leapt after Guy's backward progress, still quick. Count John got in another blow as Guy landed and tried to roll up—this one to the kidney. Then another, as if aimed, to Guy's ribs.

If Guy had suspected them broken, now 'twas no guess. Agony flared up and down his spine, poured oil over furious coals, sparked reaction into flames. Guy snarled, twisted, rolled his knees to his chest. With a quick jerk and grunt he curled his legs through his tied arms and threaded them, back to front. As Count John came in for another kick, Guy's bound hands shot out and grabbed the swinging edge of Count John's tunic. Hauling himself up, costly brocade squeaking and then ripping beneath his weight, Guy swung his right foot into ne brocade-clad hip. Then a lurch forward and a vicious shove, sending the count sailing—with Guy atop him.

They landed with a heavy, spine-jarring thud and *squelch* of mud and sodden grass, limbs tangling, pain and fury, hot breath exhausting into the night. And Count John's shrieks.

"Seize him!" Those shrieks were turning from rage into pain and terror. "*Seize him!* Get him off me, get him o—!" His voice stoppered into a gag as Guy wrenched his hands upward and shoved them against the Royal Windpipe.

It took three guardsman to pull Guy away, and two more to pin him on his back, arms and legs stretched to three points of the compass. It was then the pain finally hit, slamming behind his eyes all red-black; for long moments Guy couldn't so much as consider breathing.

Count John came stalking over, the quillion dagger extended, and placed it beneath Guy's chin. "Quite a dangerous dog We have here, it seems. Well, Templar. Since you were the one to deprive me of my entertainment for the tournament, then mayhap you should take the witch's place on the pyre."

This was greeted by silence. No one dared move, hardly anyone dared to breathe. Strangely enough, it enabled Guy's own air intake; the band of pain around his chest snapped in two and he took in a long, staggered, and careful breath.

"M-my lord!" Sheriff de Lisle stammered into the quiet, "Y-you ca—"

With the speed of a striking snake, Count John rounded on him, whipping the dagger up between them. "Are you daring to tell *me*, de Lisle, what I can and cannot do?"

De Lisle, no fool, lowered his gaze and backed away.

Guy watched him, turned his eyes to Johan. His brother also seemed stunned, but also, an unpleasant backlight had started filling his gaze. Guy had seen the look before—on carrion eaters, waiting for the top predators to finish gorging.

"Search every orifice this man has," Count John toed Guy with his boot. "He'll likely enjoy it, considering. Once you're sure you've relieved him of every weapon he possesses?" He shoved the dagger—*Robyn's* dagger—into his belt. "Throw him in the oubliette he so inconveniently emptied. And don't open it until you drag him out for the tournament."

<)

There had been a time when Marion had known the paths of the Shire Wode like the sepia map of freckles on her cheeks. But just as in the nunnery she had lost track of reflections garnered in pools of still water and her mother's looking brass, she had also lost track of woodland shadows and stirrings. As if trying to solve one of the puzzles Rob had often made from leaves and ferns, fitting them together in unlikely, instinctive patterns. She'd had to work at it then, even as she was having to work, and hard, to now make sense of this ultimate puzzle being laid before her: what remained of her life.

Now, Marion was thoroughly lost. She had moments of wondering what she had done, whether she should have trusted any of these people, what they were taking her to . . .

And found tears spilling down those freckled cheeks as she drank in the taste of *home*. It didn't matter where they took her, what happened from here. If she died, it would be free, under open sky and woodland green.

But first, they had to make sure Gamelyn was released.

Surely it held Much's thoughts as much as her own. The slight archer—John—kept them going, along deer paths barely visible to the eye, on roads overgrown with disuse. Marion became so turned around, the only way she knew they were retreating from the castle was how Much kept turning his head that way. Looking back.

Dawn crept, slowly, over the treetops surrounding them. They slogged through bog and fen, hopped fallen logs, startled deer and, once, a boar, thankfully slow and half-asleep. Finally John had deemed it reasonably safe to travel on a better road, giving the horses easier going. Several times they had stopped to hide, well off the road, when John had given the warning; therefore, 'twas no surprise when John halted again, and also a given that Much would exchange a look with Marion then glance back.

This time, though, they didn't retreat off the road. Instead, John put cupped hands to his lips. A throaty, trilling sound emerged— one that Marion and Rob had in childhood often imitated. In this place and from John, it was no game; the birdcall was nigh perfection.

A signal.

One answered, in an echo faint and seeming faraway, wafting through roseate light and tree-snagged mists.

And just like that, a small group of sombre-clad men materialised, lissom as tree spirits and thrice as menacing. First one then several, movement where there had been none, mist shaping humanity from where there had surely only been foliage. Yet . . . it wasn't magic. Marion felt no breath, no stirring in the air or within her senses, though she'd no certainty that her numbed perceptions could even detect subtle workings anymore.

Much had tensed, a hand going to his sword—pure instinct, nothing more or less. One of the newcomers, a cowl wrapped about the lower half of his face, saw the subtle motion with his own type of instinct. He lifted a longbow and pushed it to half nock.

Much, very obviously, took his hand away from his sword.

"Nay," John said to the bowman, and Marion belatedly realised John hadn't said two words tied together since they'd ridden away from Nottingham.

And then her gaze fell upon a hooded figure, swinging down from a tree branch with no little grace.

All of these people had some wrap or covering over their features after some fashion; this man possessed an equally common thing—a hood. Nevertheless, he wore it as a blatant mask. He was tall, lean and rangy as a yearling hart. He stopped once he reached the road, and she felt, despite the cowl obscuring his face, his eyes upon her. His step faltered—a thing at seeming odds with the nimble descent to earth—and he gave a heavy lean against the great bow he held.

He carried her brother's longbow.

The recognition of it struck Marion low in the belly. She had to prop an arm against her mount's crest as she watched him advance—a slow stride, faltering, even, but the cant of it, the rhythm seemed so familiar. And then he shook the hood back from his face, and all the puzzle pieces blew together, a fierce gale of uncanny impossibility.

Her arm gave way and she wobbled, grabbed at the horse's black mane to keep herself from listing sideways and pitching to the ground.

"Marion?"

His voice wasn't so familiar; even tense and climbing upward it purled deeper, a soft rumble napped with thick-night velvet. But it was *him*.

It was impossible. It couldn't be.

"Oh, bloody . . . You didn't tell her, John? Catch her, lads, catch her before she—!"

But her brother caught her; *Rob* swept her from the horse, nearly limp and resisting nothing . . . *Rob*. Hood falling back from a face gone leaner, the same tangled, too-long curls falling over his brow, yet his forelock had garnered a few strands salted uncommon silver. A close-trimmed scruff of black clung, determined, along his jaw and neck, and it made Marion smile. Rob had, after all, never totally cared for wearing a beard, had often whinged over the fact that nature had obviously decided otherwise.

"Rob," she husked. "It *is* you. It's impossible, it's you, it's—"

"Aye, it's me, I swear. Nowt but, and . . . " Robyn shot a considerable glare sideways where John had taken hold of her horse's bridle. John averted his face, thick hair falling into his eyes, but not before Marion saw the culpability in them. "Why the bloody fuck didn't you tell her, John?—she's going to faint away and—"

"I am not going to faint!" Marion protested and flipped a smack at the back of his skull before she'd even thought.

His reflexes had improved—he ducked and she didn't even get close. "Of all t' thick . . . y' daft pillock, you could've warned her!"

"I'm fine," Marion implored. "I'm fine, and . . . *Rob!*"

And then he was gathering her close, hugging her so tight she could hardly breathe, his hands hard and nigh painful upon her. Those hands were shaking, no less than his voice . . . he was *sobbing*, repeating her name in great wheezes and hiccups.

She grabbed back, hung on, glad for the pain, glad for somewhere to spend it. When Rob first tried to push her back, she clung; when he insisted, she allowed him to rock back, look at her. His eyes had changed the least of all, still pitch with embers flaring from some deep-hewn furnace, only now there were flames licking at those embers, white-hot and barely banked.

"Mari . . . ah, Mari, y' look dreadful, lass . . . What did they do to you?"

"What are you doing here?"

"'Tis a story we've no time t—"

"Robyn!" Urgent, the voice from over her shoulder, and her brother's frame jerked, and her own heart gave a huge thump within her breast as she turned to the bearer of that voice.

Surely there had been enough graves robbed this dawning . . . only this lad—this *man*—had never been dead. Only made dead to her.

Marion reached out, still wrapped around her brother, and put a hand to Scathelock's broad, leather-clad chest. "Will." It was hoarse.

Will seemed unable to speak, looking at her. Instead he covered her hand with his, gave her a smile all trembly in the corners.

At his shoulder, a burly man with a shaven head and a missing arm gave her a smile, a tiny bow, then said again, since Will couldn't, "Robyn. Horses coming."

Of course. Her brother was Robyn Hood.

Will hefted Marion back on the horse, as easily as if she were a feather's weight, and turned to take the animal's head merely to find Much already there, glowering.

In another time and place, it would have been funny. Indeed, Robyn gave her a lightning-quick smirk, but it faded as he tapped his bow on the ground.

At the signal, the outlaws melted into the trees. There was no other word for it. They were there, on the road, and then they weren't, and the horses led deep into the woodland. Marion found herself behind a thicket of gorse, surrounded by barely contained creatures—nay, weapons—of stealth. Much still insistently held her horse, but his hand fell to his sword-hilt. Will was at her stirrup, making quick work of stringing his bow, and the one-armed man beside him, hefting an impressive axe. The only one other than Much who possessed a sword had fanned out sunward at Robyn's direction. John was tying the two other horses to a tree.

A hand gently gripped her knee, brought her attention back to where Robyn had come to stand beside her. "Crouch down, Mari." He gave her knee a caress as if he had to keep touching her, reassure himself she was indeed there. "I've no bow t' give you could pull the now, so take this." He handed up a staff.

She loved her brother. Loved, loved, *loved* him. Clutching the staff to her breast, she leaned down on the horse, pulled her brown cape snug about her.

It seemed a long time before the horses came. Two mounted and a small troop afoot, dressed in the colours of the Sheriff's guard, heading north. Not until the sound of their passing had faded did any of her companions move, and Robyn first, sidling nigh silent up beside the brown-clad Templar who held her horse.

"Much?" Much nodded, a bit curt, and started to speak, but Robyn continued. "They have him. Don't they?"

"Aye." It was tight with in-held frustration.

Robyn leaned on his bow, peered into Much's eyes for a long moment. Much tried to stare back, almost defiant, but the steady, intimate gaze seemed to overwhelm him. His gaze flickered, dropped.

Confusion undermined Marion. Gamelyn... Guy de Gisbourne... he had come to Nottingham to kill Robyn Hood. Gamelyn—Guy—had not known Marion was alive until he'd seen her in Nottingham. Had he not known Robyn was alive? How...

Robyn's next words threw her further into mystification.

"He said you were worth ten of him," Robyn said, softly. "While I wouldn't go so far, he were right."

Much stayed silent.

"Those guards were after you, no doubt," Robyn continued. "This en't the main road, neither."

"We've gone and robbed Himself the Count of his... entertainment," Much said, giving an apologetic glance to Marion at the description. "And now I've seen you safe with your kin, Lady, I beg your leave." He bowed his head to her. "I'm returning to the castle."

"Nay," Robyn inserted, mild, "I don't think so."

Marion blinked. Beside her, Much stiffened, prompted, "So you say?"

John gave a hiss, obviously disapproving, and colour rose in Much's cheeks but he gave John a level gaze and shook his head at Robyn. "I know what you were to my master. I know what you are t' them." Much jerked his head to the others. "But you en't *my* master, and I've my orders."

"I'm no one's—"

"In the Shire Wode"—Arthur came up, swinging his axe to rest on one shoulder—"what Robyn says goes, 'master' or no. Which means you en't going anywhere lessen he says, man."

"Arthur," Robyn growled with a shake of his head, then tilted that head, a daunting light in his eyes, one Marion recognised so keenly it hurt her heart.

"Look, Much. I ken you're a Templar 'n all, and 'tis likely you can tie me in a knot with one hand behind you—"

"En't just likely," Much replied.

Robyn grinned. "Fine. But you en't going off half-nocked with this."

"I never go off 'half-nocked' in—"

"Can you fetch him out, all on your own?" Robyn interrupted.

"I shouldn't have to. They daren't hold a Knight Templar."

"Sure of that, are you?"

Again, Much flushed.

"And likely why you're making such a no'-so-smart case t' hie yourself back to bloody Nottingham with patrols hot on your tail?"

Much stiffened further—it didn't make him taller, but it did emphasise the obvious: he outweighed Robyn several times over.

The others instantly alerted—nothing overt, but a taut, wary *waiting*. John had come to stand next to Much, his gaze upon Robyn. Robyn merely slouched against his longbow, one eyebrow cocked and a smile teasing at one corner of his mouth. In fact, he looked as if he would enjoy it should Much pile in and attempt to pound the stuffing from him.

"Rob," Marion started.

Robyn didn't let her finish. "As it were, you almost didn't fetch my sister out, and with the two of you, Templars both."

"There were treachery!" Much protested.

"Aye." Robyn nodded.

Obviously troubled, Much fell silent. John put a hand to his arm, held Much's gaze as Much looked at him.

"You might not remember what a Motherless sod your master's eldest brother were, but I do," Robyn added softly. "And that bitch of an abbess is so blinded by the light she hungers for, she'll not see sense."

"Not t' mention Himself the Count is right mad," Much muttered.

"Much, Rob's right," Marion added. "Please don't to go back for Gamelyn alone."

Robyn's eyebrow arched even higher, this time at Marion. "The first time I called him that, he'd like to've knocked me for six."

There were entirely too many undercurrents in this wind-frothed river, and ones Marion needed to understand. She fell into uncertain silence.

"Well, no puzzle there," Will tried to joke. "Marion's always been prettier than you, Hob-Robyn."

And Much glared—*glared!*—at Will. It kicked Marion's bleak mood in the arse and told it off. She put up a hand to hide the quirk of her lip as Much furthered, "How do I know I can trust any of you?"

"You don't," Will retorted. "But we en't about t' trust you, neither."

"Match made in hell, like," Arthur groused.

"Your choice, Templar," Robyn murmured, his eyes steady upon Much. "I canna fathom he'd ordered you to fetch yourself into the gaol. I can send a man in and out without being seen."

"I can go and not be seen."

"Nay. You've given them proper reason to remember you." Robyn leaned closer, whispered, "It wain't be borne, Templar. The Oak is not theirs to bind."

Much's eyes widened. He stared at Robyn for a long moment, then nodded, bent his head.

"Aye, Lord."

- XXIV -

"Hot water! You en't serious!"

Robyn and Will both had grins on their faces, belying the effort of balancing the massive cauldron between them. Propped on a staff, they'd brought it from the fire beyond the trees to where Marion stood, wrapped in a borrowed cape and eyeing the small pool with some trepidation. Robyn had left her there, taking her bloodied, filthy habit and muttering darkly about burning rags and new clothes, but it had been a while. She had about decided Robyn had been waylaid by one of his men, and just about girded herself up for a necessary plunge into the frigid water.

"Wherever did you find such a lovely cauldron?" she marvelled as they lowered it carefully to the ground. Robyn loosed his end of the staff they'd used to balance it between them and angled a well-filled knapsack from one shoulder to the ground.

"You'd be surprised what David has hidden, here and there, all over t' Wode," Robyn said. "I've no idea where he gets it all. I don't ask."

"The man with the ferret." Marion was still trying to sort them all out.

"Aye," Will answered, shifting his gaze from her to his feet over and over. "Tess."

"Tess is the ferret," Robyn added.

There had also been a priest with David, waiting at the camp up the treed slope. Much had known the priest—had greeted him with puzzlement and relief. Another odd chance in all the ones stacking up in the puzzle, pieces between which Marion couldn't yet discriminate.

"Tis one of our favourite camps, this," Will kept muttering at his feet.

It was a strange sight, Will discombobulated. Not that Marion didn't feel as put off, uncertain, as naked in her spirit as her body beneath the cloak she so tightly clutched.

Too much frustration, trouble and should've/would've lie between you and Charming William...

Robyn had said it long ago, yet here they still were. Nothing changed... yet all too much. Marion lowered her gaze, turned it to Robyn, who in turn peered at Will with a canny and bitter understanding.

"I'll go on then, shall I?" Will furthered, quietly.

Marion looked down, a knot the size of her fist clogging her throat and ensuring she couldn't answer had she the words to utter.

When she looked up, Will was no longer there.

Robyn was, though. "Do you want me to go, too? I mean, if you want to be alone—"

"I've been alone!" It burst from her, unstoppable. "I've been alone for... for... damn! I've no *idea*—"

"Three years, seven months. And a rough fortnight," Robyn said, very soft.

Such a simple fact—the counting of the days—utterly devastated her. Yet she couldn't do anything about it but stare at him, clutching to her cape, her feet damp and cold and getting colder while tears, fat and salt-wet, filled her eyes and spilled over her cheeks.

"Aw, Mari," he said, and came over, wrapped his arms about her. She let him, curled into the warmth and the earth-spice smell of him—

That last made her pull back. "I shouldn't make anyone put themselves within reach of what's no doubt crawling on me. And I'm getting your tunic wet."

"'Tisn't the first time, pet," he chided softly, "for nits or wet." Gently, he pushed one of her greasy curls back. "And now I'm hoping it wain't be the last. But 'tis all too true you smell like the back end of a grain-fed milch cow." He gave her a tiny shake. "Go on, woman, use the water before it gets cold. There's nowt more to be had without a long wait."

While she rinsed and scrubbed and poured warm water over her, Robyn went for a swim in the pond. To clear his head, or so he claimed.

"Did you freeze the bugs off, then?" she queried as he came sloshing out, all shrivelled and shivering, but bright-eyed as the first time he'd sunk an arrow in the centre of a target prick.

"I fancy I did, at that." He bent over, shook like a sopping black dog, then queried, "Want me to wash your hair?"

He'd started on the second rinse with the luxurious warm water before she fathomed what he was doing with all the homely comforts: this place set apart from the men in their camp up the rise, just the two of them in the Wode, like it had been so many times before.

The knot formed in her throat, and she didn't want to try to speak past it for fear it would turn into another crying jag. Instead, mute and grateful, she let him wrap her in a fur, used a cloth he gave her to towel her sopping curls whilst he sorted through the rucksack he'd brought. He pulled out two tunics, soft flax for under and warm woollen for over, a pair of long woollen braies, and—again, the oddest things were knocking her over—a handful of cloth rags. Robyn had seen the bloodied, torn hem of her skirts even if the other men had kept averting their eyes—and had kept watching her enough to discern the cause.

She watched him, too, as he left her to her dressing and went to put on more than braies and a warm fur. Marion had already noticed the fist-deep hollow in his left pectoral; there were other scars, too. Some whitened with time, others still livid-new. Some invisible, no doubt. Almost impossible, to connect this confident, wiry-hard wolf with the toddler who had held to her skirts, with the lath of a lad who had seemed all hair, skinny limbs, and too-big feet. This was the brigand, the Green Man.

Robyn Hood.

Well, he still had the big feet. And, though it seemed impossible, more hair.

"You've grown into a lovely man." Marion's voice quavered; she clenched her fists and willed it steady. "Mam and Da would be so proud of you."

Robyn shrugged into his namesake, settled it on his shoulders and tied it secure. "I doubt they'd be too proud of what I've turned me hand to."

It made Marion think of Gamelyn.

Guy de Gisbourne.

The monster. The cold-eyed war machine. The twenty-year-old

Templar assassin. He was barely nineteen, if she remembered it a-right, and Robyn not even that. Yet they had left Marion behind, grown older while she, as if hung in the fae lands on the World Tree, had stayed in place. She had not borne rightful witness to their growth from lovely lads to hard-sharp men, remembered them only as innocents tangling in a sweet green Wode— only Robyn had never truly been an innocent, had always had that uncanny, quicksilver *knowledge* behind his ebony eyes, and Gamelyn had torn the innocence from his own breast, cast it from him like something weak, *unclean*.

Tears rose, sharp and stinging, filling her eyes before she could stop them. She thought she'd cried them all, in the hole. Robyn was watching her, brows puckered and unsure. Marion scrubbed a brisk palm at her cheeks and drew her knees up to her breast, laid her chin on them. Silently contemplated him as he backed off, gave her the needed space.

"What have you turned your hand to, Hob-Robyn?" Her words were quiet. "What have *you* become?"

She knew what she had heard, though she'd not recognised it at the time. Outlaw. Renegade. Killer and firebrand, the Horned Lord's vengeful avatar.

"No more than I've had to"—he shrugged—"and no less. I'm wolfshead, Mari. I've a price on me head 'twould sell fifty wolf pelts at the hundred court, but there en't many as would turn me in. The villeins and freemen as don't fear the Horned Lord's wrath fear me. Or owe me. 'The Hood's justice', they call it, and I'll give it, I will." Robyn came over to her and crouched on his haunches before her, eyes dark but not with pain, or blame. Acquiescence. "Da turned in his dearest friend; I 'spect he'd have done no less just because I were his son."

"They knew all along what t' Horned Lord would have from you."

"Nay, truly not. And what they did know, they tried to protect me from as they could. No blame to them. They knew it meant the death of their ways. Of *them*." He turned his profile to her, looking out through the trees, seeing . . . whatever he saw. His face was set, not soft with thought or wonder despite the brush of cloud- and tree-dappled sun against his cheeks. "Robyn Hood's what I am, Marion; it's all I've ever been. Mam and Da let me be Rob. And you." He turned back to her, looking at her— through her, really. "It doesn't matter, not now. What matters is you. What did that bitch do to you? Is she some sorceress herself, to keep the Lady benighted?"

"No power of her own, nay," Marion said quietly. "I don't know what kept me sleeping in me own head, but 'tweren't her. I think, even in her own way, she cared for me." She shivered. It seemed . . . obscene.

"'The Heathen she captured and tamed,'" Robyn muttered, and when she peered at him, questioning, he shrugged. "Nowt more than sommat Ga . . . Gisbourne said."

Gisbourne.

The way Robyn said it.

Gisbourne had left Nottingham with the promise to bring back Robyn Hood's head. Only he hadn't, had he?—for here stood Robyn Hood, and Much had brought her to him, while Gamelyn . . . Guy . . .

Marion shivered again. "If you're a witch of a wolfshead, then I'm a witch who's run to one. I remember, Hob-Robyn. And I *will* kill her."

"Aye, and you'll have to get in the queue for that," Robyn said, wry. "But I'm thinking you have more the right than any." He scooted closer, sat beside and wrapped his arms about her. One hand lingered at her cheek, fell to the hollow of her throat and stroked, lightly.

With a sudden hiss of surprise and a shudder of his long frame, Robyn jerked his hand away.

"Rob . . . " Her voice went faint as she turned to him, noted the strange light in his eyes as they fastened upon the hollow at her throat. His fingers, twitching as if they'd been burned and were chary of a repeat occurrence, gave a quick brush at the tiny silver cross at her neck.

She'd forgotten it was there.

Robyn took in another, halting breath, then reached out, flattened his hand just below her throat. Between his palm and her breastbone, the little cross warmed. Pulsed.

"It's his," Robyn murmured. "*His.*"

"Gamelyn." She nodded. "It were his mother's."

"His blood upon it." Robyn curled his fingers about it. "He knew *how* . . . Where are you?" Barely a breath. He lifted the silver from her throat and breathed the words again, ever so soft in the Barrow-tongue, "*Ble wy ti?*"

It sent a shiver deep within her. Marion peered at Robyn, wondering at both the sadness and affection borne upon the charm-breath.

"It's dark," her brother said, slow and heavy. "And cold." And then he gave another shudder, his eyes closing. He leaned his forehead against her temple, husked, "When did he give this to you?"

"Before I . . . " She hesitated, then put her hand over his where it still lay, curled against her breast and about the silver cross. "Before I remembered. And then I started to remember."

"Aye," Robyn muttered. "If owt could pull your spirit from darkness, this would."

"It's . . . proof, isn't it? Of where his heart lies."

"I think he en't aware what his heart *is*, no matter where it lies," Robyn said, a soft growl, then shook his head as she put fingers to his chin and tried to get his eyes to meet hers. As if he knew the questions brewing and found them . . . insupportable, at least here and now.

Yet there were so many questions she wanted to ask, so many things flitting through her thoughts, birds caught in walls and battering themselves in an effort to be freed.

Robyn held her tighter, murmured, "I have you, pet. You're home."

"Nay." She shook her head. "Home is gone, torn from us, burned and laid waste and . . . and we'll never see it again."

"That en't so, Mari. Everything comes around again, one way or t'other. That we're here, wrapped tight about each other, but proves it. Loxley's gone, but woodland's growing back over the burnt ground, and the green Wode's always been our home, our hearts . . . our *spirit*."

"It's not . . . I . . . " Marion took a deep breath, tried again. "*Three years*, Robyn. I never got to grieve. I never knew what were wrong with me. It never touched me, 'til I were in the hole in Nottingham." She choked, loath to speak of it, unwilling to let it run riot through her mind again, so soon. "Oh, I knew parts of me were . . . missing, but not why. Or how."

"And we've not nearly enough time now, for the grief." Robyn's voice sounded against her hair, rough with her pain. "I'm sorry."

Not enough time. Marion hesitated, unsure. Then said, "Because we have to fetch Gamelyn out of there."

Robyn stiffened against her, said, slowly, "Aye."

The tone of his voice invited no further scrutiny. Marion couldn't just leave it there. There was too much already she didn't know.

"He were sent to kill you."

"No difference, there, from what were meant all along."

"Yet he didn't." Marion spoke slowly, feeling her way along a slope growing slick. "Kill you."

Robyn drew away, sat up. "Mari—"

"He came back for me, and had Much bring me to you. Would have brought me back himself, did it no' go awry. To *you*."

"Aye." Robyn leaned forward, legs crossed, elbows resting on his knees. "But it's . . . tangled, lass. You en't understanding."

"*Make* me understand. D'you think I'd not ken that your lads would as soon see him dead? Robyn, whatever . . . I don't know what they think, or what you think, but he saved my *life*."

"I ken what he did. We both agreed he should do it. We gambled, mostly won."

"So he's with you. You're—"

"Mari, I don't know *what* we are, y' see?" he retorted. "Rivals, to be sure. I'm not sure there's owt left allowed us."

"Allowed." Marion leaned forward, brushed the forelock from his downturned face, tried to meet his gaze. "That en't my brother, the Rob I know. He'd not bide with anyone *allowin'* him—"

"Rob en't here no more, Mari," Robyn said softly. "Neither is Gamelyn, and the sooner you fathom that, the better." He turned to her, leaned over and brushed a kiss to her forehead, then rose.

"Come, pet. There's a fire waiting, with a hot meal." He held out a hand to her. "And plans that need making."

<)

"So once Gilly returns, we should know the lay of things." Robyn reached over the fire, cut another two slices from the roasted rabbit, handed one to Marion.

"Are you going to cut it for me?" she teased.

"I might," he retorted. "Let your baby brother spoil you for a little longer, aye?"

"He'll have to queue up behind *you* and the Templar's lackey." A grinning Arthur gave Will a hard nudge in the ribs.

"Shut your sodding face," Will growled back, under his breath.

Robyn pretended not to hear, figured no one else had, either.

Then Much spoke, proving he had. "The next to call me 'lackey' will be missing some teeth."

"Aw." Arthur grinned, showing a few gaps. "Too late, man."

Much rose, slowly. Robyn started to speak, was interrupted as Marion, seated between Robyn and Much, put a hand on Much's sleeve and stayed him. Then she looked across the fire at Arthur, grey eyes sparking, flint to steel.

"He is my guest. He saved my life."

To Robyn's amusement, Arthur cringed as if Marion had whacked him with a staff.

"I'm sorry, lass," he muttered. "Meant owt by it."

Robyn slid his gaze to Much, who looked to Marion like a cow who'd lost a calf. Next to Arthur, Will was still sulking over how Much had claimed the place beside Marion. Robyn smirked and didn't bother to hide it. Aye, watching *this* new bit of wrangling was going to be more fun than a sack of brassed-off badgers.

"Gilly?" Marion asked.

"Gilbert," Dolfin answered, steering things portside to peaceable. "One of the men sent by Robyn and John to gain us some information."

"While you were shedding the dirt," Robyn told her, and handed her another slice of meat. She declined with a smile and a tilt of her head against his shoulder. "We need to fatten you up," he insisted.

"Not in one day. I'm stuffed."

"Gilly's just hopin' he can find a way to enter the archery contest," David pointed out.

John chuckled, cross-legged between David and Much.

Humour restored, Will reached for another piece of meat. "Well, 'tis Gilly we're talking about. He gets an idea, it's hard t' shift him. Must be his noble's upbringing."

Robyn snorted into his mug. "An' we've no peasant hardheads in this lot, not a one."

Much's hackles were smoothing. Good. Arthur seemed almost as bent on baiting this Templar bear as he'd been the other. If he kept it up, Robyn would have to knock him one. Or, he thought with a smirk, just sic Marion on him. That was a surprise . . . or perhaps not. Arthur were one what wanted a wife, sure enough. And lots of bairns to climb on him. A shame, it were.

"Well, we're here. Not to mention the marks," David said, wistful. He gave Tess a goodly chuck of meat—only fair, since she'd helped take the bunnies down—and she disappeared into his cowl, making pleased, purry noises. "*Fifty* of 'em. And taking such a sweet reward from the Sheriff? He'll never live it down."

"If either of us won," Robyn pointed out.

"Sod that!" Will snorted. "There's few'll challenge Gilly, and certainly none'll touch yourself, Robyn, and you know it."

"That Saracen woman what took such a shine to the Templar might come close," Arthur pointed out. "But aye, say Gilly does come back with th' all clear. We kin go in bold as good horse-brasses, win the marks!"

Much, who had perked up at mention of the Saracen and Templar, had resumed staring into the fire. Plainly fretting, thinking too deep upon unpleasant things.

Fancy that. Robyn also had a few unpleasant things racing

through his brain, and he imagined they weren't too dissimilar to what Much was contemplating.

The sun already reached toward noon. Much was supposed to ride for Temple Hirst, did Gisbourne not show up by midday. Gilbert hadn't returned, either.

"Entering the contest sounds too much of a risk," Dolfin protested, earnest if reasonable. "With all that's gone on, I'd not put it past the Sheriff to have planned such a thing."

"Of course he planned it," David shrugged. "To honour Count John's coming, eh?"

"What if he also means it to catch the one man rumoured the shire's greatest archer?"

"Either way, thing is," Robyn pointed out, "Gisbourne took in the head of 'the shire's greatest archer'. Why would they suspect owt?"

"Guy was captured helping a prisoner escape. It's quite likely he spent the night locked away, if he isn't still," Dolfin countered. "You've snared the prize that counts from them: your sister sits with us, freed. Why take the chance?" Those too-blue eyes were fixed upon Robyn, sudden reminder of his father Adam's gaze— not just in hue, but their fierce probity.

Robyn had to look away. Surely the monk wasn't privy to his thoughts, not when Robyn's own hadn't yet kenned them. The men were pleased—cocky, even—that Marion had been rescued. The Templars would see to their own. Robyn had given Gisbourne a trust—and backed it with a second plan at the tournament if they'd had to— but they hadn't done. No need for the plan—but to go in, scoop up the marks, perhaps watch the Templars tear hell out of the place if Count John didn't let Gisbourne go soon enough? All the better.

Only . . .

"Taken the prize," aye. *Only I'm not so sure they've not replaced it,* Robyn thought. He'd put nothing past that elder brother . . . or the Black Abbess.

"We've gone in and out of Nottingham with none the wiser," Will boasted.

"If your man en't returning anon, I'll have to go on," Much said into the sudden silence. "I have my orders."

"It's a good thing to know what we're up against," Dolfin insisted.

"I fear I know that already," Much muttered.

Robyn agreed. Every instinct he had was clawing acid against his nerves, warning and revolt, demanding action. He knew better than to not heed his instincts.

But there were others to consider. His men, anxious to count skulls in regards to Nottingham. Dolfin, an unlikely ally, and one justifiably wary of a situation sprouting treachery everywhere they turned. His sister, who had just spent too many days starving in a gaol and didn't need to be dragged across the shire yet again . . . and who Robyn would bet his best bowstring wouldn't consent to being left behind did they go to Nottingham. And again, his men. His *brothers*. They'd no love . . . need . . . whatever it was Robyn had for Guy. They had come strictly for Marion, and because they would do anything for Robyn.

Yet "anything" might find a sticking point at rescuing the man who'd spend so much effort and fury trying to murder Robyn Hood.

He should stay out of this. Should listen to the kirtle-tucked, barefoot Brother Dolfin, should let Dolfin ride away with Much to fetch the Templar masters, should disappear with Marion and his men into the Shire Wode and let the Templars descend upon Nottingham like the wrath of their god.

If they would. Much seemed to think they would. But Guy had already disobeyed them, had aided the wolfshead he'd been sent to depose and kill.

Yet Templars were a law unto themselves. Robyn was daft as a brush to imagine he was needed—or even wanted, or think he could gain anything in the wanting. This wasn't some jongleur's tale, no courtly romance with a neat, tied-off ending of sunsets and silks. Guy was no simpering maid to be rescued, and Robyn certainly no huge-thewed conqueror. Robyn *was* the conquered— wolfshead, peasant, pagan—with the only power he possessed that of the woodland and his longbow. He'd little power to garner from the barren, man-shaped confines of a castle used to subjugate his people. The Green Man might die beneath scythe and fire and be reborn, but even the power of the Horned Lord couldn't reattach a head whacked off its neck.

"If we went to this archery contest," Marion was saying, the gleam in her grey eyes scoring another acidic mark against Robyn's twitchy nerves, "who's to say stray arrows mightn't fly?"

Aye, the Horned Lord murmured. *You'd have them in one place, enemies all. Your Maiden has come through the darkness to find her heart beating tandem with My own, in this.*

Yet your heart, Winterlord, in this is Mine. The Lady's breath tickled at Robyn's nape, made him shudder. *Your fair Oak has proven his heart, as well. We must take him back, from the things and plots of those who would destroy Us. You are the moment, the breath of now; he is the future.*

Robyn's breath stuttered in his throat.

"Robyn?" From the frown on Dolfin's face, it wasn't the first time he'd spoken. "Are you all right?"

The others had noticed Robyn's abstraction—save Much, lost in his own thoughts—and were, as usual, paying the mildest of attentions, just enough but not too much. Marion had put a hand on Robyn's knee—what had alerted him—and he covered it with his own, nodded reassurance to Dolfin.

Dolfin didn't seem vastly reassured. He kept the discomfiting gaze upon Robyn and Robyn, again, looked aside. The sooner Dolfin left—bloody damn, but the sooner *all* the bloody and blasted monks vacated their territory and never looked back!—the better. Celibate hounds of god had *no* place in their fecund Shire Wode . . .

Celibate? A chuckle wafted across his neck, and the Horned Lord furthered, *Your leman is, indeed, not a good monk.*

"Marion's right," Will agreed. "All our enemies in one place—"

"And that makes it acceptable to go in and take them out?" Dolfin asked. "Mark my words, if you cross a line such as this, they'll hunt you until you're all dead."

"Pardon to ye, Brother Tucked-up Robe." Will's reply came heated. "You speak all high-minded, but they've been hunting us like animals all along. Your Templar friend is part 'n parcel of it. You've no idea what has been done to us and our'n."

"I think I know more than you give me credit for," Dolfin replied, not giving an inch. "You have power here, in your Shire Wode. Your leader sits awash with it!" Again, Dolfin didn't back down from the frowns this garnered him.

They all knew Robyn didn't like to be put on display for what would claim him. Yet Robyn found himself more intrigued than exasperated by Dolfin's notice. Even more by the telling acceptance twining that notice.

"What need do you have," Dolfin continued, "to take arrow and blade to those who have nothing compared to you?"

"*They* have nowt?" Arthur growled, and lifted his maimed arm, hacked at the elbow with his own axe. "What d'you call this, then? I'd call it a proper example they've a sight more power than most!"

"You're taking my meaning and twisting it," Dolfin said. "I'm of the faith you've so set yourselves against—"

"The faith what's set against *us*, with chains!" Will retorted.

"And fire," John added, a low growl.

"I'm of that faith, and I'm not against you. Not all of us are."

"I bided with many faiths amongst my brother Templars,"

Much said suddenly. "I were wary as any, but Templars value all knowledge, call it *gnosis*, worship it as much as any god or spirit." He peered at Robyn. "It were why we came, you know. Sir Guy and myself. To take from an outlaw the magics he'd stolen from the *dryw*. Only"—he shrugged—"they weren't stolen, after all. I imagine they'll be fair swolloped to find you en't who any of us thought you were. *Including* Sir Guy."

He has been compromised by a world shifting beneath his feet. The Lady riffled misted fingers through Robyn's hair. *You must finish what you started. You cannot give up on him now. Gamelyn needs be set free, in more ways than one.*

He doesn't... want me—

He is scared. You are scared. And why not, when each of you holds the power to destroy the other in your heart and hands? Oh, Hob-Robyn, can you not see the truth when it slaps you in the face? It is only that, like you, Gamelyn has been trying to find footing in the wake of losing what he loved.

"—and in this forest lies something far beyond ordinary comprehension, something altogether beautiful and terrible—"

"Sommat they would *destroy!*" Marion burst out. "The Abbess cried war upon our people. The Church sanctioned it. She had my family slaughtered like pigs and took me away, for three years kept me from anything to remind me of *my own mind*, like some fly held in a piece of amber." Her fingers crept up to the tiny cross about her neck.

And Robyn felt the truth of it—the *charge* of it—like the sting of a knife opening a pus-pocket, letting it drain, shock and relief. He closed his eyes, gritted his teeth, and reached for the earth with both hands between his bent knees, grounding it.

Aye, this is beautiful and terrible. This is war and the scarlet knight has cried it: with his blood upon his Maiden's flesh, with your blood upon the altar stone, brought forth with his blade. Marion was pulled fully into thisworld when her consorts collided. The Horned Lord's words merely confirmed what Robyn's own reactions had begun to tell. *How could it be otherwise?*

You must free him, the Lady murmured. *You must. For the good of everyone you would care for, you must untangle this tight-snarled tynged. He is Ours. Yours. As long as the three of you stand, back to back, there is little will prevail against you.*

"She needs to be taken from thisworld," Marion was saying. "Her and those like her are proof of what's set to overrun us all. They've taken hallowed things, even our names they've torn from us, conquered our world and twisted ancient truths to claim as theirs. And you say we've no rights to fight against it? Should we just lie down and be destroyed?"

"I say nothing to rights." Dolfin answered gently. "So much of what you say is true. And too many *have* no rights. But I can speak to war, sweet lady. It is a horrible, horrible thing. You've seen yourself what war has done to Gamelyn. I'm sure Much has his own brutal stories."

Much slid Dolfin a wary glance.

"You think this en't war?" Robyn said, a soft growl.

"I have to believe Robyn Hood—the Green Man of the Shire Wode—does more by aiding those whom power abuses than warring against that power," Dolfin said. "You prove yourself better than they with every poor soul you raise up."

"Better?" Robyn shook his head. "I'm no more than most, monk, and I've never said I were. If I've a gift, well, others have their own. It en't about being better. You and your priests of the White Christ preach of another world—a *better* world, so you say—but how many truly ken their own teachings? Or follow 'em? My da believed the same as you, that life is somehow its own sacred thing. But it en't. It just *is*. If anything, it's what pours from us in the living and the doing makes the hallowing. *Including* our dying—"

"Easy to say when you've never been on the other side of the blade—" Dolfin bit off the words, realising what he was saying—and to whom.

"Aye, easy," Robyn echoed, deep-soft. "But I *have* been on the other side. Left half my wits behind, some would say. We en't sacred, or special. But what's in us and around us? It always returns."

"And you think this gives you the right to play God?"

"The difference between your like and mine, monk, is I don't *play*. I've no choice but to take it serious. You speak of rights—I'm no less a priest than you, yet still you think *you've* the rights to lecture me t' me duty, as if I'm some callow lad sneaking wine from t' vestry!" Robyn arose, earth dropping from his fingers; he flicked it into the fire with a hiss. "I'm *dryw*, Hallowed, Horned, and Hooded. I've *walked* the otherworld, treated with *ardhu* Arawn, run with t' Hunt and t' *Cwn Annwn*. The Horned Lord possesses my body as He sees fit, and the Lady my heart as She wills, and while my truth en't the whole of thisworld, 'tis the truth I 'ave, what I promise those who would walk with me. I wain't make any bend their necks or be droved as cattle; neither will I let any despoil my forest or claim it as theirs when they don't even *know* it. My god's fury is my *right*. I'll stop those who'd 'urt what's mine and care for my own. En't that all anyone can do, and not go mad with their own power?"

Dolfin watched him, still frowning. But pondering, and most carefully.

"Those who think they've the right to have charge over what en't theirs," Marion said, low, "are the sick ones. Or those as'll be sick, when it's never enough."

"The White Christ isn't the only Sacred King who's given his blood and died for his land." This from David, as he went around the circle, pouring more ale. "Have a drink, Brother 'Tuck'."

Dolfin blinked at the appellation, then gave a tiny, thoughtful smile and pointedly tucked another fold of his cassock into his rope belt.

Robyn sat back down, accepted more drink and a smile from David. Tess chittered at Robyn as David poured, climbed into Robyn's black hair and nosed at his ear. He handed her a titbit, scratched under her chin and chirruped back to her. Tess curled up on his shoulder, eyes blinking in a shaft of sunlight.

A considering, heavy quiet fell over the small group as they finished eating.

Much rose, looked at Dolfin. "Are you still bent on riding with me, Brother?" As Dolfin nodded, he said, "I'm seeing to the horses, then."

Robyn gained his feet. Tess scolded him; he poured her into David's hands and followed Much over to the horses. John was already there, helping with bridles and girths.

"Will they come for him?" Robyn asked softly.

"They will," Much affirmed. "The Master . . . well. Sir Guy is one of his own. I think, seein' what you hold close, here in the Wode, you ken such things."

Robyn nodded. "And then?"

"Then?"

"If they do fetch Gisbourne out, what of . . . *my own?*"

Much gave a slight grunt as he tightened the girth; his horse sighed, shifted in its hobbles. "You were Hunter and now Horned One. The Master of Temple Hirst treated with Cernun, once."

"And what if this Templar Master decides I'm no fitting heir to the Horns?"

Much looked away. John turned a troubled gaze from Much and back to Robyn, then sighed and slipped a bridle onto the horse Marion had ridden to the camp.

"Aye, well," Robyn said, very quiet. "Sir Guy had no answer t' that, neither."

- Entr'acte -

Robyn wasn't going to like this—nay, not even a little.
    Halfway to Nottingham, Gilbert hitched a ride on a haywain. He paid his unquestioned passage by promising to help unload the vehicle when they reached their destination, and also by telling stories to the beleaguered driver's seven young children. That some of those stories were tales of Robyn Hood merely drew the driver's curiosity into the fore; he inserted his own statements and questions amidst those from the children who sat, rapt listeners, in the hay beside Gilbert. In the process the driver imparted a few rumours before they arrived to the castle gates and were given leave to the stables.

Gilbert helped the man offload the hay as promised, grinned a goodly fare well to the children, and went to find out which of the driver's rumours were true.

Which led right around to Robyn being less than pleased. Gilbert didn't make it halfway through the crowded market stalls before he heard one of the hay farmer's rumours not only confirmed, but trebled and embellished: the Templar Knight had been flung into the Nottingham gaol.

Speculation ran rife about the cause, from whisperings of truth to outlandish fantasy. Count John had gaoled Gisbourne because the Templars refused to support John's bid for the vacant throne.

The Templars were sorcerers so Gisbourne had been under orders to free the witch. Gisbourne had placed interdict upon several villages and the Archbishop had been sent for. Gisbourne had duelled the Sheriff and wounded him. Gisbourne had profaned the sabbat of Samhain and Robyn Hood had turned him into the *mari lwyd* and drowned him in the Trent.

Spoken of in a few shocked whispers: Gisbourne had brought the Sheriff Robyn Hood's head, and so deserved to die.

Another, equally powerful one: Robyn Hood had been the one to kill Gisbourne, come to Nottingham with Gisbourne's head, riding his horse and wearing his clothes, and been caught. Robyn was half fae and half witch, after all; he would likely set himself to free a witch from prison.

One thing held clear—whichever individual now inhabited the oubliette would be punished. And the winner of the archery contest would receive an even greater reward: to decide the ultimate fate of the prisoner.

Gilbert felt rather numb from all he'd seen and heard. Despite being the one best suited for such espionage, living in the green Wode made the reality a nerve-twining sensory excess. It hadn't always been so. Once he had been the middle son of a well-to-do fiefdom, notorious for his excesses—including drunken rows, a talent for gambling, as many whores as his bits could stand, and an unseemly preoccupation with a peasant's weapon, the bow. Now, however, he found himself viewing the sensate orgy of food and violence making up a tournament with a detached distaste.

That numb overload made it easy to imagine someone followed him. But after he'd seen the furtive, stalking figure for the fourth time, intent upon Gilbert when he supposedly wasn't aware, but turning away as Gilbert would glance back... well, nay. No imaginary pursuit, this.

Gilbert managed, with a quick duck behind the fruit-seller's stall and then a roll beneath a cart, to shake the tail for long enough to duck into the smithy's back storage shed. It was dark, and noisy from the forge and work going on in the main shed, yet out of the way enough to waylay someone with little notice.

He didn't have long to wait. Sure enough, his tail approached and hurried past Gilbert's hiding place, obviously concerned over losing the quarry. The "quarry" repaid such haste with an equally rapid duck outward and snatch, then hauled his pursuer into a darkened doorway. This was no common villager, however; Gilbert's pursuer gave a quick twist and lurch sideways, free arm rounding to land a hard fist against Gilbert's jaw. Gilbert reacted with woodland-honed reflexes, ducked and grabbed, had his assailant twisted, tripped, and slammed against the wall of the tiny shed in the time it took to breath twice.

"Gilbert!" his assailant yipped—softly, and in the tongue of the Franks.

"Siham?" A frown starting to quirk his brow, Gilbert loosened his grip and started, in same, "What are you—"

She didn't let him finish, loosed a rapid volley. "I saw you in the market and followed you. I should have known you'd know you were being tailed, but when I saw you I had to . . . Are the others here? Is Robyn here—umph!"

Gilbert clapped a hand over her mouth, hissed against her ear, "Don't say that name aloud!" Giving her a warning glance the whole while, slowly he removed his hand, said, "I'm here. Listening." He kept his voice down despite the clang and bang filling the air. Frankly it was the only way to be heard in close quarters beneath such a din. Mayhap they'd picked the perfect place for an informative tryst, after all.

"Then have you heard?" Her dark eyes—all he could see of her face within the kaffiyeh she wore wrapped up close—were apprehensive.

"I've heard many things," he said, still cautious.

Siham nodded. "As many rumours as truths, but when I saw you, I hoped you and yours had heard enough to come, help him."

"So that much is true—Gisbourne has been locked up?"

Siham nodded. "I saw it myself. There was much disturbance last night, guards and cries and the alarm bell. Most stayed in their homes, unwilling for trouble, but I snuck from my pallet to see what was going on. I knew something must have gone wrong." Gilbert started to speak, she added, "I am bedded down in the stall my horse and Guy's share; the barn is crowded and no one yet realises both the mounts aren't mine. I also paid the hostler enough to keep it that way."

"What did you see?"

"Enough soldiers to take out a garrison fort in the Lebanon, both royal and the Sheriff's. I watched as they marched Guy across the bailey and to the bowels of the keep. He was bound. The Sheriff and Count John were talking afterward—in Anglic, I couldn't understand, but their intent was clear. And I've heard enough from the innkeeper beside the stable—he's Limousin, speaks langue d'oc better than Anglic. One comfort?" Siham gave a vicious smile. "Our gazelle-eyed Templar left behind a lot of carrion on the walls of Nottingham. They're still cleaning the mess."

Our Templar? Gilbert wasn't sure what he thought of that.

"I was trying to think of how I could get word to Ro—to him, and then I saw you. Gilbert, my friend, it is an answer to my prayers. *Inş'allah*," she tacked on with soft reverence and made a gesture, fingers to her forehead.

Gilbert's command of the Saracen languages was practically nonexistent, but that one he recognised, and repeated after his own fashion, "*Bendith*." She frowned, not comprehending, so he returned to Frankish. "Aye, as the gods will. Have you heard anything else?"

"Many rumours. Too many to speak of. But one word was sent out this morning, directly from Sheriff de Lisle through his mouthpiece the seneschal: the Templar is prisoner, charged with treason and sorcery. They claim also he is a sodomite—which is worse to your people for some unfathomable reason." She rolled her eyes.

Gilbert shrugged—it was an oft-used charge even when inaccurate. Though he'd bet marks it wasn't. Recently, from the look in Robyn's eyes as he'd watched Gisbourne ride away.

What a complicated mess one's heart could create.

"There is more, my friend. The seneschal announced, to the joy of more than makes me comfortable, how the Templar will take sentence from the witch's place on the pyre. The prize has not been withdrawn from the archery contest, which also made cause for celebration. Not only fifty marks, but a hundred is now offered, and the one who can prove his—or her"—she tilted her head, eyebrows raised—"'superior accuracy at the butts shall have the privilege of determining the prisoner's manner of death.'"

Gilbert stood, silent and thinking, none too keen to bring any of this back to Robyn. Deep waters, these—and Gilbert was a poor swimmer at best. Nevertheless, he had a feeling what Robyn would do. What Robyn in truth should have the right to do, no matter how uneasy it made the rest of them.

Perhaps the lure and repulsion dancing between Guy de Gisbourne and Robyn Hood, an illicit passion primed with old fetters and new knives, had frayed overmuch to hold fast. Perhaps it was even now evolving into something more, levels and layers that the two, Templar and Outlaw, could not avoid. Yet one truth remained, here and now: Gisbourne had saved Marion. At the cost of his own freedom, at risk of his own life.

Here and now. It was enough for Gilbert. Hopefully it would be enough for the others.

- XXV -

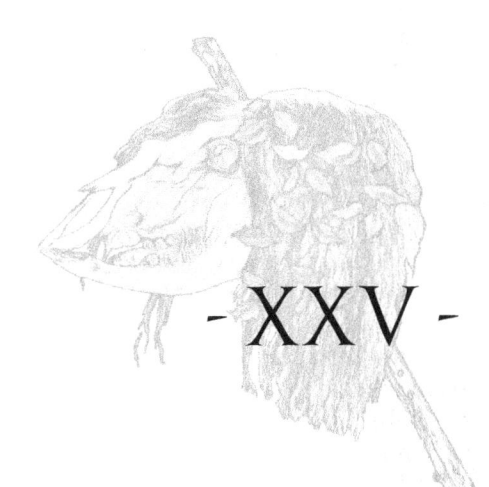

Much would never return from Temple Hirst in time.
It wasn't despair prompting the observation, but impassive reflection. Guy could only assume—hope, actually—that Much and Marion had safely escaped. From there other assumptions followed: if Much had managed to make his way back to Nottingham; if he'd avoided the patrols in doing so; if he'd discovered Guy had in fact been incarcerated and was slated for the entertainment billet vacated by Marion's escape . . .

Guy had been thrown into the oubliette, hit the muck-slimed floor hard and lain there, agony stabbing into every breath, until he'd reined pain into adrenaline. They had left his hands tied; he had quickly taken care of that, sawing them free on a sharp hinge, which had rusted and broken away from the wall. A chain still dangled, limp, from the hinge and the scavenged skeleton that had undoubtedly died in it comprised a litter of bones at his feet. Guy had left the severed rope where it had fallen atop the bony skull, found himself pacing the small confines like a caged beast. This had merely informed him of how escape, without two Templars and a rope and ladder, was indeed impossible.

And marvelled at the strength that was Marion's, coming up from days in this hole with her will still intact.

Not the most pleasant of places. He'd seen worse, and better—the better being a storeroom full of old, forgotten tomes from which he'd almost been sad to break free.

Aye, hopefully Marion was safe, and Robyn taking her deep into the Shire Wode. Hopefully even now Much galloped back to their Preceptory and the safety there.

But no doubt remained: Much wouldn't make it back in time. Over a hundred-and-fifty miles round trip, assuming Much had followed orders—and he would. He'd wait until midday, then turn his rouncey's head for the Preceptory. The rouncey was fast and fit, but one could not deny simple facts of time and distance.

The most difficult facet beneath which to remain impassive, however, was the way he would likely die.

Guy slumped—carefully—against the slimy wall and slid to a crouch in the mouldy straw. Put his head in his hands.

The dreams had started when they had first landed in Normandy. Not ones of the Shire Wode—not at first—but ones of himself and other Templars. In gaol, in the dark. Bound. *Burning*. Guy had gone to his master, disturbed. Hubert had listened, the expression on his face sliding into a strange mix of awe and pity. The realisation that Guy had somehow disturbed a Templar Master made adequate argument against confessing any future manifestations.

Particularly when said manifestations had started to conjure a past of which he had vowed to never speak.

Another vow, ground into dust, and whilst Guy now understood what had been plaguing him, had always kenned how Hubert's apprehension had reflected a fear in which Guy's dreams represented some kind of future foretelling, he had never allowed himself to imagine the burning as his own death. He had been implicit in so many things, after all, blood-soaked duties in which the Order would not so openly allow one who wore the white to indulge. The charges accrued beneath his black and crimson tabard could have filled an inquisitor's tally—heresy, disobedience, assassination, treason, sorcery, sodomy—aided and abetted by the Order's own arcane purposes or tolerated in the manner of wielded power. Altogether wasteful, to chide a weapon for being stained if it balanced light in the hand and held a deadly edge.

Yet it seemed Guy's worst fears, however egocentric, had come to realisation.

Perhaps Siham would win the archery contest and give him the same mercy she had planned for Marion.

Better this, after all, than the possible disenfranchisement of an entire Order. Richard was still King, anointed by God;

Richard's Lackland brother would end up paying hell for disregarding the sovereignty of the Knights Templar.

This was all, of course, assuming Hubert didn't wish Guy drawn and quartered and *then* burnt, once Hubert heard what his pet assassin had risked everything for.

"Your sister's safe. The two monks have gone to fetch the Templars—"

"And they'll never get to Nottingham in time."

"You don't know that, Robyn."

"Aye?" Robyn flung the hair from his eyes and glared at his companions. The fire lit all their faces, stark and pale—and, in some cases, outright fearful.

Gilbert had come back. His news was dire.

As if merely waiting for confirmation—or the waiting had slowed instincts that would no longer be gainsaid—Robyn had lurched to his feet and started pacing. Started throwing queries left and right, everything from how many arrows they had cached to lambswool and horsehair and extra clothing for disguises, then on to the logistics of breaking camp.

"Well?" he said, peering at them, expectant. "Get a move on."

And chaos had erupted.

"You en't serious!"

"We can't possi—"

"Let his own see to—"

"We've freed our own, 'tis no—"

Marion was the only one still seated. The fire warming her toes, her knees drawn to her chest, she watched, silent, with a faint smile on her face. One Robyn remembered, and knew exactly how to interpret.

I'll go with you, it said. *He's ours. We'll free him, together.*

Robyn shouldn't even be contemplating her participation. She had spent debilitating days gaoled in the dark, had not pushed a bow in years. Instead Marion's expression rose within him a fierce, feral glee his indigo-painted ancestors would have recognised.

"You seem to be thinkin' I'm asking permission, here," he snapped. "I en't. I'm telling you—all of you—what I'm after. You can go or not."

More uproar; Will shouted it all down. "If you think we'll leave you to go in there alone, you're mad. In fact, you *are* mad, risking everything for a murdering, Motherless *Templar!*"

Robyn turned on Will, grabbed his leather vest with both hands, and shoved him backward until he sprawled against a tree. He didn't know why Will was surprised. But Will was.

"Second chances, aye? We've all had them, sometimes third ones, and now you say he doesn't? Everything he's done, it's been from grief and fury."

"You're *excusing* what he is?"

"I *know* what he is!" Robyn spat. "Just as I know what *we* are! And I am not *leaving him there*, do y' hear? I en't leaving him to rot in the dark or die in the fire!" His hands trembled and spasmed, tangled so tight in Will's leather vest it creaked protest. "Sweet Lady, Will, how could you even *think* I would?"

"Robyn—"

"Or is there some truth in your taunts about 'tunic lifters', Scathelock?" Robyn sneered, shoving at Will again. "You're the one, after all, who's always got 'em ready."

"That's bloody rubbish you're talking!" Will shoved back. "It en't that! It never has been! Bloody damn, we've been over this before! None of us has any rights to court outsiders! For their safety, for ours. No matter what the fancy is, tackle in or out or several. Those are the rules as *you* made 'em, Hooded One."

"And the Templar en't of us, Robyn," Arthur agreed. "In any fashion."

Gilbert had fallen uncharacteristically silent, arms crossed, morose. David, shaking his head, ventured, "What if it's a trap?"

"They still have to spring it, aye?" Robyn snarled. "In the middle of an archery tournament, with everyone watching."

"You shoot with your left hand, and they'll have you." Arthur pointed out. "There's plenty would gleefully watch the Sheriff pitch you atop the pyre."

That one, strangely enough, hurt. Robyn's gaze slid to him, hands tremoring then stilling upon Will. "All the more reason to take back what's mine *because* it's mine. Not because some god sang it in my ear. Not because some villein accepts our help then spits on us a fortnight later. Not because you've given me your say-so!"

"Aye, let's talk of permissions, then," Will said, gruff. "What of John?" His hands grabbed and tightened, brutal, on Robyn's wrists. "What of *his* feelings in all this sorry mess your knob's landed you in?"

"Will—" From behind Robyn, Marion's protest rose, wavered.

"Do you really think," Robyn said, very quiet, "John knows nowt?"

John was standing not far from Marion, leaning against a

tree—the only one besides Marion herself who hadn't circled around their leader in overt challenge. John seemed . . . not relaxed, but unaffected. Untroubled. *Waiting.* His brown eyes met Will's and held, their clear lamp burning steadfast.

"I've allus known," John told him. "There's a deep place, here." He put a hand to his breast, looked around at his companions. "He en't Motherless. He's t' Summering lord. He *is* of us, and if you don't see't, you're all fools."

Silence.

Will looked away, shaking his head. "All of it. Mad."

"Tell me owt I don't know, Scathelock," Robyn replied.

With a fierce, keen look, Will pulled him, sudden-close. Robyn stiffened then gave, returning the embrace just as fierce.

"You bloody-minded sod," Will murmured. "Y' have to be careful, aye? I en't gonna lose you again."

Robyn averted his face, gently pounded a fist on Will's chest and quipped, "Let go, y' ginormous pillock. You'll be wanting t' tup me, next."

"Not bloody likely!" Will snorted, and shoved Robyn back. "Well, Gilly, looks as if *you're* getting what you want out of all this."

Gilbert came over, leaned against the tree, and smiled. "So, my lord," he addressed Robyn. "How long *has* it been since you've shot right-handed?"

They'd brought him up to this cell the day before, no doubt so he could hear the scaffolding being sawn and hammered into place. See it, too, should he choose, from a half-circle iron grating that gave a rather decent view of the upper bailey stretching beyond in a mix of mud and close-grazed green. At eye level, the opening; below it a wall of rock, half a man's height, led to the floor of hard-packed earth. The cell hadn't been used for human habitation in some time—no doubt because wind and rain both blew up the hill and straight into the half-circle "window."

Guy knew the latter all too intimately because he had been stripped to braies and shackled to a ceiling beam right in front of it. His hands were cold, bruised wrists manacled together and over his head to the beam. His feet were also cold, bare against the chill, packed earth—but better to have them supporting at least some of his weight. His bare torso took the brunt of the wind and wet from the wind funnel/window, his thin braies sodden and clinging to him, groin to midthigh, like a film of ice in a north wind.

The bindings gave pain—as indeed intended—but this pain bided no different than any other he had endured. It meant nothing; it did not belong to him, did not . . . *touch* him, did not sink into his soul even when the metal shackles further abraded what marks he'd garnered a mere two nights previous. It afforded absolutely no pleasure of any kind.

He was particularly relieved by that last.

A heavy tread of worn, mud- and shit-covered boots passed outside the grating on a regular basis. There were always three, sometimes four sentries at the door. The number of guards placed about his impromptu cell might have been humorous, or flattering. But Guy was in no pleasant humour, nor was he flattered. It merely meant that every time he tried to jerk at the chain lashed around the beam, someone came and kicked his feet out from under him. When he tried to swing and reach the far wall where the end of his chain fastened to a hook, they would come in, kick his feet out from under him, and tighten the chain another notch. Every time he climbed the chain, hoping to find some flaw in it, they yanked him down, then kicked his feet out from under him. And when the guards did release him, either to eat, shit or piss, there were at least four of them, heavily armed.

After they chained him back up, they—of course—kicked his feet out from under him.

At least the activity, such as it was, warmed Guy up a bit.

The only items upon Guy holding to any warmth also held no rational explanation for doing so. The superstitious guards had left those items strictly alone. One guard had drawn a dagger and put a hand to the cord knotted at Guy's hips—fully intending to strip it from him, Guy was sure. Instead, the guard had let out a choked cry, backed swift as a well-trained destrier, and forked an evil eye at Guy, muttering about sorcery. Since then, they'd left the cord strictly alone—it, and the charm about his neck. John's charm.

No rational explanation, certainly, that the things should hold . . . something. He'd felt the effects of one of John's charms before. But the cord braided thin about his hips . . . Guy had worn the girdle of the Templars since his initiation, and never felt this sort of . . . heat and energy and . . . well, whatever it was. Tingles, yes. But now? Ever since Robyn had . . . touched it—

whispered to it, drawn his hair across it, lain kisses and breath along it

—it had vibrated against his skin, a constant hum of sensation opening Guy, entirely too much, to other sensations. As if when Robyn had risen reaction in Guy's body, he had also intensified this, given it some power Guy hadn't possessed.

You give yourself too little credit, my Knight. You were sleeping, curled in the shadows long. The Maiden parted the grey curtain of your slumber, and the Hooded One has finally waked you.

Well, that was helpful. He was to be burnt for witchcraft. Until then he would have to settle for being half-naked, and damp, and cold as hell. If hell was, in fact, cold. It did look as if Guy was going to find out firsthand.

And he was going to be . . . *awake* for it. Lovely.

That night, Robyn dreamed.

No soft, misted slumber, this. Nay, these dreams bided behind his eyes as he sat awake, dry of sleep and respite, watchful in the crotch of the huge oak tree marking their camp.

The night was startlingly clear. Both the moon's sliver and the cheery flames that warmed their sleeping gave adequate light through the naked branches of his perch. Enough, anyway, to finish his task.

Of willow heartwood, pale as the virgin's moon that lit his work, it was a piece he had long ago begged leave to take for just this purpose. The Lady's vengeance should be done with Her own weapons. Perfectly seasoned, hard and light, carved slender and deadly. He had waited until everyone slept—such a work was not well done save in secret—and had spent the last hour marking it with faint runes, a spiral pattern of his own blood. Now he was tying and gluing the fletchings—good goose vanes knifed and split, marked and set—with the final touches. Peacock feathers, tufts of a goddess's eye, to guide the willow in Her purpose.

As he worked, he whispered and hummed. Breathed the spells. Wove all he was into the arrow, lithe body and fierce heart, wild instincts and stubborn purpose and strands of ebon darkling *tynged.*

This might be the last fight. He was not unaware of that. But if he was to go down, it would not be without a last, deadly blow.

Will you die for Me, Holly Lord? Would you die for your people, o King?

If I died my people would not care. But aye, for you, Lady, Robyn breathed into the arrow. *For your earthly vessel. For my brothers. For him.*

For Robyn saw him, knew Guy, *dreamed* him: first in the dark then in the grey dank-cold, bound and stretched, bruised and bleeding. Saw the fleeting things inhabiting Guy's own dreams: mists adrift within stolen snatches of sleep, horned shades and fire, darkness, starry nights of loving, pain denying contentment so long ago and far away. Suffered the stab and tingle in outraged ribs as they stretched in heartbeat and breath, the ache in arms pulled just that far into discomfort, the chafe of metal against bare, freckled skin.

The fury. The *will*.

Sweet *Lady* but his Oak was beautiful, bound and feral and seething, just waiting for the moment to strike.

Robyn considered the coming day. In the aftermath of Loxley, his wound had forced him to make himself adequate with a right draw. He could last much of the tourney with that. Gilbert had seeded, with coin and coercion, a few distractions in Nottingham proper—but Robyn was wary to trust to those. Better to rely as he could upon his men and Marion; whoever chose to help would be happy chance, nowt more.

Marion had managed, as he'd known she would, to argue her way into the raid. She'd even proven her point with a light shortbow David had taken from stores. The string had broken on her second shot, but her arrow had sung true. Some things you just didn't forget. Gilbert had twisted a new flax string for her, and their strongest arms, Will and Arthur, would be her partners. A few good meals had done much to set her to rights—but then, Marion had always been as tough as old leather. She would be good for a few choice shots, no doubt have a sore arm come the day after.

There would be a day after for her. A second chance. For her. For Guy. For himself, somehow.

Shame to come all this way and then miss the reunion.

You think you can cheat death again, Hob-Robyn?

For you, Robyn breathed into the night. *It's time to come home, Gamelyn.*

☽

Guy woke, his face wet, and when he licked his lips he tasted salt. He scrubbed his face against his shoulder, uncomprehending, looked at the mix of grime and tears on his goose-pimpled skin.

It's time to come home, Gamelyn.

Felt dread crawl into his gut and hunch there, colder than his cell and terrified.

No, he told the echoes of that low, insistent voice. *Don't come for me. I've already had you killed once.*

🜪

"Robert of Barnsdale, master clerk. And my brother, Gilbert."

The clerk glowered at them from behind his table, sucked on a tooth. "Longbows, eh? I en't seen many of those in a tourney, and for good reason—those monsters're too chancy. What's yer da thinkin', lettin you come all this way and spend his money for nowt? Too many of you lads in th' manor, thinkin' yer Robyn 'Ood, or the like!"

A woollen muffler—ostensibly against the misted, chill morn—wrapped the bottom of Gilbert's face, and a finely woven hood shadowed his eyes; nevertheless those eyes flickered nervously to his "brother" beside him, held.

Robyn merely smirked and winked beneath his own woollen cowl, kept holding out the entry fees—tuppence apiece. His voice drawled as devoid of common clip as any minor lordling when he replied, "But if we win, master Clerk, what a win, eh?"

The clerk snorted, wrote their names in the ledger, and took their money. "The first rounds will be starting anon. Pay attention; y' don't want to miss your chance. Next!" he bellowed.

A mailed guardsman, clad in de Lacy's colours and made of more granite than flesh from the expression on his face, shouldered past them. Robyn and Gilbert escaped from the crowded table. Not that it did much good. The lower bailey of Nottingham castle was packed with people, milling over the grounds and about the stalls, sellers' cries rising above the din, hoping to gain attention.

Robyn, snugging his own woollen wrap tighter about his pulled-back hair, kept grinning. "You lads, thinkin' yer Robyn 'Ood."

His mimicry was perfect, down to the whiny undertone of the clerk's voice, and Gilbert laughed, nudged his shoulder. "See, even a ripe old trout like that knows of Robyn Hood. And in the process," he added, softer, "saw only two spoilt rotters, fresh from their da's manor. Excellent voice, you're in."

"I've had good teachers, aye?" Robyn nudged Gilbert back, couldn't help a fuss at the tunic he wore—fine, perhaps, but stiff and scratchy to skin used to well-worn flax or leathers tanned smooth as butter. Even the serge breeches made more rustle than he found comfortable. Well, fussing with his appearance stayed well in character for a wealthy young git.

"Stop scratching!" Gilbert admonished, then nudged him. "You clean up adequately, my lord."

"Hm. I fancy the colour, 'tennyrate."

"'Tis the finest green dye Lincoln can produce. Proper suitable for the Hob—"

"Hsst, you." Right about now Robyn was merely grateful his undertunic and braies were of plain, soft-worn muslin.

And he was *famished*.

As if reading Robyn's mind, Gilbert skipped sideways, nabbed several skewers of roasted pork from a meat stall as they passed.

"Hoy!" the woman watching the stall protested; her outrage turned to a grateful curtsey as she saw the tender of coin Gilbert tossed her. "That'll buy you four more, gentle sir!" she called after.

"Lovely!" Gilbert circled back and started to gather his bounty, hesitating as he saw the woman. "On due consideration, I'll take two. Keep the rest—your smile is all the more lovely, and just giving it cause is well worth the payment."

She smirked, then shrugged as her man emerged from the shadowed cooking tent behind, eyeing Gilbert. It wasn't friendly. The man had more meat on a tray—and enough muscle to make a meat pie of Gilbert, who gracefully made both a quick bow and an exit.

Robyn was trying not to burst into laughter. It didn't stop him, however, from nicking his share and tucking in.

"'Tis the same the shire over," Gilbert lamented, licking at his fingers where meat juice trickled. "The pretty ones are all taken."

"Plenty in the Underkeep'll let you take 'em," Robyn pointed out. "One gives you half fee, t' boot. Were I a whore I'd charge you twice ower, all the nonsense you spout courting."

"I have no complaints." Gilbert's tone went from airy to sly, with a grin to match. "P'rhaps you should try a bit of Frankish poetry on that knight you fancy."

Robyn nearly choked on his meat, snorted, "Chance would be a fine thing!"

"Hm," Gilbert said, all sage wisdom, "more a fighter than a lover, that one. And everyone knows you love a fight."

"Cheeky," Robyn warned. "First we have to fetch him out alive."

"Then?"

"Then I'll snog the daft git legless. In front of all of you."

"Ooo, *pornographos*! Done!"

Robyn rolled his eyes, kept scoffing his meal.

All the time, beneath tally and wandering and banter and food, neither his nor Gilbert's attention strayed from their true purpose:

watching and processing everything. From the crowds milling about, peasant and noble alike, to the banner-festooned walls swarming with more guards than made them comfortable, past the busy market stalls and through the secondary portcullis—wide and raised. They both stopped, looking upward, Robyn licking his fingers and Gilbert still chewing. The back bailey rose beyond, the pathway beneath their booted feet leading to the huge stone keep, crouched heavy and menacing. In its shadow, the level sward had been cordoned off, the archery butts placed. Those would, in their turn, no doubt be cleared away after the surest arrow had flown, for the morrow's mêlée.

People milled freely past them, up and down through the gate; they sidled out of the right-of-way, gawking—Robyn was sure—exactly like the two manor-bred lads they thought to mimic.

"Ponce!" Gilbert marvelled. "Brother-mine, 'tis a long time since I've pricked an arrow in as fancy a butts as these."

"Just think of soldier buttocks and you'll be fine," Robyn suggested with a grin.

But the grin faded as they made their survey of the field. On the far side and nigh to the keep, a pavilion had been raised, uninhabited as of yet but draped with the reds and golds of the Royal Presence. As they continued up the rise, Robyn more than once tried to sneer at it. Yet each time he found the expression fading as his gaze, inevitably, slid toward another scaffolding across from it.

The wood from both constructions shone pale and new. The latter of the two had no colours, no drapings to disguise or reveal its purpose. But of its purpose there was no doubt. A goodly pile of dried brush and seasoned faggots had been piled up to one side.

"Rob?" Gilbert used the old nickname freely, snugged an arm tight into his.

"It's daft. But . . . " Robyn took in a breath. "Marion might've been there. And now? Bloody damn, Gilly."

Gilbert squeezed his arm.

(♪)

Marion leaned on her staff, peered flat-eyed from beneath the shelter of a dirty, wide brimmed hat. She kept finding her attention snared by the scaffolding, particularly focusing upon the piled faggots, upon the iron ring spiked into the fresh wood.

She shifted, uncomfortable. Not just with her garb—though it was no more comfortable to her than Robyn with his fancy tunic and breeks, which he looked fabulous in, to boot. Marion was deliberately un-fabulous. Beneath several layers of oversized tunics, she wore a well-padded, short gambeson, which not only kept her wonderfully warm, but added bulk and disguised the telltale roundness of breast and hip. It was all deucedly uncomfortable after the light freedom of hose-clad legs beneath skirts, and a hat blocked her peripheral vision more than any veil ever had. The one comfort amidst the strange lay in the quiver and shortbow harnessed to her back—the latter being the same one David had found for her. Her body hadn't forgotten that, at least.

She kept thinking, not of the possibility averted by her own escape, but of another possibility looming just as treacherous.

Gamelyn.

"It en't going t' go away by wishing it," Will said, gruff, beside her.

Dark hair didn't suit Will, but his size and fair hair had made him more recognisable than any of the outlaws. Since he couldn't do much about the first, he'd slicked the second with dark grease, tied it into a pony's tail beneath a wide hat, and had a good shave. His hat sagged, almost as dilapidated as Marion's, and a rag over one eye completed the disguise begun with Arthur's missing arm: two ex-soldiers, wounded in the wars and come to Nottingham to show their younger companion—son or nephew, perhaps—a fine time.

And there was Arthur now, appearing from the crowd milling about the food stalls, a handkerchief already sopping with juices dangling from his elbow crook. Arthur, of course, had no bow, and his two-bladed axe had been left at camp, replaced with the smaller one hanging at his belt.

Will took the kerchief-wrapped meat, passed portions around. They all fell to hungrily, unsure of when they might get another chance.

"Saw our archer lads nigh t' the meat stall," Arthur ventured as he chewed. "They passed me th' sign. They're entered, goin' for the butts."

"Seen the others?" Will asked between bites.

"Nay, but they're likely deep into the snoop. Almost time to start our own snoop of th' walls," Arthur reminded, then hummed appreciation of his meal. "Mmm, I en't had pork cooked this fair in a while. Should I fetch you more, um, *lad?*" His eyes danced as he watched Marion inhale her portion and lick her fingers to boot.

She grinned. "Mayhap. And mayhap I can cook pork that fair when we get back."

"I'm not doubting it," Will said, but when she met his eyes, looked aside and mumbled, "I remember your cooking." He still seemed unsure what—or how—to act around her.

It was strangely appealing, the awkwardness. And daunting, because Marion wasn't quite sure how to act around him, either. So she fell back on old habits—complete with plenty of *I'm not noticing you, see?*—more apropos in this situation than not.

They certainly had other things of import to focus upon. Like that cursed scaffold.

"Did y' ever think, mayhap Robyn's not making a proper choice, here?" Will said, following her gaze.

"You sound like a bloody-minded Church tither, William. Right and wrong, good and bad. Like it's ever so simple." She turned to him. "Tennyrate, how can it not be the proper choice? Gamelyn *helped* me."

"And with what the Motherless sod has done to us and our'n, 'twould no more than wipe the slate clean." Will shook his head, pitched his voice even lower. "Lass, that Templar . . . whatever he is, he en't Gamelyn no more."

"Rob said that, too. It's beside the point."

"Did he?" Will said, frowning, and peered at Arthur.

"Well, then." Arthur nudged Will. "P'rhaps he's thinking with the bigger brain, after all."

Right. Now she wanted to grab them, a hand to each ear, and bang their thick skulls together. "With his bigger brain?"

Will shrugged. "He's more like to think with the little one when it comes to that ginger-haired noble's brat. He allus has, and you know it, lass."

"I know what's between 'em a sight better than you, I should think."

"This from one who didn't ken her baby brother were diddling lads until he'd gotten well started?"

Marion bristled. "This from one talking of people changing whilst you haven't, not one *bit.*"

Will blinked.

"Why are you even here if you're so set to see an innocent man burned to death?"

"That'un's no innocent. If he were, he'd not be—"

"So I deserved to be burnt, then."

"Ssst," Arthur hissed. "Keep it down, th' both of you—"

"Well, t' fact remains, lass, you weren't innocent neither. Not of witchcraft. But burning people 'cause they believe different from you is wrong."

"So it's wrong to burn Gamelyn!"

"Gisbourne—"

"Or d'you say it's all right to burn him because he believes different from *you*?"

"That en't what I said. But happens *our* belief murders no—"

"Now *that's* a precious load of codswallop. Starting with that first soldier you sank a spelled arrow into!"

Will stiffened. "*That* bastard deserved what he got and more!"

"So you're saying Gamelyn—"

"*Gisbourne*," Will snarled.

Marion slapped him.

Their argument had been mostly held *sotto voce*, but at this a few bystanders turned, avid, to the sudden drama in their midst. Arthur groaned, pulled his hat farther over his face.

Will stood there akin to stone, red flaring high on his cheek where she'd struck. "I see."

"Nay," Marion said, just as stonily. "I think y' really don't."

"Nay, I think I really do."

"Will." Arthur tugged at his sleeve.

Will shrugged it off. "So. If yer brother en't thinkin' with his knob and what heart that noble-bred ginger bastard bothered t' leave him with, then why is he doing this?" He leaned forward. "Is he doing this for *you*?"

Marion blinked this time. "Me?"

"*Will*." This time Arthur grabbed Will's arm, hissed, "Leave *off*, you bloody pillock, before you sink us!"

Will, still staring at Marion, backed away. He hesitated, then shook his head. "Aye, well, then. We're already sunk, en't we?" Arthur frowned. Will held up both hands. "I'm off. Now. I'll take the north and east walls on me own."

They both watched him retreat.

For *her*? What was that supposed to mean? "Sweet *Lady*," Marion growled, "but he's being a first-rate git!"

"Aye, well. You weren't helping, lass."

She glared at Arthur. He grumbled a small sigh and looked off into the crowd. His eyes were clear, alert for anything. Disgruntled, but set.

"If Will's off t' north n' east," he muttered, "and John and David are checking the keep proper, then you'n I should see to our own benighted doin's."

Of all Robyn's band, this one seemed the most straightforward. Yet now, Arthur remained all the more a cipher.

"So why are *you* doing this? You obviously don't approve."

"That takes no witchery," Arthur said, quiet, then shrugged. "My approval en't necessary, eh? Robyn's done more for me than I'll ever be able to pay, he and Will both. I'll do th' job, and that's what you're needin'. What our Lord and Lady need, for whatever purposes they have. 'Tis that simple." He shrugged again. "No question I'll likely clout the sodding Templar once we're in th' clear, but only once he's ours again t' punish."

Marion took a deep breath and put Will out of her mind. Arthur was right—it was that simple. They had to fetch Gamelyn out. No matter the cost. They couldn't lose him again.

Robyn couldn't lose him again. Her brother seemed a stranger in so many ways. Was it wrong to think this risky bid for Gamelyn's freedom wasn't just to wipe a slate clean? Not just for a boyhood memory, but for what could exist here and now—and tomorrow?

Was Robyn's obligation to Guy as well as Gamelyn? And what of Guy's to Robyn?

(↥)

"I think me . . . my . . . bow is understrung." Robyn smoothed his speech midmurmur with an apologetic grimace to Gilbert as he halted beside him. Both of them, now, had made their first go. Robyn put his fist, thumb extended, between wood and the string, then shook his head. "Aye, and there's a fistmele betwixt, yet it sounds . . . off."

"'Twas over loud when you loosed," Gilbert agreed, as Robyn stepped and unstrung his bow.

"Must be all the hot air." Robyn rolled his eyes as one of the unsuccessful archers passed, whinging to his friend. "Seen John and David?"

"John's there." Gilbert nodded, nonchalant, at a group of watchers. Robyn followed with his eyes, met John's gaze. "I suspect David's still at the prowl." He anticipated Robyn's next query. "Not seen the other three since the food stall. They know to be watching by the third round, though, so no worries, eh?"

And that, as expected, might be a while yet. Over a hundred had entered, by Robyn's dirty-quick count, during which he'd wished a quick pilfering of the entry monies lay within their means. Some of the archers clearly *weren't*, unable to even hit the target pricks at twenty ells—a distance Robyn had mastered years before his balls had so much as dropped!—let alone one of the inner rings. There were a few left-handed ones—very few—but the way those were performing, it was doubtful they'd make it past a few rounds anyway. Some of the archers had made much over practicing with a provided clout, but Gilbert and Robyn were of the same opinion: anyone who had to practice before they loosed would go hungry, sure enough. In this lot, the first round would do for any tuning.

As the round ended, the ranks had dwindled significantly. Siham wasn't amongst the ones eliminated. Robyn had recognised her bow, first, then had been impressed by the clean flight of the arrow she'd loosed from that bow. Siham had not yet noticed him or Gilbert despite their bared heads—for which Gilbert had made reasonable argument on the way here. The longbows were grounds enough for suspicion; to push those longbows with their heads discourteously covered was just madness.

Robyn hadn't realised until now how altogether used he was to his hood; a badge of honour, aye, but even more a buffer against the unknown. Another thing to put him off when the outcome was entirely too important.

Instead he focused on a less discomfiting subject: how it was fortunate Siham hadn't yet seen them, particularly since she seemed to have rejoined the lord who'd sent her here, in his pavilion on the sidelines. Baron de Lacy was the Sheriff's brother, after all, and therefore someone to stay clear of.

Not that anyone had seen the Sheriff, yet, or any of the nobles who were to inhabit that fine pavilion running alongside the archery butts.

From where he'd leaned over to adjust a strap on his boot, Gilbert gave an abrupt warning hiss and rose, glancing behind Robyn. Woodland-bred impulse claimed Robyn's muscles; he nearly spun about but at the last second controlled it. Instead he ran nimble fingers over his string and twirled it. Then, with a soft grunt, he bent the bow and slipped the string over the smooth end groove of horn. As he did, he glanced over one shoulder.

Sheriff de Lisle was there, walking with Siham's nobleman. Again, fight-or-flight impulse would demand Robyn turn away, duck his head . . . only they didn't know his face. Robyn's senses tingled nevertheless, popping like rain on a well-oiled cooking iron. He reattended his bow, let his hair fall into his eyes, hunched his shoulders.

"—you say, Brian? A wager on the female? There's none in this lot can touch her, I'll warrant."

"The day a woman can—Pardon, Roger." This as a youngish man came running up to the Sheriff, muttered in his ear.

Gilbert slid his eyes to Robyn, brows knitting. He seemed uncertain of whether he wanted to faint or laugh. Robyn wasn't sure but he felt the same. Here they both stood, within spitting distance of the man who'd put the price on their heads.

Sheriff de Lisle frowned, then nodded. The young man started to retreat, the Sheriff called him back, spoke a few more terse sentences, let him go.

"My lord Count is ready for his entrance." The Sheriff's voice revealed nothing.

His companion—Roger?—shrugged, also noncommittal, then lowered his voice. "Can't you do something, Brian?"

Robyn fanned his attention outward, found John's eyes upon him. John was a bit ashen, seeing Robyn within grabbing distance of the Sheriff.

"Don't you think I've tried?" De Lisle's words were a bare murmur—probably none but Gilbert and Robyn could hear—or were bothering to. "When it comes to cases, this is his castle, not mine. I'm only the well-scrubbed tenant. You're more likely to influence him—you're Baron of Pontefract!"

Roger looked like he'd a sore tooth. "I'll tell you, Brian, I worry how little he listens to those he should. It bodes ill for the decision we're contemplating here."

Gilbert's ears fairly flapped. Of course, always onto the politics of his left-behind class, Gilbert was more a gossipmonger than Robyn ever bothered. It served them well, and often.

And wasn't that like the noblemen, not bothering to think the surrounding villeins had ears, or the brains to use them against such talk.

Baron de Lacy's next words truly iced Robyn's spine.

"Christ, Brian. If he burns a Templar, there'll be hell to pay, and you likely the one paying."

The voices faded as they moved away. Robyn looked at John, tipped his head—a command, really—and John nodded, disappeared into the crowd after the Sheriff and his brother.

Gilbert finally spoke. "So. They mean to do it."

Robyn was shaking his head. "They might mean it. But I mean to not let 'em."

♪

Guy had ceased bothering to watch what took place outside his small window, instead dozing as best he could in the position he'd been forced to. The sudden blare of trumpets jolted him awake.

As if on cue, the lock to his cell door rattled, gave a grinding clank. As the trumpets ceased and a voice began bellowing introductions to the tournament guests of honour, the door swung open with a heavy and resistant growl. His four guard dogs trouped in, plus two extra.

"Hold him," one said, and they spread out into the cell in the beginnings of a process—quite ritualised, actually—in which Guy was lowered to the ground. One held a crossbow on him, this time joined by the two extras. One grabbed his ankles. He'd once tried kicking the latter one's teeth in, had merely received four kicks for every one he'd given, felt another rib give, and pissed blood for hours after. The third grabbed his wrists as he came down, and the fourth unfastened the chain where it had been hooked onto a crude ratchet on the far wall.

As usual, Guy ended up on his back, pinned hand and foot, but this time they unhooked his wrist manacles. Once they did so and backed away—cautious, ready—Guy curled on his side atop the dank floor, pulling his arms to his torso and gritting his teeth as stabs and shards ran up and down his arms. His feet weren't much better; they felt like overstuffed sausages. He flexed them against the cool floor. No sense moving until he actually could move with something resembling intent.

A seventh guard came in, a bundle in his arms. "Get dressed," he ordered, and tossed the bundle down in front of Guy. Slowly, Guy pushed himself to sit somewhat upright, saw that the guard had thrown him his clothes—well, most of them. No chainmail. Both tunics and his black-and-scarlet tabard, one belt—not the sword-belt, of course—as well as his breeches and boots.

"I take it," Guy ventured, "it's time for the entertainment."

- XXVI -

Trumpets winded from either end of the draped pavilion, a swell of sound proclaiming Importance. In response, the people scattered over the vast open expanse of Nottingham's baileys surged upward and inward, eager to catch a glimpse of their liege lords bedecked in splendour.

On the other side of that blare and advance, it took everything Robyn and Gilbert had to not turn tail and run. The people ascending upon the butts looked like some old tale of a barbarian horde making to sack and pillage. Thankfully there were guards stationed with pikes at the field, not hesitating to brandish them if anyone intruded too far.

"Never thought we'd be grateful for the Sheriff's guards," Gilbert quipped. His laugh, normally so hearty, stretched a bit thin.

"Bloody damn, but I hate towns," Robyn grumbled, and forcibly restrained himself from yanking up his hood. "Never liked 'em, never will."

There had been three rounds so far. Each time the "brothers" had shot well enough to be in the running, but not so as to cause undue attention. As the clerk had earlier groused, there were more longbows than Gilbert could remember seeing at an archery tourney— and he had been to his share. One of the things his upwardly climbing father had despaired of, Gilbert's penchant for a mere yeoman's weapon.

Robyn smiled at the sudden memory: Gilbert had come to them with starry-eyed fantasies a-plenty of living in the green Wode. Yet he'd stayed despite having those fantasies dashed, for they'd been replaced with more—the realisation of his archer's heart. As Robyn ran fingers along the curve of his grandsire's bow, feeling the wood warm to his touch, he smiled even more and considered those extra longbows, some of them dragged, dusty and strings rotting, no doubt, from cellars and barns. Most of them would end up back there, more the pity, but the thick strum of their loose would likely awaken more than a few archers' hearts.

"There's enough sparkle on those gowns to buy and sell the Shire Wode!" Gilbert muttered, and his hand gripped the embroidered hem of Robyn's green tunic, gave a sharp tug.

Belatedly, Robyn realised he had better do as everyone else was, and allowed Gilbert to pull him down on the field to kneel in the presence of John, Count of Mortain, Lord of Gloucester, and appointed overlord of Nottingham Castle. Count John strode in, flung his robes to one side, and seated himself upon the highest dais.

"Bloody damn," Robyn repeated, staring at the thick assortment of silks, velvets, samites, and jewellery. A sombre form drifted amongst the peacock colours, making him stiffen. First a well-clad priest, seating himself in the Sheriff's half of the box beside Siham's baron patron, then, behind them . . .

The Abbess.

Lip curling, Robyn started to rise, caught himself just in time. The Abbess, through some odd coincidence—surely she couldn't sense the virulence that Robyn knew poured from him, like waves—looked his way. He ducked his head just in time.

"That's her," Gilbert murmured, "isn't it?"

Aye, and she's Ours. At last. Lady and Lord, for once in tandem, and it made Robyn break in a rash of hot sweat.

He nodded, clenched his teeth, and closed his eyes. *Not yet.*

We can wait, Hooded One. But today it will be done.

Robyn let out the breath he only then realised he'd been holding, and reached back to his quiver. He wanted to touch the spelled arrow, feel the purpose of it. It reached shorter than his normal draw, slightly thicker . . .

It wasn't there.

He kept feeling for it, his motions getting more and more frantic as he still found nothing. Count John was speaking, had been speaking for a small while—but Robyn paid no attention. An abrupt swell of noise rose, with mutterings and exclamations from the crowd, and Gilbert's hand went to Robyn's shoulder, clenching hard enough to make Robyn wince and leave off his search.

"Sweet Lady! Robyn, get up! *Look!*"

Robyn lifted his head, saw Gilbert gaining his feet—all the archers about them, in fact, and everyone beyond seemed to be rising, animated. Robyn moved to stand, followed Gilbert's wide-eyed gaze to where it had pinned: beyond the roped-off expanse of green where the archers stood to make their shots.

The missing arrow left his thoughts as suddenly as if loosed. Silence fell over the gathering.

The man stood straight-backed and tall, refusing to shuffle despite the weight of the manacles about his feet. He paused as he entered the field, tripped and nearly went sprawling as the guards shoved him inward. By some alchemy of luck and quick motion, he caught himself midfall, stiffly kept his feet. While the distinctive crimson cross upon his black tabard lay twisted, stained and rumpled, he wore it as easily as any of the nobles in the pavilion wore their gems and brocades. His coppery head, bared beneath the clear sky, lifted higher.

"Arrogant bastards, all of their like," one of the archers next to Robyn rumbled, and a snide mutter of agreement rippled through the remainder.

Aye, was Robyn's silent riposte, with a narrow sneer towards the mouthy archer. *But he's my arrogant bastard, y' daft git. You barely made the last round and I don't expect t' see you in the finals, so we know who's possessed of a poxy squint, then.*

"You're gawking, brother," Gilbert leaned hard against him and murmured against his ear. "Not likely they'll let you snog him here in the field, you know." Robyn smirked and leaned against Gilbert right back.

Guy turned, first to the pavilion and the noble watchers there, then scanned the crowd beyond. The breeze tugged at his tunic and sent ruddy strands wafting across his cheeks. He looked indifferent, almost bored. But Robyn saw a tiny gleam, banked and waiting, behind juniper-green eyes.

Those eyes suddenly met, locked with his. The gleam surged hotter. Guy's expression went shocked, slack. Robyn could all but hear it: *What in bloody hell are you doing here?*

And then Robyn's gaze dropped to what bound Guy's hands, and his heart dropped a full fistmele within his chest. "That's torn it," he muttered to Gilbert. "We're in some trouble."

Gilbert's gaze followed his, widened as he saw what was around Guy's wrists.

Such a simple thing, to foil a plan.

"Bloody fuck," Gilbert hissed. "Who'd've thought they'd be so scared of one man?"

"I can split a rope quick as I breathe," Robyn growled. "But there's no common arrow can split iron manacles."

⇧

Count John motioned Guy forward. One of the guards flanking Guy propelled him with a fist between his shoulder blades. Guy grimaced, ever so slight, as the shove caused a grating stab in his side. Bloody ribs. He'd asked for a length of muslin—ostensibly to cleanly bind up his sliced arm, unwilling to admit to the greater injury. Instead he'd used the muslin to bind his ribs firm. It didn't do much for the pain, of course, but he probably wouldn't have to worry on it overlong . . .

And *putain de merde*, what was Robyn *doing* here? Black head bare to the fitful sun, dressed fancy as some minor noble's son and wielding a bloody *longbow*? What did he think he could possibly accomplish, save being thrown on the pyre with Guy?

Despite the horror such a thought gave him, a tiny, foreign sensation wriggled into his gut and pooled warmth there. Robyn had come to win the archery tournament. Which meant he valued the offered prize. A tiny quirk teased at Guy's mouth as he turned to the draped pavilion.

Aye, Lord, She whispered in his hair. *He has come for you, proof to answer your own. Who else should free My knight but the best archer in My land?*

Guy knelt, more to Her voice than any fealty to those about to decide his fate, and couldn't help wonder: his own what? Smug hope tilted and cooled into dread. *You cannot ask this of him.*

If you think I or anyone else can constrain the Horned Lord's pwca, you are sore mistaken, sweet.

"We made a promise for this fairing, yes?" Count John walked forward on the dais, pitching his voice to carry. The crowd, curious, fell silent. "That the archers would have a say in the fate of Our prisoner—a woman found guilty of witchcraft by Crown and Church."

The count had his own, higher seat, but had gathered distinguished guests to either side of him. Courtiers, primped and coifed and rather unremarkable save what marks their appearances had surely cost them, were to Count John's right . . . and to his left, most of them familiar, enemy or otherwise.

"This Templar, Guy de Gisbourne, has broken into Our gaol and taken Our prisoner by foul, unlawful means. He has freed an accused witch, and he stands before Us today, accused of treason and sorcery."

What, no sodomy? Guy was sure Johan—or the Abbess, seated in her own state with an overly self-satisfied demeanour—would not approve of the omission.

Count John leaned forward. "Our loyal sheriff, here, worries overmuch We are set upon indiscriminately burning a Templar Knight. But it has been charged that you are a false Knight, an imposter. Nor are We indiscriminate, for We have decided these good archers will vie for your disposition. Since you took their prize, you will return it to them, take the witch's place."

Sheriff de Lisle did indeed appear rattled and unsure—an expression even more prominent in the faces of his two brothers. The Baron de Lacy in particular had never treated Guy in any fashion but kindly. Of course, the Abbess had enough antipathy directed toward Guy to make up for her brothers' lack of conviction in murdering a Templar. No doubt she thought it God's will.

You, I will strangle, he told her silently. *Slowly. For my father. For Marion. For Robyn.*

Then there was Johan. His gloating gaze upon Guy, his malingering behind the false throne—a hound licking the boots of a usurper.

Within striking distance, Guy's enemies one and all, and no reason remaining to stay a killing hand. Yet his hands and ankles were manacled like a trained bear, unweaponed. His chancy position was made all the more obvious as, at a signal from Count John, the guards dragged him to his feet.

"'E killed Robyn Hood!"

The voice rose from the gathered crowd, stridulous and angry. As if the one, bold voice had unleashed a snarling dog in their midst, others began to protest.

"Aye, kill 'im!"

"Burn him!"

"He killed Robyn—"

More and more voices rose, a surge of accusations and brandished fists. And in the small group of archers—some of whom looked as if they would like to agree but dared not, unprotected by any mob—Robyn stood, eyes wide and confused and meeting Guy's with a mix of horror and disbelief. Count John tried to outshout them, buried instead beneath the mix of angry cries.

"He threatened to burn my village!"

"Filth! Murderer!"

"Templars are—"

"Devils, they are. Devils need burning!"

"*SILENCE!*" The Sheriff's bellow carried snarling authority. It reminded the crowd where they were, and at whom they were shouting. "This is my castle, you insignificant cattle! You've no rights to demand anything!"

A tense, quivering silence ensued, the crowd weighing their numbers against undeniable influence.

Guy and Robyn kept staring at each other. Guy found himself wondering at the vagaries of fate: that Robyn Hood would hope the Sheriff could regain control of his villeins.

"Have your guardsmen arm their crossbows into the crowd!" Count John ordered, and as the Sheriff relayed it and the guardsmen obeyed, the crowd visibly shrank.

"You will have your chance," Count John said to them, almost a croon, and what had started to form into an angry mob broke into separate, cowed individuals. Guy forcibly pulled his gaze from Robyn's, settled it on the dais.

Found his attention just as snared by what Count John had shoved into his broad, jewelled belt.

The quillion dagger.

Guy took a step forward, tiny but undeniable, and one guard took rough hold of his arm. Guy slid his gaze sideways; the guard released him.

"You will have your chance," the Count repeated with a flick of his hand, dismissing the Sheriff back to his chair. "His punishment will befit such a traitor. It is plain he, like much of his Order, thinks himself above the king."

"Nay, my lord Count," Guy growled into the silence. "I am answerable only to my Grand Master and the Pope, but neither do I think myself above the king. Which you are *not.*"

Count John's face went white, then crimson. His hand dropped to the dagger in his belt—Guy had the brief hope he would throw it, at least that way he'd have it back. Instead, Count John made a sharp gesture to the guards, who promptly kicked Guy's feet out from under him.

Again, ribs stabbed and grated as he rocked up to hands and knees. He found his gaze straying to the crowd, inevitably fixing itself upon a sloe-eyed mix of admiration and fury wrapped in fine-woven Lincoln green.

Where did you steal that *from?* It came from nowhere, a non sequitur Guy was surely mad to even think up; the addition to it had him smirking. *So you dressed up for me, did you?*

Was it just as mad to imagine Robyn returned the smirk, as if he'd heard?

"Call the archers to the line!" Count John ordered. "Take this . . . filth, and chain him to the stake!"

⤴

Robyn stood amongst the first group to return. He and six others took aim for the seven butts at the field's end. Those had been taken another thirty ells farther; the better to separate the remaining forty-odd archers. He spent the time before his loose fussing with his nock, taking several deep breaths and trying to put out of his mind what he'd just witnessed.

The crowd. They would have gone for the Templar, had been put back into their cage growling and snapping . . .

Because they thought Guy of Gisbourne had killed Robyn Hood.

Nay, he couldn't brood on this, couldn't fixate on the missing willow bodkin, of Guy tied to the stake—with iron manacles!—couldn't ponder those faggots stacked and waiting. Couldn't *think*. Not now.

Arrows started to fly: one outer hit, one complete miss, two in the black, then his turn.

Breathe in with the draw, eye the target, adjust for that southerly breath of wind teasing his curls and raise the bow ever so slightly for the distance . . . exhale and *loose*. To the watchers it would seem he'd barely aimed, and they'd be right. He didn't aim— not like *that*, anyway—and hadn't since he'd been a stripling learning to hunt with his da.

He was nervous. It was not a familiar sensation. He'd never been uneasy at pushing a bow in his life, never been put off by anything. This made no sense, made his teeth chatter and his fingers tremble as they set the arrow to nock. His loose came slower than normal, careful, gave a slight aberrant wobble as it sank into the target.

Two more looses after Robyn: one more centred in the black inner ring than his own, one swerving wild. Still, he passed through to the next round with three others. Robyn had not allowed himself to even look at Guy since they'd taken him over, muscled him up the scaffolding, and chained him to the stake. This time he had to look, found Guy peering back at him.

Wanted . . . *wanted* to riffle his fingers through the tangled copper of that forelock no longer so neatly plaited back . . .

Instead, Robyn wrenched his gaze away to inspect his surroundings. Found his bearings, one at a time: Will on the wall behind several onlookers, John and David in the crowd scattered along the upper bailey, Gilbert waiting for him—was Siham talking to him?—Arthur and Marion at the opposite wall, not an arm's reach from a clutch of watching guards who had no idea what stood beside them.

Robyn came walking back to the ever-dwindling group of archers, saw it was indeed Siham beside Gilbert. They weren't looking at each other, but he could see they were speaking. As Siham's lot was called to line she came forward, giving Robyn a slight nod as she passed.

Robyn retreated to Gilbert like a bairn to its mam, uneased and humiliated by his shot. Plainly Gilbert didn't know why he was distressed, but sensed it and put a hand at Robyn's back, rubbed his palm there, gentle-firm.

"There's some fine archers in this lot," Robyn murmured for Gilbert's ears only. "You and I are the only ones left with a longbow, you'll note."

"I did. I'm sure you noted how the Sheriff is watching us."

The Sheriff wasn't the only one. Johan Boundys also watched, brows drawn heavily together. Worse, the Abbess also had begun eyeing Robyn in particular, her expression pinched even further. He'd wager it wasn't interest in his archery prowess.

"Fancy that." Robyn rubbed his thumb against his first two fingers, peering at them. "Here's hoping we live up to expectations."

"Chancy game we're having," Gilbert replied. "We'll just have to do what we always do, eh?"

Robyn peered at him, one eyebrow lifting.

"Improvise."

A grin tucked itself in one corner of Robyn's mouth. "Aye, well, we should be used to that by now."

"Precisely. One of us is likely to beat this lot, at least. Including *her*, whatever she thinks." He nodded towards Siham as she stepped to line, drew, carefully sighted, and loosed: all deadly economy and power. "The cheeky bint just told me she can't throw the tournament. Her lord has marks wagered and she won't cheat him."

Both Robyn's eyebrows rose. "Well," he admitted. "She is proper good."

"She is. She also informed me," Gilbert pitched his voice in mimicry, "while it isn't impossible to shoot adequately with either hand, 'twas unlikely any archer, however great his talent, could win even in controlled conditions with a weaker sight."

"Fancy that. Sounds familiar."

Gilbert snorted. "Guilty as murder on all counts. I, too, once thought myself convinced of the mechanics of the thing. But you showed me, eh?"

"Mm. Everyone pushes their bow as suits them, including m'self. But the lass has a point. I've shot better, Gilly."

Gilbert blinked. "You mean you didn't intend that last shot?"

Robyn shrugged, miserable.

"You're the only person I know"—Gilbert slapped his palm against Robyn's back smartly—"who gets overfaced by a crowd's support. 'Tis what it was, you know, you stroppy pillock."

"It en't just that." Robyn leaned closer, whispered, "The willow is missing."

Gilbert angled back, frowning. "The . . . arrow? The one you—"

"I've looked in me quiver. Checked the ground. It's gone, and I didn't even feel it leave."

⬆

The arrow hummed, from its place in the quiver slung along her shoulder blades; it sang dark, broken notes that she breathed still-quiet, akin to a mother rocking a bairn to sleep. As they had approached the Nottingham gates, Marion had taken the chance, fingered it unseen from Robyn's quiver. There had been the fear within her: that her talents would not be up to the task of deceit, of taking the arrow without Robyn's knowledge. Yet the spelled willow had known her, the runes cast in her brother's blood warming against her skin, lulled quiescent. The smooth wood had nestled into her hand as if she, and not the Shire Wode's Lord, had fashioned it.

Robyn was conflicted, split in twain between vengeance and a lover's fate.

She had been torn, also. Watching Gamelyn—Guy—walk to the scaffold from which he had saved her had stabbed a wound in her own heart. It was one to not be healed until they had him back, with them, in the Shire Wode where they all belonged.

Arthur had wandered away, just for the moment; he ambled back over, leaned close. "Robyn's goin' on wit' it," he murmured. "I'm no' sure what he thinks we can do—those iron shackles have us as trammelled as Gisbourne."

"He'll know what to do," Marion whispered back, and the steel in her voice smoothed even Arthur's doubting expression. "The moment will come to him, and he'll take it."

So would she. She had tied off the threads of Guy's fate; now it remained Robyn's to weave. He alone possessed the power to do so. She could not be torn—and now that the spelled arrow no longer bided in Robyn's possession, he would not be either. She could not have forged such a powerful thing, not yet. Her own breath had too long been held in stasis, unpractised. The Hooded One was instrument, embodiment, the Horned Lord's executioner of justice. Yet this life-thread was Marion's to knot and sever, even as Robyn had fashioned the instrument.

She was ready. The Lady's arrow had been defiled, Her voice held long silent in thisworld. The one who had thought to usurp it, *contain* it, would be stopped.

⇧

The sun's face hid, more and more, behind gathering clouds; as if in answer, the wind picked up. Thankfully it held, steady and slight. One target had been moved farther back; it sat, waiting, at over ninety ells.

A fair distance, one Robyn knew would give him no trouble— with his proper hand. The remaining archers were almost contemplative in their quiet. The two with shortbows were undoubtedly considering their competition; a longbow's commonly-touted disadvantage—*chancy monsters*, as the clerk had growled—was, in skilled hands, an advantage at distance. The watching crowds no longer held any doubts over the two longbows being in proper skilled hands.

So they waited, respectfully silent, as the next order of go was drawn and called: Gilbert first, then a fletcher named Fulbert, then Siham, then Robyn.

Robyn fully intended to do business with Fulbert in the future. Somehow. Those were fine arrows he'd been loosing.

Beneath cover of gauging wind and sun, Robyn gathered his people by eye. John and David had moved to opposite corners of the gathered crowd; John and Robyn exchanged earnest glances. Marion and Arthur were still on the closest wall, able to watch the postern gate as well as the dais. Unfortunately, Arthur's waiting rope ladder would continue to wait. Will had moved to his own position, opposite, where the trees grew too close to the wall and where, so Marion had said, her own escape had been aided.

The crowd waited, remarkably silent. They seemed to hardly breathe, waiting. But Robyn could feel it, as hot on his neck as ever the Horned Lord's breath . . . and his own breath escaped him, swirled in damp ceriphs glittering beneath a flash of sun. It was a chancy thing, right enough, but it just might work.

As Gilbert lined up for his turn, Robyn fingered two arrows from his quiver. One was long, light, with a blunter tip—an example of what he had been using all the while for the targets. The other was heavier, with longer fletchings and a razored tip—sharp as a bodkin but wider—more deadly and therefore unlawful for any villein to carry in the forest. With such a broadhead arrow the king's deer could easily be taken, after all.

Almost absently, Robyn yanked his thick hair from its well-combed confinement at his nape. Pulling it over his right shoulder, he knotted it and stuck the two arrows there, waiting. His fingers stroked at the broadhead point, let it trail along his finger, the sharp edge welling a bead of blood. The wind luffed at Robyn's hair.

All the while he was humming, a soft, low strain vibrating the back of his throat.

Gilbert loosed. The wind making sweet talk to Robyn took another price from Gilbert. His arrow dipped slightly; it hit two fingers off true centre.

A collective gasp—both respect at the difficult shot and disappointment it had fallen short—rose from the crowd. Gilbert gestured, gave a bow—and Robyn smirked. His Gilly-lad always did fancy an audience.

The fletcher went next, but Robyn ceased paying attention, sinking into his own being. "*Rhyddau.*" He turned his head to breathe it upon the broadhead arrow. Release. *Release.*

Instinct, never truly sleeping, alerted Robyn and pulled him from the making. Siham came into his peripheral vision. Her arms were crossed over her lovely eastern shortbow, and she opened her mouth as if to speak. Almost in the same moment she realised they could not understand each other and went silent. But her eyes spoke, obvious regret and hope. She likely had her own plans, should she win—she had liked Guy, had given Gilbert sound information. But Robyn wasn't about to trust this to any outside his own.

Gilbert also gained Robyn's side. Siham said something, quick and tense, to Gilbert; he answered in kind.

The wind calmed, kinder to the fletcher than Gilbert, but he took too long in the loose, nervous. Perhaps he wasn't accustomed to the distance. Either way, the arrow sank the outer rim of the centre black. The crowd let out a low groan of dismay. The fletcher's shoulders slumped.

Siham gave a shrug to Robyn, turned away, and went to take her own chance at the line.

"She says she'll find a way, if the win comes to her," Gilbert said.

Robyn was no longer watching, his attention once again turned inward, heeding the feel of his own breath in his lungs. A tiny crimson pearl seeped from the finger he'd blooded. Rubbing it into the inside curve of his bow, Robyn whispered into the black, felt the broad arrow-point vibrate as if in answer, felt *tynged* wrap him like a warmed wolf's pelt.

"What are you doing?" Gilbert murmured.

"Improvising," Robyn replied.

⤒

Guy had never seen Robyn nock right-handed. He remembered what Marion had told him long ago—how her parents had tried and tried to change their son's hopelessly left-handed draw.

Well, all right, he was bloody Robyn Hood, wasn't he?—and no doubt he'd had to learn at the same time he'd been surviving that great hole in his left shoulder, and certainly Guy himself could wield a sword with both hands. But the limitations were unavoidable. There remained a degree of focus that had to go into using any weaker asset, no matter how slight that weakness. Focus that would, in its turn, cause more weakness. And unless Robyn had purposefully thrown the past several looses, he was not shooting like the uncanny machine he normally was.

But even more amazing?—how one's mind would concentrate on banalities when one was bloody fucking terrified. Because Guy was. Not only of the burning—as he had told the boy in Hathersage, he had seen people burn and it was a horrific way to die—and he would no doubt see enough of it in hell, given the life he'd led.

He feared burning to death, but oddly, he feared for Robyn more. For whom he'd seen *with* Robyn. Gilbert, next to him in the tournament. John, whose amulet hung, heavy and somehow cold, about his throat. David, across from John, with a pouch at his waist that occasionally moved, betraying Tess's presence. Will on the wall up from David, and Arthur.

And *Marion*.

He almost hadn't recognised her, shabby with a hat and wrap over her head—but she had looked at him, exchanged a glance emotive as a kiss.

Guy had to turn away from it. Instead he watched, with a face set in stone and bowels set on turning to water, as the field of archers whittled down to a final four.

They each took their place: judged, nocked, held, and loosed. First Gilbert, done in by a burst of wind. Then the fletcher, holding too long. Then, Siham.

Siham stepped up to the mark then backed away, staring down the field. She knelt, tested the wind with the fringed end of her *kaffiyeh*, then stood and did the same thing, counting the ripples and their motion. She lifted her bow, put the arrow to nock, all the while murmuring to herself, taking her time. It was lovely to watch. Siham did not have Robyn's wild grace or power; she lacked the quicksilver talent that all but made Robyn one with his arrow. Yet what Siham did not possess in synergism, she made up for in sheer concentration, in focus and resolve. No doubt Robyn could magic an arrow into any target did he choose; Siham would drive hers by force of will.

She loosed. The arrow imbedded itself in the black's centre.

The watchers bawled out their appreciation. In the pavilion, Guy saw de Lacy leap up in his chair and plant a victorious fist skyward—and almost knock aside a section of roof draping. The baron was no more short of stature than skinny.

It went on for some time. As the watchers cheered, Guy found his eyes fastening to the remaining archer as he ambled forward, gave a slow nod and smile to Siham's success. Robyn turned, ever so slight, as he reached the line. His gaze flickered to Guy's then away. Focused. Waiting. Slowly the commotion wound back down, everyone comprehending what Guy already had:

If "Robert of Barnsdale" put an arrow right next to Siham's, then the two of them would have it to do all over again.

The stillness could have been cut and parcelled as Robyn stepped up to the line and tugged his hood forward. It could have been to block the wind from tossing his hair into his eyes—but Guy wondered, watching as Robyn didn't shove back either his forelock or the thick tangle of ebon at his collarbone. Guy had to smile, even if slight; in the latter lay knotted two arrows.

The amulet upon Guy's chest had, inexplicably, gone from chill to frigid, setting a fierce ache thrumming with his heart. For the first time in years, he wasn't altogether sure he wanted a cold heart at this particular moment.

Robyn stood there for moments, nostrils flaring as if he could scent the target as well as see it. With some care, he drew one arrow down and out from its hair-knot, nocked it. A slight murmur undulated through the watching people as he did so, stoppered silent as he drew. Held. Loosed.

Guy didn't realise until it had flown: Robyn had nocked it left-handed.

Then Robyn turned away, as if he already knew what would happen.

Mere seconds later, an odd *crack* echoed against the gathered crowd, altogether unlike to the normal sound of an arrow hitting the butt. Robyn turned to meet Guy's gaze once more. He smiled, a brief and brilliant thing, then tugged his cowl closer about his face.

Guy laid his head back onto the pole, let out a soft, gasping laugh.

Silence remained, a collective breath taken, none quite believing what they'd just seen. It held as a pair of Nottingham's villeins sped across the field to bring the butt forward for inspection; one let out a whoop as they came:

"He split it! He's split the arrow!"

And the dam of silence burst into bawls and cheers, staffs drumming against the ground.

Guy raised his head in time to see Gilbert nigh body tackle Robyn in a giant hug. The other archers were crowding in, offering their own respects. Guy smiled again as Siham threw an unapologetic shrug to her sponsor. De Lacy and, indeed, all the nobles in the pavilion were goggling enough to not worry over what marks they had lost to a remarkable shot from a peasant's bow. Siham then went over to Robyn and gave him a bow, very low. He returned it, both hands to his face then outward, as if blowing dandelion fluff against her cheeks.

In the tumult, Guy noticed that Robyn's band had moved. There but a moment ago, now they were simply . . . vanished. Save Gilbert, who had tugged Robyn's cowl back from his face, shaking his head. And John, who hadn't moved very far from where he'd just been, looking at Guy like a man throwing a rope to a drowning mate.

The trumpets winded again, desperate against the noise. Somewhat unwillingly, the crowd calmed, though there were still murmurings and mutterings: excited, barely contained, rippling muted from person to person as if some gleeful secret was being passed.

Count John toed the front edge of the dais, waiting with the Sheriff to his right and—Guy felt his own nerves prickle warning—Johan just behind them.

The memory came to him, then, like a rush and slap of cold water.

I've seen Robyn Hood's face...

Guy leaned into his bonds, wanting to scream a warning. The futility of it choked him: hope the disguise would, through some miracle, hold. He watched in an agony as Robyn walked across the field to the waiting nobles, once again bare-headed, bold as polished brass and his eyes twice as shiny. With the same, artless grace he had shown at the butts, Robyn stopped before the draped dais, dipped down to one knee, bent his head.

Surely Guy wasn't the only one who felt a sick tilt to his stomach, watching Robyn bare his neck as if awaiting the headman's axe. Nay, John was watching Robyn now, and he also had a distinct lack of colour to his cheek.

Count John started speaking—loudly enough, fortunately, for Guy to hear. To appease the crowd, probably.

"Congratulations, master archer. Please rise before Us, you have well earned your reward." Count John nodded to the Sheriff, who came forward with a leather purse drawn tight.

The Sheriff was smiling. Guy didn't like it one bit.

"I've rarely seen an archer shoot with both hands." A definite barb tilted the Sheriff's statement.

Guy gritted his teeth. It had been a vain hope, to think none had noticed that last shot. Robyn's smile faded, ever so slightly—had it been instinct, thinking only of the shot and not how he was making it?

"All of us have talents, my lord Sheriff."

"Some talents are noticeable, indeed. My guardsmen could use an addition such as you. Mayhap you'd be interested in their company?"

Guy also didn't fancy the way that question was phrased.

"You offer me no little honour, milord Sheriff, but I fear I must decline. My father has promised me elsewhere." Robyn let his voice carry beyond, with a lilt so cultured and precise it made Guy blink, ensure it was indeed Robyn speaking.

"And that is?" Count John asked.

A distinct smirk curved Robyn's lip. "To the monastery at Doncaster, milord."

All right, then. If Guy wasn't tied to a scaffolding ready to burn alive for sins woefully unimagined, he'd probably laugh out loud.

"A man of God!" the Sheriff marvelled, and tossed over the purse. "How lucky Doncaster will be to receive one such as you."

Robyn snatched the purse midair and regarded the Sheriff. It seemed a frown had gathered Robyn's brow; hard to tell, as it came so fleeting and left moreso.

"So." Count John stepped forward ever so slightly, waved a hand in the direction of where Guy stood upon the scaffold. "How will you take your other reward, then? Shall we fashion you an oil bodkin for the pyre?"

Robyn looked toward Guy, seemed to consider the question most carefully. "Well, milord Count, bein' a pious man—as you yourself surely must be—it doesn't seem on to murder a man tied hand and foot. Or, actually, to murder one at all."

And oh, *God*, but as Guy watched, a snide smile quirked on Robyn's lip to match the Sheriff's.

"As I recall, you said whoever won the contest should have a choice upon the Templar's fate. So." Robyn hefted the purse, tossed it into the air, and tucked it into his belt. "I choose you should set him free, and he comes with me to Doncaster to atone for his sins."

- ENTR'ACTE -

"The effrontery! The gall!"
    Silence had met the archer's request. Then another uproar had started. The odd thing: before, where the crowd had been roaring for the Templar's blood—and that for killing a filthy pagan outlaw who needed killing—now said crowd was not wholly in favour. Some, true, still were, but well over half were inexplicably siding with the archer's request. Meanwhile, the King's brother still cursed the villein's effrontery.
    Elisabeth watched. Having grown bored with the archery contest, she'd risen from her chair to spend its remainder closeted in the back area of the pavilion, all but hidden behind the drapings of Count John's dais. She had continued to watch, mildly interested, first as Count John had stalked to the back of the tent, and now as he held impromptu council with her brother and her *losengeor* of a cousin. Yes, no matter respect for her departed Uncle Ian, his eldest Johan was no more than a lackey angling whatever way the wind blew. Otho would have shown more sense. But Johan had finally gotten rid of Otho, as well, packed his household off to Pontefract. As to Uncle Ian's youngest . . .
    Elisabeth slid her eyes to take in the scaffold. *That* one was finally going to get what he deserved, no question.

Unless this archer had his way.

"You need to take care, my lord Count," de Lisle said, urgent and low. "He has taken your words—and you did say them, my lord Count—and now he has the people behind him."

"Do not think to chastise Us, Sheriff!" Count John snapped.

"I am not doing any such thing, my lord Count!" de Lisle protested. "But I must confess, I am not prepared to let Robyn Hood simply *walk* out of Nottingham!"

Robyn Hood? The archer, a young and minor noble from his dress, was Robyn Hood? She angled forward. Brian saw her, frowned then shrugged and ignored her.

She was only a woman, after all.

"*Neither* of them," Johan gritted, "should walk from here."

Only a woman. But she had ears, and a brain to process what she heard, and something foul brewed within this, niggling at her. As surely as the Templar's identity had. As surely as Marion's growing disobediences had. Elisabeth had ignored both—unfortunately—yet her underlying intuition had proven correct. And now . . .

The archer. He unnerved her. She glided over to a curtain nearer the dais, peering outward.

This, then, was the infamous Robyn Hood. Who would have expected a manor-born son to sully his hands with pagan filth? Or to risk capture in such a fashion? No doubt the forest devil had demanded the rescue of another soulless red-haired acolyte. Brian wanted his head and would finally gain it, it seemed. Only the count wanted more.

"It has played out as you said it might, Boundys," the count acknowledged. "You were right."

Right about what? Had Johan gone behind her back, given the men something of import that, by rights, he should have shared with her first?

Only a woman. Elisabeth fumed, and listened.

"Be that as it may," the Sheriff pointed out, "if we let him go, I have no leverage."

"But when I have my brother beneath my blade, begging, then you will have all the leverage you need, *non*?"

"Assuming you can get him there," de Lisle snapped.

"I taught him how to fight. I know his weaknesses. And you have already seen the lengths to which this Robyn Hood will reach to free his *enculer*."

Elisabeth blinked at the rancour of the accusation as much as the accusation itself. She knew what the Templar was, by temperament and depravity and, according to some, the sanction of his masters. But why would Johan name this Robyn Hood as sodomite as well, and with such venom?

Half hidden by the drapery, fingers twitching at it and setting the gold-edged crimson to sway, Elisabeth peered down at the outlaw. His eyes slid her way at the movement— a cunning beast, this one, missing nothing—then settled on her. He turned his head, staring at her all the while. Nothing moved in his stare, flat, black as night.

She had seen that face somewhere before. Seen those *eyes* . . .

Flames, rising into the night to cleanse a pagan ritual, and a demon boy's body sprawled at her feet. Ebon curls clenched in her fingers, and flat-black eyes staring skyward as her captain had kicked him over. . .

No. It wasn't possible. He was dead! *Dead,* and she had bent over him in the next moment, twisted the crossbow bolt deeper herself to ensure it.

As if he kenned her thoughts, he kept watching her. His eyes lit, no longer dead but suddenly burning, flames licking into blackness like fires at the dark gates of hell.

Her breath seizing at her throat, Elisabeth staggered back behind the shelter of the draperies, clutching a beringed hand to her throat.

"All of it, as you said." Count John was saying. "We will not forget your loyalty."

"You cannot let him go free, my lord Count. If you will but let me, we can take care of them both."

"The man is notorious, Boundys," the Sheriff said. "The outlaw has never held a sword in his life, I'll warrant, but you think to set yourself against a Templar assassin?"

"Yet is it not suspect?" Johan snorted. "'S truth, my youngest brother bided ever more book-loving monk than squire. He is no assassin!"

Elisabeth, heart pounding like a terrified rabbit, sneaked another gaze around the curtains. The pagan revenant no longer looked to her, but the scaffold. The Templar was peering back at him, with a gaze that turned her stomach.

"And all those dead men on my wall-walk mere luck?" de Lisle retorted. "Sir Johan, you underestimate this one at your peril—and ours. Your own lord can tell you. I'll fetch my brother Roger. He has dealt with Sir Guy and his Master both."

"Stop, now!" Count John hissed, snatching at de Lisle's arm as he turned. "I have had enough of barons and earls, enough of their meddling in the affairs of their betters! And I am this close to having had enough of *you,* de Lisle! Where does your heart lie in this? Do you wish this wolfshead dealt with or no?"

Brian stood there for a moment—Elisabeth could tell he was fuming, but none of it showed. Abruptly he lowered his head, bowed low, and backed away.

Elisabeth wanted to protest; instead she ducked farther back into the draperies, hidden.

I am sorry, mon frère. *I am sorry to see your ambitions thwarted yet again. But is not pride a sin? And they are correct. We cannot let either escape. We cannot let these beasts leave Nottingham alive.*

- XXVII -

"I en't believing it."
    Marion agreed, absolutely. From that amazing, confident moment when Robyn had turned from his loose knowing—just *knowing*—he'd done it, to the realisation he'd used his left draw and made it altogether possible their enemies would ken who he was. And now, watching him saunter up to the dais as if he owned the entirety of Nottingham Castle and *demanding* . . . Well. Her heart beat with a mix of wanting to hang her little brother up by his toes and bang his head against a stone wall, or just hug him until his eyes popped because, well, her Hob-Robyn was still, it seemed, about as predictable as a ball of lightning most days and it usually, somehow, worked.

Then Arthur leaned against the stones of the inner parapet wall and said, "Listen to 'em, lass! I en't *believing* it." Marion belatedly kenned they weren't thinking of the same thing at all. Arthur spoke of the watchers.

There were shouts and protests, still, more intemperate than the amazement and awe of Robyn splitting the arrow. But more than that: it buzzed just below the roar, tens of elated whispers growing into something stout and persistent, *insistent*.

"Robyn Hood. It's Robyn Hood!"

"He shot wi' his left—"

"I knew it. He wore th' cowl, and I *knew*."

"Had to be. *Had* to be, and—"

"But he's trying to free the Templar!"

"I knew it. Robyn Hood."

"Why would he—"

"The Templar didn't kill him, then."

"'Tis holy men, they are."

"Sure, only the Green Man himself coulda made such a shot."

Marion didn't find it odd, not at all. Her mother and father had been held with reverence. Why not Robyn? But when she said as much to Arthur, he snorted and shook his head.

"Nay, lass, your ma and da weren't firebrands, were they? Nowt to them could be seen as threat: they obeyed the rules, toed the line, and kept things secret." As if realising she might take it wrongly, Arthur quickly added, "They'd two bairns, aye?—reason to not take chances. But we're outside the law, lass, and Robyn pokes things until they bleed. Small comfort to scairt people who want to just keep their heads down and survive."

"He's the Horned Lord's—"

"Aye, that too. Reverence has two faces, and a little fear's never a bad thing to keep your nerves primed. But this?" He was grinning more than Marion had yet seen—had been sour since they'd made note of the expected ropes being iron. "This is more the thing."

More the thing. His pleasure was infectious; Marion's own smile broadened as she returned her gaze to the dais and saw the chaos reigning there. But the smile congealed as she noted a dark figure gliding from curtain to curtain. Her fingers, of their own accord, went to the arrow in her quiver. The willow whispered as she touched it, hummed soft descant as, all the while, Marion watched.

Watched as the Abbess came to the front of the dais, hiding behind the drapings. As the Abbess watched Robyn. As Robyn returned stare for stare, and the Abbess reeled back as if physically struck.

The Abbess now knew not only who Robyn Hood was—but who he had been.

Marion's fingers gave the willow arrow one last caress, then moved to her bow, began to string it.

"Hang on, now." Arthur eyed the people about them—and not many of those. Most had spilled down into the bailey. Even the guards inched as close as they could to the happenings, not so watchful. "Look to the scaffold. Guards are approaching it. We'd best be ready to move, and fast."

Marion smiled to herself, finished stringing her bow.

⊗

The people.

They were like another entity, their own magic, raising up a kind of power he'd never before experienced. Strangely gratifying—akin to the seasonal celebrations Robyn remembered as a child—but overwhelming, if you let it. Or like...

It had been a young Gamelyn who had once asked a younger Rob, half teasing and half trepidatious of his archery: "Is it magic?" Robyn's answer had been no tease: "Bloody sodding damn, not likely! This is one thing I'm happy to do on my own—mine and mine alone!"

Like the earth magic was sommat you could use—or abuse—or even lose yourself in without a thought for consequences.

As to consequences...

This time he'd thrown the gauntlet in earnest. He was in for it; they'd either shove him up there with Guy, or tell him to shove up and set fire to the arrow like they'd first offered. And he'd the arrow to shoot, hex-breath quickened from not only himself but the energy whipped into frenzy around him: the watchers, his outlaws, Marion, Guy.

Overwhelming... aye, and lovely as a bonfire. The sheer intensity; he could feel it— feel them all—wrapping about him like a cloak, and wanted to laugh with delirious, disbelieving delight.

His Royal Arse-Pain High-and-Mighty-ness just might have a riot on his hands, did he not do as he'd said.

Unfortunately, the spectators weren't the only ones who'd recognised Robyn. He'd used his left draw—he'd had to, there was doubt plaguing his right, and he knew he could make the shot without a qualm with his left. And he'd drawn up his hood—more from habit than any rational thought. So the nobles knew. Must know.

And the Abbess. It had been a moment straight from any jongleur's tale—the impact of eyes-meeting-eyes, only in hatred, not in heart's life.

The crowd's noise abated as Count John came forward. The Sheriff trod beside him, several paces behind and looking as if he'd swallowed coals. Guy's sod of an elder brother was nowhere to be seen, and that worried Robyn.

And guards were advancing on the scaffold.

Every sense Robyn possessed sprang into full alert. He knelt—

carefully and ready to launch upward—as Count John stared at him, obviously waiting until he did. Bent his neck, slid his eyes to the scaffolding.

The guards were climbing up it. They were . . .

They were unlocking the chain!

Once Robyn raised his head, Count John folded his hands in front of him. His smile curled, distinctly unpleasant. "You seem to have hoist Us, good archer, on a slight technicality."

"I am glad to see 't, milor—"

"Villein, you will address Us as my liege."

Villein. Nay, this did not bode well at all. Robyn chose his words with utmost care. "I am glad to see, my liege, that you are a man of your word."

"We are no mere man, villein, and as such Our word is no mere word."

That didn't sound promising. But if milord the jumped-up Count intended to change his mind, why could Robyn see, from the corner of his eye, the guards escorting Guy down the scaffold? With crossbows and swords drawn, granted, but that just made sense. Guy being a Templar, and all.

A smattering of approval worked its way through the gathered watchers as the guards escorted the Templar across the field to the front of the dais. Guy, of course, remained manacled. Robyn raised an eyebrow, watched him approach.

"The things I do for you, Gisbourne," he murmured as Guy was brought over and made to kneel beside him, just out of arm's reach.

A small, stifled snort was Guy's only response; that and a tiny shake of his head as he raised his gaze to the dais. Frowned.

"Where's my brother?" he hissed.

Robyn shrugged, brought his eyes back to Count John as he once more addressed Robyn.

"We have freed him, to the letter of your request. But We fear he cannot go with you to . . . Doncaster, was it? This man stands accused of treason against the Crown." The count shook his head, a mockery of chagrin. "Not to mention the problems of witchcraft and sodomy. He cannot be freed without a trial."

"You mean you were ready to put a Templar to the fire without a trial?" This, strangely enough, came from Count John's left. Baron de Lacy had risen to stand with several others, also richly dressed, chains of office hanging from their shoulders.

And His liege-ness didn't like that, nay, not one bit.

Neither did the crowd. They began muttering and shifting again, restless. Angry.

"Where did they go?" Guy hissed. "Your men and—!" He left off with a grunt as one of the guards gave a kick to his haunch.

"My lord Count." De Lacy came forward slightly. "Did this man confess to these charges? Is that why you sentenced him without a trial?"

Count John whipped about, challenged, shrill, "Do you question *me*, de Lacy?"

De Lacy wanted to. Robyn wished, fervently, he would. Some things were worth the beating.

Not to their kind, the Horned Lord whispered. *We are with you, my own. Anon, 'twill be over.*

Guy was frowning again, and shaking his head; he'd heard. Robyn looked up to catch Marion's eye . . . Nowhere to be seen, despite Arthur signalling quick reassurance. Unfortunately, Robyn wasn't all that reassured.

The baron indeed did not deem the fight worth the price. He raised his hands, bowed, and backed into his small group of supporters. They were murmuring amongst themselves, with the crowd starting to wind up again, as if de Lacy's small defiance had worked itself into the common ground, rich as cooked compost.

"You call Us to account? And this . . . villein dares to remind Us of Our word?"

Count John leapt down from the dais. His guards, after a mild near-attack of apoplexy, scrambled after, bringing crossbows to bear on anything suspect. Count John stalked over to Robyn, and Robyn braced himself for the blow; after all, he knew who most likely would fetch it, in this company.

Oddly enough, Count John merely grabbed Robyn by the hair, dragged him up to a standing position. He immediately appreciated his mistake, as Robyn towered over him by a head-and-half.

That was when the blow came, slapping him back down. Robyn went sprawling nearly against Guy, felt Guy tense, growled, "Don't. En't your fight yet."

Guy muttered a particularly foul curse. Robyn grinned, rolled back to a crouch.

"You're lucky We have allowed you to have any redress from this tournament, held within the laws of Our land and upon the grounds of Our Royal Castle. Since you have declared yourself outside that law. *Robyn Hood*."

Robyn lifted his chin. Well, then. There it was, what they all weren't saying.

"Did you think you could fool Us so easily, wolfshead? Such a talented archer— foolish enough to forget himself and wear a hood no sane archer would tolerate as possible hindrance in a contest? Or shoot with the same cursed bow arm that has made him infamous?"

From the distance, a peacock howled, as if in raucous challenge to the name echoing all around the gathering. No shouts, no overt protests. Not yet. But those who hadn't known . . .

Well, they knew now.

"*Putain de merde*," Guy groaned, softly, from beside him. "Can I not take you *any*where?"

Robyn wanted—really, *really* wanted—to snog him senseless. Right now. Instead he slid a significant glance sideways. It had Guy blinking and looking away, telltale colour splotching his cheeks.

Aye, a sharp sword to go with the dull one. If they got out of here alive, Robyn intended to see he'd more than the one dagger waiting in his furs. Speaking of daggers . . . He glanced around, scanned the crowd. Sure enough, his little John had one ready. Gilbert stood beside John. Both of them signalling they were ready when Robyn was.

"Silence!" Count John bellowed, returning his attention to Robyn. "I don't think you're a stupid man, wolfshead. Despite you swaggering into Our castle to save something you could no doubt find in some brothel." He threw a sneer towards Guy, who merely stared back, unblinking. "So I imagine you must be wondering why you're still alive."

Truly, much of what Robyn wondered was why His Nappy Greatness couldn't decide whether he made up an *I* or a *We*. The puzzlement helped clear his head, actually; not only the Horned Lord's presence rode him, but John astride that, whispering a hopeful *geas* along his knife: *Let me. Let me take him.*

Nay. Not yet.

"I will give you a chance, Robyn Hood. You can let this . . . comrade of yours fairly prove his innocence. In a language even a hired killer can understand: trial by battle. We even have Our champion ready." Count John gestured over to the pavilion, where a fully mailed man stood, dark head bared.

Bloody damn. Of *course*. Robyn slid a narrow glance to Guy.

"I understand you both well know Our champion," Count John said. "Sir Johan Boundys de Blyth."

Robyn started to speak.

Count John held up a finger, stalked over to stand right before him, bent down. "Or," he added, low and smooth and dropping all formality, "you can agree to work for me."

"Work?" Robyn angled back. "For . . . you?"

"You've spent a lot of time and energy accosting my nobles. Much of that money was meant for my brother's ransom." A pause, heavy with meaning. "Do you understand me, villein?"

Robyn's hand instinctively went to his bow and his eyes to Guy. Guy gave a slight nod: *keep going*.

"I would desire," Count John continued, "none of this ransom be paid. If you agree to work for me, at my biddance?" An iniquitous smile quirked at his mouth, and he shrugged. "Then both you and your . . . *inamorato* shall be freed. No combat. No risk of death. You can return to your little dalliance in Sherwood Forest and never be bothered again—as long as you do exactly as I order."

Robyn peered up at Count John, eyes widening.

"We will give you a moment to consider," Count John said, then stood and retraced his steps to the dais.

Robyn watched him go, mind whirling.

And you were wondering why you do what you do? The Lady ran cool fingers through his black hair. *Is it worth it, my Hob-Robyn, to have a king's brother desire your power?*

He didn't know how to answer, didn't know how to voice anything except a hoarse question at Guy, "What'd he just call you, then?"

"Nothing we haven't done." It was terse. "I heard the choices. Choose the trial by combat."

Robyn slid his gaze once again sideways. Guy was peering at his brother, eyes hot-bright.

"Do us both a favour and bloody choose the bloody trial by bloody combat," Guy said between his teeth. "*Please.*"

(X)

This was more like it.

No more nancing about, waiting. No more wondering how the bloody hell they were going to get out of this. No more having to watch that sodding royal bum-boil prance about and shriek and threaten and fling Robyn about like he was *nothing*.

That last had *really* brassed Guy off.

Not your fight, Robyn had said.

Well, it was now.

They unshackled Guy, gave him back his sword-belt and sword, along with his helm and boiled-leather arm braces, his shield, chainmail tunic and trews. Robyn, one arrow still incongruously tucked into his knotted hair, hood pulled back upward and his longbow laid carefully at their feet, buckled him into it like some squire.

Johan watched them the entire time with a mixture of contempt and disgust. Guy wanted to knock it off his face, right then. There was, unfortunately, the matter of the half a dozen crossbows trained on him and Robyn.

"Nice lot of pelf you have here, milord," Robyn murmured, nigh silent.

"Says the thief of the Shire Wode." Guy's retort came almost as quiet. "Where did you steal *your* clothes, by the by?"

"Such an accusation! And here I thought me tunic matched your eyes."

Guy rolled those eyes.

"Well. Since I'm such a thief, you'd do well t' not leave this pretty chainmail lying about camp. I've nowt *this* nice and shiny."

"Assuming we make it back to your camp. 'Pelf,'" Guy snorted. "More like a peasant's misinterpretation of style." Guy gave a slight wince as Robyn gave a yank to the links, settling them across his torso. "I fancy you've a signal for your people to 'run like hell'?"

"I fancy I do. I'm not above using it, eith—Why are you making faces?"

"I'm not."

"You are."

"A broken rib or two. Or three." Guy shrugged. "I've fought with worse."

"Aye, I'll warrant you have. I almost pity the poor misbegotten sod." Robyn glanced at Johan. "He has no idea what he's in for. Now't I think on it, misbegotten is the wrong word. There's you, after all."

"Mm. Fasten that one, too."

"You're proper bossy when you're getting ready to kill someone. This one, then?"

Robyn's hands were quick and agile, and Guy found himself contemplating how he'd not had those hands on him enough. Not near enough.

Neither was it something he *could* contemplate about now.

"By the by," Robyn said as he laced up Guy's arm braces. "I noticed his Royal Pratness has my dagger."

"My dagger, you mean?"

"*Your* dagger? You're talking rubbish. I'll give you this much; it might be *our* dagger."

Bloody hell. "Our dagger, then," Guy said, peering at Robyn.

Robyn peered back, then dropped his attention to the other wrist guard. "Well, what is he doing with it?"

Inconceivable. "What, do you want me to fetch it for you?"

"Well, aye. Please. I rather fancy that dagger, and being as how you're such a scary rotter of a Templar and all . . . " A flash of teeth, and the midnight eyes slid up to meet Guy's, lit like coals glowing in the night. "An' listen to the crowd, now. They're fomentin' revolt as we speak."

A distinct rumble had begun emanating from the gathered people, with a promise of ugly on its fringes.

"This might just work." Robyn put a hand to the crimson cross. Guy shook his head, backed away. "Not now."

Robyn held on, gripping the black tunic, as brusque as Guy. His other hand rose to the dip of mailed-over flesh between Guy's collarbones. Beneath his fingers, the amulet—John's amulet—vibrated. Robyn gave a gentle exhale across it and it heated like a metal shield on a lantern, sent Guy's spine a-shiver.

"I called the *geas* upon him," Robyn murmured, almost a singsong. "Regret, and wonder, empty nights and long days, and his dam's blood the death of him . . . so must it be."

"Robyn?" Guy queried, sharp-soft, as Robyn's gaze blurred, glimmered.

"*Alban hefu*," Robyn continued—and this *was* song, a melodic quaver. "*Anadl eich tynged, Arglwydd*."

And released Guy, backed away.

The words hung in Guy's ears . . . in his *mind*. First they tangled, then they unknotted, drifted then combed themselves into soft skeins of understanding.

Light of Summer. . . breathe your destiny, lord.

And it sank into him, filling his limbs not with shaky warmth but something even more necessary: aloof, practiced calm. Guy gave a curt nod, then, taking helm under one arm and shield in the other, turned and walked over to the dais. Behind him, Robyn bent to pick up his bow. The crossbows were conflicted, half with Robyn and half with Guy. A smile Guy couldn't halt chased over his mouth as he heard Robyn say, almost lazily, "If I meant to shoot the bloody thing, you'd be dead, y'know."

Johan watched, and waited.

Guy well knew the courtesies of such a thing, used them, spun them out. Striding to the dais beside Johan, he unsheathed his falchion, and knelt. Lowered his head, as if in prayer.

The watchers had been buzzing, the wont of such crowds. As he knelt there, silent, the watchers became just as stilled. Incitement from them, heat from the charm at his throat, breath from Robyn. And then they were no longer there, for him. Nothing, no one. Merely himself and his enemy.

There was pleasure, after all, to be had in the practice. But putting the practice into motion?

Sublime.

When he looked up, Johan also knelt. One of the priests from the retinue— Prior Willem, de Lacy's brother—stood on the dais, signing a blessing over both of them. The Abbess's head was lowered respectfully, but her gaze laid venomous watch upon Guy.

He eyed her in return. Making the sign of the cross, he took those fingers and put them to his lips, flicked them toward her. Her face paled then went florid, angry.

Guy rose to his feet. "Thank you, Father," he said to the priest, tipped his head to the Sheriff, then Count John. "My lord Count," he said, low, and held his hand out. "My dagger, if you please."

Count John looked as if to refuse, but Guy just stood there, palm extended. Count John grimaced and rolled his eyes—then handed over the dagger.

Johan rose, tipped his own head and smiled. Already mailclad, his sword lay sheathed at his hip, his shield looped over one arm. "You're going to need more than a pretty dagger, Brother."

Guy didn't bother to answer. Instead he looked at the helm on Johan's head, smiled, and tossed his own helm at the foot of the dais. Hefting his shield, he turned on one heel and strode to the field's centre.

He could feel his brother's gaze following, then he heard a small curse, and the sound of another helm hitting the ground. Then the heavy tread of booted feet, and the clink and sigh of tightlinked metal roiling together. A sword being drawn, and the tread growing faster.

The crowd gasped, no doubt at the sight of the Templar with his back turned on an opponent even now coming at him, at a good trot with sword poised.

Guy closed his eyes, took in a breath, waited until chainmail scraped in a twist instead of sighing with the charge, and whirled. Danced aside just as Johan's sword came down where he had been.

Johan recovered, spun to take the momentum of his swing, his broadsword lashing through the air. He tilted his head, smiled. "So. At last you've grown those eyes in the back of your head, *lapin*? Let's see what else you remember."

He lunged forward. Within a few steps, Guy recognised the pattern—an old training exercise—complete with a vicious, round punch. He dodged the blow, spun and delivered his own ending— a left cross, which took Johan in the jaw and sent him staggering back.

A distinct puzzlement crawled into Johan's expression. Guy almost laughed. But laughing would make his ribs ache.

A circle, slow and tactile. Several more engagements, each one growing more aggressive. Another circle.

"So," Johan said, musing. "The rabbit fucks a mangy wolf, and thinks it will give him teeth. Assuming you do, after all, fuck him. Or does he still use you like a woman whore?"

Guy smiled, with a graceful twist of wrist whipped his sword into a shining, singular circuit. "Come, Brother. Our father is not here to restrain your foul mouth. You're lord of Blyth now, and I'm a wanderer after all. Why don't you call me what you really want to?"

"Ah," said Johan. "The *gadelyng* has a tongue, after all."

Guy shrugged, lunged in. Steel rang, clattered. Shields slammed, wood and metal clashing. Johan smashed against Guy, thrice and with all the finesse of a berserker, sending him back with sheer brute force.

Then Johan broke away, panting. "I'm still bigger than you."

"Aye, true enough," Guy answered, with a smile that lit angry colour into Johan's cheek. "You're heaving like a fat old man. You're *soft*, not fit for this sort of . . . exertion, living like a lord in our father's house."

Another engagement, this one ill-considered with anger. Guy kept smiling, kept dodging, kept parrying. His obvious ease only made Johan all the angrier.

"You have no father in my house! *Gadelyng!*"

"Are you calling our mother a whore?"

"The mother you murdered?" Johan growled, tried to slam the edge of his shield against Guy's face. Guy ducked, returned the favour with a hammerblow to Johan's shield-arm.

Johan's shield dropped—a good blow. Guy eased up, ever so slightly, with satisfaction; Johan reciprocated with a surprise slash—his sword against Guy's injured ribs. Pain ricocheted sparks of crimson behind Guy's eyeballs. He tried to curse, couldn't draw the air to so much as hiss, stumbled back.

Johan followed, shield arm still hanging useless, but sword ready to do it again. "Does the Templar have a problem? What a shame."

Guy snarled, dancing out of reach. Kept moving, a large circle to gain time while he desperately fought to straighten up and huff his breath back.

"So you are not so almighty as you would have me think, are you, Brother Gamelyn? Does your mangy wolf like it when you wear those monk's skirts?"

The taunt, plainly meant to infuriate, instead nearly made Guy laugh—bad idea. His ribcage spasmed tighter. He kept moving, circling, imploring breath. Just one breath, to break the pain . . .

Johan pressed closer. "There has never been a time when you could best me. There will never *be* a time when you can best me. I taught you how to fight, and I will teach your skinny-arsed boy-whore how to watch his *enculer* die."

"How interesting"—finally, *finally*, Guy could take a breath, albeit shallow—"that you noticed his arse." Tossing his shield aside, he sucked in another breath, deeper. Then a third, still deeper. The pain seared akin to a salt-laced blade, but breathing began to dull it. By the fifth breath, Guy was drawing the quillion dagger in his freed hand; by the seventh he leapt forward. Pressing attack to Johan's weakened arm, Guy got in a cut to Johan's face and a few stiff strikes against his mailed torso, sending him reeling.

Stepped back, to wait.

And all the while Johan stared at him, bleeding and staggered, angry and disbelieving. It had never occurred to Johan that he might lose. And now, Guy knew, he was contemplating the possibility.

"*You!*" Johan could no longer cage his fury, humiliation driving it into voice. "You took from me what was mine, always! From the time you were born, when you killed our mother, and from then on! The old man *loved* you—loved *you!* You were his favourite. The *old man's son.* At least in the end he saw what you were—a filthy, buggering catamite!"

"And forgave me, Johan," Guy said, and finally—finally—knew it for truth. "Did he ever forgive you for taking his last days from him? Do you writhe at nights, remembering what you and that craven bitch up there, cloaked righteous as any of God's murderers, took from him?"

"I took *nothing!*" Johan screamed. "Save what was rightfully mine!" And lunged forward.

Guy whirled, brought up his falchion in a glittering, eloquent arc. It sent Johan's weapon—and hand—sailing in a shower of blood. Swift as thought, the falchion reversed its arc as Guy doubled it back, high and centred, to cleave his brother's head from its burgundy-clad shoulders.

"You took from him, as you took from me, the only things worth having," Guy said, soft and fierce, as the body fell, twitching and bleeding into the green.

Out of habit, nothing more, he knelt beside the body. He had no prayer to offer, no unction to give, simply a whisper against the breeze, and one only he would understand: "*Beausant.*"

Silence. Guy raised his head, saw Robyn watching him, the dark-scruffed face shadowed by his hood yet shining with too many things to count. Guy had to turn away or just go over and embrace Robyn hard enough to crack more ribs. Instead, with a tiny grimace Guy rose, shoving the quillion dagger back into his belt. And still, the silence persisted, the gatherers beyond the field stilled with shock and awe, the nobles within the pavilion watching with expressions betraying the gamut: smug to dismayed to furious.

The last reaction, in particular, belonged to Count John. Guy answered it with a nimble flip of his sword into the cradle of his arm, then strode over to the pavilion and swung the sword to rest, point to earth.

"I am Guy de Gisbourne, who was Gamelyn Boundys de Blyth. I was robbed of my hearth-right and my father's bequest for my future by the one who now lies dead. As Blyth Castle is your fiefdom, my lord Count, I ask of you as well as my lord of Pontefract, Baron de Lacy, overlord of Blyth, to stand witness to what has been done this day."

Guy met de Lacy's eyes as they narrowed upon him. Considering. Gauging. Then a slight twitch of de Lacy's mouth, a tilt of his head.

The tacit acknowledgement made Guy lightheaded. Or, Guy considered as he gave his own answering nod, perhaps just the lack of breath in his rib-sprung lungs. And surely it was inevitable, how he found his gaze sliding to Robyn.

Robyn's eyes were shining.

And, *damn*. That made him even more lightheaded. He couldn't up and faint, not now. He had one more thing to say; the most important thing.

He met Count John's eyes. The count hunched in his chair, glowering. Guy knelt, leaning heavier on his sword than he would have liked.

"Honour your bargain, my lord. You will let us go."

Still, the silence. It was the peacock who broke it with his raucous call.

"You must, my lord Count." This from de Lacy, an agreement firm and carrying. "He has reclaimed his rights by trial of battle, proved his innocence in sight of God."

"Roger!" The Abbess rounded on her eldest brother. "Roger, it had to be sorcery. God would not have let such a man win."

"Elisabeth!" De Lacy seemed taken aback. "Trial by battle is *held* in God's sight! It is one of the older and most respected—"

"It was *sorcery!*" She rose from her chair. "The wolfshead and the Templar both, evil! Unholy, unnatural *animals!*"

An ugly snarl began to rise from behind Robyn: the crowd, sensing things were trying to go awry.

"In truth, the Templar's innocence has been proven," Count John riposted. "But the wolfshead? He is outside any law."

"He is to go free as well." Guy did not have to work at setting his voice to rival stone. "Those were the terms."

"Terms?" Count John rose from his chair. "You dare speak to me of *terms?*"

"Aye, let's speak to your terms, shall I?" Robyn's voice rose above the murmurings. "About how *the wolfshead* didn't fancy agreeing to what terms you'd've laid upon him. Did he, *milord Count?*"

Oh, bloody damn, Robyn, shut it, don't... Guy turned his fiercest glare upon the green-clad figure who stalked up and halted beside him. He might as well have tried to dim the full moon, or slap manacles on the wind.

"You have no voice here, wolfshead!" the Sheriff growled, but he had no better luck.

Robyn merely laid his longbow across his shoulders and laughed. "I've no voice? Then shall I, m'lord Count, tell your fancy-dressed minions what you wanted of me? Me, a wolfshead?"

"Are you threatening me, you filth?" Count John countered. "Fine, then. If you open your mouth again"—a gesture, and the royal-clad guards went to attention, their crossbows trained on Robyn—"I'll have you shot where you stand. *Wolfshead.*"

The watchers saw it all. Reacted.

"Foul!" someone cried from the crowd, and then another.

"The Templar won the day!"

"Trial! He won!"

"Let them both go!"

"A Robyn!" Some started, and others followed suit: "A Robyn, a Robyn!"

- XXVIII -

Marion needed a better vantage point. She told Arthur so and moved down the wall, keeping the Abbess always in view. She had drawn, then relaxed, then drawn several times; the willow in her hand did not wait patiently. But the control came easier with every try, surging from deep within: instinct and will commingling to prop up the lack of practice.

She was under no illusions it would last forever.

Nor were the people going to put up with Count John's dallying forever. The growling had grown into shouts; now the shouting escalated into chants, and people pressing forward onto the field, shaking fists and staffs and whatever else they held.

They were chanting Robyn's name.

Count John rocked back a few steps, wide-eyed. The nobles were stock-still, save for the Sheriff, who strode forward and began shouting commands—at his own guards and Count John's as well.

And the Abbess. She trailed the Sheriff, arms gesturing wildly. She was furious. Marion knew all the signs, remembered—even when she couldn't remember—how such volatile outbursts had seemed ones only nobility could indulge. Again, the Abbess grabbed her brother's arm; despite him pulling away, she took hold again. Finally the Sheriff had to shove her aside, bulling his way to the dais front.

Several courtiers were already jumping ship. The Abbess's voice sounded again, shrill beneath the Sheriff's hollered commands at the guards. Fury swerving into desperation, the Abbess turned, imploring not only de Lacy but the priest who'd blessed the bout, pointing . . .

At Robyn.

Marion hissed the breath in between her teeth, let it out, started to nock the arrow. Halted, again.

"Enough!!" Count John leapt from his chair, his shrilled command rising above the din. Next to him, the Sheriff pulled aside several guards who had, crossbows at ready, come onto the lower dais to protect their liege lord. There were other crossbows being levelled onto the crowd—finishing what Count John's quelling cry had begun.

"Silence!" Count John bellowed. "We have heard your voices!"

Despite the distance, Marion could see well-oiled wheels turning behind the count's dark eyes. It did not ease her mind much.

"Since Our people so greatly desire *your freedom*." The last two words spat from between Count John's teeth at Robyn, who stood, body half poised for flight, beside Guy. Both of them, a stone's throw from the dais. "We shall show Ourselves magnanimous. Today, within these castle walls, both of you are free men. You shall—"

The Abbess gave a furious cry, more shrill than even the count's, a negation that ricocheted off the stones like a *baen sís* wail. She ran forward, fell on one of the guards; stunned, they let her rip the crossbow from them.

The moment she did it, Marion *knew*.

The Abbess swung the crossbow clumsily up to her shoulder, aimed it at Robyn.

In one smooth motion, Marion had shoved the hat and cowl from her head, lifted her bow, nocked and pulled the willow arrow. Of her, with her, from her. The spell came as effortlessly from Marion's lips as the arrow from her fingers; she loosed it screaming, shrill into the black, to the black heart of its target.

And Marion was no longer participant, but witness. Robyn had heard the willow leave its nock, twisted around to see Marion. Almost at the same moment Guy uttered a shout, lurched and leapt for Robyn. The spelled arrow screamed into the Abbess's breast just as she triggered the crossbow.

The sickening, pulpy sound of arrows impacting flesh, first one then another. The Abbess looked up, toward the battlements. Her

eyes met Marion's, wide and disbelieving. In them Marion saw—
Saw—the willow's writhings, heard the spell— *deathtakeyou... take
you*—and gave a grim smile, breathed the last throes of it as it
smoked and sparked.
   Yes. It is I. Witness whose hand has taken you.
   The Abbess fell to her knees, clutching and tearing at the
draperies. And Robyn and Guy went tumbling, sliding, headlong
across the field.

☦

Free men. Today. In the castle walls.
   Robyn noted how he hadn't said *outside* them, so they'd best
get going. *Now.*
   The Abbess screamed and shoved into one of the guards.
Another scream answered—this one higher-pitched, and from no
human throat. A tremolo of death and pain and . . .
   Tynged. Breath magic. The spell he'd laid, the *geas* he'd woven.
   Robyn twisted, scanned the upper walls. Found Marion there,
red curls bared to the sky, expression fierce, bow still vibrating.
   Almost in the same breath, Guy shouted at him, let out a harsh
grunt as he slammed full into Robyn. It was as if Robyn had been
whacked by a petrified tree stave; the air went out of his lungs
with a violent cough and he went sailing. Then another, more
painful—and airless—huff as they hit the turf, rolled and skidded.
It seemed to take forever before they finally slid to a halt, with
Robyn all but squashed by a Templar in chainmail and leather
who'd leapt for him and knocked him down as if he were afire.
The howling . . . *thing* kept screaming, not in Robyn's ears but
behind his eyes. Black and copper hair thwarting his vision, Guy's
metal-clad shoulder digging into his collarbone, Robyn squirmed
enough to look toward the dais.
   The Abbess tottered, falling to her knees, hands to her breast.
Sprouting there, blooded dark and howling against his senses, was
the spelled willow arrow.
   Everything else lay strangely silent. People watched, stricken
with horror, both on the dais and in the crowd.
   Then it broke, into shocked murmurs, into a shout from the
dais, voices raised, figures running for the fallen Abbess.
   "We have to go," Robyn whispered into Guy's ear—Guy still
sprawled atop him, not moving. "Get off me, you great heavy—"
Robyn started to shove him over only to have John appear at their
side, shove Robyn against the ground, hard. "John, what—"

"Let me help!" Gilbert knelt down beside them, voice urgent.

As if in response to that urgency, Guy lurched halfway up, faltered. He looked like he wasn't sure where he was, or what. His head bobbled forward, and Robyn saw it, then.

A thick, dark crossbow bolt, protruding from his back.

"Oh, no . . . not . . . " Robyn stammered. "Nay, you en't gonna do this to me now, not—"

Guy tried to push himself upward merely to fall against Robyn again, like a wounded buck flailing down a hill.

"Bloody damn!" Robyn whimpered, holding him, twisting and scuddering out from beneath him. "Help me, Gilly . . . *John* . . . we have to get him up, fetch him *out*!"

"Who shot the arrow?" the Sheriff's shout rang through the field. "Who shot, damn you?"

Robyn shot a glance at the dais. Count John was nowhere in sight, nor were half his guards; obviously they'd bustled him away. De Lacy and the Prior were kneeling next to the fallen Abbess. Someone pointed up at the wall, the Sheriff looking up where Marion had been . . .

Robyn looked—she was already gone.

"Robyn?" Guy's voice threaded with a wheeze. He was trying to rise again. "Robyn, I think . . . I'm hit?"

"That mad bitch shot at you, Robyn," Gilbert said. "He shoved you out of—"

"She *shot* at you," Guy protested.

"And you got in the way, you great pillock!" Robyn burst out. "I should kick your arse!"

"Later," John insisted, putting a hand to Guy's face. Guy blinked. "Y'r here, too?" he slurred, and John nodded, smiling.

"Who loosed the arrow?" the Sheriff was shouting. "Find them!"

"We have to go," Robyn said. "Guy. Listen to me. We have to go."

"Don't think . . . I can." Guy's attempts to rise were becoming fewer, weaker.

"Don't you *dare* do this to me!" Robyn hurled in his face. "I'll bloody well carry you if I have to, but we came here to fetch you out! You're *going*!"

Guy went meekly silent. With Gilbert and John, Robyn managed to get Guy somewhat to his feet. Crouching, Robyn shed his bow and quiver and started to heft Guy—carefully, mindful of the bolt in his back—over his shoulders.

The movement of anything wounded, as always, attracted predators. The Sheriff's voice rang out.

"Halt, villein!"

"Take m' bow! Disappear!" Robyn hissed to John and Gilbert; when they hesitated he snarled, "*Now!*"

They obeyed, John scooping up Robyn's longbow and Gilbert his quiver, both scattering to opposite sides of the gathering crowd. They knew as well as Robyn they would be of no help were they caught for any reason.

Robyn went to one knee, let Guy fall over his shoulder. "Bide still, now," he whispered when Guy started to stiffen, touched him and added a hex-breath to it. "*Be ye still.*"

And Guy did, head lolling and both arms sliding, frighteningly limp, down Robyn's spine.

"Your men," the Sheriff leapt from the dais, strode toward them. "Your men *did this.*"

Robyn could do little more than watch him come, watch the guards train crossbows on him, grit his teeth.

"I'll see you're hanged, you filthy pagan bastard!"

The crowd shifted, fell back, rote behaviour reacting to the force of the Sheriff's authority, his anger. Falling silent, witness.

"You'll see nowt this day!" Robyn growled back. "Come no farther! Are you sure there are no more arrows, should you attack me or mine again?"

One had to give the Sheriff his marks—he kept coming, only slowing the slightest, eyes darting back and forth. From the corner of his eye, Robyn saw John moving, a tiny dagger drawn and ready by his ear. Then he saw Gilbert, sliding around the back of the crowd. Arthur on the battlements, and Will. *Marion.*

She had shot the arrow, doomed their enemy, and her ferocity prickled hot up and down Robyn's spine, rising as they came forward. *Not yet*, he whispered, inward and upward, hoping she could sense it as easily as he could sense her wrath. *Not yet*.

Marion could receive the Lady, but Robyn had always been better at containing the Horned Lord's rage. Nothing spoke back to him; their gods were silent, sunken into their earthly vessels. Robyn mouthed it for them, swore it:

It will be over, this day.

All of them, circling like ravens, gravitating to the smell of blood and ready to strike . . .

"*Come no farther*, I tell you!" Robyn put every bit of biddance he could into the command, pulled it from the stones, the grass, only this was soft, urgent—spoken to his band as well as the Sheriff, not the threat or curse he had intended to wreak, but still heart-true. "Your grief is speaking! She shot first. You *know* she shot first. She has hit an innocent man!"

The Sheriff slowed, a frown scrawling onto his face. It had obviously not been what he had expected from a cornered Robyn Hood, either.

And Guy hung still... so still.

Guy? Robyn sent into the black. *Where are you?*

No answer; only the black, stretching out before him, a long skein of quickly fraying *tynged*.

A female voice sounded from one side, sharp and clear. Robyn recognised it, thought wildly how Marion had better not have bloody come down here, then further recognised the patter of Frankish talk.

Siham. Hands outstretched, plainly earnest—adamant, in fact, with her words tripping over each other.

The Sheriff answered, brusque. Dismissive.

Siham stepped in front of Robyn. She raised her voice, still speaking. On the dais, de Lacy rose slowly, peering at his archer. Then, at Robyn. As if the baron's eyes were a spelled brass, they reflected everything: the Saracen woman trying to talk down a man above her station, the kneeling figures beyond her, one crouched beneath the other, looking up with eyes shiny-scared big as platters, holding the black-clad knight close as skin. Stilled, cornered, with predators circling the wounded, tethered deer...

"Ro... Rob?" At least Guy was trying to speak. But he had started to shiver.

"Shh, now," Robyn told him, then added, "Unless you can tell me what they're saying."

"Saying? Someone's saying... what?"

Sweet *Lady*, he had to fetch Guy out of here, to the Wode!—somewhere Robyn could *help* him, not amidst these stone walls where it was thrice as difficult to even *breathe*...

Nevertheless, he started murmuring. He'd no cognition of what swirled over his tongue. His eyes never stopped flickering over the Sheriff, the nobles on the dais.

Siham kept talking.

From over his shoulder, the slurred-thin translation came. "She's saying... my lord Count set you free. How we didn't... shoot." Guy coughed, shuddered and let out a groan. "God, Robyn... it *hurts*."

"I know. Bide still. I'm fetching you back home."

"Home," Guy whispered. "Time... to come home, Gamelyn..."

Robyn was the one shuddering, now, dread and chill. He started to rise, slow. Every muscle in his body flexed, strained, protested;

Robyn forced himself hard, steady. The broadhead arrow, still in his hair, poked at his ear; he'd nigh forgotten it.

The Sheriff saw him moving, started forward; again, Siham blocked his way. He shoved her aside. This prompted a growled muttering from the gatherers, a surge forward. De Lacy appeared beside the Sheriff, grabbing his arm.

"Brian, be sensible."

"He . . . *murdered* her."

"He *didn't*. I saw what happened. It wasn't him, or anyone around him!" De Lacy looked around them, at the encroaching wall of uneasy onlookers, snatched closer to his brother, and hissed, "Christ, Brian, listen to me! You do this now, you'll have a *riot* on your hands!"

Robyn looked the Sheriff in the eye. "Listen to him. Count John said we were free. We're free, today."

"In these walls," the Sheriff shot back. He yanked his arm from his brother's, hurled further threat, "And once you're *outside* them . . ."

Robyn started backing, slowly, murmuring. As the movement jostled Guy, he whimpered, "Rob?"

Tucking the spell behind his teeth, Robyn answered lightly, "Aye, well, your chainmail weighs akin to a staggered ox."

"Y'r always," Guy murmured, "trying to . . . have my clothes off."

Robyn wanted to laugh—it choked in his throat and burned. He let it, put the burning into what was building, slowly, within. Felt another kind of heat, between his shoulder and Guy's.

John caught his gaze, big-eyed.

"Warm," Guy sighed. "I won't forget."

The amulet. John's amulet, the hex-breath upon it pulsing between them: *Remember who you are. What you have been. What you shall be.*

The Sheriff snatched his arm from de Lacy's grip; de Lacy caught it again, kept up his soothing talk. Siham, too, remained there, another barrier. Robyn had to turn away, though it twisted and sparked every nerve-wrought instinct he possessed. He couldn't keep backing; he might fall, and if Guy fell on that arrow . . .

Robyn sidestepped, feeling the Sheriff's gaze on his neck.

Predator. Wounded, easy prey.

Nay, not easy. You'll not hunt me long. It was nearly a whisper, vicious promise spun into the breath, building. *You'll be the prey, you and any of yours who would defile my kingdom.*

The crowd milled, still uneasy, yet parting before him and half closing behind him. The disturbed murmurs had begun to take on significance. A question. An answer. Fear. Pity. Hope.

A name encompassing all those, voicing from tens of throats: Robyn. Robyn Hood.

He kept looking over his shoulder, kept checking.

Siham came behind him, walking, bow in hand. Holding his back, or waiting for an ordered moment, at the gate?

Time would tell.

"Robyn!" A hoarse call. Gilbert paced him, barely two ells away amidst the shifting, murmuring crowd.

"Scatter," Robyn commanded. "All of you."

"Past the gates he'll *hunt* you!" Gilbert spoke for all of them, Robyn knew. Their presence was a tangible thing—around him, supporting him, as if all their hands shored him up, lightening the weight across his shoulders.

But this, he could carry. For the first time since he had seen a stranger's cruel smile tip a Templar's too-familiar mouth, he *knew*.

Back to back, nothing will stand against you...

"Scatter to the winds," he said, half-spoken, half-sung. He slid his eyes to John. "Give the signal, little John: scatter to the Wode, to await the Hode and the Horns."

John held Robyn's gaze as the words faded, hanging between them. Ducking into his hands, he blew across them. *Aye, Lord.*

Then was no longer there.

The peacock, once again, fluted his call above the strain of murmurs. Only this call floated lower-pitched, with a trill at the end. Immediately its higher avatar sounded—the real peacock this time, challenging a rival to his realm.

Arsy bugger, Robyn saluted the peacock, and kept walking. Kept calling the breath to him . . . and it surged forth, more than he'd ever thought to glean from the confinement of city walls and tamed machines of iron and wood. More people . . . more breath . . . more visions to call into the panic. Even the castle's stones—Robyn had never dreamed they would sing to him like *this.*

Raped from their dam without leave, without grace; they too wanted vengeance.

It was Gamelyn's, this. Birthed in cold stones, his first wails to sing them warm, his voice to bring them to life, carry their tale back to the green Wode always encroaching . . .

His Oak was still with him, blasting defiance, brandishing dagger and sword.

Robyn nigh staggered beneath the surety of it. He had never called a Hunt as Wild as this. It seethed and writhed in his brain, wildly eager to be set loose. *Not yet,* Robyn told it. *We need our Wode about us, our darken realm. Not yet.*

They were to the first portcullis. He checked the walls—Will and Arthur were gone. Checked the crowd—David, Gilbert had vanished with John.

"Guy," he murmured. "Stay with me, love. Stay."

Silence. Only the power pouring into Robyn's own frame, only the warmth of the amulet against his ribs, only the moist, spastic heat of halting breaths gave any clue as to whether Guy lay alive or dead. The body across his broad shoulders lolled, empty-heavy, nigh boneless.

Marion stepped from the crowd, filthy hat and cowl once more pulled forward, bow in hand.

"I gave th' signal!" Robyn hissed as she fell in just before him.

"I en't knowing any cues or t' like, master archer," Marion hissed back. "I'm new t' these parts, aye?"

He wanted to plant a boot in her ragged backside. But if he kicked her arse as she deserved, then he'd drop Guy.

Where are you, Oakbrother? Please, talk to me.

"'Tis a pretty problem you have, little brother." Grey eyes slid toward him, glimmered moon-silver. "He's Her knight, as you are Her archer. Breathe the spell, Robyn Hode. Sing the Hunt to take them. Loose the ebon hart, the crimson hind, the scarlet *capull* all cloaked grey. Call the wolves to finish it."

It was not in him to demur without one final protest. "Mari, your bow. You might have to . . . Can you?"

"I will until I canna. Then I'll club 'em with it."

(†)

Where are you, Oakbrother?

He doesn't know. It is blackness. Fire. Swords and pikes and knives waiting . . . bound by hundreds of sweating, naked demons . . . dragging him to the edge of the precipice. Heat billows up from the edge, scorching his face, singeing his hair; the smell of it reeks sharper than the demons, poking him with their pikes and knives and swords . . .

Oaks burn, eh? Burn strong, and hot, and long.

Guy—it sounds from far away—*where are you?*

No difference, really, that matters. It seems he's in hell.

(†)

Down the bailey they trudged, four figures: two with bows hefted yet unnocked, the third carrying the fourth, pace slow but exact. First the upper level, then the lower, tread heavy, careful, unwilling to falter. They were tracked, first by a semi-protective arc of villeins and then, trailing like outlier carrion-eaters, a wary group of nobles, then farther still a staggered file of guards with crossbows and pikes ready.

All of them, wary for and of the line to be crossed just past the outer gatehouse of Nottingham Castle.

"We're almost there," Marion said, hoarse.

The spell whirled in his mind, waiting. He'd little breath to voice it, but it was built, ready. The broadhead arrow kept poking Robyn in the ear, annoying and insistent—

Robyn jerked. If he'd a free hand, he'd slap himself with it. "The arrow. In my hair."

"You allus put—"

"This one. Spelled. Thought I'd have to break iron."

She was following—of course she was, Marion had more brains than he by a long shot. "The portcullis. It's on rope and chain."

"Aye. When we reach the bridge, run ahead." He kept it to short bursts, saving breath. "Look for the best way. When I get to you, run out, take the chance. It's a long one, but . . . "

She kept nodding, reached forward and threaded the arrow from his hair.

"Don't wait. Run like mad. I'll follow. You'll've bought me"—he stumbled, by sheer will staggered and kept upright—"the time for it. Stay low, no straight lines. The others will be waiting, ready to loose. Head for them. Shoot whatever shoots at us."

As they approached the gatehouse and its massive walls, guards were gathering. Waiting. Not as many as Robyn had expected, but there. And all the eyes—over, behind, beyond—following as they slid into the darkness of the gatehouse, heading for the end light. Their footsteps tapped, nigh silent, beneath the arch.

Marion ran forward, stopped just short of the portcullis.

Guy murmured, soft and plaintive as a dove announcing the coming morn.

Robyn turned, careful with his burden, to tip his head to Siham.

A smile curved her lips. She nodded back, then turned and walked away, disappearing into the shadows of the gatehouse.

⚸

As Marion ran forward, she found the heavy chains attached to the portcullis ropes— more, found one link connecting them all.

She nodded back to Robyn. Backlit from the gatehouse exit, he slid fully into the shadows, his steps hastening only by a little. Kept coming. Back into diffused sunlight, emerging from the arch, beneath the enormous wooden-and-iron portcullis hanging above them like a great-toothed maw.

"Now!" he gritted out.

Marion ran out, took aim. She could hear Robyn whispering the arrow-spell, the metal secret, could feel it tightening. She loosed. The arrow sped right over Robyn's head and sank with a dull clang into the exact link she'd spotted. Blue fire danced across the iron, sparks and cracks and hisses. It snapped, hung. The portcullis shook, gave a great and groaning tilt sideways, slid then stuttered to a quivering halt.

Shouts, screams, panic and tumult from within. Robyn gave a shudder, peered upward. Eyes rolling up into his head, he heaved up a guttural from the depths of his being. Marion felt it in her own being: an invocation. Nay, a demand. The portcullis creaked and groaned, rumbled, clattered . . . then roared down, landing behind Robyn, shaking the ground beneath their feet.

"Run!" Robyn shouted at Marion.

Instead she clung to his side, cover.

He gritted again, "Run! T' Hunt—!"

A laugh. "Do you truly think, Brother, the Hunt shall touch *me*?"

A sudden smile flashed over Robyn's face, as abruptly took flight. Eyes closing, he staggered, steadied, all the while muttering, shaking his head. Trying to control, moving forward, not buckling, adamant. Behind them, the bell had started to ring. The gate crash had set enough chaos to occupy them for a little while, perhaps enough for a loaded down outlaw archer to fetch his lover to safety. They were vivid targets against the bridge.

A shout from within the castle. The guardsmen atop the wall raised their crossbows, obedient but in question.

From the wooded surround a volley answered, slender bolts felling the crossbowmen even as they took aim. Marion drew, loosed as several came from the gatehouse arch—four of them. She felled one, another toppled into the moat with an arrow through his throat, and two dove for cover behind the entry.

Duck and run, nock and loose, draw their volley on tiring legs, with a bow arm that wouldn't let her keep this up for long. Guards falling, arrows flying, and not one crossbow bolt spent itself close to Robyn and Guy. Road dirt, then rocks and weeds, then grass against their feet. The longest meadow Marion had ever crossed in her life, then hedges, then . . .

The Wode took them in, wrapped a cloak about Her own.

Marion sank to her knees in the grass, panting. Robyn stumbled into Will's waiting arms; Will and David both barely managed to catch Robyn and Guy as they fell. The jolt made Guy lurch half-upward with a gasp, then fall back against Robyn, who rolled him gently onto his side.

"That," Guy said, very plain, "*hurt*, bugger it."

"Well, then stay awake," Robyn chided, between hoarse pants. "I'll take yon great curvy sword and whack you up your ginger head if I have to."

Guy chuckled; it choked into a grimace. "I really am going to have to teach you *how* to use a sword someday."

"I'll hold you to that, y' git. *What* were you thinking?"

"Not thinking. Like you," Guy mumbled. His eyes rolled up in his head; he was shivering violently. "Guess . . . my turn . . . to die . . ."

He gave a huge shudder, went still. Already heavy, he seemed to grow heavier, pull at Robyn's arms.

"N-n-nay, you en't. Wake up, now." Robyn's voice cracked upward. He shook Guy. "Wake up." Shook again, harder, and still no response. "*Guy!*"

Marion let out a tiny whimper. None of the others made a sound. She started to lean forward, reach out . . . hesitated as Robyn's head dropped. His hair spilled from the folds of his cowl to cover his face, spreading over Guy's like black blood. His shoulders quivered, and it spread down his body, rippled into shudders.

The breeze, light upon them all, dropped into flat-calm. Marion glanced at the others, eyes wheeling wide to match their own; they knew.

The alarm bell began to ring, then. Shouts, the clatter of hoofs and metal from within.

Robyn's hands, gripping Guy's tunic, flattened. He shoved upward, eyes a-flame upon the castle stones, nostrils flaring. As if in answer, the portcullis started cranking upward, slow, and men began spilling out beneath it.

"They're coming," Arthur hissed.

"They'll come," Marion said, watching her brother swerve, full-tilt, into the madness. "And wish they hadn't."

Robyn's head tilted back, and he spread his arms, palms to the sky. Breathed:

"*Hunt them.*"

And the wind came, then, screaming through the trees like a thousand hungry phantasms.

- XXIX -

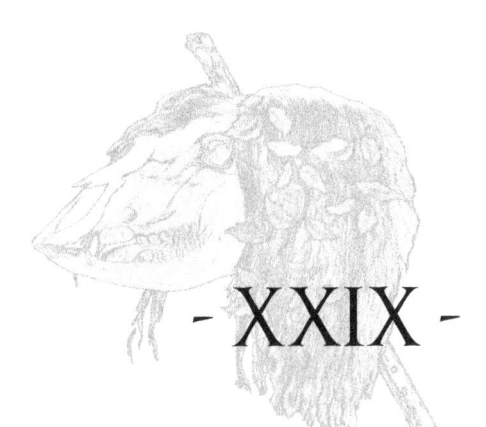

K*eening...*
   Wolves yip-yip-yipping, bounding and gathering beneath bare branches, red-eyed and black as night. They sink into their mile-eating pace, gather behind their Lord as he runs, swings up astride his mount and screams bloody vengeance into the waning sun.
   Chasing...
   The stag halts, blasts, with a twist of his great horned head, charges. Paves the way for the hooded and horned rider, the Green Man who looses arrows as he rides, scattering the people who flee the night mare he straddles, bareback and unbridled.
   Running...
   Predator becomes prey becomes downed masses to be ravaged, tossed aside. It is souls they would have this night, not meat or bone.
   Some they do not touch. Those who fall to their knees in fear or love or fealty—or all three. A female archer, dusky-cheeked, who bows before Cernunnos's anger with no fealty but great respect. Her master, whose blood smells of treachery yet does not reek with it. Another with the enemy-blood falls to his knees, praying with a heart as true as his mind is calculating—they leave him to his own god, his own fate.
   They avoid the fallen one—the goddess's arrow has pierced her.

Willow has staked Her claim, crouches upon the black-clad body and snarls when they come too near: *Mine*. For others . . .

Ghosts walk the parapets, burnt-out eyes and torn, mangled limbs. Drowned bodies, human and animal, tread from the moat. Half-eaten corpses unlock their cages and pour themselves piecemeal onto the bridge, crawling into the gatehouse. The Underkeep rings with cries of the damned and the lost, and those who are not drunk or drugged past dreamings crawl into their holes and don't emerge for days.

Robyn Hood's justice, they will call it anon—those who can give it voice—as Nottingham Castle sinks into hell.

Hell. It must be.

And there's a mad wolfshead in it.

That wolfshead approaches Guy with a swagger in his hip and a curl on his lip that, even now—chained in Purgatory to a stake by grossly-endowed demons who promise to roger Guy until he can't walk and *then* burn him—makes Guy want to shove the man up against the wall and roger *him* until *he* screams.

Only Robyn Hood could walk up to the precipice of hell bold as polished brass and shaggable as . . . well anything Guy has ever *ever* wanted to shag.

"Aye, pet," Robyn says, "you're no' so bad yr'self, all tied up and willing. And you definitely look dashing walking over to that pyre lit so hot and high, but I'm not about to let you throw yourself in."

"Why are you here?" Guy asks, voice shaking.

"It's a game, aye? All of it, a great game."

"I thought your people were the ones who didn't play games with your hearts?"

"But Gisbourne," Robyn counters, a quirk on his lip, "you don't have a heart, rememb—!?"

The arrow takes him high in the chest. Robyn grunts, staggers, looks down at it as if stunned, then sinks. It is slow, taking moments instead of seconds as if Robyn refuses, at first, to fall.

"Bloody damn, if you're going to die then get *on* with it, you pretentious git!" a voice growls and, with a whine and flash of steel, a spray of hot blood that momentarily blinds Guy, Robyn is felled. Guy struggles, but the demons hold him fast, and when he finally blinks away the thick heat clotting his gaze, he sees a black-robed figure bent over Robyn's body like some feeding raven.

"Get off him!" he screams. "*Murderer!*"

The black cloak is flung back. It is not the Abbess. Not Johan. Not the best of his nightmares but the worst of them.

It is himself.

Gisbourne rises, wipes his bloodied sword on his black cape and rams it into its sheath. He gives his chained-up avatar a wry frown, then shrugs. Smiles. Bends over, picks up the severed head by its tangled black hair.

"Robyn Hood. His head tied to your saddle, remember? What you were sent to do? We can go home now, yes?"

It's time to come home, Gamelyn...

Guy starts screaming, then, and cannot stop, cannot stop, *cannot stop*...

✝

He is the night, fed upon the stars sprayed across the sky like life itself from a goddess's milk-heavy breasts.

He is the Hooded One, the Horned Lord's shade, reaping souls beneath the horns of the moon and slipping silent into the waters. He is the stag taking flight from the arrow, the king of a breaking realm, first and last of his kind.

He is . . . lost. Bereft.

He is Robyn Hode, walking the green Wode with the grace of a panther . . . but He has never been merely that. The wolves, done with their Hunt, fawn around His heels, nip and lick His fingers with their blood-spattered muzzles, purl and growl and play. His shadow follows, gliding across the grass beneath the eyes of Her moon, more the sparkle and ebon of a night sky, truly more shade than mortal shadow. It is horned, cowled. There is a longbow at the shadow's back and a fine quillion dagger glints dully at one hip, yet the man feels no burdens, as if they are not there. Or as if they are so a part of Him they cannot be felt, in this now.

He is . . . elsewhere. Elsewhen.

Yet He is here, now, walking the forest, drawn to its heart. Drawn to *His* heart, in the last.

Marion sits on the sward, Ivy awaiting Her Holly Lord with green kirtles spread about Her, moonlight peaceful and gentle where it touches. The one lying in Her arms is clad in white and scarlet, red-gold hair flung across green. No defrocked, black-clad Knight Templar, this; curled like a babe in the womb, Summer warming, all peace and comfort beneath the Mother's heartbeat.

Yet there it ends. There is no purity of peace in Guy's face. Eyes wide and staring, dilated, his expression is fixed in a rictus of fear.

Robyn can hear it: not the howls of the Horned Lord's Wild Hunt, not the screams and shrieks of a city laid low with its own spectres, but one voice. One voice crying out, shrieking in fire and heat and hate, pale, callused hands outstretched and drenched in blood that stains the water and sets fire crackling, turning the forest scarlet.

It is a peculiar, torturous hell.

Marion bends over Guy, whispering, cinnabar curls commingling with ruddy-silk locks, rocking back and forth.

He wain't wake, Robyn says, and falls to his knees.

Marion nods, says sadly into Guy's hair, *The spell is. . . strong.*

Strong. Aye, and then some. Robyn can hear it, sung as a woman—not mother— gives a noble's babe suck. Can smell it, imprinted into freckled skin with rod and holy water, incense and prayer. Can see it—See it—marking an old soul with new penance and sin, doubt and faith, right and wrong, dark and light.

They've raised our Summerlord in a cage!

And he has tried to free himself. He knew the cage, but also love and loyalty, hope and innocence. He has sloughed it away, denied the wholeness of his being. The only thing he now believes in is hell. That he deserves nothing but. And that's where he now lies, trammelled in his own twisted, scarred otherworld. I canna find him.

We have *to find him—bloody damn, I hear him, hear him screaming!*

Finally, She looks up. Her eyes open, smoke grey bleeding into silver pennies, reflecting the thin, horn-crescent shade of His approach.

For they *are* Other, in this not-time and place.

I cannot help him. Her words are soft, but malleable as iron.

This, Robyn grits out, *is not negotiable. This is one sacrifice I* refuse *to make.*

You misconstrue, o pwca. You bear the Horns. You threw the bones 'twould claim him yours. You called the Hunt. You wear the Hood. In this moment, in thisworld as well as others. She leans forward. *'Tis thou who art his heaven. . . and his hell.*

Aye. It is the Hooded One who bends down, Holly and Horns, shadow and flame flaring in ebony eyes. *And I know how to wake him.* He cannot uncurl the figure tight knotted, half-in and half-out of Her lap, and so moves around to where Guy's back lies exposed—

Stops, breath thumping in His chest as He sees the arrow still there, obscene and real in this land of thought and will.

He pulls up the back of Guy's white tunic, finds the cord lying there, shimmering like a blood-filled umbilical at the freckled curve of Guy's back. Tangles fingers, clenches.

Nothing.

Panic laces *tynged* into jagged rents, sets embers flickering uncertain behind dark eyes, sets gold and silver metal a-dance, a peripheral jingle against horn.

Guy, Robyn growls, takes another wrap of silk about his palm. *Answer me, Gisbourne!*

But there are only screams in the black. Denial. Hell.

Guy of Gisbourne died on Samhain, beheaded by Robyn Hood. From then until now, we have been seeing his death throes. He did not die easily. Marion strokes the copper-gilt hair back from Guy's face, trails a hand down his breastbone and over his belly to cover Robyn's hand where it lies, tangled in the thin measure. She peers at Her brother/Consort. *He is not meant to die to thisworld forever, lost. But our own illusions are the strongest, the hardest to dispel. Are they not, Lord?*

It is an aimed arrow to the heart, a hot scorch of flame through the trees, a bitter season spent nearly dying from not only an enemy's arrow flight, but the despair and the *isolation.*

I am the last of my kind. I have a body. I have a soul—the Horned Lord reaches out, touches His Lady's face—*but no heart. Not without him. I cannot do this. It will not end here!*

Without endings, beginnings cannot emerge, She says. *Call our Oak to this place. Call His name.* Her hand slides back up to the amulet carven so delicately into three interlaced teardrops. *The magic cannot yet wane, as long as We stand, back to back in the Shire Wode. We will do this together. I will claim the arrow. You must claim His spirit. Say His name!*

And the Hooded One bends down, breathes it across the cord, caresses it with His fingertips. Says:

It's time to come home, Gamelyn.

☦

Banished. In hell, screaming. Burning. Never-ending, everlasting, torment for eternity and he would never, *never* be free . . .

Then a sinewy, hard hand took his own, and a soft voice called his name, and he was flung back into cool darkness, and a scream echoing into the trees—his own—and more pain scorching his nerves than he'd felt since . . .

Since Crusade. Had he been dreaming?

No. No more dreams. I can't do it again. . . please, not again.

Then a voice shattered Guy's world and set it back on its axis, all at once.

"Bloody damn, if *that* en't a nasty way to wake a fellow."

A red haze remained, clouding Guy's vision; through it he espied his own hands, clutching fur and sheepskin and . . .

A thick hank of black hair.

"Don't be such a bairn, Robyn. You've plenty and then some. Our fair knight's just had a nasty bodkin popped from his back, and you're whinging about your hair!"

It was Marion who spoke, Marion who came around and knelt before Guy. Her hands were extended; upon them rested a crossbow bolt, smeared with gore. "We got it all, clean."

The red haze obscured Guy's vision again—surely it must be some trick of light, for it seemed, as Marion held the arrow before her it . . . dissolved. Went scattering into tiny, golden pinpricks, shadows and light dancing up her arms to encircle her throat—an arrow-torc—then sinking inward.

"She is, after all, the goddess's Arrow." John's voice, this time, in his ear. John in whose lap Guy had been cradled as they pulled out the arrow.

And Robyn's hair still tangled in his fingers. Robyn lay beside Guy on the boughs and skins, on his back, head angled toward Guy, grimacing. "Can I have m' scalp back, now?"

Unsure if he were dreaming, Guy released his grip. It wasn't easy—his fingers seemed determined to hold to something, somehow.

Marion rose, walked over to the fire, and bent—there was a fire, at their feet.

Slowly the surroundings started to make sense, and the pain dulled to a small throb, with little tattered flares of outrage. Beyond, nigh to the fire, sat Arthur and Will—the latter whittling nervously at a stick. The fire smoked with green wood, its plume undisturbed by wind. There were small sounds—the pops and ticks of small animals running along bark, the pips of settling birds, the soft, mournful query of an owl not far away. Woodland sounds, as familiar to him as his own freckles when he was young . . .

It's time to come home.

Marion returned, a bowl in her hands, to kneel behind Guy. David was there, beside her; Guy realised David's hand lay against his upright shoulder, gentle but wary—as if he were contemplating bathing a cat—to hold him firm in John's lap. Tess was there, too, propped downhill on David's chest. Her front paws gripped his tunic, and she watched every move as Marion cupped fingers in the bowl and began careful layering of a gooey, warm, and foul-smelling paste to Guy's wound.

He must be dreaming. The outlaws were not trying to kill him. "Where are we?" Guy husked.

"We're home." Robyn said it almost wonderingly. "In the Shire Wode."

"Sit him up a wee more, Johnny," David said, and Marion added, "Hand me th' gauze, Gilbert." Gilbert hoved into view with the requested rags.

Guy found himself lifted to a seated position, precarious despite John and David's grips on him. Pain kept stabbing a broken-edged blade into his ribs, sending uncontrollable shudders up and down the left side of his back.

He was going to pay hell wielding a sword for a while. Guy supposed he should count himself lucky "for a while" seemed the operative phrase.

Robyn watched, all the while. "I think we've managed it so you wain't have a great nasty hole like meself." A grin, but it seemed halfhearted. "'Tennyrate, you're t' one always saying pain's good for the soul."

It demanded a like answer. "Couldn't you have fixed my ribs and closed the hole while you were at it?"

"That kind of magic'll kill you, most days," Robyn said, serious.

Guy suddenly noticed how Robyn hadn't risen from his place, either. "Are you . . . have you . . ."

"I did and have. I've been out as long as you. But not 'cause I tried to catch an arrow with me backside."

"He thought you were dead," Marion said, low. "It drove him t' put a bit more into calling the Hunt than he might should have done."

"The Hunt. The . . . Wild Hunt."

"Aye, that." Robyn smirked up at the trees. "Nottingham wain't be bothering us for a while."

"And the Abbess?" Guy had to ask. He couldn't remember.

"Dying slow. And mad." Robyn's eyes slid to Marion. "Marion stole my arrow, the cheeky bint. And sunk it."

"'Tisn't the first time. Likely not the last." Marion's mouth brushed Guy's, then Robyn's. "We're safe, for the now. And supper's nearly done. If Will en't let it burn."

"I wouldn't!" Will protested from the fire.

"Pottage?" Guy asked hopefully, and Marion smiled as she tucked the bowl of herbs in the crook of her arm, rose and retreated.

"That's that done, then," David said, tying off the gauze. Gilbert and John eased Guy back down. Gilbert rose to join the others at the fire. John lingered to stroke Guy's hair back from his forehead, then bent over Robyn, laid a kiss to the pulse point at his throat. Robyn's mouth quirked as his eyes closed, but he didn't move—likely couldn't—and John retreated as well.

But not far, only to the fire.

Guy didn't move—couldn't move had he wanted to—and didn't take his eyes from Robyn. Robyn's arms were thrown up above his head; he was naked from the waist up and the underside of his arms gleamed pale in the moonlight, sliding into the dark fur at his armpits and scattered over his chest, all shadows and flickers. The breath whistled, soft, from where his bottom lip had fallen open; his chest expanded in a sigh. Guy understood that, well enough. The pain, more and more, began to dull, undeniable but more readily dismissed. The boughs were soft, springy beneath the sheepskin.

He wanted to reach out, touch Robyn, make sure it was real. Instead he whispered, "Are we truly here? Alive? It's not a dream?"

"What are dreams, anyway?" Robyn said, his eyes still closed. "I'm not sure I know the difference, most days."

Guy nodded, closed his eyes. Over by the fire, the others were conversing in low voices, as if none wanted to broach the night's stillness.

He understood that, too.

Suddenly, Robyn spoke. "I . . . never thought the pain would be too much for you. I thought you wanted it. Needed it. Instead you decided you'd not feel again, and I . . . I dragged it out of you. All that pain, all that need . . . and it nearly killed you."

Guy opened his eyes, stayed silent for a few breaths. Then he slid his hand—very carefully—toward Robyn, tangled his fingers once again in unruly ebon and gave a tiny tug. "I think . . . " He hesitated, then said, "People like us, we're hard to kill. *Beausant.*"

"Is that Frankish?" Robyn murmured, still looking up at the tree-laced night sky.

"It is indeed."

"What does it mean?"

"It means . . . " Guy rubbed a dark lock between his thumb and forefinger. "*To be whole.*"

And Robyn smiled.

- Postlude -

When Hubert de Gisborough, Master to Temple Hirst, first galloped toward the gates of Nottingham Castle with four Templar Knights, six well-armed paxmen, and a wandering monk with a staff athwart his saddle, he came prepared for the worst.

He found it, but not in the manner expected.

The fields to the north, which should have been full of pavilions and encampment for the tournament, looked as if a huge wind had blown down half the encampments. And among those were brush flattened or gear abandoned, places that looked as if they had been inhabited but were no longer.

The portcullis was lowered. The royal flags were flown—which made Hubert sneer; he knew damn well King Richard hadn't yet been released—but there were only a few guards wearing the red and gold, and fewer still in the dark blue Nottingham favoured. They passed Hubert and his retinue in, with astonishing alacrity.

What they found inside was even more astonishing—and frightening.

Several hours later, they exited the castle and headed back north at a round gallop.

They found a lone Templar waiting for them, on the crest of the north road nigh to Papplewick.

"I have been to Nottingham, and found chaos in your wake."

"Yes, my lord Commander."

"I was brought to understand that you took a witch from their gaol, killed tens of guardsmen as you did so."

"Yes, my lord Commander."

The sun shone, imperious and brilliant. Guy knelt in the middle of the road, ruddy head brushed and braided, bared and bent. He was dressed within an inch of his life, mailed and girt as if for a formal audience, the singular mar in his appearance one arm, held too close and stiff at his side. It seemed . . . bound. And so had Guy been standing there in the road as they'd ridden up; he'd not moved from the spot since Hubert had called his company to a halt, dismounted, and walked the remainder of the way. As Hubert had approached, Guy had knelt, stiffly and with none of his usual grace, and waited in silence for his Master to speak.

"You humiliated the King's brother. Attacked him." Hubert was pacing back and forth, his agitation barely containable. Much held Hubert's horse obediently enough, but no question it was killing him to endure his master's humiliation from a distance. Even the monk—Dolfin, wasn't it?—had insisted on riding back this way, wanting to find out about Guy. Well. They both could wait, after galloping full speed to Hirst and nearly killing two horses with all this madness.

And madness it remained. "For this crime—toward which I am sure you will have adequate response—they threw you in gaol and . . . !" Hubert could scarce utter the words without nigh choking with rage. "And made plans to burn you at their witch's pyre!"

"Yes, my lord Commander."

Hubert halted, standing nearly atop Guy. "And all of this for what?"

The bowed head began to tilt up, the pale brows drawing together in consternation. At the last moment Guy collected himself, dropped his head, and asked, woodenly, "I beg your pardon, my lord Commander?"

"You will beg my pardon anon," Hubert snapped. "*Confanonier*, what of the mission upon which your Temple and your Master sent you? Have you done as I asked?"

A pause. Then, slowly, "I fear I have failed you, my lord Commander."

"Failed." Hubert drew it out, punctuated it with a click of his tongue.

"My lord. You charged me to find the wolfshead who had usurped the power of the old druid. But there is no such man."

"No such man." Hubert considered the man kneeling before him. The most talented acolyte he had seen in all his days—a talent that had for so long lain withered, stunted, unable to blossom or fruit. Yet in this moment it was plain, to anyone with trained senses and reach, that what Hubert saw before him should not be kneeling to any man.

Sherwood has stolen you from me, has She not, Guy? The thought brought a catch to Hubert's throat. Surely, he had seen it coming, but...

"What of the artefacts?" Hubert growled at the bent, copper-gilt head. "What of the Horns of the God? Where is the Goddess's Sacred Arrow?"

"They are where they belong, my lord Templar."

Hubert started, looked up to see another coppery glint—this more of pure fire than forged metal—caught in a stray glint of sun against the fallen oak. Her hair cropped short in a tangle of curls, the girl spoke their tongue like a peasant from Gascony and dressed worse, in a tatterdemalion of fine woollen, coarse linsey, and short boots oddly ill-suited to the outdoors. But she held herself like a queen, and...

Sacre tête, but how had the girl sneaked up on them like that?

"As is your vassal, where he belongs." The peasant girl/queen walked forward, slowly. "Gamelyn is too modest, my lord. He's not failed you."

Guy's head shot up at the familiarity, his gaze fastening to Hubert's.

"Neither," she added, quiet but firm, "is he merely your vassal. He has heard the voice of the Lady."

"Who are you, woman?" Hubert said, wary. Also, intrigued.

"I think you know who I am, Templar. You too have heard Her voice, though to you She speaks a different tongue."

It broke any façade Hubert might wish to hold to—not only the soft, frank acknowledgement, but the humming, deep within his chest that acknowledged the Lady's avatar on earth. Hubert found himself going on one knee, drawing his sword and touching it, point down, to the ancient Mother upon which he trod.

"Maiden, you have my sword."

With a rattle of chainmail and saddle-trappings, the other Templars dismounted, did likewise. Much was already there.

"You do me honour and grace, noble sirs." Her words were grave. "For I am Maiden to the Shire Wode, and to your most honoured of Knights. Who is wounded enough without you chastising him as if he's done the wrong," she added, sharper.

Guy started to say something; Hubert also made as if to speak.

"This is polite and all, giving my sister her due. But 'twould be more polite if you'd stop babbling in Frank. You're in my Wode, y'know, and we speak English here."

Another voice, male, floating down from the upper branches of the oak beneath where Hubert knelt. Hubert had no more heard this one's approach than the girl's. He lurched to his feet, hand on sword hilt, ready.

The Maiden, however, didn't seem concerned, and Guy, still kneeling where Hubert had left him, shook his head, albeit carefully. He raised his gaze, a slight smile on his lips.

"He does that," Guy remarked—in English. "It is disconcerting, the first dozen times or so."

The oak gave a small shudder, and a shadow quickly descended to reveal itself as a lanky young man dressed in leathers and a fine Lincoln tunic, which looked as if it had been ripped down the front then faced with doeskin. The leathern hood over his head might have belonged to any man; that, plus the huge longbow strapped to his back, gave commonplace origins the lie.

"You, then," Hubert said, "are Robyn Hood, *c'est ça?*"

"He is indeed," Guy said, and a gleam, soft and *alive*, burned in his green eyes—that life further bespeaking what changes had, somehow, occurred. "And . . . a ghost, laid to rest. He was once of Loxley, son to Eluned and Adam, as Marion was daughter. Cernun's chosen."

"I . . . see," Hubert said, a smile chasing over his face then settling in one corner of his mouth. "Oh, good Lord, Guy—on your feet. You have been wounded . . . but I truly feared I would find you dead on my return, with what was said in Nottingham." He reached down, helped Guy to his feet, held him there until he steadied.

Guy gripped him back, stood there, very close, for a long moment. "I fear, my lord, I shall never wear the white again."

"All of us have more than one purpose in life, Gamelyn," Hubert returned softly, and kissed him, first one cheek and then the other. Pushed him back, gently, and included the Hood and the Maid—Marion—with his words. "I too had a shield brother, dear to me in spirit *and* body."

Guy blinked, and Hubert smirked. But of course—the young always forgot their elders had once been that—young.

"Well, this one is *not* allowed to play shield again," Robyn said fiercely, putting a startlingly gentle hand to the bulk of bandage beneath Guy's tunic. Startling, not only because the hand—and arm—were built hard from the bow he carried, but that the animal vitality of the young man did not seem so easily gentled.

"Neither does he need to be taking any long rides up country," Marion said, just as firm. "He's not healed yet, not by a long shot."

Hubert contemplated his Templars, dismounted a small distance away, then brought his gaze back to his *Confanonier*. "Mayhap she's right. You're no use to me like this, you realise."

If the man known as Robyn Hood had possessed horse's ears, he would have pinned them. The Maid, too.

"Mayhap a good fortnight here, with Much to bear you company, would set you to rights. Keep an eye on Nottingham for me. Not that I believe they'll offer much trouble." Hubert shrugged. "I spoke with Roger de Lacy. And the count. I... ah... made it quite plain to John Lackland what shall be his lot should he take such liberties again."

"You... *threatened* him?" Marion ventured.

"Where it hurt all the more," Hubert said. "In his wallet. 'Tis useless to threaten such men with interdict, but John shan't be king long—if he ever is—without the ability to acquire funds."

The smile tucking itself into Robyn Hood's mouth played damned wicked, and Guy's not far behind. The Maiden was chuckling, nodding, and Much...

Oh, my. Much stared at the Maiden like a lovesick pup.

Well. At least Guy's paxman had sworn no vows in *that* direction.

"So," Hubert said. "A fortnight. Longer, if necessary. And I would hope the Hooded One might accept an invitation to the Temple when you return, Guy." Guy blinked. So did the outlaw.

"M-me?" Robyn Hood stammered, and he abruptly seemed quite young. "To the Temple?"

"I think we might have many things to speak about," Hubert said, and motioned for his horse.

- - - - -

END BOOK TWO

- - -

Kindly turn the page for a Preview of
Book Three

Winterwode

"What do you mean, *this en't the first time?*"

Robyn was still half-asleep and a bit tender behind the eyes from one too many mushroom caps; he'd been minding his own business and warming a pot of mulled cider. Amidst shivering. He'd woken up to a bloody cold, very empty bed.

Then Will had shown up, in a very bloody hurry, with his shoulders hunched around his ears, and had he a tail to tuck, it would have been tight-wrapped somewhere between his knob and his navel.

And right after that had Marion shown up, wielding Gamelyn's sword like a stony-eyed angel threatening parishioners from the corner of some cathedral of the Christ.

However, instead of lighting into Will as she'd clearly wanted to do, she'd flown at Robyn and begun bloody chasing him all over camp with Gamelyn's sword. All because Robyn had been half-asleep, and when she'd asked him if he'd set a watch on her, he'd been daft and told the truth.

He'd not even had a piss yet!

"What do you think I'm supposed to do? Let you wander around the forest on your lonesome?" Robyn retreated to the other side of the fire, snatching at both his unlaced shirt and the fur nigh dragging it off his shoulders.

Not that it did any good; Marion just followed him. "Let me? *Let me?* Who do you th—"

"Mari, pet, if you'd just—"

"Don't you 'pet' me—and what were you thinking? On second thought, you weren't thinking! You were just assuming! Like you've t' rights! Putting minders on me as if I were some child!"

David had already scooted out of the way, taking his precious iron utensils with him. Gilbert and Arthur dodged right, then left, then scattered as brother and sister darted around the hearth-fire, first one way, then the other.

"You en't no child, but you're a woman, and in case you'd not heard, these parts are filled with outlaws—Ow!" He skipped sideways as she swung, and the flat of the blade smacked his thigh. "What're you trying t' do, geld me?"

"You en't using 'em, anyway—!"

"I am! Just 'cause I en't after making a bunch o' bairns—"

"The likes of more of you is all we need—!"

"—like me goolies just where they are!" This time Robyn leapt over the fire. "What in hell are y' doing with Gamelyn's sword, anyway—Bloody *damn*, woman!" Robyn yipped as she swung again, too close for any comfort. He changed tactics. "Put that sword down! Right now, before y' really do cut someone!"

"Stay still so I can whack you another one, you bloody great"—a lunge—"arrogant"—another dart—"knob!" Marion overbalanced and the sword nearly went flying. Robyn skittered sideways, took refuge against the huge trunk of the hazel sheltering much of the camp, and snatched up the only weapon he could muster—a staff.

Marion glared at him for one breath. Two.

Robyn raised the staff, glaring back.

None of the others dared to so much as twitch.

Then Marion marched over, hefting the falchion over her head. It came down, a glittering arc. Robyn went staggering back against the hazel's trunk, his staff cloven in two, and the sword's curved blade rebounded against the root-laced ground with a sharp, nigh painful ring.

"Hoy! What in bloody hell are you doing to my sword?" Gamelyn's voice rose, sharp.

Marion spun around, snapped out, "So, were you in on this too? Either of you?"

Robyn took part of his attention—only part, mind—from Marion. Gamelyn stood on the camp's edge, fists clenched. Beside him, Much hovered, all dusty with road dirt. Both seemed baffled.

Join the ring, mates. Robyn barely had time for the silent reply before Marion turned back on him and growled a curse surely no novice nun should know. In the next moment, Marion flung the sword down, turned on one heel, and stalked off.

Gamelyn cringed as his sword once again made contact with the hard, root-tangled ground.

The outlaws—those who happened to be in the wake of Marion's passage—wisely scattered.

Robyn wasn't considering wisdom or anything else; he lurched upright, started after. "Mari—!"

Marion kept going, and Robyn kept following, and just before she reached the camp periphery, she whirled. Robyn nearly ran over her, halting just in time with the aid of some creative arm flailing and despite some clumsy foot sliding.

Silence. Then:

"Do not," Marion growled, "bloody follow me!" And she stomped off into the trees.

More silence, punctuated by a huge sigh of relief from Will.

It was a mistake.

"I told you!" Robyn rounded on Will. "Told you this would happen, did you not mind what I said and go aft—"

"I en't the one as is allus going after, and you know it!" Will snapped back, with a venomous look in Much's direction. "This wasn't my fau—"

"It never is, Scathelock, but you followed her this time, aye? And just like I said, you were a great lumbering pillock and she saw you."

"She never saw me," Much said, low. "I know she didn't."

"Or mayhap she prefers you to follow her!" Gilbert tried to joke.

That was a mistake as well. It was Will's turn, this time, to round on Gilbert and hiss, "Shut your gob!"

"Bloody fucking damn, William." Robyn stalked over and shoved at him. "It's not like I en't had enough o—"

"You followed Marion?" Gamelyn interrupted. Soft, almost colourless in tone—no doubt why it penetrated Robyn's growl of accusation. "Tonight? To Barrow Mere?"

An uneasy silence followed; none of the outlaws took that place lightly.

"Aye, I did!" Will broke it, defiant, and tucked his chin not unlike an angry bull. "What of it? I should think I've more rights there than any bloody Templar!"

Barrow Mere. Robyn narrowed his eyes, put off and puzzled. Will was on the defensive, no question, and Gamelyn . . . well, he was proper brassed off, because when Gamelyn did get that offended, you'd never see it in those flat eyes, but the blood would rush beneath his skin until all the freckles disappeared and his face turned into a bloody coppery idol.

"You'll push too far one day, Scathelock," Gamelyn snarled.

"I'm waitin' for 't, believe me," Will snarled back, and Robyn decided that was enough of that, here and now.

He strode into their sight line—Gamelyn was still having a

cold-blooded seethe at Will, whose own glare surely belonged on the business end of a crossbow—scowled at both of them, and crossed his arms. "Right, then," Robyn said to Much. "Where's John?"

Much's gaze darted toward Gamelyn, then met Robyn's gaze again with a reassuring nod. "He's well enough. No doubt having a bite and flagon of ale at the inn. We thought it best he bide nigh t' trouvère, considering."

"Considering."

"Aye. There's a few more branches to this tree. Just like Himself figured." Much again flicked a glance at Gamelyn, now peering into what seemed to be thin air, then Will, red-faced and muttering at the ground, then the others, still scattered in Marion's wake. "Looks to me like we could all use a good stiff drink, at that."

⊕

Want to find out what happens next?
(Because there's a lot more storytellin' to be done, here!)

You can find the entire series of
The Books of the Wode
at Forest Path Books

https://forestpathbooks.com

Interested readers can also catch up on the latest
news and releases by joining
J Tullos Hennig's Reader Group at:

https://subscribe.jtulloshennig.net
and/or by visiting
https://www.jtulloshennig.net

You might even nab yourself a free story or two!

AUTHOR'S NOTES & ACKNOWLEDGEMENTS

If, to loosely quote Frank Herbert, "Beginnings are delicate times," then I'd like to add that endings are the portal to more beginnings. For this writer they are also often a time of contemplation, looking back over the process and thinking, with equal amounts of wonder and terror: How did I ever come to this place?

You see, it has been a very long journey to this particular ending/beginning. Robyn has been with me my whole life. When I was a child, if it wasn't as Tonto or Trigger or Bambi that I was gallumphing about the woods, (I always preferred animals and sidekicks, which pleased my cousins as they liked the Hero-Type) it was Robin Hood. (And now I'm going to go back to the other spelling, well, because.) Robyn (particularly book-Robyn) wasn't quite the accepted Hero-Type. He did his share of arse-kicking, but also got his arse kicked in return, used his wits, was always vanishing in the forest and firing flaming never-miss arrows at the enemy. He was a survivor. He had his companions as well as his share of enemies—one bad Guy in particular. Literally.

Guy of Gisbourne has found himself at the forefront of Robyn's enemies. Not bad for someone who started out as a one-off bounty hunter who preferred horsey drag and ended up rather-brutally dispatched in the appropriately-named Robin Hood and Guy of Gisborne. This ballad has a later date attributed to it, but is reckoned by many to actually be amongst the earliest. It has layers and underpinnings that are astounding when one reads it thoroughly. I have always thought it one of the subtextual masterpieces of the Robin Hood ballads. No wonder it spawned a plethora of bad Guys, running the gamut from Evil Overlord to Lecher to Fool.

And Marion. From fair maiden and mere prize tossed to the hero, lover or wife or poisoner or tomboy or whip-smart partner . . . historically, she hasn't been around as long as either Gamelyn or Guy, and she did rather start out life as The Love Interest. Not being partial to strict genre romance, I wanted to do more with her, and not in the "gurrrl power" mode which, again, often has to tear down the (often male and often Robyn) protagonist to make a character strong. I did see Marion as an equal and a catalyst—an interesting enough character to have her own identity, a strong person first, and woman who could make her own place.

And the "Merry Men." So many expectations and assumptions go with them too: Much as simpleton (though he was a strapping badass in the earlier ballads), Little John the giant (including a tomb with a ginormous inhabitant), Will who wore poncy Scarlet clothing... why not twist those tails a bit too? No more outlaws blending into the "wode"-work—and after all, I'd learnt from a master when I was younger about how those "merries" could each be their own living, breathing entity. (*sends a blessing-breath to the otherworlds to a fellow writer very much missed*)

And Templars. Templars often are played as either good beyond reason, or bad beyond belief; they have as many myths and fancies surrounding them as Robyn does. My interest with them lay in the Fantastical as well as the Historical: their reputation, the quasi-sorcerous elements, the acceptance of what was considered forbidden—heresy, sodomy, ceremonial and covert ritual (all accused and admitted). Granted, torture often seems more a tool used to have victims say what is programmed into them during an ordeal, so any "confession" must be suspect by its nature... but what if there were some truth to even the smallest part of it?

What if? is, after all, what a writer of speculative fiction lives for. That, and powerful influences. Influences are, truly, *anadl tynged*. They are all about us, we can't help but feel them, their breath of destiny. We need them. I, for one, want to be influenced. I want life to hand me, every day if possible, something to broaden my horizons and enrich my writing.

There are inspirations and influences I didn't note in *Greenwode*, some I found whilst researching *Shirewode* (because really, research never stops) and some just because while my bookshelves are quite organised, once the books leave the shelves all bets are off.

I can't believe I didn't mention Joseph Campbell, because, well... go read his stuff and you'll know. Or watch the excellent series Bill Moyers did with Campbell before he died. Maurice Keen, whose books I have had for years and just recently rediscovered packed away—particularly Outlaws of Medieval Legend. Robert Hardy, whose books *The Great Warbow*, and *Longbow, a Social and Military History* are fabulous. (I also loved him in the televised *All Creatures Great and Small*.) *The Medieval Underworld* by Andrew McCall, which is chock full of sin in the Middle Ages. Stephen Knight, whom I found this past year through the amazing rochester.edu website and whose books I somehow had not yet seen but quickly caught up on. (And Mr. Knight is the one I have been delighted to hear say more than once that perhaps it "is time for a 'gay' Robyn Hood" . . . so yes, if I ever meet him I want to buy him a drink for putting that out into the ether.) Another fascinating book I came across while drafting *Shirewode* was *Robin Hood in Popular Culture: Violence, Transgression, and Justice*, edited by Thomas Hahn. There was a particular gem of an essay about adversaries Robyn and Guy—Stuart Kane's *Horseplay: Robin Hood, Guy of Gisborne, and the Negotiation of the Bestial*. This one made me smile and nod, and more than a little. It has many interesting, twisty things to say about the homoerotic and animalistic subtext of the ballad encounter; which not only makes it right up my alley (interesting and twisty being main qualifications), but the premise is indeed something I've often nodded and smiled about and, in fact, ended up writing the Wode books because the idea would just not let go. And the ballads; it always comes back to the ballads.

Carole. Rosina. You know why. And a tiny shout-out to some old RoS friends—you know who you are, and I hope someday you read the Wode books and enjoy them.

If *Greenwode* had a sense of Bildungsroman, then *Shirewode* is perhaps the heroic journey invoking separation, trials/initiation, and transformation. While Guy and Marion are the most obvious travellers of this path, Robyn has his own way as the *pwca*—not only the trickster who steals fire from the otherworlds, but the shaman who returns from the dying journey. If Marion is the catalyst and shadow, weaver of fate, Guy is the innocent and damned, possessing the conscious and judgmental will, and Robyn is the subconscious wild, the chaos of nature and instinct. Not to mention the essence of loyalty and faith in Much and John, and protection, trust and brotherhood in the ties to the outlaw band and the Templars . . .

In the meantime, I hope this tale touches you as strongly as it has touched me.

Persistent buggers, these characters . . .
I imagine they'll be back.

--JTH
Autumn, 2012

J TULLOS HENNIG has always possessed inveterate fascination in the myths and histories of other worlds and times. Despite having maintained a few professions in *this* world—equestrian, dancer, teacher, artist—she has never successfully managed to not be a storyteller. Ever.

Given a heritage of forest-dwelling peoples—Choctaw, Chickasaw, and Scots-Irish—the decision to make a home base in NW Washington State with the Amazing Spouse was a no-brainer. They live alongside a pair of equine freeloaders on retirement pensions, a wolfhound who alternates between leaping over the sofa and snoozing on it, and a press gang of invisible 'friends' Who Will Not Be Silenced.

Active in conventions and genre literature in the 70s/80s/90s, Jeanine returned to the authorial fold with the publication of an award-winning series of historical fantasy novels, as well as being presented with the Speculative Literature Foundation's juried Older Writers Grant.

Her historical series *The Books of the Wode* presents a truly innovative re-imagining of the Robin Hood legends, giving especial emphasis and reality to both pagan and queer perspectives.

https://www.jtulloshennig.net

CPSIA information can be obtained
at www.ICGtesting.com
Printed in the USA
BVHW041356060522
636304BV00022B/958/J